DYNASTY 26

The Dream Kingdom

Also in the *Dynasty* series:

THE FOUNDING
THE DARK ROSE
THE PRINCELING
THE OAK APPLE
THE BLACK PEARL
THE LONG SHADOW
THE CHEVALIER
THE MAIDEN
THE FLOOD-TIDE
THE TANGLED THREAD
THE EMPEROR
THE VICTORY
THE REGENCY
THE CAMPAIGNERS
THE RECKONING
THE DEVIL'S HORSE
THE POISON TREE
THE ABYSS
THE HIDDEN SHORE
THE WINTER JOURNEY
THE OUTCAST
THE MIRAGE
THE CAUSE
THE HOMECOMING
THE QUESTION

DYNASTY

26

The Dream Kingdom

Cynthia Harrod-Eagles

LITTLE, BROWN

A *Little, Brown* Book

First published in Great Britain in 2003 by Little, Brown

A CIP catalogue record for this book
is available from the British Library.

ISBN 0 316 86005 0

Typeset in Plantin
by Palimpsest Book Production Limited
Polmont, Stirlingshire

Printed and bound in Great Britain by
Clays Ltd, St Ives plc

Little, Brown
An imprint of
Time Warner Books UK
Brettenham House
Lancaster Place
London WC2E 7EN

www.TimeWarnerBooks.co.uk

Select Bibliography

W. R. Anson	*Law and Custom of the Constitution*
Dennis Baldry	*The History of Aviation*
Nancy Bradfield	*Costume In Detail, 1730-1930*
David Duff	*Queen Mary*
Sir Robert Ensor	*England 1870–1914*
M. G. Fawcett	*The Women's Victory and After*
J. Franck Bright	*History of England*
Bill Gunston	*A Century of Flight*
Christopher Hibbert	*Edward VII*
Jo Manton	*Elizabeth Garrett Anderson*
Keith Middlemas	*Edward VII*
Harold Nicholson	*King George V, His Life and Reign*
Martin Pugh	*The Pankhursts*
Antonia Raeburn	*The Militant Suffragettes*
Michaela Reid	*Ask Sir James*
Bruce Robertson	*Sopwith – The Man and His Aircraft*
Kenneth Rose	*King George V*
Giles St Aubyn	*Edward VII, Prince and King*
Marion Sambourne	*A Victorian Household*
Gilbert Slater	*Growth of Modern England*
J. A. Spender	*Fifty Years of Europe*
E. S. Turner	*The Court of St James's*
Ronald Willis	*The Illustrated Portrait of York*
Anthony Wood	*Nineteenth-century Britain 1815–1914*

THE MORLAND FAMILY

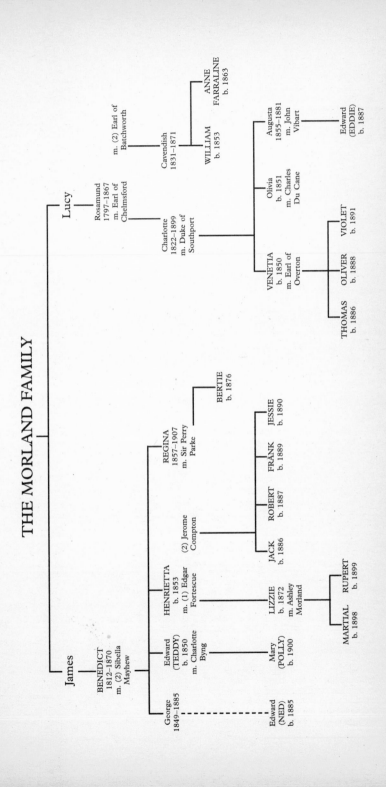

James

Lucy

BENEDICT
1812–1870
m. (2) Sibella
Mayhew

Rosamund
1797–1867
m. Earl of
Chelmsford

m. (2) Earl of
Batchworth

Cavendish
1831–1871

ANNE
FARRALINE
b. 1863

WILLIAM
b. 1853

George
1849–1885

Edward
(TEDDY)
b. 1850
m. Charlotte
Byng

HENRIETTA
b. 1853
m. (1) Edgar
Fortescue

REGINA
1857–1907
m. Sir Perry
Parke

Charlotte
1822–1899
m. Duke of
Southport

BERTIE
b. 1876

Augusta
1855–1881
m. John
Vibart

Olivia
b. 1851
m. Charles
Du Cane

VENETIA
b. 1850
m. Earl of
Overton

Edward
(NED)
b. 1885

Mary
(POLLY)
b. 1900

LIZZIE
b. 1872
m. Ashley
Morland

(2) Jerome
Compton

JACK
b. 1886

ROBERT
b. 1887

FRANK
b. 1889

JESSIE
b. 1890

Edward
(EDDIE)
b. 1887

THOMAS
b. 1886

OLIVER
b. 1888

VIOLET
b. 1891

MARTIAL
b. 1898

RUPERT
b. 1899

BOOK ONE

WEDDINGS

Come then, as ever, like the wind at morning!
Joyous, O Youth, in the agèd world renew
Freshness, to feel the eternities around it,
Rain, stars and clouds, light and the sacred dew.

Laurence Binyon, 'Invocation to Youth'

Chapter One

May 1908

In a taxi-cab rattling through London in the small hours, Jessie Compton sat up, wide awake, astonished that her two companions could be half asleep (in the case of her friend Lady Violet Winchmore) or frankly dozing (as was their chaperone Miss Miller, Violet's former governess). The girls had danced every dance since ten o'clock, but despite sore feet and prickling eyes, Jessie felt as though she could begin again in an instant. To be seventeen, in love, and in London for the Season was so exciting, it felt as though something fizzy had replaced all the blood in her veins. She leaned forward, holding the strap and staring out of the window at the dark streets, her mind a tumble of bright images.

She had never expected to have a proper London Season, or indeed a formal coming-out at all, for her parents were not wealthy. But her mother, Henrietta, was the intimate friend and distant cousin of Violet's mother, Lady Overton (Cousin Venetia, as Jessie had been told to call her) and they had always hoped that Jessie and Violet would be 'best friends' too. So Cousin Venetia had offered to bring Jessie out with Violet, which relieved the Comptons of most of the expense of it.

So here she was, coming home from the Grosvenor House Spring Ball, one of the largest public functions of the Season; and she, Jessie Compton, had been one of the privileged elite, whirling round the floor in the arms of one nice young man after another, under the wistful eyes of the lesser girls who could only look on from the sides. It had been glorious! And then, late in the evening, *he* had arrived.

He always came late. The wonder was that he had come at all, to a crowded public ball. Despite the fact that she had been chatting to her partner, Henry Fossey, and appearing to give him her whole attention, she had known the instant *he* came in at the door. He had made his usual imperious sweep of the room with his eyes (she loved the way he did that, as though he were the Tsar of Russia and could have anything and anyone he wanted!) and she had felt a squeeze of her heart as his gaze stopped a moment on her before moving on. Then he had turned away and gone into the card room. Fossey had repeated a question, making her realise that she had fallen silent for long enough for him to notice. Somehow her brain could not cope with conversation and gazing at Lord Brancaster at the same time.

She had made the effort to seem normal, not wanting anyone to know how she felt about him. He was heir to the Earl of Holkam. It was not only foolish to have fallen in love, at her very first ball, with an earl's son who was so far out of her reach, it was also wrong of her, given that the point of this London come-out was to give her the chance of attracting a better offer than she might receive at home.

Oh, but she couldn't help it! He was so handsome, so effortlessly superior to any of the other nice young men she had met. She had tried hard to stifle her feelings, but she couldn't help thinking that he liked her. He seemed to seek her out, nearly always danced with her when they were at the same ball, and when he danced with her, chatted so nicely and laughed at the things she said. She had not seen him laugh like that when he was with other girls. And they danced so well together! In his arms she felt as though she hardly touched the floor, and her body knew every move he made before he made it.

4

Energy seemed to pour through her just at the thought of dancing with him. She felt so alive she could hardly sit still. Outside the cab windows, London was wrapped in the dream-quiet of before dawn. The cobbles seemed to glisten in the dim glow of the headlights, and the small, clattery sound of the engine echoed off the high, sleeping houses of the wealthy. Shops were shuttered, and the great stores lay dark and deserted like ships in the sea of night.

Down side streets, as they passed, she sometimes caught a glimpse of another world, a second London, that existed alongside the London she and Violet inhabited. That it was so separate was what surprised her. Her home county of Yorkshire was a prosperous one, and wages were high, though there was still hardship and want when people were too old or sick to work. But at home the unfortunate were looked after. Her mother had a regular visiting round of such people. In London it did not seem to be anybody's business.

Still, Cousin Venetia, who knew about such things because of her work, said there was no longer the desperate poverty of twenty or thirty years ago; and one day it would all be gone. Science would provide the answers to all mankind's problems. Jessie believed this with all her heart. England was the centre of a mighty empire, the engine of invention and innovation, and the moral conscience of the world. They were so lucky to be English! And as Dad had said, when you were privileged, more was expected of you than of less fortunate people. You had to behave better, try harder, do more. You could be proud, but you must never be conceited or arrogant, because after all it was God who had made you English, not your own efforts.

Something caught her eye and she gave an exclamation that woke both her companions. Frantically she leaned forward to rap on the glass that separated them from the driver. 'Stop! Stop, please stop!'

The driver applied the brake, and Jessie was out even before the cab had halted properly. She heard him say behind her, 'What's wrong, miss?' She caught up the length of her skirt and ran across the pavement. In the doorway of a corner shop, beside an alley, a woman was sitting slumped, her bare legs stuck out in front of her, ending in a pair of cracked and gaping shoes. Her clothes were dirty and worn, her hair dull and straggling, and she had a sleeping baby in her lap, wrapped in a dirty red comforter.

Jessie reached her, and asked eagerly, 'What's the matter? Are you ill? Can I help you?'

The woman grunted, but her chin was sunk on her chest and her eyes were closed. Jessie crouched down and cautiously shook her shoulder. The woman opened one eye and stared at her blearily. The baby slept on. Both of them were indescribably filthy, and the smell was making Jessie's eyes water. She tried to breathe shallowly and said again, 'Are you ill?' and then, 'Haven't you anywhere to go? You mustn't sleep here. It's bad for the baby, and if a constable comes, he'll take you up.'

The woman was slow on the uptake, but now at last she seemed to grasp what Jessie was saying. She opened both eyes, lifted her head a little, and belched. Jessie recoiled at the smell of rotting teeth that came from her mouth. 'Constable? Gawd, miss, don't turn me in! I don't mean no harm.' She hacked a cough, and spat the result sideways.

The very repulsiveness of the woman made Jessie determined to help her. 'I wasn't going to turn you in,' she said. 'Haven't you got a home to go to?' Behind her she heard Miss Miller calling her, pleading with her to come back.

'I'm short my lodgings, miss,' the woman said. She reached out and caught hold of Jessie's arm with a hand so dirty that despite herself, Jessie flinched away. 'I'm a decent woman. I'd never sleep on the street, but they won't let me in without I pay in advance.'

Jessie heard the cab door open, and knew that Miss Miller's fear of harm coming to her charge would be greater than an urge towards philanthropy. Any moment now she would be dragged away. She would have to act quickly if she was to help this woman. 'How much do you need?' she asked, reaching into her reticule.

A gleam of calculation entered the woman's eyes. 'Five shillin's'd do it, miss.' She watched Jessie's hands like a sparrow watching a piece of bread. 'Gawd blesher, miss, Gawd blesher. You're an angel.'

Miss Miller's voice, breathless with anxiety, cried, 'Miss Compton, leave that person alone! Come away!'

Jessie's fingers encountered a coin and she dragged it forth. She always carried a little money with her in case of emergencies (she had imagined getting separated from Violet in a crowd, perhaps, and having to pay for a taxi home). 'Here, take this,' she said, and saw as the woman's filthy fingers closed over it the gleam of a sovereign. She felt a pang of dismay, but it was too late now to take it back.

'Jesus,' said the woman.

At that moment Miss Miller caught Jessie's shoulder. 'Come away *at once*, Miss Compton. Whatever do you think you're doing?'

The cabbie had climbed out, and was approaching too. 'Leave well alone, miss, take my advice. You don't want to do with creeturs like that one. Dead drunk, like as not.'

Jessie suspected any resistance on her part might result in the woman having to give back the money, so she stood up, turned, and said meekly, 'It's all right, I'm coming.'

Miss Miller seized her arm and hurried her along, muttering and clucking with disapproval. The cabbie sprang nippily to hold the door for them. Inside the taxi, Violet was looking sleepily puzzled. Jessie climbed in, feeling warm with satisfaction at what she had done. She was glad now that it had been a sovereign. After all, there was the baby. A sovereign would keep them both for quite a while.

The cabbie slammed the door and climbed into his

seat, and as the taxi began to move Jessie looked across at the doorway. The woman was on her feet, with the baby in one arm, staring at the coin in her other hand. But a man had come slouching out of the alley, a man in filthy clothes and a cap, and Jessie gave a cry of horror as she saw him snatch the money from the woman, at the same time dealing her a blow to the head that made her reel backwards.

'Stop him! He's taking the money!'

The cabbie had automatically braked at Jessie's cry, but now he accelerated again and the cab jerked away.

'Oh please stop!' she cried. 'We must help her!'

'Nonsense!' Miss Miller said, sounding alarmed. 'Go on, driver! Don't stop. What can you be thinking of, Miss Compton?'

'That man's taking the money I gave her,' Jessie said desperately as the taxi hurried them away from the scene.

The cabbie, whose glass was partly open, said, 'His moll, most like. You didn't oughter've done it, miss. Wasted, that's what that money was. You can't help that sort anyway. Give 'em anything, and they just drink it away.'

'It was so *thoughtless* of you,' Miss Miller said. 'Suppose you had caught something from her? Suppose she had attacked you? Why, she might have been the lure for a gang of *white slavers*!' she suggested, in breathless horror. 'What would your mother, or Lady Overton, say if anything were to happen to you? I'm supposed to be taking care of you,' she finished rather pathetically.

Jessie felt sorry for her, realising all at once how uncomfortable the chaperone's position was, how frightened she had really been. But it wasn't right to see someone lying in a doorway and not see if they needed help – she was sure about that, at least. And perhaps that man would give the woman *something*. 'I'm sorry,' she said. 'I just wanted to help her.'

'It's not your business to help,' Miss Miller said. 'Those people can take care of themselves.'

They rode in silence after that. The taxi-cab pulled up outside the Overtons' house, and Jessie and Violet stepped out of the leather-smelling stuffiness and shivered a little in the cool air of dawn while Miss Miller paid the driver. When the cab finally rattled off round the corner of the gardens, Miss Miller was still frowning, her lips moving as though she were rehearsing excuses. Jessie stepped close to her and said quietly, 'I'm sorry I upset you. You're right, it was thoughtless of me. I won't do it again. Please don't tell anyone.'

'Very well,' said Miss Miller, only too glad to agree on silence. She had not relished having to confess what she had not prevented Jessie from doing.

Jessie followed Violet up the steps of the house, content. In the east the black velvet sky was changing to luminous turquoise, with the morning star shining like a single rose-diamond, infinitely precious; and the first blackbird called, a clear and somehow enquiring thread of song, vibrating out of the dark towards the light. What Miss Miller had said was true, in a way, she reflected: it was not her business to help that woman. When she was grown up and married, she would do her part, as her mother did; but just now, for these few weeks of the Season, her business was pleasure, dancing, and falling in love. Everyone was saying it was the most brilliant Season of the past decade; and Violet was one of its leading débutantes. She was so beautiful, so graceful, and good and kind, too. Jessie felt privileged to be her friend. There was no doubt that Violet would make a brilliant marriage sooner or later; and if she didn't meet the man of her dreams this year, there would be other Seasons to come. But for Jessie this opportunity would not be repeated. She had only until August.

Of course, neither of them would accept an offer from the most desirable *parti* in the world if they didn't love him. It was love they were looking for – true love, love that lasted to the grave and beyond. They had discussed it endlessly in those hours they spent chatting in their bedrooms. They had agreed that there was one right person for everyone, and their business was to find him. And they had agreed that one would know at once, that there would be a 'sort of lightning', as Violet had put it. Jessie had felt that lightning when she first saw *him*. Oh, dancing with him was so wonderful . . . !

Her thoughts had come full circle. Tired now, she fell asleep as soon as her head touched the pillow. Outside, dawn had broken, and London was starting up, like a clockwork machine set in motion, slowly at first, clicking and whirring and gathering speed, until it became the frantic, roaring thing of full daytime. It began quietly with the first milk-horse, clopping hollowly on the cobbles, head nodding sleepily as it stopped automatically at each house, knowing its route to its very bones. Then there was the postman, rapping his way along the street; and the first maid, popping up from a basement, gummy-eyed, to beat out the kitchen mat at the top of the area steps. The early workmen appeared, in caps and shapeless jackets and big boots, walking off to their jobs; and live-out servants came hurrying in to theirs. Housemaids came out to scrub steps, footmen to polish brass door furniture, reluctant lady's maids to walk the mistress's dog. Then motor-vans appeared, delivering luxuries, flowers, wine to the wealthy, and boys on bicycles with baskets on the front, bringing meat and groceries and bread. There was the coal lorry, tipping its glistening black treasure down the little round vents in the pavements; the sweep, grey-faced and white-eyed, with his bag of brushes, to see to the other end of the process. The light broadened and the sky disappeared behind its curtain of smoke as London's countless chimneys sent up their working ribbons. The machine roared at full throttle, and the thrilling, chill silence of dawn was like a distant memory of another world entirely.

After a late night the girls were always left to sleep in. Jessie was roused at last by a faint click of the door being opened, followed by the rustling of skirts as the maid crossed the room to open the curtains. Jessie heard with amusement the soft sound of the window being closed. London maids hated open windows. They said it was because they let in smuts and smells, but Jessie thought this was only a surface excuse, and that really they had a superstitious fear, as if the devil might slip in through any unsealed door or window and take possession of their souls. Jessie liked her bedroom window open, and waged a constant, unacknowledged battle with cousin Venetia's servants on the subject.

Sanders, – Violet's lady's maid, whom they were sharing – turned from the window and, seeing that Jessie's eyes were open, smiled and said, 'Good morning, miss.'

'Good morning. What time is it?'

'Eleven, miss. Luncheon at one. Lady Violet's awake. Shall I send your tray in there?'

'Yes, thank you,' Jessie said.

Sanders went out, and Jessie lingered for a moment longer in the downy comfort of her bed – twice as large as her own at home. She loved staying at the Overtons' house in Manchester Square. It was so different from Morland Place. Here Jessie and Violet had their own bathroom – between their two bedrooms and adjoining each – and there was hot running water, heated by a boiler and pumped up. At home, baths were taken before the bedroom fire and water had to be carried up from the kitchen in great cans. Also the Overtons had the telephone, necessary because Cousin Venetia was a doctor (one of the first lady-doctors ever to qualify), and they had electric light. Cousin Venetia complained that it was not as reliable as gas and that the electric globes were so weak they were always breaking. And it was true that electricity didn't give as much light as either lamps or a gas-mantel. It was all right for general purposes, but not very good for reading. But Jessie still felt it was like a miracle simply to flick a switch and flood a room with light.

All the same, she did rather miss the cosiness of the ritual back home, when blue dusk seeped into the room, and the servants came to light the lamps and draw the curtains and settle the family in for the evening. Home was so nice, after all! And it was good to think that it would be there waiting for her, when the excitement of this Season was over.

The Season! Energy surged through her, and she scrambled out of bed. What the girls liked first thing in the morning was for Jessie to run through and jump into Violet's bed so they could discuss the previous day's marvels before dressing. There was always so much to talk about; and this morning was special, for several reasons. She went to her dressing-table and took a small package, wrapped in tissue paper and tied with ribbon, out of the top drawer, and went through the bathroom into Violet's room.

Violet was sitting up in bed looking ruffled and sweet and very beautiful, as she always did when just awake. Jessie thought suddenly and with a pang that soon Vi would get married and then she would never see her like this again. It came to her that these days of their come-out were very precious, and that they were sharing something special, which would never come again.

She got into bed beside Violet, kissed her cheek and said, 'Happy birthday, darling!'

Violet smiled. 'I didn't think you'd remember.'

'Of course I remembered. You're seventeen today. That's a milestone.' She presented the package in her hand. 'This is for you.'

Violet unwrapped it. It was a paper fan between wooden sticks, the paper painted with a watercolour scene of a lady in a crinoline with a black-and-white greyhound. The sticks were embellished with flowers and the whole was clear-varnished, and finished with a tassel of royal blue silk.

'It's lovely!' Violet cried.

'I made it,' Jessie said. 'Well, I bought the sticks, actually, but I did the painting and folding and sticking and everything. Making the tassel was the hardest part – goodness, how fiddling!'

'But, Jess, how clever of you!'

12

'Oh, not really,' Jessie said, bathed in the glow of accomplished giving. Vi was such a nice person to give things to. Despite her parents being frightfully rich, she wasn't the least bit spoilt. 'I read in a book how to do it. I've been doing it in the early morning, before you were awake. I wanted it to be a surprise.'

'It's a lovely surprise,' Violet said. 'And the painting is wonderful! You really are good at it.'

'The lady in the crinoline is meant to be you,' Jessie said. 'I was going to do her with a handsome young man, but I can do dogs better.'

'I'm glad you did the dog,' Violet said. 'I like the dog.'

'I'm not sure I'd know which man to paint you with, anyway. I was watching you last night and – well, it's not Tommy Fairbanks any more, is it?

'Oh, was it obvious?'

'Only to me. So?'

Violet sighed. 'No, you're right. Tommy's a dear, but he can't compare with – with someone else.'

'Someone else,' Jessie said, regarding Violet's face closely. 'I thought I knew you so well, but I haven't been able to guess who it is.'

'Haven't you? I was afraid I was making a spectacle of myself.'

'Not you, Vi darling. Discretion itself. So who is it? Do tell.'

Violet hesitated a moment, then said, 'George Carrick.'

'Really? I wasn't near to guessing that. Well, Tommy's handsomer, I think,' Jessie said judiciously, 'but Carrick has something about him. And he is heir to a marquisate. You have to consider that. I'm sure your parents would like you to be a marchioness.'

Violet flushed a little. 'I've only danced with him a few times.'

'But couldn't you tell at once? One ought to know, with true love.'

'Yes, you knew at once, didn't you, with Brancaster?' Violet said.

Jessie almost wished that she hadn't told Violet of her feelings, because it was harder to resist them with Violet encouraging her. But of course, they told each other everything; and besides, Violet would have guessed anyway. 'I'm a country gentleman's daughter with no dowry,' she said. 'Brancaster would never think of me. How could he?'

'But I'm sure he *does*! He seems to appear at everything you go to, and he always talks to you, and he dances with you an awful lot.'

'Lots of men dance with me – Willie Hunter and George Cooper and the rest. It doesn't mean anything. That's what they're meant to do – dance with us.'

'I'm sure it means something with Brancaster. Thomas says he's very careful about paying attention to débutantes, after that scandal last year. Mary Talbot said to me at supper that no-one expected him to come last night. And, after all, he didn't dance with anyone else, did he?'

'He danced with you,' Jessie pointed out.

'Only out of politeness, because you're staying with us.'

'And he danced with Amelia Vanbrugh.'

'But Amy Van's a cousin, isn't she? So that doesn't count.'

Jessie sighed. 'Oh, Vi. Robert Fitzjames Howard, Viscount Brancaster, and Miss Jessie Compton from Yorkshire? It's not likely.'

'You always say that, but why shouldn't he love you?' Violet saw nothing surprising in anyone's falling in love with her friend, whom she thought not only pretty but far wittier and cleverer than any of the other girls they knew.

'For one thing, because I won't have any money – which he is sure to know.'

'Why?'

'Because someone will have been sure to tell him. Now, Vi, don't look like that! George Cooper told me that Angela Burnet told him that Edith Owen's father's business is failing. He said he was really glad that you and I

14

don't talk about other girls like that,' she added with gratification. 'He said some of them are dreadful cats.'

'I don't know how they can,' Violet said, with indignation. 'But I tell you what, Jess,' she went on, 'if anyone can marry for love without worrying about dowries and such-like, it's Brancaster. I heard my father say the Fitzjames Howards own most of Lincolnshire.'

Jessie yielded to temptation. 'Oh, Vi, I know it's wrong, but when I'm dancing with him and I know all the other girls are staring at me and envying me – well, it feels so marvellous! Don't hate me, but I do love making them jealous!'

'I could never hate you,' Violet said – a little sadly, but Jessie, thinking of Brancaster, didn't notice.

'I've tried to be sensible about it, but I can't seem to help it. Every time I see him I fall in love all over again, and you must admit there isn't anyone to touch him.'

Violet did admit it.

'Do you really think he could possibly care for me? Last night at supper I said something – I forget what – that made him laugh, and he said I had a ready wit. Do you think that means he likes me?'

Violet gave her whole mind to the question, and they plunged into the débutante's customary discussion, analysing exactly what was meant by every word and gesture of the young men they were currently in love with – and, indeed, of all the other young men who might possibly be in love with them.

'I wonder if Brancaster will be at Ascot next week?' Jessie said at last. Lord Overton was a close friend of and equerry to the King, and was taking the girls on Gold Cup day, to the Royal Enclosure.

'Bound to be, I should think,' Violet said. 'He must guess you'll be there.'

Sanders came in at that moment to announce that Lady Violet's bath was ready, so Jessie was spared the necessity to reply.

★　　★　　★

There was to be a special family luncheon for Violet's birthday, and while the girls were dressing, the first guest was already downstairs in the drawing-room talking to Violet's parents. Lady Anne Farraline was unmarried and lived in London in Bedford Square, alone except for a lady companion, who had been 'foisted on her', as she put it, for decency's sake by her brother William, and whom she therefore ignored completely. Miss Vaughan had been very much put out at first, finding that Lady Anne went everywhere alone and without consulting her at all; but as there was nothing she could do about it, and as Lord Batchworth was too busy on his country estate with his own growing family ever to come up to London or enquire what his sister was doing, she soon accepted the situation. Miss Vaughan was a devotee of the theatre, and being in London, with all her living expenses paid and her time and her salary entirely at her disposal, she was able to indulge the passion to the full. So, as Anne was wont to say, the niceties were observed and everyone was happy.

Venetia worried a good deal about Anne, and thought it a dreadful waste that she had never married. Anne Farraline had been a great beauty and though now in her forties she was very striking still, tall and fair with large blue eyes that flashed fire; but she had dedicated her life and her considerable energy and talents to the Cause – the enfranchisement of women – and scorned the follies of love.

There were two main women's suffrage societies: the NUWSS, dubbed by the press the 'Nusses', or the 'nice Suffragettes', who were dedicated to peaceful and consti-tutional methods; and the militant group, the WSPU, who were called the Wasps, or the 'nasty Suffragettes' because they made a nuisance of themselves, interrupted meet-ings and got themselves arrested. Anne, much to Venetia's regret, belonged to the latter group, and had already served one term in prison for attempting to make a speech in the lobby of the House of Commons.

16

Venetia and Lord Overton were both intellectually in favour of the Cause. Venetia had herself been a rebel and pioneer. In their courting days Overton had not been sympathetic to Venetia's titanic struggle to break into what had always been a man's world, but the pain of losing the woman he loved had concentrated his mind wonderfully and he had managed to perform a right-about-face on the subject with considerable grace. During the years of their marriage his sense of justice had overcome the residual prejudices of the age and his upbringing, and he was now firmly committed to the ideal of equality for women. But his position was delicate. The King was very much against votes for women, and as a close companion of His Majesty he could not afford to be involved in any of the Suffragettes' activities, nor allow his wife to be.

Anne was talking about a recent outrage perpetrated by the authorities on the leader of the WSPU. With her, conversation always struggled to find another path. Like Alice in the Looking-glass House, it went out of one door only to find itself returning through it a moment later.

'They threatened us with a Charles II statute, which prohibits processions to the House of Commons of more than thirteen people,' she said, as she walked restlessly up and down before the unlit fire. She reminded Venetia of some great cat, a tigress or lioness, in a cage. It seemed almost unnatural to confine her in a polite drawing-room. 'So Mrs Pankhurst quite deliberately went with just twelve other women. She was completely within her rights. She was walking peaceably with a bunch of flowers in one hand and a petition in the other, and when she got to Parliament Square two policemen simply seized her by the wrists and told her she was under arrest. She had done absolutely nothing wrong, yet she was arrested and given six weeks in the second division!'

'It's very bad, I know, dear, but—' Venetia got no further.

'And the only reason she wasn't given three months was that *that* would have meant a trial by jury, and

17

Gladstone was afraid a jury might have let her off – which, considering she had broken no law, was only too likely.' Herbert Gladstone was the Home Secretary.

'Well, of course—'

'Can you imagine what the newspapers would say if a man was treated like that? But of course a man never would be. A magistrate would never dare. And this was done on Gladstone's express orders, mark you,' she added, fixing Overton with her burning blue gaze, 'and what Gladstone does is on Asquith's orders. The government has forfeited all claim to legitimacy. It flouts the law and pleases itself. You would think Asquith were the Tsar of Russia!'

Overton shook his handsome head. 'I hold no brief for Asquith – nor Herbert Gladstone. But order has to be maintained in the precinct of Parliament, you must see that. Members must not be prevented from carrying out their function through fear or because of intimidation.'

'Intimidation? A fifty-year-old woman carrying a bunch of lilies?'

'Any demonstration could lead to violence,' Overton pointed out. 'But I agree with you that the sentence was far too draconian. Asquith's policy is to use harshness towards you women as a deterrent. It's not,' he added, with a shrug, 'what I would call gentlemanly behaviour.'

'Well, he will learn how far we are deterred by such brutality,' Anne said.

Venetia stirred with anxiety. 'Anne, dear, you're not planning anything rash, are you?'

'Rash? No, not rash. You know that Asquith has refused to take Stanger's Bill any further?'

'Yes, I heard that,' said Venetia. This was a Private Member's Bill for women's enfranchisement, which had passed its second reading by a large majority.

'Parliamentary time is limited,' Overton said. 'All governments have to decide what bills to promote and what to put aside.'

'It's not a matter of time,' Anne said. 'Asquith has said publicly that no women's amendment will be made unless he sees evidence of support for it in the country at large. Well, we are going to give him his evidence. We are going to hold the biggest franchise demonstration ever seen in London: Women's Sunday, on the twenty-first of June, in Hyde Park. There'll be twenty platforms and eighty speakers. We expect a crowd of a quarter of a million – probably more. I know you won't speak,' she concluded to Venetia, 'but you will attend, won't you? It's most important that everyone turns out, especially the educated and the eminent.'

'Flattery,' Overton remarked. 'She has you now, my love.'

Venetia cast him a distracted look, and said to Anne, 'You know I can't become involved. We've been over this before—'

But Overton interrupted her. It had taken him time, and a personal struggle, to learn to see his wife as an independent woman, and not as his property; to allow her opinions and to respect her differences and even be glad of them. He sometimes felt guilty that his advancement at Court had forced her to curtail her activities and deny some of her principles. So he said, 'I think it will be all right for you to attend.'

Venetia turned to him, surprised. 'Do you say so?'

'Among so many, you won't be conspicuous. There's no reason for the King to hear about it. I'm sure you can go along for a little while. You will want to leave before things get out of hand, in any case'

'Things will not get out of hand,' Anne said indignantly. 'Everything is being planned down to the last detail.'

'Things always get out of hand when a large number of people come together in the middle of London, particularly if the day is hot.' Anne's eyes flashed angrily, and he went on hastily, 'But this demonstration is just the right sort of thing. Dignified protest – not like that silly bell-ringing business.'

During a by-election in Dundee in May, a woman suffragist had followed the Liberal candidate, Winston

Churchill, to every meeting, and rung a muffin bell continuously whenever he tried to speak. In the end he said, 'If she thinks this is a reasonable argument she may use it. I don't care, and I bid you good afternoon'; and he left. Churchill still won the seat, and the tactic had been denounced in an open letter to the Suffragettes by Bernard Shaw, who said that if letting women into politics was going to mean 'the argument of the muffin bell' he would turn against votes for women.

'We've used reasonable argument for forty years,' Anne said, 'and you men have refused to listen. The muffin bell made its point. It annoyed Churchill, and nothing a woman *said* would have had the slightest effect on him.'

'Bernard Shaw is an ass,' Overton said, 'but he's right in this case. If you annoy men you will make them dislike you, and—'

'We don't want men to like us,' Anne said impatiently. 'We just want them to give us justice. We have got rather beyond trimming our actions and fawning like dogs in the hope of winning a smile from our lords and masters.'

Venetia and Overton exchanged a glance, and Venetia said, 'Please don't speak like that in front of the girls. In fact, I'd be obliged if you didn't mention the Cause at all when they come down.'

Anne raised an eyebrow. 'Oh, I shan't, of course. I know you are set on passing them through the cattle market and into marriage, and I respect your decision.'

'Whatever you think,' Venetia said impatiently, 'the world is what it is, and marriage is the best – usually the only – life for a girl. If Violet had shown any inclination to be a doctor or anything of the sort, I should have supported her, but she hasn't. She *wants* to be married. It's the most natural thing for her, her best chance of happiness, and her only real chance of freedom. As for Jessie, this is her one opportunity to marry well, and I won't have anything spoil it.'

Anne lifted her hands slightly. 'As I said, I respect your decision. We can't all be foot-soldiers.'

'I hate to hear you sounding so hard,' Venetia said. 'Fighting for justice for women ought not to make women hate men. If it does, then it will have made things worse, not better.'

Anne laughed suddenly, and seemed much more natural, more like the eager, loving girl Venetia remembered. 'You are quite right. And I don't hate men, not at all. Forgive me if I sounded too vehement. I remember the fun of my own come-out and wouldn't spoil Violet's and Jessie's for worlds. Tell me, are they in love yet? Have they had any offers?'

Her tension eased, Venetia smiled. 'I'm sure they're in love – girls of that age always are. Violet has plenty of partners and is very much admired—'

'As she should be. She is the prettiest débutante of the Season, by my vote.'

'—but she doesn't seem to be favouring any one man over another. Jessie is very popular too. She has a nice, light, teasing way with the men. Not flirtatious, exactly, but easy and humorous.'

Anne shook her head. 'I know exactly what you mean, and it's disastrous. She treats them all like brothers. There's nothing more fatal.'

'Oh, Anne!' Venetia laughed.

'Never mind "Oh, Anne"! I know whereof I speak! Being a comfortable sister to all the suitable young men means she doesn't care about making them in love with her, and *that* means she's in love with someone *un*suitable.'

'Absurd! We don't let her meet anyone unsuitable,' Venetia said.

'In her case, unsuitable might mean too high. Who did she dance with last night?'

'No-one who might not make her an offer,' Venetia said loyally. 'Except perhaps Brancaster. Though of course if he *were* to fancy her, there's no reason why he shouldn't marry her. Money can't be an object with him.'

'Money is always an object,' Anne said, 'though it need

not be an objection. But I fancy Brancaster knows his own worth. It might be a good match for Violet, though. Holkam is old and in poor health. He never leaves Norfolk these days. Once Brancaster inherits and takes his seat, he's bound to be more active in the House. We must find out his views. He could be very useful to us. We don't have nearly enough supporters in the Lords.'

'Oh, Anne, really!' Venetia said, laughing. 'We're not going to promote matches to suit the WSPU!'

Anne smiled too. 'Of course not – but there's no harm in using what's to hand, is there?'

The girls came downstairs, and at the same time Violet's brothers arrived. The elder, Thomas, Viscount Hazelmere, was in the Blues. The younger, Oliver, had come up from Oxford, bringing with him their cousin Eddie, son of Venetia's late sister Augusta. The four had grown up in the nursery together and were devoted, and Violet was delighted to have them all there together.

There were kisses all round, and congratulations and presents for Violet. Tom had bought her a pair of gloves, Eddie a silk rose, and Oliver, who was something of a comedian, had bought her a small looking-glass with a moustache stuck to it. 'So you can see what sort of a man you'd have made.' There was a wonderful joke-shop in Ship Street, he explained, which was full of such things – he had hardly known how to choose one thing for her from among so many.

Anne's present was the greatest surprise: a beautiful sable muff with brown satin lining and a chain of gold and crystal beads. Violet could only stare at it in wonder, a blush rising in her face, while Venetia protested, 'But Anne, dearest, it's much too much! Too generous of you, really it is.'

'Every girl needs a muff,' was all that Anne would say, shrugging off her generosity.

After luncheon, when they returned to the drawing-room, Anne was asked to play for them. She played well enough to have done it professionally, had there ever been

22

any question of her having an occupation beyond being a lady, and when she was at the keyboard she lost herself entirely in the music. Her choice was, typically for her, a complex and stormy Chopin prelude, followed by a difficult late piece of Beethoven. She played with great brio, her large, shapely hands moving powerfully over the keys, her body taut with emotion.

Not all of those disposed about the large and elegant drawing-room were music-lovers, and in any case, home performances were a traditional time for private conversation. Besides, once she began playing, Anne would not have noticed anything less than raucous laughter from her audience. So Oliver quietly changed his seat and placed himself beside his mother on the sofa. 'Can I ask you something, Mama?'

Venetia was actually enjoying the music, but hearing that he was unusually grave for her merry son, turned to face him and said, in a suitably low voice, 'What is it? Don't tell me you're in trouble again.'

'Well, sort of,' Oliver admitted. His career at Oxford had not been uneventful, although because his offences all arose from high spirits, he remained liked by the dons as well as popular with his peers.

'You've been progged again. What was it this time?'

'Oh, no, nothing like that. Well, I was fined a bob last week for smoking in my cap and gown, but that's not it. I don't mean that sort of trouble. No, the thing is – well, should you mind very much if I didn't finish at Oxford?'

Venetia stared. 'Oh, Oliver! You've been sent down!'

'Oh, Mum!' he mimicked. 'Nothing of the sort! It's just that what I'm doing now doesn't suit me and I'd really like to do something else.'

Venetia felt the constraints of whispering were too much for this conversation. She rose, beckoned him with her, and went out and into the morning-room.

'Now,' she said, 'tell me all, my errant boy. What have you been getting up to? Out with it!'

'"Out with it," she says.' Oliver addressed an invisible

23

third party. 'Will she like it? Never mind – all on the one throw! Here it is: I want to be a doctor.'

It was perhaps the last thing Venetia would have anticipated. She hardly knew what to say. She searched his face, and said at last, 'When did this desire come on? It's very sudden, isn't it?'

'Not so very. I've been thinking about it for a while, but idly, you know. Well, it's in the blood, ain't it, with you and Grandmama both in the medical way? It always seemed interesting to me, though I never really connected it with myself – like something you read in a book, you know? But then last year there was that friend of mine and Eddie's at Balliol – you remember: Jemmet, who got sick and it turned out to be consumption?'

'Yes, poor young man. You told me about him at the time.'

'Well, that's what brought it home to me. Suddenly I saw your work, which had always been something remote and almost – unreal, you know? And there was Jemmet, who was as real as can be. And I put the two together in my mind and thought, Eureka! That's what I want to do! I want to know what made the poor fellow sick and what to do about it.'

Venetia shook her head. 'My love, I've been practising medicine for thirty years and researching into tuberculosis for the last six, and I haven't the least idea in the world what to do about it.'

'Oh, I understand that. But you will, one day. And there's all the other things that you *do* know what to do about. It just seems to me that the human body is the most interesting thing in the world one could study, much more than the army or the Church or the law or any of those things. A second son has to have something to do, you know. So, should you mind, awfully?'

Venetia took a moment to think. There was no financial necessity for Oliver to earn his living: she had a private fortune extensive enough to pay him a comfortable allowance all his life. But that was not a view she had

24

ever expressed to him. She remembered how she had rebelled against the enforced idleness of her youth, how her longing for work – for useful work – had been denied because she was a female; and she had seen enough of the trouble rich, idle young men got into and the misery it caused both to themselves and their families. She had always hoped and intended that Oliver would find something with which to occupy his life, even if it was only breeding racehorses. But he had always been so light, the clown of the family, taking nothing and no-one seriously. Could he *really* want to be a doctor? Surely it was just a whim, and would soon be replaced by a passion for motorcars or architecture or ballooning?

'No, I shouldn't mind,' she said at last. 'I should be proud of you, I think. But, Oliver, are you really sure? Have you thought how much studying and hard work it would mean? It would require real dedication from you, especially as you would start from so far behind everyone else. I shouldn't like you to begin and then throw it up after a few months. Do you really think you are up to it?'

Oliver looked a little disconcerted, and said, 'I know you think I'm not much of a scholar. Thomas sailed through everything, and I'm not Thomas, so everybody assumes I've got no brains.'

'I didn't say that.'

'I know. But you think it, and I can't blame you. I've always played the fool. I've *let* people think I was just a will o' the wisp. But the truth is, Mama, that I'm pretty bright upstairs when I apply myself – only I haven't found anything worth applying myself to before. And it ain't a sudden whim. I've been thinking about it for a year, since Jemmet died. In fact, this year at Oxford I've been attending some lectures and reading books, trying to get a bit of a grounding in the right subjects.'

'What subjects?'

'Physics and biology. I did try botany for a while, but it was awfully dull.'

Venetia smiled. 'All medical students find botany dull.

In my day, most of them cut the lectures and paid the porters to mark them present.'

'There, you see! You'll be able to give me so much practical advice.' Oliver smiled too, a smile of enormous charm, and Venetia suddenly saw him grown up, matured into an eminent physician and using that smile on his patients to valuable effect. She remembered the year he had taken up tennis and the determination and concentration with which he had mastered the game in a few weeks. Yes, he could do it, she thought, if he applied himself.

'You're twenty now,' she said. 'Can you really bear to go to medical school for another three years, along with boys younger than you? Will you really—'

'Stick it out? Yes, I really think I will. If you and Papa give permission. And if I can get into a school.'

'Oh, there'll be no difficulty about that,' Venetia said. 'Even if none of the other schools will take you, I could get you in at the Southport.'

'I should hope so,' Oliver said with a grin, 'seeing Grandmama founded it.'

'You were counting on that, were you?'

'Not entirely. I did think your influence would count in other places too. Do you think Papa will let me?'

'I don't think he will mind. I suppose you were relying on me to persuade him, too?'

Oliver pretended hurt. 'I thought you'd be pleased to have a son follow in your footsteps. I thought you'd be proud of me.'

Venetia hugged him quickly, wondering, as she embraced his hard, man's body, where all the years had rushed away to since he was a little boy she could pick up in her arms. 'I am pleased. And I shall be proud of you. But you know, don't you, that Society people don't regard doctors very highly? It won't give you the *entrée* into every drawing-room, like the army or the diplomatic service.'

'Oh, I don't care about that,' Oliver said easily. 'Medicine must be much more interesting than Society. And Tom and Vi and Eddie will always invite me to dinner.'

Venetia laughed, and said, 'You will always get by, my dear. But we'd better go back into the drawing-room now – it's too rude to poor Anne!'

'I'm sure she never notices anything when she's playing. Will you speak to Papa, then?'

'Yes, the first thing. But he won't decide on the instant, you know, so you will have to go back to Oxford tomorrow.'

'Will I?'

'My dear boy, moving you will involve a great deal of organisation. It won't happen one–two–three. Oh dear, there's always so much to do at the same time. I can't think how people are ever bored.'

Just as the tea-things were being brought in by two footmen and a maid, an unexpected visitor arrived.

'Mr Jack Compton, my lady,' the butler announced, simultaneously flicking a glance at the maid to scurry off for an extra cover.

Jessie was across the room and hugging her brother before he had had a chance to make his politenesses. 'Darling Jackie, it's so good to see you!'

Jack kissed her unselfconsciously, said, 'My, you do look pretty! But let me mind my manners first, Jess,' and set her gently aside so that he could address Venetia, who was his godmother – 'I do hope you don't mind my dropping in unannounced like this, ma'am?' – greet the rest of the company and wish Violet a happy birthday. He had brought her a present: a fine handkerchief, nicely embroidered with a spray of violets. He presented it with a hesitant modesty that said he knew it was only a trifling thing and not worthy of her, but she accepted it with sisterly warmth and admired the embroidery as if he had done it himself.

The footmen were carrying round tea, and with the tacit permission of the rest of the company, Jessie installed

27

herself with her brother on a small sofa a little apart so that they could talk privately.

'So how do you come to be here?' she asked, as Jack consumed bread-and-butter with an active man's hunger. 'I didn't think I'd be seeing you again until August.'

'August?' Jack queried, vaguely.

'Cowes Week,' Jessie said patiently. 'You know the Overtons always go to Cowes Week, and since I'm invited with them this year and you work in Southampton, which is only just across the water, I naturally assumed you'd take the trouble to come and see us.'

'Well, of course I will, now I know, but since you didn't tell me before that you were going to be there . . .'

'I'm sure I told you in my letter that I wasn't going home until Lord Overton goes to Marienbad with the King.'

'I dare say you did, but how was I to know when the King goes to Marienbad? I'm just a humble engineer. I say, is there any more of this bread-and-butter?'

'I'll get you some.' When she returned with it, she said, 'I was pleased that you remembered Violet's birthday.'

'I am too,' Jack said, 'but I can't take credit for it. I called in at Lizzie's, and she reminded me.'

Lizzie was their half-sister, who lived in London with her husband Ashley Morland, who was in the shipping business, and their two children. Their younger brother Frank, who was studying at University College, also stayed with Lizzie during term-time.

'Where did you get the handkerchief, then?' Jessie asked.

'It was one someone gave to Lizzie for a present that she'd never used. It was an extra piece of luck that it had violets on it, don't you think?'

'Oh, Jackie!' Jessie said reproachfully.

'I say, you won't tell her?'

'Of course I won't! But all the same . . .'

'I'd have bought her something if I'd had time,' Jack defended himself. 'But there are no shops open on a

28

Sunday in that part of the world anyway, and at least I didn't come empty-handed.'

'So you came up to London to see Lizzie, then?'

'Oh, I just dropped in, you know, as I was passing. Couldn't go by without dropping in. I thought I might see Frank but he was out with some of the university men – gone rowing at Hammersmith or something of the sort.'

'So you were with them all day, were you?'

'Ah, no, not exactly. I just called in, as I said, on my way to Pont Street. Lizzie did ask me to stay for lunch, but I said I wasn't sure how long I'd be, and as it happened—'

'Pont Street? Who's at Pont Street?'

'I was coming to that, if you'd let me finish. The Puddephats have just moved into a house in Pont Street, so I called on them to pay my respects, and as it happened they asked me to stay for luncheon.'

A smile spread across Jessie's face. 'So that's what you came up to London for! And there I was thinking it was for my sake, and Violet's.'

'Well, naturally I did think of calling on you as well – and here I am, after all.'

'After all – yes, that's just about the truth! After all the other calls, and after spending most of the day gazing at Maud Puddephat.'

Jack took on his dignity. 'They've done so much for our family, and Uncle Teddy and Mr Puddephat are such friends, naturally I owe them the courtesy of a call.'

Jessie squeezed his arm. 'I know you're sweet on Maud, and I'm glad. She's a very nice girl. Why shouldn't you go courting? It's a man's privilege.'

'Maybe so, if a man's in a position to support a wife. Until I am, I can't go courting. I just visited them, that's all. But it was lovely to see Maud again. She's the sweetest, prettiest girl in the world.'

'And you love her. Does she love you, too? She'd be a great fool not to.'

'Well, I know she likes me, but whether it's anything

more than that I can't say. I don't *think* there's anyone else, but I can't be sure since I can't declare myself. This money business is the dickens!' he added gloomily. 'I get the horrible feeling that before I can set myself up some other fellow will get in before me and snap her up.'

'Perhaps you ought to declare yourself,' Jessie said. 'If she knows you're interested, and if she loves you, she'll wait for you. Otherwise you can hardly expect—'

'I don't expect. And I couldn't ask her to wait for me when I've no idea how long the wait would be. That wouldn't be fair.'

'Oh, Jackie! If she loves you, it isn't fair not to at least give her the chance to wait.'

'Do you think so?'

'I know so. We girls are helpless until the man declares himself. It's hateful to be wondering if the man you fancy loves you, hoping he'll say something, not able to say anything yourself. Your fate is completely in his hands. It's horrid. Tell her you love her, explain your situation, and at least give her the chance to tell you what she feels.'

'Hmm,' said Jack doubtfully.

'Are you so very badly off, then?' Jessie pursued. 'I thought you were doing well at Rankin Marine.'

'Oh, I am, and Mr Rankin is really pleased with me. He's putting the motor-boat I designed into production, and he's even going to call it the JC, after me. The Rankin JC – sounds fine, don't you think?'

'Very fine. But won't he give you any more money?'

'He hasn't said so precisely, but there have been hints that if it's well received he'll increase my salary. But I'll still only be an engineer –'

'Chief design engineer.'

'– and the Puddephats are very rich,' Jack finished, ignoring the interruption. 'Maud's their only daughter. Now poor Ray is gone' – the Puddephats' only son had died in South Africa – 'she'll inherit everything.'

Jessie could not pretend she did not see the problem. But love for her brother and youthful enthusiasm surged immediately upwards. 'But if she loves you, I'm sure they wouldn't want to break her heart. It's not as if you aren't respectable. And they like you, don't they? They asked you to stay for lunch, and they wouldn't have done that if they didn't.'

'Yes, but I'm afraid that's because of Uncle Teddy. They see me as one of the family. It doesn't make me a suitable match for Maud.' He sighed and changed the subject. 'What about you, Jess? Are you enjoying your come-out? Are you in love with anybody?'

'Well, I am,' Jessie admitted, 'but he's far above me, and there's no point in hoping until – unless – he says something definite.'

'Ah, I see now why you are so eager for me to declare myself to Miss Puddephat! Well, to give you your own words again, he'd be a great fool not to love you.'

The following day, all Venetia's careful plans for the Season were thrown into disarray. The girls, after their quiet Sunday night at home, were up early enough to go riding in the morning, accompanied by Oliver and Eddie, who were not catching the train back to Oxford until noon. Venetia took the opportunity to catch up on some of her own work, and was thoroughly and peacefully engaged with microscope and slides when the apologetic butler informed her there was a visitor. She was about to remind him, tartly, that she was not at home, when he added, 'It is Lord Knollys, my lady. He says it is a matter of some urgency.'

Lord Knollys was the King's private secretary, and an old friend of Venetia's, a dancing-partner from her youth. She suppressed a sigh, put down the slide she was holding, and said, 'Very well, I will come. Show him into my private parlour and bring sherry. I'll be there in a few moments.'

Her private parlour was on the same floor, and was connected, via her small library and study, with the laboratory where she was working. She took a moment to remove her protective coat, wash her hands and smooth her hair, and then went through. Knollys was seated in an armchair, legs elegantly crossed, sipping at his sherry. He rose to his feet at once as she came in. She crossed the room and gave him her hand, saying, 'Francis, how charming of you to call. I thought you were at Windsor.'

Knollys, firm-featured, with dark, intelligent eyes – handsome still, though his hair and moustache were white now – kissed the hand she had offered with a pressure that denoted old affection. He smiled, but she could see he was in serious mood. 'I was,' he said. 'I came up to Town to see you. It's good of you to receive me. I'm afraid I've interrupted your work.'

She waved that away. 'Just some research, which has waited so long it can wait a little longer. Do sit down.' She poured herself a glass of sherry and sat opposite him. 'I gather from your expression that it's something important.'

'I've come to ask you a favour. It's a very large one, and it's damnable that I have to ask it, but I am my master's servant. I know you understand that.'

'You intrigue me. Out with it.'

Knollys sipped again, taking a moment to assemble his thoughts. 'How much do you know about the Russian situation?' he asked.

'I know we signed an alliance with them last year, and that the King worked hard for it. And that it isn't popular in certain quarters.'

'That, I fear, is an understatement. We needed the alliance to counterbalance Germany's pretensions, and naturally the Kaiser is furious about it. More importantly, the radicals in this country are outraged that we should be allying ourselves with—'

'"A blood-soaked tyranny" – yes, I saw the letters in *The Times*.'

'But Grey is determined that Russia should be re-established as a factor in European politics – and, of course, the King wants it.'

'Which is why he is paying a state visit to Russia next week.'

'You come most conveniently to the point,' Knollys said, with faint embarrassment.

Venetia's mind leaped ahead and she looked dismayed. 'Francis, no!'

Knollys ploughed on. 'The radicals were angry about the visit from the moment it was announced, but now rumours are flying round that its real purpose is to conclude a naval and military treaty. God knows where such rumours come from, but they have inflamed the radicals all over again. Ramsay MacDonald calls the visit "an insult to England", Keir Hardie talks about "consorting with murderers", Arthur Ponsonby says it "condones atrocities". The radical press is in a ferment, and the Opposition are calling a debate in the House on Thursday.'

'All the elements of a fine scandal. And so?'

'And so the King wants it made very plain that it is really nothing more than a family affair. A journey to see his niece and the Queen's nephew. They're taking Princess Victoria with them, and the King has asked me to invite you and Overton to join the party, and to bring young Hazelmere with you.'

Venetia looked her dismay. 'I am in the middle of my daughter's coming-out. I have plans from now until August. I can't possibly drop everything, cancel all our engagements, just like that.'

Knollys gave the faintest shrug. 'I hate having to ask you. But if the King wants it . . .'

'The subject has to obey? But why me? Why us? *Can't* you talk him out of it?'

'The Tsar knows you both; he regards Lord Overton in particular with affection. Your sister attended the Tsarina when she was at Windsor. Your father was well known in the Russian court. Lord Overton is a close friend of the King. As a story it holds together, and it will look much more like a family visit and less like a political one with you along, especially if your son accompanies you.'

'You could have Overton and Thomas with my blessing, but what am I to tell my daughter?'

33

'My dear Venetia, I know it is a dreadful thing to ask of you, and believe me, I have done all I can to put the objections to His Majesty. But he's determined on it, and of course he sees it as an honour to you as well as your duty. Lady Violet's Season doesn't weigh with him against the diplomatic considerations.'

'And you think it shouldn't weigh with me, either,' she concluded, and sighed. 'Well, I suppose I have no choice, but the poor girls will be so disappointed. And what on earth am I to do with them while we're away?'

'It will only be for ten days. You will still have the rest of the Season. And it will be a great opportunity for young Hazelmere to make his mark. Most young men in his position would give their eye-teeth for the chance to be noticed and make important connections.'

'You'll be going, of course?'

'Of course. And Fritz Ponsonby and my sister Charlotte.'

'Well, that's something, I suppose. At least there'll be someone intelligent to talk to. But, oh Francis, the nuisance of it!' she exclaimed in exasperation.

He finished his sherry and stood up. 'I had better not add insult to injury by taking up any more of your time. The *Victoria and Albert* sails on Saturday, from Portsmouth. I'll send you over a detailed itinerary later today. I'm sorry it's such short notice. Now I'll let you get back to your research.'

'I shan't have time for that now. I'll have to make arrangements, cancel engagements, dictate a thousand letters, and supervise the packing for a royal *and* imperial visit. That's a month's work to fit into five days. Goodbye, Francis. Please thank His Majesty for the signal honour he is bestowing on us.'

Knollys grinned suddenly. 'I knew you'd see it that way,' he said, taking his leave.

Chapter Two

On Saturday the 6th of June the royal yacht *Victoria and Albert* set out from Portsmouth for Reval, and Jessie and Violet, accompanied by Sanders, took the train from King's Cross to York. Though their disappointment at having to miss two weeks of their precious Season was acute, there was compensation for Jessie, at least, in a visit home. 'But poor you!' she said to Violet.

'No, it will be lovely to see Morland Place again. And actually to stay there, instead of in our house.' Her mother owned Shawes, whose boundary ran with that of Morland Place.

'Your house is grander,' Jessie said.

'No, it isn't. It's just a house. Morland Place is a *castle*.'

'"A fortified manor house of considerable antiquity",' Jessie said. 'That's what the old guidebooks say. From when we used to be open to the public.'

'Well, it's got a moat and a barbican and a portcullis, so that makes it a castle for me.'

'The portcullis doesn't work any more,' Jessie said, 'but you can call it a castle if you like. Oh, it will be so lovely to see Mother and Dad and everyone.'

'Will they be there at the station to meet us?'

'No, I'll bet you it will be Uncle Teddy. He loves trains, and he never misses the chance to meet someone off them.'

And so it proved. As the train came in round the curve of the magnificent station, there was Uncle Teddy standing four-square as if he owned the whole thing, splendid in top hat and frock-coat with a white rose in his buttonhole, a cigar to rival the King's in one hand and his gold hunter in the other to check the time of arrival. He was a director of the railway and such things mattered to him. Two captive porters stood patiently behind him, like courtiers to the monarch, and beside him—

'It's Polly!' Jessie cried, from her position half out of the window. 'He's brought Polly. Oh, the darling! Isn't she the prettiest thing, Vi?'

'I expect she is,' said good-natured Violet, who had no view but Jessie's back.

The train eased to a steamy, hissing stop. Uncle Teddy, without having moved, was right beside the door to their compartment. 'What luck!' Jessie said.

'No luck about it,' Teddy said. 'I simply telephoned King's Cross to find out which carriage you were in, and placed myself accordingly.'

'You are so clever!' Jessie cried, and he smiled, enjoying her reaction. His vanities were small and simple, and he loved pleasing people and arranging small surprises.

One of the porters darted forward to open the door, and Teddy helped the girls down, with a bear-hug and kiss for Jessie and a more formal salute for Violet, whom he tended to treat as though she were made of eggshell china.

Jessie was hugging Polly. 'How delicious you look! I thought I wasn't going to see you again until August, and here you are!'

'I was always here. Here *you* are,' said Polly logically. 'I'm so glad you've come back. It was *horrid* dull without you. You look pretty, too. I like your hat. How do you do, Cousin Violet?' she concluded properly, holding out her hand to shake.

'You don't have to call me cousin,' Violet said. 'And you can hug me too, if you will.'

'Turn around, Pol, let me see your outfit,' Jessie instructed, and Polly obediently twirled on the spot. She was wearing a sailor dress of white trimmed with blue with the traditional square yoke and a very full skirt, complete with a sailor hat with a blue pom-pom. Her golden hair fell in extravagant ringlets down her back, and her ensemble was completed by white buttoned boots with pointed toes. 'Don't you just look like an angel!' Jessie exclaimed. 'I especially love the boots.'

'So do I,' said Polly, with a satisfied glance downwards. She was eight years old, a late and only child of Uncle Teddy, who had given up hoping for children when she was announced. Her birth had cost her mother's life, which had made her even more precious to her father, who doted on her to such a degree that if she had not been naturally good-natured she would have been horribly spoilt.

The porters had finished getting down the baggage, and the party now turned towards the exit.

'I wish you had been here for my birthday, though,' Polly said. 'It was only last week. You could have come last week instead of now.'

'We didn't know we were coming at all,' Jessie said.

'Papa gave me a puppy. It's so sweet! I wanted to bring it to the station to show you but it's not weaned yet and, anyway, Papa said the trains would frighten it.'

'I should think they would! But we'll see it when we get home.'

Outside the station, in the favoured position right opposite the entrance reserved for railway directors, was Uncle Teddy's steam motor-car, a gleaming green and brass monster, with Simmons the chauffeur at the wheel. The luggage was stowed, the porters tipped, Teddy and the girls climbed in, Sanders got up in front with Simmons, and the motor glided away like a ship floating off on the current. Used now to London's motor-cabs, Jessie marvelled all over again at how silent and smooth a steam car was, and wondered that everyone did not have them. The road from the station had been tar-macadamed, as had Blossom Street and the Tadcaster road, so it was

37

dustless and a great improvement to drive upon. Jessie remembered the first time Uncle Teddy had brought a motor car to Morland Place – he had borrowed it from a friend – and had taken her father out on a trip. Both of them had had to cover up from head to toe in dust-coats, silk face-masks and goggles. Now they were all sitting quite unprotected, even with the hood down – though when they turned off the macadamed road on to the track, Simmons had to drive very slowly.

'I've been thinking about having our track tar-macadamed too,' Teddy remarked, 'but your mother thinks it would look horrid.'

'And feel horrid when we ride,' Jessie said.

'I suppose there is that,' Teddy said, disappointed.

When they came in sight of Morland Place at last, Jessie's heart gave a little tug, and for a few moments Polly's chatter faded into a background sound like the unheeded babble of a brook. She had only been away four weeks, but it was *home*, with all that that untrans-latable word implies. She had not been born there – they had moved there from London when her father had been made bankrupt, when she was five – but she barely remembered any other house. Even if she had, she did not think it would make her feel differently about Morland Place. There was something *about* it, the way it seemed to grow out of the ground, solid, permanent, welcoming. Her mother said that she felt that way because she was a Morland, and that all Morlands were joined to Morland Place by an invisible thread that would always tug at them. It made it sad, Jessie thought, that Morland women must always know they would one day have to leave and go and live in their husband's house. Of course, Mother had come back: when Dad had lost all his money, Uncle Teddy had offered it to them as a home. It had been standing empty then – Uncle Teddy had lived in the city – and Jessie just remembered it as it had been, dilapidated, part fire-damaged, full of dust and not much else. As well as no money, Mother and

Dad had had no furniture and no servants. It had been wonderful for Jessie and her brothers as small children to run and run about the empty rooms and up and down the staircases and corridors. She remembered how bitterly cold it had been in the winter, with only one fire lit – in the kitchen where they had mostly lived. She remembered how plain the food had been, and how often she had been hungry.

It was very different now. Uncle Teddy had moved there from the city after his wife had died, and brought his furniture and servants and money with him, so the house was now comfortable and warm and well tended, and Mother didn't have to cook and clean any more and Jessie could have had a lady's maid if she'd wanted one – Polly would have one when she grew up. It was much better all round as it was, of course, but in her memory that magically empty place lived on.

They turned off the track and rattled over the draw-bridge, sending a family of ducks scooting away down the moat in panic; passed under the cold, moss-smelling shadow of the barbican, and emerged into the warm, sunny courtyard. The great door stood open, and as soon as they stopped Mother came out on to the step – she must have been waiting for them in the hall, Jessie thought. The sight of her mother gave her the same sort of tug and upsurge of love as the sight of the house. She started down the steps towards them, smiling, and Dad appeared behind her, his dogs – Kithra and Fern – thrusting their muscular bodies past him to run up to the car, shoving their silent muzzles upwards, yellow eyes gleaming, their hard tails an ecstatic blur.

One of the stablemen came forward to open the door and hand Jessie down, and she ran the few steps into her mother's arms. 'Oh, Mama,' she said – something she hadn't called her since she was little.

Henrietta hugged her daughter close, but she heard the 'Mama', and said, 'What is it? Haven't you enjoyed your-self in London?'

Jessie straightened up, smiling. 'More than you can possibly imagine,' she said. 'But it's still good to be home.'

There was so much to do, and all at once. They had to greet Jessie's father, Jerome – a smiling, handsome man with laughing blue eyes, who lately had begun to affect Violet with a strange warm and shy feeling. Then there was Emma, who had been Jessie's nurse and was now Polly's, but more than that was just part of the family, for she had stayed with them in the difficult years when it had been doubtful if she would ever receive any more wages. The dogs were everywhere, whacking legs with their iron-bar tails, which could bruise even through the thickness of skirts, and Polly wanted them to visit her puppy in the barn and come at once to her room to see her other birthday presents.

Henrietta told her firmly that later would do and took the girls upstairs to their rooms so they could remove their smart travelling-suits and hats – 'I must say you both look very nice, and very grown-up. You look as much an expensive lady as Violet, Jess!' – and change into plain skirts and blouses. Then Jessie said she absolutely *had* to go and see her horse.

'I've missed him so much in London, though Cousin Venetia provided me with a *very* nice horse to ride; but it isn't the same as one's own darling – is it, Vi?'

And as Violet agreeably said that the first thing she wanted to do, too, was to see Hotspur, they went downstairs and out to the stable, gathering the whole crowd of people and dogs on the way. Jerome had thoughtfully brought Hotspur up to the yard stable in anticipation of his daughter's wishes, and the handsome gelding – bred by their own Arabian, Pasha, out of a thoroughbred mare – was looking over the half-door of his box when the multitude of admirers appeared. He whickered and bowed his head, and then much less elegantly banged the door with a forefoot to suggest that compliments were all very well but there should be sugar too.

And while this was going on everyone was asking questions and answering them, telling the news of home and London and asking after friends and relatives, and Polly was talking non-stop so that every pause became informed with segments of her sentences.

When Robbie, Jessie's middle brother, arrived home from York on his bicycle, having finished his half-day at the Union Bank, they all went in to have luncheon. He was a calm, placid young man of twenty, good-looking and lazy, without either Jack's energy and inventiveness or Frank's imagination and intellect. Jessie had once asked him what he did at the bank and he had seemed stumped for an answer. Jack said he just slept at his desk all day until one of the clerks woke him up and put him outside at the end of business. Bicycling home obviously gave him an appetite, however, for having greeted the girls and asked if they were enjoying their Season, he addressed himself to his plate with an air of having nothing more to say until the cheese came on.

The only person missing was Uncle Teddy's ward, Ned, who had a position at Meynell's paper mill at Layerthorpe and would not be home until the evening.

Through the soup and fish, Jessie and Violet took turns in telling what they did in London as young ladies enjoying their first Season. Polly was held rapt by the account of how they did not get up until noon most days, and either went out to luncheon at the homes of other girls, or lunched with Venetia and whatever guests she invited for them. In the afternoon, when they were not shopping or being fitted for clothes, they went riding in the Park, which distinguished them from the common run of débutantes who – to Jessie's surprise, for horses were a large part of her life at home – were not horsewomen. They visited the various exhibitions and daytime functions, the Royal Academy, the Lord's cricket match; once down to Oxford for the May Eights (Oliver and Eddie arranged a picnic party in Eddie rooms), and once to Windsor to watch polo. Then there was tea –

sometimes, when cousin Venetia was busy, at the House of Lords with Lord Overton, but more usually at the house of one of the hostesses, where they would meet the other girls and chat over the tea-cups and tiny cakes in a freer and more intimate way than they ever could when men were present. Then it was home to rest and dress for the evening's engagements: dinner, usually followed by a ball. Sometimes there was a visit to the theatre, a concert or ballet instead, but in general it was understood that the proper business of the débutante was dancing, and they undertook it with a will, rarely giving up until the band did.

'Well,' Teddy said, as the meat came on, 'I must say, it's hard on you girls – I beg your pardon, young ladies – to have your fun interrupted like this. But I suppose your papa, Violet, can't say "no" to the King. We must see if we can't arrange something for you while you're here. Not that it can compare, but we might have some little dance or what-not. There are plenty of nice young men in York, to say nothing of the officers at the cavalry barracks. And Robbie can bring some of his friends to dance with you – can't you, Rob?'

Robbie looked so blank that it made Jessie laugh. 'Well, there's Harris at the bank,' he said at last.

'The one with the pretty sister?' Jerome asked innocently.

Robbie looked confused for a moment, and then continued, 'And there's Joe Micklethwaite, I suppose, but Jessie's known him all her life, practically.'

'These smart young ladies won't want to dance with the Joe Micklethwaites,' Teddy said sternly. 'A nice chap but never has two words to say for himself. They're used to sophisticated Society fellows now.'

'Your uncle is assuming you want to dance, of course,' Jerome said. 'Perhaps you've given your hearts away already and have no more interest in the ballroom.'

'Oh, really, Dad!' Jessie protested.

'What does "oh, really" mean? Are you in love, Jess?

What's the paltry fellow's name? More importantly, has he made you an offer?'

'Don't tease,' Henrietta said, seeing Jessie's blush.

'Nobody's made me an offer,' she said.

'But she has lots of dancing partners,' Violet said loyally. 'She never sits out for a single dance.'

'Just as it should be,' Jerome said. 'This is the time of your life when you should be dancing with as many different men as possible and having lots of fun. I should hate you to tie yourselves up with the first man who addresses you. You're still very young.'

'I thought the point of coming out was to find a husband,' Jessie said, fixing him with a clear look. 'What did you send me to London for, otherwise? I can dance with people I *don't* want to marry just as well here.'

Jerome held up his hands. 'I think this is getting a little complicated. Let's change the subject. I expect you want to go out riding this afternoon, don't you, Jess? I had Hotspur taken out yesterday so he wouldn't be too fresh for you, and I've a nice little mare for Violet to try. Potter's bringing her up as we speak.'

'Oh, thank you, Dad! You'd like to ride, wouldn't you, Vi?'

'Make the most of this good weather,' Henrietta advised. 'It's lasted so long, I can't believe it won't break soon.'

'I hope not,' Jerome said. 'The hay is just about ready. I was going to start cutting next week.'

'Oh, goody!' Jessie said. 'Can I help? I love hay harvest.'

'You're too grown-up to grub about the way you used to, but I might be able to find you something to do that's not too undignified.'

'I don't mind about being dignified.'

'But think what this fellow you're in love with would say if he saw you grimed from head to foot and with hay in your hair,' Jerome said. Henrietta gave him a reproachful look and he hastened to say seriously, 'On your ride this afternoon, if you want to come round by

Twelvetrees you could look at the polo ponies. I've done a lot of work on those two bays you were schooling and I think they've come on very well.'

'And I must see darling Pasha,' Jessie said. 'I wonder if he remembers me? Oh, it'll be lovely to be around horses again. There aren't enough of them in London.'

'Horses are all very well,' Robbie said, between mouthfuls, 'but Cornwallis at the bank has something much more exciting.'

'Exciting?' Jerome said blankly. 'Is this my middle son talking?'

'It's a motor-bicycle,' Robbie said, looking as annoyed at the teasing as he ever managed to be, which was not very much.

'Like Harris's?' Jessie said. 'I didn't think that was very exciting. It made a terrible noise and it only went about five miles an hour. Hotspur could have beaten it at a trot.'

'No, no, not like that. Harris's was an old Singer Motor Wheel, practically out of the Ark. Cornwallis has a real motorcycle, a Triumph, the same sort that won at Brooklands. The modern ones have really powerful engines and go as fast as motor-cars.'

Henrietta shuddered. 'Why do you men always want to go everywhere faster? What are you going to do when you get there?'

'It's not the getting, but the going,' Jerome said. 'Women don't understand. Once we progressed beyond our own two legs, we always wanted to go faster. It's man's nature to excel. Setting a new record only challenges others to try to break it.'

'That's right,' said Teddy, for the honour of the sex. 'Now we have railway trains and motor cars, we will always be trying for greater speed.'

'And with engineering and technology expanding all the time, achieving it,' Jerome finished for him. 'What a wonder of an age we live in! And Jack tells me it will be powered flight next.'

44

'I think that's a long way off yet,' Teddy said. 'It's a flight of fancy at the moment. And talking of flights, I have decided I really must install a lift in Makepeace's.' This was the draper's shop in York which he had inherited and which had been expanding both sideways and upwards at a rapid rate in recent years, metamorphosing into a department store. He had opened a second Makepeace's in Leeds, which had been new-built on a vacant site and had every amenity, and was planning a third in Manchester; but the original in the crowded heart of York could only grow piecemeal.

'A lift, Teddy? How grand!' said Henrietta.

'I know it's only two storeys, but there are so many staircases now it's like a rabbit warren. And some of my customers are quite elderly. Besides, smart people expect a large store to have a lift these days.'

'Will it be a really grand one?' Polly urged. 'With a page in a uniform to run it? A uniform with lots of buttons?'

Teddy hadn't thought as far ahead as that, but he would deny his darling nothing. 'As grand as can be,' he said. 'Panelled inside and gilded gates and crimson carpet. Two of them, in fact, side by side, to cut down the waiting at busy times.'

'I think the uniform should be blue,' Polly said happily. 'Not dark blue like a policeman but—'

'Blue like your eyes,' her father concluded for her.

Jerome laughed. 'A new shade for the dressmakers – Polly Blue.'

'That's quite a thought,' Teddy said, taking him seriously. 'I must get them to work on that at the mill. Would you like a colour named after you, chick? And it needn't stop at that. Why shouldn't we have our own complete line of colours, sold only in our shops? It would be something to make people come to Makepeace's rather than anywhere else.'

'Everyone in York already comes to Makepeace's,' Henrietta pointed out. 'You have no rivals.'

'But we do in Leeds and we will have in Manchester. And if I open one in London there will be plenty of competition.'

'In London? Do you really mean to do it, then, Ted?' Henrietta said. It had long ago been mooted, but as a dream rather than an intention.

'It's the next logical step,' he said.

'Now see what you've started,' Jerome said to Polly.

She beamed. 'I should like to go to London, and if Papa had a shop there, well, I would,' she said, with a logic of her own.

Violet was not as dedicated to horses as Jessie, and on the following day, after church, when Jessie wanted to go riding, Violet said she would be happy just to stay at home and talk to everyone. Jessie was always surprised that anyone could waste any opportunity to be on horseback, and would have gone alone, but Ned offered to go with her, and she was glad of his company.

Ned was the illegitimate son of the late George Morland, the elder brother of Teddy and Henrietta. He had been born posthumously, and when he had been orphaned by the death of his mother, George's housekeeper, Teddy had first taken him in and then, despairing of children of his own, had adopted him. George had died otherwise childless, and Teddy had inherited the estate which in happier circumstances might have been Ned's, so there had been a general thought that Teddy might mean to make Ned his heir. The idea was strengthened by his paying to send Ned to Eton and then Oxford. But though the birth of Polly had not changed Teddy's affection for him, everyone privately believed that it must have changed Ned's prospects. This might have caused resentment in some young men, but Ned was unassuming, good-natured, and grateful for all that had been done for him – and since in fact he had never, even in pre-Polly days, thought he would have Morland Place, the 'loss' of it did not affect him.

To Jessie he was like an extra brother, and since her favourite, Jack, had left home, he had come to an extent to take his place as confidant.

'So, tell me, what's the most exciting thing that's happened to you in London?' he asked, when they had finished their first canter and were walking the horses side by side. He rode very well, and Jessie noticed his good seat and quiet hands with a sort of proprietary pride, remembering some of the horrors she had seen in Rotten Row, where many of the young men were all show and no substance.

'Oh, meeting the King, I think,' she answered. 'It must be that.'

It had been on the Thursday the week before, when they went to Ascot races for the Gold Cup. It was the day on which traditionally everyone dressed to a dizzy height of elegance and perfection, keeping the best of the week's outfits back for it, and 'everyone who was anyone' was there. The Overtons had a private box, agreeably near to the Royal Box, and though it was not properly a débutante's outing, Jessie and Violet both had new gowns and hats for the occasion, and were breathlessly excited as they strolled between the Royal Enclosure and the paddock and back, part of the illustrious crowd, the élite of Society.

The King was there, of course, beautifully dressed and very genial, seeming enormous to Jessie – 'Not fat, you know, but just bigger than everyone else, the way you'd think a king should be,' she told Ned. 'And beautifully *clean*.' With his white hair and beard and the fat cigar between his fingers he had looked just like his picture in the illustrated papers. But the pictures could not convey the *presence* of him, the aura of magnificence and kingship he carried about him like a golden aureole. 'A bit like Pasha, you know. You just *had* to look at him.'

He had stopped to speak to the Overtons, of course, and had some conversation with them about the forthcoming trip. He had looked kindly at Violet and she had curtseyed and he had said something agreeable to her. And then, though she had not been presented at Court, he had noticed Jessie.

'I thought I should die,' Jessie said. 'I was frightened out of my wits. He asked Cousin Venetia who I was and she said, "May I present," and I just managed to remember to curtsey, though I felt as though my brain was frozen solid, and my heart was stopped in my chest so I thought I was going to faint. But he was so nice, and he smiled, and looked just like an uncle – do you know?'

Ned nodded. 'I can imagine.'

'Only of course a terribly *grand* uncle. His eyes were so bright and blue – like Polly's but paler. He asked was it my first time at Ascot and I said, "Yes sir," and he said he hoped it wouldn't be my last and I said I hoped not, too, because the horses were so beautiful. And he said did I like horses and I said yes, and that my father bred them, and then Cousin Venetia said something about Morland Place and, do you know, the King *knew* it?'

'He knew Morland Place? Has he been here, then?'

'I don't know. I don't think so, but he said he had bought a very nice horse once from Uncle George a long time ago, and Cousin Venetia said that we didn't breed racehorses any more but army horses and polo ponies and the conversation changed from there and he didn't look at me again, which was a good thing because my legs had turned to jelly and if he'd gone on looking at me and talking to me I think I would really have fainted dead away.'

'I'm sure you wouldn't have,' Ned said, amused. 'Not our bold Jessie.'

'But you don't know how paralysing the King is,' Jessie assured him.

'So, are you in love, Jess?' Ned asked casually. Glancing sideways he noted her expression and said, 'I see you are. Do you want to tell me about it?'

So she told him about Brancaster. She hadn't really meant to tell anyone, but Ned was so nice and so sympathetic, and she wanted so badly to talk about it. There wasn't much to tell, only a few dances and pleasant conversations, but fresh in her mind was the incident at Ascot, which she now recounted. They were all standing near the paddock rails when Lord Brancaster appeared and, having made his bow to Venetia and Lord Overton, addressed himself to Jessie and Violet, saying how nice it was to see them there and mentioning the weather and so on. Violet soon excused herself from the conversation to talk to George Carrick, leaving him to Jessie, and he had said that he had noticed her speaking to the King.

'I didn't think you had been presented at Court,' he said.

Jessie wondered how he knew, but as he must know that the Overtons were close to the King, she explained instead that the King had once bought a horse from her uncle.

'Ah,' he said, 'so horses are in your blood, so to speak. Perhaps you'd give me your opinion for the next race.' He pointed out the horse he was proposing to back. 'Do you think it will win?'

'No,' Jessie said. 'Bad hocks, and too light in the shoulder.'

Brancaster had been amazed at this reply, and after a moment he had laughed and said, 'You are an original, Miss Compton! I've never met a débutante like you.'

'Then he quizzed me about the rest of the horses in the paddock,' Jessie told Ned, 'and asked me which one I thought would win, and why; and then we talked a bit about Morland Place and I told him about the polo ponies I was helping Dad to school, and he seemed very interested. And he said, '"You are really a country person, aren't you? Do you find living in Town tiresome?" So I said no, that I was enjoying it, but that I couldn't imagine living permanently in Town, and there was more to do in the country. And he said, "You interest me. Your opinions are all so decided for a young woman."'

She looked appealingly at Ned for comment on this remarkable piece of conversation, but he only said, 'Go on.'

'Then he asked me whether Vi felt the same way about living in the country, and I said I thought she felt exactly the same but the other way round, so to speak. Then we had to go back to the enclosure for the next race, and Cousin Venetia asked him if he would like to join us in our box for luncheon, and he said he would, and he bowed and went away. Anyway, when lunch came he came to the box, and almost the first thing he said was to thank me for recommending the horse for that race because it had come in first and he had won a hundred pounds on it.'

'A hundred?' Ned exclaimed. 'He must have put a large stake on to win so much. Or was it an outsider?'

'Oh, I don't know,' Jessie said impatiently. 'But listen.'

She went on. In the box the Overtons and their various guests – they were twelve at the table – lunched on lobster and salmon mayonnaise and strawberries and cream and champagne, and Brancaster had been seated between Jessie and Violet and made himself agreeable to them both; though Violet never seemed to have much to say in his company, so it was Jessie who had most of the conversation. Towards the end of luncheon, Jessie had mentioned that her stay in London was to be interrupted, and that when the Overtons went off to Reval, she would have to go home to Yorkshire.

'I'm very sorry to hear it,' Brancaster had said. 'I hope you will not miss the whole of the rest of the Season?'

No, Jessie had replied, she would stay down for two weeks and then would be able to come back to London.

'And does Lady Violet go with you?' he had asked. And then he had said, 'I may be away myself. My father has been asking me to take care of some business for him, and if I am to go out of London it might as well be next week.' And then he had asked if Lady Violet had any particular young man who would regret her absence, but

50

in the middle of Jessie's listing Violet's more prominent partners, Cousin Venetia had stood up and all conversation came to an end.

Her narrative finished, Jessie was silent. The horses walked on, tossing their heads against the flies. Their bit-rings jingled, and Ned's mare, Compass Rose, who was an inveterate mouther of the bit, spattered both riders lightly with foam.

'So this fellow, Brancaster is making up to you, is he?' Ned asked at last.

Jessie concentrated hard on her hands. 'I rather thought you might be able to tell me. You're a man—'

'Yes, I am, aren't I?' Ned said blandly.

She looked at him. 'Don't tease. I'm serious. Do you think it meant anything, what he said? Saying he was sorry I was going, and then that he might as well go away himself?' Ned, who was feeling a murderous rage towards the unknown nobleman, who to his mind was clearly toying with Jessie for his own amusement, was silent, and Jessie went on in a small voice, 'I try not to think too hard that he means anything, but it did seem rather – particular. Don't you think?'

'Well, I wasn't there, so it's hard for me to guess what he might mean. It may *sound* particular but, you know, Jess, men often say complimentary things just to be polite.'

'Do you?'

'Never,' he said. 'But I'm not a Society smart, and I'm not an earl.'

'Nor is he, yet.'

'Oh, Jess, do be careful.'

Jessie's lip trembled briefly before she caught it under control. 'So you think he *doesn't* love me?'

Ned couldn't bear to take anything away from her, even the hope of what seemed to him a hopeless passion. But he was afraid that she was going to be hurt. He said gently, 'I don't think it's likely. Do you?'

She didn't answer at once. Then at last she said, 'You'll keep what I've said secret?'

'Of course, if you want me to. You can trust me.'

'Yes, I know.' Another silence, and then she said, 'I've tried not to fall in love with him, I've tried to be sensible, but I don't know how you stop when it just happens. I don't suppose you understand.'

If she had looked at Ned at that moment she might have seen how well he understood, but by the time she looked up at him again, he was staring peacefully at the horizon.

'Let's canter again,' he said.

The royal yacht anchored off Reval on the Tuesday morning, the 9th of June. It was a beautiful day: bright, hot sunshine falling from a crystal sky, the gently rocking sea reflecting its deep colour and dazzling with diamonds. Across the water, at anchor, was the Russian Royal Yacht, the *Standart*, and already a pinnace was heading from her towards the *Victoria and Albert*, flying the imperial standard. Fritz Ponsonby, standing beside Venetia on the afterdeck, said, 'Well, now, that is pleasant! Protocol requires the King to pay the first visit, but the Tsar is evidently dispensing with that in compliment to his aunt and uncle.'

'He did seem very fond of them, if one may judge from the one occasion I witnessed,' Venetia said.

There were many connections between the British and Russian royal families. The most pertinent was that the Tsar's mother was Queen Alexandra's only and beloved sister: the Queen and the Dowager Empress were still so close that they holidayed together in Denmark every August, when the King was taking the cure at Marienbad. Secondly, the Tsarina was the former Princess Alix of Hesse, child of Queen Victoria's daughter Alice: not only a niece of the King, but one who had spent a great deal of her childhood at Windsor, and who had been a great favourite of her grandmama. Furthermore, one of the Tsarina's sisters, Princess Elizabeth, had married the Tsar's uncle Serge; and the King's brother Prince Alfred had married the Tsar's aunt Marie. It should not have been difficult for anyone to believe that this was a family visit, with so many connections. Venetia wondered again, rebelliously, if the Overton presence was really necessary.

The imperial party came on board, and there were warm and affectionate greetings all round. The Tsar was wearing the uniform of a Russian admiral, and Venetia saw the King's eyes running over it with his usual keen interest. The examination concluded with a minute nod, so she presumed the Tsar had managed to get all the details rights. The King, in compliment to his nephew, was wearing the uniform of the Kiev Dragoons. The Tsar was popularly claimed to be the spitten image of the Prince of Wales, but to Venetia's eye the resemblance lay solely in that they wore the same beard and moustache: underneath it their features were quite different.

The Tsarina was in her mid-thirties, but though still beautiful, she seemed to have aged a great deal in recent years, and beside the Queen, who was in her sixties, she looked the older of the two. It was a peculiar sensation to look at them together: never had Venetia more keenly appreciated the Queen's uncanny unchanging youthfulness. The Tsar was all genial smiles, but the Tsarina seemed distant and cold. Venetia had been told that this was only her dreadful, paralysing shyness; but still, she thought, after so many years of public life she might have learned to dissemble a little more.

The imperial children had accompanied their parents, and they were a sheer delight. The four grand duchesses were as pretty and gentle as a basket of kittens. They were all in white muslin with blue sashes, their long hair in ringlets of varying shades of golden brown, and they had delightful, smiling, unassuming manners. The little Tsarevich was a beautiful boy with dark blue eyes, dressed in a white sailor suit and Russian sailor hat with the red pom-pom. The eldest girl, Olga, was thirteen; the boy, whose hand she held fast the whole time, as if to stop him running off, was four.

The Tsar asked for the King's suite to be presented to

him, and then he invited everyone to come back to the *Standart*. Protocol, Venetia reflected, as she took her turn at stepping down into the pinnace, required some time-consuming activities, like this double journey by small boat. It was fortunate that the sea was calm and there was virtually no wind.

Aboard the *Standart* there was a guard of honour drawn up, which came to attention in a crashing salute as the King arrived on deck. Ever the master of form, he greeted them with the traditional Russian 'Good morning, my children,' and they replied with a roar of 'God save the King!' though because of their accents Venetia would not have understood it if Fritz had not told her what they were saying. The Tsar then escorted them to the after-deck where a band struck up, and liveried servants appeared with silver platters of caviar sandwiches. Venetia thought with amusement that they tasted like a saltier version of the fish-paste sandwiches that had sometimes been served in her nursery at tea-time: one had to know that caviar was fabulously expensive to appreciate it. More servants offered them small glasses of a clear liquor which she expected to be vodka but which turned out to be kirsch.

As the group stood chatting and listening to the band, the Tsar and Tsarina made the polite rounds, finding something to say to everyone. When he reached them, the Tsar greeted Overton warmly as a friend, and declared himself happy to see Venetia again. 'It was at Buckingham Palace that I met you last,' he said. 'I am delighted to see that you have not changed in the least since then. This surely cannot be your son – this tall young man? The uniform of the Blues, is it not? Very becoming. I remember, ma'am, when we last met, I complained to you of having to wear Windsor uniform,' he added. 'I have a much wider choice now, I am glad to say.'

It had been many years since that meeting, and Venetia was surprised at the minute detail of his memory. Thomas, unexpectedly, seemed overwhelmed by the notice of the ruler of half the world, but after a little application of the Tsar's professional charm, he entered into a lively description of a play he had seen recently.

'Ah, the theatre in London!' the Tsar said. 'I enjoyed it so much. How I envy you! But you haven't our ballet. You must come to Petersburg and see it.'

Thomas, flattered, stammered that he would love to.

When the Tsarina reached them on her separate circuit, Venetia saw close up that she was both tired and nervous, and her face seemed drawn, as if she had lately been either ill or very unhappy. To begin with she seemed at a loss for something so say, but then, with a visible effort, pulled herself together and said, 'Lady Overton. Yes, I had the pleasure of knowing your sister. How is she?'

'Very well, thank you, ma'am.'

She seemed to warm a little as memory came back. 'She was very kind to me. It was at Windsor, in the year I became engaged to my dear husband, and she listened most patiently to all my foolish babblings. I have the warmest memories of her.'

'I'm sure she was honoured to be of service to Your Majesty,' Venetia said.

The Tsarina's large, sad eyes moved to Thomas's face. 'And is this your son? Oh, how lucky you are! Have you other children?'

'Another son, and a daughter. My daughter had her début last month.'

'That is a pleasure still to come for me,' she said. 'The Emperor sometimes says that if he were a private man he would be ruined, having to find dowries for four daughters.'

'They are lovely and charming girls, Your Majesty,' Venetia said, injecting as much warmth as she could into her voice, since the Tsarina was so obviously trying hard to be conversable. 'They must be a great joy and comfort to you.'

'Comfort, yes.' The Tsarina's eyes became remote again. 'I try to give them as happy and ordinary a home life as possible. I was so happy as a child. They ought to have that, at least, don't you think? Everyone ought to have a happy childhood.'

The unhappiness just below the words was so palpable to Venetia that she hardly knew what to say. It made her want to shiver, as though in a warm and brightly lit room she had passed the open door to a cold, dark cellar. On this sunny deck under the clear sky, with the background of a cheerful band and pleasant chatter, the pretty ship, the bunting, the rocking blue sea, this woman seemed to stand apart, locked in a trouble all her own, from which she stared out unseeingly like a prisoner through bars. Venetia had a strange sense of foreboding: the Tsarina seemed for a moment limned in a doomed light; the very sunshine seemed to cool.

But Court habit made her mouth some acceptable, commonplace answer, and the moment passed as the Tsarina, in an ordinary voice like an ordinary mother, said, 'Do you dread your daughter's getting married? It is what every mother hopes and plans for, and yet to think of them going away, perhaps not to see them again for years and years – it is very hard.'

'It must be different for Your Majesty,' Venetia said. 'Your daughters, I suppose, must marry kings. Mine, I hope, will marry someone who will not take her very many miles away.'

'Yes, of course,' she said. 'It is the fate of princesses. But if they have husbands as kind and loving as mine, I shall be content for them.' She smiled as she said it, and her face was transformed. She looked for that moment the beautiful princess she had been. It was plain that she really did love her husband.

Soon the reception was over and the royal party was once more descending into the pinnace for the journey back. Francis Knollys, standing beside Venetia, said, 'State banquet aboard the *Standart* this evening. We shall know this stretch of water tolerably well by the time we reach our beds tonight.'

'Thank heaven the weather is calm,' Venetia murmured. 'It wouldn't do to arrive at a banquet feeling seasick. What will we be given to eat, Francis? Russian food or English?'

'Oh, I think you will recognise most dishes,' Knollys said. 'And champagne is champagne the world over. What did you think of the kirsch?'

'It didn't seem to me to have much taste.'

'Fritz said it tasted like boot polish to him. But at least it served to take away the taste of those vile fish sandwiches!'

Once back aboard the *Victoria and Albert*, there was no time for anything but to dress.

'Thomas is so lucky,' Venetia said, as she and Overton went to their cabin. 'He only has to be sure his uniform is put on correctly. No other decisions to make. He can wear the same thing every night and never have an eyebrow raised at him. And you only have to put on your black and white. It is very hard to be a woman.'

Overton grinned. 'Poor darling! And you've always hated clothes, haven't you? But I love to see you dressed up. You're still the most beautiful woman in the world to me.'

'Hmph!' Venetia said. 'I'm fifty-eight and as gaunt as a winter crow. It must be my beautiful character you are thinking of.'

They were inside their cabin now, and alone for a moment. He took her in his arms. 'Everything about you is beautiful,' he said. 'Your eyes – your face – your mouth—' He kissed each as he mentioned it, and the last kiss lengthened as she responded to him with the great love that seemed only to grow as the years passed. 'Not gaunt at all,' he murmured, his lips moving to her neck. 'Just slender as a young girl.'

That made her laugh. 'Oh, Beauty!' It was her old pet name for him, from when he was a lieutenant in the Blues, the age that Thomas was now. 'You are absurd!'

'No, just in love,' he said. The door behind them began

57

to open and they had to draw apart. 'Damn,' he said, under his breath. 'Why is it that whenever one starts to make love to one's own wife . . .?'

Her maid and his man appeared with the full gravity of an imperial banquet in their eyes.

Venetia looked at her husband tenderly as he allowed himself to be led meekly away to the dressing-room. 'We can continue this conversation later,' she said, and was rewarded by the corner of a smirk on his disappearing mouth.

The grand saloon on the *Standart* was everything that rich panelling, thick carpets and glittering chandeliers could make it, and without the very slight rocking motion underfoot there was nothing to betray that one was in a ship. Venetia was wearing the best evening gown she had that the King had never yet seen, which she had been saving for an expected invitation to Sandringham. It was of a soft, mauve-blue silk crêpe-de-Chine, in the latest high-waisted 'Empire' revival style. It was so close-fitting over the hips that in spite of her natural slenderness she had to wear one of the new corsets, which were boned from below the bust almost to mid-thigh, and instead of drawers, cambric knickers which gave a smoother line over the hips. The gown had deep inverted pleats at the back to give the fullness which swept down to a demi-train; the bodice was draped and trimmed with braid of silver-gilt thread embroidery on net, edged with the fashionable ball fringe. Evening sleeves were being worn long that year, of which Venetia was glad, feeling that a woman's upper arms were not her best feature once she had passed fifty. The sleeves of her gown were of an almost transparent blue silk, ruched and gathered on to the white silk undersleeve, ending in cuffs of the same braid.

And for an Imperial State Banquet, of course, jewels were *de rigueur*. Venetia wore the tiara she had inherited from her mother, a very pretty piece (which also happily solved any question of how to dress the hair), and a sapphire necklace, also her mother's, together with matching diamond and sapphire earrings and bracelet, which were a present from Overton, bought for her in Coronation year when he had received his earldom. When they had gathered on the *Victoria and Albert* beforehand, she had noted the King's quick, comprehensive inspection of her appearance, and her relief that she apparently passed muster made her feel a surge of affection for him. It might make one anxious beforehand, to know one would be inspected, but at least when it was over one could be sure that one was perfectly appropriately dressed for the occasion.

The dinner was, as such things are, a long succession of dishes, all elaborate and no better than lukewarm, for gold plates always seemed to suck the heat out of food. The Russian suite included the Prime Minister, Peter Arkadyevich Stolypin; the ambassador, Count Benckendorff; and the Foreign Secretary, Baron Alexander Isvolsky. Isvolsky was the principal architect of the entente with Britain: he and the King had met at a royal wedding in Denmark and had taken an instant liking to each other, which had started the whole thing off. Venetia got Benckendorff as a dinner partner, which ensured a pleasant evening for her, since he was witty and amusing. In the course of conversation he asked her about her experiences in Berlin during the Franco-Prussian war.

'However did you know about that?' Venetia asked in astonishment. 'I can't imagine how long ago that was. I was just a girl.'

'It is an ambassador's business to know everything,' he replied. 'Or, at least, everything about those with whom he finds himself in company. You formed part of the Crown Princess's nursing corps, I believe?'

'Yes. Princess Victoria was so very kind to me – a lovely and intelligent lady.'

'It is the greatest possible pity that the Crown Prince

died so untimely,' Benckendorff said. 'Perhaps the influences on the present Kaiser might have been mitigated if his father had lived longer.'

Venetia eyed him with interest. 'Do you think the Kaiser mad?' she asked bluntly.

'Not yet, but he soon will be. However, that is not for general consumption, but for your ears only. It would not do for someone in my position to suggest that power corrupts.' He twinkled at her, and she smiled at his calculated indiscretion. 'The Kaiser believes he is being "encircled" by France and England, and now Russia – though what else he could expect when he alienates his neighbours and allies himself with Austria, our chief rival, one cannot imagine. But he will never believe that this present meeting is not a political one.'

Venetia said, 'Overton and I are here specifically to prove that it is a family reunion,' she said.

'Indeed,' said Benckendorff. 'But the Kaiser is one of those who, once a bee is in his bonnet, will resist all efforts to dislodge it. He suspects a secret agreement between the emperor and the King, and therefore such an agreement there must be, persuade him otherwise how you will.'

'Then I might just as well have stayed at home,' Venetia said ruefully.

'I am very glad you did not,' Benckendorff said gallantly.

'Thank you,' Venetia said, a little absently, for she was thinking of other things. 'You know, it is the common opinion in our country that the Kaiser is a friend to Britain, and whatever passing annoyance he feels over this or that action, he will never behave aggressively towards the country of his grandmother and his uncle.'

'Germany has immense military power, and increasing naval power. Sooner or later, he is going to want to use it. What child could bear to have a fascinating toy, and leave it for ever in its box?'

'The Kaiser is not a child.'

'I wonder,' said Benckendorff gravely, 'whether you think that makes him more, or less, dangerous?'

The rest of the visit was surprisingly pleasant to Venetia, who had not expected to enjoy it. It was restful to be on board one or other of the yachts, too far from home to worry about what was happening there, and with no decisions to make but what to wear. The weather remained benign; the Tsar and the King were both happy, genial and at ease, and had the knack of making those around them feel the same.

The King had long interviews with Stolypin, who was impressed with the range of his knowledge and his grasp of Russian affairs, from agriculture, railways and banking to foreign relations and internal politics. He said afterwards to Venetia that he was 'fascinated' by His Majesty and that '*On voit bien qu'il est le premier homme d'état de l'Europe.*' The King's meeting with Isvolsky was that of old friends, and Benckendorff told Venetia at dinner on the second evening that it was entirely the King's doing that the atmosphere of Russian feeling towards England had changed from suspicion to cordial trust.

On that second day the King made the Tsar an Admiral of the Fleet; a compliment which so surprised and pleased the Tsar that at dinner that night on board the *Victoria and Albert* he returned it by making the King an Admiral of the Russian Navy. Admiral Fisher, one of the English suite, who was sitting by Venetia on that occasion, whispered to her that it was a very honorary honour, since the entire Russian fleet, bar one cruiser, had been sunk by the Japanese in the recent war and now lay at the bottom of the Pacific Ocean.

Admiral Fisher seemed to be enjoying himself very much, and showed an unexpected turn for clowning which kept the company amused. One evening he told the band to play the waltz from *The Merry Widow*, and danced to it with Grand Duchess Olga with his hands behind his head in imitation of the Russian manner. 'How about Siberia for me?' he asked her loudly, over the music. The King told him he must remember he was no longer a midshipman, but even the sad Tsarina smiled at his foolish antics. On another occasion he danced a horn-pipe, which caused a storm of applause and successive demands for encores until he was too exhausted to go on.

One morning Venetia was taking the air alone on deck, enjoying the quiet after the previous evening's festivities, when Francis Knollys appeared by her side, leaning on the rail like her and staring down at the water. They were silent for a while, as old friends may be, and then Venetia said, 'It all seems to be going well, don't you think? Even the weather is holding.'

'Hm. There are stormclouds at home, however,' Knollys said. 'Asquith is furious that the King made the Emperor Admiral of the Fleet without consulting Parliament.'

'I thought it was done on the spur of the moment,' Venetia said.

'So it was, but that's not an excuse that would recommend itself to Asquith. He even plans his sneezes several weeks ahead.'

Venetia smiled. 'Absurd! However did he come to marry Margot Tennant, do you suppose? She's pure quick-silver. I can't imagine him proposing to her.'

'Perhaps she asked him.'

'I can imagine that more easily. Is it true you once proposed to her, Francis?'

'She says that I did, and it would be ungentlemanly for me to contradict her.' He glanced sideways at her. 'She says that when she refused me, my expression was one of pure relief. I would certainly not contradict that part of the story.'

'Yes, I can't see you being happy with her. But, then, I'm not sure who would be – except that Asquith seems content enough, for all that one can tell.'

'My expression was not one of relief when you turned me down, Venetia my dear,' Knollys said.

She raised her eyebrows. 'I never did! I mean, you never asked me.'

'Have you really forgotten? On the day after your sister's coming-out ball, when I called on you at Southport House?' Venetia continued to look blank, and he smiled ruefully. 'There was quite a crowd there, but I hoped you might have remembered.'

'Oh Francis, you didn't really propose, did you? Oh, my dear!'

'Well, you were far above me then, a duke's daughter. It was sheer impertinence on my part. You were rather fond of Cocky Lansdowne, as I remember.'

'I was never serious about Cocky.'

'I don't think you were serious about any young man. We were all rather afraid of you.'

'Nonsense!'

'Your intellect, you know – it had us all in quakes. And you had a way of delivering the most cutting remarks, with a smile by way of anaesthetic. One could see even then you were destined to become a surgeon.'

She laughed. 'Now I know you are teasing.'

'Am I? I wonder why you think I remained single all those years. No, don't answer that. I'm glad you were persuaded to come along on this trip, for my own sake, though I'm afraid it will not have answered, as far as the official reason is concerned. The Kaiser is never going to believe it was a family visit, now HM has made the Tsar an admiral. He'll be bound to think there's a secret military agreement being made, especially as we have Fisher with us.'

'But the Kaiser can hardly believe there's a naval pact being forged,' Venetia said, 'when the Russian navy is down to one ship.'

'You underestimate the Kaiser's ability. He believes three impossible things before breakfast every day,' said Knollys.

Though the trip was not unenjoyable, Venetia could not help feeling a little annoyed, as they cruised homewards, that her time had been wasted and that she had been snatched from the important business of bringing out her daughter for no good purpose. One afternoon, as tea was being served on the afterdeck, the King strolled over to her, where she stood at the taffrail watching the wake.

'A good game last night,' he said by way of opening. 'The cards were not kind to you, Lady Overton, but you put up a spirited defence. How do you find Fisher as a partner?'

'As good as any partner could be against such a run, sir,' Venetia said.

'Your husband had all the luck at the other table.'

'Husbands and wives should never play together,' she said. 'It causes strife.' She was glad that the King had had lucky cards, for he was not a very skilled player, and he didn't like to lose. When the rubbers went against him he would begin to scowl and drum his fingers. She did not care much for bridge in any case, but playing against someone who needed to win was a strain on the nerves.

'Have you enjoyed yourself these ten days?' the King asked her, and while she was assembling an answer, a little unnerved by his keen blue gaze, he went on, 'I am aware that it was not convenient for you to come. You must not think I do not know what you gave up, or that I am not appreciative. And as well as the inconvenience to you there was the disappointment to your daughter – and the other young lady, Miss Compton, wasn't it? Your ward, is she?'

'No, sir – just the daughter of a cousin. Her mother and I are old friends, and we hoped from the time they were born that our daughters would be friends too.'

'Just so, just so. Girls who come out together, eh? Well, I have done them a great injury in interrupting their first Season. I hope they will find it in their hearts to forgive me.'

'There can be no question, sir.'

'Do you think not? But I must not show myself ungrateful. Perhaps you will give them these. Here – just a trifle, token of my appreciation of their sacrifice. Do you think they'll like 'em? Think they'll go down all right?'

He drew from his pocket two small boxes and handed them to Venetia. She opened them, and found each contained a small diamond brooch in the shape of a basket of flowers.

'Pretty, eh? Do you think they're pretty?' he asked anxiously.

'Quite beautiful, sir. The girls will be overwhelmed. You are very kind.'

'Oh, not at all. It's nothing at all,' he said, looking pleased. He turned the conversation then, to prevent her thanking him any more. Later, Venetia reflected that he must have brought them with him, since there was nowhere he could have obtained them once he was on the yacht. He loved to surprise people and to give them presents, and sometimes, she thought, a surprise took quite a lot of planning in advance.

Chapter Three

The preparations for Women's Sunday had been occupying those at the centre of the WSPU for four months. At their headquarters at Clement's Inn two extra rooms were opened up, extra help was taken on, and five thousand pounds was set aside for advertising. Posters were pasted onto hoardings all over the country, depicting in life-size the twenty women chairmen of the rally. Handbills were circulated with the details of the seven processions that were to converge on the park, beginning from Euston Road, Paddington station, Marylebone Road, Kensington High Street, Albert Bridge, Victoria Embankment and Trafalgar Square. Thirty excursion trains were to be laid on to bring parties in from the provinces, and a quarter of a million mock train tickets were printed and distributed as advertisements to encourage people to make use of them. Seven hundred banners were made at various locations to be carried in the processions, each eight feet by three and attached to two six-foot poles. Thousands of flags were made up, to be carried by the marchers and distributed to the crowds.

Anne Farraline was very much involved. Along with other luminaries such as Mrs Pethick-Lawrence and the Pankhurst sisters – Christabel, Sylvia and Adela – she was to have her own platform, and was responsible for keeping it manned throughout the afternoon. Twenty such platforms would need eighty women to speak and there were not so many orators in the organisation. Sylvia undertook to train more speakers, and Anne asked Lizzie to be one of them.

Lizzie was already engaged in the preparations. As one of the society's typewriters, she was busy at Clement's Inn every day, typing letters, answering the telephone, dealing with printers, dispatching messengers and doing her best to think up new ideas for advertising the event. Her husband, Ashley, had to call on large reserves of his patience as his wife could talk about little else when he came home from the office, and their telephone rang several times an evening with calls that were not for him. Her half-brother Frank, who was lodging with them while he was at university, was happy to be engulfed by the WSPU, and went out daily with Harry Pankhurst to chalk pavements and stick up fly-posters. He recruited other students at University College, and the Ashley Morland drawing-room in Endsleigh Gardens frequently resembled a meeting-hall as four or five large cheerful young men gathered with Lizzie around a table to discuss tactics. The house was just around the corner from the college, and Ashley often suspected that it was the prospect of exchanging Spartan lodgings for its comforts for an evening that inspired Frank's friends, rather than a burning desire to see women enfranchised. His suspicion was enhanced by the fact that Lizzie, who with two sons of her own knew how hungry boys always were, made sure the meetings were always attended by lavish refreshments.

For a long time Lizzie had spent a few hours twice or three times a week at Clement's Inn, but as Women's Sunday drew nearer it became six hours every day, plus the evening activities. Ashley was driven to complain mildly one day at breakfast that he wished she was as solicitous of his well-being as that of the students, for his dinner the night before had consisted of cold soup, cold meat, and the remains of a blancmange from Sunday.

'Oh, dearest, I'm sorry,' Lizzie said. 'I forgot it was Cook's day off and I hadn't told Aggie what to prepare.'

'That's all very well, but you know you promised the society would not interfere with your duties at home. What would you think if I allowed some outside interest to prevent me from going to the office, so that I had no money to bring home at the end of the week?'

Lizzie jumped up impulsively and ran round the table to kiss him. 'I'm so sorry! I promise I will do better in future. You are the most understanding man in creation, but this will all be over soon.'

He patted her arm, sending her back to her seat, and said, 'I don't begrudge you your campaign. But do try to remember you have a household to run as well. It is very hard for a man to come home from a long day at work and not find the comfort he has been used to and has looked forward to all day.'

Lizzie said, 'Yes, I know. I'm sorry,' and remembered that she hadn't yet checked the laundry which had come back the day before, and that there were buttons off a multitude of shirts, including two of Ashley's. Why were men – and boys – so hard on buttons? There was no need for her to sew them on herself. Ashley had always told her she could have more help if she wanted it, but in normal times she didn't need more help and was quite happy to do a little sewing in the afternoons or evenings. It gave her pleasure to sew on a button for Ashley and know herself to have been material to his comfort in that small way. It was just that at the present time there was so much to do for the Cause, and when anyone – particularly Anne – asked her to do something extra, she found it difficult to refuse on the grounds that there were buttons to be sewn on or asparagus to be purchased for dinner. They did not exactly *say* that they regarded such tasks as beneath the educated woman, but she always felt they thought it, which was just as bad. She had better see about engaging a sewing-maid, at least until the present rush was over. If she found herself with time on her hands, she could always get rid of her again – though probably she would only have to wait for the girl to leave. London servants were notorious for their impermanence. They moved from place to place with the restless improvidence of gypsies, and it was rare for one to finish her six months. It was a wonder she had kept their present cook so long. She was a good cook, and Lizzie had felt obliged to bribe her with a whole day off per week instead of a half, but she was afraid even that would not hold her much longer.

So when Anne asked her to be a speaker, she said no, very decidedly. 'I really can't take on any more, Anne dear. I've already had to refuse Mrs Drummond when she asked me to be a railway-station steward on the day, and with "crusade fortnight" coming up I shall be as busy as I can be. You must remember I have a home and family to take care of.'

Anne gave her a cool smile. 'Yes, with a husband at his office all day, children at school all day, and a flock of servants to do any work that needs doing, your home and family must be a great drain on your time and resources.'

'There are things I have to do myself, and servants still need to be supervised,' Lizzie said, hurt. 'You don't seem to want to understand.'

Anne relented. 'I'm sorry. That was very wrong of me. Forgive me, Lizzie dear. Sometimes I am so involved that my tongue runs away with me. I do so want this to be a success.'

'I do too. But we must each do what we can, you know. Besides, I'm quite sure I couldn't be a speaker. I'd never know what to say if anyone heckled me, and my voice is too soft to carry.'

'Oh, Sylvia would have brought you up to the mark. But if you can't, you can't.'

One of Emmeline Pethick-Lawrence's ideas was for official Suffragette colours to be designated, and for all the marchers and speakers to use them. After long discussion (everything women undertook, Lizzie thought, seemed to involve long discussion) the colours decided on were purple for dignity, white for purity and green for hope. This gave a wide new field for advertisement and

Lizzie was made busy ordering sashes in the colours for the speakers and marshals, and favours in the colours to be sold to onlookers and marchers. But enterprising traders and manufacturers, given the hint, developed a wide range of goods, such as hats and babies' bonnets, motoring scarves, dolls and china mugs, matchboxes and playing-cards, even iced gingerbreads, all striped with the three colours and emblazoned with 'VOTES FOR WOMEN'. A manufacturer of uniforms presented Mrs Drummond, who was to be chief marshal on the ground, with a peaked cap and epaulettes in the colours and a tricolour sash lettered with the word 'GENERAL', which soon became her nickname.

The last two weeks before the day, dubbed 'crusade fortnight', saw an intensification of effort. WSPU canvassers visited shops, hospitals, factories, even restaurants, calling on women to join the demonstration, to bring their friends and families and to wear the colours. Others stood in railway stations handing out the mock tickets. Every evening bands of cyclists rode out to the suburbs on decorated and illuminated bicycles to distribute handbills. Pavement chalkers renewed their advertisements as fast as they were obliterated and the fly-posters papered the walls, especially in areas around factories and workshops. In variety theatres the cinematographic advertisements featured scenes from the campaign and invited the audience to join them. Frank recruited ever more friends to canvass around the colleges and medical schools to persuade students to turn out on the day. And three days before Women's Sunday, Flora Drummond hired a steam launch and a brass band, and she and Anne took it up the Thames and moored opposite the terrace of the House of Commons. While the band played to attract the MPs' attention, Flora and Anne unfurled between them a banner on which were the words: 'Women's Sunday – June 21st – CABINET MINISTERS SPECIALLY INVITED'. Soon men were pouring out of the House onto the terrace to see what was going on – MPs, officials and various House

70

servants – and first Anne and then Flora Drummond addressed them through a megaphone. Most of the men seemed to be amused, though whether it was supportive laughter or derisive it was impossible to tell from a distance. But before Mrs Drummond had finished her speech the river police appeared and the launch was chased away down the river.

For a wonder, Sunday the 21st of June turned out to be a brilliantly sunny day of the clear, limpid kind, and the sky that hung over the green grass and full-leaved trees of Hyde Park was a flawless blue. By arrangement with the police, a quarter mile of the park's railings had been temporarily removed for safety's sake. The twenty wagons serving as platforms had been arranged at hundred-yard intervals around a central furniture van which was to act as an information centre, and which Fred Pethick-Lawrence, who was to man it, had dubbed 'the conning tower'. From its roof a changing selection of reporters and VIPs were invited to get an aerial view of the whole event.

The seven processions, comprising thirty thousand marchers, converged on Hyde Park in the early after-noon and, true to her word, Venetia walked at the front of the one that started from Marylebone Road. With her were twenty female medical students and three lady doctors whom she had recruited herself for the occasion, together with Lizzie and Ashley and their two boys, Martial and Rupert, who were aged ten and nine and thought the whole thing most wonderfully exciting. Lizzie wore a white dress with a sash and scarf of the colours and a tricolour ribbon round her straw boater. Venetia, as befitted her dignity, wore the favours more subtly. On the jacket of her cream linen suit she wore a WSPU pin, and she had a posy pinned to her large hat made up of violets, a gardenia and green leaves. The little boys wore sailor-suits with ribbons of the colours on their bonnets. Ashley declined to 'make a figure of himself' with white

71

or the colours, and wore his ordinary clothes, but he walked at the end of the front row and carried one pole of the enormous banner. Frank was in the procession that started at Euston station, along with the most dedicated of his fellow-students, wearing boaters with tricolour ribbons and carrying a banner of their own make. Jessie and Violet had naturally wanted to walk with Venetia, but she had absolutely forbidden it, and Overton, who agreed with her that it was not something he wanted them mixed up in, got them out of the way by taking them for a picnic ride in Richmond Park and inviting a number of other young people to make up a party.

The processions were very well organised, with stewards at every main-line station to muster the groups as soon as they stepped from the train and place them in sections of ten, each with a leader, so that everyone knew what to do. The parties from the provinces had brought their own lovingly created banners, often elaborately embroidered with long mottoes; most of the women wore white with trimmings in the colours, and the men wore rosettes. Two thousand extra police constables were on duty for the day and they all seemed to be very good-tempered and helpful as the processions wended their way towards the park, keeping junctions clear and holding back the crowds that were lining the streets. Londoners had always loved a parade of any sort, and the fine weather brought them out in thousands. When the marchers had passed they fell in behind to follow them to the park; others had gone straight there to see the processions arrive, to stroll under the trees, enjoy the brass bands, and to hear the speeches.

People came – and came and came. Women in summer muslins and enormous hats, women in plain skirts and blouses and boaters, poor women bare-headed leading dirty-faced children, factory girls in shawls, scrawny sweat-shop girls with pricked red fingers, well-fed servant girls in their off-duty best, men in light suits and dark suits, bowlers and boaters, men in working clothes and caps. Vendors took up station, selling ribbon favours and souvenirs, gingerbreads and toffee apples, peanuts and oranges, pies and buns, matches and newspapers and tracts. The smell of trampled grass and hot bodies was spiked with the tang of oranges and pipesmoke; underfoot a litter slowly spread of peanut shells, orange peel, paper, fallen ribbons and lost gloves. Around the edges of the mass hardy souls sat down to picnics of sandwiches, biscuits, hard-boiled eggs, bottled beer, lemonade. Others simply sat on the grass to rest their feet, wipe their children's noses or feed their babies. In the very centre, up on the conning tower, Fred Pethick-Lawrence looked down on the crowd and directed the policemen through a megaphone to where they might most be needed.

And still the crowd grew and grew, solidifying into a dense mass of humanity that barely moved, only milled slowly, with sluggish streams trickling between the stationary islands that coagulated around the platforms. The numbers were already great by the time Venetia reached the park at the head of her procession, and having fulfilled her promise she did not feel the slightest urge to stay.

'I'm going home now,' she said to Lizzie, 'and if you're wise you'll go too.'

'But I can't,' Lizzie said, surprised. 'I'm part of the committee. I've worked for months for this.' And in any case, as Venetia could see quite well, she didn't want to: her eyes were bright and her cheeks flushed with excitement.

'Very well, but you had better look to your boys,' Venetia said. 'They're too small to be jostled in this crowd.'

'Lots of people have children here,' Lizzie said. 'And I think it is an important experience for them. We must bring up the new generation to understand the issue of women's rights, or nothing will ever change.'

Venetia left it at that. Lizzie was not her responsibility and, in any case, Ashley was there with her and would presumably take care of them all. She made her farewells and slipped away. It was impossible to get a cab with the roads full of pedestrians making their way to the park, so she walked, and felt nothing but relief when she finally got into quieter streets and no longer had to thrust her way past a solid mill of bodies. It was hot, and her feet were tired and her head ached from the noise and the glare. She wondered how the stalwarts like Mrs Pankhurst could go on and on feeling enthusiastic year after year and doing things that would always mean crowds and noise. I've grown too soft, Venetia thought. But I've had my own struggle and done my part. She had never been able to care deeply about the vote. Intellectually, of course she wanted it; but even as a young woman her passion lay elsewhere, and long, long ago she had said to Anne, 'You must get the vote for us. I have to give my energies to becoming a doctor.' She had not been entirely serious when she said it, but Anne had taken her at her word, rather to her regret. *You mean*, she quizzed herself wryly, *that you would be happy to accept benefits won by other people, as long as you and your dear ones did not have to suffer in the cause?* But when you thought about it, the majority of the population felt like that. Martyrs were few and far between, and most people were content to ride along on the achievements of the few.

Besides, she clinched the argument with herself, I've two girls to bring out, and that takes up all the energy *I* can spare. Relieved with that conclusion, she turned into an empty street and walked more briskly, thinking longingly of tea.

At the park, the crowds were mostly benign: they had come out of interest and curiosity, and were in general well disposed towards the Suffragettes. But there were two elements out to cause trouble: one was the usual gang of roughs, idlers and East-End men who would always make a nuisance of themselves if they could, just for the fun of it; the other was the settled opposition, the *antis*, who hated the very idea of women's suffrage and would do everything in their power to spoil the day and stop the speeches through barracking, ridicule, and even physical attack.

To begin with, as Ashley edged a way through the crowds for himself, Lizzie and the boys, there was no sign of rowdiness. The bands played, the sun shone, people strolled, children munched, and up on the platforms the Suffragettes addressed their largely indifferent audiences to no more than good-humoured ribbing. It was around platform number eight, where Christabel Pankhurst was to speak, that the crowds were thickest, and here there was an air of excitement, for she was a rousing speaker. As well as being good to look at – young, slender, attractive and feminine – she had a strongly intellectual mind that could present an argument logically, and an enormous vigour that actually seemed to enjoy the heckling. She would always give as good as she got, and do it with patent relish.

A factory girl made room for them as they reached number eight, smiled at the two little boys, and glancing at Lizzie's sash said, 'Come to 'ear Chrissie, mum? My eye, she can't 'alf talk! I'd go anywhere to 'ear 'er. Sweet an' pretty as a flar, she is, but when them blokes starts up 'eckling of 'er, she shuts 'em up just like a man!'

'Yes, she is wonderful, isn't she?' Lizzie said. 'Nothing seems to floor her.'

'Goin' to 'ave a rough ride t'dye,' the girl responded, gesturing to the other side of the platform. 'Them East-End toughs over there is out for blood.' On the other side a gang of young men had pushed themselves to the front of the crowd, grinning and looking around them and nudging each other in the way of their kind.

The crowd was so dense that a way had to be forced through for Christabel by the police, and when she climbed up onto the wagon platform, dressed in academic cap and gown, a roar went up from the crowd and the 'toughs' began chanting, 'We want Chrissie! We want

Chrissie!' Those nearest the platform took hold of the edge of it and began rocking it. Christabel started to speak, her clear voice cutting through the babble and the chanting, but she had not said more than a few words when one of the toughs shouted, 'All tergevver nah!' and at this evidently prearranged signal, they burst into roaring song.

'Put me on an island where the girls are few,
Put me 'mongst the most fee-rocious lions at the Zoo,
You can put me on a treadmill and I'll nev-ah fret,
But for pity's sake don't put me wiv a Suffering-gette!'

Christabel paid them no attention, and though her words were drowned, she walked about the platform, addressing the crowds on all four sides in turn, making her characteristic gestures with outflung hands. The roaring song petered out at last, and now she could be heard. People pressed closer to hear her; more of those filtering past gathered around number eight. Christabel flung off her gown and cap as though they hindered her, and carried on, walking here and there in her plain dress of holland, answering the heckling with quick repartee.

But though she held the crowd for a while, those who wanted to hear her were outnumbered by those who wanted to shout her down. The heckling became almost continuous, the language deteriorated, and the bursts of shoving and fighting became increasingly violent.

'We had better get the boys out of this,' Ashley said to Lizzie, his mouth right by her ear so that she would hear him. But it was easier said than done. The crowd was packed tight, and movement was near impossible. Somebody threw something – it looked like an apple core – at Christabel, missing her, but raising the temperature another degree. Somewhere nearby a child started crying shrilly. Behind them two men began swearing at each other, and then came to half-wrestling blows, their elbows and feet inflicting inadvertent damage on those who could

76

not move enough to leave a space round them. A surge pushed Lizzie into Ashley; someone knocked the factory girl's hat over her eye – 'Watch what you're bleedin' doin'!' she shouted angrily – and someone stepped on Rupert's foot, making him cry out and then burst into tears.

A working man in a shapeless jacket and greasy cap who was standing in front of them turned and caught Lizzie's eye, and he said kindly, ''Ere, missus, better get them little lads out o' this. Pass 'em up the front, put 'em on the platform, 'fore they gets trampled.'

Someone else had had the same idea, and she saw anonymous hands lifting up a small, grubby, howling girl onto the platform edge. There was no way out backwards. She picked up Rupert and handed him on to the man, who seemed a decent sort. Ashley picked up Martial, and a moment later she saw them lifted and seated safely on the platform. The pressure from behind was still growing, and Ashley put his arm round Lizzie to support her. No-one could hear what Christabel was saying now, but she carried on speaking notwithstanding, swaying and gesticulating, moving from one side to another of the platform, which now had a fringe of little children sitting with their backs to her and their legs dangling over the edges.

The fight behind them was growing more violent, gathering more combatants as people got jostled or accidentally hit and took their revenge. The language was the worst Lizzie had ever heard, and even with Ashley's arm round her, she was beginning to feel frightened. But help was on its way. Presumably Pethick-Lawrence up on the conning-tower had seen the problem, for now there was the sound of a police whistle and in a moment the pressure eased as two mounted policemen began to work their way in, loosening the crowd and separating the fighters. The gang of toughs ran off, scattering through the park, and were pursued for a little way and then left go. Lizzie and Ashley were able to collect the children and made their way out to the perimeter of the crowd, where suddenly all seemed peaceful by contrast and they could straighten their clothes and hair and catch their breath.

Things had gone better round other platforms. The younger, unknown speakers had been allowed to talk with little interruption, and when Lizzie and Ashley made their way to Anne's station, they found her addressing a mainly self-controlled crowd, with ordinary heckling rather than abuse or nonsense being thrown at her. Like Christabel she was happy to answer hecklers and had her arguments and facts well mustered so that her opponents were the ones who ended by looking silly. The rest of the rowdyism seemed to be concentrated on Mrs Pankhurst and Mrs Martel. A group of sailors constantly interrupted the former, while the latter's wagon was almost overturned by toughs.

But most of the massive crowd was well-behaved, and there was a fair sprinkling of famous figures to give weight to the occasion and attract the attention of the press. Lizzie saw H.G. Wells and Thomas Hardy, and Ashley pointed out George Bernard Shaw to his boys. Shaw's wife had marched in the procession with Mrs Pankhurst and was a prominent suffragist.

The afternoon ended with what was called 'the Great Shout'. At five o'clock buglers on the conning-tower were to give the signal, at which point the speaker on every platform would lead the crowd, saying, 'One, two, three – VOTES FOR WOMEN!' However, though the shout was taken up in an amorphous roar from the platforms nearest the tower, from the outlying ones there was too much other noise going on for anything to be organised. Even so, a resolution calling on the government to give votes to women was carried at every platform, and soon afterwards the crowds began slowly to disperse in happy holiday mood, leaving behind the organisers, the diehard supporters, and a great deal of litter.

The reports in the press the next day were glowing, speaking of the 'impressive spectacle', and when the illustrated papers came out they showed photographs of Hyde

Park completely submerged beneath a sea of humanity. Estimates of the numbers varied between a quarter and half a million people, but there was no doubt that it had been overwhelmingly well attended, more so than any franchise demonstration ever held before.

A triumphant letter was sent to Asquith, pointing out that public demand for women's suffrage had been clearly demonstrated, and asking what his government meant to do about it. Asquith replied with a typically dry and terse letter, saying that he had nothing to add to his statement of May the 20th.

'You see,' said Anne angrily to Venetia, 'how it is. The demonstration in Hyde Park was the largest anyone could have organised. It is impossible, unfeasible, to do anything greater in that line. He could not expect it. We have shown the support he asked for, and he has snubbed us. There is nothing for it now but militant action.'

'Oh, Anne!' Venetia said in dismay.

Anne's face was implacable, her eyes flat and hostile. 'It's no use, Venetia. They won't listen to reasoned argument. So we must make a different sort of argument that they will *have* to listen to.'

'What do you mean?'

'We must attack the one thing that men care about – their property.'

Venetia did not say anything. She knew it was pointless to try to argue with Anne in this mood; but she wondered whether she had any idea of how really determined the great body of public men was to keep women from sharing their privilege. For Anne to be plunging into trouble and danger for the Cause was one thing, but to be doing it for a cause that could never be won was quite another.

Jessie had enjoyed her time at home, seeing her family, riding her darling Hotspur, visiting the home farm and the stables at Twelvetrees. Uncle Teddy and her mother between them had ensured that they were entertained

79

with dances and young men to dinner. Some of the young men were friends of Robbie's, some were the sons of Teddy's or Jerome's acquaintances, some were young officers from the cavalry barracks. Jessie got on with them all very well. As a lone girl brought up with three brothers (four, counting Ned), she knew what interested the male sex, and could talk to them about horses and dogs, hunting and shooting, cricket and motor-cars, so that, where they were often tongue-tied around young ladies, they could be natural with her and enjoy her company rather than suffer in red-faced silence. Because of this, and because of her liveliness and prettiness, there were quite as many admired her as the lovely Lady Violet, and one of them was so overcome by the excitement of finding Jessie easy to talk to that he thought he must be in love and proposed marriage to her during an interval between chukkas at a polo match at Fulford.

Jessie enjoyed being popular, as any girl would; she even felt - unspoken and sternly suppressed - a rather unworthy satisfaction at finding herself the equal in popularity to Violet, who was her superior in every way in eligibility; but her heart was not touched by any of these boys. She was in a dream of love, and the secret hope that the love might not be hopeless tickled and jigged inside her and would not be denied. Being home was just an interval in the voyage of discovery that was London, the Season, and Lord Brancaster.

The first event after their return to Manchester Square was Women's Sunday, and Jessie was disappointed that they were not allowed to go to it, and even more disappointed that Brancaster was not one of the company invited by Lord Overton to the picnic ride in Richmond Park. By dint of what she hoped was subtle questioning of Henry Fossey – a serious young man who was secretary to an MP and seemed to know the movements of everyone with the slightest connection to the Houses of Parliament – she learned that Brancaster was still out of London.

'He went down to Lincolnshire – something to do with his father's estate. It's pretty run down, I understand. Lord Holkam's been in poor health for years, so I imagine things have got out of hand.'

'Is it a large estate?' Jessie asked, after a brief struggle not to. Fossey was such a nice young man and evidently liked her. He was bound for a seat himself one day, and Cousin Venetia had made it plain enough to her right at the beginning of the Season that she thought him a very suitable match for her. Jessie liked him, too, and did not want to rub his nose in the fact that he was not Lord Brancaster. But it was becoming increasingly difficult for her not to talk about him, since he was so constantly on her mind.

'Oh, yes,' Fossey said. 'But, then, everything in that part of Lincolnshire is large. Have you never been to the fens? Curious place. Everything flat and bare, divided up by the great drains and dykes that run straight as rules from horizon to horizon. Nothing but sky and wind and water. Not everyone's idea of pretty country.' He eyed Jessie thoughtfully. 'Nothing like the North Riding. They say if you're not born to the fens you never know how to love them.'

'Oh,' Jessie said. They rode in silence for a little, Jessie noticing, without at all wanting to, that Fossey was not a very good rider – and, indeed, why should he be, being Town-born and Town-bred? The Fossey money was all in stocks and shares – they had a country place, but it was in Surrey, which to Jessie was practically the same as London, and in any case humbug country as far as hunting was concerned. Did they hunt in the fens, she wondered, with slight anxiety. But of course it was only a hop and step from Lincolnshire to Leicestershire, and Lord Holkam was bound to have a hunting place, wasn't he? The anxiety dissolved.

'It's probably a good thing that Brancaster's still away,' Henry Fossey said, after a moment. 'The Women's Sunday in Hyde Park would have made him mad.'

81

Jessie looked at him. He was gazing into the distance as though he had said nothing of importance. 'Why?' she asked, trying to sound uninterested.

'Oh, because Holkam is one of the diehard anti-suffragists – worse than Lord Curzon and Asquith put together – and Brancaster is bound to feel the same, isn't he?'

Jessie thought it best not to answer that, but inside her head she dissented. Young men did not always think the same as their fathers. Often they seemed to think the very opposite. And Brancaster – even thinking his name brought his face before her, his mouth, his eyes, the swooning feeling she had when he smiled at her – Brancaster must surely support the Cause, which was so just and fair and obviously right. She felt Fossey's eyes on her, and for a variety of reasons changed the subject.

'Are you going to the Eton and Harrow match? Who do you think will win?'

'Well, I have to say Harrow, because my little brother is playing,' Fossey said, with discernible pride, and Jessie took up the thread and led him – and her own thoughts – firmly away from the Earl of Holkam's heir.

It wasn't until the first weekend of July that she saw him, when the Overtons were invited with Jessie and Violet to spend Saturday-to-Monday at Wolvercote, the seat near Oxford of the Earl of Aylesbury. Aylesbury was Venetia's second cousin: her grandmother had been sister to his grandfather. She had spent considerable time at Wolvercote during her youth, her mother and the previous earl being close friends.

The present earl had sons of twenty-one and nineteen and a daughter of eighteen, so the house party comprised plenty of young people of just the right age for Jessie and Violet, including the Seavill sisters, Florence and Amalfia, who had become good friends. The invitation to the Overtons had advised that the King was spending the weekend nearby with Lord Avens and would be motoring over with his hosts and Mrs Keppel on Saturday to dinner, so it would be a very grand and formal meal (tiaras and orders to be worn). Venetia had made sure the girls took their diamond brooches with them so that the King could see them wearing them.

They went down after luncheon on Saturday by train, and were met at the station by one of Lord Aylesbury's motor-cars (he was apparently very motor-minded, an interest he shared with the King). Country-house visiting was something quite new to Jessie, and she was so excited she could hardly notice anything about the great hall into which they were admitted, except that there were flowers everywhere and the air smelt of spice. The earl and countess and their children greeted the visitors, and there were kisses and hands shaken and introductions, and a certain amount of what seemed to Jessie rather pointless chattery from the grown-ups, and then Lady Aylesbury said, 'I'm sure you'd like to see your rooms, now.' A footman was beckoned forward to lead Lord and Lady Overton away, and then a maid smiled and bobbed to the girls and led them off in a completely different direction.

'What happens now?' Jessie whispered to Violet, as they followed the maid up stairs and along corridors. Wolvercote was a large and rambling house, and she thought despairingly that she would never find her way down again.

'We change for tea and the maids unpack,' Violet whispered back.

'Unpack? Where are our things?' She hadn't seen either the luggage or the servants since Paddington, except for a glimpse of them at the other end of the platform at Oxford station.

'They'll be there when we get to our rooms. That's why we take so long saying hello downstairs, to give them time to get up there.'

The Aylesbury maid finally showed them to two rooms almost opposite each other on a narrow corridor with panelled walls and a very worn carpet underfoot. It was the Tudor wing, she informed them. Jessie was startled to see a white card in a holder on the first door on which

83

was written in careful script and Indian ink, *Miss Jessamine Compton*. There was a similar card on the other door, which said, *Lady Violet Winchmore*. She thought of some servant making up the cards beforehand, sitting at a table down in the servants' hall and copying her name from a list. It made her feel rather important.

The maid closed the door behind her, leaving Jessie alone in the room and rather anxious, for though her luggage was there, as promised, Violet was now out of reach in her own room and she did not know quite what to do. Change for tea, Violet had said, but how, precisely, and when did you go down, and how did you find your way?

She thought that at least she would take off her hat, and she had only just done that when the door opened and to her great relief Wilson came in. She was one of Venetia's housemaids, who had come along as lady's maid to Jessie since, Venetia said, there was so much changing of clothes at a country house weekend that Sanders could never have maided both girls.

'Oh, I'm glad to see you,' Jessie said. 'I thought I was going to have to manage alone.'

'I'm sorry, miss,' Wilson said. 'There was so many of us all arriving at the same time down there that it took a while for the housekeeper to get to me and tell me where you were, miss. But I see your luggage is here all right, and your tea things are right on top.'

'Must I really change?' Jessie asked, as Wilson crossed to open her box. 'It does seem a waste. I've only worn this to travel down in, and I suppose I'll have to change again for dinner.'

Wilson had not done a great deal of lady's maiding, but Venetia's Hayter had trained her and she took her duties very seriously. 'Oh, yes, miss, of course you must! You can't be wearing a travelling-costume to afternoon tea. Wouldn't do at all.'

'Well, it all seems rather foolish to me,' Jessie said, with a sigh.

Wilson twinkled at her. She had a soft spot for Miss Compton, who tended to treat servants like personal friends rather than staff. Some of the Overton servants disapproved of that sort of informality, but Wilson liked her for it. In her view a real lady always knew where to draw the line, and you could tell Miss Compton would never let anyone take advantage. 'I did hear something down in the servants' hall, miss. Lady Elizabeth's maid – which is Lord Aylesbury's daughter, miss – happened to mention just as Sanders and me were coming in that Lord Brancaster will be a guest this weekend, and should be arriving in time for tea.'

'Indeed?' said Jessie calmly, though inside she was wondering frantically whether Wilson had guessed about her feelings for Brancaster – and, if so, how. She submitted without another word to having her costume and blouse removed. She washed her face and hands in the bedroom basin and then Wilson dressed her in the afternoon gown of thin pale green silk trimmed with dark green velvet, which she wore over a cream lace guimpe. Wilson did her hair, and then Jessie dismissed her and went across to Violet's room. Sanders was a more deliberate worker than Wilson, and was still arranging Violet's hair. Jessie met Violet's eye in the looking-glass and unable to keep it to herself for another instant said, 'They've invited *him*. He'll be there at tea.'

It said much for Violet's sympathy that she understood at once and did not ask any embarrassing questions.

'Oh, good. I'm so pleased for you,' she said, though Jessie thought that for a moment she did not look pleased, only rather put out, almost dismayed. But then she smiled, and the thought was gone on the instant.

'Not that anyone is likely to notice me when you are in the room,' Jessie said. 'You are so beautiful, Vi, and that tea-gown is so pretty.' It was of mauve chiffon over silk, a colour that suited her to perfection.

Sanders finished Violet's head, and left them.

'But you look lovely, too,' Violet said.

Jessie touched the scar on her cheek. 'With *this*?' she said simply.

Violet turned right round to face her. 'It barely shows at all, and I'm sure no-one would ever notice it unless they were looking for it. Besides, if someone loves you, things like that don't matter.'

It was what mothers always said, and their children never believed.

Jessie only smiled and said, 'I'm glad your room is near mine: I'd never find my way back down on my own. Are you nearly ready? Because I'm starving. I don't know why trains always make me hungry, but they do.'

Brancaster was not present when they stepped into the great hall, and for a moment Jessie's disappointment was acute. But she really was hungry, and the most wonderful tea was spread on a large table for everyone to help themselves, while two footmen and a maid poured and handed cups of tea. Violet was claimed by Aylesbury's eldest son, Lord Calder, and swept off to one sofa, while Jessie was cordially pressed to join his sister, Lady Elizabeth Chetwyn, on another, where she sat between her and Florence Seavill. Between their happy, inconsequential chat and the consumption of hot muffins and Battenburg cake, Jessie was so comfortably occupied that when Brancaster did arrive she genuinely did not notice him for a moment and was able to appear satisfyingly self-contained.

He was the last of all the guests to arrive, and he went first, of course, to his host and hostess, who were seated on the other side of the great hall with the Overtons. He made his bows, was provided with a cup of tea by a footman, and stood with them for some time talking, while Jessie answered her own companions increasingly at random and found it difficult to keep her eyes away from that fascinating back. Tea was almost over – it was nearly time to dress. At any moment they would all be on the move, and suppose he went straight to his room without seeing her? Yes, the Overtons and the Aylesburys were standing up now. They were obviously preparing to leave the room.

And then he turned, scanned the hall with that lordly gaze of his, and finding Jessie's eyes on him, he bowed in her direction; located Violet and bowed to her; and then at last – at last! – walked over to the sofa where Jessie sat.

'Miss Compton,' he said. 'What a very great pleasure to find you here. I was afraid you meant to stay in Yorkshire for ever. London was very dull without you and Lady Violet.'

In her happiness and excitement, Jessie laughed and said, 'Now, really, how would you know that? You've been out of London yourself. In fact, we were back before you.'

He looked taken aback for a moment, and then smiled. 'I had forgotten how very frank you always are. That sort of commonplace compliment won't do for you, I see. I must be careful what I say.'

She blushed a little. 'I didn't know it was a compliment,' she said, and then thought that was a stupid thing to say.

But he laughed and said, 'Quite right. A compliment must be sincere or it is nothing. I shall say London *must* have been dull without you. Will that do?'

'I don't know,' she said. 'I shall have to think about it.' She meant just that, but he seemed to find her answer amusing.

'You are such a droll, Miss Compton. *À bientôt.*' And he bowed again and went away to speak to Violet.

Watching him go, Lady Elizabeth Chetwyn leaned to Jessie and murmured, 'How do you manage to think of things like that to say to him? I do admire you! He simply *paralyses* me.'

Jessie looked at her, surprised. 'Does he?'

'Oh yes! He's so grand and handsome and so – so *sure* of himself. I had to dance with him once last year when I came out and I couldn't think of a thing to say. When he spoke to me I just turned red and stammered like an idiot.'

'He is very handsome, isn't he?' Jessie said, watching him stoop over Violet's dark head, seeing his wonderful profile, his smile, watching his lips kiss Violet's hand, wishing it were hers, remembering exactly what the touch of his lips on her hand felt like.

Florence Seavill, who had been out a year already, said, 'Mama says he's too handsome for his own good.'

Lady Elizabeth nodded. 'He was supposed to be in love with my cousin Helen last year but it didn't come to anything. Her mother made such a fuss, saying he'd treated her badly.'

'They say Lord Holkam has told him he must get married this year, so I suppose that's why he's going everywhere,' Miss Seavill said.

'I say,' Lady Elizabeth exclaimed, as something seemed to strike her, 'you don't think Mama invited him here to look at *me*, do you?'

Jessie hardly knew what to say. She had spent so long telling herself to be sensible and not to hope too much, but Elizabeth's words had revealed to her how far she had come to believe that Brancaster was interested in her. Yet Elizabeth seemed to think he was still entirely unattached. Evidently no rumour of such interest had reached her. She watched him straighten up and leave Violet, walk towards the door; Violet's head turning after him as though fastened to him by a string.

'I don't know,' she managed to answer at last. 'Should you – should you like to marry him?'

'Oh, no,' Elizabeth said decidedly. 'I don't want to marry anyone for ages yet. And I wouldn't want to marry someone who makes me feel like that. I'd like to marry one of my cousins, someone I've known all my life, so I shouldn't be scared of him. It would be so horrid to marry someone and have to think what to say all the time, and always be afraid of saying the wrong thing and have him think you a fool.'

'Oh,' said Jessie. In her dream of romance she had never considered what it would be like actually to *be* married – it was the *getting* that seemed to matter. That was all she and Violet had ever discussed.

'That's the dressing-bell,' Florence said.

'It's early today because of the King coming,' said Elizabeth. 'Oh dear, I wish he weren't. It's so much more comfortable when it's just family. I shall be paralysed all over again.'

Despite meaning not to be, Jessie was awed by the grandeur of the evening. After all, he *was* the King, and everybody made such a fuss about it that it was impossible to keep pretending it was not going to be daunting. Wilson was in a froth of excitement, and came to dress Jessie babbling of servants' hall struggles over the use of irons and brushes, and the jewels she had seen being taken out of the safe for various ladies. Jessie let her chatter, but felt herself being wound up like a watch spring by Wilson's nervousness. By the time she was ready to go down, with her diamond brooch pinned prominently to her shoulder, she felt hollow with apprehension, and not at all sure she could control her train well enough not to fall headlong in front of the company. She envied Violet her apparent composure; but Violet was always quiet, and if she was a little more so this evening, who was to notice?

They were twenty-four at dinner, and as the King liked strict precedence to be observed, Jessie was paired off last with a young Mr Russell, who seemed as nervous as she was. Even the younger Seavill girl, Amalfia, went ahead of her because her father, Colonel Sir Harry Seavill, was a baronet. There was a long period of standing around in the drawing-room while they waited for the King. No-one was allowed to smoke, and there were no refreshments served, and since everyone had been quietly forbidden to move around, there was nothing to do but talk to one's partner. Mr Russell had nothing to say for himself, so Jessie was able to stand quietly and watch Brancaster talking to Cousin Venetia, with whom he had been paired. He seemed to be charming her, and several times Jessie saw her smile. Was it possible that he was making himself agreeable *for her sake*? She tried to shake the thought away as too flattering. Violet, on the other side of the room, had been paired with Lord Calder, and Jessie saw her watching her mother and Brancaster too. She looked tense and unhappy, and Jessie guessed that she was indeed more nervous than she had seemed.

When the King arrived with Mrs Keppel and Lord and Lady Avens, there was a flurry of excitement and tension, but as far as the lesser people like Jessie were concerned it proved to have been worry for nothing, for though he passed smiling down the line and had everyone's name mentioned to him, he did not stop and speak to her, nor even seem to look at her particularly, and by the time she was rising from her curtsey he had passed on and the moment was gone. The King was offering his arm to Lady Aylesbury and heading for the dining room, his big booming voice bouncing ahead of him, and everyone was falling in line behind him. She laid her hand on Mr Russell's arm, gathered up her train, and they took their place at the end of the procession. Two footmen held open the double doors to the dining-saloon; beyond them the room was long and lovely and candle-lit, shadowy in the corners, the table beautifully decorated with flowers, the silver and crystal glinting in the moving light. There was the same spicy smell in the air – Jessie had learned by now that it was pot-pourri – together with a hint of scent from some of the ladies.

Jessie had been afraid that her partner would not know where to take her, that there might be some potentially embarrassing ambiguity about the seating arrangements; but of course as they were last and least there were only two places left by the time they entered the room, in the centre of the table on the right. She walked with Mr Russell past the silks and bare shoulders and glittering jewels, the broadcloth and white linen and orders, the heads that moved and swayed to a soft murmur like the distant sound of the sea, and felt at last the pleasure of being there, in this fine company, in this great house. How many people could say they would be dining with the King of England tonight?

That anticipatory pleasure was the high point of the evening for her. Dinner was really rather dull. Her companion on the other side, though perfectly pleasant, was a quiet and thoughtful young man who liked to listen rather than talk; while Mr Russell could not seem to shake off his nervousness sufficiently to initiate conversation. As Lady Aylesbury was rather strict about formal dinners, there was no talking across the table – which in any case was so wide it would not have been possible to do so without raising one's voice to an unseemly pitch. So there was little for Jessie to do but eat. The food, though elaborate and delicious (there were ten courses, hors d'oeuvres, soup, fish, entrées, relevés, game, roasts, savoury, entremêts and dessert), was no compensation for having to be on her best behaviour, concentrate on using the right implement, eat in tiny, ladylike nibbles, and be sure not to spill or splash. Her greatest pleasure, as the seemingly endless succession of dishes was handed and cleared, was that as Lord Brancaster was seated at the opposite side of the table from her, she was able to look at him. He was further up the table, of course, so she could not hear anything he said.

The only voice one could hear clearly at the table was the King's: from years of trying to make himself heard by the Queen, who was very deaf, he had acquired the habit of speaking very loudly, and pronouncing each syllable of a word separately – 'em-u-late' and 'par-li-a-ment' and 'in-ter-est'. He had Cousin Venetia on his right and seemed to enjoy her conversation particularly. Lady Aylesbury, in consequence, let him talk to her much longer, only turning to her own right-hand companion half as often, which meant in turn that Jessie had twice as much of her silent as her not-so-silent partner, and was also facing the wrong way to look at Brancaster.

At last Lady Aylesbury stood up, the females all filed

out into the drawing-room, and the doors were firmly closed on the gentlemen, the port and the cigars. It seemed a very long time before the company was reunited, but even then the evening was not redeemed from dullness as the King wanted bridge. The tables were made up and Jessie was left to the company of the other young people who did not play, Mr Russell, Amalfia Seavill, and a brother and sister who, while perfectly pleasant, seemed to Jessie not over-endowed with intellect. Conversation between them did not flourish, and in the end Mr Russell picked up a newspaper, Amalfia *Strand* magazine, and the brother and sister sat side by side staring at nothing in particular and occasionally making a remark about something at home, which meant nothing to their companions.

Jessie was driven to pick up a book about birds, which was lying on the table nearby, and her only moment of pleasure came when Lord Brancaster, taking the advantage of being dummy, got up to walk about and, having paused to look idly at the music lying on the piano-top, finally strolled over to where Jessie was sitting.

'Are you pleasantly occupied, Miss Compton?' he said. 'You are passing your time more usefully than the rest of us, at any rate. You don't play bridge?'

'I've never learned it,' she said. 'But at home sometimes I play cribbage with my father and brothers.'

'I have never learned cribbage,' he said. 'On the whole I find card games rather a waste of time, don't you?'

'I like them sometimes. Violet and I used to play when I stayed with her, when we were little.'

'What a pretty image that makes in my mind – you and Lady Violet playing cards together as children. Let me guess that it was generally you who won.'

'I don't remember,' she said. She dared to look up directly at him and felt the surge of rapture wash over her. Oh, if only she could think of something witty to say!

He went on, lowering his voice. 'I noticed at dinner you seemed rather grave. Was the menu not to your taste?'

'Everything was very nice,' she said, 'but I couldn't help thinking I would have had more pleasure from eating bread and cheese out in the fields at home.'

He raised his brows. 'One can have enough of rich food, I suppose.'

'Oh, it wasn't that,' she said, 'only that one could have been comfortable and eaten as one pleased and not worried about one's clothes and what knife and fork to use.' Immediately she felt she should not have said it, that she had sounded gauche and stupid, but he seemed to find it amusing, and smiled at her in the way that made her spine shiver.

'You are so very droll, Miss Compton. I never know what you will say next. I can't tell you how much you have added to the pleasure of the Season! Oh, but the hand is ending; I must return to my table.' He gave her a little bow, and said very softly, 'I leave you to your companions. Perhaps you should try shocking them: I doubt if anything less will rouse them.'

The rest of the weekend, once the oppressive honour of the King's visit was over, was more enjoyable. On Sunday morning after church Lord Aylesbury conducted everyone on a walk round the gardens and the hothouses. After luncheon, those who wanted to went riding, while the non-riders were taken on a carriage-drive to visit the model home farm. Then came afternoon tea, then changing for dinner, and after dinner the young Chetwyns organised a game of charades. The enormous dressing-up basket was brought down into an ante-room by two of the footmen, and the company divided into two teams. Jessie was sorry that she was separated both from Violet and Lord Brancaster; but the game was fun even so. The other team went off into the ante-room, and there were shrieks and laughter and hilarious conversation for what would have been a tediously long time had not Jessie's team been making similar noises as they discussed their 'word'.

Everyone entered into the spirit of the thing, and Jessie was enchanted to see dignified grown-ups making themselves as foolish as the young people in the service of the charade. The maids threw themselves into it wholeheartedly, and were always scurrying off to fetch this or that item or suggesting a solution to a problem; and when the plays were enacted all the servants gathered, by permission, at the back of the room to watch. Jessie acted well, for she and her brothers had been 'getting up plays' at home all their childhood, and she loved putting herself into another character, and never felt in the least self-conscious. She played a gypsy in her team's charade, and danced around an imaginary camp fire with great gusto. Violet had never been much given to acting, but in her play she only had to be a queen and sit on a throne and look gracious, which she did very well, and looked, Jessie thought, very beautiful in a velvet mediaeval gown from the dressing-up basket and a pointed headdress made of cardboard rolled into a cone with a chiffon scarf hanging from it. Brancaster, as her suitor, flung himself to his knees before her very convincingly.

After the charades there was a period of pleasant confusion while things were being put away and the rooms set to rights. A lot of greenery had been borrowed from Lady Aylesbury's conservatory for the last play, and some of the young gentlemen helped to carry it back. Jessie had not seen the conservatory, so she followed them. It was a large one, and she took time to look round it, thinking how much her mother would love to have something like this, and how living in a fortified manor house had its disadvantages. In one corner she discovered a large ginger cat curled up on the cushion of a chair, and stopped to stroke and talk to it. The young men went out again while she was so engaged, but the cat was enjoying her ministrations so much that she lingered, stroking its cheeks and saying, 'Now I really have to go, puss. Oh, yes, I know, but I can't stay here all night with you.'

And then there was a soft footfall behind her, the hair

rose on the back of her neck, and she straightened up and turned to find Lord Brancaster had come in. He had brought back a potted fern that had been borrowed, and now, putting it down, he came towards her.

"'I can't stay here all night with you,'" he quoted her. 'My dear Miss Compton, what a great pity! But we can take advantage of the few moments we have.'

Being alone with a young man was not something that ever happened to well-brought-up girls, and Jessie would have blushed and been tongue-tied even if she hadn't been so in love with him.

'Shall we?' he said. 'I think the unconventional Miss Compton may dare anything.'

He took a step nearer and her heart raced, and every nerve ending seemed to tingle. Her eyes were resolutely down, but she was so overwrought that her mental image of his face seemed to be what she was really seeing, and not the marble floor.

'Miss Compton!' he said, very close and very low.

Now she looked up into his face, and the difference from imagination was so vivid it made her draw in a quick little gasp. His eyes were very bright, and he seemed to be breathing rather quickly. She thought he had never looked so handsome, and she yearned so much for him that she had lifted her face to him without even knowing it. He put his arm round her waist, pulled her to him and kissed her.

The shock was like a bolt of lightning to Jessie: it was the forbidden thought she had resolutely not been thinking, but in her innocence she had not expected it, not really. The feeling of his lips against hers was something so electric, so thrilling, that her heart seemed to contract almost in fear, and her legs trembled so that she thought she would have fallen down had his arm not been round her. But it lasted only a few seconds. Long, long before she had the slightest wish for him to stop, he did. He straightened up, gently withdrew his arm from her, and said, 'I thought I was not mistaken.'

She opened her eyes. There was a little smile of satisfaction on his lips. He put his hand up to tweak his necktie straight and said, 'Thank you, Miss Compton. I must go before anyone else comes in, or both our reputations will suffer.' He looked at her consideringly for an instant, and then said, 'I need hardly say that this must be our secret.'

She tried to say, 'Yes,' but though her lips moved, she had no voice.

He touched her chin with one finger. 'For your sake as well as mine. Do you promise?' She nodded. He smiled and went quickly out.

Jessie felt her face flaming, and waited a while to let her cheeks cool, staring at the dark windows, hearing in the background the cat still purring hopefully. He had kissed her! *He had kissed her*! He must love her, then. But why had he come and gone so quickly? Oh, what did he mean by any of it? She knew that a man was not meant to kiss you before you were engaged, but that sometimes they might want to. She and Violet had discussed at great length whether they would ever allow a man to kiss them, and had agreed seriously that they probably would if they loved the man very much and meant to marry him. But he had not asked her if he could, and it had all happened so quickly that there hardly seemed to have been any moment when she could have exercised judgement or made a decision.

She was not sorry she had done it, but she was glad he had made her promise to keep it secret, for otherwise she was afraid she would not have been able to prevent herself telling Violet about it. It was better as a secret, something delicious to hug to herself, to take out and relive and polish and daydream over in the quiet time in bed before sleep.

When she felt she could keep her countenance she went back to the drawing-room, and found the same pleasant confusion reigning, as if only a few moments had passed since she had left, rather than an aeon. No-one seemed to have missed her, and no-one seemed to notice her re-entering. So that was all right. The rest of the evening passed somehow. She did not have an opportunity to speak to Brancaster and he did not look at her, involved as he was in a conversation with Lord Aylesbury, apparently about farming improvements.

She went to bed at last to dream, rather disappointingly, of gypsies and dressing-up and hothouses and a large number of people none of whom bore the slightest resemblance to Brancaster. In the morning, at breakfast, over her eggs and haddock and fried tomatoes, as she waited for him to appear, she learned that he had already left to go back to Town by an early train, having, he had told his host the night before, business with his bank. Violet met her eyes and made a face expressive of sympathy and disappointment, and Jessie felt a strong urge to tell her about the kiss after all; but before they were alone together with enough privacy for such confidences, she had control over herself again, and her promise to Brancaster remained inviolate.

Chapter Four

Venetia had been out with the girls all afternoon, paying 'morning' calls and then going for tea at the Seavills'. She returned home with them to dress for the evening, but was still only discussing with Hayter what she would wear when her husband came into her dressing-room and indicated with nods and eyebrow raisings that he needed to talk to her privately. She dismissed Hayter, and said, 'Well, Beauty? Your face is portentous.'

'I've had a visitor this afternoon. Brancaster has been here.'

'Lord Brancaster? Is it something I should know about?'

'He wants to marry Violet.'

Venetia stared. 'That accounts for the determined effort to charm me when we were at Wolvercote. I did wonder at the time whether there was anything behind it.'

'And did he?'

'Charm me? Yes, up to a point. He seems a nice enough young man, but surprisingly – well, dull.'

'Dull?'

'Oh, not dull, exactly. Commonplace, I suppose,' Venetia said. 'One hears so much about him being the *premier parti* of the Season that one's expectations are raised, but he didn't say anything of great interest or penetration.'

Overton smiled. 'When did you ever hear any young man say anything of interest or penetration?'

'I remember you did, to me.'

'That is the flattery of memory. Besides, you were not my potential mother-in-law.'

'True. Well, he's handsome and he smiles a lot. What else? He has the reputation for a flirt. There was that business last year with Helen Arlington.'

'He mentioned that. He said it was a misunder-standing.'

'Well, probably it was. I don't think we ought to make too much of it. Emily Aylesbury told me she never thought there was anything in it but Lady Arlington's pique at being thwarted and having him slip her net.'

'You're arguing both sides together.'

'So I am,' Venetia discovered. 'As to flirting – young people spending time with each other is what the Season is all about. How are they to find out who they love if they don't talk and laugh with lots of different people? What do you think of him?'

'Well, it's a good-ish offer for Violet,' Overton conceded.

'Only good-ish?'

'Holkam's estate is much more encumbered than I thought. As far as fortune goes, she could do better. But his title is good—'

'Yes, it's an old one. And Holkam's health is such that there would be no long cadetship.'

'Cold-blooded woman! He hinted at that, too.'

'Did he, indeed?'

'He was quite frank. He has the title and the land and we have the money. Fair exchange is no robbery.'

'Beauty, he didn't say that!'

'No, not in so many words, of course, but that's what it comes down to. As I said, in terms of fortune she could do better, but when it's a case of a love-match, different standards apply.'

'So he spoke of love? I'm glad to hear it.'

'He said he loved Violet, and that he was sure she loved him. He said she was everything he admired in a woman and that he had singled her out at the first meeting as his ideal of a future wife.'

'Well, that sounds all right. But I had no idea he was interested in her,' said Venetia. 'He didn't seem to pay her any particular attention.'

'It seems he was being deliberately circumspect, because of that Arlington business last year. He said he did not want to expose Violet to gossip until he was sure she loved him in return.'

'Well, I suppose that's laudable. Caution in a young man is quite unexpected.'

'My thoughts exactly. Can he really be in love, and behave so circumspectly?'

She smiled. 'You were not like that. You didn't mind who knew it, my poor Beauty. But Brancaster's situation is different,' she added fairly.

'I suppose so. But it strikes me as damned conceited,' Overton confessed.

'Conceited? Well, he'd be a fool if he didn't know his own worth in the marriage mart.' Venetia cocked an eye at him. 'Are you "agin" him?'

'I don't know. No, I can't be agin him on so little evidence. And after all, we thought him suitable enough to invite him to Violet's ball, so we can hardly cross him off the list now. It's just—'

'It's just that you don't want to part with your darling daughter, and any man who asked for her would be bound to fall short of your exacting standards.'

'You always did see through me.'

'Well, look, Beauty,' Venetia said sensibly, 'he's a handsome, well-mannered young man of good family, with extensive lands – albeit mortgaged – and heir to an earldom. If Violet loves him, as he seems to think she does, what reason would we have to refuse him?'

'No reason. And if Violet does love him, there's nothing more to be said.'

'And if she doesn't, you'll take pleasure in kicking him out like the cur he is?'

Overton gave a rueful smile. 'Am I overreacting?'

'Just a little, I fancy.' Her expression changed. 'Well, I

suppose it is a triumph for a mother to have her daughter marry straight out of the schoolroom, but I half hope she turns him down. She's so very young. Still, a good match is what everyone wants for her.'

'We have to find out first whether she wants the fellow or not,' said Overton. 'Better get it over with, do you think?'

Venetia took pity on him. 'We'll do it together, love. Ring the bell.'

Summoned to her mother's dressing-room, Violet went with the simple surprise of a clear conscience. Fortunately she had not started to undress, so the 'at once!' in the summons caused her no difficulties. She was even more surprised to find her father there, at a time when he should be in his own dressing-room.

'Have I done something wrong?' she asked, with artless innocence.

'No, darling, not at all,' Venetia said. She exchanged a glance with her husband and seeing his resolutely closed mouth she carried on. 'Papa has had a visit from a young man, concerning you.'

Violet knew what that meant. There were several of them who had been courting her. None had asked her to marry him, but though it was unusual these days for a man to be so correct as to ask permission of the parents *before* proposing, it was nice that he should want to do things properly – whoever 'he' was. It would be a feather in one's cap to have an offer before the end of one's first Season. She wondered which of them it was. Carrick? Fairbanks? Perhaps that nice Viscount Calder, Aylesbury's heir. He reminded her of her own brother, Thomas. Perhaps it might not be disagreeable to be married to him. She might be married before she was eighteen – that would really be something to be proud of.

Venetia was observing her daughter's tranquil face and air of gentle enquiry with concealed surprise. No blush, no conscious look, no hopeful flutter. This surely could not be a girl in love? Was Brancaster mistaken, or dissembling? 'You don't ask me who it is,' she said. 'But then, I'm sure *you* could tell *me*.'

Violet shook her head. 'I can't guess.'

'Can you really not? It was Lord Brancaster who called. He told your father he is very much in love with you and—' She broke off as Violet turned pale, and swayed a moment as though she might faint. Overton, who had been leaning against the dressing table with legs crossed and arms folded, was across the room in an instant, slipped an arm round her and put her gently on a chair. She looked up at her mother with a face of such trouble that Venetia did not know how to interpret it.

'He – loves me? Surely – did he really say *me*?' She appealed to her father. 'He said me by name?'

Overton laid a gentle hand on her shoulder. 'Yes, my love, of course he did. What is this? You look so shocked. Had you no idea?'

'No – none – that he loved me.'

Overton shook his head a little, glancing at his wife; and then he said gently to his daughter, 'He has never given you any idea of his feelings? He seemed quite sure of them himself. But does the idea of marrying him upset you? You can't think I or your mother would ever try to persuade you, if you don't like him.'

'Oh, but I do like him!' she cried out, and then bit her lip, looking from one to the other with tears sparkling in her eyes, ready to fall. 'I love him – so very much! But I didn't – I never expected—' She stopped. 'He loves me?' she asked again.

'He said he loved you as much as he was sure you loved him,' Overton said, 'and it seems he was right, though I said to him that I had not seen any sign of a preference in you for him.'

'I tried not to show—' The tears spilled over and her lips trembled. Venetia thought how lucky Violet was, though she didn't know it yet, to be able to cry so elegantly, without spoiling her looks. The tears lay on her cheeks like diamonds on a porcelain rose. 'He was always very kind to me,' she managed to say through little indrawn sobs. 'And spoke to me so gently, and looked at me as if he – cared for me. But I thought it was – I tried not to love him because—' She stopped again. Overton gave her his handkerchief and she pressed it against her eyes and struggled for composure. 'I thought he loved someone else,' she concluded.

Venetia thought she understood. 'He has paid attention to other young ladies, but not more than was proper, I think. And you know it would not have been right for him to make you look particular until he was sure of his feelings – and yours.' There was a faint question mark on the last two words, but Violet did not respond to it. Venetia went on, 'He assured your father that he had never thought of anyone but you. He said he loved you and wanted to marry you, and that he believed you loved him.'

'I do,' Violet said, half muffled by the handkerchief. 'Oh, I do.'

'If you are sure of that, you must consider what your own wishes are.'

'I want to marry him,' Violet said, in a low voice, almost inaudible.

'All you need to decide,' Overton said, 'is whether you would like me to give him permission to address you. You don't have to decide yet whether you want to marry him. There's no hurry at all. You can take your time to get to know him better.'

She looked up, her face suddenly blooming, the colour coming back into her pale cheeks. 'Oh but I do know him, and I want to marry him more than anything! I love him, Papa! I don't need time to think about it. I'm very, very sure.'

'Very well,' Overton said, suppressing a pang. This was why you brought girls out, and it was an eligible match, but still she was his little girl and he would have to part with her. 'I shall send for Brancaster tomorrow and tell him that he may speak to you.'

'Thank you, Papa.' Violet hesitated. 'May I tell Jessie?'

'Yes, of course, if you want to,' Venetia intervened. 'But you must dress as quickly as possible. We shall be shockingly late for dinner as it is.'

It was hard, very hard; more especially as, since she had been with her parents, Wilson had slipped in to tell Jessie that Brancaster had been to see Lord Overton. When Violet got back to her room, Jessie was there, restless with excitement and with all her hope in her face.

'Did they mention him? I wonder why he wanted to see your father. Could it have been anything to do with me? Did they say anything about it?'

Violet took hold of Jessie's hands, trying to still her, and the expression on her face made Jessie suddenly nervous.

'What is it, Vi? Something bad?'

Violet sought for words, and then thought that the only way was to say it straight out. 'Brancaster wants to marry me. He came to see Papa to ask his permission. He said he loves me.'

Jessie stared. 'Loves you? No, there must be some mistake. They must have misunderstood. He never said he loves you?'

'There's no mistake. He asked Papa for my hand. Oh Jess, I'm so sorry!'

Bewildered, Jessie tried to follow the story in Violet's face. 'Sorry? But – but you don't mean —? You haven't said you will marry him?' Violet nodded. 'But you don't love him!'

Violet's cheeks burned. 'I do. I didn't mean to. I tried not to, because you loved him. I knew I shouldn't – but I couldn't help it. I tried to fall in love with someone else, but it was no good. I've loved him all the time. All the time.'

'No. It's not true,' Jessie said stonily.

'I've tried not to show it. And I didn't encourage him – I promise you I didn't. But I'm dreadfully in love with

104

him, and now it seems he loves me too, and . . .'

Jessie was thinking hard. Little pieces dropped into place. She remembered when she had guessed Violet was in love with someone, how Violet had hesitated before saying it was Carrick; her look of unhappiness when Jessie spoke about Brancaster; how quiet she had always been when in company with them both. Her love for her friend made her sympathy quick, and she thought how awful Violet's dilemma must have been, to fall in love with Brancaster, knowing how Jessie felt.

But then the reality hit her. He had asked for Violet, not her. 'It can't be!' she cried helplessly. 'He always danced with me and sat with me. It was always me he came to speak to.' But he had danced with them both, hadn't he? And sat with them both. 'The things he said to me!' He had said he'd never known a débutante like her. He had called her droll and original and said he never knew what she would say next. But he had never said he loved her. Had he only been flirting with her? Had she misread the signs? Lately she had been almost sure – but he had offered for Violet, that was solid, concrete, un-get-overable fact.

One last, miserable surge of feeling pushed the words, 'But he kissed me!' up into her throat, but she managed to choke them back. She mustn't tell – she must never tell. Thank God she never had. She saw in Violet's happy face – happy under the concern for her – the truth of the situation. Violet must not be made miserable by any shadow over this miracle of hers. 'Vi, do you really love him?'

Violet nodded and pressed her hands, and then blurted, 'I do. Oh, Jess, I do love him. I tried not to, for your sake. I wanted you to have him. I tried to keep out of the way. I even pretended to myself about Tommy Fairbanks and then George Carrick, but I can't care for them, not in the same way. They aren't a shadow to him. Oh please, please try not to mind! Even if I refused to marry him, it wouldn't make him marry you, would it? And – and it would break my heart to say no.'

For a moment rebellion welled up in Jessie, and she wanted to tell her friend that she did mind, that Violet must refuse him, that if she refused him Jessie still had a chance with him. But pride came to her rescue. If he had offered for Violet, either he did not love Jessie, and had been trifling with her; or he did love her, but did not think her high enough to be married by him. In either case, she must not make a fool of herself by letting anyone see her disappointment.

And then love for Violet said that if she cared for Brancaster she should have him, and nothing Jessie said should spoil it for her. She must have been mistaken about him, she told herself. The alternative was too horrible, for it would mean that he was not marrying Violet for love. Of course he loved Violet! Who would not? She was everything Jessie was not, beautiful, gentle, good and nobly born. Only a fool would have thought Brancaster could ever prefer her to Violet – and she was that fool. Her heart was like a lump of lead in her chest, making her feel sick, but it was all her own fault and she must not let Violet suffer for it.

'Of course you can't say no,' she said, and her voice came out very strangely, but steadied as she spoke. 'Don't be a little idiot, Vi! If you love him and he loves you, of course you must marry him.'

'But – you won't hate me?'

'How could I ever hate you? You're my friend – practically my sister. I shall be very happy for you.'

'Oh, Jess! Will you really?' With tears of relief she put herself into Jessie's arms and they hugged each other.

'Of course,' Jessie said, her cheek against Violet's hair. 'I'll have a little weep and then that'll be over with. I want you to be happy, darling. That's what matters.'

'I want you to be happy, too. And you will be. You'll find somebody else. Lots of people admire you. That nice Henry Fossey, for instance – and lots of others. You'll find someone before the end of the Season. There are so many nice boys.'

Staring at the wall across Violet's shoulder, Jessie thought: *Yes, but they are just boys. Brancaster is a man.*

'We'd better go and dress,' she said at last, releasing herself and turning away.

'Will you be all right?' Violet asked anxiously.

Jessie turned back to smile vividly – perhaps a little too vividly, but it was a first effort. 'I'm over it already,' she said. 'It was just a silly fancy of mine. I shall dance at your wedding with a light heart. If I'm invited.'

'Of course you'll be there. I won't get married unless you are.'

When the news of Violet's engagement reached Henrietta at Morland Place, she had no-one to discuss it with. Teddy was away on business in Manchester – a not infrequent occurrence since he had textile mills there, and was also planning to build a new department store. Unusually, Jerome was also away. He had gone to visit his sister, who had lived in France for many years and was in failing health. Henrietta and Mary had been close friends once, and it was through her that she had met Jerome, something for which she would always be grateful. But later there had been a cooling between them, and Henrietta had had little contact with her for some time even before she left the country. There had been something behind that emigration – some trouble Mary had got into in London, Henrietta thought – but she had no idea what. Disgraced people always went to live in Paris (or Italy if the disgrace was really bad) but she had never heard anything, and if Jerome knew – she supposed he must – he had not told her. She assumed it was Mary's secret and did not ask him.

Jerome had kept up an infrequent correspondence with his sister – like most men he was not a great letter-writer – but now she was ill he had felt it incumbent on him to go to her. The journey to Paris by train and boat was so easy now that he had intended to be away only a week, but he had said on departing, 'It depends what I find when I get there. Mary doesn't complain much, but reading between the lines I suspect that she may need my help in several ways.'

And Henrietta had said, 'Take as long as you need. Don't worry about anything. I can manage here until Teddy gets back.'

So there she was, queen of all she surveyed – the house and grounds, the home farm, the stud, the rest of the estate, Teddy's York businesses and his eight-year-old daughter Polly – and the only help she could call on was Ned, who was away long hours at the mill, and her son Robbie who, Jerome sometimes joked, had reached his full capacity when he learned to tie his own necktie. But things pretty well ran themselves, with only a light touch on the tiller from time to time, and her duties about the house were considerably eased by the absence of the menfolk and Jessie in London. She even found time to take Polly out riding most days, which was a great pleasure for both of them.

But it did mean she had no-one to share the news with. The heir to an earldom seemed an entirely appropriate prize for Violet, whose father was an earl and whose mother was a countess in her own right and the daughter of a duke, and it was no wonder Venetia sounded pleased about it. Henrietta had never had high worldly ambitions for Jessie. Her own marriage had been for love and had been a very happy one, despite various troubles and a period of severe financial constraint. What she wanted for her daughter was a comfortable income, and love like her own for Jerome. If those things had come wrapped up in an earl's son, she would have been no more happy than if they had come guised as a banker's or a lawyer's or an engineer's.

Venetia's letter said that Violet was very much in love with Lord Brancaster, and was eager for an early wedding. It was mooted for the end of September, as Overton went to Marienbad with the King in August, and he and Venetia were both expected at Balmoral in October. The end of September would give Venetia seven or eight weeks for preparations, and Overton two or three immediately before the wedding for all he needed to do. So Jessie would be able to finish her Season, and Violet would enjoy it with her, her last chance to be a girl.

The original plan had been for Jessie to go home to Morland Place after Cowes Week, when Overton went abroad with the King. At that time Venetia usually came up to Yorkshire and opened up her house, Shawes. There she would spend three weeks with whichever of her children decided to stay with her; Lizzie and Ashley and the boys timed their summer visit to Morland Place to coincide. This annual 'get-together', as Ashley sometimes called it, had become a high point in the year for them all.

But with the wedding to arrange [Venetia's letter continued], I think the family holiday must be given up. I shall have to stay in London, especially as I shall have to do almost everything without Overton's help. If you want Jessie at home, I can send her back to you by train after Cowes Week, but since Violet naturally wants her to be a bridesmaid, I shall need her in London at some point to be fitted, and if you can spare her, I know the girls would like to stay together until the day. It will be wonderful for them both, to be able to share the preparations and excitement. What do you think? I can assure you Jessie is in good health, and if the rigours of the Season have taken their toll on her bright cheeks, it's no more than can be said of any girl in London at present! I shall see to it that there is some time spent in the country during August, for them if not for me – perhaps even a few days by the sea – to restore those roses. And of course you know that you are welcome any time to come and stay. In fact, you will be more than welcome to *me*, as I should value your help and advice about several things. I have never married off a daughter before, and two heads are better than one.

So it looked like being a happy and busy summer in Manchester Square, Henrietta thought, folding the letter. It would be nice to spend some time with Venetia and help her with the wedding. They had always wanted their two girls to be friends, and it was good that the friendship had ripened so much during the last weeks. She hoped it would endure after marriage. Henrietta remembered her first marriage, and how strange and isolated she had felt, and how much she had needed a female friend. She had been able, luckily, to call on her younger sister Regina; she guessed how much Violet, with no sisters of her own, would need Jessie. And for Jessie, it would be a good opportunity to widen her experience and her acquaintance, to be asked to stay with Violet.

On the day after receiving the letter, she had a cable from Jerome to say that he was staying on a week longer; so it would have to be with Teddy that she shared the exciting news. However, when he arrived home from his trip she could barely interest him in it beyond a 'well, well', and a 'pleased for her', because he had news of his own.

'I haven't just been in Manchester this time,' he told her, taking his favourite chair in the drawing-room and stretching out his legs comfortably. 'I've been all the way to Ireland.'

'Ireland? What for?' Henrietta asked. 'Something to do with the horses?' She brought a glass of sherry and set it on the small table beside him, then took her own chair and automatically picked up her sewing, which always lay there beside it in her work-box but never seemed to get very far ahead these days. She was not a natural needlewoman and sewed without great pleasure, but equally she felt odd sitting down with nothing to occupy her.

'Nothing to do with horses at all,' Teddy said, 'though it's natural you should think so. No, I've been to Belfast, to the dockyard of Harland and Wolff, and a most interesting time I've had of it, I can tell you! Pity old Jerome's not at home. I've been keeping this a secret for weeks, and now I'm having to tell it only to half an audience.'

Henrietta gave a private smile, knowing how he felt, but said, '*I'm* here. And I'm very interested. What were you doing at this dockyard?'

'I was there at the invitation of Lord Pirrie, the managing director, and a fellow named Ismay, managing director of the White Star Line.'

'You've mentioned him before, haven't you?' Henrietta said, head bent over her work, trying to find where she had left off the last time.

'I may have done. More likely it was his father, though – Thomas Ismay. He was head of Ismay, Imrie and Company, and I met him quite a few times in Manchester at public meetings and so on. He bought the White Star Line for a thousand pounds when it was bankrupt – oh, thirty or forty years back – and built it up through hard work and good sense until they were able to sell it, back in '02, to an American company for ten million pounds!'

'Goodness,' Henrietta said, beginning to unpick some stitches. She remembered now that it had been late at night when she put them in, and they were large and crooked. I must have been tired, she thought. These are bad even for me!

'Well, by that time Ismay senior had died and it was the son who was in charge. After the sale of the company he stayed on as chairman of White Star, and they thought so well of him they made him a president of the American company too.'

Henrietta looked up, a little surprised. 'He's President of America?'

'No, no, that's what they call a director over there. *A* president, of the American company – International Mercantile Marine. He's married to an American lady – met her when he was working over there for a while. Awfully nice fellow – very clever cove, like Jerome, and completely the gentleman. Went to Harrow, apparently – like Jerome again. They wouldn't have known each other, though – Jerome was well before Ismay's time. Anyway,

111

what happened was that Lord Pirrie and Ismay have a notion to build some new ships, and they invited me to Pirrie's office in Belfast to look at the plans and discuss a little business.'

'Oh, that's nice,' Henrietta said, drawing out the last of the old thread.

'Dash it, Hen,' Teddy said, a little agitated, 'I don't believe you're listening to me at all! Put that old sewing down, can't you?'

'I am listening. You said they are going to build some new ships. And I listen better when I sew.'

'Yes, but these aren't just going to be ordinary ships. They are going to be the biggest, most luxurious ships ever to sail the seas!'

'I thought Cunard had those already,' Henrietta said. 'The *Lusitania* and the *Mauretania*.' She was not completely ignorant of shipping matters because one of Teddy's mills had the lucrative contract to provide linen goods to the Cunard liners.

'Yes – so far. But these chaps mean to outdo Cunard and beat them at their own game – challenge them for the North Atlantic run, where the real money is. So these new ships are going to be half as big again as the *Lusitania* and more luxurious than the most expensive hotel you can imagine. They'll be like floating palaces. Pirrie and Ismay agreed that money should be no object in the fitting out. They're going to cost one and a half million pounds each to build – that'll tell you!'

'One and a half million?' Henrietta's imagination was caught at last. 'And they want you to be involved with them?'

'They want me to provide the linens, as I do for the Cunarders; and not only that, but all the internal fabrics, the curtains and bedcovers and upholstery materials and so on. They even want me to advise on the carpets. It will be the biggest contract I've ever had, worth I don't know how many thousands. And what an advertisement! I'll be able to name my price to other customers when

112

they know I did all the woven materials for White Star's new giant liners! Little Polly is going to grow up a very rich girl indeed! She'll be able to marry anyone she wants – the King of England, if she likes!'

'It sounds wonderful, Teddy dear. I'm so pleased for you! But won't Cunard mind?'

'They have a contract with me, Hen, they don't own my company. I can make linen for anyone I want to.'

'Tell me more. What happened at this meeting?'

'Well, I travelled over with Ismay from Liverpool, and we were met at the docks by Pirrie's motor-car and taken to a very splendid luncheon in the directors' dining room. Then to his office to look at some plans. The managing director in charge of design was there, Thomas Andrews – he's Pirrie's nephew, by the by, nice chap – and the general manager, Alexander Carlisle, who will be in charge of all the decorating and equipping of the ships. They're going to be enormous, Hen, nine hundred feet long – a hundred feet longer than *Lusitania*! They'll be so big that Harland and Wolff are having to build new slipways and gantries for them. Ismay was telling me on the journey that he has had the idea for a long time, but had to hold fire because none of the piers in New York is long enough, and the New York Harbour Board were hard to persuade to build a new one.'

'Have they got names for them yet?'

'Oh yes, giant names for giant ships. They'll be the *Olympic*, the *Titanic* and the *Gigantic*. They expect to lay the *Olympic*'s keel in December, and she'll be two years to build, and will take probably another year to fit out, so she'll be launched some time in 1911.'

'That's a long way off.'

'Gives me more time to get the designs worked out, the samples made and approved, and the machines tooled. Everything will have to be perfect. I'm thinking of giving one whole mill over to the work – the quantities will be enormous, with over a thousand passengers, and of course they will need constant replacements.' His eyes were bright and his face flushed with excitement now, and Henrietta was reminded of him as a youth, on his first visit home from Oxford, describing the skylarks he and his new friends had got up to. 'I shall have to look again very carefully at the workload as it stands now between the mills. I may have to buy or build a new factory entirely. Carlisle showed me some preliminary lists of what they may need. These ships will have every luxury, you know, even down to a gymnasium, Turkish baths and a swimming-bath. Think of all the towels they will need, just to begin with!'

Henrietta laughed, infected with his pleasure. 'It does sound very exciting.'

'There's nothing like it yet in existence,' he said solemnly. 'I've seen the plans and I know. Cunard will be furious when they find out. They can hardly try to build anything still bigger. I got the idea Pirrie and Ismay were a little peeved because Cunard was given all that money by the government to build *Lusitania* and *Mauretania*. Unfair competition, you know! So they are determined to wipe Cunard's eye and steal the North Atlantic prize. Cunard can hardly hope for Asquith to cough up again, just for the pride of the nation.' He chuckled. 'I can't wait to tell Ashley about it. He'll be so interested! When do he and Lizzie arrive? They are still coming?'

'Oh, yes, I can't see that they'd change their plans because of Violet's engagement. They will be here next week, when Jessie was supposed to be coming. Ashley only stays a week, but Lizzie and the boys will stay three weeks at least, four if I can persuade them. And Jack comes at the same time, of course, for his week. He'll be disappointed not to see Jessie.'

'We must have a grand celebration dinner for their first night,' Teddy said eagerly. He loved giving dinners and parties.

Henrietta was doubtful. 'Oh, I don't know that they would want something like that the very first night. Wouldn't it be nicer to have just a family dinner?'

114

'Well, that's all I meant,' Teddy said. 'A grand cele-bration *family* dinner. With lots of champagne. And I'll ask Ned and Robbie if they'd each like to bring a young lady, and one for Jack too, and perhaps have a little dancing after dinner, just by way of a lark. And I'll ask Mrs Meynell – she's practically family.'

Alice Meynell was the widow of an old friend of Teddy's. Ever since her bereavement he had been visiting her, first to commiserate and then to help with the various problems that faced an unprepared woman who had always been looked after by men. Alice had been a great deal younger than her husband and was still only in her thirties and very pretty, one of those gentle, helpless women who always seemed bewildered by life. It was six years since Meynell had died, and the widow might be supposed to have recovered by now; but the marriage had been childless so she had no son or even daughter to support her spirits, and no family of her own. Teddy's visits might well have become irreplaceable to her. Still, wanting to ask her to a family dinner seemed rather pointed, and Henrietta could not shake off the idea that he had suggested young ladies for the boys out of some instinct for symmetry, which hinted at an interest in Mrs Meynell that was more than charitable.

Of all the many activities of her coming-out Season, Jessie thought that she liked Cowes Week best. It had been hard, the last few weeks before it, coping with Violet's engage-ment, trying to be wholeheartedly glad about her radiant happiness, concealing her own pain and disappointment. It had been hardest of all to meet Brancaster for the first time, to offer her congratulations and shake his hand, and feel the utter blankness of his eyes as they rested briefly on her. He had smiled and said all the right things, that he would always welcome her as a sister, knowing how Violet loved her; but the smile and the words had been like knives to her, in the face of what she had allowed herself to dream of and hope for.

He had never loved her, she was sure of that now. It was all a painful and shameful mistake on her part, a shocking self-delusion in one who prided herself on her good sense. He treated her with smiling indifference, and she believed now that his previous attentions to her had simply been for Violet's friend, perhaps hoping for her advocacy in his cause – or perhaps, as Wilson had suggested with a shake of the head, to divert attention from his real object so that Violet would not be subjected to too much talk. There remained that kiss, which was something she was unable to explain to herself. She buried it deep in her mind and did not revisit it, afraid of what she might think about it if she did.

It was painful to be in company with him and Violet together. He was very attentive to Violet, sat by her, fetched her cup, picked up her fan when she dropped it; engaged her in conversation; paid compliments both to her and about her to others. He said to everyone, when they congratulated him, that he was the luckiest man in the world. Violet, now licensed, plainly adored him, and the Overtons were pleased and content with the affair.

When the news was first announced, Jessie had supposed he would be around them all the time, and had braced herself for near-constant pain; but in fact it was not nearly as bad as she feared. He did not visit every day, nor stay all day when he did, and many of her and Violet's engagements continued as they had before, except that he was, of course, a constant subject of conversation. When Violet, anxiously, asked Jessie if she minded her talking about him all the time, Jessie assured her that her own feelings for Brancaster had been the idlest of whims, and that she was over him already; and she said it with enough conviction for Violet at last to believe her. She did not want the slightest shadow to fall over Violet's happiness.

There was still pleasure to be had for Jessie in the rest of the Season. Since Violet's engagement was announced, Henry Fossey had been much more particular in his attentions to Jessie, and she liked him very much, and found his conversation witty and amusing. One evening in the loggia at the opera house, during the interval, he proposed to her. She felt a thrill at the words, and was pleased and grateful to receive an offer, but she had not hesitated before refusing him. She knew she had been sent to London to find a match, and that Fossey would be a good husband, but though she liked him, she was not in love with him, and this close to her passion for Brancaster, she could not shake off the feeling that one ought to be in love to say yes.

Usually an engaged girl went to stay with her future husband's family for a week or so before the wedding so as to become acquainted with them; but as Brancaster's mother was long dead, he had no brothers or sisters, and his father was in poor health, this was not appropriate in Violet's case. Instead, Lord Holkam came to London for one night and entertained Lord and Lady Overton and Violet to dinner at Claridges. Violet came back from that engagement rather subdued, and when Jessie asked her what Lord Holkam had been like, she could only say rather stern and frightening.

'But Mama says he is ill and that might make him seem disagreeable, and one should make allowances.'

'Didn't your mother like him, then?' Jessie asked.

Violet looked a little troubled. 'He seemed almost not to like *her*,' she said, as if stating the impossible. 'But perhaps he was in pain, poor man. I think from what Brancaster said it was a great trouble to him to come to London at all, in his state of health.'

Jessie hoped she had acquitted herself creditably since Violet's engagement, but it had been hard for her. Sometimes she felt as though her jaws would snap with the strain of smiling and smiling. So it was a relief to leave London and Brancaster behind and go down to Cowes with the Overtons. She had never been on a yacht before, nor seen a yacht race, and she was looking forward enormously to both. Lord and Lady Overton stayed on the Sandowns' yacht, *Tutamen*, and rented a cottage on the island for the children. It was a charming house only a few dozen yards from the sea, and this year Colonel Sir Harry Seavill had taken the cottage next door; so in addition to the three boys, she and Violet would have the company of Florence and Amalfia. And Jack had promised to come over from Southampton for at least one day, and perhaps for longer if work permitted.

Jessie enjoyed the week enormously: watching the wonderful yachts skim like birds over the water, their sails braced like wings to the breeze; strolling about the Royal Yacht Squadron gardens, listening to the bands, taking tea on the lawn; reading her name listed the next day in the newspaper among the guests present! She loved the sea, the smell of it, the buoyant sparkle of it under the sun that made you feel it was foolish to be unhappy about anything. She loved the sound of the seagulls and their whiteness against the blue sky. She loved the harbour sound of water slapping against the hulls, and the clink of rigging against the masts.

And at the cottage they all had great fun. Jessie went sea-bathing for the first time, and after the initial shock of the cold and the strangeness of the water, she took to it with delight and even learned to swim a stroke or two. The boys hired rowing boats and took the girls out on the water, and tried to teach them how to fish. There were drives in a selection of governess carts and dog carts to see Osborne House and Carisbrooke Castle. They played cricket in the garden, and foolish card games, paper games and charades in the evening in one parlour or the other. And there was, all the time, a wonderful, inexhaustible flow of easy, comfortable conversation.

Oliver talked to Jessie at length about his plans to become a doctor – with everything else Venetia had had to do, she had found time to write the necessary letters and conduct the necessary interviews, and he was to start as a medical student in October at the Middlesex. He was to spend the summer 'cramming' with a tutor to try to get his basic subjects up to scratch. The tutor his mother had arranged for him was an old friend of hers, a rather impoverished general practitioner. Mark Darroway had helped Venetia to study when he was a student and she was barred from medical school. He had a practice in Soho and had never been well off, partly because of the number of poor people he treated, and partly because he had a numerous family. He was glad of the extra money for cramming Oliver, and Venetia was glad to do him a good turn, and to know that Oliver was in safe hands.

Oliver had met him, and thought him a trump. 'He sees such a variety of cases in his line of practice that I know he'll be really useful to me. And he has such a clear way of explaining things – useful to a duffer like me!'

'You aren't a duffer at all,' Jessie said. 'You've just never been interested before.'

'It's nice talking to you,' Oliver said. 'You're so sensible, and so interested in everything.'

Perhaps the best thing, Jessie thought afterwards, was that Brancaster was not at Cowes. For the week, Violet was her own special property, just as in the old days. She cherished every moment, realising that it was perhaps for the last time. All too soon they had to go back to London, to be engulfed by the increasing frenzy of the wedding preparations. Violet became the affianced of Lord Brancaster again, and a public figure. Her picture was in the illustrated papers, speculation about the wedding filled the gossip pages, the important wedding gifts were listed, photographers hung around the door in Manchester Square, and a stream of visitors called to offer their felicitations, or sometimes just to stare. Violet sailed through it all on a tide of happiness and requited love, and at night, after they had gone to bed, often trotted through to climb on Jessie's bed and talk and talk. The engagement did not change her: she was just the same Violet, and Jessie loved her just the same. But she was not entirely Jessie's Violet any more, and soon would be very much someone else's.

★   ★   ★

119

Lizzie and Ashley and the boys reached Morland Place in time for lunch. They were the first of the visitors to arrive: Jack's journey from Southampton was rather longer and he was expected by the middle of the afternoon. Martial and Rupert were excited to be back at Morland Place, which was so different in every way from their tall, narrow London house in Endsleigh Gardens, and wanted at once to be released from the iron grip of their nurse, Nana, who had accompanied them, so that they could run and inspect every part, from the shadowy cellars up to the mysterious attics. Polly wanted them to come with her at once and play with her dog, Bell, and go and see the family of kittens that was living in the Easter Barn. Nana wanted them to greet their grandparents and the rest of the company with polished politeness and remain quietly while the grown-ups talked, the better to display the fruits of her training. Emma, tears of pleasure in her eyes at seeing them again, wanted to take them to the kitchen and feed them cake, despite the imminence of luncheon; and Kithra and Fern wanted to wash them.

Compromise was reached by sending all the children upstairs with Nana and Emma, to see their bedroom (the old night-nursery, from which Polly had been promoted to the Red Room), to be changed out of their smart travelling outfits of Norfolk jacket and knickerbockers into sailor suits in which they could play, and to have luncheon in the day-nursery. Martial immediately said to Polly, 'Race you to the nursery,' a challenge he was likely to lose, and the three of them rushed away, with the dogs bounding after them and Emma and Nana following more sedately, talking comfortably of nursery things, coughs and laundry, naps and diets, rashes and home remedies.

When the thunder of feet had died away, Teddy asked if Lizzie and Ashley would like to go straight to their room, but Lizzie said she would sooner sit and chat until luncheon was ready, and they went into the drawing-room.

'It's so much nicer than the way I remember it when

we first came here,' Lizzie said with satisfaction, looking round the panelled room and the elaborately patterned plaster on the ceiling. 'I can't think how anyone could want to cover up the panelling with wall-paper.'

'Well, that was the fashion then,' said Henrietta, whose late elder brother George – or, rather, his wife Alfreda – had been responsible for many 'modernising' changes to the house, which Teddy over the years had been unpicking. 'Besides, Alfreda thought the panelling was ugly and gloomy.'

'But it's so magnificent. Most people would give anything to have something like this in their house.'

Henrietta said, 'I like it but, then, I grew up with it. Some people do think panelling gloomy. Though it's very practical. Wall-paper does *mark* so.'

Lizzie laughed and said, 'Practical? Oh, Mother!'

Henrietta smiled. 'We're lucky that Alfreda didn't have it removed, but only boarded over. It's the original linen-fold, you know, from the fifteenth century. It could never have been replaced. If it had been pulled out it would probably have been burned.'

'It makes me feel quite faint to think of,' Lizzie said.

'Perhaps at the last minute George had a conscience about it,' Henrietta said.

'Look here,' Teddy interrupted plaintively, 'this is all very well but I have some news to tell.'

'And so have we,' Lizzie said, and seeing her uncle's stricken face hurried on, 'but you be first.'

They were very interested, as Teddy had predicted, in his news. Ashley worked for a shipping line, and was American by birth – as was his principal, Mr Culpepper – so he understood and appreciated every point Teddy had to make. Not only that, but he had met Lord Pirrie, briefly, at the offices of the Culpepper Line, and both he and Lizzie had dined in company with the Ismays at Mr Culpepper's house.

'Oh, yes, I remember him very well,' Lizzie said to her mother. 'He was a striking man, with a big, handsome head – the sort of person you can't help looking at when he comes into a room.'

'Never mind that,' Ashley said, amused. 'What does it matter what he looks like? He's an intelligent man, with a forthright way of talking – didn't you think, sir?'

Teddy agreed. 'Precise. Says exactly what he means, no flowers and curlicues. Sort of man it's good to do business with, because you always know where you are.'

Lizzie said, 'I had a long chat with his wife while the men were at their port. Such a nice lady, and not a bit assuming, considering they are millionaires. She was so easy to talk to.'

'That's American manners, my love,' Ashley said. 'We sometimes find English manners rather too stiff and formal.'

'I think Mrs Ismay felt that. She said some people, especially in America, did not like her husband's direct way of speaking, and thought him cold, but that he is really very shy and that's his way of hiding it.'

'Oh, you women do talk nonsense,' Teddy said. 'Why shouldn't a man be exact in his speech?'

'I agree,' said Ashley. 'Flowery language is all very well for poets and drawing-room *roués*, but a man of business should use words as an engineer uses tools.'

'Quite. To say that speaking precisely makes a man cold and unfeeling—'

'*I* didn't say he was cold,' Lizzie said indignantly. 'Mrs Ismay said other people sometimes thought he was. She said she took a while to get used to it when she first met him. But she said he's the kindest man in the world and always anxious to help anyone in trouble.'

'It makes me turn cold to think how you women will talk about us behind our backs,' Ashley said. 'Here's a lady you've only just met . . .'

'I didn't tell her anything about you, my love, so you needn't worry.'

'I think you are all wandering off the point,' Teddy interrupted. 'The point is that Ismay and Pirrie are going to build the largest and most luxurious moving objects ever seen upon the face of this earth, and that I, Edward Morland of Morland Place, was their immediate and unhesitating choice to provide the soft furnishings.'

'Quite right, Uncle Teddy,' Lizzie said. 'That is a fine and wonderful thing and worthy of celebration.'

'I'm glad you see it like that, because I've planned a special dinner tonight when the boys are all here, and I promise you the champagne will flow like water.'

Henrietta said, 'But, Lizzie, darling, you said you had some news, too.'

She looked at her husband a moment and then said, 'Yes, I have. It may sound rather small beer besides this ship business, but – well, Ashley and I are expecting another child.'

Lizzie went up early to bed, while Ashley looked settled in for a long conversation with Teddy about business and politics, so Henrietta took her chance and followed her daughter up to her room for a private conversation.

'You look tired, darling,' she said. 'Let me maid you.'

'Oh, would you?' Lizzie said. 'Darling Mother. I feel all fingers and thumbs tonight.' Henrietta undid all of her many buttons and helped her off with her dress, and then Lizzie turned her back and she began on her stay laces.

'Who does this for you at home?'

'Oh, one of the girls. Or Ashley, sometimes.'

'I like it when Papa does mine. It's a special thing.'

'Mother!'

'Darling, I'm not so very old yet, you know.'

'I know but – well, you are my mother.'

Henrietta laughed, and planted a kiss on the back of her daughter's neck. 'I hope you have a little girl this time,' she said. 'I would like you to know what it's like to have a daughter.'

'It won't be a girl. I'm the sort of person who has boys,' Lizzie said, and she sounded so despondent that Henrietta looked thoughtful.

123

She removed the corset and dropped it on a chair, and said, 'Sit down at the dressing-table and I'll brush out your hair. That always used to soothe you when you were a girl.'

Lizzie obeyed, and said, 'How did you know I need soothing?'

'I know there's something wrong,' Henrietta said, feeling for pins and pulling them out. 'It's not just tiredness from the journey.'

'I *am* tired,' Lizzie said. 'Dreadfully tired. I'd forgotten how awful the beginning of pregnancy is. Or was it this bad the last time? I can't remember properly from ten years ago.' Henrietta maintained a receptive silence. 'Ten years!' Lizzie went on. 'I'm thirty-six, Mother. I thought I'd done with all this. Now I've to begin it all again – the sickness and the backache and feeling like a badly packed piece of luggage for month after month. And then at the end of it all, the agonies of childbirth.'

Henrietta picked up the hairbrush and began on the length of Lizzie's tumbled hair – curly like Jessie's, but not so fair now. 'At the end of it all,' she suggested, 'a dear little baby.'

'Oh yes, I know,' Lizzie said. She stared at nothing, not meeting her mother's reflected eyes. 'You might as well know,' she announced defiantly, 'that I don't want this baby.'

'Oh, Lizzie!'

'I can't say so to Ashley, of course. Now it's coming he's delighted, and he expects me to be, too. But men always are, aren't they? It's not them that have to go through it.'

'I know, darling, but Ashley's a good man and a kind husband, isn't he? And a baby can come any time to a married woman. It's in God's hands.'

'Not in our case,' Lizzie said, and now she did meet Henrietta's eyes – still defiantly, but with a splash of colour in her cheeks. 'Did you never wonder why we stopped after the two boys? Or, rather, *how* we stopped? We take precautions. We didn't mean to have any more. This baby is – is a mistake.'

Henrietta did not speak at once, feeling deeply embarrassed about the turn the conversation had taken. Of course, she *had* wondered; she had even suspected; but it was not something she could ever have brought herself to broach with her daughter. It was not so very long ago that contraception was absolutely taboo. It was considered disgusting and immoral, and the public verdict was that a woman practising it made herself a prostitute. Twenty years ago doctors could be struck off for advising on it, and two people had been imprisoned for publishing a book about it. Decent women did not talk about contraception, and if there were some who secretly practised it, they would never have dreamed of admitting it to anyone.

It had not even now become completely accepted, and women of Henrietta's generation had difficulty in shrugging off the attitude of the times they had lived through. But she was aware (though she did not quite know *how* she was) that younger married women these days did not want to be perpetually pregnant like their mothers and grandmothers, and that they and their husbands were using artificial methods to limit their families.

Lizzie said, 'Are you shocked?'

Henrietta gathered herself. 'No, not shocked, precisely.'

'You are. You think I'm wicked.'

'No, darling, of course I don't.'

'Well, what, then?'

'It's – it's not something I feel comfortable with. But you are old enough to make your own decisions – you and Ashley.'

Lizzie looked gloomy again. 'That's what *we* thought. But here I am, pregnant again!'

'Your *precautions* didn't work?'

'Sometimes they don't. That's what they tell you. But we never thought it would happen to us. Oh Mother, I don't *want* this baby!

Henrietta was shaken out of her embarrassment. 'Oh,

Lizzie, don't say that! Please don't say that. All babies are from God. He means you to have this child, and when it comes, you'll love it.'

'Will I?' she sighed.

'You will,' Henrietta said firmly. 'And it's best that you should never have to remember you said anything to the contrary.' Lizzie remained unconvinced, she could see. Henrietta resumed her brushing.

After a moment, Lizzie said, 'You had five.'

'And one I lost.'

'I'd forgotten that.'

Henrietta smiled slightly. 'I wouldn't expect you to remember. But I often think about it, and wish it hadn't died.'

'You'd have wanted more children?'

'Oh, yes. But of course Papa and I started late. I was thirty-two when I married him. I always wanted a large family.'

'Like Aunt Regina, and her eight.' Lizzie shuddered.

Henrietta smoothed the length of hair down Lizzie's back, laid down the brush, and said, 'You will love the baby when it comes. You'll see. When you hold it, you'll wonder how you could ever have doubted it for a moment.'

'I hope you're right,' Lizzie said, with a sigh. 'Just now I feel too tired and horrible to believe it.'

Chapter Five

Jack was sitting at his slope in his office, daydreaming. This was a pleasant room on the top floor, with a window stretching along most of one wall, giving an airy view of the small tributary of the estuary, which ran along the back of the building. When the tide was out, the water became a narrow trickle running in a deep groove between wide mudflats, where redshanks and oystercatchers plied their busy trade. There were curlews on the marshy land on the far side, whose rippling cries always raised the hairs on Jack's neck, and further off a few red-brown cows grazed the tangy grass in pace with flocks of lapwing. It was a fine September day, with that soft sunshine of early autumn that Jack always thought was more golden than summer sun; with his window partly open, a delicious air wafted gently in, warmly tinted with salt and sea, mud and grass and leaves.

There was a tap on his door immediately followed by a rattle of the doorknob. It was loose and did not catch easily, which gave Jack just enough time to come back to himself and pull the top sheet across what he had been dreaming over. The door opened, and a young man came in: a stranger, a year or two younger than Jack, in a rather battered tweed suit. He had thick, dark-brown, somewhat unruly hair, and the most pleasant, friendly face Jack had ever seen. He began to smile automatically just at the sight of it, and the young man, who had been hovering politely in the doorway, beamed in response, his face alight and eager.

'I say, I hope I'm not disturbing you? Mr Rankin said to come up.'

'Not at all,' said Jack.

The young man advanced, hand held forward. 'Thomas Sopwith,' he said. 'You are Mr Compton?'

'Yes, that's right. Jack Compton. How do you do?'

'Mr Rankin told me you are the genius behind the new motor-boat, and I very much wanted to meet you,' said Sopwith. 'You'll excuse the informality? He said I could come straight up. He and my pater are old friends, so I'm something of the "son he never had".' He made a charming and expressive face. 'I fancy he has quite a number of them.'

Jack laughed. 'Yes, I think I may be one, too. Luckily for me, of course.' He waved a hand round the office. 'I don't know where else I would have been given so much leeway.'

'Oh, rot,' said Sopwith. 'From what I hear you are the jewel in the company's crown – and now I see you in the flesh, I can tell you must be brilliant to be chief engineer and designer already. I was expecting a fellow of my father's age at least.'

'Are you interested in the JC?' he asked.

'I've had a look at her and she's beautiful. I mean to take her out for a trial, but I had to come and meet the lady's father first.'

'Are you thinking of buying one?' Jack asked, mindful that wages had to be paid.

'Quite likely. My father gives me a shockingly large allowance, and I love all things mechanical: motor-cars, motorcycles - I've a motorcycle of my own, a Triumph 450. Goes a bit when she gets a clear stretch of decent road and I can let her out. And I've done quite a bit of sailing, but I've never driven a motor-boat.'

Forgetting to be a salesman in the warmth of Sopwith's interest, Jack said, 'The JC is really rather a first effort. There are things about her I'm not satisfied with, which I hope we'll do better in the JC2 – if Mr Rankin lets me redesign her.'

'What sort of things?' Sopwith asked, and when Jack hesitated, wondering how simple he needed to make the explanation, he added, 'If it helps, I'm an engineer too – well, training to be one.'

'Indeed?'

'Yes, I'm at Seafield Park.' This was an engineering college a little further down the estuary, at Lee-on-the-Solent. 'I'm just about to start my last year.'

'I was at Manchester,' Jack said.

'Oh, I've heard good things about that place. They turn out very bright chaps there. My father's a civil engineer, so it's in the family, you know.' He smiled suddenly. 'As the only boy in a litter of girls, I suppose I pretty well had to follow in Father's footsteps – it would have broken the pater's heart otherwise. How about you?'

'No, there's no history of engineering in my family: farmers and horse-breeders since time immemorial. My only connection with machinery is that my uncle Teddy is a manufacturer. Textiles. He makes all the linens for the Cunarders,' Jack said, and added with a touch of pride, 'He's going to make all the soft furnishings for the new giant ships White Star is building. Have you heard about them?'

'Have I not!' Sopwith said. 'There's little else talked of all along Southampton Water!'

Now Jack laughed at himself. 'It's a very faint sort of reflected glory for me, isn't it? But I can be proud of the JC, at any rate. Come and have a look at the drawings, and I'll explain what I want to improve on her.'

He spread the drawings out on his desk, and the two young men lit cigarettes and pored over them. 'The shape of the hull isn't quite right,' Jack said. 'There's too much turbulence under the bow. I think I can make her much faster if I can get rid of the backwash, by increasing the taper *here*. And then there's the propellor. I've a lot of theories about propellor shape . . .'

There followed an enjoyably technical conversation, and the initial liking between the two warmed by the minute. Several cigarettes later, Sopwith said, 'So, is it because of your uncle's connections that you decided to design boats – rather than, say, motor-cars?'

'No, not really. I did work on motor-cars for a while, but the business closed down and then it was a case of taking the positions that were offered. The best opening for me in Manchester was with a boat-building company, and that led on to Rankin Marine. And after all, an engine is an engine, no matter what you put it in.'

'That's true enough. But you're designing the whole craft now, not just the engine.'

'If you want to know where my heart really lies, come and look at this.' He went back to his slope, and turned up the top sheet, letting it drop over the back, to reveal what he had been daydreaming over when Sopwith first came in.

Sopwith stepped up close. 'I say, an aeroplane! Are you actually building it?'

'No, this is just a fancy model,' Jack said. 'But there are lots of things that are similar, to my mind, between driving a body through the water and through the air. The lines, the effect of turbulence – the propellor, of course, does the same job. I'm sure the shape of the propellor is crucial to performance.'

'First get your boat into the air,' Sopwith said. 'There is that small problem. It's never been done yet.'

'Oh, but it's happening already,' Jack said. 'Powered flight isn't just a dream any more. There's a fellow in France – an Englishman, called Henry Farman – who actually flew a box-kite biplane about two thirds of a mile this year, back in January. Of course, there's a lot more work to be done on it – it was very unstable in manoeuvring, apparently – but there's no doubt he got daylight under the wheels, and kept it in the air for several minutes.'

'But flying is not really a practical possibility, is it?'

'There's not a doubt in my mind that it is. There are scores of people over there working on various kinds of

130

flying machines, and it's only a matter of time before they iron out the problems. There's a French magazine all about it. Mr Rankin gets old copies sent him and he lets me see them.'

'By Jove, I'd like to have a look at those!'

'And there are two brothers in America who claim to have stayed up for half an hour at once.'

'Yes, I've heard of them – Wright, isn't that their name? – but nobody believes them really, do they?'

'I know there's a lot of scepticism – my sister's husband is an American, and he says the American papers scoff about it and call them liars. The *New York Herald* said it was difficult to fly but very easy to say "We have flown".'

'That's true enough.'

'But one of the brothers has brought his machine over to France this year to demonstrate, and I don't believe he would do that if he weren't confident he could get it up. I don't think he has actually flown it yet, though I haven't seen the most recent issues of the magazine. But I'm quite certain in my own mind that powered flight is not far off now.'

Sopwith's eyes glowed with enthusiasm. 'My word, wouldn't that be something? I've done some ballooning, and that's good fun, but one's completely at the mercy of the wind. You never know how fast you'll go or where you'll land. But an aeroplane, now! If you could steer it, and take off and land at will . . . ! You really think it's coming?'

'I've no doubt at all.'

'Well, when it does, I mean to be one of the first flying men up there!'

'Me too! Think of being up in the sky with the birds, looking down!'

They grinned at each other exuberantly, and at that moment Mr Rankin came in. He was an austere-looking, thin, elderly man, but the sight of the two young men, handsome with all the vigour of youth, softened his face almost into a smile.

131

'So, you've been making friends, have you? Young Sopwith here is the son of a very old friend of mine, Compton, and he's interested in our motor-boat. Going to take it out for a trial spin, aren't you, my boy? It's all ready for you now, if you'd like to come along.'

'Right-oh!' said Sopwith. 'Well, it was a great pleasure to meet you, Mr Compton.' They shook hands again. 'Once I'm back at Seafield, how about getting together one Sunday, and taking a spin out into the country? I know where I can borrow a motor-car. We could find some inn or other for a spot of grub.'

'I'd like that very much,' said Jack.

'Good. I look forward to it.'

'I hope you like the JC.'

Sopwith followed Mr Rankin out, and Jack returned to his legitimate work, feeling that he had made a real friend.

The consequence of this visit manifested itself a few days later when Mr Rankin summoned Jack to his office. This was at the front of the building, overlooking busy Southampton Water and the boatyard itself, and was luxuriously panelled and carpeted, with a large fireplace, extensive bookshelves, and a display of scale models of some of Rankin's best lines. Over the fireplace was an oil painting of Mr Rankin's wife, who had died giving birth to their only child, a stillborn son. He had never married again, dedicating his life to his business. Jack thought he looked unexpectedly small, dwarfed by the big room and the enormous desk, and rather alone. He remembered Sopwith's words about 'the son he never had'. Rankin had been very good to Jack, and a warmth of gratitude filled him, which was almost like affection.

'You sent for me, sir?'

'Yes, Compton. You'll be pleased to know that young Sopwith is going to buy a JC.'

'I'm glad to hear it, sir.'

'He is very well connected, and visits with many leading families in Hampshire, and of course knows all the sailing folk. I think we may hope for some favourable advertisement from this sale. Indeed, I have already received in the post this morning an enquiry from Lord Ruthven about a JC for his son, who is a friend of Sopwith's.'

'I'm very pleased, sir.'

Mr Rankin examined Jack in silence a moment, and then added, 'I must confess that it was in my mind, when I sent young Sopwith up to see you, that you and he might take a liking to each other. He seemed very impressed with you, Compton, and I believe you may take the credit for this sale all to yourself.'

'Thank you, sir.'

'I am very pleased with your work, very pleased indeed. Perhaps I don't express myself sufficiently on that subject. I believe you have great abilities.' He gave his infrequent, rather grim smile. 'Compliments are all very well, but man cannot live by compliments alone, eh? I mean to increase your salary, Compton, with immediate effect, by one hundred pounds per annum.'

It was almost the last thing Jack had expected. 'Thank you, sir!' he gasped.

'I know you will justify my faith in you.' The effort at personal contact was proving a strain on Mr Rankin, and he now dismissed Jack – 'That is all' – and began reading the papers in front of him to emphasise that no more should be said.

It was several weeks later, when Jack and Sopwith met for the proposed 'spin', that he learned the background to this little scene. The friendship between the two blossomed, so that within a few hours they felt as if they had known each other all their lives. Jack was eighteen months the elder, but Sopwith's more varied experience of life made up for that, and the two had similar tastes and interests and the same warm, friendly nature.

As they chugged noisily along in the borrowed motor-car, Jack told his new friend about the raise in his salary. Sopwith grinned mischievously. 'Ah, I was hoping something might come of it!'

'Come of what?'

'Well, I know old Rankin pretty well, and he's a decent old bird, but not the readiest when it comes to shelling out. So I thought as I was in the right place that I might as well try and do you a bit of good. Told him how bright you are. Said I thought you had great talents. Hinted that you might be tempted away at any time by a rival firm offering you more money.'

'Good Lord, you didn't really?'

'Oh, I didn't make you out disloyal, don't worry about that. I just told Rankin he was jolly lucky to have you and hoped he was doing all in his power to keep you. Mentioned what high salaries good designers could command: companies virtually coming to blows over the best chaps, and so on. Laid it on with a trowel, rather, but it seems to have worked.'

Jack laughed. 'And there I was, thinking I'd won it on my own merits.'

'So you did!' Sopwith said. 'Rankin wouldn't have stumped up if he hadn't known all those things were true. I was just the catalyst, that's all.'

'You obviously have a genius for that. I can imagine you now, going through life catalysing people right, left and centre.'

'Well, someone has to make things happen, and people are shockingly inert on the whole. And having seven sisters teaches you something about methods of getting your own way. Have you plans for spending the extra, if you don't mind my asking?'

'I'm going to save it,' Jack said.

'Sounds dull.'

'Not when you have an object.'

Sopwith brightened. 'A motor-car?'

'No, a lady named Maud.'

'Nice name. Someone local?'

'No, her people live in London. Pont Street. So I don't get to see her very often. I'm not the official suitor, you see, so I can only "call in", as it were, when I'm in London for a reason.'

'Oh, really? Well, as it happens, my family live in Kensington. You must come and visit me at home one weekend, and that'll give you the perfect excuse to call on the lovely Miss – what's her name?'

'Puddephat.'

'I wonder if my people know them? Might be a way to advance your cause if they do. I shall make discreet enquiries.'

'Thanks awfully. You really are a friend,' Jack said, pleased and surprised at the warmth of his interest, and his instant desire to help.

'So I should hope,' said Sopwith, shrugging off the thanks. 'Shall we see how fast the bus can go? There's a straight stretch just coming up. Would you like to take the wheel?'

'I'd like to, but I don't know how.'

'What? You've never driven a car before?'

'Well, don't sound so astonished! I should think most of the population never has.'

'I'm not concerned with them, old chap, only you. Right it is! The first suitable field we come to, I shall undertake to make a driver of you. It's quite easy, you know, only a matter of being able to do two things at once. If you can ride a horse, you can drive a motor-car. At least a motor doesn't go into hysterics at the sight of a cow or a sandwich bag blowing in the wind.'

Violet's wedding seemed to Jessie, both at the time and afterwards in reflection, a thing quite unreal, somewhere between a dream and a play in a theatre. And, like the heroine of a dream, Violet became, as the day drew nearer, both more vivid and more distant.

To the *ton*, it was the Wedding of the Year; but the population of London at large had also taken Violet to their hearts. She was, to begin with, not only very young and ravishingly pretty but sweet and good into the bargain: remarkably for the most written-about débutante of the Season, there was no-one who had anything but good to say of her. Then there was the fairy-tale quality of her having captured the heart of the most sought-after *parti* in London. It was a story to warm the heart of *Daily Mail* readers. The gossip columns hastened to remember that Brancaster had attended Violet's launch ball and had chosen her as his first partner. (In fact, he had danced with Jessie first, but no-one remembered that now.)

This would have been enough for the newspapers and illustrated weeklies to 'take her up', but there was a gratifying newsworthiness to her family and connections. Her mother was the daughter of the Duke of Southport and had been one of the first lady doctors, a story that in itself had all the elements of romance; and her father was a close friend of the King, who, it was fervently believed, would attend the wedding and the breakfast, making it the event of all events to be seen at. As the appetite of clerks and housemaids was whetted rather than satisfied, journalists probed deeper into the family, and came up with the story of how the present duke had been a suburban civil servant when the failure of the direct line hurtled him into the title and wealth. Was there no end to the romance of this family? Thomas (handsome brother in the Blues) was photographed at the Changing of the Guard and his current mild interest in Lady Jane Culverkeys was inflated into an *affaire du coeur*. Oliver and Eddie were dogged by hungry 'news hounds', and one of the less scrupulous papers hinted darkly at some exciting mystery in Eddie's origins.

So there were pages every week about the family and the wedding plans. Photographs appeared everywhere of Violet looking beautiful stepping out of a taxi-cab in Manchester Square, riding in Rotten Row, attending a military review, arriving at the opera, visiting a gallery. There could hardly have been more excitement if it had been a royal wedding; and the instinctive desire for some privacy, which made Venetia refuse to give details of what her daughter would be wearing on the day, set the popular press into a ferment of speculation over what soon came to be known simply as The Dress. Sanders, who was to go with Violet when she married, cut out everything she found about the wedding, and began to make up a scrap book.

Jessie had to grow used to seeing her own picture in the papers, as a companion or background to Violet, and even sometimes to having her name mentioned, as one of the bridesmaids. It added to the sense of unreality for her. As the day came closer there seemed more and more to do and less time for the girls to be alone together, so what Violet was feeling about the whole affair became an unknown quantity to her. She thought her friend was looking strained and not as radiantly happy as she would have expected; she came to the conclusion at last that poor Violet was 'scared stiff' – and who wouldn't be? Jessie thought that to have to walk down the aisle of the great cathedral with thousands of eyes on her, and thousands more waiting outside, would be enough to put anyone off the idea of marrying at all. The whole thing seemed to promise to be stiff and magnificent and terrible. Only the prize of Brancaster at the end of it could make it all worth while.

But Lord Brancaster, the handsome prince of the fairy story, seemed more unreal, too, as the days passed. He and Violet were never alone – and, in fact, they saw less of him than when he had been courting her. Jessie met Lord Holkam, who came to dinner at Manchester Square (a return engagement for the Claridges dinner) and he seemed to her old and ugly and frightening, his vast face an unnatural colour, his eyes small and congested like those of the bull back home. He was pushed by a manservant in a wheeled chair, his right foot propped up and hugely swaddled, and when he was helped out of it and on to an ordinary one at the dinner table he seemed to come up all-of-a-piece like a horrid misshapen marionette. There was a strange smell about him, too, which Jessie noticed when she went up to curtsey to him. He hardly spoke during dinner, glared about him as though disliking his surroundings, and left immediately afterwards, declining to sit over port and cigars with the gentlemen or join the ladies in the drawing-room. His health was again advanced as the excuse. Violet and Brancaster were to live with him after their marriage, in his country house. Jessie imagined her friend disappearing into the ogre's den like a sacrificial victim: Violet so slender and pale and delicate, the ogre so huge and grim and hideous. How could handsome Brancaster have sprung from those loins?

The great day came at last. Wilson and another housemaid dressed Jessie while Hayter helped Sanders with Violet – or The Bride, as Jessie sometimes found herself thinking of her. The process, she imagined, was something like the elaborate feats undertaken in the kitchen by a master chef – somewhere between creation and decoration. Jessie herself had gone to a peak of excitement and then over the top, and now felt tired and somehow remote from what was happening to her body, as though she were floating outside herself and merely observing. It meant she stood unprecedentedly still while the maids dressed her, earning their faintly surprised praise for her patience: usually Wilson had to fling clothes on to her as she passed, so to speak. All the bridesmaids were wearing cream satin with pale pink sashes and headdresses of pink rosebuds. When Wilson turned her to look in the long glass (lent for the day) she thought, from her remote, floating position, that the girl in the reflection looked beautiful.

Then Sanders came to say that Violet was ready and would like to see her, so moving carefully and rather stiffly (satin demanded a very efficient corset), she went through the bathroom to Violet's bedroom. Violet was standing in the middle of the room looking even stiffer than Jessie felt. She turned rather jerkily on the spot to face her as Jessie came in, and Jessie stopped for a long moment to gaze. Violet's wedding gown was of white lace over a silk slip, and the slim, high-waisted style suited both the material

and the girl, making her look tall and slender and eth-
ereal. Her face was perhaps rather pale, but her eyes were
enormous and bright, and with the headdress of pearls
and diamonds interwoven with white rosebuds in her dark
hair, she seemed crowned with stars.

It was necessary to speak. Jessie said, 'You look . . .'
and then since no more suitable word came to her unready
brain she concluded ' . . .beautiful.'

Violet's lips trembled. 'Oh, Jessie,' she said, and held
out her hands. Jessie went to her, and took them. They
were icy. 'I'm so scared,' she said, almost in a whisper.

'You'll be all right,' Jessie said automatically.
'Everything will be all right.'

Violet's eyes filled with tears. She stared desperately
into Jessie's. 'I don't want to marry him,' she whispered.
'I don't want to marry at all.'

'Vi, darling . . .' Jessie began, but could think of no
way to continue.

'I wish I'd never seen him. I don't want to go away
from Mama and you and home and the boys and everything. I don't want to be all alone in a hotel with him. I
keep thinking about – about what's going to happen, and
I'm scared.'

Jessie knew what she meant. It was not a subject they
had ever discussed – that was unthinkable – but she had
thought about it often and guessed Violet had too.
Naturally, any girl would. Did Violet know how the thing
was done? Cousin Venetia was a doctor – had she told
her? Jessie had grown up on a stud farm and she knew
some things about breeding in animals, though she didn't
quite see how they could be applied to humans. But
when you were in love, she thought, you did not think
of that unecstatic end to the romance. She had loved
Brancaster and hoped to marry him without ever contemplating what it meant. Now she considered him briefly
in that agricultural light and found the prospect both
thrilling and terrifying, and had to snatch her mind
hastily away.

She had to say something to Violet. 'But you do love him, don't you?'

'I don't know,' Violet said. 'I thought I did, but this morning it doesn't feel like it.'

Jessie pressed the hands that were beginning to warm a little in hers. It was impossible for Violet to scratch from the race now; what Jessie must do was somehow help to bring her up to the mark.

'It's just nerves,' she said. 'You do love him really, and everything will be all right. You're marrying the man of your dreams – your handsome prince. You're the luckiest girl in the world. Just think of all those other girls envying you, and enjoy it.'

A faint smile was her reward. 'Do you really think it will be all right? I mean – everything?'

'Yes, I do. You love him and he loves you. It will be – wonderful.'

'Thank you,' Violet said, after a moment, and leaned forward to kiss Jessie's cheek, leaving a tear there, like a touch of chrism that Jessie never wanted to wipe away.

'I have something for you,' she said. 'I was going to give it to you afterwards, but I wonder now if I'll be able to get near you afterwards, so perhaps I'd better give it to you now.'

It was a brooch, made of coral in the shape of a hand, holding a mother-of-pearl rose.

'It isn't much,' Jessie said, 'but it comes with my love. My best love, always.'

'It's beautiful,' Violet said. She knew better than anyone how little money Jessie had and what effort this represented. 'I shall treasure it always. Pin it on me, darling.'

'Vi, not on your wedding dress!'

'Yes, yes, I want you to. I want something of yours with me, today of all days. Pin it here for me.'

So Jessie attached the cheap little brooch to Violet's fabulously expensive lace just at the base of her throat, where she had indicated, and kissed the pale, velvet cheek with love. Then she stepped back, and the girls looked at each other for a long moment. This was the real ending, they knew. They would never be alone together like this again.

'Goodbye, Jessie,' Violet said.

'Goodbye, Violet darling.'

The wedding took them over. Afterwards Jessie remembered the photographs in the illustrated papers of the Coronation, and thought it was a bit like that, for the bride's party travelled in a train of carriages drawn by white horses. Violet and her father brought up the rear; ahead of them, like outriders to a princess, Jessie and three of the bridesmaids (the Seavill girls and Lady Elizabeth Chetwyn) rode in one carriage, the other four bridesmaids in another. The last part of the route was attended by policemen, holding back the enormous crowds who lined the pavements hoping for a glimpse of the 'Society bride' who had filled the gossip pages for so long. They teetered on tiptoe and waved and cheered and beamed as if they knew her. The bridesmaids arrived at the Abbey just sufficiently ahead to be ready when the bride's carriage halted to help lift Violet's twelve foot train down, carry it up the steps and arrange it behind her. Jessie as chief bridesmaid put the bouquet of fragrant creamy roses, myrtle and white heather in her lace-gloved hand, rearranged her veil, tweaked her gown into place, and then took up station in the procession, treading behind the shimmering, ghost-white figure into the shadowy spaces of the Abbey.

Music soaring out, echoes clashing among the ribs of the fan vaulting. Red carpet, thick underfoot and feeling treacherous, as though it might catch at one's feet; rows and rows of smart people, big hats, flashing orders; faces turning – sometimes a familiar face, seen fleetingly in passing, as if from a moving train. There up ahead was Brancaster, tall and solid-looking, like a goal to be reached, with his groomsman beside him – Amy Vanbrugh's brother Cedric. Brancaster turned to watch his bride approaching. Jessie could not see his face: it was oddly indistinct, as if seen through a mist. Still she felt a pang, and thought, *What if it had been me?* She heard little of the service itself, coming to almost with a start as the processional music burst out to tell her it was all over. Her friend Violet was now Lady Brancaster. The bells began to peal in confirmation of the fact. The couple went smiling down the aisle towards the doors; the brides-maids fell in again behind. Outside the patient crowds had their chance to cheer again, and the carriage horses fretted their feet and champed their bits. A multitude of photographers crowded forward, flashbulbs bursting like fireworks, the restraining policemen smiled fatherly smiles, and a sharp little wind drove a scatter of brown leaves underfoot from the great trees in Parliament Square.

It had been a dull, overcast, though dry day. Now as they drove away from the Abbey a few spots of rain began, but held off just long enough for them to reach their destination before setting in heavily with every appear-ance of permanence. The wedding breakfast could not be held at Manchester Square since the dining-room was not large enough, but these days it was becoming quite respectable to hold such affairs at hotels. Rather daringly, the Overtons had chosen the Savoy instead of Claridges – the 'safe' choice, where once Queen Victoria had called in person on the exiled Empress Eugénie. The Savoy had a somewhat more showy, even perhaps theatrical repu-tation. The King, when Prince of Wales, had often dined there, and there the famous chef Escoffier had created unique dishes for the likes of Sarah Bernhardt and Lillie Langtry. Just a few years before, in 1905, it had put on the fabulous Gondola dinner for the millionaire George Kessler: the forecourt transformed to resemble old Venice with four hundred Venetian lamps, operatic arias sung by Caruso, a five-foot birthday cake and, for reasons no-one now remembered, a prominent appearance by a baby elephant.

That the wedding breakfast should be held here was the perfect final touch of out-of-the-common stylishness, which sent the newspapers into ecstasy, and even the rain did not dampen their enthusiasm. When the meal was over, the couple withdrew to change into travelling-dress (the Savoy was famous for the modern comfort of its rooms, including electric lighting and a quite startling number of bathrooms), and then the motor cars were outside waiting to take them, their servants and the luggage to Victoria to catch the boat train.

The newspapers were full the next day of detailed descriptions of the new viscountess's rose-fawn silk going-away costume trimmed with smart black lace and braiding, her large hat trimmed with black ostrich feathers, the full-length sable coat (a present from the bride's father), which matched her enormous sable muff. But what Jessie remembered best was that when Violet darted aside to bestow a parting kiss on her friend and chief bridesmaid, she was wearing on the silk lapel of the expensive costume a little coral brooch in the shape of a hand.

Back home at Morland Place, everything was the same, except that dear old Kithra had died, a quiet old dog's death, in his sleep; and Polly had a governess, a Miss Mitchell, who seemed nice but rather downtrodden.

'I hope you won't find home dull now, after so long in London,' Henrietta said, when Jessie had unpacked.

'Oh, not dull, Mother. It's never that,' Jessie said.

'But you seem out of spirits. It was the thing I worried about, that having a London Season might make you discontented with everyday life.'

'I expect she's just worn out with all the gaiety,' Jerome said, coming to his daughter's rescue. 'Burning the candle at both ends, and so on. All she needs is fresh air and healthy exercise. I'm glad you're back, Jess. I need your help with the polo ponies. No-one understands them better than you.' Jessie knew it was flattery with a purpose, but she smiled anyway. 'I think the bay with the white snip is ready for backing now. Would you like to come and help me with it this morning?'

Hard work, Jessie had read somewhere, was the best medicine for a broken heart; and horses, she had always felt, could soothe any pain. If you had to be disappointed in love, the very best place to be was Morland Place. There was always something to do with the horses, which involved being out in the open air until you were so tired you could hardly stand; and if it wasn't the horses it was the farm, or visiting the tenants and villagers with, or on behalf of, her mother. There were 'morning' visits to be paid with her mother; shopping to do in York or Leeds; and a whole variety of social engagements. Uncle Teddy was very affable, had a wide acquaintance, and loved both to entertain and be entertained. So there were supper parties and musical evenings, dances private and public, visits to the theatre and to concerts which, if they did not equal London's in quality, seemed to Jessie just as enjoyable.

Morland Place hosted two weekend parties for shooting, got up to a standard of luxury in keeping with Teddy's rapidly increasing wealth. They involved an enormous amount of organisation, into which Jessie threw herself with gusto; and when the guests arrived, she did her part in entertaining them, chatting to the gentlemen about their guns and dogs, and keeping the ladies amused while the men were out. And pretty soon the hunting season would begin, which would happily fill up a large part of every week – and once hunting started it was not long until Christmas.

There were the family concerns to keep up with. Robbie was conducting a courtship of Miss Harris, sister of his colleague at the bank, which was not going smoothly. Miss Harris was a capricious, as well as lively young woman. For her sake, Robbie had learned to play tennis, but now, of course, tennis days were over, along with bicycling days (at least for dainty young ladies – Robbie would have cycled through a blizzard and not noticed), and he did not shine at indoor pursuits. Miss Harris did not ride or hunt, either, which boded ill for the winter. Robbie's place at her elbow was being usurped by what seemed to him a pallid, undersized young man who merely excelled at card games and could reduce Miss Harris to tears of laughter while playing Consequences. Robbie had always been something of a joke to his own family, and he was glad to discover at home a newly sympathetic Jessie who had time to listen to his woes and even give him advice.

There was Lizzie's forthcoming new baby to think about, and letters from her every week to look forward to; and Jack's letters home now always included a separate sheet for Jessie, in which he recounted his progress with Maud Puddephat. The difference his new friend Sopwith had made was remarkable. It turned out that his parents did know the Puddephats slightly, enough to give him something to work on. He had somehow engineered an acquaintance between Miss Puddephat and one of his many sisters, which opened a whole new range of ways for Jack to be in her company. If only he had lived in London rather than Southampton, he might have seen her several times a week. As it was, he could only get up to Town on Sundays, which ruled out occupations like roller-skating and tennis.

However, the Puddephats were glad that Maud had a new friend: until he had settled in London Puddephat had moved about the country a great deal and in consequence Maud had always been a rather solitary girl. They were glad to encourage her to go out with Miss Sopwith, and if that meant that Miss Sopwith's brother and Jack Morland were in attendance, they had no objection. Both were decent, reliable young men who could be depended on to behave themselves and take care of the young ladies. So on one or two bright Sunday afternoons the four went bicycling together, and on others for a spin in the country in one of Sopwith's borrowed motor-cars. Occasionally one or more

145

of the Sopwith girls was prevailed upon to visit their brother down in Hampshire, and then it was natural for them to invite Miss Puddephat along for the outing, and to ask Jack to join them for a Saturday-afternoon sail on the Solent, perhaps, or a walk in the woods above Swanwick.

To Jessie, Jack confided that Maud seemed fond of him – though she was always quiet and reserved, so it was not easy to be sure of her feelings. But he had hopes, now that his salary had been raised, of being able to declare himself to her as soon as he had saved enough to make marriage a possibility. Sopwith was a great encouragement to him. He liked Jack and thought him extremely clever and able, and therefore could see no reason why any young woman should not favour him. His cheerful, sanguine temper worked on Jack's doubts until even Jack felt that he was not such a bad match for Miss Puddephat after all, and that 'nothing venture, nothing gain' ought to be his motto.

So Jessie had plenty to do and think about; and she was happy to be home, even though there was something missing, just the very top edge of joy in life, which she had always felt before she went away. She did her best to regulate her thoughts, and it was only in bed at night, in the drifting time before sleep, that she caught herself imagining the progress of the Brancasters. They were travelling through France and Italy for six weeks, and then Scotland for another two or three so that Brancaster could have some shooting, before going down to the family seat for Christmas. Violet's letters seemed as remote as Violet herself, full of descriptions of where they had been and what they had seen, but never of how she felt, or what it was like to be married. She barely mentioned Brancaster at all, which ought to have been a help. But still Jessie would slide into sleep with the image of his face before her mind's eye, and dream complicated dreams of searching for something she had lost.

One day she and her mother and Polly were in the kitchen, working at the big scrubbed table in the middle of the floor. It was Christmas-pudding time, and Henrietta always liked to make her own, to an ancient recipe that had been handed down through the ages from time immemorial, 'Or at least,' she added honestly, 'for a hundred years or so, because I know my mother said she had it from my grandmother.'

There was all the washing and stoning of fruit to be done, the peel to be cut, the suet to be chopped, and the almonds to be blanched, before any mixing and boiling could be started. Emma normally helped with it too, but she was laid up with a feverish cold and Henrietta had made her stay in bed, refusing even to allow her to have the mending basket brought up to her.

It was the cook's afternoon rest time, when she went to her room to doze over a picture-paper until the kitchen maid took her up a cup of tea; and the rest of the servants were about their afternoon tasks, so they had the kitchen to themselves, except for the girl in one of the sculleries finishing the washing-up, and the kitchen maid who was pottering back and forth tending the stoves and laying the table in the servants' hall for their tea. Polly had begun well, stoning raisins, but the idea of Christmas was not quite enough to make the work exciting, and after a while she wandered off to play with her dog. Jessie and Henrietta carried on, chatting at first; but then Jessie fell silent. Henrietta, finding her comments unanswered, looked across at her daughter and saw that she was in a deep reverie, cutting candied lemon peel by instinct alone, her eyes fixed unseeingly on the distance.

'What's the matter, darling?' she asked. Jessie started and looked at her enquiringly. 'I know you're not quite happy. Can you tell me about it?'

Jessie felt guilty to have been caught daydreaming and said briskly, 'I'm quite all right, Mother, really.'

'Yes, I know you try hard, because you are a good girl. But I can't help seeing that you've lost your sparkle. Is it – ?' She hesitated delicately. 'Are you in love with someone?'

147

Jessie held on for a long moment, but her dear, gentle mother was looking at her so kindly. 'I was in love with someone. But it was all a mistake. I thought he loved me but he didn't.' It burst from her like water breaching a dam. 'Oh, Mother, I made such a fool of myself!'

'In what way, darling?'

The knife and the piece of peel lay unnoticed under Jessie's still hands as she stared in anguish down the corridor of memory. 'This man – I ought to have known he could never care for me. He was far above me in every way. All the time I thought he loved me, it was someone else he wanted.'

'How do you know it was someone else?'

'Because he married her,' Jessie said starkly.

'Oh, darling,' Henrietta said, 'I'm so sorry. It's very hard to love someone and not be loved back. But the pain won't last for ever. You will get over it, you know.' Jessie shook her head, and Henrietta went on, 'I know you won't like me to say it now, but please believe me, this will pass. You're very young, and young hearts are strong. Someone else will come along and you'll fall in love again and then you'll wonder how you could ever have cared about this man.'

Jessie sighed, and began cutting peel again. 'I don't feel as if I'll ever be happy again.'

'I know, darling. But at least he's out of your way for ever. You've discovered it was all a mistake on your part, and he's married to someone else. It would be worse if you still thought he loved you, if you could torture yourself with hope that he might come back some day. This way, it's all over, and you know there's nothing to hope for.'

Jessie's curiosity was aroused. 'Did you love someone like that? And hope they would come back?'

'Yes, I did,' she said. 'It was a long time ago, and I was very wrong to hope, because I was married to Lizzie's father at the time, but I couldn't seem to help it. I loved him, and even though he had gone away, I kept wondering if

148

he was thinking of me, and if I would ever see him again.'

'And what happened?'

'Well, he did come back. And I married him – but that was long afterwards.'

Jessie laughed. 'You don't mean *Dad*!'

'You needn't say it in that tone. I was a girl once, you know, just like you. Why is it young people think their elders have always been the same age?'

'I'm sorry.' She felt silent again. 'If I see him again,' she said, after a moment, 'how will I bear it?'

'You'll bear it very well,' Henrietta said firmly. 'And, you know, if you do meet him, you may find him very different when he's no longer a gay bachelor. Most men become very dull when they get married.'

'Mother!' Jessie cried, delightfully shocked.

'Well, not your father, of course.'

'But how can you say that, when all you've ever wanted me to do is get married?'

'Not *all*. If you had wanted very much to do something else, I would have encouraged you. But even if you had wanted to be a teacher or something like that, I would still have wanted you to marry as well. Old age can be very lonely for a woman unless she has a family.'

'I don't think I will ever marry now,' Jessie said.

'Of course you will, darling.'

'I don't mind, really,' Jessie said quickly. 'It means I can stay here, and I would hate ever to have to leave Morland Place.'

Henrietta wondered if she ought to warn her daughter against attaching too much affection to the place, given that it belonged to Teddy, and that one day he would die and pass it on to someone else. But Jessie had enough on her mind just now.

'What I feel worst about,' Jessie went on, 'is that you spent all that money on me, sending me to London to get a husband, and I've come back without one. I'm so ashamed that I've let you and Dad down.'

'You haven't let us down. How can you think it?'

'You don't know the worst,' Jessie said in a small voice. 'I did receive a proposal from a man, but I refused him.'

'You never told me that.'

'He was very nice, and he liked me a lot, but I didn't love him, and he couldn't compare with – well, the other one. I'm sorry, Mother.'

'Jessie, dearest, I wouldn't have wanted you to accept a man you didn't love!'

'But you sent me to London. And it must have cost the earth!'

Henrietta shook her head. 'Oh, my dear, is that what you've been thinking? In the first place, it didn't cost so very much, and in the second place, we wanted you to have the pleasure of a Season, and the opportunity to meet a wider circle of people, but there was never any question of your *having* to find a husband. In fact,' she added, 'your father was rather relieved that you didn't come back engaged. You're so very young, and he wasn't quite ready to part with you yet.'

'I'm older than Violet. And you were younger than I am now when you married for the first time – you've told me so.'

'Yes, well my first marriage wasn't a happy one, so don't take that for an example. Don't be in such a hurry to grow up, Jessie darling. Enjoy being a girl while you can. You have a few years to romp and be free, and to dance with as many young men as you can, and fall in love with a different one every week if you like, before your real love comes along and you settle down to being a grown-up.'

'But isn't it nice being a grown-up? Don't you have fun, too?'

'It's different. A different sort of nice, and a different sort of fun. You'll see.'

They continued with the pudding making, in silence at first, and then chatting more comfortably. Jessie felt a little better, seeing – just faintly – her mother's perspective, that what had happened was not the end of the world, nor even

150

the end of all pleasure in life. She did not feel it yet, but she was able to believe that she might feel it one day, in years to come, perhaps when she was an old woman of twenty-three or something.

Polly came back in time to help with the mixing, when traditionally everyone who stirred the bowl could have a wish. The pudding batter was so stiff that it had to be put on the floor for Polly so that she could stand over it and use both hands on the long wooden spoon. She screwed up her eyes and wished so hard her face went quite red. Jessie thought she was probably wishing for something like red shoes or a pony-phaeton or ice skates, something she was quite likely to get if only she dropped the hint to her adoring papa.

When Jessie's turn came she stirred industriously, and could not immediately decide what to wish for. The childish part of her mind still believed in pudding wishes – enough, at any rate, to make it matter what she said in her mind when she closed her eyes. She could not wish for Brancaster – that would be wicked and wrong. She did not quite yet want to wish to forget him: the pain was sweet as well as troubling, and it was all she had left of him. In the end she wished that, if she could not have Brancaster, she would one day have another love. *I wish for true love to come one day*, she said in her mind, with her eyes closed.

'Now you, Mother,' she said, passing the spoon. Mindful of the importance of these ceremonies, Henrietta took it and stirred with due gravity. Usually she just stirred and closed her eyes for the children's sake; but today, at the last minute, she was inspired to make a wish herself. *I wish for love for Jessie one day. Love as good as mine has turned out to be.*

The art of wishing, she thought, when she put the spoon aside, is to wish for something that probably will happen.

'What did you wish, Mother?' Jessie asked, curious about her expression.

'It doesn't come true if you tell,' said Henrietta.

*   *   *

Christmas preparations were in full swing, with only a few days to go, when a cable came for Jerome from Paris to say that his sister was very ill.

'I shall have to go,' he said.

He looked bleak, and Henrietta was prompted to say, 'Must you go now? Couldn't it wait until after Christmas?'

'Of course it can't wait. Mary would never have allowed this cable to be sent unless she were really ill.' Or, his mind added, unless she were too ill to know about it.

Henrietta relented at once. 'I'm sorry. Of course, you are right. I only wanted to save you the journey at this time of year.'

'It will be the same time of year after Christmas,' he said, touching her cheek with a forefinger to show he was not angry with her. 'I'm sorry too. But I have a hollow feeling that this may be the last time I see her. Missing the Christmas celebrations can't weigh against that.'

'You go and look up the trains,' Henrietta said contritely. 'I'll start packing for you. I do hope you won't have a rough crossing.'

Her hope was vain. The sea was so rough that only a point more of wind would have cancelled the crossing altogether. Jerome stood at the window of the deckhouse as the packet stood first on her nose and then on her tail, while the spray and rain lashed the glass so hard it was impossible to see anything beyond it. But what he was seeing was not in the present but in the past. He had retreated thirty years to the time just before he had first met Henrietta, when he and Mary had shared a house in Bishop Winthorpe and enjoyed all the pleasures that freedom, youth and a comfortable income afforded. He saw her, dark-haired and handsome, riding one of her fiery horses: she always liked a mount that was a challenge, preferably of the sort that never had more than two feet on the ground at the same time. Laughing, witty, energetic, independent Mary. She had never cared two straws for any man, judging the freedom of doing what she pleased when she pleased worth more than any security marriage could offer. It made it all the more strange that when she did lose her head, it was so badly and with a married man whom Jerome had always thought rather dull. The man's wife had discovered the affair and a shocking scandal had ensued, so that Mary had had to leave first London and then the country. *Why* had she done it? Not, surely, for love; surely not for lust? Had she simply come to an age when she saw her lack of a male companion as a stigma? Had she grabbed in a panic at an imagined last chance for happiness?

Her exile had been long and, he guessed, painful, though Mary would never complain or allow anyone to pity her. She had written, always, in lively terms about the pleasures of living in Paris; but he remembered her as she was when he had last seen her, so suddenly frail, clasping his hand at the last, when he was leaving, with a look in her eyes he had never seen before, not even in the worst of her trouble. She had looked afraid.

One benefit of the wind was that the crossing, though unpleasant, was short, and he was able to catch an earlier train from Calais and was in Paris a whole hour before his time. He took a cab to the house where she had her apartment, and surprised the concierge, Madame Bolfass, coming downstairs with a covered basin to take out to the privy in the yard. Though sophisticated in many ways, the French had never really got to grips with plumbing.

'Oh, M'sieur, you are here already!' she cried in French. 'Madame will be so glad. She has looked for you ever since I sent the cable. I think,' she added confidentially, 'she does not understand the clock any more. I hoped you would be here today but I dared not tell her so.'

'What is it? What is her illness?'

'A stroke, M'sieur. Last Friday night, when she was coming in from the theatre. Thank God I was on hand when it happened. She fell in the hallway, and I had to get Bolfass and the boy to carry her upstairs. But only think if I had not been in the hall at the time, she might have lain there for hours.'

153

'I am sure you have given her every care. She could not be in better hands.'

'Not so, M'sieur, it is always better to be with one's family at such a time. But I have done what I could. Dr Ediers has been to see her but gives no hope, alas. That is why I sent for you. He says she might have another stroke and be taken off at any moment. Madame understands this. But I think she has been clinging to life, waiting to see you,' she added sentimentally.

'Can she speak?'

'Yes, M'sieur, though it is hard to make it out. One side of her mouth is pulled down. But she can understand what one says. Will you go straight up, M'sieur, or can I get you something first? Did you dine on the train?'

'No, I had nothing, but I will not wait.'

'Coffee and bread, perhaps? You must be faint with hunger.'

'No, I must go to her at once.'

'*Bien sûr*, M'sieur. But I will bring some coffee for you, at least.'

He thanked her and said he would show himself up. He found Mary in her bedroom, propped up on four pillows in her high white bed, looking strangely small and shrunken. Her eyes leaped to him at once with recognition and painful relief, but she did not speak or move.

'Mary, Mary, my dear,' he said, and crossed quickly to her side. He took up her hand. It was cold and felt slightly damp, and was disconcertingly limp, like that of a corpse. The other was warmer, and he felt the faintest response in it to his squeeze.

'I came as soon as I could. Oh, my dear, I'm so sorry you have had to be alone.' He forced a smile on to his face. 'Now I'm here, we'll soon have you well again.'

She pressed his hand slightly again, and said something, which at the third attempt he distinguished as 'No lies!'

He let any attempt at a smile fall away. 'No,' he said.

'What am I thinking of? This is Mary. You deserve the truth from me now, just as you always did.'

'Dying,' she said.

He understood that when she repeated it. 'I think so. The doctor said it could be any time. But doctors don't know everything,' he went on, unable to help himself – and, after all, that *was* the truth. 'People do recover from strokes, against all the odds.'

She shook her head, sparely, once each way against the pillows. '*I* know.'

He was getting better at deciphering her mumbles, and caught it first time.

'Well, I won't argue with you on that. We shall see. But at all events I will make you as comfortable as I can.'

She looked anxious, and squeezed his hand to emphasise the next effortful communication. 'You won't leave me?'

'No, no. Don't be afraid. I promise I won't leave you. I shall stay here until – as long as you need me.'

She seemed to relax a little at that. But she had other things to say, though it took time for her to speak them and for him to understand them. Madame Bolfass brought him coffee and fresh bread, which he consumed avidly, having had nothing all day; as she left them she whispered there would be something more substantial waiting for him below when he was able to leave the sick-room.

Over the next couple of hours he listened to Mary and wrote things down. When he had visited her earlier in the year she had been having financial difficulties, not because she had not enough to live on but because some problem had arisen over her drawing the money from the bank. He had been able to rectify that for her, simplify procedures, pay some bills that had become overdue and interview some tradesmen who had been taking advantage of her situation. Now she wanted to be sure that everything would be settled on her death, that her accounts would be paid and the Bolfasses, who had been kind to her, rewarded.

155

Talking tired her, and at last she fell asleep, and he was able to leave her for a while. As he stepped out onto the landing, a delicious smell wafted gently up from below, something with a hint of garlic and herbs and the strong suggestion of meat bubbling gently in savoury juices. He shivered suddenly, feeling exhausted, chilled and hungry.

Mary seemed a little better the next day, a little stronger, and Jerome's hopes were revived, though he did not trouble her with expressions of them. She wanted him to write out a will for her, and take detailed notes of her wishes for disposing of various small trinkets and mementoes to friends and those who had served her. The doctor came again, shook his head to Jerome, said that he should engage a nurse to sit with Mary when Jerome was out of the room, and to sleep in her room during the night. Even if it was only for a few days, it was right that she should be properly attended, and Madame Bolfass had too much else to do, and was too old to be running up and down stairs.

So Jerome interviewed a few girls the doctor sent round and chose a quiet, sensible one. He went to the bank again, and to various tradesmen. He sorted through Mary's papers and possessions. He consulted a lawyer about the proper form of a will. And in between he sat with Mary, sometimes listening to her slow and painful sentences, or making notes of her wishes, sometimes talking himself, beguiling her weary hours with memories of their childhood and gilded youth. As he held her hand and summoned up images for her, she seemed to drift in and out of consciousness, and he hoped that it might be thus that she would finally quit: gently, upon a sea of words.

It was hard for Henrietta to feel enthused about Christmas with Jerome away, and on such sad business; but plans had been made and she did not want to be the cause of spoiling the fun for everyone else, so she put on a bright face. Christmas Day was, of course, quarter-day, the time for tenants to come up to the house to pay their rents and receive their instructions for the coming year. In the past, it had been traditional for them to bring their families and for the Master to distribute presents to all, and to serve mulled ale and mince pies. Many of the old traditions had lapsed in the latter days of George Morland, and afterwards all but the home farm had been sold. But since Teddy had come back, he had found himself more and more attracted to the history and traditions of the Morlands, and wanting to be Master in the old sense. For eight years now – all of Polly's lifetime – he had been buying back the land, restoring the house to the way it was when he was a boy and resuming the pleasant little traditions he and Henrietta remembered.

So as Christmas Day would all be taken up with the tenants, church and the family dinner, Christmas Eve was to be the day for celebrating with friends. It began before dawn with the expedition to fetch in the Yule log, which he had marked on one of his rides and had had cleared of brambles and trimmed ready. In the end all the young Morlands went with him to fetch it, though Jessie had had to go herself to Robbie's room and roust him out, telling him Uncle Teddy would be heartbroken if he stayed behind. Ned had resigned himself to rising in the dark and had left word with the kitchen maid to call him. Polly was thrilled with the whole expedition, as were Martial and Rupert (Lizzie had come down with them the day before, escorted by Frank, to stay a week). To them, everything about being at Morland Place was magically different, and the romance and novelty of rising in the icy darkness of before-dawn far outweighed any unpleasantness.

Jessie forced herself to get up, shivering, in a room in which the fire had not yet been kindled, out of a sense of duty to her uncle; but once up, dressed and out, she was glad she had done so, and was quietly seized by the magical quality of the occasion. The snow had been settling for a week, and there was a good foot of it on the ground. Christmas Eve morning was very still, penetratingly cold, and though dawn was hours away, there was a three-quarter moon still up, hanging low in the sky, looking like a half-sucked lemon drop. The frozen sea of snow was crisp and glittering, the trees stood decked and stately as if only waiting for candles to be lit on them. The dogs rushed about, excited at this departure from the norm: Jerome's Fern and his new bitch-pup Brach, Uncle Teddy's two pointers Digby and Danby, his spaniel Muffy, and Polly's young dog Bell. They bounded through the snow, springing high like deer, running out ahead and coming back and circling the humans to hurry them along. The big hounds were mute, expressing their excitement with lashing tails and wide grins, pointing their muzzles up at the children's faces; Muffy barked, and then barked again at her own echo coming off the trees and laden hedges; Digby ate snow in great mouthfuls, and Danby shoved her nose into it, then had a sneezing fit, pawing at her muzzle and shaking her head until her flapping ears rattled like castanets.

The party tramped across the drawbridge, over the moat patched with skeins of ice and posh, up the track and then over Low Field, crossing the deep cut of Askham Lane, and across Chapel Field to the wood just south of the Wetherby Road. Uncle Teddy led the way, carrying a lantern which was redundant now but which would be needed on the return journey when the moon was down. Ned and Robbie carried the dragging tackle between them and Jessie walked behind arm in arm with Frank, while the little ones frisked about like the dogs, and threw snowballs at each other.

When they reached the place where the Yule log lay, Uncle Teddy commanded a silence and said the traditional prayer over it. Then the boys fitted the tackle round it and stood into the harness like horses and tugged it free. It was a mile back to the house, and Jessie thought Frank and Uncle Teddy would probably have to take a turn at dragging it. She wished her father and Jack could have been there, not for that reason but to share the joy of it. The children and dogs were quiet on the return journey, having run off their excess energy. The moon slid away, down behind the trees, and in the wonderful vibrant darkness of before-dawn, the stars became suddenly visible, and between the pinpoints of their blue-white brilliance and the crushed diamond of the snow, the air seemed almost to crackle with cold, clean emptiness. They were all alone in the world, marching through a silent landscape behind the bobbing yellow smudge of Uncle Teddy's lantern. Polly came up beside Jessie and slipped a hand into hers; and then Frank began singing in his pleasant, mellow tenor:

> '*It came upon a midnight clear,*
> *That glorious song of old —*'

And the others joined in:

> '*From angels bending near the earth*
> *To touch their harps of gold:*
> *"Peace on the earth, good will to men,*
> *From Heaven's all-gracious King."*
> *The world in solemn stillness lay*
> *To hear the angels sing.*'

Their clear young voices filled the air like bells; it was not midnight, Jessie thought, but the world did seem to lie in solemn stillness. She suddenly felt absolutely happy, and for that moment could not have wished for anything more than to be where and who she was.

When they got back to the house, it was astir, and the servants and Henrietta and Lizzie were waiting in the hall to receive them for the ceremony of lighting the Yule log in the fireplace in the great hall. There was a scent of pine and myrtle on the air from the greenery with which the hall had been decorated; and a hint of spice and oranges, those essentially Christmas smells. When the fire was alight, there were mugs of hot chocolate for all, with little spiced biscuits; and then Jessie and Uncle Teddy went out again for the next part of the tradition, taking jugs of hot lamb's-wool down to the cowhouse to regale the early milkers. When they returned there was a splendid breakfast with great burnished sausages, and by then the Yule fire had burned up so well that the carpet of dogs spread belly-forward before it was beginning to groan with too much pleasure.

The rest of the day was taken up with preparing for the dinner and ball that were to occupy the evening. They would be twenty-eight to dinner; and afterwards all their friends and neighbours would be gathering to dance in the great hall. The small orchestra would be set up in the gallery and there would be a supper at eleven thirty in the dining-parlour, and hot soup after the post-horn gallop at two. Jessie wore one of her London gowns, and danced until her feet were sore, finding herself wonderfully, flatteringly in demand by the local young men, now she had the unmistakable aura of a London Season about her. She enjoyed herself very much, and in particular found herself taking pleasure in the conversation and skilful dancing of a young man named Peter Firmstone, whose family owned a fleet of barges that carried cargo between York and Hull port. It was pleasant to be whirled through the steps again by someone who knew what he was doing, and to have a man's strong arm around her.

Miss Harris had come, and seemed to be being nice to Robbie for once. Kind Ned made a point of dancing with all the least popular girls – a little solemnly, perhaps, but he was a good, if correct, dancer, and was handsome in his way, and must have given many an otherwise wistful heart a small flutter. Frank danced with a different girl every time, and whenever he was not dancing, seemed to have a little knot of them around him, helpless with laughter, while he maintained a faintly surprised air, as if he could not imagine what was amusing them – which only made them laugh the more. Even Uncle Teddy danced – twice with Alice Meynell, once with Henrietta, once with Mrs Chubb and once with Lady Lambert.

During the supper interval, Henrietta came up to Jessie as she was eating cold chicken and hot pasties in company with Peter Firmstone, and said, 'Enjoying yourself, darling?'

'Oh, yes,' Jessie said. 'This is as good as any ball in London.'

'And you don't have to go out into the cold at the end of it to get to your bed.'

They smiled at each other a moment, and Henrietta saw that her daughter was contented, and was glad. Young Mr Firmstone was extremely handsome – tall, lean, blue-eyed, and with pale fair hair that went well with his tanned face – and a nice boy too, and she hoped that he would go a long way to curing Jessie of her sickness. And then something cold and hard jabbed itself at her hand, and she jumped and looked down into the smiling yellow eyes of Fern. 'Oh dear,' she exclaimed in dismay, 'somebody's let the dogs out from the kitchen! They'll be all over the buffet if we don't catch them.'

'I'll help you,' Jessie said. 'Oh, look, Bell's stolen a pasty! And Danby's got her paws up on the table. Won't you give a hand?' she added to Mr Firmstone. 'We can only grab two each.'

He put his plate aside at once and said, 'Of course I'll help. Don't worry, Mrs Compton, it's the kind of thing that could happen to anyone. It only proves how excellent your supper is.'

They had just managed to catch six collars between them when the clock in the hall struck midnight, and simultaneously Teddy at the far end of the room tapped a fork ringingly against a glass and called out, 'May I have your attention, please?'

The chatter died away, and everyone turned towards him. Jessie, glancing at her mother, saw that she had no idea what he was going to say. Trays of champagne glasses were being brought round by the servants, two of whom were summoned by Henrietta to put down their trays for a moment and remove the dogs. There was to be a Christmas toast to friends and neighbours, Jessie supposed.

'My dear friends, neighbours and family members,' Teddy began, in oratorical style. 'Firstly I would like to say thank you to all of you for doing me the honour of being my guests this Christmas Eve. Morland Place is a very old house, and we Morlands have been here on this spot for over four hundred years. There must have been many fine celebrations during that time, but I can honestly say that I have never enjoyed anything more than I have enjoyed your company here tonight.'

There was a little laughter, and a few calls of 'Hear, hear!'

He went on, 'And there is another reason for my great happiness tonight, which I would like to share with you. To the blessing of a loving family and a multitude of dear friends, I am now about to add the greatest blessing of all: the hand of a lovely and gracious lady in marriage. Mrs Alice Meynell has this evening consented to be my wife, and I hope and trust you will now charge your glasses and raise them to her, and wish us well. And a merry Christmas to you all.'

There was a burst of comment and a spattering of applause, out of which confusion of noise Ned, perhaps surprisingly, found his head first and stood on a chair to say, 'Ladies and gentlemen, the toast is Mrs Meynell, health and happiness to her and my father, and a merry Christmas!' With laughter and cheerful additions and God-bless-yous, everyone drank the toast.

'What a wonderful crown to the evening's pleasure,' Firmstone said to Jessie. 'Had you any idea of it?'

'Not the least,' she said. 'He has been helping her with this and that ever since her husband died, and of course Mr Meynell was a great friend of Uncle Teddy's, so there was no surprise about that. But I had no idea he was in love with her or wanted to marry her.'

'Good for him,' Firmstone said, raising his glass. 'I am all for matrimony: an excellent excuse for celebration. I wish them every joy.'

'Oh, so do I,' Jessie said. 'Mrs Meynell is a very nice lady indeed, and I'm sure they'll be very happy together.'

And she looked then at her mother, who was still standing nearby, and was surprised to see a rather frozen expression on her face, as if what she had heard had been a shock to her, instead of a surprise.

'You had no idea, then, Mother?'

'No,' said Henrietta. 'None at all.'

Chapter Six

Mary died on the 28th of December. All that day she had seemed to struggle to come to consciousness. During the afternoon her breathing grew gradually more laboured. Once she seemed almost to wake, but then she sank again, and as the early dark of midwinter set in and the snow began to fall, she stopped breathing.

There was much to do to settle her affairs and arrange her interment, and it was not until the 8th of January that Jerome was able to leave to come home. Weary and grieving as he was, the journey seemed very long to him, and though the crossing was less rough than on the way out, it was bitterly cold. When he reached London, he debated whether to stay the night with Ashley and Lizzie and travel on the next day; but in the event the lure of his own bed and his own family was too strong. He took a cab from Victoria, but the traffic was heavy, and as the snow began again it ground to a complete halt. The cab was stuffy and freezing inside; his feet were like blocks of ice, his breath clouded the air. When the traffic eventually allowed them to move again, they crawled for some distance before passing the overturned cart that had held them up. He knew he had by now missed the train he had been intending to catch, and arriving at the station at last he discovered it was almost an hour and a half before the next one.

He might still have gone to Ashley's house, which was only five minutes away now, but he felt too tired to change his mind. He bought a meat pie and a cup of coffee at a coffee stall, hoping they would warm him up, and then in desperation entered the licensed refreshment rooms and bought a large whisky. But still he felt cold right through, and spent the long, tiresome railway journey, as the train crawled through the snowy darkness, alternately dozing and shivering. At York station he realised he had forgotten to telegraph ahead for someone to meet him, and as he emerged into the icy air of the station fore-court, he found that the only cab left was a horse-drawn one, with a horse that looked in a worse state than he was. The cabby was unwilling to take him outside the city. It was black as Newgate Knocker out there and snowing besides, so Jerome could hardly blame him, but he was desperate now to get home, and offered him double fare and a fine tip on top.

The cabby got him as far as the gibbet, where the track for Morland Place turned off, but when he saw the billowy snow off the main road, he decided against going any further.

'Ah'm sorry, maister,' he said to Jerome, his watery eyes screwed up against the cold air, 'but Ah dursent risk it, not in't dark. T'awld horse is all Ah've got, and if Ah stray off t' track and brek 'is leg in a ditch, it'll be t'workuss for me an' t' missus. Will Ah tek ye back t'th' station? Ye can stay the neet at th' Hotel.'

But Jerome was not much more than half a mile from home now, and he could not bear any further disappoint-ment. The snow had stopped, he knew the track as well as he knew his own hand; at the end of it was Henrietta, and great roaring fires, and hot food, and his own bed.

'No, I'll walk the rest,' he said. 'Take my luggage back, will you, and leave it for me at the station, and tell them I'll send for it tomorrow? The name is—'

'Aye, Maister Compton, Ah knaw ye well enough,' Cabby said with a nod. 'But are ye sure?'

'Quite sure. Just hand me that small bag. That's all I need for now.'

He set off with determination, but it seemed a long way under an absolutely dark sky – the moon was not up, and the stars were obscured by clouds. The snow glimmered faintly all around, the air was deadly cold, and he was very tired – his legs felt like lead. Though the snow on the track was not terribly deep, he was not booted for it, and when his feet and lower legs were wet through, the cold in them became actually painful. He had time to regret his stubbornness before the first light of Morland Place gleamed yellow through the darkness. Then at last he was stumbling across the drawbridge, under the sudden, snowless oblivion of the barbican, and into the yard. The yard dog barked sharply, and then stopped as he realised who it was, came out with a rattle of chain from his doghouse, shook himself briskly and then bowed and yawned with pleasure. Jerome caressed him briefly in passing, noting that his hands were so numb he could not feel the dog's head. He trod up the steps to the great door, and at last, at last, he was home.

By the time Henrietta, summoned by a startled servant, reached him, he was shivering uncontrollably and looking very ill. She suppressed any of the useless exclamations, questions or reproaches she might have voiced and saw instead about getting him warm, dry and fed. A hot bath before the fire in their bedroom, a brisk towelling, and then, she said, he might as well get into his nightshirt and straight into bed. The fact that he agreed to told her how badly he felt. The nightshirt had been warmed before the flames, and she had had a hot brick slipped between the sheets while he was bathing. A bowl of steaming soup was ready for him as soon as he was in bed; and by the time he had finished that he was almost asleep.

He was restless in the night, and his body felt to her like a furnace. By the morning he was obviously feverish and ill. He did not resist her advice to stay in bed. He would not eat, though he drank a little hot tea; then he just lay against the pillows, his eyes shiny with fever, racked now by sneezing fits, now by a harsh cough.

The symptoms developed with alarming rapidity, and after Teddy had looked in mid-morning, he agreed with Henrietta that the doctor ought to be sent for. Dr Hasty's dog cart was outside within two hours. Jerome's fever was over 100°, his face was flushed, his throat sore, and he ached all over. Dr Hasty examined him and told him cheerfully that he would soon be better; but when he left the room and faced Henrietta and Teddy outside on the landing, he looked grave.

'It's an influenza,' he said. He was a brisk little man, much in keeping with his name, though with children he had a wonderful calm patience. 'Keep him warm. Try to get him to take some light nourishment. Warm milk or beef-tea, that sort of thing. Little and often, that's the idea. Even if it's only a few spoonfuls every couple of hours, it will help. And on no account let him get up. He must rest absolutely. Influenza puts a great strain on the heart, so he must lie as quietly as possible until he's well again.'

'But he will get well?' Henrietta asked anxiously.

Hasty did not answer directly. 'Influenza is always serious, and I must say I don't like the look of him. It usually runs its course in a week or two, but it's very debilitating. A patient may be weak and listless for months afterwards.'

'Is there nothing you can give him?'

'I'll send something round to ease the symptoms. But nursing is the answer. Keep him warm and quiet, try to get him to eat a little, as I've said. And influenza is very catching. You must take precautions to prevent it spreading right through the house. Keep everyone out of the room. I'll send round a tonic, as well – make sure everyone has some. Have you someone reliable who can nurse him?'

'I'll do it myself.'

He frowned. 'Are you sure?'

'I could not be happy leaving it to anyone else,' Henrietta said firmly.

167

'Very well,' he said. 'But I recommend you have a trained nurse to help you. You must keep up your own strength and that means getting proper rest. I know a suitable person who is free at the moment. A Nurse Sawyer. Very nice young woman, quiet and sensible.'

Henrietta agreed to this, and Nurse Sawyer was in residence before the day's end. As Hasty had said, she was sensible and quietly spoken, with an air of cheerful efficiency that did Henrietta good. She was glad she had agreed to have the nurse, because Jerome grew rapidly worse, and nursing him day and night would have been too much of a strain on her. Jessie would gladly have helped, but Henrietta would not allow it. His temperature rose to 101° and then 102°; the doctor diagnosed that pneumonia had set in. By the end of a week Jerome was too ill to know who was around him.

Since his arrival home he had been too ill to be told any of the news, about Teddy's betrothal to Alice Meynell, for instance, or the death of Henrietta's brother-in-law, Sir Peregrine Parke. Henrietta nursed Jerome with a grim determination, almost afraid to leave him for a moment, even with the excellent Nurse Sawyer. She was haunted by the old saying that deaths always came in threes. Mary and Perry within a week of each other – who would be the third?

Perry Parke had been virtually a recluse since his wife had died a little less than two years before. Henrietta and Teddy had tried to keep contact with him, for Regina's sake, but he had refused all overtures. Seven of his eight children were grown up and gone, and the youngest, Walter, was away at university, so he lived all alone in the Red House, a great Georgian red-brick barn in the village of Bishop Winthorpe, on the other side of York. Henrietta's first husband had been rector there.

Teddy had heard the news of his death when he went into York on New Year's Day to attend to business and to visit Mrs Meynell. He dropped in at his club and was asked by Henry Russell, the solicitor, if he had heard that Sir Perry Parke had quit his lease on the day before. Russell had heard it from his neighbour who was brother to Parke's physician.

'Luckily his boy hadn't gone back to Cambridge yet, or he'd have been all alone but for the servants.'

Teddy hastened to the writing room to dash off a note of condolence to Walter, promising to call very soon. But before he could redeem the promise – indeed, shortly after he arrived home that afternoon – Walter came to Morland Place to bring the news in person. He drove himself in an old and rickety gig, drawn by the elderly cob who had been eking out a retirement pulling the lawn-mower. It was a sign of how far things had gone at the Red House that this was the best equipage he could assemble for the task.

Though grave, Walter seemed calm and not over-whelmed with shock or grief. He was a slight but good-looking young man of twenty-one; of Perry's children, Henrietta thought he most resembled his father.

'I had to come into York to do various things, so I thought it better to call on you than write,' he explained.

'What was it?' Teddy asked.

'His heart. He hadn't been well all over Christmas, but nothing one could put one's finger on. Just said he felt a bit seedy, you know. Well, simply being in that house is enough to give you the whim-whams – so big and dark and empty with only the pater and me there. And cold! Those fireplaces downstairs burn a ton of coal and still they'd hardly warm a mouse. Anyway, at breakfast yesterday he complained of indigestion, said it was giving him a pain in his chest. Hardly ate a thing. And then when he stood up, he just keeled over. Gave me the dickens of a shock, I can tell you. Of course I sent for the sawbones right away, but it was all over there and then, even I could see that.'

'Oh, my poor boy, I'm so very sorry,' Henrietta said. She had cried when Teddy told her, and now her pink

169

eyes were filling all over again, with pity for Perry's lonely death, and for what Walter might be suffering.

Walter's eyes seemed to grow moist by contagion. 'It was very quick, that's my comfort,' he said. He drew out his handkerchief and blew his nose. 'And, after all, it was a sort of release for Papa. He's never been happy since Mama died. I think he went a bit strange in the head after that. Well, he had been a little odd for a while before, as *you* know. Aunty Patsy tried several times to make him see sense about you and Uncle Jerome, but he never would.'

'Oh, my dear, that's all forgotten now,' Henrietta said.

'*De mortuis*, you know,' Teddy said uneasily. It was not the time to remember that Perry had cut Henrietta out of his life after she had married Jerome, on account of his being a divorcé.

Walter shook his head. 'Of course, Uncle, all due respect to my father and so on, but it has to be said he wasn't the easiest man to understand. I mean, virtually driving Bertie out of the house and all that.'

'He had a great many worries on his mind,' Henrietta defended him.

'Yes, I know,' Walter said sadly. 'I'm afraid the poor old pater was stony broke. I haven't heard the worst of it yet – Greaves, the solicitor chappie, is going to call tomorrow but he let me know that much straight away. I'm afraid there won't be funds for me to finish my doctorate now.' Walter had been studying mathematics at Cambridge, looking forward to a donnish life.

'Are things really so bad?' Teddy asked.

'It rather seems that way. I shall have to go out and earn an honest living. Oh, I shan't mind it too much,' he added quickly, for fear that his words might be construed as criticism of his late father. 'I shall get a post as a schoolmaster somewhere, and continue my studies in my spare time. Perhaps they might take me back at the old school. I think I could be as happy at Eton as anywhere. And the others are all settled. It's poor old Bertie one feels sorry for.'

'I suppose he will come home now?' Henrietta asked. Perry's eldest son had always been her favourite. As he had got on so badly with his father, he had spent a great deal of time at Morland Place in his youth, so that she sometimes thought of him as her 'extra son'. He had been living in India for the past seven years, at first as an agent for Mr Puddephat, but later also breeding and training horses on his own behalf.

'I suppose he'll have to, even if it's only to wind things up. Of course, he's Sir Percival now,' said Walter. 'Funny to think about that!' Bertie hated his first name so much he had always used his second. 'And the house and estate and so on are entailed on him, though whether there'll be anything but debts to inherit I don't know. I sent off a cable to him this morning when I was in York. I don't know how long it'll take to reach him. If he's "up country" on one of his jaunts it could be months, and that'll mean everything will be left to me.'

'We'll do everything we can to help you, my dear boy, you know that,' said Teddy.

'Thanks, Uncle. I was hoping you might say that. Of course, I shall take responsibility until Bertie gets home, but I would appreciate advice. I've never done anything like this before,' he finished, a little bleakly.

'What will you do about a funeral?' Henrietta asked.

'It can't wait for Bertie, because even if he sets off at once it will take him weeks to get here. So I thought I had better get on and arrange it myself.'

'Quite right,' Teddy said. 'At St Mary's, I suppose?'

'Yes, sir,' said Walter. 'The rector came to see me yesterday, and said he'd hold himself in readiness.'

'Chase is a good fellow,' Teddy said. 'He'll set you straight about form and so on.' He hesitated a delicate moment and then said, 'Have you enough money for your immediate wants?'

'Oh, yes, sir, thank you, as far as I know what they are. I mean, there's food and coal in the house, and the servants haven't deserted. But I'm not just entirely sure about the funeral expenses – the coffin and carriages and the sexton's and organist's fees and so on. If Papa really did have nothing left but debts, can I order things that might never be paid for?'

Henrietta was shocked. 'It can't be that bad, surely?'

'I hope not. But I just don't know. I want to give the pater a proper send-off but it seems wrong to risk bilking the tradesfolk.' His eyes were wet again, proving that inside he was younger than his outward calm suggested.

'Don't worry about that,' Teddy said at once. 'Any expenses incurred for the funeral I will guarantee if the estate fails altogether. You can tell anyone so if they ask – though I'm sure they won't. Greaves will be the only person who knows the state of affairs, and he won't talk about it, you can be sure.'

'Oh, thank you, Uncle. You are a trump!' Walter said, evidently enormously relieved. 'Well, in that case, it might as well be sooner as later, don't you think? Perhaps on Monday or Tuesday next week?'

'So soon?'

'Well, I don't mean it to be anything elaborate. I don't think that would be appropriate. Just family and tenants, and such of the villagers as want to turn out. It's not as if Papa ever had any public office, or went into society.'

'I suppose you're right,' Henrietta said. 'But don't have it on Monday. That might mean people having to travel on Sunday.'

'Very well, Tuesday, then. And – you will come? Please? I know Papa was rather unkind to you, Aunty, but—'

'As I said, that's all forgotten,' Henrietta said. 'Of course we'll come.'

'And if you want to borrow any of the servants—' Teddy began.

But Walter said, 'Oh, no, sir, thanks, but that won't be necessary. Our own people will want to do it all.'

And so the simple funeral had taken place on the 5th of January. Perry's family had gathered from various quarters. His three daughters, Edith, Adelaide and Amy

172

Patricia, were all married, Edith to a local farming gentleman's son, Addy to a headmaster from Harrogate and Amy Pat to a man with a printing business in Leeds. The two elder came with their husbands; Amy Pat was still lying in with her first child, and could only send a letter. Lucas, the second son, came up from Bath where he was attached to the diocesan staff; Peregrine, known as Peg, and Arthur travelled down from London together. Perry's sister Amy and her husband were abroad and could not come; Amy's twin, Patsy, now Lady Laine, travelled up from Leicestershire where she and her husband, the Society painter Sir Vivian Laine, had been staying with a fashionable house party.

By Henrietta's advice Walter had ordered the servants not to stint the coal, and enough large fires were burning at least to take the cavernous chill off the house. The rector, Mr Chase, did the service beautifully, and the church was one of the loveliest in Yorkshire; but January was a sad time for flowers, and Henrietta felt the lack of them keenly, as poor Perry's coffin was lowered into the ground to a background of bare chestnut trees, grey sky, and the chilly cawing of rooks.

Back at the Red House afterwards, Henrietta found herself beside Patsy.

'Well, that's the end of an era,' Patsy said, looking round the drawing-room where they stood near the fire, trying to get warm. 'Poor Perry! I had forgotten how shabby the old house was. It was all right when we were children and it was full of noise and movement. I suppose Bertie will sell it. But Vivian says it will be hard to find anyone who wants a place like this nowadays, especially so far from London.'

'Have you heard from Amy recently?'

'About six weeks ago. She and her husband are in India somewhere.'

'Oh? Not far from Bertie, then.'

'That's what I thought, but it turns out that India is a pretty big place, and they're in a different part from him. On the opposite side, Vivian says.'

'It's a pity Sir Vivian couldn't come today, to support you.'

'He didn't want to,' Patsy said plainly. 'He hates funerals; and besides, Lord and Lady Rutland are at the house where we're staying, and he's hoping to get a commission to paint Lady Rutland's portrait, so he wants to stay close to her and butter her up.'

'Oh, Patsy!' Henrietta laughed despite herself.

'You must be sorry Jerome isn't here. It's so sad about Mary. I wish now I had gone to see her in the autumn when we were in Paris, but there never seemed time, with all the parties and receptions Vivian was invited to. I feel very bad about it. Poor Mary. We were so close once, she and Amy and I. It's strange to think about it now. She seemed to change so much.'

Lucas drifted over to join them. 'I must say Walter's done very well, arranging all this in such a short time. I did offer to help him,' he added defensively, 'but after all, he is the only one of us without responsibilities, and it would have been very difficult for me to absent myself for several days. The Bishop wasn't too pleased at my leaving him today.' Like Patsy he stared around at the shabby room, with the tell-tale pale patches on the walls where paintings had been sold. 'It looks as though things had got pretty bad. Has anyone heard from Bertie yet? I suppose he'll sell the old place.'

Peg joined them in time to hear the last words, and added cheerfully, 'Well, none of us wants it. Horrid old heap.'

'Your grandfather would have been sad to think the family would leave the Red House after all these years,' Henrietta said.

'It happens to the best families,' Peg said easily. 'No-one cares for history in these modern times.'

'I can't think Bertie will want to live in England anyway,' Lucas said. 'He's never shown any sign of wanting to come back. Anyway, what could he do here?'

'He could breed horses, as he does in India,' Henrietta suggested.

'Not so profitably, I suspect. I imagine he has a pretty easy life of it over there.'

'Besides,' Peg had added, 'I expect he's got a dozen black wives by now. It *would* cause a stir if he brought them back to Bishop Winthorpe with him!'

'Don't be disgusting,' Lucas had snapped. 'And in front of your aunts!'

Patsy had felt it prudent to change the subject, and had asked Henrietta when she expected Jerome to come home.

'There was a cable yesterday to say he hopes to be able to leave by the end of the week. I hope the weather doesn't worsen. He had a dreadful crossing going out.'

'You'll be glad to have him back.'

'I shan't feel easy until I have him at Morland Place, safe and sound.'

She thought about those words often as she sat by Jerome's bedside, watching over him helplessly as he struggled with the infection. There was nothing to do – that was almost the worst thing – but be near him, sponge his face, stop him throwing off his covers when the delirium took him. She and Nurse Sawyer took watch and watch through the night, four hours on and four hours off, and during the day each made sure the other took time off for a walk out of doors and to eat proper meals. Jessie begged to be allowed to help with the nursing, but Dr Hasty would not say that the likelihood of infection was definitely past, and Henrietta refused her. She hung around the draughty passage outside the door, pining like Fern for a sight of Jerome. Henrietta was afraid she would make herself ill; but Ned came to the rescue, gently insisted on her removal to the fire, and kept her occupied, playing cards and backgammon with her hour after hour through the evenings, and taking her out riding whenever he could during the day.

Jerome's condition grew worse, his temperature climbed to 104°, and a numbness of exhaustion and despair came over Henrietta, so that she seemed to move in a dream, watching her hands doing things as if they were miles away and not just at arm's length. Her beloved husband was dying, and yet it seemed to be happening to someone else, not to her and the warm, laughing, loving man she had lived with and slept beside all these years. The terror and struggle were going on in some distant part of her mind, as though in another room, and she could only watch in a kind of apathy as he seemed to sink deeper into himself, growing more gaunt and strange as the days passed, unreachable, fading away from her. It was like one of those dreadful dreams where you are unable to act to prevent some tragedy, where your hands and feet move with underwater slowness, and no matter how you try, you cannot scream.

There came the night when she was sitting with him through the darkest hours. Nurse Sawyer was sleeping in the trestle bed on the other side of the room. The firelight made a red cave of light and shadow, and the candles ran their ripples like water across the ceiling. Jerome had been restless; now he had fallen quiet, his breathing harsh, stertorous and regular. Henrietta sponged his flushed face, moistened his dry lips, smoothed back his hair with an automatic hand, just as she had done these things hundreds of times; and suddenly, as though the shell around her had cracked and spilled her out, she was *there* again. She saw him, she knew herself, she felt the pain like a terrible pressure in the chest that rose up her throat until it was as rigid as a tube of iron with her unshed tears.

'Oh, my darling, my darling,' she whispered, in breaking grief. She knew what this harsh breathing was. It was the end. He had struggled until he had no more strength, and now he was failing, fading, leaving her. 'Oh, please,' she whispered, 'please don't leave me.' She held his insensible hand in both hers. *I never said goodbye*, she thought. It was two days since he had been properly conscious. *I can't live without him*, she thought; but she knew she would have to, and saw in a brief flash the long path of years that she would have to trudge without him, never again able to be with him, see him, touch him, confide in him, lie close to him in the night.

The sound of his breathing changed, grew slower, more laboured. He seemed sunk in a dead unconsciousness. It could not be long. She ought to call the nurse, perhaps; but what could she do? No, his last moments should be hers alone; he was not to die in anyone's arms but hers. She leaned over him and laid her lips to his brow and cheek, unresponsive as a block of wood, as if he had gone already. *I love you,* she said in her mind. *Only ever you.* And then there was nothing left but the waiting.

Just before four in the morning he seemed to give a great gasp, and his hands tightened as though he were snatching at life; there was a beat of silence, and then the breath he had drawn in went out in a long sigh. A terrible pain seemed to embed itself in her heart, and she could not move, as though it had impaled her to her seat. Across the room she heard a rustling sound and then a soft footfall as Nurse Sawyer woke and got out of bed. She loomed up out of the flickery darkness and went to the other side of the bed. Henrietta wanted to speak, to tell her what had happened, but her throat hurt too much and she could not make a sound. Nurse Sawyer bent over him, laid a hand against his brow and cheek, and then took up his other hand to place her fingers against his wrist.

'I think the fever has broken,' she said.

Henrietta only looked at her, her poor wits gone completely.

'He's had his crisis,' the nurse said. 'The fever's broken. He's quite cool now, and his pulse is steady.'

Henrietta made a sound of enquiry, all she could manage. Nurse Sawyer smiled. 'The worst is over, ma'am. I think he's going to be all right.'

Jerome's convalescence was long. The illness left him so debilitated that for weeks he could only lie propped against his pillows, taking nourishment like a baby and

177

staring at the patch of changing sky outside the window. The life of the house went on, and the wider life of the seasons, but his compass had shrunk to one room and the events of his bedside. He slept a lot to begin with, and Hasty said it was the best thing for him, and that when he was awake he must be kept very quiet, and not troubled or excited. Everyone wanted to be allowed to visit him, but too many faces and too much talk tired him out. Visits were restricted to five minutes per person, and no more than two a day. For the rest of the time, either Jessie or Henrietta sat with him, and Nurse Sawyer was retained as night nurse so that Henrietta could sleep.

Jessie was glad to be able to help her mother, and profoundly relieved to be with her father again. Being shut out of his room while he was – as everyone thought – dying had been dreadful to her. Now she could be useful to him, caring for him with the quietness and gentleness he needed. She found she could anticipate his few wants, understanding instinctively when he wanted her to talk and cheer him with news from outside, when he wanted her to read to him, and when he just wanted her to sit by him quietly. She had always been a lively, active girl, tomboyish and noisy about the house, more interested in riding and climbing trees and playing cricket than any maidenly pursuits. But now at her father's bedside she found a womanly grace and a tenderness she had not needed before. He liked to have her there, and often smiled at her and called her 'his gracious silence'.

'You've grown up, my Jessie. I'm glad I survived to see you become a woman.'

Dr Hasty said that it would be many months before he regained his strength. Henrietta still did not feel able to leave him to go and stay with Lizzie for the birth of her baby. It was born on the 24th of February, and Venetia was present in Henrietta's stead, understanding how her friend would feel torn between the two needs, to be a wife and to be a mother. The birth was not attended by any great difficulty, and by two in the afternoon Lizzie was resting on her pillows with a small, red-faced baby girl in her arms.

Ashley was thrilled: having two sons to carry his name and satisfy his male vanity, he had secretly hoped for a girl, and was now prepared to give her his entire heart and be as fond and foolish a papa as was ever wound round a small finger. Lizzie was moved by his evident delight, and found her own feelings unexpectedly being stirred. She had not wanted another baby, had carried it unwillingly, and had both hoped for and expected another boy. She knew how to be a mother to boys. But now, holding this tiny, vulnerable thing in her arms, she felt her heart seized by it. A daughter! She had a daughter – a little girl to pet and love; to be to her what she had always been to her mother. Sons grew up and went away, but a daughter you had always.

'What shall we call her?' Ashley asked, gazing enchanted at the sleeping face, lifting the tiny fingers to his lips to kiss them.

'We didn't think of any girls' names,' Lizzie said. 'I was so sure it would be a boy.'

'It ought to be something delicate and pretty,' said Ashley.

And so they called her Rose. Jessie was the one who read Lizzie's letter to her father, recounting the news. 'Every mother ought to have a daughter,' he said. 'And every father, too,' he added, with a fond look at Jessie. 'A daughter to wind herself round his heart. I like the name Rose.'

'Another flower name,' Jessie said. 'Like mine and Violet's.'

'I hope I shall get to see Miss Rose,' Jerome said.

'Why shouldn't you?' Jessie said quickly, feeling the cold touch of fear on the back of her neck. 'Lizzie will come and visit as soon as she's out of bed, and bring the baby.'

'Yes. But sometimes I feel so weak and tired—'

'You've been very ill,' Jessie said. 'It will take time. Be patient.'

179

'To think of my Jessie advocating patience,' he said, with a faint smile.

At the end of another month, he was spending most of every day out of bed, though on Dr Hasty's recommendation he returned to it for a couple of hours in the afternoon. He had not yet left the house, and was so easily tired that he still did little but sit. But it was pleasant to have a change of scene, and to be part of the life of the house again.

Teddy had been shocked when Jerome first came downstairs at how feeble he seemed, but once he had got used to the sight of him, he began to feel he had waited long enough for his wedding, and revived the subject with Henrietta one day. He followed her out to the wilderness, where she had gone to pick daffodils for Jerome, to bring a little of spring in to him, since he couldn't go out to it. It was a blowy day, with watery clouds on the horizon threatening rain, but overhead was a patch of blue sky and the sun was shining in a diffident, practising sort of way. Daffodils grew all around the edge of the wilderness, and Teddy found Henrietta with her basket and scissors standing by a patch of them, watching them nod and curtsey in the breeze.

She started when he spoke her name, and he said, 'You were in an absolute reverie. What were you thinking?'

'Oh, just that the daffodils look so bright and cheerful, it seems a shame to cut them.'

'Was that really all?' The sun, shining in her face, showed the strain she had been through lately. 'Poor Hen, you do look tired. But he's getting better now. And Lizzie's had her baby and they're both doing well. The hard times are over.'

'I hope so,' she said. The thought of that third death still hung over her, but she would not speak of it, in case words gave it power. 'Did you want me for something?'

'Yes, I wanted to talk to you about Alice. Take my arm and walk a little. You shouldn't stand still in this cold wind.' She slipped her hand under his elbow and he took the path round the outside of the wilderness, so they could keep in the sun. 'When I announced at Christmas that Alice and I were going to be married, I meant it to happen pretty well straight away,' he said. 'But first Perry died, and then Jerome got ill. Well, naturally I didn't press matters in those circumstances. But Hasty says Jerome is really on the mend now, and – well, I'm anxious to get on with it. I mean, there she is, all ready to be my wife, and she wants it, and I want it, and – you do understand?'

'Of course,' Henrietta said automatically, but her heart sank at the revival of this worry – on top of everything else! She did understand that Teddy, who was a warm-hearted man, should want a wife, and want her sooner rather than later; but wasn't he being a little insensitive, given how ill Jerome had been and how weak he still was? 'I know you don't want to wait any longer,' she went on, 'but I really don't think Jerome is strong enough to be disturbed yet. You know Dr Hasty said he mustn't be worried or upset.'

'Oh, the wedding won't disturb him, don't worry about that. I've talked to Alice about it, and she agrees with me that we're both too long in the tooth for any fancy celebrations. We mean it to be very quiet, no fuss, just a nice little ceremony between us and such of the family as want to come. No outsiders, no large party, nothing of that sort. I'd like it to be in the chapel, and Alice would like that too. If we had it there, it would mean that Jerome could be present, if he felt up to it.'

Henrietta struggled for the right words. 'It's not so much the wedding itself I worry about, but what comes afterwards.'

Teddy's eyebrows shot up. 'My dear girl, what can you mean?'

'You know what I mean. We've always known that we would have to move on at some point, and I know that Jerome has something put aside for that. But how can he face the upheaval in his present condition? How would we even find a place? I don't know how to go about it, and he couldn't be troubled with that sort of thing yet.' Her eyes filled with tears. 'The worry might well kill him. You *can't* ask it of us, Ted, really you can't. You've been so kind to us for so long, surely you could wait a little longer, just a few months, until he's stronger?'

Teddy stopped and turned to face her; pulled out his handkerchief, put it into her hand and guided it to her face. 'What is all this? Now don't cry! You can't think I mean to turn you out? Whatever gave you that idea? Did I ever say a syllable of anything like it?'

'But if you marry Alice—' Henrietta began, muffled by the handkerchief.

'Yes, if I marry Alice – what then? Don't you think Morland Place is big enough for all of us? Why on earth should I want you to go? I never even hinted at such a thing.'

'You – you mean—'

'I love having you here, you simpleton! What would the old place be like without you and your brood to keep it lively? The more the merrier, I say. I've always dreaded the boys and Jessie getting married and moving away.'

'But what about Alice? Surely – surely she'll want to be mistress in her own house? She won't like having me here, to say nothing of my children. She'll want her house to herself. I'm sure any woman would feel the same.'

'Don't worry your head about Alice. She knows the set-up here, and she's perfectly happy with it. To tell you the truth, she rather dreaded having to be mistress of Morland Place when I first proposed to her – didn't think she could manage a big house and tenants and all the rest of it. But when I said you'd be there to do it all, she was relieved and said in that case she would have me. If you insist on leaving,' he went on with a teasing smile, 'you'll make me go back on my word, and I shall look no-how.'

'Oh Teddy,' Henrietta said, with a watery laugh. 'You can't mean it? She wouldn't really want to share the house with all of us?'

'Honestly, Hen, I wonder about you sometimes. Did you really think I was proposing to throw you all out, with Jerome still so tottery? What do you think of me?'

She squeezed his arm, and reached up to kiss his cheek. 'I think you are the best and kindest brother in the world.'

'So I can go ahead and choose a date, can I? I'm getting awfully tired of that journey out to Layerthorpe.'

'Just give me time to break it to Jerome.'

'Of course. And assure him from me that it won't make a jot of difference to any of you.'

But whatever she said to Teddy, or he said to her, Henrietta still worried. Mrs Meynell might have agreed to share the house as a condition of marrying Teddy, but what did she really think? And how would it turn out in practice? The abstract idea was one thing, but reality might throw up all sorts of conflicts and frictions. Even if they did not lead to a demand to remove the Compton brood wholesale, the tension they would generate would not be good for Jerome. He had his pride, too, and if he felt they were unwelcome, he might well insist on leaving.

The first difficulty was telling him about it in a way that would not alarm him. She walked about the gardens for a long time after Teddy had left her, going over and over it in her mind and trying to assemble exactly the right words. But when at last she broached the subject with Jerome, he said only, 'Getting married? I thought that might be in the offing. I'm very pleased for him. A man ought to have a wife, and your brother especially. He's a fellow who likes to look after people.'

'He announced it at Christmas,' Henrietta explained, watching him carefully for any sign of shock, 'but it had all to be put off because of your illness. Now they want to get on and tie the knot, but you're not to worry that they want us to leave on that account. Quite the opposite.'

He smiled at her. 'I couldn't think your brother would toss me out at a moment's notice, in my frail state.'

'Of course not. But that's not what I meant. Teddy has been at pains to assure me he wants us to stay for ever, and so does Alice.'

'As to that, we shall see,' Jerome said. He took her hand and pressed it. 'Darling, he is very kindly reassuring us, given my state of health. But we will have to leave eventually, when I'm well again.'

'No, really, that's not what—'

'Hush, dearest. Don't worry. We knew we would have to leave one day, and it doesn't trouble me at all. I'm quite prepared for it. When the time comes, we'll find somewhere else and be just as happy there as we have been here, I promise you. I'm not afraid, and you shouldn't be either. I shall tell Teddy I couldn't be happier for him, and he shall have the wedding as soon as he chooses.'

Ned, Robbie and Jessie had no feelings about the wedding except gladness on Teddy's behalf. They liked what little they knew of Mrs Meynell, who seemed gentle and sweet-natured, and since it had never been suggested to them that her arrival might mean their departure, they had no fears on that score. Polly had been very excited at Christmas when it was announced, but when nothing more was said she forgot about it. Now the scheme was revived, her concern was not for the marriage – which was beyond her to speculate about – but the wedding.

'I hope I shall be a bridesmaid,' she said to Jessie. 'I've never been one, and if I can't be one for Papa's wedding, I shall think it great fudge!' She applied to Jessie for every detail of how a wedding was conducted and the glorious part a bridesmaid might play, ignoring Jessie's warnings that her own experience was not at all typical. When the very modest plans were revealed to her by her father, she was dreadfully disappointed.

'Not even in a proper church? Jessie said it wouldn't be Westminster Abbey, but I thought you would at least do it in the Minster, which is nearly the same. Couldn't you? Oh, please, Papa!'

Afterwards she grumbled to Jessie that it was all going

to be very *un*glorious, and that though her father had said she could be bridesmaid, it would hardly be worth while when there'd be no-one there to see her. 'No crowds, no carriages, no train to carry, and no scattering flowers or anything. When I think it might be the only time I ever am one! It's not fair!'

Henrietta was glad to discover that Polly had no apprehensions about acquiring a step-mother, no fears about being usurped in her father's affections. That side of it did not seem to have occurred to her at all. She had been beloved by her father all her life, and it simply did not cross her mind that that could ever change.

If it had not been for her own fears, Henrietta would have liked everything about the wedding, its warmth and simplicity. Even as things stood, she could not help being drawn into the preparations and finding herself enjoying them. Teddy wanted no fuss, but there was a minimum that had to be done: an extra cleaning of the house, and particularly the chapel; some rearrangement of rooms, and the accommodation of Mrs Meynell's possessions and such furniture as she wanted to keep with her. Provision had to be made for the housing of the two servants she would be bringing with her: her lady's maid, the exotically named Miss Sweetlove, and a laundry maid whom, she said, she could not do without on account of her delicate ways with silk underwear. Henrietta was aware of some speculation among the servants about whether Sweetlove would prove to be difficult and above her company, but on the whole they were so intrigued and pleased about the master marrying after all these years that they were willing to give her the benefit of the doubt.

Then there was the wedding luncheon to plan, which, though it would only be a family meal, Henrietta was determined should reflect the status of the master of Morland Place and her own pride in her housekeeping. She did not have to worry about Polly's dress, which was being made by the head woman at Makepeace's; Mrs

185

Meynell's costume was in the hands of her usual mantua-maker.

The days passed in a flash, and the morning came when Ned went off in Teddy's motor-car to fetch the bride: in the absence of any relatives, she had asked him to give her away. Jessie and Miss Mitchell dressed the extremely excited Polly, while Henrietta did her best with such flowers as the season could provide to decorate the chapel. The Reverend Mr Grantby arrived from the village to perform the ceremony, and took a glass of sherry in the drawing-room with Robbie, chatting easily about the lambing. Two couples, particular friends of the bride, the Spindlows and the Winningtons, arrived looking faintly embarrassed at the modesty of the arrangements, and encountering Henrietta crossing the hall still in her apron from doing the flowers, took her for the housekeeper and embarrassed themselves still further.

But everything went off perfectly. Jerome was well enough to stand at Teddy's side as groomsman; the servants filled up the back of the chapel and made up the congregation. Alice Meynell walked up the aisle on Ned's arm, looking as radiant as a bride should, in a pretty outfit of rose-buff silk trimmed with blue velvet piping, and a fashionably large hat. Polly walked behind in an agony of self-conscious dignity, dressed, as a brides-maid ought to be, in her own view, in pink satin. And very soon afterwards, Alice Morland was walking back down the aisle on her husband's arm, and Polly, forgetting herself entirely in her excitement, followed them in a series of jumps, using the chapel's paving stones as hopscotch squares.

Luncheon followed, with plenty of champagne, and Jerome, excusing himself from standing up to do it, made a very funny speech. There were toasts, much laughter, a few tears, and then the motor-car was at the door to take them to Scarborough for a few days. It was only at that point that Polly realised someone else was now coming first with her father, and her lip began to tremble ominously as the car pulled out under the barbican. But Jessie saw the gathering tears and hurried to distract her with a promise, if she got out of her pink finery right away, of taking her out riding. Grantby modestly took his leave; Jerome went upstairs to rest; and Henrietta saw off the guests, and then went to her writing-desk to compose letters to Venetia, Lizzie, Jack and Frank about the day's events. Her desk had had to be moved to a different position in the drawing-room to make room for Alice's piano; the mantelpiece now held an assortment of Alice's china ornaments, and Alice's favourite chair now stood at the other side of the fireplace from Teddy's. No matter what Teddy said, she thought as she lifted the lid of the inkwell, things were bound to be different from now on.

Jack took the news of the wedding to the Puddephats on one of his Sunday afternoon visits, explaining, in case Mr Puddephat should be offended at not having been invited, that it had been a very quiet affair on account of his father's health.

Mr Puddephat said, 'When a man of your uncle's age marries, it had better be a quiet affair! Anything else would risk looking ridiculous. But I am very happy for him, very happy indeed. I shall write and offer my congratulations. The lady, I suppose, is younger than he?'

'I believe so, sir, quite a bit younger.'

'It will do him good. Well, well, I wish him every joy. I expect you're sorry you could not be there?'

'Yes, very sorry. I am very fond of my uncle. He's the kindest man in the world.'

'He's an excellent fellow in every way. I shall be up that way some time this summer, so I shall be able to see for myself how happy they are. He has known her a long time, I imagine?'

'Yes, sir, for many years.'

'Quite right. Marriage is not something to be jumped into hastily,' said Puddephat, and returned to his newspaper.

Maud, sitting beside Jack, was as calm as always, and did not show any sign of having taken a personal interest in the conversation about marriage. He wished he knew how she felt about him. She never either encouraged or discouraged him and, despite all that Sopwith said, he could not help feeling that she saw him in the light of a brother. His own feelings for her were unchanged by any of the other young women he had met in recent months. It was Maud he loved. She was so pretty with her pink cheeks and blue eyes, her soft brown hair dressed wide as the new fashion was, parted in the centre and draped at the sides, with a large chignon at the back. He felt he could look at her for the rest of his life and never get tired of it. Her fawn afternoon dress was simple but elegant; under the cream lace guimpe her breast rose and fell with her quiet breathing, and he could imagine the flutter of her pulse under the tender skin of her throat – but thinking about that was rather too heating, especially on a Sunday, and he stopped himself.

Maud, perhaps feeling the obligation of the hostess towards him, said, 'How are things at work? Are you doing anything interesting at the moment?'

'Oh, still working on the JC2. The prototype went into the water last week, so there's lots to be learned from the trials. The new propellor seems to be working very well. I'd love to try out my ideas about the shape in an aeroplane. I'd give anything to be able to go over to France and talk to some of those fellows. I can't think why we're not doing more over this side of the Channel.'

'But it's only a passing fad, isn't it? Don't you think?'

'Oh, no, far from it!' Jack said. 'If that Wright fellow proved anything last year, it was that flying is not just a fidget, and his aeroplane is not just a toy. His first flight was a sensation. It only lasted a few minutes, but it was quite different from anything seen before. He had *absolute* control over his machine. He took off, flew about, banked and turned, and landed in the exact place he'd taken off from, and as gently as a feather. There was no doubt at all that he knew exactly what his machine was going to do.'

'You speak as if you were there,' Miss Puddephat said, with a gentle smile.

'Oh, well, I read all about it,' Jack said. 'You see, before Wilbur Wright, other men had managed to get a machine into the air, but it was a matter of luck, and no more than a long hop with an engine attached to it. Simply getting daylight under the wheels was an achievement. They had very little control when they were in the air, and if they managed to do anything at all, they had no surety of being able to do it twice. But Wright has been flying again and again, ever since that first flight last August, doing the same things every time, with complete control. He's even taken passengers up with him. He's shown that flying isn't just a fluke, it's – it's the *future*.'

'It's not the future as far as I'm concerned. Even if flying were possible, I shouldn't like to do it myself. Too dangerous – and I dare say very dirty and noisy. I can't see the point of it.'

All the things Jack wanted to say at the same time rendered him speechless, which was probably just as well.

She went on, 'Papa says if we had been meant to fly, God would have given us wings. That's so true, isn't it?'

Jack restrained himself. 'You might as well say, if we had been meant to travel on railways, God would have given us wheels.'

She wrinkled her nose. 'Oh, that's just silly. Railway trains are quite ordinary and sensible.'

'They weren't a hundred years ago. Don't you see? In a hundred years' time, we shall be flying all over the world without thinking twice about it, in aeroplanes that travel at speeds we can only dream of now.'

'Well, I don't believe it,' said Miss Puddephat. 'I shouldn't want to go up in the air in one of those things, and I don't see why anyone else would want to, either.'

Jack did not want to quarrel with her. 'I expect it will

only be foolish young men who want to fly,' he said peaceably. 'But you must admit it is exciting that they have discovered how to do it.'

'*If* they have. I know it was in the newspapers,' she forestalled him, 'but newspapers make things up all the time. You can't trust what they say. And why would this Mr Wright do it in France and not here, which would be the natural thing to do, if it was all open and above board? I'll believe it when I see it for myself – which is likely to be never, because I don't hear from you that Mr Wright is going to bring his machine over here and *prove* that he can fly.'

He suppressed a smile at her evident belief that a thing demonstrated only before Frenchmen did not count. 'I don't think it will be long before we have flyers in this country. Things are moving along so fast in France, they are even talking about holding a flying show in the summer, with large cash prizes for speed and height and manoeuvring and so on. That sort of thing always stimulates invention. Goodness, I'd like to be there, though!'

He paused for a moment, his eyes bright and far away as he thought how wonderful it would be. One of the differences about the Wrights' aeroplane, it had emerged, was that instead of revolving at engine speed, the propellor had been geared down, which allowed it to 'grip' the air and create much more propulsion. This idea had fired Jack's imagination. He had hundreds of drawings of propellors, as well as pages and pages of diagrams of new kinds of engine. He longed to be able to discuss them with real flyers, even if there was no chance he would ever be able to try them out.

But he knew the subject did not interest Miss Puddephat, and he must not bore her. He shook the images from his mind and asked her instead if she had been to any concerts lately. She was very fond of music, and was soon telling him with enthusiasm about the performance she had attended of a first symphony by Edward Elgar, which was proving so popular that it had

had thirty performances already since its première in December. This naturally led to other musical topics, and a request from Jack for Miss Puddephat to play the piano. It was a Sunday occupation to which Mr Puddephat did not object, if the music were seemly, and the evening ended pleasantly with Jack and Maud singing folk songs together to Maud's accompaniment, until it was time for tea, and Jack's departure to catch his train.

Henrietta spent the four days of Teddy's honeymoon bracing herself for the entry into the house of Alice Morland as mistress. While outwardly calm and going about her usual routines, she was inwardly rehearsing endless explanations and apologies, anticipating problems, and dolefully planning the Compton departure down to the packing of the last box. She tried to remain quietly cheerful with Jerome, but she should have known she could never hide anything from him. She was sitting with him one day, knitting while he read, when he looked across at her and said, 'You look as if you are doing particularly difficult sums in your head. What is it, my love?'

She was not quick-witted enough to toss out an excuse, and while she was wondering what to say, he went on, 'We'll be all right. Haven't we always been? If we have to leave, so be it. Don't you trust me to look after you?'

'Oh, dearest!' she said, in a rush of guilt and love. It should be her looking after him!

'I've had plenty of time to think in the past few weeks, lying here weak as a kitten and with nothing else to do,' he went on. 'And what I've mostly been thinking is how good it is to be alive, and to be with you. Nothing else counts. I'll live here, or I'll up sticks and move, but as long as I'm with you it really doesn't matter. We faced destitution long ago, and now we've faced death. What else is there to worry about? So don't fret, my love.' He held out a hand to her, and she took it, and cradled it contritely to her cheek.

'I'll try not,' she said.

'You should rather worry about Jessie, if you have to worry about anyone. My being ill has meant a very quiet time for her. She ought to be having fun and dancing and flirting, not sitting with her old father. Where is she now, by the way?'

'Out riding,' said Henrietta.

'Alone?'

'No, with Ned. He's such a kind boy. He's really taken care of her since she came back from London.'

'Hardly a boy. He's twenty-three now.'

'I wonder what he thinks of Teddy's marrying again?'

'I don't expect he thinks anything. He seems quite contented to me.'

'I suppose he'll get married one day and set up in a home of his own. I wish I could say the same about Jessie.'

'Don't be in such a hurry to marry her off. I can't do without her yet.'

'I suppose eighteen is still very young, these days. I just want her to be happy.'

'There'll be no lack of suitors for our little girl, don't worry,' Jerome said. 'I'm glad she didn't marry straight out of the schoolroom, without a chance to look around, like poor Violet.'

'*Poor* Violet married an earl – or the heir to an earl, anyway. But she married for love, of course.' She paused while she knitted the difficult bit round the pattern of holes, and then said, 'I wonder she hasn't sent for Jessie to visit by now. I thought there were all sorts of promises made at the wedding.'

'They haven't long been married, and you said it was a love match. I should have thought the less of myself if my new bride started hankering after other company so soon.'

She smiled. 'Foolish! But now I come to think of it, I believe they're still down in the country. Venetia said in one of her letters that they hadn't come up to Town yet.'

'Why shouldn't she invite Jessie in the country?'

'Oh, no reason, particularly, but it would be more fun

for Jessie in Town. Violet could take her about, now she's a married woman.'

He laughed at that. 'Little Violet, chaperone our Jessie? A great deal of control over her she'd be likely to have!'

'I don't suppose Jessie would go just at present anyway,' Henrietta said. 'She wants to stay here with you.'

'Exactly what I said before – my being ill is keeping her from fun and dancing.'

'I'm sure she doesn't see it like that,' Henrietta said, coming to the end of a row and switching needles. Talking with Jerome always calmed her, and the effect lasted for some hours before she began worrying again.

But when Teddy and Alice arrived home, it wasn't a bit the way she had expected. Just at first Henrietta was very nervous and tried to defer to Alice, asked her wishes, paused an instant before giving an order to a servant in case Alice wanted to do it. But it soon became plain that Alice had no desire at all to run the house. She was gentle and shy and self-effacing, and seemed to think it the most natural thing in the world that Henrietta should give all the orders. She was unused to having so many people about her, and at first tended to flinch rather when Polly shrieked or the dogs barked, when there was a hullabaloo or even a lot of noisy fun. But she grew used to it, and was soon able to go about her little concerns in serene disregard for the human and canine bodies hurtling around her.

She didn't appear to Henrietta to have many interests in life, but what she had seemed to satisfy her. She did a great deal of delicate embroidery; she played the piano; she liked very much to arrange flowers, and discovering this, Henrietta encouraged her to consider the floral decoration of the main rooms her special duty. She visited, and was visited by, a small circle of York ladies. She liked to be nicely dressed, and spent a lot of time and money on acquiring new clothes. She was not fond of dogs, but soon after her installation in the house, Teddy bought her a little canary in a cage, and she doted on that, and petted and talked to it for hours.

The rest of her life was taken up with Teddy, whom it was plain she loved very much. He adored her, and liked nothing better than to sit and tell her the details of his day, and she liked nothing better than to sit and listen to him. Because Jerome needed rest and quiet, they did not yet entertain at home, but they were popular invitees amongst York society, and went to many dinners, soirées and bridge parties; and they went quite often to the theatre, because Teddy liked a play and Alice liked to be anywhere that required her to dress up.

Even Miss Sweetlove proved no trouble. She was mollified by the size of her room (Henrietta had nervously given her one of the best ones) and impressed by the grandeur of her new surroundings, to which the Meynell villa had not held a candle. The other servants warily put her on probation until they should see how *her* mistress treated *their* mistress, but when it became obvious that Henrietta was not to be usurped, they unbent and took Miss Sweetlove to their bosoms. She responded, so Henrietta learned through the usual roundabout route, by revealing an unexpected talent for comic monologues, which sat so oddly with her rank and dignity it increased the fun enormously. The servants' hall became a much jollier place.

So all in all, the acquisition of Alice proved remarkably easy. She seemed to Henrietta far more like a house guest than the mistress – a permanent, and not at all troublesome house guest. Henrietta began to think that Teddy had chosen the one woman in the world who could make it possible for them all to live together at Morland Place. She had expected the turning upside down of her whole world, but in the event it was much less exciting than Jerome's first outing since his illness, when she took him for a half-hour's drive in her little pony-phaeton with the staid old pony Dunnock between the shafts.

BOOK TWO

JOURNEYS

Out of the earth to rest or range
Perpetual in perpetual change,
The unknown passing through the strange,

Water and saltness held together,
To tread the dust and stand the weather,
And plough the field and stretch the tether

John Masefield, 'The Passing Strange'

Chapter Seven

Jessie was not surprised that Violet had not yet asked her to visit. It was for the same reason that her letters from honeymoon mentioned nothing but the scenery and the museums. Since she had returned to England, the letters had been much less frequent. They were still non-committal, and Jessie supposed that she had so much to do in settling down in married rapture with her beloved that she had no time to miss her friend. To be setting up home with Brancaster, she thought, would be the apogee of bliss – even if it was in Lord Holkam's house, which Violet described cautiously as 'very large, very old, and rather cold'. Jessie missed Violet very much, but she thought it would be too painful to see her and Brancaster together yet. She thought Violet wise not to ask her, and would not have wanted to go, even had things at home been different.

But she could not yet have left her father. Though it had never been said out loud, she knew how close he had come to death. It was marked in his face, in his continuing weakness and lethargy. He was like a ghost of himself, only the inward essence of his intelligence and humour still shining, though dimly – not as if there were less of it, but as if it were much further away. She gathered from Dr Hasty's manner that he was still worried about him; and though she was not party to what Hasty said to her mother about him, she sensed when she was with him that some fundamental change had taken place. So she

197

did not want to leave him, both for her own sake, and because she was useful to him. He liked to have her read to him and talk to him; as some of his strength came back, to play at cribbage with him. When they were sitting together, and she was making him laugh, it was easy to forget his illness; but when he stood up or walked, his weakness was frightening. The least exertion exhausted him. When he came downstairs he had to be carried back up, which he disliked with all his old pride. Jessie had heard Uncle Teddy suggest a wheelchair to her mother, and had seen her mother shake her head ruefully.

She was useful to him in another way, too. At the beginning when he had been desperately ill, the head man from the stud, Lelliot, had come up to the house with a query, and by chance Jessie had been the only person available to talk to him. He had apologised, knowing how sick Mr Compton was, but it was a question of which yearlings were to go to the January sales and which kept for breaking, and if a decision wasn't made it would be too late and the sales missed. Jessie had been in her father's confidence before he left for France, and was able to answer Lelliot firmly.

'Well, miss,' he had said, looking doubtful, 'but is that an order? Begging your pardon, but I take my orders from Mr Compton, and I shouldn't like to do the wrong thing.'

Jessie had understood his dilemma – she was only the daughter of the house and, she supposed, seemed very young to Lelliot, whose beard-stubble at the end of the day came through white so that it filled the creases of his face like a heavy frost. She was quite confident that she knew what was to be done, but he would be reluctant to trust her. So she sent him away and told him she would speak to the master about it.

When Uncle Teddy came home she recounted the incident to him, and he said, 'Lord, yes! In all the worry I'd forgotten the stud. I've no idea what your father was planning before he took ill. I always leave all that to him. What's to be done, Jess? We can't ask him, poor fellow.'

'But, Uncle, *I* know. Dad discussed everything with me. I told Lelliot, but he wouldn't take an order from me.'

'Oh, I suppose that's fair enough. You'd better tell me and I'll write a note for him.'

Jessie hesitated a moment, and then, 'It could be done another way. You don't want to have to keep writing notes and being bothered, not with everything else you've got to do.'

'No, certainly not, but how can it be helped?'

'Because I know just what Dad had planned about everything, and I bet I can answer nearly every question – the day-to-day ones, anyway. If you would write a note to Lelliot saying he must take his orders from me—'

Teddy looked doubtful. 'Oh, I don't know, Jess. Not that I don't trust you,' he added hastily, 'but Lelliot's a stubborn man, and proud. He'd not like to be told by a mere girl.'

'Oh, Uncle!'

'Yes, yes, I know you're a grown up woman, but that's what he'd think. But I tell you what, I'll write him a note saying I'll relay my orders through you, how would that be? Then you can tell him what you like, and pretend I said it.' He saw her frown, and added, 'There's no point setting his back up. If he were to give his notice we should really be in the bag!'

And so that was the way it was arranged, and it did at least give Jessie something to think about during the worst time of her father's illness. When he began to recover, one of his first worries was what was happening with the horses, and she was able to reassure him and ease his mind of that concern. As time passed, she paid daily visits to the stud, and reported to her father. She passed on his instructions, but often when it was something too trivial to bother him with she would make up her own mind, and bit by bit the stud men grew used to her, and took her orders, and even Lelliot no longer pretended everything she said was relayed from a higher authority.

It was another reason for her not to want to go away: if she absented herself, it would all come down on Uncle Teddy, who had enough to do; and it would make Dad fret not to have her there as his proxy.

So she had plenty to keep her occupied, and real, proper work to do, which was much better than any make-do occupation that merely filled time. Now and then Uncle Teddy would have her on his conscience and insist she attended some dance or social gathering where there would be young people, and she enjoyed them, and danced and indulged in a little light flirtation like any other eighteen-year-old. She had regular admirers – Peter Firmstone, George Ayliffe and Frank Winbolt – which meant she never lacked for partners or had to sit alone at evening parties. And at home, Ned was always willing to entertain her when he came in from work, to play cards with her or, as the evenings grew lighter, to go out riding with her. She liked his company because they knew so many of the same things; and because, unlike her admirers, he knew about Brancaster, so she could talk about him if she wanted. But though the ache of it remained, she found as time went on she didn't want to talk about him any more. There were too many other things to talk about with Ned who, now she came to notice it, was really rather a good-looking young man.

Ned had been at Eton, which had given him a certain polish; and his job at the paper mill obviously entailed responsibility, which gave him an air of maturity. Now, as a result of Uncle Teddy's marriage to Alice, the owner-ship of the mill became effectively Uncle Teddy's, and he had made Ned manager, with a promise that the mill should belong to him entirely one day. Jessie knew that her parents approved of this arrangement, which would give Ned an independence and proper status, and she saw how it had changed him already, given him a weight and seriousness he had not had before. She thought it made him more attractive. He was very grateful to Uncle Teddy, and to Jessie expressed a humility that added to his charm, for though he called Teddy 'Father', he was very well aware that he was only adopted and that his mother had been a servant-girl and his birth illegitimate. He could say things to her that he could not say to other, unrelated girls, just as she could talk about Brancaster to him, but not to Mr Firmstone or the others. But as they went on their long rides together, or shook the backgammon dice at the drawing-room table, it seemed that what they mostly talked about was work – his at the mill and hers at the stud – which was really much more satisfying to both.

Anne Farraline had not been on hand when Lizzie's baby was born. On that very day – the 24th of February – she had taken part in a deputation to the House of Commons. The King's Speech on the 16th had made no mention of votes for women.

Before Parliament resumed, WSPU members had made a point of following cabinet members wherever they went, addressing them when the chance offered and interrupting their meetings wherever possible. As a result, Liberal meetings were now banned to all women, and extraordinary measures were taken to protect cabinet ministers – especially Mr Asquith – when they ventured abroad. Mr Churchill, that implacable enemy of women's suffrage, had been waylaid everywhere on a two-day visit to Newcastle, so that now the mere proximity of a female not of his acquaintance filled him with unease and rage. When Mrs Drummond happened to encounter him on the way to the House and greeted him politely, he waved his fist at her and said, 'Get away from me, woman, or I'll have you put in charge!'

The deputation to Parliament on the 24th of February was to be led by Mrs Pethick-Lawrence, and as it was assumed that she would be arrested, no future engagements had been arranged for her. Anne had not intended to join the deputation, but almost at the last minute her plans changed. The WSPU had received a new recruit in the shape of Lady Constance Lytton, whose brother, Lord Lytton, was one of the Cause's advocates in the Upper House. She was a gently raised and rather delicate young woman, and when she offered herself for the deputation and certain imprisonment, she did not dare tell her family what she was doing. As she was nervous about what she had decided to do, Anne quietly volunteered herself as well, to support 'Lady Con', as everyone called her, through the ordeal.

They lunched together at Clement's Inn with the others involved, and it was obvious that the strain of anticipation was already taking its toll: Lady Constance seemed pale and almost dazed, and when she confessed to having 'a cracking headache' she was taken up to the Pethick-Lawrences' flat to lie down.

'You had better stick close to her,' said Mrs Pethick-Lawrence, when Anne came downstairs again. 'Poor thing, she's very apprehensive.'

'Is she really up to it?' Anne asked. 'She doesn't look well.'

'She has a weak heart,' Mrs Pethick-Lawrence admitted. 'It's an old condition. But she's immensely brave and quite determined, and if she wants to do her part for the Cause, it's not for me to try to stop her.'

'It will cause a stir to have her arrested,' Anne admitted, 'provided the police don't recognise her and let her alone.'

'The same applies to you.'

'Yes, two "ladies" in Holloway. What a coup! A little light disguising for both of us is in order, I think. An unfashionable hairstyle and a drab coat should pass us in a crowd.'

Lady Constance came downstairs in time to have supper with Anne, but she was unable to eat much, obviously feeling rather queasy with her nervousness. A cab arrived to take them to Caxton Hall, and as they stood up, she said, 'I've just realised, I've no idea what part I am to play. What does one have to do?'

Anne thought briskness the best antidote for her

companion's nervousness. 'Oh, you don't need to worry about what you'll do: it will all be done to you. The one thing you need to remember is that you must not on any account be turned back. If the police become too violent you can cut matters short by getting yourself arrested.'

'How – how do I do that?'

'Create a breach of the peace. Pretend to make a speech, or collect a crowd round you. The police will arrest you and take you off at once.'

After the gathering at Caxton Hall, the members of the deputation set off in a column of twos, with Anne and Lady Constance bringing up the rear. 'If we do get through,' Lady Constance asked suddenly, 'what do we do?' She looked a little better now they were on the move: there was a touch more colour in her pale face.

'Make a speech,' Anne said.

'What about?'

'It doesn't matter, really. They won't be listening, and you won't be allowed to utter more than a few sentences.'

Lady Constance looked round at the crowd of people come to see the fun – Asquith had told the press the deputation was coming and that he would not receive it, to make sure the crowds would gather and impede the women. She said, 'Do you see how the white collars and shirts of the men almost shine in this grimy dusk? They are the work of women who have no advocate. Women who are despised and ignored, who have no rights and no-one but us to fight for them.'

'Excellent,' said Anne. 'Work that up, and you have your speech. All those men in Parliament have women to wash their shirts for them, from the ministers down to the police officers.'

The crowd and the police were gradually hemming in the procession, and soon forward movement was impossible. Even breathing was difficult as they were pressed closer together. Anne linked arms with Lady Constance. They were being shoved backwards, however they resisted. Seeing her companion pale and breathless, Anne said, 'This is hopeless. We aren't even in Parliament Square yet. We had better try another way.'

She held on to Lady Constance's arm and began to work them out of the crush backwards and sideways, and as soon as they were clear of the police they found themselves in a looser-knit crowd who seemed friendly and rather sympathetic to the Cause. Anne was alarmed at the condition of her companion, who seemed so breathless she could hardly lift her head, and who seemed to get herself along with enormous effort, as though she were trying to walk through heavy mud. But Lady Constance did not suggest turning back, and when Anne suggested it, she fixed her with a fierce eye and shook her head vehemently, though unable to speak.

Slowly and persistently the two women worked their way through the mass of bodies, which of course grew more dense the nearer they came to the House. Sometimes they had no control over their direction, being shoved by the weight of the crowd. Lady Constance was carried a little away from Anne in this manner and pressed up against the broad serge form of a policeman. Summoning her courage, she looked up into his face and said, 'I know you are only doing your duty, and I am doing mine.' If she had hoped her emollient words would touch him, she was soon disabused. He shouted at her, 'Go home, you hag! You've no business here!' And then he seized her round the ribs, lifted her up and threw her bodily away from him. All policemen were big and burly, being chosen for their size and strength; Lady Constance was small, slight and thin. She flew through the air and cannoned into some bystanders, who staggered but did not fall under the impact, and were able to set her on her feet.

Anne struggled to get to her, remembering how shocked she had been the first time she had been manhandled. Indeed, this was probably the first time in Lady Constance's life that anyone had raised a voice to her, let alone touched her in anger. Even being jostled in a crowd could be frightening and upsetting to someone from a sheltered upbringing; and Anne knew how those policemen liked to hurt. When they grabbed you, they did it roughly, and did their best to squeeze the life out of you while they threw you with all their strength. She reached Lady Constance, expecting to find her weeping, but though pale and struggling for breath, she seemed in control of herself.

'Are you all right?'

'Yes,' she gasped. 'But – why do they hate us so?'

'Because they're afraid of us, I think,' Anne said. 'Look here, it's going to get worse. Don't you think you should give up?'

A hint of steel showed in the large, rather pale eyes. 'No! I must go on.' And then, 'Worse?'

'You did not hit the ground that time. You've no idea how much it hurts. And not just the body. It makes *me* want to cry.'

Lady Constance shook her head, but said again, 'I must go on.'

So they resumed the struggle. Twice more Lady Constance was thrown; Anne three times. They hit the ground each time, and the third time Anne went down there was a flash and explosion of light near her, which told her a press man had photographed her in that degrading posture. It was as she had said to Lady Constance: the bodily hurts of crashing into the pavement from a height were as nothing to the mental pain of helplessness, humiliation and injustice.

She got to Lady Constance and helped her up after her second throw. A stout couple of bystanders added their assistance, and the woman kept saying, 'What a shame! What a shame!' With their help she got Lady Constance to some railings, where she leaned, gasping, her face deadly white and her chest labouring to draw in air. And such dank, foggy air, Anne thought: it was a real February night.

Now Lady Constance seemed almost done. 'I can't go on,' she said. 'I simply can't.'

'Wait a little,' Anne said. 'Take your time. You'll be all right presently.' Lady Constance shook her head, gulping like a fish on a bank. 'Look, we're almost there now. There's the Members' Entrance. If we can just get to it and walk in! Let me straighten your hat, my dear, and tuck up your hair. Try to look normal, and we may get right inside. Think of that!'

Lady Constance nodded now, closing her eyes for a moment, and then straightened up, trying to bring her breathing under control. Together they started forward again; and then suddenly, in that mysterious way crowds have, the throng parted and fell away, and the two women were at the gates, with no-one near them, and the two policemen on guard looking the other way. Anne slipped her hand under Lady Constance's elbow, straightened her back and walked forward with her head held high, keeping a steady, unhurried pace. Lady Constance took her lead, and they were past the policemen and through the gates.

But that was as far as they got. Instantly four other constables came running, saying, 'You're under arrest.' They flanked the women and took hold of their elbows, but quite gently, and Anne saw Lady Constance's eyes close in relief. Her head sank forward on her chest, and it was plain that the policemen were having to support her. Despite her frustration at not having got further, Anne also felt relief at being arrested. It meant the end of struggle, and that struggle was so hard to keep up, however much one's mind was determined.

For that night's work, she and Lady Constance were each given a month in the second division; and so as Lizzie was introducing her new baby into the world, Anne was behind bars and quite unable to pay the usual visits, or even to write her congratulations.

By the time she was out and able to go to see Lizzie, little Rose had recovered from the ordeal of birth, lost her wrinkles and become a more pleasing colour.

'What a pretty baby,' Anne said politely, more or less meaning it.

'Pretty? She's beautiful!' Lizzie cried. She was out of bed, but had not yet left the house, and Anne had found her reclining on a day-bed in a fine, delicate cream net and lace négligé. 'Wouldn't you like to hold her?'

'Not really,' Anne said.

'Well, I will,' Lizzie said, and was soon cradling the infant and gazing into her face as if it was her first baby, not her third.

'So, are you well?' Anne asked, finding it was for her to start the conversation.

'Oh, yes, quite well. Only very tired. This one took it out of me a great deal more, I don't know why. But I don't feel like getting up and bustling as I did after the boys. I'm quite content just to sit and hold her. Don't you think she's the prettiest baby in the world?'

'Yes, dear, but we've already said that,' Anne said. 'I never thought you'd become such a doting mother.'

'Perhaps it's different with girls,' Lizzie said unrepentantly. She was still gazing into Rose's face. She was sure the baby was trying to smile.

'Perhaps. But one mother's cherished little girl has just had a very unusual and unpleasant experience.'

Lizzie looked at her at last. 'Oh, yes, of course. You've been in prison. I'm sorry, I should have asked how you are.'

'Oh, I'm very well. A month is not so bad, once you're used to it. But I wasn't referring to myself.'

'Goodness, yes – Lady Constance Lytton! Everyone was very surprised.'

'Her brother most of all, I fancy.'

'Yes, it seems he didn't know beforehand. Ashley says he's been making the government very embarrassed about it.'

'I fancy the magistrate was embarrassed when he sentenced us. Lady Con and I were both given one month, but Mrs Pethick-Lawrence was given two, though the circumstances were identical.'

'I know. There's been a lot of comment in the press

about it – another embarrassment for the government.'

'We're going to have a big procession to meet Mrs Pethick-Lawrence when she comes out, to make sure the government doesn't forget. Of course, she's the one who usually arranges the pageantry, but as she's inside I am to take it over. We'll have lots of children and young girls in white – that always pleases the public. Lady Con and the others from February the twenty-fourth are going to ride in a carriage, and I have an idea of riding at the head of the procession – a horsewoman catches the eye so well. Especially if I hire a white horse.'

Lizzie said idly, 'You ought to do it dressed up as Joan of Arc. Now she's been made a saint, it's very topical.'

But instead of laughing, Anne looked inspired. 'Yes, and she's Mrs Pethick-Lawrence's great heroine. Nothing could be more appropriate!'

'Oh Anne, I didn't really mean it,' Lizzie protested.

'Why not? I do. I can hire armour from a theatrical costumiers – or at a pinch, we can make it ourselves out of cardboard and silver paint. However, it must look right – nothing shabby or we shall be laughed at. And I can wear a short wig – we've plenty of those at Headquarters – and carry a lance with the colours flying from the end. It will look very well indeed!'

'I'm sure you would look magnificent but, really, have you thought about it properly?'

'What is there to think about?'

'Well, for one thing, as Joan of Arc you'd have to ride astride. In public. What would people think? It wouldn't be proper at all.'

'Oh, Lizzie!' Anne said, laughing, her prison-thin face lighting at the absurdity. 'I've just been released from Holloway gaol where I was shut up as a common felon! How proper do you think that was?'

The procession duly took place on the 17th of April, and Anne, as Joan of Arc, in silver armour and riding a white horse, looked magnificent at the head. The whole thing went off beautifully, except that one bystander, being handed a leaflet just as the horse went by, waved it above his head and shouted out, 'All the winners! All the winners!' The procession marched from the West End to the Aldwych where a grand public meeting was held in the Aldwych Theatre – appropriate since the column of marchers had been enhanced and enlivened by a deputation from the Actresses' Franchise League. The reports in the press were favourable and extensive enough to satisfy the leadership – though Anne was beginning to have doubts that these peaceful demonstrations really achieved anything.

But Lizzie's caveat did prove to have been right in one regard: Anne's appearance in public as Joan of Arc prompted a protest from her brother William, the Earl of Batchworth, who made an unprecedented journey up to London on purpose to remonstrate with her. He disliked leaving his home and family and hated the dirt and noise of the capital, so his mere presence was proof of how exercised he was.

Anne listened with as much patience as she could to his lecture on the unseemliness of Lady Anne Farraline's riding across in a public place, to say nothing of dressing up like a common actress and disporting herself about the streets as if she were in vaudeville. But at last she interrupted, saying, 'Really, William, you do choose the oddest things to complain about. Don't you know I've just come out of prison? Isn't that rather more shocking to your sensibilities than my heading a procession on horseback?'

Her brother's cheeks seemed to grey at this reminder, but he said seriously, 'No, it isn't. At least in gaol you are out of public view. And there's – some *sense* to it, I suppose. People have gone to prison for their beliefs, and been honoured for it – though I never thought to see my *sister* expose herself in that way. But this – this parading about in costume is simply vulgar and disgusting!'

'Oh, William!'

'You don't seem to think how it must affect me,' he went on bitterly, 'to have a sister who continually brings shame on my name. It hurts my standing with my friends.'

'It hurts my standing with my friends to have a brother who does not support my struggle. You are never seen in the Upper House. You should be there arguing for the Cause.'

William stared at her. 'Argue for the Cause? But I don't *want* votes for women. I don't understand why you do. It's all such nonsense!'

'Is it?'

'What would a woman do with the vote? Women don't understand politics.'

'That's just like my tying your legs together and then saying, "Why should you want to go outside? You can't walk."'

Lord Batchworth looked utterly baffled. 'Go outside? What are you talking about? Tie my legs together?'

'It was an illustration, William,' Anne said patiently.

But he had no wit and had never used a metaphor in his life. 'Why are you talking to me about illustrations? What the devil do they have to do with anything?'

She tried again, 'Look here, you know your neighbour, Sir John Redding?'

'Of course I know him. What of him?'

'Would you say he was a clever man? A sensible man?'

'Biggest fool in Christendom.'

'Would you say he understood politics?'

'Of course not. He hasn't an idea in his head.'

'Does he have the vote?'

'Of course he does! Whatever are you talking about him for?'

'My point is that for a man to have the vote doesn't depend on his understanding politics, so why should it for a woman?'

'But women don't *have* the vote,' William said, lost and exasperated. 'I don't know what you're talking about.' She gave up. 'But look here,' he went on, 'I want you to promise me you'll give up all this nonsense. Think of me. Think of my family.'

'I can't give it up,' Anne said, rather sadly, bcause she had loved her brother when they were children. 'I'm sorry, William, but that's too much to ask.'

'Then will you at least try to be more circumspect?' he pleaded pathetically. 'The *Manchester Guardian* takes a delight in reporting everything you do. People look at us in church.'

'I promise I won't dress up as Joan of Arc again – how would that be?' she said.

He eyed her doubtfully. 'But what else *will* you do? I suppose you've got some devilment planned?'

'No, no, the next thing is a very nice, ladylike Women's Exhibition in a hall in Knightsbridge. You know the sort of thing – stalls of millinery and bric-à-brac and nicely dressed people walking about and buying things.'

He looked relieved. 'Do you mean it?'

'Certainly. It's from May the ninth to the twenty-fifth at the Prince's Skating Rink. I hope you will come and support us, brother. I shall wear my largest hat and my most fashionable costume and look every inch a lady.'

'I think you are teasing me,' he said doubtfully. 'Of course I cannot come – you know I hate to be away from home – but if that is really what you are going to do, I must say I shan't mind it after what I have been through. Stick to that sort of thing in future, and I dare say I shall have nothing to complain about.'

When he had gone, she thought, Yes, as long as I don't embarrass you, you will be able to ignore me entirely, which is what you most wish to do. And what applied to William individually applied to the whole male population. That was why the peaceful demonstrations would never get them the vote. The only way, in the end, to make men give them the vote would be to make *not* giving it unbearably uncomfortable for them. And she felt, for a moment, rather tired.

Marriage was not at all what Violet had expected. Her disillusion began on the very first night, with the things that Brancaster seemed to want to do to her. They shocked and disgusted her so much that just at first she wondered if he had got it right – well, not the general principle, she supposed that must be more or less what happened, but the detail. The general principle was bad enough. It didn't seem possible that people had fallen in love and got married generation after generation – and in some cases, like her parents, stayed in love – with this awful secret behind the bedroom door. Then she wondered if it was perhaps her fault – if it was something that she was doing or not doing. But if that were the case, surely Brancaster would tell her, or at least indicate in some way how it might go better. But he never said anything about it, not during or after, so she had to assume that it was what he had expected. And indeed, the idea of actually talking about it to anyone, least of all him, was so horrifyingly embarrassing that she could only be glad of his restraint.

Her passion for him withered and faded during the first few days. Those longings she had felt to be held and kissed and she knew not what else disappeared like a burst soap bubble when she discovered what the 'what else' was. She set herself instead to endure it. Awful (and at first dreadfully painful) as it was, it was at least mercifully brief. He did not kiss her (though he did caress her in ways, or at least places, that she did not much care for) nor tell her he loved her, though he did grunt a bit and make strange gasping noises. And when it was over he would roll off her and lie for a moment or two until his breathing slowed, clear his throat, give a sniff or two, and then with a 'Goodnight, my dear,' he would get up and go off to his own room. It was her consolation that they did not sleep in the same room (her parents, she knew, slept in the same *bed*!) as she often cried afterwards because of the awfulness of it, and she would not have liked him to hear her.

But if her passion died, her love endured. During the day he was the Brancaster she had fallen in love with, and the honeymoon was a wonderful experience. He

212

seemed to know every place they visited, and was full of interesting facts about the scenery and the buildings. She loved the travelling on strange foreign trains and ferries, loved the waiters bringing her coffee in thick white cups, and delicious bread so unlike that at home. She loved the labels saying 'Lady Brancaster' on her trunks and bags. She loved the fluid foreign tongues she heard all round her. When they got to Italy, she loved the southern blue skies and the tall dark cypresses, the people who seemed to smile all the time, the dark, gold-gleaming churches and the fabulous collections of paintings.

Most of all, she loved being with Brancaster, and seeing people turn their heads and stare as they went by because they were such a handsome couple. She loved to dress in her wonderful new clothes and go to receptions and dinners and balls with him, knowing that of all the girls in London, she was the one he had chosen. She loved just to sit and gaze at him while he talked. And, yes, outside the bedroom, he did talk. She was sure he knew everything, and she felt she could never tire of the sound of his voice. He talked to her over breakfast of what they were to see, and over dinner he talked of what they had seen. He was not just her handsome prince, he was her protector, provider and mentor. During the weeks of their honeymoon she learned to put the bedroom thing into a separate compartment in her mind and simply not think about it. It was, she told herself, a small enough price to pay for being his wife the rest of the time.

When they came back to England, she saw her parents only briefly as they passed through London – a disappointment, as she had assumed they would stay in Manchester Square for some days at least. But Brancaster had said, without explanation, that they must catch a train that day, and after a few hours only with her mother, and not having seen the boys at all, she was whisked away to Scotland.

She did not enjoy the shooting parties. The men went off all day, and the women were left to lounge around the house and gossip all morning, before being obliged to pile into open brakes and be driven to a freezing field to partake of luncheon with the gentlemen, who did nothing but boast about how many birds they had killed. Then, after standing about for a deafening battue or two, they would take their frozen feet, numb fingers and red noses back to the house, where they would lounge and gossip until the gentlemen came back. Then there was tea, changing for dinner, dinner itself, and more lounging and gossiping until bedtime. She knew nobody in the party, and as she and Brancaster were much the youngest guests, she felt like a child with the other women. She never knew what they were talking about. They used nicknames, code words and slang to an impenetrable degree. The only variation in the evenings was cards, and once or twice her being asked to play the piano and sing. When she obliged, they listened only to the first few bars before continuing with their conversations, but at least, she thought, playing and singing entertained *her*, and she was happy to do it for her own amusement.

After Scotland they went straight to Brancaster Hall in Lincolnshire, where they were to spend Christmas. She had thought her family might be invited to spend it with them, but her mother and father were already engaged at Sandringham for Christmas itself, and they were not asked for any other part of the season. Brancaster Hall was large, rambling, mainly Tudor, and desperately cold. It sat in the middle of the fens, with the wet lands reaching away in all directions as flat as a sheet of paper. The icy winds whistled across these plains unimpeded, and after a week Violet concluded that there was very little about the house that impeded them either, and that they might just as well have been living in a sieve. The house was very dilapidated, none of the windows fitted, and when it rained, which it did a lot, the servants fell into a well-practised routine of placing receptacles under the leaky places, and changing them when full without thought, as though they could do it in their sleep.

The house was old and smelt musty, of mould and mothballs. The furnishings were old, featuring much heavy Jacobean oak, faded grey-green tapestries, and dark carpets with holes that caught her feet until she learned where they were. The servants were old, and they smelt of mould and mothballs too. They shuffled about, whiskery and watery-eyed, so set in their routines that she half expected to look down and find that their bent old legs ended in wheels that ran on rails. It was hard to get them to do anything different, and often her requests went unheeded, not, she felt, because they disliked her or were defying her, but because they found it impossible to break the habits of a lifetime.

And Lord Holkam was old – the oldest of all: old and ugly and frightening. He smelt of mould and mothballs and tobacco and brandy and sickness. She was terrified of him. His brooding silences were bad enough, but when he interrupted them with a sudden barked question, ending in an imperious 'Hey?', glowering at her under his bushy eyebrows, she felt ready to faint. Mostly he ignored her, for which she was grateful. The party he had assembled for Christmas consisted of people almost as old as himself, some distant cousins, some friends of his youth or relatives of his two wives. He didn't seem to like any of them much, and glowered at them and did not answer their conversational gambits. Then when they got to talking among themselves he would suddenly pounce, roar at them for ignoring him and chastise them for rude-ness and ingratitude. He fell into dreadful rages for no apparent reason, and was so contrary that he even contra-dicted himself, demanding a four of bridge to be made up and then, as soon as the table was ready, cursing the game as a blithering waste of time and demanding music instead. Violet felt sick with fear when music was called for, because it was usually her duty to go first, and she never knew if he would listen quietly and give her a curt nod of approval or roar with fury over her choice or performance. It was the uncertainty, she felt, that was the worst thing. If he had always disapproved, she might have braced herself for it, and borne it better.

It was a dismal party, and what with the bitter, penetrating cold of the house, the discomfort of the beds and the indifferent food (always cold, on account of the distance of the kitchens from the dining rooms: vast blackened joints of meat, bloody inside, stuck to the platter with congealed fat, everything either burnt or raw, as if the cook had a faulty clock in his head) Violet was amazed that it lasted so long. But the sad old guests (the men so bent and whiskery! the women so wrinkled and ugly!) seemed to stay and stay, as if however bad Brancaster Hall was, where they came from was even worse. She was so out of place among them that even they seemed to notice it, and sometimes they would try to be kind to her. The men would call her a pretty puss and invite her to sit by them, and the women would ask her about her family, which made her want to cry. She was homesick, her back hurt from the lumpiness of her bed, and she had chilblains on six of her toes, which burned and itched and drove her to distraction.

But when the party finally broke up, things were a little better. She was free now to wander and explore, and being alone was better than being with people she didn't like. Lord Holkam withdrew into his private suite of rooms and she hardly ever saw him – a distinct improvement. Brancaster she saw little of. In the daytime he was busy about the estate, which she gathered was in a state of almost terminal neglect; and in the evenings he often went into his father's rooms to consult or be given instructions. Oddly, Brancaster was the one person who loved Lord Holkam. He held him in esteem, and seemed almost pathetically eager to win his approbation. Violet thought that the earl perhaps cursed Brancaster slightly less unkindly than everyone else, which might pass for affection with him.

To her, Brancaster had changed. While they were on honeymoon he had talked to her all the time, told her things, sometimes elicited her opinions, smiled at her, seemed to be pleased with her. Now, at home in Lincolnshire, he barely seemed to know she existed. He wore a permanent worried frown, and if they met in passing in the house he would look at her as from a great distance, sometimes acknowledging her, sometimes not. At dinner he would talk to his father, if Holkam were dining down; if they dined alone together, he would often bring papers to the table to read, and if he did speak to her, it was vaguely and rather impatiently, as if he had been dragged from some eminence of thought to 'do the polite'. Occasionally neighbours or local friends of his would dine, and then he would talk all right, for hours together, but to them, not to her.

She told herself he was worried, and that she ought to make allowances, but she often cried at night, comparing this strange, lonely life with her dream of marriage. She loved him still, but she began to think that he did not love her. He did not seem really even to like her very much. He visited her bed almost every night, and it was so brief and businesslike she was able to bear it very well, though it still puzzled her. Once she almost thought she felt something, that a sensation somewhere in her body was on the point of beginning, which might have been very important and even delightful; but he stopped doing whatever it was that had caused it, and the sensation stopped too. It was rather like having someone open a distant door just a crack, so that wonderful music made itself heard for an instant, before the door was slammed shut again. Afterwards she thought she had probably imagined it.

The February weather was frightful, rain, sleet and snow by turns, and always the relentless wind, so that outside exercise was usually impossible. She went out into the wet shrubbery whenever she could, and coming back into the damp house caught one cold after another. Indoors, she had little to occupy her. It had never been suggested that she take over the running of the house,

217

and her terror of Lord Holkam prevented her volunteering to do anything. Besides, it seemed to bother the servants when she spoke to them, and the idea of changing anything seemed beyond possibility. She discovered the library, though its books were mostly as old and musty as everything else in the house. There was no modern reading, but she found a cache of eighteenth-century novels – Fielding and Richardson – and took them to the warmest corner she could find. She had never been a great reader, but she was so desperately in need of diversion she was glad now of their prolixity, for it meant they lasted longer.

March blew in grey and windy. She ached for company. Her parents had been much engaged with the King in February, and had been included in a royal visit to Berlin, but they would be free now, and she longed to see them again, and the boys, and Jessie. But it was not suggested that she should visit or invite, and she was afraid to ask. So she wrote her letters, and wrote cheerfully, mentioning nothing she could not praise, not allowing her lonely disappointment to show in a single word. She did not want to worry her parents; and besides, she had pride. She had married Brancaster for love – had 'stolen' him from Jessie to do it – and she would not now let anyone see that she had been a foolish girl with a head full of fairy stories. She would keep up her shop-front. It wasn't so bad. No-one was really unkind to her – Lord Holkam shouted at everyone – and in time she might learn how to make a difference to her surroundings, and be comfortable.

Spring came, and things got a little better. She was able to go out more: the wind had lost its keen edge, and sometimes, in a sheltered spot, the sun was almost warm. Now, with nothing to distract her, she fell in love with the extraordinary, other-worldly beauty of the fens, the great sky so full of subtle colour, the windy clouds blowing across the upturned bowl of it, the eerie cry of the curlew, the tumult of sheep and lambs, and everywhere the rushing sound of water in the dykes. In the neglected, tangled pleasure-garden in the lee (such as it was) of the house, she found hidden jewels of flowers, under tangled brambles or struggling through mats of long, dead grass like witches' hair. One day, finding a nest of primroses gasping for air, she cleared away the dead matter from around them, and the action and the pleasure it gave her inspired an idea for something she might usefully do with her time. At first hesitantly, and with nothing but her bare hands, she began to tidy the garden. Then one day, she came across an old lean-to shed, half covered in ivy, resting up against the tall red-brick wall that divided the pleasure garden from the kitchen garden, its rotted door fallen off and lying flat on the ground. Venturing inside she found some tools – secateurs, a rusty pruning knife, a trowel and a hand-fork. Now whenever it was fine she went out into the garden and did a little, here and there, snipping back, uncovering, unchoking. Small squares of garden came to life under her care. It gave her a sense of achievement.

Lord Holkam never came down to dinner now. She gathered he was unwell – or more unwell than he had always been. It was not his gout, but something more serious. Often Violet ate alone as Brancaster remained in his father's rooms all evening. She began to feel almost light-headed with solitude, as though she had become invisible. When she did her gardening, she sometimes found herself chatting to the flowers as if they were younger brothers and sisters.

Then one day in May, when the sun was really warm for the first time, and the skylarks were making love to the great fen sky, it suddenly occurred to her that something that had been puzzling her for some time – just faintly, in the back of her mind – ought not to puzzle her at all. Across the nearest dyke the sheep were scattered like blown petals over the new green of the grass, the pretty lambs dancing about near their mothers, whisking their long tails in the breeze that had grown miraculously warm. She made the mental connection between spring, lambs, skylarks, and her own faint question mark, and thought, with mild surprise, that it was more than likely that she was going to have a baby.

By the end of April Lizzie was fully recovered from the birth and was up and about – or 'so's to be 'round', as Ashley jokingly put it. So she was able to take part in the preparations for the Women's Exhibition. Its purpose was to educate the public about the Cause and the advances women had made, but it was also intended as a fund-raising event, so it had to be attractive and enjoyable. As Lizzie had been good at drawing in her school days, Anne recommended her to Sylvia Pankhurst, who had been put in charge of decorations and had come up with an ambitious scheme entirely to cover the walls of the whole hall – which measured 150 by 250 feet – with murals on twenty-foot-high canvases. Sylvia took her on with her usual enthusiasm, but Lizzie felt rather out of her class when she discovered that the other helpers on the 'murals committee' were former students of the Royal College of Art. She hung back diffidently at first, but there was so much work to do that she was soon in the thick of it, plying a brush with the rest of them, with white paint in her eyebrows and burnt umber and gamboge tint on her knuckles.

The theme of the murals was 'They who sow in tears shall reap in joy', and the designs drew on the style and motifs of William Morris and Walter Crane. There was a pattern of arches and pillars interlaced with vines, and under each arch a symbol of hope and self-sacrifice: a woman sowing seed, angels playing harps and viols, flights of doves, an almond tree in blossom, and so on.

Among the exhibits, one was a history of the movement in photographs, a remarkable collection got up by the WSPU's press photographer. Another was a pair of replica prison cells, one a bare, comfortless second-division cell in which a Suffragette prisoner could be seen scrubbing the floor or labouring at sewing; the other, twice as large, a first-division cell in which a male political prisoner took his ease, read books and enjoyed far greater comfort. There were the usual stands selling refreshments, sweets, souvenirs, fancy goods, bric-à-brac, and a very smart millinery stall to which some of the best milliners in London had contributed hats. There was a screened-off photography booth, where one could have one's portrait taken, and another in which a relay of palmists told fortunes. A graduate of the Royal College did instant sketches; one of the WSPU's foremost chalkists demonstrated pavement art.

Each day there was an orchestral recital, an exhibition of morris dancing by Mary Neal's child dancers, and a display of Grecian dancing by some lady students from University College London; and the Actresses' Franchise League gave a different one-act play every day about the Cause. The Suffragette drum and fife band gave displays of marching – in which they had been drilled to proficiency by an actual army sergeant – wearing smart military uniforms in the WSPU colours. There was a display of gymnastics led by Miss Kelley and, perhaps most exciting, a lecture and demonstration by Edith Garrud, the first British woman ju-jitsu instructor.

The exhibition was a great success, and raised almost six thousand pounds for the Cause. Ashley was impressed by the efficiency of the organisation. 'This is really businesslike,' he said, on more than one occasion. The millinery stall with its first-quality wares attracted a number of wealthy and important ladies, including the Countess of Aylesbury, and Lady Forrester, who was the daughter of Ashley's employer, Mr Culpepper. The Culpepper family's involvement was a matter of great pride to Lizzie, because it was through Ashley's advocacy that Mr Culpepper had paid for the installation of a real American ice-cream soda fountain, the first of its kind ever seen in England. It proved enormously popular, especially with Frank's university friends. Ashley, in loyalty both to the Cause and his master, made a point of visiting it every time the family went to the exhibition. This proceeding met with the full approval of Martial and Rupert, who declared that there was no nicer food in the world, and begged to be taken to America, where such wonders abounded, and if possible to be allowed to live there for ever.

'We really should take them some time,' Ashley said to Lizzie, as she sucked a malted-milk drink through a straw, a surprisingly pleasant experience, she found. 'I'd like to show them New York – it's one of the wonders of the world. And I'd like to see my brothers again.'

'I'd love to go,' Lizzie said. 'But we'd never be able to afford it, would we? And how could you spare the time? Would Mr Culpepper let you go for so long?'

'That would have to be arranged, of course. I'm glad the exhibition was so well organised, because it has created a favourable impression all around. If it had been a slapdash show, he would have been annoyed with me for involving him in it, but as things are, I dare say we might manage it one day.'

'Perhaps when Rose is a little older. It would be a shame for her to miss it.'

'True. That would mean waiting about ten years, which should give me enough time to work out how to arrange it.'

Lizzie smiled. 'Do you think we should bring her here tomorrow? We could have her portrait taken in the photograph booth.'

'She'd hate the noise and bustle. You can have her photograph taken at home any time.'

'I suppose so. I just don't like leaving her behind.'

Ashley smiled too. 'I've seen the most wonderful baby's perambulator in the window of Bartlett's. If we bought it, we could walk her in the gardens together on Sundays.'

'A father, walk his baby? Whatever next?'

'In America fathers often walk their babies.'

'In this country, the nanny does it. However, I'm willing to give it a try, if you think we'll enjoy it.'

'We might start a fashion,' Ashley said.

'Or a revolution,' said Lizzie.

Lord Brancaster was not at breakfast. Disney, the ancient butler, told Violet as he shuffled to the table with a pot of cold coffee that he had breakfasted early and gone into Lincoln on business. When Violet passed through the hall later that morning on her way to the garden she found Brancaster evidently just arrived, being relieved of his coat by Disney, and giving orders that the land agent be sent for.

Violet approached him. 'May I speak to you, please?'

Brancaster's frown deepened. 'Excuse me. Not now,' he said tersely.

Violet's eyes filled with tears. She did not want to cry and annoy him, but he had spoken to her so brusquely – *and* in front of a servant – that she could not help it.

Disney coughed, and it might or might not have been a signal to his master, but at all events Brancaster seemed to look at her properly, and he said more gently, 'Forgive me, but I must attend my father at once on a matter of urgency. Can it wait until luncheon?'

Violet was piqued enough to say, 'I did not know I was to see you at luncheon.'

Brancaster seemed to restrain an impatient gesture. 'If you will be patient until then, I shall be able to give you my full attention.'

She bowed her head in assent and walked away, not to betray herself further. But as the hour for luncheon approached, she found her spirits rising. He had promised to lunch with her, he had promised his full attention, and she had such news to give him that must make him happy. She found she was looking forward to it as to a festive occasion – which in her present depleted state of entertainment it really was. When she came in from the garden she sent for her maid (not Sanders, alas, who

223

had not been able to bear the cold, solitude and lack of young company and had given her notice, but a local girl who had chilly hands and a permanent sniff but at least was used to the hardship) and dressed with particular care in her prettiest day dress. She had Sibsey do her hair again until she was satisfied that she looked irresistible. Then she went down to the morning room, where luncheon was served, and waited impatiently, walking about the room and humming a tune.

Brancaster came in like a cloud threatening rain, but when she ran up to greet him, smiling and holding out her hands, the scowl gradually faded and he looked her over with interest and dawning pleasure.

'You – er – you look very pretty today,' he said. He took both her hands – largely because he could not leave her with them stretched out for ever, and when she squeezed them and turned up her face to him, he stooped and kissed her cheek.

'Thank you,' she said.

'Quite blooming, in fact. Is there some reason?'

'I am having lunch with you. Isn't that reason enough?'

His smile faded a little. 'Ah. I have been much occupied with business, as you know, and—'

She released one of his hands and drew him towards the table. 'Of course,' she said quickly, not wanting his mood to darken again. 'I understand perfectly. Shall we sit down?'

The two places had been laid, as usual, at either end of the table, but she had spent some of her waiting time moving one cover so that the places were cater-cornered to each other. He stopped when he observed the arrangement and said, 'What's this? Disney surely never set the table this way?'

'No, I did it,' she said boldly, though her heart was fluttering with apprehension. 'I have something in particular to say to you, and I do not wish to shout it the length of a table.'

He looked at her in a startled way, as though a mouse

had roared. He seemed to take some time to consider whether a crime had been committed, and she felt like giggling, which was not at all like her. Eventually he said, 'Well, I suppose there's no harm in it, as it will be just the two of us.' He pulled out her chair for her, and then sat himself, looking uneasy. 'Well – er, my dear?' he invited.

He doesn't even know what to call me, she thought a little sadly. But she jumped straight in, as she had planned to do. 'I think I am going to have a baby,' she said.

He blinked. 'Only think?' he said at last.

'I'm sure, really.' A blush rose up her neck as she was forced to refer to something unmentionable. 'It has been three months since—' There was a slight blush on his face too, which surprised her, but embarrassed her all the more because it occurred to her that it was something he should have known. 'Three months,' she concluded.

'Ah, yes,' he said. He cleared his throat. 'Indeed. I had not – that is, I suppose – of course, you must be right.'

There should be something more than embarrassment, she thought. 'I hope you are pleased?'

He gathered himself with an effort. 'Yes, yes, of course, very pleased.' And even as she watched, it caught up with him, and pleasure entered his expression. 'I am delighted, in fact. Delighted. You are quite well?'

'Oh, yes. I understood there would be some disagree-able symptoms but there's nothing of that. I feel very well.'

'Good, good. Well, well.' Now he positively beamed at her, and she felt a flutter of love for him. It gave a person power to be able to create pleasure in another. 'You will want to be examined by a doctor, of course. And we must tell my father. This is what he has been waiting for. He will be so glad!'

The door opened at that moment, and Disney came in with two footmen, bearing the trays on which the dishes sat covered with lids from which the silver had worn around the edges. Violet eyed the lids with disfavour. They were meant to keep the food warm, of course, but they failed dismally: all that happened was that the rising steam condensed on them and then dripped back onto the food, imparting a metallic taste.

The process of serving was always slow, and now the poor butler looked quite bewildered by the different arrangement of the covers, and did not seem to know what to do with the dishes. When the food was on their plates, the junior footman took the trays away, and Disney and the other footman prepared to take their places back against the wall behind the chairs, where they would remain throughout the course. But Violet made meaning and impassioned gestures with her eyes at her husband, and after a moment Brancaster caught up with her and, a little irritated by the necessity of it, said to Disney, 'You may leave us now. We can manage for ourselves. I will ring when I want you.'

Disney was so dumbfounded he almost argued, but recollected himself in time and with a gesture to the footman made his slow and creaking exit. Violet almost sighed with relief when the door closed behind them. Brancaster took up his knife and fork and said, 'Well, madam?'

It wasn't exactly inviting, especially the 'madam' where she had recently been 'my dear', but her need was urgent. 'I want to see my mother,' she said. 'I miss all my family so much, and I haven't seen any of them since November, and the boys not since the wedding, and now I have this wonderful news to tell them—'

'Surely you can tell them that in a letter?'

'But I want to tell them in person. They'll be so happy and I want to be there to see it, and I know they would expect me to tell them myself and – and I *so* want to see them! Please let me go.'

'My dear,' he said, 'I'm afraid it is out of the question at the moment. I have too much business and I cannot leave my father.'

Violet's heart sank, but she continued bravely, though

in a smaller voice. 'I might go by myself, perhaps?'

'That would not be fitting. My father would not approve of a lady travelling alone.'

'But I would take my maid.'

'That would not do. My father does not believe any lady, and especially the future Countess of Holkam, should travel without the escort of a male relative. He is very protective of ladies.'

Violet thought it sounded less like protection than imprisonment, but it was a fleeting thought and she did not voice it. She had accepted rules all her life, and if her new family's were more restrictive than her old family's, it was not for her to quibble. She ate some cold damp mutton and cold wet cauliflower and tried to think through the problem.

'Perhaps they could come here, instead of my going there. I expect Mama would be glad to come and visit me, Papa too if he is not too engaged.'

Brancaster shook his head. 'Out of the question, I'm afraid. My father could not bear the disturbance of a visit at present. I'm a little surprised you should suggest it, given his state of health.'

'I'm sorry,' she said humbly. 'I don't really know what his state of health is.'

'It is very frail.'

'I'm sorry,' she said again, and there was silence as she choked down some more of the horrible luncheon, along with some unruly tears. She seemed close to them so often these days. Perhaps it was something to do with her 'condition'.

After a while Brancaster said, more gently, 'I'm sorry you should be disappointed. Things have fallen out in such a way – at another time I might have taken you, but as it is . . . I hope you understand.'

Then the idea came to her, and her face lit. 'One of my brothers might come for me! If Tom or Oliver were to fetch me and bring me back, that would satisfy your father, surely? I'm sure one of them would make himself

227

available. Please, sir, don't you think that would do?'

But still he shook his head. 'Even with a male escort, my father would not allow you to travel in your delicate condition. He would think it most improper, especially as I would not be with you. No, I'm sorry, my dear.'

'Perhaps,' she said carefully, 'we might not tell him about my condition.'

'What? Lie to my father?'

'No, no, not lie to him – just delay telling him for a week or two. Just until I have seen my family.'

'It wouldn't be right.'

'Why not?'

'He's my father. He's the Earl of Holkam. We are living under his roof. It would be dishonest and ungrateful.'

The tears now scalded up and she could not stop them. They spilled over onto her cheeks, the hottest things in the room. She sobbed, 'I want to see my mother!'

Brancaster made a sound that might have been alarm or exasperation. He threw down his napkin and rose to his feet, and stepped round to her side and put his arm round her shoulder. The touch was too much for her. She turned and pressed her face to his jacket and cried, while he patted her awkwardly. At last he said, 'There, there. Please don't cry. Come, my dear. Here's a handkerchief. Please try to stop. Think of the servants.'

Thinking of them seemed such an odd thing to be bid at that moment, and brought the image of Disney's bent old legs and shuffling walk to her mind, and she began to giggle at the same time as crying, which was very strange.

It alarmed Brancaster, who said, 'You are hysterical. Please try to calm yourself. Violet, I beg you, have some control!'

His use of her name touched her, and she made a great effort. She swallowed down the tears, straightened her shoulders, used his handkerchief to dry her eyes and blow her nose. Her mother had once remarked that she was lucky to be able to cry and not look ugly afterwards, and now, apart from a flush to her cheeks and a slight pinkness to the end of her nose, she was as pretty as ever, only slightly ruffled, which was rather attractive. Brancaster was moved, by her tears, by her obedient effort to control them, and by her loveliness, which he had forgotten about since they had got back from honeymoon.

'I did not mean to distress you,' he said, in the most subdued voice he had ever used to her. 'I quite understand that you must want to see your mother, even at this time. Or,' with an effort of imagination, 'especially at this time. Perhaps it would not hurt to keep the news from my father for a little while longer. You have not told your maid?'

'No. I've told no-one but you.'

'Very well, if you can arrange for one of your brothers to escort you, I will undertake to get my father's permission for your visit. Of course, your family must keep the secret until we have informed my father. He must believe he is the first to be told. Do you think they will be able to do that?'

'Oh, yes,' Violet said eagerly. 'Mama is a doctor and Papa is a courtier. They both understand how to keep secrets. And the boys—' She thought of Oliver, the rattle, and well-meaning but not-very-bright Eddie, and said, 'Perhaps I won't tell the boys. Just Mama and Papa.' She thought of seeing them again, and her face shone. 'Oh, *thank* you, Brancaster! I've missed them so much! You are very kind.'

And perhaps it was the realisation that he had not, in fact, been very kind that prompted him, a little guiltily, to say, 'I think there is something that perhaps I ought to explain to you.'

Chapter Eight

Venetia had had no anxiety about not seeing Violet for so many months. She had missed her, of course, and would have been glad of a visit, but there were plenty of letters from her daughter, saying all was well. She might have expected to be invited at some time over the Christmas season, but she knew that Lord Holkam was old and unwell and she had learned, during the short time she had spent with him before and during the wedding, that he was reclusive and bad-tempered. Of course, he suffered from gout, a complaint so painful it would try anyone's temper. At any rate, she saw nothing sinister in his not wanting his in-laws around him.

In any case, her own life was as busy as ever. Her operating lists did not grow any shorter, and though she saw few medical patients now, she was still following her research into lung tuberculosis. She had recently been asked to join the committee of the National Association for the Prevention of Consumption, which had been founded by the King himself. And in February her carefully planned diary had been thrown into confusion by a request from the King that she as well as Overton should accompany him to Germany.

Relations with Germany were taut and the Kaiser seemed to be growing ever more volatile. In 1905 in Bremen he had spoken alarmingly of the coming of a 'world-wide dominion of the Hohenzollerns' and had almost started a war with France over Morocco where he had claimed 'great and growing' German interests. He upset the King by talking openly in yachting circles about the looseness of English morals in general and the King's relationship with Mrs Keppel in particular. On a visit to England in 1907 he gave vent to fierce tirades against Jews, of whom there were, of course, a number among the King's close friends. He further trumpeted that it had been purely thanks to him that the British had not been disgraced in the Boer War, claiming that he had sent Lord Roberts a strategic plan for the British Army without which they would have been defeated, and that he had single-handedly prevented an international coalition from forming against Britain.

In 1908 the *New York Times* had sent W. B. Hale to interview the Kaiser, but had said afterwards that the Kaiser's remarks were too 'strong' to be published. A rival paper, however, printed a censored synopsis of the interview, in which the Kaiser said that war between England and Germany was inevitable, and the sooner it came the better, because England was degenerate and the King corrupt. As a background to all this, Germany was continuing to build more and larger and better-armed battleships, claiming that the Anglo-French-Russian entente was a threat to Germany, against which Germany was entitled to defend herself.

So the present State visit to Berlin became inevitable. The Emperor must be placated. Ever since the State visit to Russia, the Kaiser had been agitating for a visit by the King and Queen to Berlin. Why should Cousin Nicky be singled out for the honour? When would it be his turn? If Uncle Bertie and Aunt Alix did not come, it would be a snub to him and proof that the visit to the Tsar was not a family visit after all, but part of a military plot against him.

'Whether he really believes it, or whether it is just part of his public act, it's impossible to tell,' Lord Knollys said to Venetia over tea, when he visited her with the request.

'We all know he says one thing in public and another in private,' Venetia agreed. 'Personally, I believe he's mad rather than devious, but the effect is the same.'

'The King doesn't at all want to go. He said to me, "I know the Emperor hates me. He never loses an opportunity of saying so behind my back, though I have always been kind and nice to him." And the Queen, of course, is furious about being "dragged" to Germany, as she puts it. But the Kaiser won't let it rest, and his hints have become rather pointed and threatening now. He says a visit would have useful results for the peace of the world.'

'Which means that the corollary is—'

'Precisely,' said Knollys. 'You don't need me to interpret for you.'

'No indeed. Have some teacake.'

'Thank you. I always say you have the best tea in London.'

'Will the King take the opportunity to talk to the Kaiser about naval armaments?'

'It is intended as a goodwill visit only. He loathes tackling important subjects with the Emperor, because he's so irrational, and there's such an undercurrent of hostility whenever they stray away from family matters. Ponsonby says there's always a feeling of thunder in the air when they're together. It's natural the King should want to avoid provoking him.'

'It doesn't help that the cabinet is so divided over Germany,' Venetia said thoughtfully.

'Quite. Lloyd George and Churchill have their faction, and Asquith does nothing to check them.'

'I suppose one is not surprised by Lloyd George's attitude, given his background. One visit to Germany to look at their National Insurance system, a few ladlesful of flattery from the Wilhelmstrasse, and he rushes home to extol the Kaiser's virtues and tell us we should stop building battleships and put the money into social reform! What is the point of trying to reform a country that you can't even defend from an invader? But Churchill, on the other hand, ought to know better.'

For the last year, Mr Churchill had been making

232

vigorous speeches denouncing 'the braggart call for sensational expenditure on armaments', pouring scorn on the 'fear-all school' and the 'agitation of ignorant hotheads' for an 'aggressive and Jingo policy'. He had nothing but contempt for the growing belief that war between Britain and Germany was inevitable, and asserted that the two countries had nothing to fight about, no prize to fight for, and no place to fight in.

'The King is afraid that the Chancellor's faction will lull people into a false sense of security,' Knollys said. 'Grey agrees with him. He told Hardinge that Churchill and Lloyd George between them would ruin the party, and that Churchill's speeches were ungentlemanlike.'

'His behaviour towards the Suffragettes is certainly ungentlemanlike,' Venetia said.

'Ah, now, don't begin on the suffrage question,' Knollys said, with a placatory smile. 'You know how I'm placed.'

'My poor Francis! Let me refill your cup, and do try the macaroons.'

'Thank you. I'm very fond of a macaroon.'

'That's why I ordered them.'

'Your cook has a light hand,' he said, after an appreciative bite. 'So, with regard to Berlin – you will come?'

'Are you suggesting I have a choice? Of course I will come – though it is very inconvenient. I have so much to do, and it will disrupt my lists dreadfully. But if it will help . . .'

'Even if it only postpones war a little, that's a worthwhile aim. I do believe the King may be a check on the Kaiser. Perhaps only a very slight one – but it's certain that nothing else is.'

The King normally spent the month of February on the Riviera, and it was a sacrifice for him to give it up, because he was not at all well. He had a nasty cold and a constant, racking cough: the chill damp of Germany and the strain of an official visit were not what Venetia would have prescribed for him. She thought he looked very poorly: tired, and a bad colour, and beginning to be

233

really old. The weight he had lost after his operation in '02 he had quickly put back on, and more; obesity and his constant cigar smoking exacerbated his chronic bronchitis. Observing him on the boat crossing the Channel, she realised with a sudden chill that his time was running out, and it was a frightening thought. What would they, and indeed the world, do without him?

Little things went wrong from the beginning. On the train going to Berlin, the driver applied the brakes suddenly and violently just as dinner was being served and a footman lost his balance and tipped a dish of quails over the Queen. There was a shocked silence, especially as one of the little birds was left caught up in her hair; but the Queen made light of the incident and even made everyone laugh by saying that she would arrive in Berlin 'coiffée de cailles'.

The next incident was when the train reached the frontier station of Rathenow ahead of schedule. The bandmaster had been told to strike up 'God Save The King' as soon as the train stopped and to keep playing it until the King stepped onto the platform. But the King was not yet dressed, and for ten long minutes the royal suite had to stand to attention as the tune was played over and over again until they wanted to scream. The King appeared at last, looked flustered, and to make up for lost time walked much more briskly than usual as he inspected the guard drawn up in his honour, which led to breathlessness and a violent coughing fit.

Matters went no better when the train arrived at Berlin. The Kaiser had gone to great lengths to arrange everything about the visit with military efficiency: knowing his uncle's passion for ceremony and protocol, he wanted to show how well Germany could do those things. The welcoming party for the royal train had been carefully selected and rehearsed, and was assembled on the platform exactly where the King's carriage would stop. Unfortunately for the Kaiser, the King had gone back to sit with the Queen, and it was from her carriage that he alighted, many yards away. Venetia thought she would explode from suppressed laughter, seeing the welcoming party still saluting and gazing fixedly at the wrong door, while the King stood completely unattended, looking round him with mild curiosity. Eventually, of course, the mistake was noted, and the Kaiser, Kaiserin, other royals and official dignitaries had to hurry down the platform, the men clutching their swords and the women their hats, military boots clumping, medals banging, looking very undignified indeed.

As if that were not humiliation enough, when the party left the station to get into the coaches waiting to take them to the palace, the sudden combination of booming cannon, cheering crowds and waving flags frightened the horses. Some reared and threw their riders, some walked backwards into the crowd, scattering them hastily. Then at one point on the route the horses harnessed to the carriage in which the Queen and the Kaiserin were riding suddenly threw up their heads, rolled their eyes and refused to go any further. The ladies had to transfer to the carriage behind, which meant that everyone else had to do the same in a sort of General Post, leaving the occupants of the last carriage to walk. It was all very undignified, and the Emperor was in an absolute fury at having been shown up before his uncle.

But the Kaiser had done his best to make his guests comfortable. To make them feel at home, he had had pictures of Sandringham and Copenhagen hung in the Queen's rooms, and books in Danish, and a concert piano placed there for her use. In the King's rooms were a portrait of Queen Victoria and a series of prints on 'British Naval Victories'. Even in Venetia's room, there was a painting of an English country scene on the wall, English stationery on the writing-desk and English biscuits in the tin on the table. Her suite was very imposing as well as comfortable, and even the King's physician, Sir James Reid – an old friend of the Kaiser's – had three rooms to himself, which he confided to her when they met before

235

dinner he thought were 'most luxurious'. Reid was also pleased and excited that he had been presented by the Kaiser with the Order Grand Cordon of the Crown. Venetia was as impressed as Reid that the Emperor should thus remember an old but very humble friend. The Kaiser was such an odd mixture of parts that she was more than ever sure he was mad.

There was a gala dinner at the Palace that evening, at which the King seemed to have difficulty in getting through quite a short speech, coughing constantly. Unusually, he did not speak from memory but read a prepared text: he had been so worried about what the Kaiser might say that he had insisted each saw and approved the other's speech beforehand. The Queen had been placed, much against her will, at the Kaiser's table, and Venetia, lower down the same table, watched with trepidation as the meal progressed. It was hard enough that those two who disliked each other so much should have to sit together, but given the Queen's deafness, their conversation, such as it was, had to be carried on at full pitch, and often remarks that had better never been made in the first place were obliged to be repeated.

There was a family luncheon the next day, at which Venetia was not required, and – another example of the Kaiser's intermittent thoughtfulness – she found he had arranged for her to pay a visit of inspection to the hospital where she had helped out during her time in Berlin as a girl. It was a happy thought, though Ponsonby told her afterwards that the King was not best pleased as he was known not to approve of women stepping out of their traditional rôle. He thought that the Kaiser had done it to annoy him.

In the evening of that day there was a Court Ball, which reminded Venetia again of her time in Berlin in the suite of the Kaiser's mother. In those days there had always been an atmosphere of tension between the two courts, of the Kaiser's father and his grandfather. It seemed there were still difficulties between the generations: at this ball

236

two of the Kaiser's sons asked the band to play a two-step, at which the Kaiser exploded in fury, for he had ordered that no modern tune was ever to be played.

The week dragged on. There was an evening at the Opera, at which the Kaiser had commanded a spectacular performance of the last act of *Sardanapalus*, which filled the stage with fire and smoke. Unfortunately the King, who was looking very drawn, had fallen asleep, and woke with a start to believe there was a real fire, and demanded of his nephew where the firemen were and why they were not evacuating the house. The Emperor laughed at him, which did not help matters, and the Empress had to calm and reassure him.

There was one successful event, when the King was invited to a reception at the Rathaus by the city's businessmen and dignitaries. The burgomaster's little daughter presented him with a golden goblet of Rhenish wine, which he received with such charm as to reassure the nervous child and delight the assembly. He then made a speech in faultless German, proposed a toast to the people of Berlin and, to judge by its reception, won the hearts of all present with his easy charm, geniality and warmth.

On the same day the King held a return luncheon at the British Embassy for the imperial party. He was always an excellent host, and Venetia felt that good will was at last being built up, though whether it would outlast the visit was another matter. Afterwards they withdrew to the drawing-room. While they were waiting for coffee to be served, and the King was sitting on a sofa chatting to Princess Daisy of Pless, one of his large cigars between his thick fingers, he was suddenly seized with a coughing fit. It had happened before, of course, but this time he did not seem able to stop. The dreadful noise went on and on – it sounded, someone had said, as if he was going to break in two – and he began to choke. He fought for breath, his face turning an alarming puce, and at last fell back on the sofa unconscious; the cigar dropped from his fingers and fell on the carpet, burning a hole.

Princess Daisy, her eyes enormous with horror, began struggling feebly with the collar buttons of his tight Prussian uniform tunic, but her fingers were too shaky to work properly. Venetia could not help herself, but crossed the room and took charge, pushing a cushion under the King's head to position it better, working the tight collar undone, taking his pulse. It was irregular, and his face had become dusky. She was afraid that this might be the end. A consideration of the protocol involved if the King were to die here crossed her mind briefly.

But in a moment he drew a gasping breath and opened his eyes. His pulse steadied, and as he looked at Venetia, she felt his embarrassment at finding himself in such a predicament with a lady doctor, and prudently let go of his wrist.

'Where's my cigar?' was the first thing he said.

'You dropped it, sir. Someone picked it up and put it out.'

'Help me to sit up,' he said.

She gave him her arm and he used it to pull himself, pushing with his other hand, until he was sitting upright.

'Damned embarrassing thing,' he muttered to her. 'Don't make a fuss.'

'No, sir.'

'Smoke went down the wrong way, that's all.'

Their eyes met and she felt a brief intimate contact with him, which prompted her to say, 'You know you should not smoke them, sir. They are making you ill.'

The pale eyes did not flicker. He was not angry with her; he almost smiled. 'And you know that they make no difference at this stage. No-one lives for ever, Lady Overton. Ah, here's the Queen.'

Someone had gone to fetch the Queen, who was in another room with the Kaiserin, and word had been sent for Sir James Reid. Venetia moved quickly away as the Queen glided in, outwardly calm and beautiful as always, whatever went on inside her. Venetia thought that she was, in her way, the perfect queen, as Edward was the

238

perfect king – affable, genial, dutiful, methodical, and able to put everyone at ease from the highest to the lowest. Truly, the country was lucky to have them.

Reid hurried in and asked everyone to withdraw. Venetia went with the others into the next room, but only a quarter of an hour later the doors were opened again and they were readmitted. The King was on his feet and assured everyone that there was no cause for alarm, that he was perfectly well, and lit a fresh cigar. Reid announced that it was just a form of bronchial attack, and in no sense dangerous. There were some doubtful looks at this, in particular from the Princess of Pless, who had been frightened out of her wits, and Sir Charles Hardinge, who plainly thought that Reid was treating the incident in far too casual a manner. But Venetia caught Reid's eye for a moment before he looked away, and understood that he had been given his instructions by the King. He was doing as he was told, as she explained to Overton afterwards, when he repeated Hardinge's opinion.

'He's in a difficult position,' she said. 'Obedience to the King's wishes may well cost him professional prestige. Those who don't understand may think him negligent.'

'You don't think he is being negligent?' Overton asked.

Venetia shook her head. 'What's to be done? If the King were an ordinary person and could be persuaded to retire, go and live in a warm, dry climate, worry less, give up smoking, and eat more moderately, his health might improve. But he's the King, so the first three are impossible for him; and nothing Reid says will persuade him to the last two.'

With difficulty, Overton asked, 'Do you think the end is near?'

It was with equal reluctance that she answered: 'I think we are into the final furlong.'

Overton met her eyes. 'Do you think he knows?'

Venetia remembered her brief exchange with the King, and the almost kindly way he looked at her. 'Yes, I think he does.'

Perhaps it was that breath of mortality that led the King at the last minute, on the day of departure, actually on the station platform, to broach the subject of the German navy with the Kaiser. Venetia learned of it afterwards from Ponsonby: all she saw was a short and earnest conversation, before King and Kaiser embraced each other in farewell and the King climbed up into his carriage.

'I wonder what changed his mind,' Ponsonby said, when they met on the deck of the homeward-bound yacht. 'It was never intended that he should mention anything like that. It was supposed to be a social visit only.'

'Indeed, that's why I am here,' Venetia said. 'Do you think it did any good?'

'The visit, or talking about the navy?'

'Either. Both.'

'Probably not.'

'Francis thinks that the King does act as a check on the Kaiser, just a little.'

'Perhaps so. The Kaiser really did seem to want to make it all agreeable,' said Ponsonby, 'but I have the impression that most of the German people hate the English as much as the Queen hates them.'

On her return to England, Venetia had much to do to catch up with her work, and hardly noticed Overton's absence when he accompanied the King on his delayed spring holiday in the sun. She had got back to her routine by the time May and the Season began, and she half expected that the Brancasters might come to Town – whatever Holkam's state of health, it was usual for a newly married peeress to be presented at Court. But instead she got a letter from Violet proposing a solo visit, and asking for the escort of one of her brothers, on Lord Holkam's insistence. This did not surprise Venetia, given Holkam's age. In her own youth, it had been deemed disgraceful for a lady to travel in a train alone (or in a taxi or omnibus at all) and though Violet was married, she was very young, and a man of Holkam's generation might well think a maid's attendance not nearly enough. Thomas was busy with his military duties and she did not want to take Oliver away from his studies, so she asked Eddie to undertake it. He had finished his university time without taking his degree, and the King, true to his promise, had given him a position at Court, which provided him with just enough income to live respectably. But his duties were few, and on her approach he professed himself able and willing to oblige.

At last Venetia was able to welcome her married daughter and, as soon as she had removed her very large hat, hold her in her arms, shedding a few tears of happiness on Violet's dark head.

'Let me look at you! Darling, you look thin in the face. You are well? You have been well?'

'Yes, I'm very well, Mama, really I am. I did have a lot of colds in the winter, but I'm over them now.'

'There's something about you,' Venetia said, scanning her face closely. 'What is it?' before Violet could say anything, it came to her in a flash. 'You're pregnant?' Violet blushed and nodded. 'Oh my darling, I'm so pleased! When?'

'In October, I think. But, Mama, I must ask you to keep it secret for a little while, until we've told Lord Holkam. He would be so annoyed if he thought he wasn't the first to know. We didn't tell him because he wouldn't have let me travel at all if he had known and – oh, I did so want to see you!'

'What could be more natural? A girl wants to be with her mother when she has her first child. We had better arrange for you to have it in London, so that I can be on hand. From what your letters tell me about Brancaster Hall, it is not a very comfortable place to have a baby.'

'I'm afraid that won't be possible,' Violet said. 'Lord Holkam would never let me have the baby anywhere but Brancaster Hall. The heir to the earldom and so on.'

Venetia frowned a little, but said, 'Well, old people have

their fancies, I suppose. It will be more difficult, but I can arrange my work so that I can come down to Lincolnshire and stay with you instead.'

Violet looked anxious. 'I wish you could, so very much, but that won't be possible either.'

'Why ever not?'

Violet told her.

What Brancaster had confessed to Violet on that day at luncheon was that Lord Holkam deeply disapproved of Venetia, both on account of her being a doctor, and her having been involved with the Suffragette movement. He had seen the photograph of her marching at the front of the column on the so-called Mud March, and at the time had deplored that a duke's daughter should so far forget herself. But it was all one with the unnatural behaviour of a female who abandoned woman's natural sphere and pitted herself against men in the medical world - surely the profession that, to follow it, entailed the worst violation of woman's nature. Holkam disliked any attempt of women to achieve anything outside the home, and medical women were the most unladylike; but the Suffragettes were his worst anathema – harridans and man-haters every one, who ought to be put down like mad dogs.

It was natural for Violet to ask him falteringly at that point how Brancaster had persuaded his father to accept the match between himself and the harridan's daughter – for she had observed enough to know that Brancaster would not have proposed to her without permission.

His answer was, 'Oh, well, as to that, the blood lines are all right, and there are not many heiresses whose fortune is in cash rather than property. In fact, it was my father who suggested you to me in the first place, as soon as he saw your name in the Court lists.'

It was very hard for Violet to assimilate this. She had assumed Brancaster had seen her, fallen in love, and then proposed her to his father. Now it seemed she had been selected on very different grounds and not by Brancaster

242

at all. Was there no love in it whatsoever? Her rather shocked silence impinged itself on Brancaster, and he said, defensively, 'Come, my dear, you know how these things go. Marriage for people of our rank is a bargain. I offered a title and land, you had a dowry. It was a fair exchange. Your parents thought so, or they wouldn't have agreed. And, as I said, most heiresses bring part or even most of their dowry in land, which wouldn't have suited our purposes. Your parents are unusual in having most of their wealth in portable investments.'

And he went on to explain that through long neglect by Lord Holkam – partly, no doubt, a result of his ill health – and through the terrible downturn in agriculture over the last twenty years, the estate was in desperate case. Holkam Castle, the original seat, was a virtual ruin, and the dilapidation of Brancaster Hall was evident. Rents were pitiful, drainage was breaking down, and the land was in poor heart. In addition, the part of the Holkam income that came from West Indian estates had fallen dramatically, and he would have to pay a visit there before too long to try to revive it.

'So you see,' he concluded, 'I had to marry an heiress with cash money, and most of them are American girls. My father would never have stood for that – he loathes foreigners.'

'You mean,' she said in a very small voice, 'it was me or no-one.'

'Exactly,' he said, and seeing her expression, amended it to, 'What I mean is that I never thought of another girl. Now what is it? Please don't cry. I should have thought it would please you to know I never considered anyone else.'

'I'm not crying,' Violet said, and it was very nearly true. 'But I thought – I thought you loved me.'

He looked a little blank at that; and then he said, 'Of course, I'm very glad that I was able to marry you. You were the prettiest girl of the season and you have all the qualities I looked for in a bride. But it would be foolish to pretend that I would have been able to marry you if your circumstances had been different. It was very – very *lucky* that everything came together as it did, your fortune and yourself both being so attractive.'

It seemed all the reassurance he could give her, and she swallowed the tears that still threatened to rise, and said, 'You really – *love* your father, don't you?' She was aware that the word 'love' might have different connotations for him, but she couldn't think how else to say it. Indeed, his first answer was that surely everyone loved their father, suggesting a very different emotion from the one she meant. But she could see that it was something that he wanted to talk about, and so she encouraged him with questions, and soon the whole story came out.

Brancaster had not been his father's original heir. Holkam had been married before, to a woman of impeccable beauty, breeding and dignity. She had borne him a son, Robert, who had been like her in beauty and accomplishment, and whom Holkam had adored. Two other births had been unsuccessful, the infants dying before their first year, and when, twelve years after their marriage, Lady Holkam had died, the earl had invested all his love in his son, not caring to marry again. But at the age of eighteen the heir had died in a tragic accident: he and his horse fell at a dyke while out hunting. Though there had been only a foot or so of water in the dyke, the horse, being on top of him and cast, had trapped him so that he had drowned before rescue could reach him. Holkam had been almost mad with grief, and for many months locked himself in his room and saw no-one.

But in the end stern duty had braced him, and he had determined to marry again, because the estate and title needed an heir. He had found a suitable young woman, and she had borne him a son. He had called him Robert, too. Violet reflected with pity that Brancaster had not even had his own name. His mother had died when he was only five, and he had been brought up by a series of nurses under his father's stern eye.

As he told the story, a great many things became clear to Violet. It explained why Lord Holkam was so old for a father, so set in his ways and so tyrannical. She understood, though he did not say so in plain words, that Brancaster was almost pitifully anxious to please his father, longed, indeed, to be loved by him as well as approved. He had had no-one else to love, after all, and difficult shoes to fill. Though he never said so – Violet merely understood it – Brancaster wanted his father to say that he loved him better than his predecessor. From what she had seen of Lord Holkam it was a hopeless wish, and she pitied Brancaster from her heart.

At the end of the exposition she understood her husband and his situation a great deal better, but the truth about her own situation was not very palatable. She was on approval, as far as Lord Holkam was concerned, and if she annoyed him in any way, Brancaster would never take her side against him. By presenting an heir she would justify her existence to both, so she had better hope she had a boy; but she would always have to do as she was told – certainly for as long as Holkam lived – and would similarly have to take second place with Brancaster to his father; if she had a son, perhaps third place.

But the optimism of youth revived, and she considered that Holkam was old and ill, and that he surely could not last much longer. When he was dead and out of the way, things would be different. She still loved Brancaster, and had been touched by his story. She hoped, from the fact that he had confided all this to her, that he did love her, in his way. She had no rival but the old man. When he was out of the way, surely Brancaster would turn to her? She was married to him and had to make the best of it, but optimism said that with understanding on her part and departure into death on Lord Holkam's, it would all turn out well.

She did not talk to her mother about 'making the best of it': she gave her to understand, without precisely saying so, that all was well, and that love flourished just as expected. But it was necessary to tell Venetia of the earl's dislike of her, which was difficult and painful for them both. Her mother took it the way she had hoped, and said that old people, particularly sick old people, had their fancies. She comforted Violet that it could not last long.

'I'm glad you told me, darling. I feel much better for knowing, and you need not worry that I shall take offence or do anything to make it more difficult for you. But if I am not to be there when the baby comes, I must be satisfied that you are properly looked after. Who will attend you?'

'I don't know,' Violet admitted. 'No-one has said anything about it.'

'That probably means no-one has done anything about it either. The result of being in a household of men. I know it's embarrassing, but you must ask when you get home, darling. You must have a good physician on hand, and an experienced midwife and a month nurse after-wards. I could arrange it all if you think it would not offend anyone – and, really, I can't see why it should. The earl must want his heir delivered safely.'

'I suppose so. But – I don't know – perhaps, as Lord Holkam feels—'

'I think you are being over-sensitive,' Venetia said; but she knew her daughter was shy and diffident, and after all, she was only just eighteen. What she needed was someone on hand whom she could rely on, someone with common sense who would bolster her confidence. 'What is your maid like? I wish Sanders had not left you – I was very disappointed in her. Your present girl seems rather dull.'

'She's nice, but not very intelligent.'

'She's not what I would expect a future countess to have for a dresser. How if I found you someone better and sent her down to you? Do you think Lord Holkam would mind that?'

'I don't suppose he would even know. He hardly leaves his room now.'

'And Brancaster would not object? He must want you to appear creditably dressed.'

'I think – I think he would not mind it. He doesn't seem to have anything to do with household matters.'

'Why should he, indeed? Most men care nothing as long as you don't bother them about it. Very well. I shall find you someone and send her down, and it will be someone who knows how to look after you properly, in *all* circumstances.'

'Thank you, Mama,' Violet said. 'You are so wonderful and understanding.'

'Your happiness, my love, is all that matters to me.'

'Oh, I am happy,' Violet said. And in spite of everything it was true, not least because at the last minute, when Violet was taking leave of Brancaster to come to London, he had touched her hand and said, as if he would miss her, 'Don't stay away too long.'

There was a passage in the Bill of Rights that said, 'It is the right of the subject to petition the King, and all commitments and prosecutions for such petitions are illegal.' The WSPU planned to present a petition to Parliament on the 29th of June, and when they were arrested, to challenge the arrest in court on those grounds. The petition was to be carried by a deputation of the most distinguished Suffragettes, because it had been noted that it embarrassed the government to have to imprison women from the upper classes.

Anne did not believe this new ploy would have any effect. 'If they do not care about the law – except to use it improperly as a weapon against us – why should they care about the Bill of Rights?' she said to Lizzie.

'But I should think it will get us a great deal of popular sympathy,' Lizzie said. She was holding Rose on her lap facing her, smiling and receiving smiles. These days, the vote seemed strangely unimportant to her compared with her daughter's gummy delight in looking into her mother's face. Besides, childbirth this time had really 'knocked the stuffing out of her', as Ashley put it, and she did not seem to have the energy left over after household and motherly things to want to campaign.

'What use is that?' Anne said impatiently. 'Popular support has no power to effect the change we want.'

'But we have to prove to Asquith that the majority of the country supports us.'

'We will never do that, because it doesn't. What is right is not always what is popular. Popular support is a comfort, but it is the government which denies us our rights and they have already proved they are not susceptible to reason or logic. They are concerned only with their own comfort. So we must make them *un*comfortable.'

'And how will you do that?' Lizzie asked. Her eyes were locked on Rose's, she smiled and the baby smiled. It was a delightful experience. She could not remember if she had ever had so much pleasure with the boys. Why did mothers hand over their babies so completely to the care of others?

Anne regarded her thoughtfully. 'I think I had best not tell you that,' she said.

As she suspected, Lizzie was not really listening, and only answered, 'As you please. Anne, don't you think a baby's smile is the most perfect thing in the world? Look how her little bare gums show when she does it. Isn't she enchanting? Yes, she is,' she added, to the baby. 'Oh, yes, she is. She's my Rosy-posy-tosy. Yes, she is.'

Rose, smiling and blowing spit-bubbles, seemed to agree. Anne took her leave.

More than two hundred rank-and-file members had offered themselves for the Bill of Rights deputation, and as only a handful of the distinguished were to form the actual deputation, the others were divided into groups of seven or eight, each with a leader, and on the night the groups gathered in offices scattered around the area of Westminster, so they could approach the House from different directions in support. But Anne, with a following of some of the younger 'hot-bloods', was planning a different kind of protest. When the time came for the groups to march, they were going to make their way to Whitehall and smash the windows of government buildings with stones.

The action was not authorised by the WSPU, and when Christabel Pankhurst got wind of it she tried to talk Anne out of it.

But Anne said, 'We cannot always be on the receiving end of violence. It is time we fought back. It's no use, Christabel, you won't change my mind. We must make them sit up and take notice, and you know perfectly well that this deputation will have the same effect as all the others – that is, no effect at all.'

'But we must have unity. We have to act together. We must show discipline inside the ranks or we will be despised by the men.'

'We are despised already.'

'But think, Anne! So far we have done nothing criminal. Our offences have been merely technical—'

'And we have been gaoled for them. If they treat us like criminals, we had better behave like criminals.' Christabel looked uncomfortable, and Anne added, 'Come, it is only a few panes of glass – the very minimum of violence. This government praises Russian demonstrators when they throw bombs and kill people.'

'It will change the game entirely. I am afraid it is a mistake, Anne.'

'Well, you can pretend you didn't know about it beforehand. We won't contradict you. Or, if you really think the appearance of unity is important, you can support us. I leave it to you.'

Though Anne looked forward with relish to this new departure, and to giving the enemy some of its own back, it still frightened her, and she understood very well the feelings of the women under her charge who, though determined to carry it through, viewed the prospect with great apprehension. They were gently born and carefully raised, women of refinement, and for such a female deliberately to throw a stone, let alone to do it with the intention of breaking a window, was a violation of her nature and upbringing.

In the office where her group assembled, she could see they were unnaturally quiet and some seemed depressed and close to tears. She herself could sense in the back of her mind a powerful little tugging that said, 'Forget all this. Don't do it. Go home.' Home and safety and peace – the temptation was strong. But for years now she had subdued her feelings by the operation of her intellect, and having promised herself that she would not stop until women had the vote, for her own pride she could not go back on her word.

So she rallied them, talked to them, exhorted them until they looked more cheerful. Then she went over the plans again, trying to get them into a practical state of mind where they would concentrate on the details of the campaign rather than think about what they were doing. Each was supplied with a dolly bag made of denim containing stones wrapped up in brown paper and string, which she hung from tapes tied around her waist under her skirt so that there was nothing to raise the suspicion of a policeman. The bag could be reached through a side placket, and when the signal came to 'smash up' they would slip their hands in, pull out the stones, and let fly at the appointed target. Anne knew that it would take enormous self-will for each to do her part, and she was afraid some of them would fail. When the time came they would simply not be able to force themselves to an act so unnatural and shameful.

There had been plenty of advance warning about the deputation. At public meetings and in letters to the newspapers Mrs Pankhurst had said, 'Mr Asquith, as the King's representative, is bound to receive the deputation and hear their petition. If he refuses to do so and calls out the police to prevent women from using their right to present a petition, he will be guilty of illegal and uncon-

250

stitutional action.' This struck a chord with many people, and there was widespread sympathy for the position. Other elements felt it promised a good evening's fun, and for both reasons there were enormous crowds gathered, and a heavy police guard all around the House and patrolling the wider area.

At half past seven Vera Holme, an actress and singer who played in Gilbert and Sullivan productions at the Savoy Theatre, set out from Caxton Hall on horseback with a message for Mr Asquith. Her appearance was greeted with great enthusiasm by the crowds, and as she rode towards the House she was followed at a run by a mass of excited youths, shouting and cheering. At St Stephen's she met a line of policemen who blocked her way, while a mounted inspector seized her bridle to stop her. She gave him the letter to Mr Asquith and asked him to deliver it. He dropped it contemptuously and told her to go away.

She returned to Caxton Hall with the news, cheered all the way by the crowds, and on her arrival the deputation set out. It was led by Mrs Pankhurst, who was not only tiny but was now beginning to look rather fragile, accompanied by eight distinguished suffragettes, two of whom were frail, white-haired elderly ladies. As they set out, marching briskly, a shout of 'Here comes Mrs P!' ran before them, and willing bodies cleared a path for them through the cheering masses. Behind them came the fife and drum band, while the other groups converged from their different directions. At the Strangers' Entrance they were met by Inspector Jarvis and Inspector Scantlebury, the House of Commons detectives, who handed Mrs Pankhurst a letter from Mr Asquith's secretary saying he would not receive them. Mrs Pankhurst read it out loud, and then demanded entrance. The police began to push them back, and aware that some of her colleagues were too frail to endure the rough handling that always followed, Mrs Pankhurst decided to force an immediate arrest. She slapped Inspector Jarvis's face. He looked shocked and surprised at first – he was a kind man and had had a very good relationship with the Suffragettes until now. Then his face cleared and he said, 'Ah, I understand why you did that.'

'Then you must act on it,' Mrs Pankhurst said.

'I don't want to arrest you,' said Jarvis.

But the pushing and jostling was getting worse, and the seventy-six-year-old headmistress, Miss Neligan, had already had her bonnet knocked askew and was breathless from the crush.

'I'm afraid you must,' Mrs Pankhurst said, and slapped him again. He shrugged and took her in charge.

At nine o'clock, when it was calculated that the uproar in Parliament Square would be at its height, the stone-throwers, in two groups, set out for Whitehall. There were plenty of policemen about, but though they received one or two suspicious looks, no-one tried to stop them. When the moment came, they took out their stones and threw them at the chosen windows. They were not practised at throwing: some of the women did not throw hard enough, so the stones fell feebly short; others missed their targets; and two of the women could not in the end bring themselves to do it at all. Anne's first stone hit the window frame instead of the glass, doing no damage. She heard a shout and saw a policeman running towards her, and suddenly the blood was hot under her skin, and, with a wonderful sense of exhilaration, she threw her second stone with all her strength and heard the shocking, exciting sound of tinkling glass as the pane disintegrated.

A meaty hand grabbed her arm as she drew out a third stone, pulling her round; with his other hand the policeman grabbed her wrist and twisted it until she cried out with pain and the stone dropped to the ground. 'All right, you!' he shouted, his face so close that flecks of spittle touched her cheek. 'That's enough of that! What the bloody hell d'you think you're doing? You're nicked, my girl!'

Another policeman came pounding up and grabbed

her other arm, and she felt the thick fingers biting into the tender flesh of her upper arms. 'Are you going to come quietly,' the second constable asked, 'or do we have to drag you?'

'I'll come quietly,' Anne said. 'There's no need for violence.'

They seemed taken aback at her accent. The painful grip on her arms loosened a little, and the second-comer said, 'I don't understand it. What's a lady like you doing mixed up with this here? Breaking windows? Whatever possessed you? Where's that going to get you?'

'Our rights are being violated,' Anne said. 'We have to protest in whatever way we can.'

The first policeman, much less sympathetic, said, 'Oh, don't give her the excuse to start jawing! All these blasted Sufferingettes can talk the hind leg off a donkey. Just get her back to the station and be done with it.'

The other constable fell in on her other side and they marched her off briskly. Though Anne was a fast walker, they were so much taller than her and their strides so much longer that she could not keep up, and she was dragged along in the usual humiliating way, with them half carrying her, their massive hands wrapped around her upper arms, so that her toes only just touched the ground. She knew she would carry the black marks of their fingers for above a week, but it was the feeling of helplessness she hated most.

As they neared Cannon Street there were more enormous crowds gathered to see the arrested brought in, and each one was cheered mightily as she was borne past, skimming along with her frantic toe-tips scrabbling for the pavement. Many of the onlookers applauded. Some shouted, 'Well done!' and 'Votes for women! Keep it up!' As Anne was hauled up to the door she heard someone say, 'That's Lady Anne Farraline – the Earl of Batchworth's sister,' and immediately afterwards there was a flash and a muted explosion as a photograph was taken. Of course, it could only be a journalist who would recognise her in her present dishevelled state. A nice photograph for poor William to brood over, she thought.

And all the time, in Parliament Square, a battle royal was raging, as group after group of Suffragettes struggled to reach the House and were thrown back by cordons of police, some of them mounted. By the time order was restored, fourteen men and a hundred and eight women had been arrested; of the stone-throwers, thirteen had been taken in charge.

The following day the Parliament Square arrestees appeared in Bow Street charged with obstruction, assaulting the police and malicious damage. Mrs Pankhurst was put up first as a test case, and pleaded that under the terms of the Bill of Rights and the Tumultuous Petitions Act, they were legally entitled to petition Mr Asquith as the King's representative. The magistrate was uncertain how to proceed, and all the cases were adjourned until advice had been taken. The stone-throwers were bound over to be heard separately at a later date, on the 12th of July.

Venetia, of course, heard of it. On the day before, the 28th of June, she and Overton had been at a reception at the Foreign Office given in honour of the King's birthday, where there had been another disturbance. One of the Suffragettes, Theresa Garnett, had got into the reception using a ticket passed on by a sympathiser, and during a pause in the background music she climbed up onto a windowsill and began addressing the company on the subject of votes for women. A silence of horror had fallen over the assembled cream of Society, who had read about Suffragettes in the newspapers but had never expected to find themselves so close to one. Inspector Jarvis, who had been on duty at the door, ran in and apprehended her and as she was led away through the glittering throng, which parted like the Red Sea to let her by, she nodded and smiled to left and right and said genially, 'You will see that we get votes for women, won't you?' It was so well done that Venetia had difficulty in keeping her countenance, but as everyone else in the room was stony-faced and silent she dared not appear sympathetic. In the morning a newspaper described Theresa Garnett as 'a Suffragette disguised as a lady', which did make Venetia laugh; but she found nothing amusing in the news that Anne had been arrested again – and, moreover, for breaking windows.

On her way back from the New Hospital for Women on the 2nd of July she called in at Bedford Square and found Miss Vaughan in a flutter of distress. Lady Anne had gone to Clement's Inn but she expected her back very soon. Would Lady Overton care to wait? Venetia accepted the offer, and as soon as she had sat down, Miss Vaughan jumped straight in with 'Oh, your ladyship, have you heard the news? It is so dreadful! I can't bear to think of it, I can't indeed! Whatever will Lord Batchworth say? It was bad enough last time when she was arrested for making a speech in the House of Commons lobby, but this! Whatever could have persuaded her to do it? I've been in such a state of nerves ever since she came home that dreadful night. I am sure Lord Batchworth will blame me for not taking better care of her and, indeed, I blame myself! But who could have thought of such a thing?'

'I'm sure no-one will blame you,' Venetia said, and, sacrificing politeness for reassurance, added, 'It is not to be supposed your influence could ever prevent Lady Anne from doing what she wanted.'

This did not seem immediately to comfort Miss Vaughan, who continued to mourn aloud. It was so shocking, so shameful! For a lady to deliberately break a window, a government window at that, in a public place, in full sight of anyone who happened to be passing—

Venetia enquired whether doing it secretly when no-one was around would have been better.

Miss Vaughan was shocked. 'Your ladyship can't have considered! Oh, I beg your pardon! But it is not a subject for levity. The Farraline name – Lord Batchworth – the newspapers—'

Venetia was very glad when Anne came in and, in her brisk way, got rid of her.

'Ah, I see Miss Vaughan has been entertaining you in my absence. Thank you, Maria, but I need not keep you. Would you be so kind on your way to your room as to ask Ellen to bring up some tea for Lady Overton and me?' When they were alone, Anne said, in a light, tight voice, 'Have you been lectured on my moral turpitude? Maria has been in a ferment. She can't understand – literally can't understand – how I could bring myself to do it.'

'It does challenge the imagination,' Venetia said mildly. She examined her cousin carefully. 'You look pale and strained. I think, perhaps, you are not taking this as calmly as you would like it to seem.'

Anne sat down rather heavily. 'It was more difficult than I expected,' she admitted, in her normal tone. 'And, of course, being wound up so tightly beforehand always leads to a reaction afterwards. I have been at Headquarters this morning, explaining myself to the committee. It was an unauthorised action, you know.'

'Ah! I did wonder. It was such a departure. You thought of it yourself, then?'

Anne nodded. 'We have got to find new ways of making our point. They don't care about our peaceful protests.'

'But I wonder if it is wise to – to escalate the violence? Won't that give them an excuse to do the same?'

'They will do that anyway. Asquith and Gladstone are cold-hearted brutes. They hate us. But as Caesar Tiberius said, "Let them hate me as long as they fear me."'

'Oh, Anne,' Venetia said, seeing through the defiance.

Anne's lip trembled and she caught it under her teeth to still it. Then she said, in a low voice, 'I dread going to prison. *Dread* it. I'm so afraid I shall break down and cry and beg and shame myself before the others.' She met Venetia's eyes. 'You can't think how terrible it is to be locked up. The confinement, the smells, the terrible food are bad enough; but far worse is the humiliation of being insulted and given orders and looked at with contempt by the wardresses – women who in any other circumstance I would not permit even to address me. And worst of all is the feeling of helplessness. When I think of it, I almost believe I would rather die than go back there again.'

'Is it really worth it?' Venetia asked.

'I've gone too far to turn back now,' said Anne. She was silent a while, and Venetia sat looking at her, wondering what she could say. But at last Anne straightened her shoulders and forced a smile and said, 'Well, now you've seen me at my worst. I hope you are not ashamed of me for being poor-spirited.'

'On the contrary, I admire your courage,' Venetia said.

'When I've just been telling you how afraid I am?'

'It would not *be* courage if you weren't afraid,' Venetia pointed out.

Anne shook her head, and then got up and walked about the room. 'Well, I have annoyed them into arresting me, and I have no doubt whatever that I shall be sent to Holloway. We must see what we can think up by way of annoyances while we are inside. Something that will embarrass them and, if possible, make them feel as helpless as I do.'

She did not look afraid now. She was wearing the expression that had always said she was planning some devilry.

'Oh, Anne, do be careful,' Venetia said.

And she laughed. 'Too late for that, Venetia dear!'

On the 9th of July another Suffragette prisoner, Marion Wallace Dunlop, was released from prison. She had been arrested on the 22nd of June for printing the famous words from the Bill of Rights on the wall of St Stephen's Hall with a rubber stamp, for which she had been given one month. She had demanded first-division status as a political prisoner but it had been denied, and on the 5th of July she had hit on the idea of going on a hunger strike. After a little less than four days she was released. When Anne heard this, she knew she had found her way to

257

cause the government annoyance and embarrassment from inside prison. She got the other stone-throwers together and put it to them.

'We must refuse to obey any second-division rules. Refuse to wear the clothes. Refuse to keep silent. Block up the peepholes in the cell doors. Break the cell windows. Anything we can think of to rebel. And if they still refuse to treat us as political prisoners, we must refuse to eat. What do you think?'

Most of them had half expected it, knowing Anne, and having heard the talk about Miss Wallace Dunlop. Still, it was a shock, and it took a great deal of talk before they had all prepared their minds for it, and agreed a plan of action.

'It will be a grand gesture,' Anne concluded. 'But we must all swear to each other that we will stand firm. If we all hold out they will have to release us, and do you know what that will mean?' They looked at her hopefully. 'It will mean that in future, no matter what we do, they will not be able to imprison us for more than a few days. We will blunt their sharpest weapon. But every one of us must stick. If one gives in, it will spoil it for all.'

She got them all to agree to that, and after some more conversation, she saw they were all looking less pale and frightened. To hold out for the Cause, or the WSPU, or women at large, was one thing, but to hold out for the sake of the others in this room, for one's particular comrades in arms, was much more personal, more comprehensible, and therefore more bracing. Anne looked at them with affection, nice ordinary women, brought up in comfort and gentility, none of them particularly strong, clever or brave, but all determined to do their best in a sphere for which life's experience had not fitted them. They would bend their natures until they cracked, but they would not break. And so, now, neither would she.

'We are all truly sisters now,' she said, holding out her arms to them. 'Everyone who does this with me is my sister from now on.'

And they looked pleased. Lady Anne Farraline was beautiful, inspiring, exciting. Apart from Christabel there was no-one in the movement so charismatic. And she was from one of the best families in the land, far out of their normal social sphere. To be called her sister was flattering and thrilling.

Teddy always had a great deal to do and, having been idle all his youth, had learned in middle life actually to enjoy being busy. There were his various business interests, his stores, his mills; he was a director of the railway and on the Board of Governors of St Edward's School; and since Jerome had been ill, there was more for him to do about the estate at Morland Place. He had a land agent, a bailiff and two secretaries, but it was not the same as having a brother-in-law for keeping an eye on things. Jessie helped a great deal, of course, and as Jerome grew a little stronger he was able to resume some of his supervisory duties. But Teddy knew that, according to Hasty, his heart had been damaged by his illness, and he must not take on too much. So he did everything he could not to rely on him, though he sometimes had to bite his tongue not to ask Jerome's opinion, for it had become such a habit with him over the years.

In addition Teddy had made several trips to Belfast to consult over the fittings for the new ships. The building of them was coming along now. Keel number 400 for the first ship, the *Olympic*, had been laid at number-two slipway on the 16th of December the year before, and keel number 401 for the *Titanic* had been laid at number-three slipway on the 31st of March. There was not much to see yet, but the sheer size, especially the length, of the keels was an eye-opener. It made one realise, as figures on paper never did, how enormous these ships were going to be. Everyone involved seemed to feel it: the atmosphere of excitement seemed always palpable whenever he visited those busy, noisy, teeming dockyards. And a visit to Harland and Wolff always required a visit to Manchester to pass on the information and inspect and modify the plans for making the goods. It meant being away from York and Morland Place when really he needed to be at home more than ever, and there were times when he wished his darling Polly had been a boy and ten years older.

But with all that he had to do, he still managed to keep an eye on his late brother-in-law's estate. Pobgee, Micklethwaite and Exelby, the solicitors, were the executors, but in Bertie's absence there were things it was more proper for a member of the family to do, such as collecting together Perry's more intimate personal belongings, and settling with the servants. Walter had gone back to Oxford to make the most of the time he had left, his fees having been paid until the end of the year; Lucas, Peg and Arthur were not inclined to take an interest in what their father left, since it seemed doubtful there would be much of it and it would all go to Bertie anyway; so with his usual good humour Teddy had stepped into the breach.

Bertie had been away on a buying trip in the mountains when his father had died and there had been no contact with him for months. But in April a letter had come saying that he was back at Jungaipur, his hill-station about thirty miles north of Darjeeling, and had received the news. Then in June he had written to Exelby, and in a separate letter to Teddy, that he would be coming home. It would take a long time to sell up and settle his affairs out there, so he was not expecting to be in England until the following summer.

In the mean time, he was grateful to his uncle for overseeing matters, especially in regard to the servants. All of them had been in his father's employ for years, and most of them were old. Bertie was anxious that they should be well treated, and wrote to Teddy, 'I know that probate takes the dickens of a long time, and that the law does not take account of the loyalty of servants and such other matters. If it should be a question of requiring some immediate outlay to secure their comfort, I wish you would be so kind as to undertake it, Uncle, and apply to

me for the money. I can arrange for a sum to be transferred to your bank quite quickly.' Exelby was more than
happy to accept Teddy's help and advice, and so a skeleton
staff was chosen to keep the Red House and its grounds
in minimum order, and the rest were turned off or helped
to find other positions, with appropriate recompense.

That Bertie was to come home at last caused enormous interest throughout the district. Speculation was
wild as to how he would have changed, whether he would
have become like an Indian himself, whether he might
arrive with a string of exotically dressed black wives and
a swarm of half-native children. That he would be fabulously rich seemed to be a given: some of the younger
element believed – or perhaps rather hoped – that he
would come riding into Yorkshire on an elephant with a
camel train behind him laden with boxes of gold and
gemstones, ivory and tiger skins.

It amused Jerome to hear the stories that various family
members brought back to him, which were eloquent of
the shortcomings of free education. The patchwork of
speculation included identifiable elements from China,
ancient Egypt, darkest Africa, the cannibal isles of
Polynesia, the Tales of Ali Baba and Aladdin's Wonderful
Lamp. Though he did not say so aloud, he did think it
possible that Bertie might bring back a native woman –
he had been out there and unmarried for some years,
after all – but he had enough opinion of his nephew to
suppose that he would be discreet about it. He wondered
how Jessie would react to the return of her former hero
– she had had quite a crush on him a couple of years
ago – but though she was as interested as anyone else,
and as amused as he was by the various wild rumours,
she discussed it with him with an underlying calm. She
remembered Bertie with fondness and looked forward to
seeing him again, but the special shrine in her heart now
held a secret statue of Lord Brancaster. She had forgotten
the reality of Bertie, though she did remember with a
small pang that it was actually Bertie who had given her

261

her first kiss – though of course as he was her cousin it didn't really count.

She had settled down into a new sort of life, one with a great deal of work and responsibility, which she found she relished. She spent a lot of time with her father, and their discussions ranged over a wide variety of subjects. Henrietta saw that Jessie was taking the place with her husband that Lizzie had occupied before her marriage, and was content that it should be so: it satisfied him, and gave invaluable education to her. Besides that, Jessie had enough balls and parties and other outings to keep her amused, and enough gentlemen admirers to salve her pride; though it was often Ned who escorted her, for she found his company soothing and safe. It was he who took her for the first time to see the moving pictures at the Hippodrome: it had once been the New Street Chapel but had been bought by the Yorkshire Bioscope Company when it closed for worship.

And when Uncle Teddy sold his Gardner-Serpollet steam-car, because his motor mechanic Simmons said it was becoming difficult to replace parts, and bought instead a petroleum motor-car, a blue and silver Benz, for the fabulous sum of seven hundred and fifty pounds, it was Ned who suggested Jessie should learn to drive.

'It will be a lark,' he said. 'And you never know, one day it might come in useful.'

'I can't think how it ever could, but I must say, now you've put the idea into my head, I should rather like to. It looks so big and powerful – it would be rather like driving a four-in-hand. Do you think I could?'

'Simmons says it isn't difficult, only takes concentration.'

'But I wonder if they would approve – Mother and Dad and Uncle Teddy? Is it a thing a girl can do?'

'Why not? I read in the papers that the Suffragettes have a motor-car, and of course they have a lady driver. Chauffeur, I think they call it.'

Jessie was about to protest that few people regarded the Suffragettes as the template of proper femininity, then realised he was teasing her. 'But seriously, do you think I might?'

'I don't see why they would object. After all, you do work at the stud that most girls don't do, and they don't seem to think that's unladylike.'

No objection was made – in fact, Jerome, laughing at the thought of little Jessie controlling the monster of a car, said it would do her good and strengthen her wrists for riding – and though Teddy was doubtful about a girl's being able to drive, he did not think it would be improper if it was only on their own land. Jessie tried it, and loved it, and the feeling of power was, as she had imagined, rather like driving a team of horses. It was only a pity the motor car was so noisy and smelly in comparison with horses; but she acknowledged the fascination.

Recently Robbie had fallen out of love at last with the disagreeable Miss Harris, and was now courting a Miss Cornleigh – Ethel – whom everybody liked. Miss Cornleigh had a younger sister, Angela, who was just Jessie's age, and when they met they took an instant liking to each other. Angela was mad about tennis, but had never ridden; Jessie had never played tennis, but the Cornleighs had a tennis lawn behind their large house in Clifton. So Jessie gave Angela riding lessons in return for tennis lessons, and promised to take her hunting next winter if she got on well enough; and as soon as Jessie got the hang of tennis, she was invited to Clifton Lodge where they had frequent tennis parties. So Jessie now had a female friend for the first time since Violet's marriage, and a new pastime that enabled her to meet nice young men. The Cornleighs had three sons as well as four other daughters, and Mrs Cornleigh was on Alice's visiting-list. All in all, the summer passed very pleasantly for Jessie.

Chapter Nine

On the 12th of July, Lady Anne Farraline and the other stone-throwers were tried at Bow Street and sentenced, some to four and some to six weeks, in the second division. In the Black Maria, sitting in the dark in the 'upright coffin', Anne reviewed the covenant she had made with the others, and the instructions she had given them. It would be hard, painful, and would require great courage to do what they had agreed, but it was right and necessary. Somehow the public's attention must be seized and held.

At Holloway prison they were taken to the reception room and lined up for the roll to be taken. But Anne said, 'Before anything else happens, we would like to see the governor, please.'

The senior wardress, a hard-faced woman with strong arms and surprisingly blonde hair, snapped, 'The governor? It isn't likely. Answer your names when you are called.'

'We will not. It is our right to see the governor, and it will save a great deal of time and trouble if you send for him at once, because we will not do anything until we have seen him.'

The wardress scowled and muttered under her breath, but perhaps she was unused to dealing with someone like Anne, who was so obviously out of her usual surroundings, because she left them with the other wardresses and went out of the room. In a little while she returned with the matron, who said briskly, 'What is all this nonsense? You women must remember you are prisoners now, and must obey orders. I will call out your names and you will answer "yes", and then you will undress.'

Anne interrupted. 'We will not answer the roll, we will not give up our clothes, we will not obey any of your orders. We have asked to see the governor, as is our right, and we will not move until we have seen him.'

'What's your name?' the matron asked angrily.

'I shall not give it to you. Send for the governor.'

One of the wardresses whispered to the matron and she raised her eyebrows, and turned back to Anne to say, 'You're Farraline, aren't you? You've been inside before. You know the rules. Don't make it harder for yourself and these others. You'd do better to set an example. Some of 'em will be in tears before long.'

Anne didn't doubt it, but this was not the time to show weakness. 'We are all of one mind, and you will not shake us. We demand to see the governor.'

And so, in the end, he was sent for. He came, rather a pathetic figure, Anne thought: almost she was sorry for him. His clothes were shabby, his shoulders stooped, his hair thinning, his face careworn. He looked along the line of women with a weary apprehension, as if he would rather have been training lions in a circus than having to deal with Suffragettes in Holloway. Anne did not wait for him to ask, but stepped straight in with her statement.

'I am Anne Farraline and I speak for all of us. We have been sentenced to serve in the second division, although our offences were political. A man committing the same offence would have been put in the first division. This is inequitable, unfair and unjust. We therefore demand that we be treated as political prisoners and transferred to the first division.'

The governor drew a tired sigh. 'There is no such thing in this country as political crime. You have all been committed for malicious damage.'

'I am not here to debate the law with you, sir, or how it should be changed,' Anne said. 'I know that is not your province. I merely inform you that we intend to rebel against all second-division rules until we are given first-division status. To begin with we will not give up our clothes and possessions, and if you attempt to force us, we will resist. Think how *that* will look in the papers.'

The governor shook his head in a goaded way. His job was to run the prison in an orderly manner, but they kept sending him these women whose whole purpose was to be *dis*orderly. He could quell the ordinary woman felon with a glare, but what was he to do with – well, for the want of a better term, ladies? After a pause for thought he said, 'Very well. You may keep your clothes and bags for the time being, on condition that you answer the roll and then go quietly to your cells. I shall have to communicate with the Home Secretary about your status. It is not something I can decide on my own authority. Will you go quietly?'

'Yes,' said Anne.

He looked enormously relieved. 'Very well. You will not be allowed to go to chapel or to exercise: it would damage discipline for the other second-division prisoners to see you dressed as you are. You will have to remain in your cells until I have an answer from Mr Gladstone.'

This was rather a blow: chapel and exercise were at least a relief from the confines of the cell. But the main point had been acceded and she said, 'We understand.'

A short time later she heard the heavy, metallic clunk of the cell door closing behind her. The elation of the struggle, the buoyancy of comradeship dissipated, and she could not escape the cold feeling of dread which that sound laid on her. But at least the cell was quiet and private; and they had won the first round: she was still in her own clothes, and with the writing materials and books she had put into her bag in anticipation. Despite its being summer outside, it was cold in the cell; and she was hungry, but it was already after prison supper time, and there would be nothing more brought until the morning. It was after 'lights out', as well, but it was still light outside, so she got into bed for comfort and read a little until she fell into a sleep of emotional exhaustion.

One of the troubles with prison, as she had found the first time, was that the day started so early. It was hard to sleep once it grew light outside, and once one was awake, there was nothing to do but think. She tried to distract herself with reading, but her mind continually wandered. She listened to every slight sound and tried to interpret it: footsteps, clanking of metal, distant voices, hollow with the echo of bare walls and floors. Breakfast was brought at last, a loaf of the usual brown bread and a pint of tea. She found the coarse bread as unpleasant to eat as wood shavings, but was so hungry she managed to choke some down. There was a battered tin knife on the tray, and when Anne picked it up she found some previous prisoner had painstakingly scratched a message on it:

> Courage, brave heart, victory is sure,
> Help comes to those who work and endure.

It was a comfort to remember how many had come this way before, and she was contemplating scratching something on the other side for the next person when the wardress came in and took away the knife. Feeble and blunt as it was, the prisoner was only allowed to keep it for long enough to cut the bread, for fear it might be put to other use.

Later she was taken to the lavatory (a horrible experience for someone gently born) and on her way back, to restore her spirits, she knocked on each cell door as she passed and shouted, 'Courage! Victory!' Though the wardress breathed heavily and growled her disapproval, she did not try to stop her, perhaps not wishing to start another battle so early in the day. Anne heard the women inside call back to her, and the sense of connection heartened her. She saw that they had each blocked their peephole from inside, as agreed – a small act of defiance but one that annoyed the wardresses out of all proportion.

Back in her own cell, she did the same, and then, longing for the least sight of the outside world, she pushed

267

her chair under the window and stood on it. On tiptoe, pulling herself up by the bars, she could just see out. It was rather overcast, but the sky was high enough not to threaten rain, and it was warm. It was good to see the green of trees out in the real world. Pipes ran along the wall under the window and, still holding the bars, she managed to get a toehold on them and lift herself a little higher so that she could look down as well as straight ahead. There were the prison grounds, a series of enclosed yards and various outbuildings. She could see prisoners in brown dresses wheeling barrows of dirty clothing towards a building that she supposed was the laundry; others were taking rubbish out to the ash pit. Then there was the outer wall, and beyond it an ordinary street, with houses opposite, and gardens, and trees – some planted along the pavement, some peeping over the roofs from the back gardens. Her cell was on the top floor of the building, and as she stared out, a pair of pigeons came flying over from one of the trees and landed on the roof just above her window. She heard the scratching of their claws on the edge of the guttering, and then the male cooing and burbling in courtship.

Another of the women had been taken to the lavatory and knocked at each door as she passed, as Anne had done, and shouted, 'Votes for women!' In the distance Anne could hear voices as two prisoners in adjacent cells shouted to each other at the door, and then were told to be quiet by a wardress. The doctor came and asked some brief questions about her health, took her pulse, and pronounced himself satisfied. The wardress who accompanied him pulled the paper out of the peephole with an exasperated sound. When they had gone, Anne blocked it up again. She looked at her watch and found that it was only five to ten. She had thought it was almost lunchtime. Time passed so horribly slowly when you were locked up. She vowed not to look at her watch again, and tried to settle down to read; but she found herself looking up from the page all too often, staring at the walls. She knew it was her imagination, but she had the feeling that they were nearer than they had been, that they were very gradually closing in. The cell would become smaller and smaller until she was crushed, as she had seen a working man crush out the flame on a match with his thumb and finger.

Come, she told herself, this is foolishness. If you are imagining things already, on the first day, what will you be like tomorrow? She went to the door to listen, and heard Miss Appleby – one of the youngest of them, and about whose ability to endure she had had doubts – singing. It was a Suffragette song, of course, one set to a hymn tune. Mrs Pankhurst did not approve of anything that might seem sacrilegious, but the melodies of old favourite hymns were so well known and so amenable to new words that it was impossible to prevent their being used. In her sweet, childish voice, Miss Appleby sang:

> *'Asquith's reign has passed away,*
> *Winston Churchill's had his day,*
> *Suffragettes have come to stay,*
> *Therefore give them votes.'*

It sounded more wistful than militant, but the sound cheered Anne, and put something else in her head apart from the circular thoughts that had been oppressing her. She began to sing herself, and went again to stand on her chair so that she could look out, instead of in. Out in the real world it was so easy to talk about going to prison, to plan the actions that would take one there, to swear that no consideration of personal danger or inconvenience would stop her until the foul injustice was corrected. But out in the real world it was easy to forget the reality of prison. It was as if there were two Annes, the one who campaigned and fought and dared and risked all, and the other who had to take the consequences and serve the sentence. It was lucky that they were inextricably linked together, she thought.

Dinner was brought: a hard-boiled egg, potatoes and

a pint of tea. Shortly after the tray had been removed, the governor paid her a visit, accompanied by the matron. He seemed even more stooped than the day before, even more grey, and there was a smell of whisky about him, as if he had been bolstering up his spirits. He told her that he had sent a message to Herbert Gladstone the night before, reporting the women's demands, but had received no reply.

'So the situation is unchanged,' Anne said.

'As far as I am concerned, there is nothing I can do. I cannot move you into the first division without authority.'

'Then I have to advise you that I and the other Suffragettes will not co-operate with second-division rules. We are determined on resistance until our request is met.'

The governor looked depressed, but he did not attempt to argue. 'Very well. For the present you may continue to wear your own clothes. But if an answer from the Home Secretary is not forthcoming or is unfavourable . . .'

He did not complete the sentence. He and Anne looked at each other. They both knew what Gladstone would answer, if answer he did. And she found herself saying, 'I'm sorry.'

He seemed a little surprised; and then he said, 'This is not a situation any of us would choose.'

When he had left, she went to her door, removed the paper from the peephole, and called to the women in the adjacent cells, Miss Appleby on one side and Miss Roberts on the other.

'The governor's been. No message from Gladstone. Are you ready for the next stage?'

They both called yes to her. 'Very well, pass the word along for the smash-up. Begin when you hear my window break.' Their assent came back, Miss Appleby's sounding rather frightened. 'Good luck,' she called. 'Be brave. Votes for women!'

She gave time for the word to be passed, and then took off her shoe, climbed on her chair, and hit the window glass as hard as she could with the heel. It was surprisingly resistant; and of course there was that something deep inside a woman that did not *want* the glass to break. She tried again, harder. On the third blow the glass broke with the satisfying, frightening sound she remembered. From either side she heard the sounds of hammering and smashing. She managed to break six of the small square panes. She had started in the middle so she now had a nice oblong of fresh air, which smelt wonderfully good to her. In one of the houses opposite the prison, a woman had come to the open window to see what was happening. Anne took off her tie, which was in the colours, put her hand carefully through the gap and waved it so that she would know what it was about. The woman waved back, and then her husband joined her and stared too. Then the woman stooped out of sight, and reappeared with a baby in her arms, which she held up, taking its fat little wrist to make it 'wave'. For some reason, this brought Anne close to tears. Then the wardresses burst in, white with either fury or fear.

The next day the visiting magistrates came and the Suffragettes were each charged with mutiny and sentenced to seven days' close confinement. The punishment cells were below ground level, cold and damp as tombs. They contained nothing but a block of wood fixed to the wall for a chair, and a plank bed and pillow. They had double iron doors and an opaque deadlight of unbreakable glass onto the corridor where a gas jet burned, giving the same dreary, dim illumination day and night. The women were forced to strip and put on prison dress, and their possessions were taken away from them. This, for Anne, was almost the worst thing, for without books she knew the days would be hard to bear, especially as they had agreed at this point to begin a hunger strike. For a moment she wondered what she had done, whether she had been right to lead these women into this trouble, to put them in such a position. It was all useless, wasn't it? The men would never yield. They might all die down here and Asquith and his colleagues would hardly care.

And then she heard, coming down the corridor, the sound of singing. Someone had begun it and others had taken it up. She could not hear the words, but she knew the tune well enough: 'O God, Our Help in Ages Past'. Tears flooded to her eyes; but she knew her next-door neighbour would be waiting to hear her voice, and forced them down and, after a moment, rather shakily, joined the singing.

The next day was Thursday, the 15th of July. The breakfast tea and bread were brought, and Anne was so hungry that they almost looked inviting. She said she did not want any but the wardress left them anyway, only looked rather sharply when she came to take the tray away. The morning dragged by. What with no daylight, no sounds from outside, and the watery smell of mould, Anne thought it was rather like being at the bottom of the sea. She felt as if they had all been drowned and forgotten. Was anyone up in the world of sunlight thinking about her? Had anything been put in the papers? Did anyone know what they were doing or was it all quite wasted?

The doctor came and took her pulse, and tried to argue her out of the hunger strike. 'It's irrational and unreasonable. What do you hope to achieve by it? You hurt no-one but yourself. What good will it do to make yourself ill?' She thought he seemed rather perfunctory, and supposed he must have already said the same thing to several of the others, without success.

'It is my treatment which is unreasonable,' Anne replied. 'I shall continue the strike until I am removed to the first division and given the status of political prisoner.'

'You should be ashamed of yourself,' he snapped. 'I know you are the ringleader. You are a woman of rank and education, but these others are not like you. Some of them are just foolish, ignorant girls. They follow your lead, and you are leading them into senseless risk.'

'I do not tell them what to do,' Anne said. 'They are acting of their own free will, just as I am. We are all quite aware of the risks, and we are also quite determined that we will not submit to injustice.'

'Tcha!' the doctor said in disgust. 'You deserve all you get – the lot of you. A pack of hysterical women! I wash my hands of you.'

The next visitor was the chaplain, a frail-looking, elderly man who was like milk after the doctor's vinegar. He seemed quite an educated person, though his clothes were threadbare, and he looked at Anne with sympathy. 'I am sorry to see you in this predicament,' he said. 'Is there anything you want?'

'A good many things,' Anne replied, 'but I don't suppose you can supply any of them.'

'If you mean removal from this cell, I'm afraid not,' he said with a faint smile, 'but if there is anything more immediate?'

'I don't suppose I would be allowed a library book?'

'I can't say for sure. I imagine not, but I will see what I can do.' He hesitated a moment and then, 'I knew your father, just slightly. I was an army chaplain before I became a prison chaplain.'

'Did you indeed? You know who I am, then?'

'Yes, of course. If you will forgive me the liberty – I believe your father would have applauded your stand.'

Anne was touched. 'I was only a little girl when he died, but I loved him dearly. I hope he would have been proud of me.'

The day dragged past, with the pains of hunger growing ever sharper. After dinner had been brought and rejected (even the potatoes began to look attractive, despite their black marks and bluish sheen) a wardress came in with a copy of the Bible. 'The chaplain sent you this,' she said. She was younger than some of the others and eyed Anne with wonder, as if she could not think why a lady should want to do such a thing as get herself jugged. 'I should think he reckons you need it.'

It was a great deal better than nothing, and Anne was grateful to the chaplain. She began at the beginning, devouring the familiar words as though they had been food, and had got as far as the serpent when the door was unlocked again and the governor came in. He asked her first of all if she would eat.

'I will have something sent in straight away if you will.'

'Thank you, but no.'

He almost pleaded: 'I wish you would. This will do no good, and will certainly damage your health.'

'Being shut up in this damp cellar will damage my health,' Anne said sternly.

'I wish you need not be.' He lowered his voice. 'I know you are in the right, but after the window-breaking you had to be punished. Prison rules must be kept, or where should we be?'

Anne shrugged, feeling too tired to argue. 'I suppose the fact that we have been brought down here is to be taken as Mr Gladstone's reply.'

'No, no, that was an internal matter. The visiting magistrates act independently.'

Anne gave a short laugh. 'I think we both know that the visiting magistrates have their orders from Herbert Gladstone. I saw that my sentence was written down before I entered the room.'

'Mr Gladstone has yet to reply to my message,' he said stubbornly.

'You see the contempt in which we are held. Do you think a man would be treated as we are treated?'

He took a step closer. 'For God's sake, ma'am,' he said in a low voice, 'do not do this. Take some food. I will have some broth, or hot milk sent in. Or jelly. Would you not eat some jelly?'

She looked at him sadly. 'I cannot be bought off with dainties. Come, sir, you must understand that I am determined. What do you think of me?'

'I think it is a great pity to see a lady – to see any female – with a man's determination. You are the gentler sex.'

'Your sex has done this to us,' Anne said, and at that he turned abruptly and walked out.

The next day the hunger had gone past the gnawing

stage, and had settled like a nausea, which she seemed to feel not only in her stomach but curiously in various other parts of her body. There was a foul taste in her mouth and her head ached abominably. She felt so weak she could not bring herself to get out of bed at the usual hour. Bed was also the warmest place, and she was feeling the cold very much now she had nothing in her stomach. But the wardresses came in and told her to get up and get dressed, and then took her bed away. It was obviously an attempt to put further pressure on her, for there was nothing else in the cell but the short seat fixed to the wall: nowhere to lie down but the floor, nothing to do with her body but sit on the wooden slab or walk about. They brought no washing water either, and when she asked for it, they said curtly, 'Use your drinking water,' and went out. They are trying to humiliate me, she thought. It must be on Gladstone's orders, to try to get a speedy end to the strike. God rot him! She would not yield. It stiffened her resolve just when she needed it.

When she woke the next morning, she realised at once, and with a horrible panic, that she could not remember what day it was. It seemed of vital, overwhelming importance, but though she racked her brain she could not work it out, and it brought her to the verge of tears. When the door opened and the wardresses came in, it was her first question.

'It's Saturday,' said the senior – the hard-faced blonde. 'Get up, we are taking out your bed.'

Anne tried to get up, and could not. Her limbs would not answer her.

'Are you ready to give up this nonsense now?' the wardress demanded. Her eyes gleamed with satisfaction, Anne thought, to see her brought so low.

'No. I will not,' she said. Her voice seemed faint, as though it were coming from someone else, a long way off. She made a huge effort, pulled herself over on her knees, and then managed to get to her feet. When she stood up she became very dizzy and the wardress had to catch her arms to stop her falling. They sat her on the wooden seat, and the younger one pushed her head down to her knees.

'Don't sit up, or you'll go queer again,' she said.

Anne sat like that, holding her head in her hands, while the dizziness had its way with her. There were black swooping things behind her eyes, and the nausea crawled up from her stomach to her throat like a sick animal and died there. She felt she could not swallow; could not breathe. Through the tumultuous roaring in her head she could hear the sounds of her bed being taken out, and she wanted to weep. Another day of this, God help me! How shall I get through it?

Then there was a hand on her arm and something was pushed under her nose. A savage smell seemed to jolt her brain in her head, but almost at once it settled down more in its accustomed space. She sat up slowly and the younger wardress slipped the smelling-bottle back into her pocket. 'Thought you was going off, then,' she said confidentially. 'Will you take breakfast?'

Anne could only shake her head, afraid that if she spoke she would cry.

It was her worst day yet. The faintness, nausea and headache persisted, to which was now added a feeling of breathlessness, and palpitations all over her body, as if she had grown a dozen extra hearts and they were rushing about inside her like panicking birds, knocking to get out. She longed to lie down but dared not risk the floor; she longed to walk about but had not the strength to get up. Her legs ached intolerably; her hands were icy cold.

After dinner-time, the governor appeared, with the matron. He looked grave, and worried. He said that he had had a reply from Herbert Gladstone.

'What is it?' Anne asked, in a voice that croaked. Her tongue and lips were swollen.

'He says he has fully considered the position, but sees no reason why he should take action in the matter,' said the governor, his eyes anywhere but on Anne.

'Which proves,' Anne croaked, 'that he could if he would.'

The governor did not answer. He stood where he was, his eyes fixed on the floor, seeming to debate some inner argument. But at last he only said, 'I am very sorry,' and went away.

On Sunday the 18th of July, Anne could not rise from her bed. The wardresses tried to rouse her and she tried to get up, but she had no strength left. When they left her again, she lay there, staring at the ceiling and feeling oddly warm and relaxed, as though she were in a warm bath. The nausea and headache of the past few days had left her. She felt light and empty and curiously serene, and her thoughts drifted in and out, as though she were floating out of herself for short periods. She wondered if perhaps she were dying, and found she did not much care. Gladstone will be sorry, she thought, but it was a distant and unemphatic thought. The doctor came in and tried to persuade her to give up the hunger strike and take some food, but she only looked at him dreamily and said, 'No.' He harangued her for a while, and then went away.

During the morning they sent in a cleaner to sweep out the cell, and she smiled at Anne kindly and said, 'Dear dear. What a thing. What a thing.' Later on – she had no idea how much later for time had ceased to exist – she heard someone singing. It was 'Rock of Ages', and she thought, Yes, of course, it's Sunday. But the hymn stopped in mid verse and fell into a sound of weak sobbing. That wasn't someone in church, she thought, then remembered where she was, and wanted to cry herself.

On Monday the 18th she woke to pain. Every part of her ached; she thought she could feel each separate bone in her body, as though her skeleton were trying to get out through her skin. She wanted so desperately to get up, to move about, that she thought she might scream with it, but she was too weak to do more than raise her head. When she did try to struggle up, it only brought on the palpitations again, the pulse knocking in her chest, then her throat, then her head, then her armpit. It frightened her, and she panted for air and wanted to call for help, but could not summon the breath.

She must have lost consciousness, for it was with a sense of coming back from somewhere that she saw there were people in her cell.

'We're taking you to the hospital,' one said. It sounded like the matron, but speaking from a long way away. Why was the room so dark – dark and swirling with red and black spirals that impeded her vision? She was lifted up – oh, how the hands hurt her bones, which were now on the outside of her skin, where even the air hurt them – and put into a chair, which was lifted and wafted her away. At one moment her vision cleared and she saw that it was two rough-looking women in prison dress who were carrying her. She wanted to ask them if she knew them, but her voice would not work. The only thing that would seem to come out of her mouth was a whisper of 'Votes for women.' The women looked at each other and one of them sniggered.

The matron tutted and muttered, 'At a time like this! Shameless, shameless!'

By the time she reached the hospital she was shivering violently. They put her to bed and brought her hot water bottles and extra blankets, and when the shivering fit passed they brought beef-tea and hot milk, which she refused, wearily. She did not care any longer whether she lived or died. She only knew she must say no and go on saying it.

The doctor came and harangued her again. 'You may very well have damaged your health permanently. If you carry on with this nonsense you certainly will. Is it worth it to you, to be bedridden for the rest of your life, a misery to yourself and burden to others? It is utterly senseless, what you are doing. It would be senseless if it were for a good cause – but for this! For the vote! It is only lunatic women like you who want it. Even if you succeeded no-one would thank you – and you will not succeed. For God's sake be reasonable, give up this ridiculous protest and eat something. Who is the better for what you are doing?'

'My soul,' Anne whispered.

'Ha!' said the doctor, and stamped away in a rage; but at the door he turned and came back and leaned over the bed pushing his face close to hers, glowering. 'You will be dead tomorrow. Where do you want what's left of you sent?'

'To Mr Asquith,' she whispered; and then he did leave her.

She drifted then, down long, horribly red-and-black tunnels, with walls that thudded irregularly and with a force beyond sound, as if there were a huge engine somewhere nearby whose vibrations she could feel. In the tunnel there was a smell, too – or was it a taste? Perhaps something between the two. It was foul and cloying, and she thought it was the taste of death. She thought of her brother, of Venetia, of Lizzie, of poor Miss Vaughan, saw them all in black, at her funeral. None of them was crying. She wanted to sleep but there did not seem to be sleep, only this horrible, pounding tunnel.

And then someone called her, and slowly but inexorably she turned back and drifted towards the voice. She opened her eyes and saw light, proper yellow light. There was fading daylight at the window, and lamps were lit. Someone had hold of her wrist and was taking her pulse – one of the nurse-wardresses. And the person who had called her called her again. It was the governor, leaning over her.

She focused on him with difficulty, frowning a little. 'What time is it?' she whispered.

He straightened a little, pulled out his watch from the fob, and said, 'Almost half past six.' He looked at her, and added, as though he knew he had not said enough, 'In the evening.'

'Monday?'

'Yes, still Monday. Well, now, are you feeling miserable?'

'No,' she said, 'I'm very comfortable.' And she was, almost. The aches had stopped, and as long as she kept her head still, there was no dizziness or nausea. She felt only very light, very weak, very – transparent, as though a breath could blow her straight off the edge of the world.

'Are you still obdurate? You will not eat?'

'I will not,' she managed to say.

He stared at her a moment, and then said, 'Well, I have some good news for you. You are to be released. Do you understand? You are going home.'

She could not speak, could only look her feelings.

'Now, you must be very careful and quiet. Move slowly, or you will faint. I'll have you sent some milk and beaten egg with a little brandy in it, and that should help to get you up. A wardress will help you dress, and then we'll fetch you a cab. Where will you go? Is there someone at home to care for you?'

'Yes, Miss Vaughan,' she said, trying not to cry. They had won, she thought – but the words had no triumph for her. She felt only weary to death with the whole thing. 'Thank you.'

He began to turn away but she called him back with a croak. 'The others?'

'No, only you,' he said. 'I have no orders about the others.'

'I will not leave without them,' she said.

His face creased a little more, and he sighed. 'I was afraid you would say that. Well, I shall telephone, and see what I can do. I think the Home Office will agree now. We really can't have someone like you here, in this condition.'

She drifted again, she did not know for how long. And then he was back, his face registering his extreme relief. She focused on him with difficulty, and made an enquiring noise.

280

'All of you,' he said.

'Thank you,' she said. And then she closed her eyes and thought, *Thank God*.

Lord Overton had heard about the impending releases in the House, and he had gone home on purpose to tell Venetia. A telephone call to the governor and another to Bedford Square meant that when Anne was assisted down to a waiting taxi-cab at about half past eight that evening, Miss Vaughan was sitting in it, looking extremely apprehensive under her hat and clutching a smelling-bottle tightly in her gloved fist in case of need – her ladyship's or her own. Anne did not normally care for Miss Vaughan's company, but on this occasion she was glad to have her there, rather than make that journey alone.

When they arrived at Anne's house, everything was prepared for her reception, a good fire in her bedroom and hot bottles between the sheets, a maid ready with hot water, nourishing broth simmering in the kitchen – and Venetia, stethoscope at the ready, to examine her.

'I am not an invalid,' Anne protested, though in a voice so weak as to contradict her.

Venetia was shocked at the sight of her. She had worked enough among the poor to have seen far worse in the matter of pallor and loss of flesh, but this was *Anne*. 'How could you do this to yourself?' she said, forgetting for an instant that she had vowed not to argue with her cousin on this occasion.

'*I* did not. This is Asquith's doing,' Anne said with a little return of vigour. She longed for a bath, but felt so weak she made do with a wash in hot water, and allowed herself to be undressed and put to bed. But once there, she insisted on sitting up and holding court. 'All sorts of people will be coming to see me,' she said. 'I must receive them.'

Venetia told her sternly to be quiet while she examined her thoroughly. Anne, who had had some broth and was feeling much better, submitted impatiently. 'I am very strong,' she said. 'I have done nothing but lose a little fat.'

Venetia straightened up and said, 'I think you are right. Your heart seems in good order, that is the main thing.'

'A little fasting is not enough to damage the heart of a Farraline,' she said grandly, and then added with something of her old, mischievous look, 'We beat Miss Wallace Dunlop's record, however. Five days! There's something for the book.'

'All the same, Anne,' Venetia said seriously, 'you must never do anything like this again. You escaped unharmed this time, but fasting of this sort, under such conditions, is very injurious. It puts too great a strain on the heart. You have done your part, now let some of the others take over. You are not a young woman.'

'Bosh! I'm only forty-five. Miss Neligan is seventy-six.'

'Miss Neligan did not go on a hunger strike.'

'She would if required,' Anne said. 'I shall do what is needed, and there's no point in asking me not to, because you know I will pay no attention. And in any case, it is my own life, to do as I like with.'

Venetia sighed. 'Well, I've said my piece, delivered my warning – I can do no more. You know that I only say these things because I care about you.'

'Yes, and I do care about you,' Anne replied, more naturally than anything she had said to Venetia so far. 'I am sorry that I worry you. I wish you could feel as wholehearted about the campaign as I do, though I know you don't. But this is my life now. It's all I live for. Try to understand.'

'I understand with my mind, but my heart protests,' Venetia said, and then, at the sound of knocking down below, 'That must be your courtiers, come to pay homage.'

'The first of them,' Anne corrected, a touch of colour coming to her cheeks. 'Let them come up,' she decreed. Her maid went to the door, and Anne called out to her, 'Oh, and tell Simpson to send up champagne.'

'Champagne?' Venetia queried, when the maid had gone.

'Certainly. This is a great victory. We did not sit down under unjust penalty, we forced them to set us free! My friends won't be coming up here with Sunday faces and hushed voices – they will be welcoming a victorious hero.'

Venetia thought of the effect of champagne on a starving body, then shrugged inwardly and let it alone. She had no wish always to play the wet blanket, especially when it would do no good.

And when the first of the friends arrived in the room, she saw that Anne was right: they were bubbling with excitement. One was carrying flowers, another played 'See The Conquering Hero Comes' on a jew's harp, and a third danced round the room shaking a tambourine fluttering with ribbons in the colours. They clustered round the bed, gazing at Anne with hero-worship, begging for her story of what it had been like, eager to tell her of the press coverage there had been and what Mrs Pankhurst had said and how Christabel would be calling on all the hunger-strikers during the evening. There were six of them, all young women, members of the Hot Bloods faction, who looked to Anne as their inspiration.

Anne sat upright against her pillows, beautiful still, perhaps even more ethereally so since her five-day fast; and received their homage with flushed cheeks and bright eyes, lips parted in pleasure. Venetia noted that two of the girls were wearing their hair in the style Anne used; and that Anne was wearing a négligé of silk and lace over her nightgown, unusually feminine and elaborate for her.

Jack Compton had become a regular reader of the *Daily Mail*, not because it had anything interesting to say about the politics or the economy, but because its owner, Lord Northcliffe, who believed very firmly that a newspaper should make the news, not just report it, was a great enthusiast for aviation, as flying in powered aeroplanes was now called. When Wilbur Wright had proved in France the year before that flying was a practical possibility, Lord

Northcliffe had announced in his own newspaper that he would put up a prize for the first man to cross the Channel in an aeroplane. He offered five hundred pounds at first, but when the challenge began to catch hold of public imagination, he increased the prize money to a thousand, and sold a great many extra copies as a result. The details of the competition were published in newspapers all over Europe and North America, heightening the interest and excitement, but it was the *Daily Mail* which had the detail Jack craved, about the likely competitors and their machines.

The attempt was to be made during the month of July, and the crossing was to be at the narrowest part of the Channel, starting from the cliffs of Sangatte, just outside Calais, where, on a clear day, you could just see the white cliffs of Dover. As July progressed, however, the likelihood of a clear day, even a moderately fine day, seemed to diminish. The inhabitants of the French coast of the Channel were philosophical about the familiar blight of rain, wind, and cloud so low as to constitute fog. Still, as every hotel and pension within reasonable distance filled up with aeronauts, engineers, journalists and would-be spectators, everyone, except perhaps the hoteliers and restaurateurs, prayed for a spell of fine weather.

By this stage there were three declared contestants with enough faith in their machines to make the attempt. Twenty-one miles was a long way, especially when an emergency landing would find nothing but salt water beneath you. The French navy had agreed to provide a warship to accompany the attempts, but the dangers were still evident. One competitor was the Comte de Lambert, who had been taught to fly by Wilbur Wright the year before and would be flying a Wright biplane.

The others were Hubert Latham and Louis Blériot. Latham was a very wealthy adventurer of Anglo-French descent, who had already exhausted all the thrills of ballooning, speed-boat racing and big-game hunting, and had begun flying only in April. Blériot was an engineer who had made a fortune in the motor-car business and used it to experiment with heavier-than-air flight.

The interesting thing to Jack was that their aeroplanes were very different from the now-familiar Wright biplane. Both were monoplanes, to begin with, and Jack had conceived a bias in favour of the monoplane, which he was convinced would prove the more useful and viable form once the difficulties of wing-strength were got over. Secondly, the propellor, instead of being behind the wings, was in front (so in a sense was not a propellor at all but – what? – a tractor?) while the tailplane, elevators and rudder were rear-mounted. If the Wright biplane had made a sort of triangle with the point to the front, so to speak, the aeroplanes of the other two competitors made a triangle with the point to the back.

Blériot would be flying a machine of his own design, the Blériot XI, which had an adapted three-cylinder motorcycle engine of 25 horse-power. This, Jack thought, was modest to the point of foolishness, and would never carry the machine and its passenger across the Channel, particularly if there was any wind, which seemed all too likely. His vote was therefore with Hubert Latham who, though he had not been flying long, had great talent and a supremely steady nerve. He was to use the elegant Antoinette IV, which was not only powered with a Levavasseur 50 horse-power engine, but also looked graceful and beautiful. Jack, with his experience in designing speed boats for commercial sale, was now of the view that something ought not just to work but to look as though it was going to.

The 19th of July was the first day on which the weather moderated enough for an attempt to be made. Hubert Latham took the chance, and at a little after half past six in the morning he took off in his pretty Antoinette, watched by an enormous crowd of journalists and enthusiasts. The report in the newspaper said that the mechanical bird dived 'into the light fog that blurred one's view of the uncertain horizon', and described Latham as a new

Icarus. Sadly, like that of Icarus, the attempt was soon over. Shortly after the Antoinette had flown over the accompanying warship, the engine spluttered, coughed, and died. Latham glided down and made a smooth landing on the sea. It was reported that when the French sailors arrived to rescue him, he was seated on top of his machine calmly smoking a cigarette, just as if he was sitting on a garden bench enjoying the sunshine.

The Comte de Lambert had set himself up near Sangatte at Wissant, but his attempt was even shorter-lived, for he crashed during a test flight and was out of the race. That left only Monsieur Blériot, whose aeroplane had been delivered to a nearby farm where it was assembled by his mechanics. The papers reported that the flyer himself was limping heavily, having badly burned his foot in a previous flight when hot oil from the engine had spilled on it. The weather, however, had closed in again, and flying was impossible. On Saturday the 24th of July it was so rough that it looked as though there would be no chance to take off for days. But in the early hours of the Sunday morning, the weather suddenly cleared, and Blériot tested his engine, informed the French navy that he was going to try, and waited for dawn.

At half past four it was light enough to see all around, and Blériot took off at maximum revolutions and flew towards the cliff. It was still very windy, and the sea was rough; visibility was poor, and the flyer had neglected to provide himself with a compass, a watch or a map. The heroic story reported in the papers afterwards told how Blériot had passed over the warship and then, ten minutes or so later, found himself completely alone, with nothing to see in any direction, no destroyer, no France, no England; no way of knowing where he was or, with the sun invisible in the murk, whether he was even going in the right direction. It was a great struggle to keep the aeroplane level; the gusty wind tugged the fragile thing this way and that; the waves seemed to leap for its throat as if trying to bring it down. He flew on until at last he saw the coast of England and, realising he had drifted off course, changed direction. But the wind was adverse and on this new course he had to battle every inch towards the cliffs.

A reporter for the Parisian newspaper *Le Matin* was waiting for him on top of the cliffs near to Dover Castle, and waved him in with a tricolour flag. The aeroplane was caught in gusty side winds and almost turned over, and then Blériot misjudged the landing, switched off the engine too soon and fell the last sixty feet, breaking the propellor and smashing the undercarriage. But he was unharmed, and the prize was his. Official timekeepers announced that he had made the crossing in thirty-seven minutes and twelve seconds.

It was not to be supposed that Lord Northcliffe would allow any particle of newsworthiness to escape his grasp, and very soon Blériot's face, with its dark eyes, jutting nose and long drooping moustaches, was as familiar as the King's. The modest aviator had gone straight back to France by boat, but was obliged by Lord Northcliffe to return to attend a lavish prizegiving and dinner at the Savoy Hotel, take a drive through the streets of London, where large crowds cheered him past, and pose for many photographs, both indoors and on the cliffs of Dover. When he returned again to France, *Le Matin* whisked him off to Paris where he was similarly fêted and cheered, while the French newspaper went one better than the *Daily Mail* by suspending his aeroplane outside its office for the passers-by to wonder at. In both countries the souvenir industry went at once to work, and the face and the tiny, frail aeroplane soon featured on cigarette cards, postcards, matchboxes, plates, mugs and scarves; the magazines and illustrated papers got out special editions and souvenir booklets; his own account, in his slightly stilted English, was printed in full in every publication, and a number of song sheets were rushed out, decorated with imaginative engravings of aeroplanes crossing violently stormy waves. The *Daily Mail*, perhaps not surprisingly, announced that Blériot's flight marked 'the dawn of a new age for man'.

It was not immediately apparent, even to Jack, what this event had to do with his proposing to Maud Puddephat, but there was no doubt that it was the surge of excitement over the whole thing that sent him rushing up to London the following Sunday. Though overcast it was a warm and dry day, so he asked for and was given permission to accompany Miss Puddephat on a walk in the park. They strolled together up Sloane Street, through the Albert Gate and down to the Serpentine, and most of the way he was enthusing to her about Monsieur Blériot's achievement and describing the aeroplane in far more detail than she could, or wanted to, understand.

'I suppose it was very clever of him,' Maud said at last, as he escorted her across Rotten Row, 'but I can't see the point of it. He had to go back to France by boat, didn't he?'

'Only because he crashed his aeroplane on landing. Otherwise he could have flown back there in it.'

'Do you really think he would have wanted to attempt it? From what I read in the papers it was touch-and-go whether he would get across at all.'

Jack had to admit that was true. 'But the aeroplane's engine was really too small. There was nothing wrong with the other fundamentals, and with a larger engine—'

Miss Puddephat was bored. 'Well, I do think he's rather a dreadful-looking little man, with that comic moustache and those glaring eyes. And besides, he's French. I don't see that all this flying is so exciting when it only happens in France.'

'It *started* in France,' Jack corrected, 'but it won't stay there. Now people have had a chance to see what can be done, it will be starting up over here, too. In fact, I heard someone say that Lord Northcliffe means to offer another prize next year for a long flight in England – from Manchester to London, or something of the sort. Lord,' he added fervently, 'I should like to have a crack at that!'

'You, drive a flying machine?' Miss Puddephat exclaimed.

'I'm sure I could learn, if I only had the chance,' Jack said, a little hurt.

'I expect you could,' she said indifferently, 'but I shouldn't like you to take the risk. You might be hurt, or even killed.'

Jack felt the blood rush to his head. 'Should you mind if I were hurt?'

'Of course I should,' she said. 'I've known you a very long time.'

'Are you – fond of me?'

'Of course I am,' she said calmly, but with a touch of pink coming to her cheeks as well.

They turned on to the path that ran along the edge of the Serpentine, and Jack felt there could hardly be a better moment. The birds were singing, the sun was almost shining, and all along the bank little children were feeding ducks in a timelessly romantic way. And, most importantly, the maid – who, like most London servants, hated walking – was dawdling a reasonable distance behind, out of earshot.

'There is a very good reason for my wanting to try for Lord Northcliffe's prize,' he said, a little breathlessly, for his excitement and nervousness were making his chest tight. 'Apart from wanting to fly, that is. It's because if I won, I would have something very particular that I should like to do with the money.'

'With a thousand pounds? It is such a huge sum, I should think anyone would have an idea how they would spend it.'

'Don't you want to know what mine is?' And before she could answer either way, he hurried on, 'I would like to spend it all on you – on us – on setting up. That is—' He untangled his tongue, turned to face her, and said, 'Oh, Miss Puddephat – Maud – will you marry me? You must know I've been in love with you for years and years, and even without Lord Northcliffe's prize, I've something put away, and very good prospects in my career. I'm not rich yet, but I mean to be one day. Will you? You said you cared for me.'

In what looked rather like a defensive gesture she put up her parasol and, from the safety of its shade, said, 'I don't know what to say.'

'Say "yes",' he prompted.

But she didn't smile. 'I am fond of you, but I hadn't thought about marriage.'

'Think of it now,' he urged.

'But I don't want to,' she said. 'No, please don't say any more. I do like you but I'm not sure if I want to marry you. And I *am* sure I don't want to marry anyone just yet. I'm happy as I am, living with Mother and Father and seeing my friends and doing all the things I like—'

'But you could still do all those things if we were married,' Jack said. 'We wouldn't have to live in Southampton. I could move up to London – there are plenty of companies and plenty of openings for design engineers.'

'But I don't want to *be* married – not yet – not for a long time,' she said. 'I don't see the point of it.'

It was the deadly phrase with which she had condemned aviation. He said slowly, 'Is there someone else? Forgive me but – I know you will be honest with me. Are you in love with someone?'

'No,' she said, and she sounded almost cross. 'Why should you think so? Why should a person *have* to want to get married, when they have a comfortable home and everything they need just as they are?'

Jack didn't answer. The maid had almost caught up with them. They turned side by side and walked on. After a bit, his spirits rose again. If she *wasn't* in love with someone else, and she *did* care for him . . .

'Well, then,' he said quietly, 'I won't tease you, but if there isn't anyone else, I reserve the right to go on loving you, and to keep hoping that you will change your mind. Will you allow me to propose to you again one day? And if you find you begin to feel differently about marrying, will you tell me?'

She did not answer at once; and then she said, 'I might as well tell you that I don't think Father would allow me to marry you anyway. You see, now that poor Ray is gone, I'm his only heir, so everything will come to me. I think there will be an awful lot of it, too.'

For some reason, Jack did not find this discouraging. He walked on, shortening his stride to fit in with her feminine steps, and looked hopefully towards the horizon. 'Oh, don't worry about that. I shall find a way to persuade your father when the time comes. And as I said, I mean to be rich one day. Engineers will be much in demand from now on, you'll see. I'm going to design the best aeroplane engine there's ever been, and people will be flocking to my door. In fact, I mean to design the whole aeroplane.'

'I can't see who is going to want to buy them,' Miss Puddephat said – rather shortly, finding the subject had gone back to those infernal machines again.

'Aviation is the future,' Jack said; and to be fair to him, he had been saying it since he was fourteen. Miss Puddephat herself had heard him say it many times when she had stayed with her parents at Morland Place. He had said man would fly one day and he had been proved right about that (if the newspapers could be believed about Monsieur Blériot's feat, which she felt she must reluctantly accept this time as so many of them agreed on it). Perhaps he would be proved right again, and that some practical use might one day be found for flying machines, unlikely as it seemed to her. In the mean time, as the beloved only daughter of a rich man, living in London and enjoying its many pleasures, she saw no reason to want to change anything about her life.

The following week brought a dramatic change to both their lives. Jack had no invitation to the Puddephats the next Sunday, but he went up to London to visit Lizzie and Frank. He took as a present for the boys, who had been aeroplane mad for two whole weeks now, a construction kit of a model Blériot XI, which he had seen prominently displayed in the window of a shop in Southampton, surrounded by Blériot souvenirs and beside a large photograph of the man himself in a frame draped in red-white-and-blue ribbons and rosettes. After luncheon, having helped Martial and Rupert begin the construction, having told them over again everything he knew about Blériot's adventure, with quite a few embellishments of his own, and having sufficiently dandled, smiled at and admired his little niece, he felt it was only polite to pay his respects in Pont Street before catching his train home.

When he reached the house, however, he found the downstairs front blinds were drawn, and with a terrible foreboding he trod up the path and knocked at the door. After a long wait, it was opened by a young maid with red eyes and a swollen nose, who looked at him in bewilderment before belatedly seeming to recognise him.

'Oh, Mr Compton!' she said. 'I didn't know – was you expected, sir?'

'No, I just called in as I was passing. But, Hannah, what's the matter? I see the blinds are drawn. It's not – not trouble, is it?'

Her eyes filled with tears, obviously not for the first time that day. 'Oh, sir, it's the poor mistress! She passed away in her sleep last night. Dawkins found her this morning when she took her tea in. It was such a shock! I'm sure no-one expected it, for she was right as rain last night, only a bit tired, Dawkins said, when she undressed her. But I saw her after dinner when I took the coals into the drawing-room, and she seemed all right then. And now – and now she's gone!' The tears spilled over and her face crumpled. Jack tentatively patted her arm, and then in a rush of chivalry pulled out his handkerchief and gave it to her.

'Thank you, sir, ever so much. Oh, the poor mistress! And now we're all at sixes and sevens, the house in an uproar, the master and Miss Maud prostrated in their rooms and the cook weeping her eyes out, if you'll believe me. I put the blinds down myself this morning, only I haven't had a minute to put crape round the knocker. When you knocked, I thought it was the – the *undertaker's man!*' A fresh burst of tears accompanied the horrid words.

Jack was very shaken. He had always liked quiet Mrs Puddephat, and he knew how deeply Mr Puddephat was attached to her, to say nothing of Maud.

'I'm so sorry,' he said quietly.

Hannah blew her nose and gained a measure of control. 'I beg your pardon, sir, but I don't think the master can see you now, or Miss Maud.'

'Of course not. I wouldn't expect it.' He drew out a card and gave it to her. 'Please don't disturb them now, but when the master comes down next, would you give him my card and my very deepest sympathies to them both? Can you remember that?'

'Deepest sympathies, yes, sir.'

'And tell him – and Miss Maud – that I will write my condolences. I am so very sorry.'

He touched his hat and walked away, abandoning his handkerchief and any immediate hopes of renewing his suit. Only a cad would think of courting a girl while she was in mourning, which meant six months at least before he could make anything but the most formal of calls. Still, perhaps it was as well, given what Miss Puddephat had said when they last met. When mourning was over, she might find there was a hole in her life that had not been there before, and which a dear friend might fill by becoming, over time, a lover. In the mean while, he felt sincerely sorry for them in their loss, and he spent the journey home on the train beginning the composition in his mind of a suitable letter of condolence.

At Morland Place, the news of Mrs Puddephat's death came as a surprise, and all were very sorry.

'It was her heart, apparently,' said Teddy, who had a mysterious way of always knowing things. The letter from

Mr Puddephat had only said 'suddenly', but his friend Havergill knew someone who knew the doctor who had attended Mrs Puddephat for years and had said it could have happened at any time.

Teddy and Jerome both wrote letters of condolence; Teddy planned to attend the funeral on the family's behalf, and ordered a very large and expensive wreath to express the sadness of everyone in the house. 'Puddephat will be at a terrible loss,' he said. 'He doted on her. And that poor girl, little Maud – what will she do without a mother?'

'She's not such a little girl now,' Henrietta reminded him.

'Still, there's no good age for a girl to lose her mother,' said Alice, feelingly.

Henrietta agreed; but later, when they were alone, Jerome said to her, 'What was it you were thinking when we were talking about Mrs Puddephat's death?'

'What can you mean?' Henrietta said; but her expression betrayed a consciousness.

'Oh, I don't know precisely,' Jerome said, 'but I was watching your face, and there was something. I know you very well, and there was something on your mind.'

'You will laugh at me if I tell you. Or, worse still, think badly of me.'

'Don't be silly. Why should I?'

'It was a silly thing to think. And not very nice, perhaps. But I couldn't help it.'

'Tell me. I shan't let you alone until you do.'

She looked at him, resting on the sofa with his feet up, as he did every afternoon now; saw the sunlight from the window striking his face – such a pale face, and the eyes so deep set. He was better than he had been, but Dr Hasty had gently prepared her for the idea that he would never be really well again. He was still here, though, that was the main thing. She loved him so much that she wanted to seize hold of him, so that nothing could snatch him away from her.

'I was thinking,' she said slowly, 'that poor Mrs Puddephat made the third death.'

'The third death?'

'You know the old saying, that deaths always come in threes. There was Mary, and then Perry – and now Mrs Puddephat makes three. I'm very, very sorry – I liked her very much – but the horrid, superstitious part of me is glad that it was her and not—' She didn't finish.

He looked at her with tenderness; with amusement and, underneath it, sadness. 'Oh, my poor love, is that where you are? You've been waiting ever since January for me to hang up my tile?'

'No!' she protested.

But he held out his arms. 'Come here!' And she crossed the room, and he swung his legs to the ground and took her on to his knee, holding her close in their familiar way. She felt the warmth of his arms around her and her heart swelled with a desperate love and longing. Just now she couldn't get close enough to him. 'Well, darling,' he said, resting his cheek against her hair, 'I'm still here, and glad to be. I suppose I'll have to go one day—'

'No,' she said, and he hugged her tighter.

'—but don't let's spoil the present by worrying about the future. I love you so much, my darling girl.'

She was long past girlhood, but she felt like a girl wrapped inside his love. 'I love you too, so very much.' And after a moment, in a very low voice, 'Please don't leave me.'

'Not for a long time,' he said. 'Not ever, if I can help it.' They sat entwined like young lovers for a long time, not speaking; and when a footman came in to light the fire – for the afternoons were cold, this damp, stormy summer – they did not move, and he backed silently out again, hoping they had not seen him.

Chapter Ten

Since Monsieur Blériot's feat had filled the newspapers, all of France had gone aeroplane mad: now at last they had something they could crow about, having taken the lead in aviation over the rest of Europe, America, and most of all the old enemy, Britain. 'France leads the world!' the newspapers cried. Rich sportsmen were putting in orders for their own personal Blériot and flying lessons to go with it, and any article that could manage to get the image of him or his machine on to its packaging or into its advertisements was sure to have an advantage over its rivals.

But the event that took place in Rheims in the August of 1909 had been long in the planning, though it received a fillip from the Blériot excitement. It was called the 'Grande Semaine d'Aviation de la Champagne' and was sponsored by the great champagne houses, who knew the value of a popular craze as well as anyone selling matches or sheet music. It was to take place between the 22nd and 29th of August on the bare open plain of Bétheny, outside Rheims, the capital of the champagne country. In anticipation of a huge number of spectators, the sponsors had even built a railway branch line to bring them from Rheims to the showground. Large prizes had been advertised to ensure that all the leading aviators and aeroplane designers would find it worth their while attending. Restaurants and bars had been built on the site for the convenience of spectators, and enormous grandstands for the wealthy to watch in seated comfort.

Jack read everything he could find about it, and longed inexpressibly to be able to be there. It astonished him that in only a year since Wilbur Wright had first demonstrated the possibility of controlled flight to the French, aviation had progressed so much that a complete air show was possible, at which it was rumoured thirty flyers would compete in forty different aeroplanes. As late as the previous October, newspapers had still been doubting the word of those who reported having seen the Wright plane leave the ground; now there was to be an aerial display so important and respectable that the former President of America, 'Teddy' Roosevelt, would be attending it, along with the President of France, Armand Fallières, and from Britain, the Chancellor of the Exchequer, Mr David Lloyd George.

There would also be a large number of high-ranking military officers from countries all around the world, though not from Britain. This struck Jack, even through his general excitement, as worrying. If Blériot could cross the Channel in something powered with a motorcycle engine, what might an enemy not do with something bigger? That strip of water, commanded by the invincible British navy, had protected the country for centuries from invasion, but given how rapidly aviation had progressed in one year, how long would that hold true? That a fleet of aeroplanes might one day land an army in the heart of England did not now seem impossible and, what Jack could imagine, plainly a German warmonger might.

To design and build aeroplanes now seemed to him not only something he longed to do for his own pleasure, but something that ought to be done for the safety of the country. It was another reason for his wanting to go to Rheims, but he assumed that it would be impossible, until the day when he called in Pont Street and learned that Mrs Puddephat had died.

Late August was a quiet time, when those who wanted to sail had already bought their boats, and the plans for the next season had not yet begun; a time for clearing one's desk, tidying one's drawers and sharpening one's pencils. Suppose he asked for two weeks' leave of absence from Mr Rankin? He would not be able to see Maud for some time, and he had quite a bit saved, which he would not now need in the immediate future. He could easily forgo two weeks of his salary, and a ticket to Rheims and two weeks' accommodation in the cheapest kind of boarding house would surely not cost so very much.

He made enquiries and discovered that there was an excursion ticket on offer from Victoria Station, which was quite surprisingly affordable; and so he made his approach to Mr Rankin. Though his master had always treated him well, he was not the sort of person one would ever enjoy asking favours of, and he expected disapproval, perhaps a downright, unsoftenable 'no'.

But Mr Rankin did not even seem to think a great deal about it before he said, 'I don't see why you should not go. In fact, I have been pondering myself whether there might be anything in it for us. There are points of similarity in the principles of sailing and flying, are there not?'

'Oh, yes, sir. The engine and propellor perform much the same function, and engine weight is even more important to the aeroplane than it is to the speed-boat. And I have been thinking lately that the stream-line will be important to a body moving through air as it is in a body moving through water – though, of course, that is for the future, when speed becomes important.'

'So you think it might prove instructive to attend? Perhaps useful to future designs for Rankin Marine?' Jack had not thought in those terms, and was too honest to pretend that he had. While he hesitated, Mr Rankin went on, 'You have often spoken about the future of aeroplanes, and I have seen some of your sketches. Do you really think there will be a demand for aeroplanes?'

Jack answered carefully. 'Things seem to be developing very quickly, and I believe if we could look forward five years, we would find a steady and increasing market for serviceable aeroplanes.'

'Hm,' said Rankin. 'Well, I am not so old that I can't embrace a new idea, and I have great faith in you, my boy. Suppose you go, then – and, what's more, I will contribute to your expenses. Learn everything you can, make notes, take sketches, talk to the other engineers, find out if there are any commercial applications that might benefit us. You had better leave on the day before it begins so that you can be there from the start.' His eyes were bright, and he rubbed his hands. 'I rather begin to take to the idea. I almost think of going myself instead.' Jack's heart sank, but his master went on at once, 'However, you understand more about aviation than I do, so you will get more out of it. It had better be you.'

'Yes, sir,' Jack said happily.

As he was going out of the room, something struck Mr Rankin. 'Do you speak French, Compton?'

'I learned it at school, sir, which is rather a long time ago now. But thanks to those magazines you have been letting me read, I have kept up with the technical words for things. I think I can manage.'

'Take a good dictionary with you,' Mr Rankin advised. 'I was in France once years ago – it was on my honeymoon, as it happens – and I found the French extremely stubborn about understanding what one said.'

'I will, sir. Thank you,' said Jack.

It was the first time he had been abroad, and everything about it was exciting. He enjoyed the train ride and the Channel crossing. Coming in at Calais and seeing the porters on the dockside with their blue smocks and funny caps and very French moustaches, he realised properly for the first time that this was foreign soil. The French train was different from an English one, with much harder seats and a very queer notion of what constituted a sandwich, though the coffee was excellent. He looked out with interest at the flat French countryside and the stations they passed through with the unknown French names and the low platforms. France was certainly not pretty like England, and the little villages they passed all seemed strangely deserted and the houses all shuttered up. But some of the larger towns looked interesting, though he was surprised that they had not more churches: you never went a mile in England without seeing a spire or a tower. In his carriage there were two other aeroplane-mad young men, with whom he soon struck up a conversation. They talked aviation all the way to Rheims, and though his knowledge outstripped theirs, he was happy to have someone to talk to, and answered their questions with great good will.

Arriving in Rheims, he had his first significant conversations in French, and found that the native people did not speak it at all like his teacher at school. In fact, the very name of the town turned out not to be pronounced as it was written, or in any logical manner at all. It also proved unexpectedly hard to find cheap lodgings, though he supposed afterwards he should have expected the town to be full. There were places still at the more expensive hotels, but though Mr Rankin was paying his fare, his other expenses were his own and he was not eager to part with too many guineas for the mere provision of a bed to sleep in.

He tramped the streets for some time without success, until at last, driven by hunger into a bakery where he bought a roll of bread from the remarkably pretty girl behind the counter, he thought to ask in his hesitant school French if she knew of anywhere with a bed to spare. She supposed that Monsieur was going to the *exposition d'aviation*, to which he concurred, and when she learned that he was *ingénieur* she at once and generously assumed he was also *aviateur*, an impression his French was not good enough fully to correct. The idea that he had something to do with the building of aeroplanes made him a hero in the present circumstances, and she took his plight very much to heart. She racked her brains, tapping her teeth with a fingernail, and having regretted that the *pensions* with which she was acquainted were *tous*

300

pleins, she at last demanded of herself whether Tante Marie might be willing to offer him *le lit de mon cousin Henri*, who was away in Paris on some business Jack never managed to understand.

There followed some rapid exchanges (in a French that was like a raging torrent to Jack's sluggish trickle) with a woman who came out from the back, wiping her hands on her apron, and interventions from a man as tall, gaunt and white-whiskered as an old horse, who followed her and looked Jack over with a thorough and very frank appraisal. At last the pretty girl took off her apron, put on her coat and hat and, with an enchanting smile, held out her hand to Jack and invited him to accompany her to Tante Marie's house. A brisk – and it seemed to him very long – walk through the streets brought them to a small dwelling in a not-very-prosperous street on the outskirts of the town. Here the young woman conducted a long conversation, of which Jack did not understand one word, with the lady of the house, a plump little matron with a strong look of the pretty girl in her face. At the end of it, Tante Marie smiled, shook Jack's hand vigorously and said that of course he could have Henri's room for the week. It would be an honour to accommodate an aviator at such a time. Jack did not even attempt to argue about it this time, accepting the benefits of his false identity. The room he was shown to was tiny and the bed narrow and hard, but the house seemed clean and he was beyond being over-nice in his requirements. When the pretty girl had taken her smiling departure, Tante Marie came down to business and in a slow and careful French, so that he would be sure to understand, she drove a hard bargain for the price of his occupancy, together with breakfast and supper in the evening, supposing that he would be all day at the *exposition* and therefore not want dinner at midday.

That settled, she took him back downstairs, showed him where the lavatory was (out of the back door and through a yard full of chicken coops) and sat him at the kitchen table with a bowl of *potage* and a chunk of bread while she went upstairs again to put clean sheets on Henri's bed. The soup was a *mélange* of vegetables and white beans, the bread was excellent, and the meal was enhanced by what seemed the cheeringly automatic addition of a little brown pitcher of red wine. A man whom Tante Marie had introduced as '*mon mari*, Georges' sat meanwhile in a tall-backed chair by the kitchen range reading the newspaper and occasionally making remarks about what he was reading to Jack. He repeated them slowly, with many civil and encouraging nods, but Jack could make little of it, and was reduced in the end to smiling and saying '*Oui*' and '*D'accord*' as if he understood. Georges was a small man who had the same long drooping moustaches as Monsieur. Blériot. He was in his shirtsleeves and, remarkably, his cap – Jack was never to see it off his head in a whole week – but he did his best by his unexpected guest, unfailingly tried to engage him in conversation and refilled his little pitcher as often as Jack would allow it.

With the problem of his accommodation solved, Jack was free to enjoy the *Grande Semaine d'Aviation*. Everything at the showground had been beautifully arranged. There was a racecourse just over six miles long, around a number of small towers, called pylons, from which observers, judges and timekeepers could watch the events. There was a large grandstand for the wealthy spectators, and a smaller one for dignitaries and guests of the sponsors, both of which were supplied with buffets serving cold food and champagne all through the day. There was yet another for press men and photographers, while the holders of cheap tickets stood in the open behind the ropes marking off the course. There was a gigantic restaurant seating six hundred where the *haute cuisine* was of the highest standard, and several smaller ones serving sandwiches and other snacks, and bars with wine and beer as well as the ubiquitous champagne. Over the week, two hundred thousand spectators passed through the gates.

Thirty-eight aeroplanes had been entered for the various competitions, and there were twenty-three flyers taking part, some of whom shared aeroplanes, others of whom were able to fly several different ones. The flyers were mostly Frenchmen, and included Hubert Latham and Henri Farman (both of whom, Jack thought proudly, had English blood), the Comte de Lambert and, of course, Louis Blériot, the hero of the hour, as well as another darling of the crowd, Louis Paulhan, a mechanic who had recently won an aeroplane in a newspaper competition and had taught himself to fly it (thereby selling an enormous number of extra copies and tempting a number of other newspaper proprietors to think about competitions of their own). There was one English flyer, George Cockburn, and one American, Glenn Curtiss. The Wright brothers were not present. Having proved to Europe that flight was possible, they seemed to have lost interest in the old world and gone home.

More interesting to Jack even than the flyers were the aeroplanes. Of the thirty-eight machines entered, only twenty-three eventually managed to take off – yet still that was an astonishing number for a science only a year old. Eight of them were 'tractor' monoplanes with the propellor to the front and the elevator to the rear, most of them Blériots and Antoinettes; fifteen were 'pusher' biplanes, with the elevator in front and the propellor behind, and they included Wrights, Voisins and the Henri Farman III. There was one oddity, which interested Jack very much, which was a tractor biplane, designed by a man called Louis Breguet. Jack's prejudice in favour of the monoplane acknowledged that the weakness of the single wing was a drawback, and he wondered whether the tractor biplane might combine the best features of both. Though the Breguet did not do more than a few hops at Rheims, Jack was able to have several long and stimulating conversations with the designer himself. He was soon discovered to be an engineer and not just an enthusiast, after which the flyers and their engineers and mechanics made him welcome around their machines, answered all his questions and listened to his ideas with interest. Soon he was helping to run the planes up, turn them, hold them ready for take-off; and, even more interestingly, was often to be found with a spanner in his hand, specks of oil on his face, and the inside of an engine exposed to his view.

The engines were the universal weak point of flying, being unreliable, and not powerful enough to compensate for their weight. A lightweight, powerful engine was obviously the priority if flying was to become practical, and Jack began to have an idea where his talents ought to take him. The most promising development he saw at Rheims was the Gnôme rotary engine that was mounted in the Henri Farman III. Instead of having fixed cylinders around a rotating crankshaft, the cylinders themselves spun round with the propellor, which generated more power as a ratio of the weight. The drawback was that it created a gyroscopic effect, which made the aeroplane difficult to control, but that, he thought, was something he could work on back home in his leisure moments.

The other great problem at Rheims was the weather. The cold wet summer continued with rain and strong winds, and aeroplanes could only fly in good weather. The first day of the meeting had such torrential rain and gusty wind that nothing could take off at all, and the excited crowd grew gradually more bored and restive as the hours went by with nothing to see. But late in the afternoon the rain stopped and the wind died down enough for three Wrights to start up their engines, run along the track and leap into the air. Most of the spectators had never actually seen an aeroplane fly, and for all that they had heard and read in the papers, the actual sight was an astonishing one. A composite gasp rose as from one throat, and there were startled cries, cheers and applause, and a babble of delighted conversation as the Wrights swooped up and down and banked to turn round the pylons.

Jack, of course, was among those who had never seen a demonstration of flight, and though he had been dreaming of it since his youth, and had probably read more about it than most people there, he was still stunned with excitement and wonder. He watched in silence with a dry mouth, one part of his brain still hardly able to believe that there was a man up there, being carried through the air, twenty, thirty, even forty feet above the ground; flying like a bird, as man had longed in his secret heart to do since the dawn of time. He felt he could stand and watch it for ever; more than that, he conceived a fierce desire to do it himself.

As the week progressed, the weather continued to cause problems, but now that the reality had been established the spectators were willing to wait patiently through the long periods of inaction for the fascination of another display. There were many crashes, caused either by engine failure or a mistake by an aviator, none of whom had much experience, given how new flying was. Some tried to make too tight a turn, some to climb too steeply, others flew too close to the ground and struck some irregularity. To see an aeroplane drop out of the air and strike the ground was a shock, but also a thrill, and added to the excitement of anticipation. Sometimes the ground was littered with the fragile wreckage of crashed aeroplanes; one burst into flames because of a ruptured fuel line.

Landing was the most difficult manoeuvre and the most likely to lead to a crash, as the flyer had not only to come down at the right, gradual angle, but had to cut the engine just at the right moment to reduce his speed enough to land: too soon, and he dropped out of the air like a stone; too late, and he would plough the nose into the earth. An engine cutting out at height was, oddly enough, less of a danger, since the aeroplanes were light and glided well, so it was generally possible to make a reasonable landing. Towards the end of the week, a further difficulty revealed itself as the weather improved and the air warmed up. This created areas of turbulence and when an aeroplane entered one it might suddenly drop a dozen feet or more, as though the supporting air had suddenly disappeared from underneath it, or be flipped up and over in the air like a coin. There was one area of the racecourse where this happened so often that by the end of the week it had become known as 'the graveyard' and was marked out by a litter of wood, wire and canvas from crashed machines.

But despite all the accidents, no-one was badly hurt. The prizes for the highest speed over two laps and, the following day, three laps were both won by the American Glenn Curtiss, much to the disappointment of the crowd. However, they applauded him sportingly for his achievement of 47m.p.h. and 46½ m.p.h. respectively – though not as much as they applauded Louis Blériot for his 47⅔ m.p.h. over one circuit. The distance prize was won by Henri Farman, who flew a remarkable 112 miles – a record – before running out of fuel. The distance was done by circuits of the track, and by the end of three hours the crowd was applauding and cheering each extra circuit with an enthusiasm bordering on hysteria. The altitude prize was won by Hubert Latham at a terrifying 509 feet in his Antoinette, and was perhaps the most impressive of the competitions to watch. All other flights took place close to the ground, for the reason that if you were going to crash it was better to do it from no more than twenty feet up; so to see the tiny aeroplane dwindle into a speck as it climbed higher and higher into the blue sky was breathtaking.

But for Jack the most exciting thing of all was the incomparable moment when Henri Farman took him up in his biplane. He could hardly believe he had under-stood correctly when the laconical bearded flyer, with his cigarette always jutting nonchalantly from between his lips, made the offer, and he had to have it repeated before he delightedly, stammeringly accepted. The Farman II was a box-kite biplane, and there was no passenger seat, of course – there was barely a seat for the pilot, just a

little basket at the front edge of the centre of the wing –
but there was a small space behind that, between the
pilot's place and the radiator.

'*Vous n'aurez pas peur?*' Farman enquired, and when
Jack hastily disclaimed anything approaching fear, he
advised him to button his coat at the neck and turn his
cap around so that the peak was to the rear, and invited
him to climb up. Jack had to scramble up on to the wing
and crouch down in the space behind the pilot's seat,
holding on to one of the struts for balance. Farman
climbed up and wedged himself in front – with his feet
on the rudder bar, his knees were up to his chest – tested
the controls, and then shouted to the mechanic to start
her up. The mechanic disappeared behind to swing the
propellor; the engine, which was warm from a previous
flight, caught immediately; and they began to trundle
forward along the track.

'*Ça va?*' Farman shouted back to him.

'Yes! *Oui*! Go on,' Jack shouted back, too excited to
remember the French for things. The ground underneath
the large, light wheels was hard and rough, and as their
speed increased he expected to be jolted about, perhaps
even jerked from his perch, but in fact the motion was
unexpectedly smooth. They tore along, the ground a blur
beneath them; the radiator against Jack's back became
uncomfortably hot; the air rushed past his face. And then
suddenly there was a new sensation, something extraordinary, something it would not have been possible to
imagine beforehand. He had had time over the days of
watching flyers to wonder whether one would know the
moment when one left the ground, and now he had his
answer. There was a feeling of lightness all around him,
together with the merest sensation of tug somewhere in
the very centre of himself, as though the earth on which
he had been born and would one day die and to which
until now he had been fixed had not quite wanted to let
him go. And then they were flying – they were flying!
They were not touching the ground any more, there was

air all around them and under them, and they were dashing through it in this inexpressibly effortless way. He looked down. The ground was dropping further away beneath them, twenty feet, thirty feet, and he felt an instant's stab of fright, which was his old earthbound self telling him that if he fell from this height he would be hurt, perhaps badly. But the rapture of the experience was too strong for fear to have any chance with him. The feeling of lightness was intoxicating. He felt as though he could have left the aeroplane and flown by himself. He wanted to go higher and higher. He wanted never to stop. He felt as though he had been only half alive before. He gulped the air as it rushed past him, drunk with bliss.

'*Ça va?*' Farman shouted to him again.

'It's wonderful!' he shouted back. '*Incroyable! Magnifique!*' There were no words for the wonder of it. He looked down and felt no fear now, only a sort of amusement that the earth and the things on it could look so small and unimportant. This was how birds must see things. How odd the top of people's heads looked, with their bodies foreshortened underneath; motor cars looked like toys. If you got high enough, he thought, you would feel like God. It occurred to him that you could make wonderfully accurate maps by looking down from an aeroplane and drawing what you saw. No, better still, photographing it. He wondered if the maps they had always relied on would actually prove to be right when they were checked from the sky.

And then, all too soon, it was over. They were lower, lower, the earth came rushing towards them greedily, eager to claim them back. The engine was cut, the air-rush filling the silence; the wheels struck the ground, they bounced with an amazing springiness back into the air, and then struck a second time, and this time were held by the earth, which allowed them to run along its surface but not to leave it again. As they slowed with the friction of the rough ground the mechanics came running alongside, to catch hold of them and bring them to a stop.

Jack found his arms and legs shaking from the strain of his crouched position, his face and fingers burning from the cold. It was always cold on an aeroplane, he had read that somewhere. Someone was helping him to scramble down across the wing, and then his feet were on grass, and he could almost feel old Mother Earth hanging on to him, an errant son returned.

'Well, *mon vieux*, you have enjoyed it?' Farman asked in French, jumping down lightly and at once lighting a cigarette.

'It was the most wonderful experience of my life,' Jack answered fervently, finding his vocabulary now. 'Thank you! I can't thank you enough.'

Farman smiled. 'Perhaps we shall make a flyer out of you.'

'I should like it more than anything,'

'I have tried bicycle racing and motor-car racing and I have been up in a balloon, but nothing compares with flying.'

'I agree with you,' said Jack, and then he laughed. 'I *can* agree with you now. I always thought it would be wonderful, but now I know!'

'Ah,' said Farman wisely, 'you have been infected with the lust to fly. You will never get rid of it now!'

It was not quite possible for Violet to engage a new maid without telling anybody – someone, after all, would have to pay her wages and allocate her somewhere to sleep, if nothing more. So when her mother wrote to say she had found exactly the right person – someone, moreover, who was originally from the north of Norfolk and would understand the weather – it was necessary for Violet to summon up her courage and approach her husband on the subject.

She enquired of one of the footmen, and learning that Brancaster was alone in the library she hurried there as fast as her size would allow to catch him before he left or someone else arrived. She entered the library quietly and saw him at the large writing-table at the far end. The room was on the north side of the house and therefore always cold, and the smell of must was stronger in here than anywhere else: the odour of quietly rotting books that no-one would ever read again. If it were hers, she thought, she would have a fire lit in the library every day to keep the books dry, as they did at home. There was an enormous fireplace at either end of the long room but fires were never lit except in the rooms in common use – and even then, she always thought, grudgingly, for no-one ever came to make them up unless she rang. At home, once a servant had lit a fire they came automatically to refresh it at intervals.

But she told herself she should not think about home too much: it was disloyal, and it might start up her home-sickness again, which she had conquered with such effort. Brancaster had not heard her come in, it seemed, for his head remained bent over the papers he was reading, and as she came closer she saw he was frowning. He looked careworn, and she felt a little surge of love and sympathy for him.

'I beg your pardon,' she said, and he started and looked up.

'Oh! I didn't hear you come in. Is there something you want?' The question was cordial enough, but he kept his finger on the place where he had stopped reading, as if he meant to start again very soon.

'I should like to speak to you about something,' she said. It began firmly inside her mind but by the time it reached the air it sounded wistful.

Brancaster seemed to think for a moment before removing his finger, straightening his shoulders and saying, 'Yes, of course. What is it?' He seemed belatedly to realise something was lacking, and rose to his feet. 'You had better sit down,' he said, coming round the table to take up one of the chairs standing against the wall and place it for her. She sat, and he stood for a moment, looking down at her. 'You are well?' he asked.

'Oh, yes, thank you, quite well,' she said. The minor unpleasantnesses of pregnancy were not what she would discuss with him. 'It's not that. The thing is, that I am not quite satisfied with my maid. She is a good girl but not very clever, and she hasn't much experience.'

'Your maid?' he said blankly. 'Did you not choose her yourself?'

She looked at him doubtfully, unsure what the question involved. 'Well – no. She just came.'

'Just *came*?'

She tried going a little further back. 'My own maid, the one I had when we were married – Sanders – she didn't like it here and she left. And on the same day Sibsey came.' He shook his head, still puzzled. 'I think she is a local girl,' Violet added.

'I suppose Disney must have arranged it,' he said. 'He has grown rather dictatorial over the years, and runs the servants' hall like a private fiefdom. Since my mother died, I dare say my father was happy enough for Disney to recruit any servants that were needed without the bother of being consulted. No doubt this girl is a relative or the daughter of a friend.'

'Oh,' said Violet. There was nothing really *wrong* with Sibsey, only that she was stupid and sniffed because her nose ran all the time; and Violet did not want to upset Disney because she was afraid of him. He not only seemed the paradigm of all the oldness and ugliness and twisted-ness and mouldiness of the household, but had a ferocious temper and a cold, satirical eye as well. And he had been with Lord Holkam for forty years. She knew that Disney and his lordship enjoyed a very close relationship, and she was afraid now that criticising Sibsey might imply criticism of her father-in-law. She said carefully, 'I don't mean to complain. I'm sure Sibsey is a very nice girl, but—'

'She's a little rustic?'

Relief flooded through her that he was being sym-pathetic. 'Yes, that's just it,' she said quickly. 'And when I was in London my mother thought she would not quite do for someone in my position, and she writes today that she has found the perfect maid for me, who is willing to come, and I would like very much to have her, so I wondered . . .' Her sentence petered out.

But Brancaster said, 'There's no reason why you should not have a London maid. Quite the opposite, in fact. A local girl does not—' He stopped, obviously having thought of something. Violet looked at him enquiringly. He went on, 'Disney needs taking down a peg. It's not good for servants to have too much of their own way.'

'Then shall I speak to him?' Violet asked, not relishing the thought.

'No, no,' Brancaster said hastily. 'I will do it. Do not mention the matter to him at all – in fact, you had better not talk to him about any of the servants. He can be touchy – and you would not want my father to feel you were dissatisfied with his arrangements?'

'No, indeed!'

'I'll speak to Disney today, and you can arrange for the girl to come down as soon as you like. There is no need for my father to know anything about it. He never leaves his room now.'

'Thank you,' Violet said fervently; and, seeing that he was disposed to be kind, she thought it a good time to raise the other question. 'May I ask you something else? Do you know what arrangements have been made for my – um – my lying-in?'

'Arrangements? What sort of arrangements?'

'About a doctor and midwife and nurse and so on,' she said, in a small voice. It was obvious he had not given the matter any thought.

'Ah! Yes – well – I suppose something had better be done. I don't know what is usual in these matters. I have never—'

'No, of course not,' Violet said.

Brancaster pulled himself together. 'I shall speak to my father about it. You will have the best of care, you need not worry about that.'

312

It emerged that, although it had not occurred to Brancaster that medical attention was usual during childbirth, his father had the matter well in hand. Lord Holkam wanted to see the succession secured. He was hanging on to the bitter lees of his life on purpose to witness the event, and had no intention of allowing the slightest avoidable risk to be taken with the baby. He had already made all the arrangements for doctor, midwife, month nurse and nursemaid. It had not, of course, occurred to him to inform the mother, any more than it had occurred to Brancaster to ask.

Violet was glad to know that she would not be giving birth all alone and without proper help, and was even gladder to be able to write to her mother with the reassurance. And when her new maid appeared, she felt she could face the trial of childbirth with some confidence. Scole was exactly what she wanted. She was in her thirties, a nice-looking, active, capable woman with a warm smile and humorous eyes. She was a trained nurse, but had been in service in a large house in her extreme youth, where as a housemaid she had often had to maid young lady visitors, so she knew what to do.

Venetia had gone to a great deal of trouble to find her, and had made sure that she knew what she would be up against, and exactly what was expected of her. She had had Hayter put her through a quick course of retraining in a lady's maid's duties, so she should not be at a loss at Brancaster Hall, and had herself refreshed Scole's knowledge of matters obstetrical. And finally she had given her a supply of stamped envelopes, to make sure there was nothing to stop her regularly reporting on her new mistress's state of health and happiness.

It was customary to call a lady's maid by her surname but, at least when they were alone, Scole very soon became Martha, and as much a friend as a servant, which was exactly what Violet needed in her state of isolation. Scole was efficient and energetic, but was also possessed of considerable tact, and managed to wring a number of concessions out of the servants' hall without putting up anyone's back. Even Disney, who despite Brancaster's personal intervention had been plainly resentful at first, was soon found to be asking Scole whether there was anything her mistress needed to make her more comfortable; and on one occasion was reliably reported almost to have smiled at her.

Sibsey remained on the staff, as maid to Lady Brancaster, doing the more menial tasks of the bedchamber, and under Scole's direction proved handy enough at fetching and carrying, leaving Scole more time to attend to her lady's inner needs. Violet felt she now had a friend and ally, and another connection with her mother and home, and spent the last weeks of her pregnancy much happier than she had anticipated. Scole helped her to prepare, calmed her fears, and kept a sharp eye on her for the first sign of labour starting. So it was that the doctor and midwife were called in good time, and Scole stayed with Violet the whole while, holding her hand, encouraging and soothing her until, after a long but straightforward labour, she gave birth at six in the evening on the 16th of October to a fine baby boy.

There was tremendous excitement among the elderly staff. Servants never usually seen in that part of the house found excuses to hang around near her ladyship's chamber, until the passage outside her door reeked of mothballs and liniment. Others gathered round the table in the servants' hall to wait for the news, relating over endless pots of strong tea other happy events of their past service – and quite a few unhappy ones, too, in ghoulish detail. Lord Brancaster, not having thought at all about it before the event, suddenly found himself caught up in the current of emotion that ran through the house, and paced up and down the drawing-room during the labour, worrying about whether everything would go well, and wondering whether the child would be a boy.

When the news was brought to him – by the butler himself, creaking in at a previously unknown speed and with the Disney equivalent of a beaming smile distorting his face – Brancaster went upstairs at once. But he still did not beat his father to it. When he arrived at the bedchamber door it was to see Lord Holkam being pushed through it in the wheelchair he had previously despised and refused to use, under the motive power of the youngest footman. The doctor, knowing who paid the bills, had gone himself to tell the earl first, and the earl had been all ready and waiting in his chair for the last four hours.

In the bedchamber Violet had been hastily tidied up and was lying, tired but happy, against a heap of pillows, with her tiny, red-faced son tightly wrapped and resting in the crook of her arm. She felt a little bewildered still, and it was hard to believe he was really hers, but the first sight of the baby had filled her with tenderness and a powerful desire to protect him. When the earl entered she was too tired to be much afraid of him. He demanded to be given the child to hold, and her first instinct was to refuse and to snatch the baby close to her; but she need not have worried. Holkam had wanted this child more than both its parents put together, and when the doctor prised it out of Violet's grip and laid it in the earl's arms, he held it with great care, and looked at it with such pride and tenderness he seemed for a moment not nearly as ugly as Violet had remembered him.

'A boy!' he said. 'The next generation of Fitzjames Howards. He will be the tenth Earl of Holkam one day. Is he healthy?' he demanded of the doctor.

'He seems perfect in every way, my lord.'

'Excellent! Well, Brancaster, here's your son. What do you say to that, eh? Robert Fitzjames Howard! Little devil's tight asleep, don't mean to wake up for his grand-papa.' Brancaster leaned down, prepared to pick up his son, but the earl had no intention of relinquishing him. 'I've waited a long time for this moment, by God,' Holkam said, almost as if to himself. 'Far too long. Sometimes thought it would never come. But here he is. A boy to carry the line forward. By God, it's a day to remember!'

He turned his head and saw Disney, who had hobbled as fast as he could in Brancaster's wake and was hovering in the doorway, trying to catch a glimpse of the baby. 'A boy, Disney!'

'Yes, my lord. God is good,' Disney said, with unexpected humility.

'Champagne, Disney, at once. The 'ninety-eight that we've been keeping.'

'Yes, my lord.'

'Doctor, you'll take a glass with us? Four glasses, Disney.' The earl seemed at those words to remember the mother. He looked across at Violet. 'You did well, madam,' he said. He met her eyes with a kind of reluctance and said, 'Thank you.'

It touched Violet too much for her to be able to speak. She had never heard him say thank you to anyone for anything. Her arms ached to hold her baby again, but she did not ask for him, understanding in that moment how important he was to the old man. At the far end of his own life, Holkam held his grandson in the first minutes of his; his head bent so that no-one should see the tears in his eyes, he said very quietly what Disney had said, 'God is good.'

The harvests had all been late, because of the poor weather, and in October in a brief and blessed spell of fine weather they were cutting the oats at Huntsham.

'I remember when I was a child,' Henrietta said, 'it was all cut by hand – hay, wheat oats, everything. It was a sight to see, the scythe men spread out across the field. It was like a ballet, beautiful to watch. Now it's all cut with the mower.'

'Progress,' said Teddy, spreading marmalade – Henrietta's own, from her grandmother's recipe, made in January when the wonderful bitter oranges arrived from Seville. Despite all the extra servants Teddy had taken on over the years, she still liked to see to some things herself. It made her feel housewifely.

'But there was a dignity and skill to it,' Henrietta said. 'It makes people happy to know there's skill in their work.'

'I like the mower,' Jessie confessed. 'It reminds me of a windmill. And at least it's quiet, not like the horrible steam-thresher. I don't know how those threshing teams can bear to work with it day after day, week after week.'

'They get used to it,' Jerome said. 'All work has its penalty as well as its reward.'

'Except for horses,' Jessie said. 'Everything to do with horses is delightful.'

'So speaks the young lady who was bitten almost to the bone yesterday by a delightful horse,' said Jerome with a teasing smile.

Henrietta looked across in alarm. 'Jessie, were you? You never told me. You must let me look at it after breakfast.'

'It's nothing, just a bruise. It's a bit stiff, that's all. It will wear off once I start using it.'

'Who bit you, Jess?' Teddy asked with interest. 'It's not like you to get nipped.'

'It was one of the youngsters we're breaking. The chestnut with the four white socks. He has a bit of ginger about him.'

'You know the old saying,' Teddy reminded her. '"One white sock buy a horse, two white socks try a horse, three white socks look well about him, four white socks leave a horse."'

'I've always thought that was unfair,' Henrietta said. 'A horse can't help its colouring. It's the handling that makes it gentle or otherwise.'

'And the blood,' Teddy said. 'Bad blood will out. A bad-tempered stallion should never be allowed to breed.'

'Well, Pasha is the sweetest-tempered horse in the world,' Henrietta said.

'And Nagira, too,' Jessie said. This was the new young stallion being brought on eventually to take Pasha's place. 'But the chestnut's not one of Pasha's. He's one of the foals we brought from Ireland. I'm breaking him for the army.'

'You should encourage him to bite,' Jerome said. 'Then the army can put him in the front line and he can bite the enemy.'

Jessie looked stern. 'Now, Dad, you know we never send out a horse from Morland Place that bites, kicks or rears. Even to the army. We have our reputation to consider.'

Jerome laughed at her. 'That's my little businesswoman!'

'My father had a chestnut with four white stockings,' Alice said suddenly. 'It used to pull his gig. It looked very smart. I think that's why he chose it. I remember the groom holding it at the gate, waiting for my father to come out. I used to go out and stroke it, and give it sugar. It never bit me.'

'If a horse bites, it's a human's fault,' Henrietta said firmly. 'What are you doing today, dear?' she asked Jessie.

'I thought I'd go out to Huntsham for a bit,' she said, looking apologetically from her father to her uncle. 'I do love a harvest, and there's nothing urgent wanted at Twelvetrees.'

Teddy lifted his hands. 'My dear girl, you don't need to ask permission. It was never my wish that you should labour in the stables day in and day out.'

'It's not labour to me,' Jessie said. 'But it would be fun to help the harvesters, just for a bit.'

'Make the most of it,' Jerome said. 'This fine weather won't last. The quicker the oats are got in the better.'

'That's true,' Teddy said. 'I'd like to start fleet ploughing while the ground's soft.'

A footman came in with the post, which he laid before Teddy, who distributed it and examined his own. 'Ah,' he said, seeing one from Tanbury, a land agent in York, 'I know what this is. This is something I've been waiting for.' He opened it and scanned it quickly. 'Yes, I was right. White House Farm is to be sold. I had a hint from Tanbury a couple of weeks ago, and I told him to keep an eye on it. I don't want anyone else snapping it up.'

'Is the price right?' Jerome asked. 'I gathered that land

prices were beginning to go up again, at least in Yorkshire.'

He had recently had the probate through on his sister's estate. She had left everything to him, and he had a nice little capital sum that he must find a home for. Would it be sensible to sink it into Morland Place, or look to buy a small place of his own; or to invest it somewhere else entirely, in shipping or engineering or whatever?

'Oh, the price doesn't signify,' Teddy said, and as Jerome lifted an eyebrow, he qualified, 'What I mean is, Tanbury will see I'm not cheated, but my other businesses are doing so well, I've no doubt I can afford it. And once I have it,' he went on with relish, 'I shall make an approach to Lord Lambert about Eastfield Farm, persuade him to sell that to me, and then we shall have all our lands back – all the core lands, I mean, before poor George started expanding them. Won't that be something?'

'Wonderful,' Henrietta said. 'Do you think Lord Lambert will sell?'

'I don't see why not. I'm sure he only bought it because it was cheap. He's never done anything with it. The lower fields, down to the Bogs, badly need draining, the buildings are all going to rack, and the tenant he has in there is a fool. Do you remember old Pike, Hen, who used to farm Eastfield when we were children? There was a man who knew the land!'

'I was always afraid of him – he was so big and gaunt and grey.'

'Yes, and he was a fierce old boy – clipped me around the head many a time, for all that I was the master's son,' Teddy said, with fond remembrance. 'But he gave me an apple or a bit of toffee just as often, when I came across him in the fields, leaning on that big stick of his – d'you remember, Hen? – with his dog sitting there beside him. A queer, ugly little terrier it was.'

'Whistler,' Henrietta supplied.

'Yes, that was its name. Thought the world of that dog, old Pike did.' As if reminded by the words, he slipped a corner of toast under the table and into Muffy's soft, waiting mouth. 'And I remember George told me he gave him a bit of chewing baccy once. Made him sick as a cat – Georgie, I mean – because he felt honour bound to chew it like a man. He worshipped old Pike after that.'

'Men are such strange creatures,' Henrietta commented. To the background sound of crockery and cutlery, and Jessie asking her uncle for more tales of the farmers of his youth (she was becoming very interested lately in the estate as a whole, not just the horses, Henrietta thought, with a spare fraction of the back of her mind) she opened the first of her letters. It was from Jack, and she read quickly through it to make sure all was well, then folded it to be read properly at a more leisurely moment.

Now Teddy was telling Jessie about the shepherd, Caleb, who had looked after the Morland sheep when Teddy was a boy, and how during lambing he had lived out in the fields for weeks at a time in a little wooden hut on wheels, not much bigger than a – sentry box, he concluded, changing the word at the last moment (Henrietta guessed), for Alice's sake, from privy. Alice must feel rather left out of these conversations, Henrietta thought. Her father had been a lawyer and she had never lived further outside York than Clifton, or in a house with more than a front and back garden. Henrietta opened her second letter, which she saw from the handwriting was from Venetia. In a moment she was interrupting the conversation with a cry of 'Oh, how delightful!'

Teddy's toast-and-marmalade was put down, Jessie's coffee cup was suspended in mid-air, Jerome abandoned the last of his egg (how little he ate these days!) and Alice stopped fidgeting a piece of her roll into crumbs. They all looked at her enquiringly.

'Violet has had her baby,' she said. 'It was born on the sixteenth, and it is a boy.'

'Now that *is* good news,' Teddy said. 'Given that her husband will be an earl some time soon, he must have wanted a boy very much. Clever Violet!'

'And is she well?' Jerome asked.

'Yes,' Henrietta said, looking at the letter. 'Venetia says, "The labour was apparently a long one, but without complications, and of course Violet has the vigour of youth and will soon throw off any effects."'

'"Apparently"?' Jerome queried. 'Wasn't she with her?'

'No. I'd have thought she would have wanted to be there, but perhaps it came on suddenly. She says, "Violet had all possible attention, with a physician as well as the midwife to attend her. The baby is strong and vigorous, and all concerned are very pleased. I understand champagne was called for at once, and Violet had her share, which must have soon sent her off to sleep and – " Oh!'

'What is it?'

'Oh! Well, it's just that she goes on – "and will have put the baby to sleep as well when it got into her milk".'

'Is that all?' Jerome said, laughing, but Alice blushed deeply and began destroying another morsel of her breakfast roll, and he was sorry, and rescued her by asking, 'Have they decided on a name for the child?'

'Yes, Venetia says he's to be Robert, like his father and grandfather. That was decided before Brancaster even met Violet. I don't know what they would have called it if it had been a girl. He's to be Robert Arthur Andrew Louis Fitzjames Howard – all family names, it seems.'

'A large burden for a little mite,' said Jerome.

'Well, I'm dashed pleased about it,' Teddy said. 'We must have champagne ourselves tonight, to celebrate, and a special dinner.'

'Little Robert, et cetera, et cetera, is not our scion,' Jerome reminded him.

'But Violet is Jessie's particular friend and Hen's unofficial god-daughter and she's visited here and we all love her and—'

'And you would accept any excuse to hold a celebration,' Jerome finished for him. 'My dear old chap, I have no objection at all to a fine dinner and champagne. Let us wet the baby's head by all means, even if there's no likelihood that he'll ever set foot in Morland Place, or even meet any of us face to face. You've held celebrations for less worthy causes.'

'I can give you a cause for celebration,' Alice said, and then, finding everyone had turned instantly to look at her, added nervously, 'I think.'

She spoke so little that her quiet voice always commanded attention. Now a blush crept up from under her collar and she did not seem able to continue. Teddy leaned across and touched her hand, looking at her with tender encouragement. 'What is it, my love? Do tell us.'

Alice was regretting now having begun her announcement in such a public way, but since everyone was waiting it was plain she would not be able to avoid going on, and so she summoned up her courage and said, 'I think I am having a baby.'

There was a moment's silence, and then everyone broke in with congratulations. Teddy jumped up, throwing down his napkin, and came round the table to kiss her cheek, then take her hands and kiss them. 'That's wonderful! Wonderful!'

'I can't tell you how pleased I am,' Jerome said.

'I'm so happy for you.' Henrietta said.

A rather bewildered smile was beginning on Alice's face as she realised that having a baby was not simply something for her and Teddy but, now she was part of this large family, for everyone. Teddy cried out, 'D'you hear that, everyone, I'm going to be a father again! Sawry –' to the butler who had just come in to check the coffee-pot '– do you hear that? I am going to be a father again. Mrs Morland is going to present me with a child.'

'I am very pleased indeed, sir,' Sawry said. 'My heartiest congratulations, sir, and madam. I know all the staff will be delighted – if you will permit me to share the news with them?'

'Yes, yes, by all means tell them! I want everyone to know. All the staff must have something at dinner to drink Mrs Morland's health.'

'Thank you, sir.'

Teddy turned back to his wife and bent over her solic-itously. 'Alice, my dear, are you feeling quite well? You must take care of yourself. Plenty of rest. Have you seen Dr Hasty? He shall recommend a specialist for you. You must have the best of care. Oh, this is such good news!'

When the first excitement had worn off, there were other considerations that came into people's minds. Foremost in Henrietta's – and she did not suppose she was alone in this – was that Alice was thirty-six and had never had a child before. Any childbirth involved a risk, but a first child at such an advanced age was always more dangerous. Her previous husband had been a good deal older than her, and perhaps that was why she had never conceived. She would not, of course, say any of this to Alice – worry would be the worst thing in her condition – but she resolved to watch her closely.

Teddy was making the same resolve, but even as he determined that Hasty, for all his skills, would not be good enough for Alice and that she must have the best specialist he could find, he could not help remembering that his first wife, Charlotte, had had every attention, and had still died. The physician Havergill and the specialist Milton and a very experienced midwife had not been able to prevent or staunch the haemorrhage that had ebbed away her life. But it could not happen again. Surely it could not happen again. God would not be so cruel as to take away a second wife in exactly the same way, would He? Much as Teddy longed for another child, he would not trade Alice for a son, or a dozen sons. Mingled with his joy and elation, there was a shadow of fear, and the guilt it generated.

Jessie did not think about these things, being young enough to suppose childbirth would always go easily. Everyone was born, people had babies every day of the week. She knew that Polly's mother had died giving birth to her, but it was an historical fact, that was all, and did

323

not impinge on her any more than that Richard III had died at Bosworth. She was old enough, however, to wonder whether a new baby for Uncle Teddy would have an effect on Polly. Polly was used to coming first with Uncle Teddy, and when the new baby came there was bound to be a fuss made of it. Jessie privately determined to keep an eye on Polly, be extra kind to her, and if necessary talk to her very seriously about the whole thing.

Jerome thought about all these things – having by far the most leisure, in his poor state of health, to think – and to them added another consideration, that perhaps it would be wise *not* to invest Mary's inheritance in Morland Place. Indeed, it might be the moment to ask Teddy to liquidate some of his previous investment. He had always seen the possibility that Teddy and Alice might have children. If they had a boy, that would be a very different matter from either Ned or Polly. Though not in Teddy's class of wealth, Jerome was not a poor man any more, but he was devilishly tangled up with Morland Place, and he had his dependants to think about. Jack was provided for, and Robbie was earning a respectable living. In another year Frank would have finished at university and would be capable of supporting himself. Lizzie was married and Ashley was doing very well. But what of Henrietta, and what, most of all, of Jessie? He must make provision for them. Mary's money, he thought, ought to be kept accessible so that no matter what happened they would be safe. And he must make a new will. If only he didn't feel so damned tired all the time! Perhaps the lawyer would come out to Morland Place to talk to him. But that might alarm Henrietta. No, he must make an effort to get into York. Perhaps one day, when Teddy wasn't using the motor-car, he might get Simmons to drive him in.

Alice was enjoying all the extra attention Teddy was lavishing on her, but there was a nuance of anxiety that hung about him almost tangibly, and played on her own fears. She wished that she had the courage to talk to

Henrietta about it. Henrietta had had five children. She would know everything there was to know. Alice had had a sheltered upbringing, her mother had died when she was very young and she had no brothers or sisters. From the household of an elderly father she had gone to the household of an elderly husband, and though there had been children born to some of their acquaintances over the years, no-one would have dreamed of discussing the more intimate aspects of their experience with her. There was about her an innocence, the almost startled gentleness of a fawn, which made everyone want to protect her from harsh reality. For much the same reason, she had never had an intimate friend, only acquaintances. The only female she was close to, her maid Sweetlove, who would have died for her, was a middle-aged virgin.

But she liked Henrietta, and felt that, given sufficient encouragement, she could have talked to her. It would have been horribly embarrassing to begin with, but her urgent need would have overcome that. But as it happened, Henrietta was preoccupied with worries of her own, and so anxious about Alice's having to give birth at such an advanced age and so determined not to let the anxiety appear to Alice, that she did not realise that Alice wanted to talk to her. Without some encouragement, Alice was unable to lower the barriers of shyness and *pudeur*.

When Ned came home from the mill, the happy news met him at the door, and he smiled with all the warmth of his nature. He had such trust in and gratitude towards his adoptive father that it did not occur to him to wonder how the arrival of a new Morland might affect him. It was only when, having changed for dinner, he met Jessie on the stairs that a possible consequence was put to him.

'You look nice,' she said. 'I always think men look nice in evening dress.' And she reached up an automatic, sisterly hand to tweak his necktie into a better shape.

'You look beautiful,' he replied. 'But, then, you always do.'

He was looking at her so intently that she blushed a

little, to her annoyance – for it made the scar on her cheek more visible. She put up an automatic hand to hide it, pretending to brush back a strand of her hair – she had developed a dozen of these little gestures for the purpose. Ned saw it, and it touched him, and only made him love her more. He caught the hand and drew it towards him and, not understanding what he meant to do, she let him. He curled the fingers over the edge of his hand and kissed them. 'You don't need to hide from me,' he said gently.

She pulled back her hand, not roughly, but with determination. 'Don't,' she said. 'No mushiness, please.'

'But you must know—'

'Don't, Ned. Tonight is Uncle Teddy's and Aunt Alice's night. Think about them. I'm awfully pleased, aren't you?'

'Yes, tremendously,' he said, obediently allowing her to change the subject and starting down the stairs beside her.

'I hope Polly will be all right about it. She's terribly excited now, but when the baby comes, she might feel pushed aside, and be jealous.'

'Why ever should she?' Ned asked, in surprise.

Jessie glanced sideways at him. 'You haven't thought how it might affect you, too,' she observed.

'How?'

'Well, Uncle Teddy said he was going to give you Meynell's mill. But if the new baby is a boy, he may want to keep it for him.'

'Oh,' said Ned. 'No, I hadn't thought of that. But, after all, it is his to do as he likes with. Father's always been good to me. I shall be all right.'

'You are a nice person, aren't you?' Jessie said, and then, not wanting to encourage him again, went on quickly, 'I wonder what's happened to Robbie. I passed Sawry just before you came out, and he said he's not home yet. He's awfully late.'

'I expect he's called on the Cornleighs on his way

home,' Ned said, with a faint smile. 'Time flies when a fellow is with the woman he loves.'

'He won't have time to dress if he doesn't come soon,' Jessie said.

In fact, Robbie burst into the drawing-room just as Henrietta was deciding (having come to the same conclusion as Ned) to give him up and start without him.

'I say, everyone looks very grand,' he said, halting in surprise. 'Best bib and tucker? Champagne? Have I forgotten something?'

'No, but you haven't heard the news,' Teddy said at once. 'Alice and I are going to have a baby.'

'Oh, I say! Good show! I'm very pleased for you,' Robbie said, and stepped forward to kiss Alice's cheek and shake his uncle's hand. 'When's it to be?'

'In May, so we understand,' Teddy said.

'Well, well! So we're having a celebration? What a day this is turning out to be! As it happens, I've got news of my own.'

Henrietta, looking at her son's flushed face, bright eyes and unusual state of stimulation, began to have a suspicion. 'Yes, where have you been, Rob? You're very late.'

'I was at the Cornleighs, and guess what? I asked Ethel to marry me, and she said yes!'

There were cries of pleasure, and everyone gathered round Robbie to congratulate him.

'I'm really glad for you, Rob,' Jessie said, kissing his hot cheek. They had fought like furies as children, but in recent months had become better friends. 'I like Miss Cornleigh very much.'

'Thanks. I know you do – and who wouldn't? She's an angel! I say, Uncle Teddy, will there be any more champagne coming round? Because now we have two things to celebrate. This is really going to be a day to remember!'

Chapter Eleven

In September 1909, while Mr Asquith was on holiday at Lympne Castle in Kent, a group of Suffragettes made it their business to disturb him. They approached him after church on the Sunday, waylaid him on the steps of the golf club when he had just finished a round with Herbert Gladstone, and in the evening shouted slogans under the dining-room windows while he was at dinner, finishing off with a few rounds of stones through the glass.

There was protest in some parts of the press about the Prime Minister's holiday being interrupted, and one or two senior WSPU members resigned their membership, saying these were not methods they approved of. The editorial in *Votes for Women* responded that arguing that Mr Asquith's holiday must not be marred by Suffragette protests was like arguing that an army must not attack the enemy if he was playing cards.

> *If he had left to us the choice of battle-ground, we should elect to pursue the conflict with him at great public meetings, and at St Stephen's, but since he refuses to meet us at these, the appropriate places, we are compelled to meet him at any other place in which he can be found.*

The Suffragettes were as good as their word and followed Mr Asquith wherever he went. Scotland Yard took to sending detectives to accompany him whenever he stepped out of his house, and smuggling him to meetings by indirect and sometimes undignified routes. But apart from irritation at the inconvenience, it seemed to have no effect on him at all. The man was made of ice, Venetia thought, and wondered how Balfour, who was nervous and highly strung, would cope with it if the Conservatives came to power.

Later in September Asquith travelled to Birmingham to address a meeting in the Bingley Hall. He was conveyed from the station platform in the lift that usually transported mailbags, snatched away in a motor-car and smuggled into the hall by a back way to avoid the protesters at the barrier in the front. Though women were now barred from attending any Liberal meeting, twenty male supporters of the Cause were there and got up in turn to interrupt the Prime Minister's speech with questions about female suffrage. Each time, proceedings were suspended while stewards hurried to seize the protester and evict him forcibly from the hall, but then as soon as the meeting settled down again, another man would pop up.

Meanwhile, two women had climbed up on the roof of the next-door factory and were throwing slates down on to the glass roof of Bingley Hall. It had been covered with a tarpaulin in anticipation of something of this sort, and did not break, but the constant thuds overhead not only made it hard to hear the speech but made the audience nervous and distracted. The meeting was effectively ruined.

When Mr Asquith left the hall to go on to another meeting, a hail of slates came down from the factory roof on to his car, breaking a window and one of the lamps. When he had driven off, fire hoses were turned on the two women, but they hid behind a chimney-stack and would not come down. Policemen pelted them with bricks and stones, scoring some important hits, but eventually it was necessary for three constables to climb up and drag them down by the fire escape, soaked to the skin, bleeding and exhausted. Later as Mr Asquith's train left Birmingham station, stones and an iron bar were thrown and a carriage window broken. Altogether nine women were arrested for the disturbances connected with Bingley Hall and sent to Winson Green prison.

A week later a horrifying report came out of Birmingham, that the women had gone on a hunger strike, and that the prison authorities had decided to resort to what they called 'artificial feeding'.

'You know what that means,' Anne said to Venetia, almost stamping round the room in her agitation. 'Forcible feeding, by tube! It's appalling!'

Venetia was shaken. 'I'm shocked that anything so horrible should be done in a British prison – and to women! What can the governor be thinking of?'

'The governor? You can be sure he had his orders from Gladstone. We found a way to evade their outrageous sentences, and now they think they have blocked it. But this! This! By God, it makes me angry enough to kill someone!'

'Do you know how they are doing it?' Venetia asked.

'Most of them by a tube through the nostrils, but three of them by stomach pump.'

'But that's extremely dangerous!' Venetia cried. 'The nasal tube is horrible enough, but the stomach pump can cause internal damage, particularly if it is resisted. The women could die! In fact, I believe a man did die – oh, back in the seventies. I read about it when I was a student. That's why it has never been used since.'

'Well, it's being used now. Asquith is a devil! Thirty-seven of us so far have forced him to release us through the hunger strike, and pretty fools we made him and his government look, too. Now he wants an exemplary sentence for the women who dared to interrupt his sacred meeting, and he means to make sure they don't get out of it in the same way. This is spite and vindictiveness, that's all, because we dared to challenge *him*, the great H. H. Asquith! He hates us because we don't bow down and worship him.'

'Oh, Anne! Try to keep a sense of proportion. I'm sure

Asquith doesn't think he is a god, and as to hating women, I think rather that he despises us – when he thinks about it at all. Actually, I'm sure he doesn't think about us as a sex from one week's end to the next, just as we don't think about flies unless they annoy us.'

'You think despising us for flies is better than hating us?'

'It's not him I'm thinking about, but you. I don't like to hear you talking about hatred. And when you said you were angry enough to kill someone—'

'They will kill one of us before too long,' Anne said, suddenly calm. 'It will happen, Venetia. It is the logical end of this persecution. Perhaps many of us will have to die before they give us our freedom.'

The calmness was almost worse, smacking of martyrdom, and Venetia tried to turn the conversation to more practical and down-to-earth things. 'What is being done about the Winson Green women?' she asked.

'Mrs Pankhurst and Christabel are going down to Birmingham today, and taking a solicitor with them. They don't believe the forcible feeding can be legal, and if it isn't, and the prison authorities continue with it, there must be an action for assault against them. Meanwhile, we must make sure as many people as possible know about it, and are revolted by the idea. We need your help, Venetia.'

'Now, Anne—'

'Don't say "no" until you've heard what I'm asking. We need a round letter from the medical profession to the Prime Minister—'

'A memorial, you mean?'

'Is that what you call them? Yes, a memorial from as many doctors as can be persuaded to sign, saying that forcible feeding is dangerous and condemning its use. That's just a medical fact, isn't it? It's not political. Besides, I'm sure the King couldn't approve of torturing women, especially women of refinement, even if they are Suffragettes.'

'I'm sure he doesn't believe Suffragettes can be women of refinement; but I don't believe he would approve of forcible feeding. I will think about it and see what I can do. But if you want male doctors on the list it will take time.'

'It's essential that most of the doctors are male,' Anne said. 'And the memorial should be led by a male doctor, too. If it appears to come from you, or any other woman doctor, it will be ignored.'

'It will probably be ignored anyway, you know that, don't you?'

'You can't have a last straw without all the other straws that come before it,' Anne said unanswerably. 'Besides, do you really advocate inaction? Do you want to sit down and do nothing about this horror?'

'No, of course not,' said Venetia. 'It's an appalling thing to do, and there are grave dangers attached to it. Apart from the immediate danger of choking, and damage to the oesophagus, it puts a terrible strain on the heart; and unless the apparatus is properly disinfected, it can import all sorts of bacteria and dangerous microbes into the body. Well, I'll do what I can.'

'Use your Society connections,' Anne advised. 'Male doctors may listen to you more readily as a duke's daughter than as an MD.'

On arrival at Winson Green, Mrs Pankhurst, Christabel and their solicitor were denied access to the hunger-strikers. All communication with Suffragette prisoners was forbidden, and no solicitor was to be allowed to see them unless they made a formal request for legal representation. Since no communication was allowed, it was not possible to establish whether any of the women had asked for a solicitor or not. It took a week before the Pankhursts could instruct a lawyer to take proceedings for assault.

The Labour MP Keir Hardie raised the question of forcible feeding in the House; and was horrified and sickened as other members began to laugh, and then to applaud and cheer. The laughter was so loud and raucous he could hardly be heard as he mentioned the man who had died from forcible feeding in 1872. Afterwards, much shaken, he wrote a letter to *The Times*.

Had I not heard it, I could not have believed that a body of gentlemen could have found reason for mirth and applause in a scene which, I venture to say, has no parallel in the recent history of our country.

Venetia recruited her close medical friends to the service of the memorial, and one of them persuaded Sir Victor Horsley to lead it. In the end it was presented to the Prime Minister with no fewer than 116 signatures of doctors, almost all of them male, condemning the practice.

Two prominent Liberal journalists, Henry Brailsford and Henry Nevinson, resigned from the *Daily News* in protest at the newspaper's refusal to condemn forcible feeding, and also wrote to *The Times* about it.

We cannot denounce torture in Russia and support it in England, nor can we advocate democratic principles in the name of a party which confines them to a single sex.

But all the protest was ignored by the government. The Home Secretary, Herbert Gladstone, told the House that there was no danger involved in forcible feeding. He said that it would be inhumane to allow the prisoners to starve to death – which, moreover, would expose the prison authorities to a charge of manslaughter. Furthermore, suicide was a criminal act, and it was the duty of the prison medical officers to prevent inmates from committing suicide by hunger strike.

On the 5th of October one of the Winson Green prisoners, Laura Ainsworth, a schoolteacher and the daughter of a school inspector, was released. Then it was that details of how the forcible feeding was carried out first came to be known, and were swiftly given as wide publicity as possible. Her account described, in very calm language, how she had been held down by wardresses while two prison doctors tried to force a feeding tube into her nostrils. Her nose was bruised and swollen after having been hit by a stone during the protest and penetration proved impossible.

I was raised into a sitting position and a tube about two feet long was produced. My mouth was prised open by what felt like a steel instrument, and then I felt them feeling for the proper passage. All this time I was held down by four or five wardresses. I felt a choking sensation, and what I judged to be a cork gag was placed between my teeth to keep my mouth open. I experienced great sickness, especially when the tube was being withdrawn.

Another of the prisoners, Mary Leigh, was also released and added her own account of being fed by nasal tube. She was forced down on the bed and held down by a number of wardresses while two doctors inserted the tube, which had a funnel at the other end and a glass section in the middle to see that the liquid was passing. A pint of milk, or sometimes milk and egg, was used. She told how the matron and two of the wardresses were in tears during the process, which was very painful, both mentally and physically.

The sensation is most painful – the drums of the ears seem to be bursting, a horrible pain in the throat and breast. The tube is pushed down about twenty inches. The after effects are a feeling of faintness, a sense of great pain in the diaphragm and breast bone, in the nose and ears. I was very sick on the first occasion after the tube was withdrawn.

It was to the background of this knowledge that a new group of Suffragettes prepared themselves for battle – this time a disruption of a meeting to be held by Lloyd George in Newcastle, accompanied by stone-throwing. Twelve women volunteered for the occasion, in the full knowledge that they would be arrested and imprisoned, that they would then go on hunger strike, and would be subjected to forcible feeding. They were, in fact, preparing to martyr themselves for the Cause.

Among them were Lady Constance Lytton, Emily Davison, Dorothy Pethick – sister to Mrs Pethick-Lawrence – and Jane Brailsford, the wife of the journalist Henry Brailsford. Lady Constance had asked Anne to be one of them, because she had found her presence so comforting the last time, and Anne had fully intended to volunteer, but she had cracked a bone in her arm, which would put her out of commission for two or three months.

'If I had only done it in some good cause,' she mourned. But in point of fact she had slipped one rainy evening on a patch of wet horse manure while stepping into a taxi-cab and had fallen, hitting her arm on the step of the cab. It was a common enough accident. Though horse traffic was gradually giving way to motor traffic, there were still plenty of horses in London and the roads were hazardous when wet.

Feeling that she was one of them in spirit, even if she would not be there in body, Anne travelled up to Newcastle with Lady Constance on the day before the Liberal rally, and went with her to the meeting that was held for the volunteers in a lodging house. Already barricades had gone up all around the Palace Theatre, marking off a large section of Haymarket, and the roads approaching it, and detectives were searching every adjacent building for Suffragettes in hiding. The purpose of the meeting was to plan the action carefully, with exact timings if possible, to make sure that full use was made of the volunteers. But there was another purpose: Christabel Pankhurst would be there, armed with everything she had learned from the

Bingley Hall protesters about the forcible feeding.

'It is better that everyone knows what they are going to face,' she said, as they settled down around the small room, some on chairs, some on the bed, the younger ones on the floor, all faces tilted towards the leader. 'I will answer any questions you have, and if anyone feels she wants to withdraw, she may do so. There is no shame in it: I assure you no-one will blame you for a moment.'

And so, in bald, unemotional terms, she described the process, and the women listened gravely. Then they asked questions, and Christabel answered patiently. Anne, sitting on the bed with Lady Constance, saw that there was a need actually to talk about it, to name the horror, to use the words. It was their way of getting to grips with it. The discussion went on for a long time, was repetitive, even rambled sometimes, but little by little these gentle, sensitive women were coming to terms with the fact that they were going to face what amounted to torture. It was not just the physical pain and distress that they needed to anticipate and conquer: there was what for many was worse, harder to bear – the humiliation, and the moral pain of enduring a forcible operation.

There was one young woman there – one of those sitting on the floor – who caught Anne's eye in particular. She had curly fair hair with a hint of ginger and the fair eyelashes and eyebrows that went with it, pale blue eyes and a very white skin. She was young and pretty and the near transparency of her brows gave her the rather startled look of a rabbit surprised by a fox. There did not seem to be about her the granite determination that marked the rest of them as ready for the battle. She asked a great many questions of Miss Pankhurst, leaning forward and spilling them out in her rather breathless, shy tones. When she asked if the wardresses would be disagreeable, and whether they would pull down her hair and take away her tortoiseshell combs, the question both touched Anne and made her uneasy. She resolved to talk to Christabel about her afterwards.

When the questions came to an end, and the plans had been gone over in detail, Miss Pankhurst wished everyone good luck, and they stood up to take their departure. In a matter of hours only they would be going into action, but there was no air of excitement, only a quiet determination. Henry Brailsford had accompanied his wife to the meeting, and he wrote about it afterwards: 'I have seen men do brave things on the battlefield – hot-blooded and angry – but I never could have imagined the cold and lonely bravery of this women's war.'

Under cover of the movement, Anne asked Lady Constance who the fair girl was.

'That's Winifred Jones. Mrs Pethick-Lawrence met her recently at a bazaar, and she joined at once and volunteered for this soon afterwards. Why do you ask?'

'She looks so young and gentle, not the sort at all.'

'Yes, I was watching her myself and thinking I ought perhaps to get her out of it if I can. There are enough of us without subjecting such tenderlings to the horrors to come.'

They waited until the room had cleared and they could speak to Miss Pankhurst alone. She listened, and then said briskly, 'Of course, if she does not feel up to it, let her stand aside. One can never tell how one is going to feel, and she has never done anything before.' Anne thought she sounded almost impatient: a general on the eve of battle petitioned on behalf of a private. There was so much to do before the time came.

But Miss Jones, when the two ladies went to her, was surprised, and quite determined, in her faint, breathless way. 'Oh, no, I will do it, I must do it. I understand what will happen. Thank you, but you need not worry about me. I'm not afraid.'

Anne inspected her face closely. 'You are,' she asserted.

Miss Jones turned her pale eyes up to Anne's. 'I expect we all are, really,' she said quietly, 'but it doesn't make any difference, does it?'

And when the time came, Anne was close enough to

Miss Jones to see what she did. Her part was played early on, when the men were just beginning to queue outside the Palace Theatre for the rally. Pretending to sell *Votes for Women* near one of the side doors, she quietly drew a stone from her pocket and threw it with a girl's clumsy, unpractised jerk through one of the door's glass panels. One of the men seized her arm, a policeman came running up to take her in charge, and it was all over. Anne watched her being led away: she seemed quite calm, and made no sound, her eyes fixed in a remote way on some mental horizon as she trotted beside the constable, tiny beside him, like a lamb accompanying a bull.

Lady Constance and Emily Davison paired each other and waited in the crowd for Lloyd George's car to arrive. As the police cleared a way for it, Lady Constance stepped out and threw her stone at it, aiming low so as not to hurt anyone, and hit the radiator. She and Miss Davison were arrested at once, before the latter had had a chance to throw her stone. Others broke the windows of the theatre, the Liberal Club and the General Post Office, and Mrs Brailsford struck one of the barriers with a small axe she had carried hidden in a bunch of flowers. Within hours all twelve had been rounded up and taken to the police station.

Anne learned what had happened after that from Lady Constance, who came to see her on her release.

'The police cells were filthy, with just a urinal in the corner, and very dark with only a small, high window, but we were all feeling emotionally exhausted and were glad just to be left alone. But of course when it came to eleven o'clock there was no more peace and quiet, because as it was Saturday night, they began to bring in all the drunks and disorderlies and prostitutes and so on, and then they were shouting to each other and swearing and singing.' She gave Anne a faint smile. 'I suppose it would have looked rather funny if one had been able to view the scene from outside – Dante's inferno, with nice English ladies added.'

'But why weren't you sent home?'

'Because Lloyd George was staying in Newcastle for the weekend, and he didn't want to be disturbed. They kept us there until Monday morning when we were taken to court.'

'Outrageous! If I'd known I would have stayed in Newcastle and made his Sunday horrible.'

'I'm glad you didn't. You must give your arm time to mend. But listen to this. When we came up before the magistrate, Emily Davison was dismissed because she hadn't actually done anything, which was right, but disappointed her terribly, because she had been so determined to go to prison. But Jane Brailsford and I were given much lighter sentences than the rest, and in the second division, while the others were sent to the third.'

'They knew who you were.'

'Of course. And when we got to the gaol, we were met by the matron who was very polite to us, and gave us cells next to each other, and the doors were left open all day, only closed by a barred gate, so that we could talk to each other. And we were allowed to exercise alone together – you know that's unheard of.'

'Preferential treatment. Gladstone didn't want the embarrassment of your names in the papers.'

'Quite so. I must say we both felt very bad about it, especially when we were exercising on the second morning and saw that some windows had been broken, but when we shouted, "Votes for women!" up to them there was no reply, so we knew they had already been taken down to the punishment cells. We had only just got back to our cells when there was a sound of hurried footsteps and doors slamming and then we heard a terrible shrieking. It went on for about half an hour. I can't describe to you how terrible it was.' She shuddered.

Anne could imagine: not only the horror of knowing one's friends were being tortured, but the ghastly anticipation of knowing one's own turn must come soon.

Lady Constance went on. 'After a while I heard footsteps again and two doctors in white jackets came past in the corridor. I called out to them, "So you have been feeding our friends by force?" and one of them said, "Well, yes. We were bound to have a food trial with one or two of them." It was said so carelessly, you know, as if they had been doing nothing out of the ordinary. I guessed it would be my turn the next day. Jane and I talked about it, and agreed we would resist by all possible means and make them use as much force as possible. Jane said if we crossed our arms and used our fingers to plug our mouths and noses, they would not be able to feed us without a great struggle. So that's what I did the next day when the doctors came in. But I saw at once they had only the matron with them, and no feeding equipment, and they looked embarrassed at my posture and said they just wanted to listen to my heart. And an hour or two later a specialist was sent from the Home Office to examine me, and a few hours after that Jane and I were released.'

'So you only served three days of your sentence?'

'Not even three days. It makes me very angry. They will do as they like to the other women, because when they come out of prison no-one will listen to anything they say, or care about it if they do listen. They are not "important" as Jane and I are. They have no-one's ear, and therefore they may be abused with impunity. They simply don't exist.'

'You are right to be angry. I wish we could teach them a lesson,' Anne said. 'If I weren't tied by this arm! But when it has mended . . .'

'Yes, we must think what can be done,' Lady Constance said musingly.

Emily Davison, who had failed to get herself sent to prison at all, managed it a fortnight later when she broke the windows of the Liberal Club in Radcliffe during Sir Walter Runciman's visit. She was sent to Strangeways gaol, and after several days of hunger strike and forcible feeding she managed to barricade her cell door. After commanding and then pleading with her to open the door, the authorities got a fire hose up to the cell window, broke the glass, and turned it on her. She was deluged for a quarter of an hour until she was frozen and could hardly breathe – she almost drowned, in fact, and said later that she thought the time for the ultimate sacrifice had come. But then they turned off the hose, and managed to burst in the door and catch it before it fell on her. She was taken to the prison hospital, and kept there for three days, still being forcibly fed, and was then released. The hosepipe incident had caught the attention of the newspapers, and questions were asked in Parliament.

The escalation of violence both by and against the Suffragettes was something that Venetia observed with dismay. She was afraid that sooner or later someone would be killed, and on whichever side the fatality happened, it would have disastrous consequences for the WSPU in particular and women in general. She knew that there was nothing she could do to dissuade Anne from hurling herself into the thick of the battle – it took the place for her now of home, husband and children and every other normal passion and preoccupation of life – and she was only glad that Lizzie seemed to have removed herself from the fray.

Lizzie was utterly absorbed in her new child. Though Rose had a nursemaid, it was more often her mother who took care of her. Jack, when he paid one of his regular formal visits to his godmother, was very amusing on the subject of Lizzie's monomania. He painted a vivid picture of her laboriously cutting out and sewing (for Lizzie had never been a needlewoman) new clothes for the baby. He described the pricked fingers and the sighs as a clumsy stitch or crooked seam had to be unpicked, the pride and pleasure when the pretty baby was put into her new dress and displayed before anyone who happened to come in: before Jack, or Frank, or Frank's large student friends, or any of the servants, or Mart and Rupert (who had learned glumly that they were not, after all, lords of all creation) or the piano-tuner, or the man who came to

341

see whether the gas-mantles could be adapted for electricity.

Lizzie fed Rose herself, and often prepared the food with her own hands, much to the annoyance of the cook whose sister had had twelve children and who regarded herself therefore as an expert on infant nutrition. It was Lizzie who 'put Rose down' for her nap, singing her to sleep; and when she was asleep, hanging over the cot gazing fondly at the curly head, straightening the drapes, and arranging and rearranging the room. On weekdays it was Lizzie who took Rose out for her walks; Lizzie again who performed the ritual of the bath, which Rose early learned to love, delighting in the effect a really vigorous splash could produce.

Now when Ashley arrived home from work Lizzie greeted him not with news of the Cause but with news of the baby – a change for the better in his view. He never minded the happy relation of his daughter's progress over the months, of her gains in weight, of the first definite smile, the first indisputable tooth, of how she had learned to turn herself over, had been able to sit up unsupported, seemed to be trying to pull herself up. He was as glad to go with Lizzie to gaze at the sleeping child, and discuss grandiose plans for her future.

On Sundays, Rose was entirely his. Being an ingenious American, he liked to bring home new-fangled toys and patent devices, none of which ever seemed to capture his daughter's fancy or ease the nursery labour. What Rose liked best of all was to be carried around in her father's arms, or enthroned on his knee in the drawing-room, to play with his watch-chain and exchange smiles with him. Her ambition seemed to be to pull off one of his coat buttons; her greatest delight was to pull her father's large blond moustache. When she did so he would cry out, 'Oh!' which always made her chuckle. Sometimes as she reached for it she would say, 'Oh!' herself in anticipation. It was the first recognisable sound she learned to make. She loved speech, and would listen enraptured while her father talked to her, telling her of his week at work and the political situation. It was often to this background of adult affairs that she fell asleep, rocked on a sea of conversation, her rosy face smiling even in sleep.

Lizzie brought Rose to visit Venetia quite often, and Venetia had to admit that Rose was a remarkable child: extremely pretty, good-tempered, and very forward in her development. Her milk-teeth arrived with great promptness, her alertness and intelligence were patent, and at nine months, having tried and failed to achieve forward momentum by lying on her belly and flailing her arms and legs – a process Lizzie called 'swimming' – she got to her hands and knees and rapidly built up a speed across a carpet that evidently gave her great delight.

Venetia enjoyed these visits. It was good to see Lizzie so settled and happy and kept out of mischief; and latterly, a little dose of Rose helped to mitigate the disappointment of not seeing her own grandson. She received long and detailed letters from both Violet and Scole, but it was not the same. She missed Violet, too, but as Overton said, philosophically, 'She doesn't belong to us any more, my love; and the boy is Holkam's grandson rather than ours.' It was true, and it was quite usual in their rank in society, but she did often think how nice it would have been if the Brancasters had lived in the next street instead of a hundred and fifty miles of bad road away.

But thinking about Violet and worrying about Anne and the horrors of forcible feeding had to take their place in a life that seemed more full than ever. Her own work took up a good deal of her time. At the New Hospital for Women, since Mrs Garrett Anderson's retirement in 1902, she had been the senior surgeon. She also operated at the Southport, the hospital founded by her mother, whose portrait in its great front hall smiled down on her whenever she passed through. (Her own portrait, by Sargent, hanging in the entrance hall at the New, embarrassed her as much as her mother's pleased her: Venetia was a brisk and angular woman and Sargent had made her soft, flowing and somehow billowy – 'like a very good eiderdown,' as she complained to Overton.)

In addition there was her research work on pulmonary tuberculosis. She had become very interested first in Roentgen rays, and then in Becquerel rays, for whose action the Polish-French physicist Marie Curie had coined the word 'radio-activity'. Venetia had attended a series of lectures by Madame Curie and her husband when they visited England in 1903. At least, given British medical and scientific sensibilities, Pierre Curie had done the actual lecturing, but he had referred honourably to his wife's separate work and given her the proper credit for it. They had won the Nobel Prize for physics that year jointly with Henri Becquerel. He had first discovered that the element uranium emitted rays that would fog a photographic plate even in the dark.

Madame Curie was working now on isolating the radioactive element, which she called radium. Venetia had read her papers and was fascinated by her idea that the emission of rays was an activity of the atom. Since the atom had previously been assumed to be the smallest and ultimately indivisible part of nature, the notion that Becquerel rays came out of the atom was provocative, to say the least. On a practical basis, there was now much discussion of whether the effect of radium on cells could be harnessed medically to provide cures for various diseases, among them cancer and – Venetia's interest – tuberculosis.

And in addition to all this there were two other preoccupations, which continually pushed into the foreground. One was the King's failing health. Because of Overton's position, it was something that was bound to impinge more on her than on the average citizen – who generally went on the understanding that as the King had been on the public scene for so long, he must be indestructible. But Overton brought worried frowns back from Court, and both Francis Knollys and Sir James Reid, who over the years had each formed a pleasant habit of 'dropping in' on her whenever there was an opportunity, talked to her about their master's state of health. From her own observations, she saw that his bronchitis was chronic and that there were now periods of bad and worse rather than bad and better. He looked tired and old, and his magnificent appetite sometimes failed him, and though he never ceased to be active, she sensed that it was determination rather than energy that drove him on.

That he knew his time was limited received confirmation of a sort in November when, in the Birthday Honours, he made Venetia's nephew Eddie a baronet, and shortly thereafter gave him a small estate in Hertfordshire. Nazeing Manor, near Broxbourne, had a pretty little house and pleasure grounds and a home farm, which had benefited from the King's interest in modern farming. It would produce a modest but respectable income, and was, moreover, pleasantly accessible from London. Sir Edward Vibart, Bt, was now comfortably settled, and while this was something that the King could have done at any time, Venetia thought it significant that he had done it now. Eddie was still young – only twenty-two – and his Court service had not yet been so extensive as to merit the award. But if the King really thought his time was limited, it would explain why he had taken this opportunity to make provision for his unacknowledged son. Venetia was happy for Eddie, who had grown up a pleasant young man of unremarkable talents, though with a great deal of his father's charm and a distinct look of him, too. She believed that he could expect a Court appointment under the next king, who adored his father and counted loyalty as the highest virtue (King Edward had reappointed most of his mother's courtiers on her death). Thus respectably occupied, and with his title and Nazeing Manor to his credit, he might marry a nice girl and be happy ever after.

Eddie's good fortune was a pleasant relief from the worry about the King's health, and from the other great preoccupation of that year: the constitutional crisis that had been boiling up ever since Lloyd George had presented his budget in April.

It began with the government's proposal to introduce an old-age pension. An Act was to be brought to provide, out of central revenue, a pension of five shillings a week for those aged seventy or over who had no more than eight shillings a week of their own, and a lesser amount to others on a sliding scale.

There was immediate condemnation of the proposal from many quarters, because the pension would effectively penalise the thrifty who saved for their old age, and reward those who took no account for the future. It would demoralise the working classes and take away the incentive for independence, which was what gave the human soul its character and made any man's life worth living. Moreover, as Lord Wemyss argued in the House of Lords, families would cease to regard it as an obligation to care for those of their members whose working days were over. The structure of the family would be weakened, self-reliance would be diminished, and dependence on the state would lead to an overall degeneration of moral fibre.

Mr Asquith told the King in March that he would need to raise taxes to pay for this pension, and it was with the Budget that trouble really spilled over. When Lloyd George presented what he called the 'People's Budget' to the Commons on the 29th of April, he declared, 'This is a War Budget. It is for raising money to wage implacable warfare against poverty and squalidness.'

The words struck a chill into many hearts. This was a new departure. The purpose of taxation, it had always been accepted, was solely to defray the cost of government; but now the Liberals were implying that taxation had a second purpose: to redistribute wealth. It smelt suspiciously – frighteningly – of Socialism.

The tax-raising contrivances were many. The duty on tobacco and alcohol was to be raised, as was that on liquor licences, to the outrage of the brewing fraternity who had only just persuaded Lord Lansdowne to abandon the Licensing Bill, which would have further limited the common man's right to buy a drink. Death duty – that most hated of taxes – was to be raised again, as was income tax, and a new supertax was to be imposed on incomes over £3,000 a year – a direct disincentive to enterprise and effort. Futhermore, the interest on savings was to be taxed more heavily than 'earned' income, which was a further punishment of thrift.

But what most inflamed the opposition and the Lords were the land taxes. The Budget proposed raising a tax of twenty per cent whenever land changed hands on sale or death, and a reversion duty at the end of a lease, a development tax of a halfpenny in the pound and a mineral rights duty of five per cent, all to be calculated on the value of the land. A land register would have to be set up to achieve this. The Lords erupted in fury. Lord Rosebery denounced it as 'inquisitorial and tyrannical' and not so much a budget as a revolution, underlying which it was plain to see the 'deep, subtle, insidious danger of socialism'. Lord Lansdowne called it 'a monument of reckless and improvident finance'. Lord Tonbridge said it was 'the beginning of the end of all rights of property'.

'It is certainly a vindictive piece of legislation,' Overton said to Venetia. 'Lloyd George may want the money for old-age pensions and such, but Asquith wants it for building more dreadnoughts, and since there are plenty in his party – in his cabinet, indeed – who don't think we *ought* to be building more dreadnoughts, he hopes to make the expenditure palatable to them by raising the money in a way they'll enjoy – through class warfare.'

'But is it so *very* bad,' Oliver asked, 'to take from the rich to give to the poor? There does seem to be so much poverty around. I see it every day – and I dare say you do too,' he added, to his mother. His medical school was, of course, attached to a hospital, where the most wretched of humanity were always to be found.

'I hope, my boy, that you are not beginning to think along socialistic lines?' Overton said, looking at his second son rather severely.

347

'I won't if you don't like it,' Oliver said equably, 'only, why?'

'Because it's pernicious,' Overton said. 'Each man is put upon earth with certain abilities, advantages and disadvantages, and it is his duty to make the best of them, and of himself, that he can. That's what forms his character, strengthens his soul, and improves the condition of mankind as a whole. But if you take away his reason to strive, you will very quickly take away his ability, and in the end even his right to do so. He will live in miserable, dependent apathy, not a free man but a slave to the whim of whoever happen to be his political masters.'

Oliver said doubtfully, 'Some of the wretched creatures I see really have no hope of helping themselves.'

'That is what we have charities for, and why the more fortunate among us have a duty before God to help the helpless. But remember this: the right of enjoyment of private property is guaranteed to us by Magna Carta; and it is private property alone which guarantees us our freedom. Duke of Marlborough or poor cottager, the principle is the same: a man has the right to keep what he owns without interference from the state, and it is that which makes him free.'

'Isn't the duke a little freer than the cottager?' Oliver asked.

'Freedom is indivisible,' Overton said. 'Do you know what would happen if we once allowed socialism into this country? Socialists want to seize possession of everything in the land, so that they can parcel it out as they see fit. Don't you see? First there would have to be an inquisition to find out what we own, then force to effect the confiscation. The sharing out of the spoils would be done by politicians and petty clerks, who would quickly form a single class to protect their powers. We would have the worst sort of police state. Corruption, oppression, pettifogging, bribery, false witness. Neighbour would denounce neighbour, sons turn against fathers. Falsified elections, secret police, spies, paid informants, imprisonment without trial—'

'But *why* all this, sir?

'*Why*? With the wealth of the whole nation as the prize? Don't you think men would do anything to seize power when it meant being able to dispose of such wealth as they pleased? And don't you think they would use that power to favour their friends and families, and spite and oppress their enemies? The next stage would be to make sure they could never be ousted from power. Parliament would go, the law would be subverted, rivals would be imprisoned on trumped-up charges. Factions would rule, and as for the individual – what man, owing his very subsistence to the whim of some jack-in-office, let alone his advancement, would dare to speak out? Where is your freedom then?'

Oliver looked thoughtful, impressed by his father's vehemence. Venetia took advantage of his silence to ask, 'What will the Lords do? Will they oppose the Budget?'

'It will be difficult,' Overton said. 'Lloyd George presents his attack on property as an attack on poverty, and resisting that will inevitably look like self-interest.'

'What *can* the Lords do, Father? Can they reject the Budget?'

'We have the legal power of veto over any Bill,' Overton said, 'but it has not been used against a Finance Bill for over two hundred years.'

'Why is that?'

'Because the principle has been established that only the Commons can terminate the life of a government. If a Budget is vetoed it leaves a government without finance and therefore powerless. To veto a Finance Bill would bring the government down, which is against the constitutional convention.' He sighed. 'I foresee great trouble. Damn these people! Why must they continually interfere?'

So the battle had begun, Commons against Lords. Throughout the summer it had been fought with increasing bitterness, inflamed by the sensationalism of some of the newspapers. Land values fell steeply. Lloyd George and

Winston Churchill made inflammatory speeches at public rallies, jeering at the Lords and whipping up class hatred. The King was furious that two ministers of the Crown should use such undignified language; the Duke of Marlborough was astonished at such words coming from the mouth of one of his close relatives. On their side some of the Lords talked intemperately of robbery and brigandage, and put pressure on the leader of the Upper House, Lord Lansdowne, to reject the Bill. The King was distressed by the attempts of his government ministers to 'inflame the passions of the working and lower orders against people who happen to be owners of property', and equally by the peers who had made 'foolish and really *mean* speeches', and were threatening to precipitate a parliamentary crisis. Between the two he held his head in his hands, did what he could to cool tempers and avert disaster, and took the toll on his health. He said miserably to Overton one evening at Windsor that party politics had never been more bitter.

By October it seemed that the Lords had decided to reject the Bill. At Balmoral two ministers, Haldane and McKenna, told the King that this would be utterly unconstitutional, while Lord Cawdor advised that the 'People's Budget' itself was unconstitutional, such a departure from all precedent that it required the specific sanction of the electorate. To avoid a general election's being fought on such an issue, the King asked Asquith to offer the Lords a January dissolution if they would only pass the Finance Bill, but Asquith refused. A headlong collision was what he wanted: if the Lords could be provoked into committing a constitutional outrage, it would give the Liberals the excuse to bring forward the long-planned reform of the Upper House – to restrict its veto and perhaps even redefine its membership.

The Budget passed in the Commons on the 4th of November by 379 votes to 149. It was rejected in the Lords on the 30th of November by 350 votes to 75. Failure of the Finance Bill meant that the government was without funds and unable to act. On the 2nd of December Asquith moved in the Lower House a resolution: 'That the action of the House of Lords, in refusing to pass into law the financial provisions made by this House for the service of the year, is a breach of the Constitution and a usurpation of the rights of the Commons.' It was carried by 349 votes to 134. The King had therefore to dissolve Parliament, and a general election was called for the 14th of January 1910.

Lord Overton went with him down to Sandringham immediately afterwards, and on the train the King told him despondently that 'he had never spent a more miserable day in his life'.

At Morland Place, as in many other places far away from Westminster, the struggle over the Budget seemed remote. Of far more immediate interest were the preparations for Robbie's wedding. Once he had been accepted by Miss Cornleigh, he was eager to make sure of her before she changed her mind, and said to his father that there was nothing to wait for, so why should it not go ahead straight away? Jerome had his own reasons for not wanting to delay, though he kept them to himself.

The Cornleighs were delighted with the match – for both the Comptons and the Morlands were old armigerous families – and said so in pleasantly frank terms at the two dinners, one at Morland Place and the other at Clifton Lodge (Robbie referred to them as 'Home' and 'Away'). It was for them to arrange the actual ceremony, and since a bride marries from her own home, it was to take place in the parish church in Clifton, which somehow struck Henrietta as odd.

'I can't help feeling Robbie ought to be married here,' she confessed to Jerome. For a Morland not to be married in the chapel at Morland Place . . .'

'He isn't a Morland, my love, he's a Compton,' Jerome said gently. 'I'm rather hurt that you have forgotten that.'

She was instantly contrite. 'Oh, I didn't mean—! Of

course I hadn't forgotten. But he's *half* a Morland, and living here makes it seem . . .'

'Don't tangle yourself up,' Jerome said. 'I know perfectly well what you mean. And I suppose it would be nice to see him married in the chapel. But it would be cruel to the Cornleighs to rob them of their fun. I'm sure they mean to invite the whole of York to the wedding. And as things are it is better that neither you nor Alice should be burdened with the organisation – both of you in delicate conditions.'

Henrietta raised her eyebrows. '*Both* of us?'

'Well, you have me to look after, and I'm as helpless as any baby.'

Once the engagement had been announced, Miss Cornleigh came to Morland Place to stay for a Saturday to Monday, and fell instantly in love with it. She had visited before, of course, but had never had the opportunity to see all over it, and when she expressed an interest Robbie was only too glad to show it off to her, taking her everywhere from cellar to attics with a proprietorial pride, and with Jessie beside him to supply the facts he had never bothered to learn. Miss Cornleigh, rather like Alice before her, was thrilled to the core by the romance of it, having been brought up in a modern villa, and at dinner that first Saturday night she could talk about nothing else, and was happy to be regaled with as much history as Henrietta and Teddy could remember, and all the ghost stories and legends they had loved as children.

'Oh, I do hope I see a ghost tonight!' she said, clasping her hands in excitement.

'I don't think that's very likely,' Henrietta said. 'Your room is in the newest part of the house. There's no reason why any of our ghosts should walk there.'

'Oh dear! What a pity! Oh, Mrs Compton, you are *lucky* to be able to live here, with the moat and the chapel and the spiral staircases and everything, and all your ancestors buried underneath. So cosy, don't you think, having them to hand? Much nicer than stuck out in a churchyard miles away. Poor Robbie! If I were you I would never want to leave here.'

Robbie said, 'Well, I shan't let you off marrying me on that account, so you needn't think it!'

On the Sunday after church Henrietta showed her round the gardens, and then Teddy took her on a drive around the estate, making sure to finish up in the tack-room at Twelvetrees where one of the cats had produced a litter of white kittens, which were just at the age of irre-sistibility so that he could present one to her with a courtly bow. On the Monday morning when Robbie had gone reluctantly to work, she asked Jessie if she would give her a riding lesson as she had done to her sister. 'I was so envious of Angela.'

'She's getting on very well. I think she might be good enough to try a hunt this winter, if she likes to.'

'I'm sure she will. I think it must be wonderful to ride, but living where we do there never seemed any point in learning. If only I lived here, I should ride all the time, just like you – and hunt, too. It does look such fun!'

Jessie lent her something suitable to wear and got her up on her mother's mare, Elida, who was old and quiet, and took her out on a leading rein. She did not seem at all afraid, and obviously enjoyed every minute. Jessie thought she would soon be proficient if she had a few more lessons; but as she had said, there didn't seem any point when she would be living in York. The days when everyone learned to ride automatically were long gone in these modern times of railway trains and motors.

On the Monday afternoon Miss Cornleigh thanked everyone profusely for the wonderful time she had had, and with her white kitten in her arms climbed with Teddy into the back of his motor and was driven home to the unromantic comfort of Clifton Lodge.

On his return to Morland Place, Teddy found Henrietta alone in the drawing-room, doing her sewing to the back-ground trilling of Alice's canary, whose cage in the window had caught a stray bar of sunshine. Teddy said,

'Look here, Hen, does anything strike you about Miss Ethel?'

'Only that she's a dear girl and I'm sure will make Rob very happy. What had you in mind?'

'Well, that she seems very attached to Morland Place. Talked about it all the way home. Now, I know Rob is looking about for a house to rent in York, but they will have to live in a very small way, given that he only has his salary from the bank.'

Henrietta said, 'Robbie earns enough to support them both, if they're careful.'

'Careful – that's what I meant. I don't suppose Jerome is in a position to give him anything very great?'

'Not very much. He has put aside a sum for each of the boys when they marry, but he has to keep back most for Jessie.'

'And I don't suppose the Cornleighs have a great deal to settle on Miss Ethel, given what a large family they have.'

'No, not a fortune, but she will have something, enough to keep her in pin-money. But Teddy, what is all this? It's natural for young people to start off in a modest way. I'd rather Robbie had saved more before he got married, but as he and Miss Cornleigh are in love, there doesn't seem to be any reason to wait, as he said.'

'No, no, let them get married by all means! I shouldn't want to wait in his position. But, you see, it strikes me that she likes Morland Place so much, and said so many times she wished she lived here – so why doesn't she?'

Henrietta stared, her needle slowing. In front of the fire Muffy, in sole possession for once of the favoured spot, sleeping with her muzzle on her paws, twitched her eyebrows and wuffed as she pursued a delicious dream. 'You mean – after the wedding – for her and Robbie to live here?'

'Yes,' Teddy said eagerly, 'why not?'

'Well – they're sure to want to be alone together, especially at first. It's part of the fun of being married, isn't it? It's very kind of you, Teddy, but—'

'Not kind at all. I *want* them here. I hate the idea of Rob leaving, that room empty, one less face at the breakfast table. I hate anyone to go – wish Jack hadn't gone down south – hope Frank comes back when he finishes at university. The more the merrier, as far as I'm concerned. I like a houseful. And I like little Miss Cornleigh so much – she's such a pretty, cheerful girl and she would bring so much life to the house. She'd bring all her friends home, too. Lots of running about and laughing and chattering. Cheer the old place up!'

'Do you think it needs cheering up?' Henrietta asked, in surprise.

'Oh, it ain't gloomy, I don't mean that. No, I'd just like to have them here, that's all. There's plenty of room. They could have the North Bedroom – that's plenty big enough, and it needs redecorating. They could have it done up to suit their ideas. And, you see, it would give Robbie time to save more towards a place of their own, so they would be more comfortable when the time came. Of course, if they found they didn't like it here, well, no harm done, eh? They can still find a place to rent in six months or a year or two, just the same as they can now. What do you think?'

Henrietta put down her work and looked at him with an affectionate amusement. 'What do I think? Well, my dear, I've no objection. What mother wants to part with her son? And it's your house to do as you like with. But I don't know if the young people will like it.'

'If they don't, they can say so. I think I shall ask them.'

'And Alice,' Henrietta prompted.

'Oh, Alice won't mind. Why should she?'

'Ask her all the same.'

He went off in high good humour, and Henrietta went upstairs to see if Jerome (who had been having his afternoon sleep) was awake. She told him what Teddy had said. He laughed and said, 'Teddy, collecting people again! What a fellow he is!'

'I hope he won't be too disappointed when the children turn him down.'

'Better that they should. The situation here is complicated enough as it is.'

'Complicated? I don't see that it's complicated. Lots of people live with their families. It used to be the rule rather than the exception at Morland Place. You've only got to read the house books to see that in the olden days Morland sons brought their brides home rather than living apart.'

'Well, this is not the olden days and—'

'And Robbie is not a Morland son, I know,' she finished for him. 'It would have been nice for Jessie to have a friend on hand, though. I sometimes think she must be lonely as the only girl. Polly's still too young to count in that way.'

But when the suggestion was put to the young people, to Henrietta's surprise and Teddy's delight, they both jumped at it. Robbie was comfortable at home and had secretly been dreading the upheaval and having to 'live in a small way'; and Miss Cornleigh could think of nothing nicer than to live in a moated manor house with ghosts. They both saw the prudential argument, and both were used to living with a large family and had no dislike of having lots of people around them.

'It needn't be for ever if we don't like it,' Robbie reminded her. 'Any time you want to take up housekeeping, you just tell me so, and we'll find a house to rent.'

'I'm sure I shall be happy here,' she said, 'and it will give me a chance to learn all about housekeeping and so on without it mattering if I make mistakes.'

Robbie thought it unlikely he would ever be in a way to provide her with a home for which housekeeping at Morland Place would serve as a model, but he forbore to say so. The North Bedroom was inspected, with some awe on Miss Cornleigh's part on account of its size; and approved, and in choosing the decorations and curtains and disposition of furniture she was able to enjoy the most pleasant part of home-making. On Robbie's salary and her own small dowry they would probably have had to make do with a cook, a maid and a daily cleaner, and while there had been a certain attraction in the idea of 'playing house', the romance of Morland Place was a much greater allure and she was happy to put it off for a while.

The Cornleigh parents saw the sense of the arrangement, and had nothing to object to it. It would not have been surprising if they did not also think that such affection on the part of an uncle as rich as Teddy might in the future lead to more solid gestures towards the Robert Comptons.

So then there was just the wedding to look forward to. Both Jessie and Polly were to be bridesmaids, along with Angela Cornleigh and the other four sisters and a female cousin, making eight in all. The wedding was going to be *very* grand, Jessie concluded, for Clifton parish church, and would probably be talked about for months. She and Angela went with Ethel to all the fittings for her wedding gown: it was to be of cream striped satin, with a draped bodice of chiffon and net sewn with tiny pearls, and a very long train of figured satin, quite worthy of its eight attendants. All the bridesmaids were to be in pink net over white satin, with wreaths of artificial roses on their heads, and in compliment to Uncle Teddy the dresses were being made by Makepeace's – though Miss Ethel's gown was being created by York's leading mantua-maker.

Robbie asked Ned to be his groomsman, and Jack and Frank were both coming home for the occasion. There would be over a hundred guests. Mrs Cornleigh confided happily to Henrietta that even though Clifton Lodge was of a good size they would be *very* crowded. As there was not room for everyone to sit down in one place, there would be a buffet-table meal, and Mrs Cornleigh happily accepted the offer of a loan of Morland Place housemaids and footmen on the day to help serve. Teddy also offered his motor-car to convey the bride to the church. The Cornleighs kept a carriage, but both Mrs Cornleigh and Ethel agreed it could not compare with the glory of arriving at the church in a shiny Benz with a uniformed chauffeur.

Nothing could be expected of the weather in November in Yorkshire, but in fact when the day dawned it did its very best for the young couple, and provided a dry, crisp morning with a blue sky and golden late-autumn sunshine to show off the pageantry of the occasion and brighten the hearts of the guests. Teddy's car took Polly and Jessie over to Clifton Lodge early so that they could dress with the others; then it took Henrietta, Jerome, Alice and the boys to the church before going on to collect the bride and her father. The bridesmaids followed the bride's car in two carriages so that they could arrive at the same time and not be kept waiting outside the church in the cold.

Robbie and Ned were there in plenty of time, having come from Morland Place by cab. Robbie looked very nervous, and wider awake than anyone ever remembered him. The church was beautifully decorated with greenery, and crowded with friends and relations, all whispering and nodding to each other and looking over the famous Morlands with interest. Then the door opened, the organ struck up, and Mr Cornleigh walked in with Ethel on his arm, looking almost ethereally beautiful, and a bevy of pink bridesmaids of varying sizes behind.

Second time, Jessie thought, as she walked behind, holding her side of the train opposite Angela Cornleigh, and aware that Polly, behind her, had been unable quite to suppress her excitement and was hopping rather than pacing with dignity. Second time a bridesmaid – and will I ever be a bride? Ned, at the altar, turned his head to watch them approach, and she thought how handsome he looked, especially when, as now, he smiled at her, making his eyes crinkle in that nice way. Robbie looked round too, and seemed quite awestruck at the sight of his Ethel transformed into this white and gliding vision. He gazed at her in a besotted way all through the ceremony and made his vows in a tone that almost suggested amazement that anyone should have to *ask* him if he did, and would.

There were photographers outside the church from all the local newspapers, as well as from Wetherby and even

Leeds where the Cornleighs had relatives, so there was a gratifying number of flashes, and cheering from the crowd of onlookers that always gathered when there was a chance of seeing a bride. A chimney-sweep was lurking near the motor car – much to the annoyance of Simmons, who was afraid he might touch the gleaming coachwork – and at the urging of the crowd he was allowed to kiss the bride's cheek for luck and given a sovereign by Teddy, who accompanied it with a discreet shove to send him on his way. The sweep smelt of drink, and was well known around York. Drunkenness had forced him to give up his profession, and he had found an easier way to live by haunting weddings; but there was no real harm in him.

Back at Clifton Lodge it was rather a crush, but some judicious removal of furniture and flinging open of doors made it a pleasant rather than an intolerable one. There was a superb banquet laid out on the buffet, with everything from roast turkey and pheasant and a gigantic ham down to jellies and ices; and as much champagne as anyone could want. A very jolly atmosphere prevailed, a sea of eating and drinking and talking on which Uncle Teddy seemed to surge about like a great ocean liner, always with Cornleigh friends and relations bobbing round him like tugs. He was a Great Man in York, and it amused his family, who were tolerably used to him, to see him being revered and enjoying it in a rather shame-faced way. Alice was taken under the wing of the bride's mother, who whisked her away to a chair in a quiet corner, arranged a footstool for her, had food and drink brought to her, and then settled down beside her for a comfortable chat about confinements. Henrietta and Jerome found their own quiet corner where they could watch undisturbed and, when no-one was looking, hold hands.

'Our first child married,' Henrietta said.

'How do you feel? Pleased? Proud?'

'Of course. I think he has chosen well.'

'Poor Rob! You needn't sound surprised.'

'Oh! Well, but you know Rob. Think of Miss Harris!'

359

'Yes, we had a lucky escape.' He turned to look at his wife of twenty-four years. 'I had a lucky escape all those years ago, too. When I think you might have turned me down . . .'

'We've been happy, haven't we?' she said. She loved him so much, and with her hand warm in his, she felt safe and cherished. 'In spite of everything, they've been good years.'

He lifted her hand to his lips and kissed it. 'If Rob has anything a quarter as good, he'll be a lucky man.'

Robbie and Ethel – Mrs Robert as she would now be referred to at Morland Place – were to have a week in a hotel in Scarborough for their immediate honeymoon, postponing a longer trip until next summer when the weather would be more favourable. When they were seen off in a taxi-cab for the station, a gold and ruddy sunset was going on like a stage-production in the background, and it was becoming very cold. Jessie wished them well of Scarborough, which had the coldest wind in Yorkshire, coming in off the sea straight, as her father had told her, from the steppes of Russia. But perhaps they would not notice: they seemed very much in love and besotted with each other.

When the cab had drawn away and they returned indoors, Jessie found Ned beside her. The young Cornleighs and their friends wanted dancing, and there was just enough space for it in the garden-room, if the older people obligingly squashed themselves in elsewhere.

'Dance with me, Jess?' Ned asked her. The music being played was of the modern sort, where you danced in couples, not the old country dances. The young Cornleighs had all the newest sheet music. 'You look so pretty in your bridesmaid's dress,' he said, when they had been dancing a minute or two.

'Thank you,' she said.

He eyed her with sympathy. 'You seem rather – depressed.'

'Oh, no, not at all,' she said, rousing herself to smile. 'I expect it's just the reaction to all the excitement. Weddings are rather tiring, don't you think?'

'Other people's, perhaps. Wouldn't you like to try it for yourself, though?'

She looked up at him, and was caught and held by the expression in his eyes.

'With me, I mean,' he elucidated kindly. 'So that you aren't in any doubt.'

'Oh, Ned!'

'Don't say "no". Not right away. Think about it for a little while.'

'But I don't—' She had been about to say, 'I don't love you in that way,' but it occurred to her that in fact that was just the way she loved him. He was handsome and nice and she liked being with him; and in particular being held in his arms while they danced made her feel excited and a little shivery. It confused her, because that was the way you were supposed to feel towards the one true love of your life – she and Violet had discussed it endlessly during their come-out, and had agreed definitely about that. But she had felt it towards Brancaster, which meant that he was the one true love of her life, even though he had married someone else. Surely you could not feel it towards more than one man? Or if you did, didn't that make you a bad person? She wished she knew more about that sort of thing. It did seem that a young woman was supposed to make extremely important decisions with hardly any information at all to guide her.

While she was struggling with all this, Ned, watching her face, said, 'You don't love me?'

'I do love you, but—' She still did not know what she wanted to say.

'Is it still that other fellow? You're still in love with him?'

'Yes. Perhaps. I don't know. Oh Ned, I don't know anything, except that I don't *think* I want to marry you, though I'm very fond of you.' She hated to disappoint him and, searching for some reason for him that would not hurt his feelings, she said, 'We probably ought not to think of it anyway. We are cousins, you know.'

He smiled, as if he knew it was only an excuse. 'Lots of cousins marry. We're both healthy, and there's good sound blood on both our other sides. Plenty of mongrel strength in *me*, anyway. It shouldn't cause any problems.' She said nothing. 'Any other excuses? You don't have to make up your mind now, you know. I can wait, if there's hope. Is there, Jess?'

'I don't know,' she said wretchedly. 'I don't know. Don't ask me, Ned, please. I just don't know what I feel or what I ought to do.'

'All right. But you like me?'

'You know I do.'

'We'll leave it at that, then. For the time being.'

Jessie was relieved not to have to talk about it any more, but it did not stop her thinking, wondering what it was she felt, wishing there were someone she could talk to about it. Someone older and more experienced, but still young. It was not something to be discussed with Mother, or someone like Cousin Venetia, kind and sensible though they were. Lizzie, perhaps? She knew that Lizzie had been engaged to someone else before Ashley. Perhaps she would be able to explain things. She would be coming to stay at Christmas: perhaps Jessie could talk to her then.

Ned continued to revolve with Jessie in his arms, content to be silent, feeling he had advanced his cause just a little, just enough. He was not entirely inexperienced with women, and he felt sure that what he had sensed in Jessie was attraction on her part for him. She was still confused about the fellow who had married Violet. When she finally got over him, all would be well. It needed a little time, that was all.

BOOK THREE

CONSEQUENCES

Dreams without sleep,
And sleep too clear for dreaming and too deep;
And Quiet, very large and manifold
About me rolled;
Satiety, that momentary flower,
Stretched to an hour:
These are the gifts which all mankind may use,
And all refuse.

John Swinnerton Phillimore, 'In a Meadow'

Chapter Twelve

It was a happy Christmas at Morland Place. As Christmas Day fell on a Saturday, Mr Rankin had given Jack the Friday off as well, so by taking a late train on Thursday he was able to have three whole days 'at home', as he still called it. Frank travelled down with Lizzie and the children a week beforehand; Ashley would follow on Christmas Eve.

Mr and Mrs Robert were installed in the North Bedroom and the arrangement was working very happily so far. On Jerome's insistence, Teddy accepted from Robbie a sum equivalent to the rent he had expected to pay on a small house, but he secretly put it aside to accumulate, plus interest, against the time when they would want to move away. But since they had no other expenses, Robbies's salary and Ethel's pin-money went a long way, and they were very comfortable. The house and grounds were so large there was never any difficulty in finding a way to be alone together when they wanted, but for the most part their bedchamber was enough, and they were glad of the company the rest of the time.

Teddy had been right that Mrs Robert would brighten up the place. She was full of fun, brimming with energy, and sang about the house all day long. She helped Henrietta so much that Henrietta began to wonder how she had ever managed without her, and was able to slip some duties and have more time with Jerome. Mrs Robert brightened the house in a physical sense, too. She showed an excellent taste in arranging the furniture to better and more elegant effect, prompted the purchase of new curtains for the drawing-room, and the repainting of its ceiling, which had got very dark and dingy from all the fire and candle smoke. She enjoyed arranging flowers, and shared the task with Alice, showing some ingenuity in supplementing the hothouse flowers Teddy had delivered from a florist in York with green leaves and berries and whatever she could find in the hedgerows and gardens. It gave her a good excuse to be out, and one of the things she liked best about living at Morland Place was the freedom she suddenly had to go out and about alone. At home, living in a suburban street, she had never gone abroad without one of her sisters or a servant to accompany her – and there had been nowhere much to walk anyway, except to the shops. But in the country a girl might walk or ride alone as long as she was on her own land, which here effectively meant unlimited freedom.

But she quite often took Polly with her when she went for one of her walks, because Miss Mitchell hated the outdoors and always had colds, and Polly was consequently lacking exercise. Polly had liked her from the beginning, having a prejudice in favour of beauty, and soon positively hero-worshipped her. Jessie, who had been her favourite person before, was too well known and often too busy, and in any case she was not really beautiful. Ethel had all the allure of novelty, and was as lovely and as kind as an angel. Soon Polly's conversation was decorated with 'Ethel says' and 'Ethel thinks', and if anything puzzled her in her school work she would no longer apply to Henrietta or Jessie or even her father, as before, but it was 'I'll ask Ethel. She's sure to know.' As Ethel had only a very moderate education, this was flattering, but she did her best to disabuse her young worshipper by telling her that she really didn't know anything at all, and that Polly ought to ask Jessie, who had been to school.

But it was in the evenings that the difference Mrs

Robert made was most apparent. Robbie came home from the bank full of eagerness to see his bride. He was deeply in love, and there was a quality of faint surprise to it, which Henrietta found touching. Now in the evening there was always lively conversation between Robbie, Ethel, Jessie and Ned, to which the older ones could listen with amusement, or join in as the fancy took them. Ethel played the piano (which Alice had rather given up since she became pregnant) and there was often music in the evenings, with the young ones gathering round to sing a mixture of old folk songs and the new popular ballads. Robbie was always buying his wife fresh music, one of the little luxuries he could afford, and a new song only had to come out in York to appear in Morland Place the next day. Ethel also had a positive genius for games, making up the rules as she went along, and whether it was cards, or pen-and-paper, or something foolish that involved dressing up, or sticking spills into one's hair, or standing on one foot and reciting, she could always think of a new way to make everyone laugh.

And as Teddy had anticipated, there were more young people around Morland Place too, in spite of the early darkness and inclement season. The other young Cornleighs liked to visit, and brought friends with them, and the fact of there being young people at Morland Place attracted others, especially Jessie's suitors (whom Ethel secretly encouraged to visit, much to Ned's chagrin). With so many after-dark comings and goings, Ethel suggested to Teddy that the track from the road ought to be marked in some way, and suggested a series of white-painted stones or posts on either side. Teddy was amazed he had never thought of it himself (especially after Jerome had struggled so badly to get home last January) and had the work put in hand at once.

So this Christmas promised to be the best ever, with the house as full as Teddy could possibly want it. That, and Alice's continued fair state, would have been enough to secure his happiness. For Henrietta, it was good to have all her children around her, and to be safe in her beloved home. Polly had Mart and Rupert to play with, Jessie had her darling Jack to pet, and everyone had delicious baby Rose, who became the focal point of the whole season as she explored as much of Morland Place as she could reach with her hands, feet, eyes and mouth. She had tired of the limitations of crawling, and would now pull herself upright on anything sturdy enough, and could walk a couple of wavering steps before sitting down with a bump. Given a finger to hold, she could walk across a room, and delighted in the ability. Her chuckles and crowing laugh, her constantly pointing finger, and the intermittent dashes of various adults to remove unsuitable things from her mouth, were what most of them remembered best about that Christmas.

Jessie had a long conversation with Jack about life in Southampton, and about his romance with Miss Puddephat, which was stuck fast in the mire of deep mourning. He had paid several visits of respect to Pont Street, but never saw Maud alone. Mr Puddephat had decided to give up his business, having made his fortune, and retire to a life of leisure, so he was never even called out of the room when Jack was there. And in any case, talk of love or marriage was out of the question at such a time.

'But she does love you?' Jessie asked, so much wanting one of them to be happy. They had wrapped up well and were walking about the rose garden together for privacy. There had been a hard frost the night before, which had created a fantastic scene where every twig and leaf and lingering rosehip was rimed, dusted and outlined in dazzling silver-white.

'I don't know,' Jack said despondently. 'I don't know any more how you tell. I thought she did, and of course one can't expect her to be thinking about that sort of thing now, with her mother having just died, but I sometimes think she ought to show it more if she did, or at least that I ought to *know* it more. If she loved me, wouldn't she turn to me for comfort? Or at least be glad that I was there? But she seems so calm, as if I were just another visitor, just anyone at all; and she never looks at me. When I talk to her, she won't meet my eyes. I used to think that was a good thing, meaning she was shy, but now I'm not sure. *Do* girls look at fellows they're in love with?'

'I don't know,' Jessie said. 'I don't know what to tell you. It sounds hopeless, but then, as you say, she is in mourning. When that's over, perhaps . . .'

'But if I'm honest, it wasn't much different before. Perhaps I'm just being a fool.'

'No, Jackie darling, not a fool,' Jessie said, squeezing his arm. 'If you love her you must try for it. Think if she loved you and you didn't!'

He squeezed back, and smiled at her. 'Dear old Jess! You're always on my side. And how about you? Is there anyone for you yet? Mrs Robert seemed to be suggesting last night that you are surrounded by suitors.'

'Oh, there are young men that I dance with, but . . .'

'You don't fancy any of them?'

'I don't know. I feel restless and – oh, sort of . . . unsatisfied, but I don't know what that means or what I want. I feel as if there's something that I'm waiting for, that's going to come, but I don't know what it is or when it will be.'

'Yes, I think I know what you mean.' They walked in silence a while. Brach came and found them, jumped round them beating her tail against their legs to tell them how glad she was to have tracked them down, and then brought them a stick to throw. Jack obliged, and said, 'By the way, I don't know whether you've heard, but Bertie has booked his passage home, and he'll be in England in June.'

'No, I didn't know. Where did you hear that?'

'Oh, from Mr Puddephat, of course. He and Bertie are in correspondence with each other. It seems from what he says that Bertie is coming home for good. I thought

369

perhaps he'd just clear things up and then go back to India, but Mr P says he's selling his hill-station, and just bringing back some of his horses.'

'Is that all?' Jessie said slyly, freeing her arm from Jack's to throw the stick for Brach again. 'No string of Indian wives, or concubines, or anything?'

'Jessie Compton! Such language from a lady's mouth,' Jack said, with mock severity.

'Well, it's only what I hear people asking. He has been out there a very long time. He's not married, then?'

'I don't think so. Nothing was said about any wife. A good thing too – can you imagine the fuss if he turned up with a black Lady Parke? Though of course there are white girls out there too – army officers' and planters' daughters. He could have married one of them. But Mr P just said he was bringing back some horses.'

'Oh, well, we shall see, I suppose, when he arrives. I shall be glad to see him again.'

'Me too. I say, you're shivering. We'd better go in.'

'Yes, once the sun goes off the garden you can feel how cold it is.'

Henrietta's only sadness that Christmas was that Jerome was not at all well, having caught a cold two weeks before that he could not seem to shake off. She worried about him a great deal, though like all of them she had grown used to his invalid status over the year, so that it no longer struck her every time as unnatural to see him sitting down, or resting in the afternoon, or walking so slowly. The Jerome who had been out from dawn to dusk, riding and working without sparing himself, seemed as remote now as the darkly romantic Jerome she had danced with all those years ago at the Red House. The essence of him was what she loved, and that was still there, unchanged, smiling out from his tired blue eyes. She cared for him and worried over him, but he was *still there*, and that was the important thing. She would take him in whatever form God allowed him to stay with her. He seemed to be enjoying Christmas as much as anyone, and made a very funny speech at Christmas dinner, though he stayed sitting down to make it. And in the evening when, as a change from games, Ethel played the piano for the young ones to dance, Jerome suddenly got up and offered her his hand, and they danced a waltz together. It was hardly more than a slow, sweet walk in each other's arms, but Henrietta laid her head on his shoulder and felt the warmth of his presence, and it was one of the best moments of the whole Christmas for her.

Violet thought often of Morland Place as Christmas approached. What fun they would all have, with all the happy, loving faces round the table; games and carols. She could imagine just how it would be. And Jessie had written to her a graphic account of Robbie's wedding: so now there would be a new face at the table – loved and loving and happy. It did not surprise her at all that Teddy had asked her and Rob to live there or that they had accepted. A house could not be too full of people one loved.

She had no expectation of pleasure from Christmas. It would be, she supposed, just like the last one, with a number of elderly relatives creaking slowly along the corridors and the smell of mothballs round every corner. At least, she hoped, if there were visitors there would be a few more fires lit, which might do something to mitigate the cruel cold. It set in early that year, and by December had sunk to a degree of chill such as she had never experienced before. Outside, under an iron sky, the bare land starved. The dykes filmed over and then froze solid, and hardy children came out to skate along them like little Dutch boys. The dead grass and bracken and the weeds in the ditches stiffened into fantastic shapes, like fans frosted with diamonds; the earth was like a stone; the frost lay along branches thick as snow; birds fell dead from the hedges in the night.

And inside Brancaster Hall it seemed hardly any warmer than outside, as the cold air fell in through the gaps around ill-fitting window frames and down unused chimneys, and draughts hurtled along corridors and under doors, cutting round the ankles like knives. Every morning the windows were covered with the kaleidoscope patterns of ice-crystals, and the water was solid in the drinking-flasks. Violet began to feel, despairingly, that she would never be warm again. But now she had Scole to work for her behind the scenes. She requested and was granted use of a small sitting-room on the south front of the house – the more sheltered side, for one could not call it warmer exactly. In this small room Scole made sure there was always a good fire. She enlisted the help of one of the younger footmen to move some thicker curtains from an unused bedroom, and persuaded him to bring up a small tapestry she had found rolled up in a store-room and hang it over the wall furthest from the fire.

Here, with the gap under the door well plugged with a rolled blanket, Violet spent her days in a deep chair beside the fire, with Scole on the other side, and quite often with Sibsey, on whom Violet took pity because she always seemed to have a cold, and was such a skinny, shivering thing, stitching away in the background. Violet's full-length sable coat came into its own now: she wore it almost all the time, especially when she scurried from her bedchamber to her sitting room. At night she spread it over her bed. Thus muffled up and holed in, she wintered like a fieldmouse, tucked away from the bitter weather.

All day she read and sewed and talked to Scole, wrote letters, daydreamed. Little Robert was brought in at regular intervals, and she liked to have him there. She was nursing him herself, which was not something she would have contemplated beforehand, but when she enquired about a wet-nurse she was told that Lord Holkam desired her to feed the child: it was the custom in his family. Once she got used to it, she was glad she had been obliged to, because it made her feel very close to him. It was a strange and marvellous thing to know one had been of direct physical use to another creature.

And feeding him gave her an excuse for doing nothing. Scole said a nursing lady needed to rest a great deal, and it suited her in her present mood. She felt remote from the world, as though the string that held her had come untied. She looked out of the window, but the scene outside did not seem to be anything to do with her, and she had no desire to go out into it. Her baby was much more interesting. Often she held him on her lap while he slept, and just looked into the fire and thought about him growing up, and wondered what he would be like and what he would do in the world.

Scole brought her her breakfast on a tray in bed now, and she had her luncheon, such as it was, in her sitting room, so she only saw her husband at dinner, and not even always then. When there were no guests, his father often wanted him to dine in his rooms. When they met, Brancaster always asked her how the boy was, and then, politely, if she had heard from any of her family; and then with an air of relief he would talk about the current political situation, or the estate, or the plans he had for improvement. Violet was happy to listen, having nothing to contribute. His manner towards her was gentler since she had had the baby. He seemed to want to be kind to her, though having little idea how the thing was to be done. She honoured the intention, and smiled encouragingly on his efforts. As she was nursing their son, he had not resumed his visits to her bedchamber. She understood that one son was not enough, not allowing for accidents or misfortunes, so he would be calling on her again at some point in the future. In her state of semi-hibernation, the possibility seemed as remote as everything else. She did not care whether he did or not. She felt as though this present state would go on for ever, unchanging. She felt like the Sleeping Beauty.

Then one day just before Christmas, with the first of the creaking relatives due to arrive the following day, there was an unprecedented sound of hurrying footsteps in the house – some of them actually *running* – and voices raised, and some distant bustle of activity. She looked across at Scole, who put down her sewing and went to the door. She opened it a crack – the cold air leaped in from the corridor like an assassin taking his chance – and listened, and then slipped out, closing it behind her. She was gone a long time, and came back in with a grave face.

'It's Lord Holkam, my lady.'

Violet looked up. The tone of her voice suggested something extreme. 'Dead?'

Sibsey at once let out a moan. 'Dead? Oh, no, oh, no! I knew something was coming! There was an owl on the roof above my window last night, a-hooting away. The owls always hoots when a Fitzjames Howard dies!'

Scole gave her the withering look of a London servant. 'His lordship isn't dead, so stop your yammering. Owls, indeed!' She turned to her mistress. 'He had a stroke, my lady, a pretty bad one. The doctor came, and a specialist is being sent for. Lord Brancaster hasn't left him for a minute. But his lordship hasn't recovered consciousness yet.'

Sibsey moaned again. 'And the tower clock struck thirteen last night,' she said in a ghastly voice. 'I heard it. He'll die, sure as sure.'

'Will he?' Violet asked Scole quietly.

'There's no knowing, my lady. He's not dead yet, that's all I can say.'

It wasn't until late that evening that official news reached Violet. There was a tap on the door and it began to open – with difficulty because of the blanket. Sibsey jumped up and ran to move it, and Lord Brancaster came in. 'Do I disturb you?' he said politely; and then, 'So this is where you sit. It is very cosy in here. I think you have the warmest spot in the house.'

'Come and sit down,' she invited, and dismissed the servants with a flick of her head. Brancaster came to the fire as if to sit down, but then sheered away and began to walk about the small room.

'I came to tell you,' he said at last, 'that my father had

374

a stroke this morning. He is unconscious, but the doctor said he is in a stable condition. A specialist from Norwich has been here this afternoon, and another from London comes tomorrow.'

'Will he . . .' She was going to say 'die', but changed it, as being more tactful, to '. . . will he get better?'

'That is what I hope Sir Charles Brenchley will be able to tell me. The other two doctors are full of don't-knows and can't-says. They tell me that after a stroke a person may lie unconscious for hours, days or weeks, may never recover from it, or may come to suddenly and with very little damage, or a great deal. Also that they frequently suffer a second stroke which may carry them off.'

'I'm so sorry,' Violet said, feelingly. It must be awful to be in such uncertainty about a parent.

He stopped his prowling and looked at her. 'Yes, I see you are. You are a kind person.'

'I know you love your father,' Violet said.

'Love?' The word seemed to surprise or puzzle him. He walked again, and then said, 'Yes, I suppose I do love him. It is not a word one associates with the proper feelings between father and son.'

'I do,' Violet said simply. 'Why shouldn't a boy love his father? I hope little Robert will love you.'

'If my father dies, he will be Lord Brancaster,' he said.

It seemed a fantastic thing to say, and Violet saw he was numb with shock. As he came near her in his restless circuit she put out a hand and caught his, and said, 'Of course he will. But that may not happen for a long time. Try not to worry. People do recover from strokes.'

He stood, captured by her hand, but not submitting. 'You must hope he does not.'

'No, why should I?' she protested quickly.

'I know you don't like him. You're afraid of him. Most people are.' He sighed. 'I think I must be the only person who . . .' Long pause. ' . . . loves him,' he finished.

'He is lucky to have a son like you,' Violet said, trying to find some way to reach him.

'I wish he thought that. He has never said so.'

'He will say so when he wakes up,' Violet said.

Now she had gone too far. He pulled back his hand, on his dignity again. 'Thank you. I came only to tell you what had happened. I must go back to him. I regret I shall not be able to dine with you this evening.'

He turned and went away quickly, before she could tell him that it was well past dinner time.

For the next few days Violet was busy, deputising for her husband in writing to the people who were expected for Christmas, telling them not to come; and in greeting, taking care of and getting rid of those who could not be contacted in time (some, she suspected as the days passed, had received their letters and had come anyway in the hope that once there they would not be turned away). Lord Holkam lay unconscious, unmoving, with the doctor and a relay of nurses always beside him, and the specialists visiting from time to time to feel his pulse and shake their heads. Sir Charles had not been of any more use to Brancaster than his inferior brethren. Until Lord Holkam recovered consciousness it would not be possible to assess the damage the stroke had done; one did not know when that might be; he might never recover it. His pulse was steady and strong, that was all that could be said for certain.

For three days the earl lay as if dead, and then the coma began to lighten. His eyes moved behind the closed eyelids, he made faint noises, not so much mutterings as weak moans. On the fourth day he opened his eyes briefly, and closed them again. On the fifth day his eyes were open a good deal of the time, but he did not seem to see anyone or anything, certainly did not respond to anything said to him, though the doctor said he was certainly conscious.

'I'm afraid the stroke may have done quite severe damage. He seems to be paralysed over most of his body, though his right hand twitches from time to time, and he can move his lips and his eyes. But he may well be both blind and deaf, and incapable of understanding.'

'He can't be blind,' Brancaster said, from the depths of his shock. 'His eyes react to the light.'

'Indeed,' said the doctor humbly, 'but being able to see does not end with the eyes. The message, as it were, has to be delivered to the correct part of the brain, and if that part has shut down, so to speak, then there is nowhere for the message to be delivered, and thus no sight.'

Brancaster waited for Sir Charles to confirm this before believing it. The specialist agreed it was so, and added that the brain was a mighty and mysterious organ, and had astonishing powers of recovery. 'As we speak the damaged part may be knitting itself up again; other parts, until now dormant, may come into play – for it is believed we normally use much less than our whole brain capacity. Your father may regain his faculties to some extent, or even fully, over time.'

'Over time?'

'Unless he has another attack, of course. It is always a possibility – even a likelihood, I am sorry to say.'

'And if he doesn't?'

'Ah! It has to be said, my dear sir, that it is possible for your father to lie here like this for a long time.'

'How long?'

'Impossible to say. Days, weeks – even months. It is not unknown.' He looked at Brancaster's bitter face, and misinterpreted it, thinking the young man was anxious to come into his title and fortune. 'Complete paralysis cases usually end in pneumonia, which fortunately carries them off quite quickly.'

'Fortunately? You call it fortunate?'

The specialist blenched a little, and said, 'It is by way of being a merciful release, that is all I meant.'

'But I don't want him to die,' Brancaster said starkly, and then, aware he had exposed himself, turned away.

Lord Holkam did not die. Christmas passed, the New Year came in, the January snow fell and sealed off Brancaster Hall from the world so that relays of men had to keep digging out a road for the doctor to come. And Lord Holkam continued to lie inert, eyes open, but apparently as sealed off from the world as if he were buried in his own personal snowdrift. Violet, for her husband's sake, went in to see the old man once a day, and wondered what it must be like to be him. What did he know? Was he aware, inside his sealed prison? Did he sleep and dream? Did he hear them, like someone walled up against their will, and shout and shout inside his head, unable to make them hear? She hoped very much that Lord Holkam was *not* aware, that it was like sleep for him. She hoped, for his sake and no-one else's, that he would die rather than go on like this.

Her pity was so intense that more than once it made her cry, and Brancaster looked on her tears with wonder. And one night he came to her bedchamber, entered hesitantly, not his usual confident, businesslike self. He came to her bedside and stood looking down at her, seeming uncertain of his welcome. Then she realised that he needed something from her, some encouragement. She folded back the covers, silently inviting him in. He hesitated a moment longer, and then slipped off his dressing-gown and slid in. He was not naked, but wearing his nightshirt – that was what gave her the clue. In the darkness she opened her arms to him, and he moved into them, rested his head on her shoulder, gave a shaky, troubled sigh. He wanted comfort, she thought; he wanted the sort of love and kindness one seeks from one's mother, not one's lover; but he had come to her. She folded her arms round him, holding him tenderly, her heart singing with triumph. He had come to her! 'I love you,' she whispered into the darkness. He did not answer, but she felt him relax in the safe, warm darkness of her embrace.

Christmas at Sandringham was gloomy, with the King in wretched health, and everyone worried about the constitutional crisis.

Francis Knollys said to Venetia one day, when he was

escaping for a few minutes in her sitting-room, 'I wish the Lords had been persuaded to pass the Budget.'

'I thought to the last moment that Cocky Lansdowne would get it through,' Venetia said.

'Balfour got to him. They rejected it on a point of principle – that the Liberals had no socialistic mandate, and that if the Lords did not force them to put it to the people they were not doing their job. But it was a gamble and, as Esher says, gambling in politics rarely succeeds.'

'But wasn't Balfour right – in principle? What if they'd let the Budget go?'

'It would have proved unpopular with all classes. The poor would have seen it was a sham and didn't make them better off, and the middle and upper classes would have writhed under the army of "inspectors" and the sheaves of "returns", and in a couple of years there would have been a large Unionist majority and a repeal. As it is, the Lords have provoked the Liberals to tamper with their powers. Once you start that sort of thing, there's no stopping it. In the long run, the House of Lords as we know it will disappear.'

Venetia tried to lighten the atmosphere a little. 'Oh, surely not? After all, what would replace it?'

'There are only two alternatives: either the second chamber would be nominated by the Lower House, which would mean party placemen who would do whatever they were told; or it would be elected by the people, which would result in continuous crisis over whose was the proper authority. Either way, we would end up with a House of Commons on which there was no check. A government with a large majority would effectively be a dictatorship.'

'Oh dear! Beauty seems to think the same way as you. I've never heard so much serious language from my nearest and dearest.'

'Language is all I have,' said Knollys. 'The King asked me not to vote, because I am so close to him, so I could not oppose the veto. I think the Lords have gone mad.

They have played right into the Chancellor's hands.'

'So what will happen now?'

'If the Liberals win they want the King to pledge to create enough new peers to swamp the Upper House and pass their legislation. It was what happened in 1832 – Esher was telling me. It's unforgivable, though, that they should ask the King to give the pledge *before* the result of the election is known.'

Venetia sighed. 'Well, I can't believe that the Tories will win.'

'No. And the King will be put in a dreadful position. If he agrees to make peers he will be favouring the Liberals and if he refuses he will be favouring the Tories. It will be the end of the Crown's impartiality either way – embarrassing, humiliating and possibly fatal to the future of the monarchy.'

'Damn these socialists?'

'I beg your pardon?'

'You were going to say, "Damn these socialists"?'

'Not in front of a lady,' he said, with a faint smile. But then, seriously, he added, 'What the world needs is a trial of socialism in some country so that everyone can see the results.'

'All this worry doesn't help the King's health.'

'No. I wish he could get away from it.'

'What happens after Christmas?'

'Brighton for a bit, staying with Arthur Sassoon, and then shooting with the Duke of Westminster. Aren't you and Overton coming to Eaton Hall?'

'No, thank heaven. Beauty begged us off, and we are going to stay with my sister instead.' Venetia's sister and her husband lived in a small house on the edge of the Ravendene estate, owned by their distant cousin, the present Duke of Southport.

Knollys said, 'I understand that Westminster has invited Sir Edward Vibart for the shooting. That's why I thought you and Overton would be going.'

'No, Eddie is going to do the honours for the family.'

'He's a nice young man – and a good courtier. The King is really very fond of him.'

'I'm very fond of him – especially when he lets me off a shooting party!' said Venetia.

The constitutional crisis and the general election were not welcomed among the Suffragettes. Though the WSPU put a brave face on it, it was obvious that the Woman Question would be quite washed away by the issues of the Budget and the House of Lords, and that whatever the result, the incoming government would have other things to think of than female emancipation. Electioneering was already going on on the basis of 'Who shall rule – the Commons or the Peers?' and, even more revolutionary, 'Who made ten thousand people owners of the soil, and the rest of us trespassers in the land of our birth?' It was matter so inflammatory that more than once Lloyd George was almost engulfed by the outrage he deliberately provoked. On one occasion, in Grimsby, he was forced to leave by a side door, climb a wall and cross a railway line to escape a crowd who wanted to burn down the hall with him in it.

In the midst of all this sound and fury, the women's voice had no chance to be heard. Still, they took advantage of the general election campaign to demonstrate, and harry the candidates whenever possible. This led to an incident that brought Lady Constance Lytton to a decision and, one day in January 1910, to Lady Anne Farraline's house in Bedford Square to explain it.

Just before Christmas one of the Suffragettes, Selina Martin, was arrested in Liverpool for breaking a window of Asquith's car. As it was Christmas, there was no court sitting, and she was remanded for a week awaiting trial. But bail was not granted, and she was sent to Walton gaol. When she refused to comply with any of the prison regulations, she was knocked to the floor and her hands were handcuffed behind her back. She was dragged across the floor face down by her hair, then hauled upstairs and forcibly fed with some violence. Afterwards she walked by herself to the top of the stairs, but when she refused to go to the punishment cell, she was kicked from behind by one of the wardresses, dragged half-way down by others, and then pushed down the rest of the flight. With her hands still handcuffed behind her, she could not save herself and fell forward, landing on her head. Stunned and helpless she was carried to a cell, thrown down and locked in.

'And all this while she was still on remand,' Lady Constance said. 'Under the law, she was still innocent, unconvicted of any crime. But Gladstone denies all allegations, and now that the election is coming, the press are not interested in us any more. You and I have some influence in the world, though it is very little; but people like Selina Martin are quite unknown. No-one cares about them except their own friends. The prison authorities can do anything to them with impunity, and when they come out, no-one will believe them, or even listen.'

'What is it that you want to do?'

'I want to strike a blow for all those like Miss Martin. You know the shameless way in which I was given preferential treatment in Newcastle, because of my rank and connections.'

'Yes, of course.'

'Very well. I mean to try whether they will recognise my need for exceptional treatment without my name, without knowing who I am. Are you with me?'

'Disguise, you mean?' Anne's eyes brightened. She was restless for action, especially since she had missed being imprisoned at Newcastle. Her arm had healed well; and the idea of disguise appealed to her active imagination. 'Dress ourselves up as lower-class women?'

'Exactly. But it must be a secret between us. No-one else must know, because if it got back to our families, they would tell the prison authorities and it would all come to nothing.'

'By God, if they should treat us badly!' Anne exclaimed with grim triumph.

'I expect they will,' Lady Constance said, with less relish. 'Are you prepared for what may follow?'

'Of course – just as you were before Newcastle. For our purposes, the worse they treat us, the better. If we are to whip up enough outrage to be heard in this political clamour, it had better be pretty bad.' She noticed that her companion looked pale. 'Will your heart stand it, Con?' she asked bluntly.

'It will have to,' said Lady Constance, and her quiet determination struck Anne again. She might be pale, and her hands might tremble a little, but what she undertook she would see through, with a courage made all the more remarkable by her sex, her health and her privileged upbringing. It made Anne angry to think of the men who would oppress people like Constance, men who hadn't a fraction of her worth, courage, or moral stature.

She laid a hand on her friend's arm. 'What's a Gladstone to you, an Asquith, a Lloyd George – a Churchill? These men are pygmies beside you. Confusion to 'em!'

Lady Constance laughed – a little shakily, but it was a laugh all the same. 'I shall feel so much better having you beside me. Are you never afraid?'

'Oh, often, when I'm alone, in the stilly watches of the night. But the rest of the time I'm just too blazing with anger to be afraid.'

'God bless that fire in you. I feel I can warm my hands by it.' She folded her cold fingers round Anne's dry, warm ones, and squeezed.

They discussed what form their arrestable action should take.

'I think we should demonstrate outside Walton gaol,' Lady Constance said. Suffragettes had made a tradition of demonstrating weekly outside prisons where women were being forcibly fed. 'It would be appropriate to what we mean to prove.'

'But the WSPU has suspended prison demonstrations during the election campaign,' Anne reminded her.

'Yes, but I mean to ask the Liverpool organisers if they will have one more. I'd like to persuade the crowd to follow me to the governor's house and demand the release of the Suffragette prisoners.'

Anne laughed. 'Oh, yes, that would be perfect! But it will mean taking the Liverpool organisers into our confidence.'

'I'm sure they will keep our secret. And it did occur to me that *someone* ought to know about us, in case – in case something happens.' She meant, Anne realised, her death in prison.

The Liverpool branch organisers agreed, and the date was set for Friday the 14th of January. Both Anne and Lady Constance rejoined the WSPU under false names and were given new membership cards. Anne chose the name of Dabs, because her brother had once had a terrier by that name, and became Miss Ann (without the 'e') Dabs. Lady Constance became Miss Jane Warton.

'Why that name?' Anne asked.

'Oh, when I came out of Holloway I had a letter from a distant relative called Warburton, praising what I'd done, so I decided then that if I ever needed an assumed name I would honour him by using his. But I thought it sounded too distinguished for this campaign so I left out the "bur".'

'It's perfect. What could be plainer than plain Jane Warton?'

'Plain indeed,' said Lady Constance. 'You know that everyone says pretty women get treated better in prison than those of unprepossessing appearance? So we must make ourselves not only look poor and undistinguished, but ugly too. I'm afraid that may be difficult for you, Anne.'

'Oh, I shall manage something, don't worry! Dye my hair, wear glasses, affect a stoop. We shall be a couple of caricature Suffragettes out of *Punch* magazine! They'll hate and despise us!'

'We must be careful not to be discovered,' Lady Constance warned. 'We must arrive in Liverpool already in character, and carry nothing with us that will betray us when we are stripped and searched.'

'Yes,' said Anne, 'like an initialled handkerchief with the wrong initials!'

'Oh, well thought of! I have initials on my under-clothing.'

'We had better buy nametapes and sew them in. We must leave nothing to chance.'

In the afternoon of the 14th of January, Miss Warton and Miss Dabs took the train from Manchester to Liverpool. Miss Warton was a little, frail-looking person in pince-nez. She wore a dark cloth coat that trailed on the ground and yet was too short in the sleeve, the deficiency being made up with coarse grey woollen gloves. Her hat was a forlorn and shapeless thing with a bit of tape with *Votes for Women* written on it, interlaced with the cloth plait that went round it, and on her lapel she wore a number of small china brooches, portraits of Mrs Pankhurst and other WSPU luminaries.

Miss Dabs was rather taller and seemed stronger, but she had a crooked look, with one shoulder higher than the other, and she dragged one foot very slightly as she walked. Her hair was a mousy colour and had a dull and lifeless texture, and was screwed into a tight bun that stuck out at right angles below the brim of her ancient and battered hat. She wore steel-rimmed eyeglasses with one stem clumsily mended with tape, through which she perused a well-worn copy of *Votes for Women*, screwing up her eyes and moving her lips as she read. Her ill-fitting brown coat had an uneven hem and her cotton dress underneath had shrunk a little and showed her scuffed boots. She wore a cockade of the colours in her hat, and a large brooch on either lapel, one saying 'Votes for Women!' and the other 'Glorious Christabel!'.

Both carried spinsterish net reticules, within which, out of sight, were several stones wrapped in purple WSPU handbills.

The Liverpool organisers had done their part, and there was a thriving demonstration going on when they reached the gaol. There was a crowd of several hundred, and two speakers, Miss Flatman and Mrs Baines, were addressing it on the subject of the Suffragette prisoners. Miss Warton and Miss Dabs mingled with the crowd, trying to work their way to the front.

Anne was very excited, especially as no-one seemed to recognise her, despite the fact that she was in close proximity to many WSPU members whom she knew very well. She had first dyed her golden hair black and then washed the dye out, which had left not only the mousy colour but the dullness. The glasses she really could not see through very well, so she did not have to remember to screw up her eyes, and the crooked shoulder and slight limp made her look less tall. As they worked forward through the crowd, Miss Dabs began to take her over, and she felt less and less like Lady Anne Farraline. Just in front of her, Miss Warton was absolutely the part – all except her sweet, clear voice, which she could not disguise. Anne, who was something of an actress, had decided to affect a lower-class accent when she was required to speak.

In that sweet, clear voice, Miss Warton, having reached the front, now addressed the people, reminding them of how the men of Dundee had recently protested against forcible feeding of women, and inviting the men of Liverpool to do the same, and go with her to the governor's house to demand the release of the Suffragette prisoners. The plan had been that Miss Warton should speak first and Miss Dabs take it up afterwards, but Miss Warton's speech was so moving that when she made a move towards the governor's house, the crowd was obviously ready to go with her, so Miss Dabs saved her voice.

The governor's house was a separate building surrounded by a small garden. As the mass of people started to move towards it, there was a danger of the two misses being engulfed, and that would not do: they must be at the forefront so as to make sure of being arrested.

Anne caught Lady Constance's eye and made a gesture to her, and began to run, so as to keep ahead of the crowd. The police were hurrying to intercept them, and they met at the hedge dividing off the governor's garden. The women were seized, but the police did not arrest them, only pushed them back and let them go.

'Smash up!' Anne said to her companion. They dragged the stones out of their reticules. Lady Constance lobbed hers gently over the hedge, afraid of hurting someone in the press of bodies. Anne, taller and stronger, could throw further and managed to break an ornamental plant pot in the garden; but one of Lady Constance's touched the shoulder of a man nearby, and that was enough to get her arrested. Two other women, who had recognised her voice, and were determined she should not go to prison alone, also managed to break windows, and were arrested. When they arrived in the police cells and got close enough to Miss Dabs, they discovered who she was, too, and were taken into the plot. One of these women was the wife of a local magistrate, and of distinguished appearance. She was useful in distracting attention from the two ladies, for she had given a false name and the police were obviously curious and a little nervous about who she really was.

The next morning the four came up for trial. The identity of the magistrate's wife had been discovered and she was released. The other Suffragette had previous convictions and was given six weeks' hard labour. Miss Warton and Miss Dabs, with no criminal record, were given fourteen days' hard labour in the third division – an outrageous sentence for the throwing of a few stones, with little damage, and a testament to their disguises and the hatred of the system for an ugly spinster.

When they arrived at Walton gaol, the difference in their treatment continued. It was not so much that the rules were different for two undistinguished women, but that they were enforced with a cold-eyed indifference, as if they were not human beings at all, but animals. Neither was given even the most cursory medical examination: Lady Constance's chronic heart disease was not discovered, nor was any enquiry made about the cause of Anne's crookedness or limp.

They refused food from the start, but no attempt was made to persuade them, or warn them of the danger to their health of fasting. The hunger at first lent Anne a sense of euphoria, and she felt elated over the success of the plan and looked forward to the further trials that were in store, if not exactly with keen anticipation at least with the fierce determination that prevented her feeling any fear. But after four days of the hunger strike, as the time approached when the forcible feeding must begin, she lost the euphoria and began to feel a sick apprehension. When, finally, the doctor burst into her cell, dangling the hated equipment from his hand, and accompanied by six wardresses and the matron, her stomach dropped away from her in fear, and she felt her mouth dry and her hands grow clammy.

The doctor's face was grim. 'Right, Dabs,' he said, 'we'll soon settle with you!'

She had no time to protest or resist: this was obviously now a practised routine. Four of the wardresses seized her and shoved her down in a chair. Two crouched on the floor and held her by the ankles, two pulled her arms back behind the chair, one held her head in a vice-like grip, and the other stood by, ready to help if necessary. There still had been no medical examination to see if she was fit for this treatment. The doctor then put one knee up on hers and began roughly to force the tube into her nostril. The pain was intense: no lubricant had been used to make the passage easier. She felt the tube scratching down her throat, and a terrible panic set in, for she felt she must either choke or suffocate, and in a completely involuntary reaction she began to struggle.

'Keep still, or it'll be the worse for you,' the doctor growled, while the sixth wardress lent her weight to the others to hold her down. The liquid was poured in through a funnel, and Anne felt it passing down the tube. There was a sharp pain behind her breastbone, and a griping cramp in her stomach, but the worst thing of all was the helplessness, being held down, being forced. She wanted to scream, but it was all she could do to breathe. It seemed to go on for ever. The only comfort in this hideous world she now inhabited was that the matron, whom she could see over the shoulders of her tormentors, was looking deeply unhappy, and quite often turned away her head as if she could not bear to look.

At last the thing was done. The doctor dragged the tube out, with no care not to hurt her in the process, and as he removed his weight from her knees he slapped her face and said, 'That'll teach you.'

As soon as the tube was out Anne was violently sick. The wardresses had quickly to let her go or she would have choked, but the two holding her legs were not quick enough to avoid the expelled feed splattering them. She was roundly abused by them, and then, despite the fact that she was trembling violently from reaction, a bucket and cloth was brought and she was made to clean up the mess herself. She tried to hurry about it, longing to be alone, but her hands shook so much she had difficulty in holding the cloth. Her nose burned and throbbed, her throat was sore, there was a pain in her head like a band of iron round her brows, and a sharp pain in her chest and stomach; but more than all those things, it was the mental pain that brought her close to tears. The doctor had slapped her! Never in her life before had she been deliberately struck, and it shocked her and cut her to the quick. Though it had not been a hard blow, it seemed to speak all his contempt for her, the contempt of the man for the woman in his power, the contempt of society for women in general and Suffragettes in particular. He despised her, and felt he could do as he pleased with and to her – and no-one in the world would take her part against him.

When at last she was left alone, she could not resist the tears any longer. She wept, not only for her own pain and humiliation but for Miss Dabs and all her like, the forgotten and powerless, who were tortured for daring to protest about their helplessness.

The days dragged by. Anne's natural strength sustained her at first, but without nourishment she weakened, and in her weakness her fear grew. Each feeding was more painful than the last, and the rest of her days were spent in apprehension, unable to think of anything but the ordeal to come. She had a constant, grinding headache, her nasal passages were inflamed and raw and it hurt to swallow; and she trembled nearly all the time. Now it was a struggle not to burst into tears at the sight of the doctor in the doorway. She wondered how Lady Constance was surviving, and had she ever seen the matron alone she might have asked, but she never had the opportunity.

She did not think she could bear much more; and yet her pride would be mortified if she gave in. She began to wish for death, as the only honourable escape from this torture. One evening, in deep despair, she broke a window pane with the intention of using a piece of broken glass to cut her wrists. But as she sat on the cell floor with the shard in her hand, she realised that she must not do it. It was her duty to the Cause and to all the forgotten women to suffer: that was what she had come here for. If she died, it must be at the hands of the authorities, so that the blame could be used against them. Fleeing them into death at her own hands was cowardice, and no-one should say Anne Farraline was a coward.

But release was nearer than she thought. The governor had already begun to wonder about the identity of Miss Warton and Miss Dabs: rumours had come in from outside, and the matron had become suspicious about Miss Warton's voice, and a certain something about both prisoners that spoke the lady rather than the woman. Also Miss Warton's health was at last alarming even the callous doctor. The governor therefore came to her, asking her if she would like to write to her mother, hoping in that way to discover who she was.

Lady Constance finally agreed to write, and composed a letter on the slate that was provided for her. But it was never sent, for the same rumour that had penetrated the prison walls also reached the Press Association, which then sent a message to her brother, Lord Lytton, to ask if it were true. By the next morning both Lady Constance and Lady Anne had been identified and were released.

Lord Lytton and Henry Brailsford wrote letters to the Home Office and the newspapers about the treatment Miss Warton and Miss Dabs had received. Anne and Lady Constance also wrote, and addressed meetings, describing the difference in the way ordinary women were treated from women with powerful friends and relatives. But a week after their release, Lady Constance collapsed and took to her bed, seriously ill as a result of the strain put on her heart by forcible feeding. Anne struggled on a little longer, but it was a heartbreaking effort: the general election took up all the attention of the press and the government and there was little or no public interest in the Suffragettes, even eminent ones. Gladstone denied there was any truth in the allegations; and after the election he was elevated to the peerage and became Governor-General of South Africa, so was spared any necessity to explain the actions of his former department.

The new Home Secretary was Winston Churchill, which Anne described as 'out of the frying pan and into the fire'. Yet Churchill was a personal friend of Lord Lytton, and through constant pressure was finally persuaded to look at the papers on the case. He found a transcription of Lady Constance's letter to her mother, which she had composed on the slate. When she had written it she had not wanted to worry her mother, and so had made no complaint of ill treatment. With that as background, Churchill said, there would be no point in attempting to take any action.

In the mean time, Lord Lytton and Henry Brailsford had conceived another plan, which was to form a 'Conciliation Committee', a group of fifty-four MPs from all parties, to bring forward a compromise Bill on women's franchise. It would not give the vote to women on the same terms as men, but would enfranchise women who were heads of household and occupied premises worth ten pounds a year. This would overwhelmingly mean single women, and it was thought only about one million would qualify. The idea was to push a wedge into the door and hope to widen the crack later, but Anne and many other Suffragettes were furious about the dilution of their claim to equality. However, the leaders of the WSPU agreed to support the Conciliation Bill and to suspend militancy for the time being, reverting to purely peaceful and constitutional means of demonstration.

Anne raged bitterly about it to Miss Vaughan, her captive audience. She was close enough to the centre to know that the capitulation had more to do with personal reasons than tactical ones: Mrs Pankhurst was tired out, and heavy with sorrow, having recently lost both her mother and her son Harry; and Christabel knew that sooner or later the membership would expect her to undergo imprisonment and forcible feeding, something she was naturally anxious to postpone as long as possible. It was, however, true that the movement as a whole was battle-weary, and that things had been getting dangerously out of hand during 1909. Sooner or later, it was feared, someone would be killed, and while those like Anne saw the logical necessity of it, and others like Emily Davison even burned for it as religious martyrs, the leaders felt responsible for the membership and preferred a period to cool off, restore strength and regroup.

After the general election the Liberals got back in, but with a reduced majority. They had lost over a hundred seats – hardly a ringing endorsement for their revolutionary budget – but with 275 seats to the Conservative Unionists' 273 they still had an overall majority, and could also generally count on the support of the 40 Labour and 82 Irish Nationalist members. There was no mention of women's franchise in the King's Speech, and the Liberals had other more pressing interests in the curbing of the House of Lords; but the WSPU stood by the truce, and pinned all their hopes on the Conciliation Committee's persuading Asquith to allow their Bill its time in the House.

Anne, partly in disgust and partly in physical and emotional weariness, left London and went down to stay with the cousins at Wolvercote to see what peace and country air could do for her health and spirits.

Chapter Thirteen

The journey to Brancaster Hall was a long one, and was made longer by the thick fog that had descended over the fens, and forced the coach that carried Jessie and her maid from the railway station to crawl at snail's pace. The carriage was old and dilapidated: the seat-covering was torn in places and tufts of the stuffing had been pulled out – obviously the work of mice, and there was such a strong smell of mice, too, that Jessie was afraid they might still be there inside the seat and had horrid visions of a sudden outpouring. The straw on the floor looked dirty, so she didn't like to push her feet into it, though her toes were gradually growing numb. Violet had warned her, in her invitation, to dress warmly, but still the cold was penetrating. She was, besides, extremely hungry: the luncheon package, of which dear old Emma had overseen the preparation, to make sure there was enough for Miss Jessie's healthy appetite, now seemed a distant dream. She looked out of the window to distract herself, but there was nothing to be seen except the cold white fog and the occasional wraith of a tree or cottage half-appearing and then disappearing again into the milky murk. She hoped they would not miss the road. She hoped the horse was up to the journey. The glimpse she had had of it at the station had not been reassuring: it was as old and gaunt and white-whiskered as the coachman.

But at last they made a turn that gave her a glimpse of tall gates on either side, and the horse picked up speed to a brisk walk. The occasional trees now included 'park' trees like hemlock, cedar and juniper, and there were no buildings to either side. So Brancaster Hall had large grounds, she concluded. The carriage swung round again and halted, and she saw a welcome glimpse of lamplight. It seemed a long time before the carriage door opened and an elderly servant let down the step and held out a hand that trembled alarmingly to help her out. She had not thought the carriage was doing anything to mitigate the cold of the day, but as she stepped down the clammy air struck her and she realised that by comparison it had been warm inside. She did not pause to look around her but hurried towards the light, almost in a panic to get indoors. The short March day was closing and the invisible sun must be setting now, removing its slight influence for warmth. Soon it would be dark, and she could only imagine how cold it would be then.

A butler who made the coachman and footman look quite juvenile was waiting to greet her in a rather dingy panelled hall with a flagstoned floor and walls hung with portraits in oils so dimmed with the smoke of ages it was impossible to make out the features – or sometimes even the sex – of the subjects. The butler was only half way through his speech of greeting, had got as far as 'I'm Disney, miss, his lordship's butler, and if there's anything that you—' when there was a sound of quick, light feet on the uncarpeted oak stairs, and Violet came into sight. She ran – practically jumped – down the last few steps and was across the hall in an instant, and Jessie found herself clutched in a close embrace, to the obvious disapproval of the butler, who belonged to a generation not given to such displays.

But Jessie hugged back as hard as she was clutched, suddenly overcome with all the feelings of love and loss that she had suppressed for so long. Violet took her hands and stepped back with a 'let me look at you' gesture, and they gazed, smiling but close to tears, at each other.

'You don't look a bit different,' Violet said at last. 'Darling Jessie!'

'Darling Vi, you do look different, but still just as beautiful as ever. More beautiful, if that's possible.'

Violet laughed at that and said, 'Such nonsense.'

'You still have my brooch,' Jessie noticed, touched. The coral hand was pinned to the breast of Violet's blue wool gown.

'Of course,' said Violet. 'I wear it all the time. It helped me to feel you were with me, in spirit at least; but now here you are in the flesh! Come and see your room,' and she turned and linked arms with Jessie and headed for the stairs. When they were up the first short flight and turned the corner she added, 'I couldn't wait for you to be shown up. Disney moves so slowly, you'd have been perished before you got to me. All the servants are ancient, but we can't pension them off because the house and everything in it belongs to Lord Holkam. We're just guests here. I've had you put in a bedroom near my sitting-room. It's small, but it's easier to keep warm than one of the grand bedrooms. I hope you approve? You can't think how cold it is here. I'm getting used to it, but coming from lovely Morland Place it will probably strike you to the marrow. I had a good fire lit in your room this morning, and told Sibsey to keep it up all day, so the chill should be taken off by now. And Scole took the sheets downstairs and ironed them herself to make sure they were dry. But this cold is tolerable, I promise you, compared with what it was a couple of months ago! I used to wear my sable coat all day, even sitting by the fire, just to keep from freezing solid like an icicle.'

This was a new, chattery Violet, Jessie thought, as they walked together up stairs and along corridors. She was not entirely at ease – which reminded Jessie of the complications that had arisen in their relationship and made her a little uneasy too. But her overwhelming feeling was of gladness to be with her friend again.

'I've missed you so,' she said, as soon as there was a pause in Violet's flow.

Violet stopped abruptly and turned to look at her, her

eyes bright with tears again. 'I've missed you, too. You can't think how much! I'm sure much more than you've missed me, because you've been with your mama and papa and the rest of the family, and I've been all alone.'

'Not quite all alone,' Jessie said. To be sure, Brancaster had not featured much in Violet's letters, but she assumed that had been merely tact on Violet's part.

But now Violet said, 'No, of course, not since Baby came. You must see him as soon as you've taken off your hat, darling; you'll love him so! But a baby isn't the same as a friend. Oh, Jess, I'm so glad you've come! We're going to have such a nice time, just talking and talking.'

The bedroom was as old and dark and shabby as everything else Jessie had seen so far, but it was obviously recently cleaned and smelt of lavender-wax with a faint undertone of ammonia. There was a good fire going, on a deep bed of red embers, and though you could not have called the room warm, the air was noticeably less Arctic than out in the corridor, and there was a hemisphere of warmth immediately around the fireplace. There were candles alight in well-polished silver candlesticks, the old furniture glowed with recent vigorous rubbing, the sheets on the bed were scented with lavender, and there was a little jug of tiny wild daffodils on the bedside table, along with a well-worn leather-covered copy of *Gulliver's Travels* and a biscuit tin. Jessie smiled with pleasure at the obvious care that had been taken to see to her comfort.

'Do you like it?' Violet asked anxiously. 'I picked the daffodils myself this morning.'

'It's lovely,' Jessie said. 'I'm sure I'll be comfortable.'

'You will as long as the fire is kept up. I've given instructions, but if it should get low, ring and ask them to make it up. It ought to be kept in all day and night, or the damp will come back.'

Jessie's luggage was not up yet – she supposed it would be a while before elderly legs could catch up with their young, strong ones – and there was no hot water, but in any case Violet said, 'Just take off your hat, Jessie darling,

397

don't wait to change or anything, and come and see my baby. I'm immensely proud of him.'

They walked along more chilly corridors and up increasingly narrow stairs, but when they reached it the nursery was warm and well lit with lamps. 'The one room I never have to argue about – everyone in the house agrees that Baby has to be kept warm,' Violet said, giving another unintended hint about the state of affairs. A pretty, bosomy nursery-maid was presiding, and brought forward the young scion at once – a red-faced mite in a long, lacy dress. When he saw his mother, he smiled at once, and waved his arms up and down, and Violet in response held out hers automatically and took him from the nurse.

'Isn't he beautiful?' she said to Jessie. 'Did you ever see anything like his cheeks? Just like perfect red velvet! And his hair is beginning to curl. I think it's going to be dark like mine.'

Jessie was not greatly taken with babies, feeling that foals, puppies and kittens all had great advantages over human young, but she had to allow some interest in the offspring of her best friend. Little Robert, comfortably held against his mother's shoulder, allowed his blue gaze to wander to Jessie, and examined her face solemnly. He had, Jessie thought, a marked resemblance to his mother, as well as having a faint and ghostly – to Jessie, disturbing – look of his father somewhere in there. It struck her forcibly then that a baby really was an amalgam of its parents – as though their features had been melted down together, well mixed, and then moulded into this new person. Violet and Brancaster. If she had had any doubt anywhere in the unthinking part of her brain, it was dispelled now: they were married, a married couple, never to be parted, and Brancaster was out of her reach for ever. It was as well to be convinced now of this, before meeting him, she thought; and she felt a sudden affection for the younger Robert Fitzjames Howard. She must have smiled on the thought, for the baby suddenly smiled at her, a beaming, gummy thing of surprising delight that made her feel strangely moved and flattered.

'He likes you,' Violet said, with satisfaction. 'Would you like to hold him?'

Jessie took the child with residual reluctance, but he seemed strong, not breakable, and was surprisingly heavy in her arms. He had got to the age of being able to support his head, so she did not have to deal with that terrifying broken-flower-stem wobbling that was the most unnerving thing about small babies. He seemed quite contented with the change of arms, and at once grabbed hold of the chain of the cross hanging round Jessie's neck and hauled on it lustily.

'He's very advanced for his age,' Violet was telling her proudly. 'He can sit up now if you steady him, and he's beginning to try to sit up on his own. And Betsey says once they can do that, they'll be crawling any moment.'

'That's right, my lady,' Betsey said earnestly. 'He's such a lovely baby, miss, ever so sweet-tempered. It's a real pleasure to look after him. And the picture of his lord-ship, if you'll excuse the liberty.'

Violet waved the servant away, took the baby back from Jessie and went to sit down with him on her knee.

'I think he looks much more like you,' Jessie said, following.

'Oh, Betsey thinks the world of Brancaster,' Violet said; and thus the forbidden name was easily arrived at between them. 'It was he who found her for me, as a matter of fact. I couldn't have been more surprised, because he doesn't bother himself with the household as a rule. But before Baby was born, Lord Holkam wanted him to be looked after by Brancaster's old nanny, who's nearly sixty and hasn't any teeth and is *far* too old to take care of my little one. I was in a terrible worry about it, but I didn't dare say anything for weeks, and then Brancaster said there was nothing we could do about it. But after Lord Holkam had the stroke, Brancaster said he wouldn't know anything about it any more, so he brought in Betsey. It was such a weight off my mind. Now Nanny just supervises the nursery – and she dozes in her own room most of the time, so she doesn't even do much of that.'

Sitting in the nursery and passing the baby from hand to hand like something good to eat, Violet asked for and Jessie told the news from Morland Place. Alice was very hearty and expecting the baby in April, and seemed quite comfortable with the idea (though it was always hard to tell with Alice, she showed so little of her feelings) but Uncle Teddy was like a mouse on a hot brick, and plainly wouldn't know a moment's peace until it was all safely over. Robbie and Ethel were very happy, and Robbie had quite changed since the marriage, and become lively and almost talkative. Ethel was a dear and fitted in so well it was hard to remember Morland Place without her. Dad had had a bad cold, which had pulled him down dreadfully and Mother had been very worried about him, but he seemed to have shaken it off now, only the least thing tired him and he hadn't been out of doors for weeks. Oh, and there was news of Bertie: he had tied up his business more quickly than he expected and was taking an earlier passage. He would be in England in April instead of June, but he was to stay with the Puddephats at first, and did not expect to come down to Yorkshire until late May, so it would work out the same as far as they were concerned.

'Everyone looks forward to seeing the dear fellow,' Jessie said. 'But no-one knows what he means to do. I suppose he will go and look at the Red House and the estate and decide then. I expect he has money of his own from his business in India. Dad seems doubtful whether he'll want to spend it on bringing the estate back – he didn't get on very well with his own father, Bertie didn't, I mean, so he probably hasn't much affection for the place.'

When the immediate news was told, Jessie was about to ask Violet for hers, but Violet looked at the nursery clock and said, 'Look at the time! We must go and dress. We've been sitting here much longer than I thought. Betsey! Come and take Baby.'

As they went back downstairs Jessie asked Violet how she should dress.

Violet said, 'Oh, wear your best, darling. Brancaster dines with us tonight, and I want him to see how pretty you are. I'll come and fetch you when you're ready and we'll go down together. You'll never find the dining-room on your own. Did you pack a warm shawl, as I suggested? You'll need to wear it between rooms.'

While Mary Tomlinson, the maid she had brought with her from Morland Place, dressed her, Jessie contemplated her feelings about the fact that she was about to meet Lord Brancaster face to face for the first time since the wedding. She had been delighted when Violet invited her to come and visit at last, but though there had never been any question of refusing, she had had a reluctance to overcome on the score of seeing Brancaster again. It would be painful, no doubt; it might be embarrassing. She imagined that Violet had delayed inviting her for so many months because of those feelings. She was glad that Brancaster had not been there to greet her when she arrived, that she had been able to have those hours alone with Violet, for them to get over the initial awkwardness and feel their way back to the love and intimacy they had shared. Of course, they could never be *quite* as intimate as before – there would always be Violet's experiences as a married woman, an area of her life that Jessie could not share, whereas when they were girls there had been no secrets between them. But the old Violet was still there, though more assured and grown up in her manner and – puzzlingly – perhaps a little more sad. Still, living in this dreary, cold house might well account for that, to say nothing of the presence upstairs of the paralysed old lord who clung on against all expectation to the life that must surely be a terrible burden to him.

But Brancaster – would he be the same? How would she feel about him? He had kissed her once, and she had never been able to decide to her satisfaction what that had meant. Would he remember it now, when he saw her again? She was afraid there would be awkwardness between the three of them. She didn't know whether he and Violet had ever talked about her, whether he knew that she had thought he meant to marry her. She would have trusted the old Violet to keep her secret for ever, but she did not know how married people were together, and whether perhaps there had to be a sacrifice on the altar of Hymen of former secrets, in the interests of a stronger union.

But when she and Violet entered the drawing-room together, where Lord Brancaster was waiting, standing before the fire and reading the newspaper, all her speculations were blown away by his absolute calmness. He greeted her politely, neither with warmth nor coldness, asked if she had had a good journey and found her room comfortable, prognosticated a fine day for the morrow, and generally behaved as if she were the most common, albeit distant, of acquaintances.

As for her own feelings, there was a pang at the sight of his undiminished handsomeness, but as he showed none of the warmth and interest in her that she had found so delightful, his physical beauty had to stand alone. He made no effort to charm, either her or Violet. His conversation was plain, about local matters and the political situation, and outside those manly topics he had nothing to say, and frequently sat eating his dinner in silence as if there were no ladies present at all. She and Violet carried most of the conversation, and when he added something it was generally on a completely different subject interesting to him: he almost seemed to disregard their chatter as if they were children.

It was a surprise to Jessie, for at home everyone listened to everyone else. Both Dad and Uncle Teddy were as interested in what she and Mother had to say as what they said to each other. Even the old Robbie had listened, though he had rarely added anything. To find herself and Violet almost dismissed in that way – discounted, if you like – was, well, not nice. You could not exactly say that he was impolite, but he was clearly not interested in them. By the end of dinner her being in love with him had dimmed to a faint ache. She almost – she acknowledged it to herself with amazement – found him *dull*.

He did not join them in the drawing-room for coffee, having excused himself when they left the table because he had to go up and see his father, and Violet did not seem to find this unusual or disappointing. Over their coffee they chatted freely, but Violet did not mention Brancaster at all, and he did not come to the drawing-room before they went to bed.

In bed that night Jessie puzzled over it all, and tried to guess the feelings of the principal players. As to her own, it was as though there were now two Brancasters, the one she had danced with in London, the handsome, charming romantic one she was still in love with, and the present one, who only looked like him, and did not stir her. It was a comfortable solution: she could be in love with the mythical Lord B quite safely without betraying her friendship, and leave the real Lord B to Violet. But did Violet find the real man as delightful? She hoped desperately that she did.

The following day dawned foggy, but it gradually lifted during breakfast and revealed a sunny day. Brancaster did not breakfast with them – Violet said he rarely did, taking his breakfast much earlier and going about estate and other business straight afterwards. After breakfast the two young women went for a walk together, and Violet showed Jessie her garden and described her plans for it for the future. Despite the sunshine, it was very cold out, and they did not walk for long.

As they returned indoors, Violet said, 'I always go up to sit with Lord Holkam at this time. Would you like to come with me?'

'You sit with him? But I thought – isn't he in a coma?'

'No, not exactly,' Violet said. 'It's hard to describe. He wakes and sleeps, in the sense that he lies with his eyes open sometimes, and closed at others, but he doesn't speak and it's impossible to say whether he knows anything that is happening around him. The doctors can't tell us for sure. But sometimes . . .' She frowned a little. 'It may be my imagination. Perhaps it is. But sometimes I've thought that I could see a gleam of recognition in his eyes when I speak to him.' She was silent a moment, and then went on. 'You see, I keep thinking, what if he *is* aware? What if his mind is normal, and he's thinking and feeling away all the time inside his head, while his body is quite paralysed and he can't do anything to let us know what he wants to say? It would be so terrible, don't you think?'

'Yes, really terrible.'

'I feel such pity for him, especially as he was so – so domineering before. Worse for someone like that to be helpless, than for someone who had always been meek and unimportant.'

'I suppose so,' Jessie said.

'So I go and sit with him and talk to him a little, just as if he could hear me, which he may do. And sometimes I think how bored to screaming-point he might be – though unable to scream, of course, which makes it worse – and I sit and read to him from what his man says were his favourite books.'

It seemed the oddest set-up in the world to Jessie, who could only marvel at her friend's tender heart – especially as she knew how Violet had disliked and feared Lord Holkam before. She declared herself ready to go with her to visit him now, though she thought it might be horribly bizarre and unpleasant.

Violet seemed glad. She smiled and said, 'Just behave as if he saw and heard everything. It would be awful to offend him now he's helpless to object.'

It was indeed very strange at first. Lord Holkam's room was enormous, bigger even than the great bedchamber at home, and seemed gloomy, with the old dark panelling and small windows of the Tudor period. There were portraits – of ancestors, Jessie supposed – all round the

404

walls, and some paintings of horses and dogs, which she would have liked to examine more closely. The carpet was dark red, and most of the space was filled with furniture, and the furniture covered with ornaments and framed photographs in the Victorian manner. The bed was enormous, and stood on a sort of raised dais; it had heavy red velvet drapes and the posts were decorated at the top with coronets from which sprang bouquets of black ostrich feathers.

And in the midst of all this dark, heavy, Victorian splendour, the earl lay immobile, propped against his pillows, and looking strangely small and wooden, like a particularly ugly marionette. Paralysis had begun to smooth out the lines of his face, while the flesh had melted away, leaving it shiny and skull-like. His hands lay on top of the sheet, and Jessie noticed that his fingernails were very long: his nurse must have forgotten, or not cared, to cut them. He seemed to stare at nothing, and though his eyes moved sometimes, it was not in any intelligent way.

Violet spoke to him cheerfully, though without familiarity, and begged to introduce Jessie just as if he were holding court. At Violet's gesture she went closer to the bed and, feeling odd about it, spoke to the wooden effigy, thanked it for having her to stay. There was a smell of sickness in the room, which intensified nearer to the bed, and she was glad to step back and let Violet carry on with her dutiful conversation. *Did* the old lord hear anything, understand anything? It was hard to say. If Violet saw anything in those random movements of the eyes, it was either wishful thinking on her part, or a greater familiarity that allowed her to discern a pattern. Jessie could not help wondering, if Lord Holkam did understand, whether he might not be inwardly squirming under coals of fire.

They did not stay long, though Violet promised to return later. When they were safely out in the corridor and Jessie was trying not to appear as relieved as she felt, Violet said, 'Thank you for coming with me. It's no part of your duty, of course, so I'm grateful for your support.'

'It's no part of *your* duty,' Jessie could not help pointing out.

'Perhaps not, strictly speaking. But, you see, I've so often caught myself thinking that when he dies, Brancaster and I will be able to have a normal life, and I'll be able to see my mother again, and we can make the house comfortable and so on. It was like wishing him dead, and then when he had the stroke and we thought he would die right away, I felt so guilty. So I can't help feeling that I've been given this time to make it up to him. Is that foolish?'

'*Very* foolish,' said Jessie, slipping her arm through Violet's. 'But very like you, darling Vi.'

The visit passed peacefully, one day being very much like another. They walked in the gardens and, when the weather permitted, for longer distances across the park, though Violet was not a dedicated walker, so they never went as far as Jessie would have liked. Violet ordered the carriage sometimes and they drove out so that Jessie could see something of the country – which she found very unappealing, flat and watery and full of straight edges, most unnatural. The highlight of the visit was perhaps when they took a trip by train into Lincoln and looked at the cathedral and the shops. For the rest they followed Violet's own daily round, which meant sitting by the fire and talking and sewing, playing with the baby, picking and arranging flowers for the house, and reading to Lord Holkam.

Compared with the energetic busy-ness of Jessie's days at home, it was dull, but Violet seemed used to it. Jessie could see how lonely she must have been, though. They saw little of Brancaster, who apparently led his own separate life, and there were hardly any visitors – perhaps because of Lord Holkam's condition. The vicar came once to enquire dutifully after his lordship, and was pressed by Violet to stay to tea; and once there was a very dull dinner party, where the guests, all neighbours, spoke in hushed voices about the earl, and then discussed farming with Lord Brancaster, deferring to his opinions in a very obsequious way.

One thing that surprised Jessie was that Violet did no poor-visiting, which her mother had always impressed on her as an important duty of the mistress of the house. It could not be because there were no poor to *be* visited: their drives showed her a very depressed countryside, dilapidated dwellings, thin and shabby people with the bowed shoulders of rural poverty. She wondered if Violet, having been brought up wholly in London, was unaware of the duties of a country chatelaine – but then she remembered that, strictly speaking, she was not the chatelaine, not as long as Lord Holkam lived.

The weather grew milder, the days lengthened, other flowers joined the daffodils and primroses, and the sky seemed always filled with skeins of ducks and geese arriving from foreign parts to begin their breeding season. Jessie acknowledged that the fens had their beauty. She had fallen into the rhythm of Violet's days, and no longer felt confined and restless; but she began to think of home, of how Alice was faring, of her father's health, and whether her own particular horses were being schooled properly in her absence. She wished she could take Violet with her for a return visit, and wondered whether, when Lord Holkam finally gave up the ghost, it would be allowed.

One day she had been walking alone in the park, from a need for more vigorous exercise than would have suited Violet. On returning indoors she went to look for her and, finding the sitting-room empty, she went up to the nursery, thinking she might be there. She could hear young Master Robert crying before she reached the room. On opening the door, she saw him sitting up in his cot and bawling with red-faced frustration. The servant Betsey was not to be seen. Jessie advanced into the room, wondering what had happened, for it was not to be expected that the sprig of the house should be left unattended. The door to the inner room, the maid's bedroom, was partly open, and Jessie saw the shape of two people within. As she came closer, she saw that they were locked in an embrace, and she had only a moment to think indignantly that the wretched girl was ignoring her charge while she carried on an *amour* with a footman (and to wonder which of the unprepossessing fellows it was) before she recognised the height and form of Lord Brancaster.

As horror leaped into her mind she beat a hasty retreat, her cheeks burning with embarrassment and shame. She heard movement behind her, realised they must have seen her, and almost ran out of the room, slamming the door behind her, in a panic that he might come after her and confront her. She ran down to her bedroom and shut the door after her, leaning against it while she caught her breath and tried to stop herself trembling. Violet's words came back to her, that it had been Brancaster who recruited Betsey for the household. Could he have done it with this in mind? But why, *why*, when he had a wife – and a lovely young wife at that, beautiful Violet? Jessie was not so absolutely innocent in the ways of the world now that she did not know there were men who liked to debauch servants, and men who were not faithful to their wives. But Brancaster had married for love only eighteen months ago. Could he have fallen out of love and found himself so dissatisfied so soon?

Or was it – she wondered, with a dreadful sense of a weight descending on her – that he had never been in love with Violet, that he had been dissembling, and that it had been a marriage for quite other reasons? Violet had had a large dowry – oh, surely it could not have been that? She remembered Brancaster's apparent indifference to Violet whenever she had seen them together. Was that, then, not just civilised behaviour, concealing passion in public? Oh, poor Violet! Pity surged through her, and she wondered, with a fresh access of horror, whether she knew.

She wondered how she would ever face him again: if he had seen her, he knew that she knew. It would be agonisingly embarrassing. She longed to go home at once – and at the same time could not bear the thought of abandoning Violet to this horrible situation. Perhaps she didn't know – and then, should Jessie tell her? How could she bear to hurt her? But if she didn't, it would be like protecting Brancaster.

It was a long time before her mind was sufficiently composed for her to leave her room and go again in search of her friend. She met a maid just ducking into one of those concealed doors that gave onto a secret warren of servants' passages and stairs that ran behind the family rooms (did Brancaster use them on his clandestine visits?) and asked her where Lady Brancaster was.

'She was with his lordship earlier, but I think she's just gone out in her garden, miss.'

So Jessie went slowly out to find her, and found her peacefully pruning and tying in a rambling rose, refreshing herself after the distress of reading to Lord Holkam. Jessie could not bring herself to say anything just then. That afternoon, when they were alone and comfortable in Violet's sitting room, she looked at the lovely dark head bent over her sewing (she was making a dress for the baby) and decided that she could not be the one to shatter Violet's dream, if dream it was. If she were asked, she would tell, but otherwise . . . And yet, she longed to know if Violet did know. If so, she might welcome a chance to talk about it.

So she said, 'Can I ask you something? Something rather personal?'

Violet looked up, a quick glance that might have suggested apprehension, and then down again at her moving fingers. 'If you can't, I don't know who can,' she said.

'I just wanted to know,' Jessie said carefully, 'what is it like, being married? Is it the way you expected?'

Violet didn't answer at once. The pause was so long, Jessie thought she was not going to; but then she said, 'No, not really. Not at all, in fact.' She sighed, and put down her needle. 'I thought it would be like you and me, only with something more added. Do you know what I mean? That Brancaster and I would do things together and talk and laugh and – and *feel* the same things, the way you and I did. But I suppose it was silly to think that. Men are not the same as women, and they think differently about things. Men and women can't be friends the way you and I were.'

Jessie thought of her parents. Weren't they friends? She thought they were – but perhaps they might be exceptional.

'What about,' she asked diffidently, not sure if Violet would answer this, 'what about married life? I mean – you know. The married thing.'

Violet answered quickly, as though she had been waiting for the question: 'I know what you mean. And it was horrid at first. I can't tell you how horrid. But one gets used to it. And it doesn't happen often, thank God. I forget all about it in between whiles.'

Jessie remembered their hesitant conversations on this subject when they had been débutantes together. They had agreed, in their profound ignorance, that it would be bliss, once one got used to it, because of loving the man and his loving you. It seemed, disappointingly, that this was not so. There was nothing in Violet's voice or face to suggest bliss had ever been on the agenda.

Jessie had to ask, daring the step towards the forbidden, 'But he does love you?'

'Oh, yes,' Violet answered with reassuring promptness. 'It's not the way we thought it would be when we were girls. Not all flame and passion. It's more calm and – and detached. But I'm sure he does love me. And he's very proud of Baby.'

'And you're happy?'

'Yes,' Violet answered. 'Things will be different when the earl goes. It's bound to be a little strange and diffi- cult at the moment. But when Brancaster inherits we'll be free to come and go and entertain and do all the things we want to do. We'll have a house in London, and I'll be able to see my family and everything will be all right. So you see—' She stopped, staring into the flames. Jessie feared she was close to crying, but when she spoke again it was in a normal voice. 'There has to be compromise. Perhaps things don't turn out as one imagines, but marriage is for ever and one has to make the best of it. And on the whole I'm quite content.'

Jessie did not dare to ask any more. Violet had made her decision, she saw, and it would be cruel to stir up any doubt about it. But afterwards, in bed, she thought that surely it *couldn't* be all there was, this calm, passionless compromise, or what had the poets and novelists been talking about down the centuries? Surely there must be bliss somewhere? Well, perhaps the marriages of titled people were intended to fulfil other criteria, and they could not expect the sort of union Dad and Mother had. If that were the case she, Jessie, was much luckier than her friend.

But at least, she thought – she hoped – she doesn't know about him and Betsey. Please God she never did find out. In this case ignorance, at least, could be bliss.

A few days later the official term of her visit was over, and though Violet wished, rather wistfully, that she could stay longer, Jessie wanted very much to go home, and only wished she could take Violet with her. 'But I'll come again, if you'll have me,' she said.

'Will you?' Violet said, sounding relieved. 'I thought you must have been so bored you'd never want to visit here again.'

'I could never be bored when I'm with you,' Jessie said. 'I'll come and visit you here or anywhere else. You only have to ask.'

Going down to dinner on the last evening, the thing she had dreaded happened: she met Lord Brancaster on the stairs, and they were alone together, with no-one else in sight or earshot. They looked at each other for a moment, Brancaster with a sort of calculation, Jessie wondering desperately what he was going to say and

411

whether he was going to ask for her silence.

But he said, 'Your last evening. I hope you have passed your time pleasantly?'

'I've had a very nice time,' she said. 'Thank you. I love to be with Violet,' she added, hoping it might be a warning to him.

He smiled – oh, how that smile jogged memories she wished she did not have! – and said, 'It was kind of you to visit us. We live in such a quiet way at the moment. For reasons which I'm sure you understand, we weren't able to offer you much by way of entertainment. But I hope you will come again.'

'Whenever Violet wants me,' she said.

He offered her his arm, and she put her hand on it, feeling very awkward. They started down the stairs together. He felt much too close to her: she could feel the heat of his body. He said, in a low voice, as though this were not a continuation, but a quite different conversation, 'Do you ever go up to Town, Miss Compton? A lively young woman must find country life palls after a time. I'm sure you have much more freedom to come and go than Lady Brancaster has, in the present circumstances. I am in Town from time to time, though she prefers to remain here at home.'

Jessie's mouth was dry, her tongue seemed stuck to the roof of it. Was he suggesting what she thought he was suggesting? She *must* have misunderstood him. But why else would he mention Town at all? 'I don't know. No. I haven't been there since the wedding,' she answered almost at random.

'You have relatives in London, I believe. Perhaps you will be paying them a visit in the near future?'

Fortunately they had reached the bottom of the stairs and she was able to take her hand from his arm, as though she had only needed it to descend. But as she drew it away he caught at it and pressed it briefly, and smiled down at her with the same smile she remembered from the conservatory at Wolvercote.

412

Touch and smile were over in a second, and they were walking on towards the drawing-room like the commonest of acquaintances. He did not pursue an answer to his last question – or perhaps he felt he had had his answer in her silence. Jessie's mind was burning with shame and resentment. She felt she understood now: understood Brancaster and everything that had ever passed between them, and she was bitterly humiliated by the knowledge. He had flirted with her, not courted her, during her London Season – flirted because he thought her a different kind of girl from Violet. He had kissed her in the conservatory, not because he loved her but because he thought he *could*. She was pretty much on a par in his mind with Betsey the nursery-maid. And he thought that, if the opportunity arose, Miss Compton would drop into his hand like a ripe apple, just as Betsey had.

It was the hardest thing she had ever had to do, to behave normally at dinner that evening, but stronger even than her personal pain was the determination to protect Violet at all costs. Trying not to show her resentment towards Brancaster in front of Violet perhaps led her to sparkle more than she otherwise would – which doubtless, she reflected later, would only reinforce his opinion of her as *fast*. She was never so relieved as when Violet finally stood up.

Brancaster stood, too, and said, 'I take my leave of you now, Miss Compton, as I do not join you in the drawing-room and will be away before you get up tomorrow.'

She said goodbye and bowed slightly from the far end of the room, in case there should be any thought of shaking hands, and escaped after Violet to the drawing-room. She was too distracted really to enjoy the last evening with her friend, kept watching the door, afraid that Brancaster would change his mind and come in after all. She slept very ill that night, and the next day was really almost glad to go. She pitied Violet deeply, and hated to leave her, standing on the gravel before the porch, looking so small and alone against the background of the great rambling house, and waving forlornly as the carriage jerked into motion and crunched away down the drive.

She spent the whole journey home in deep and unsatisfying thought. One of the things that troubled her most was that the mythical Lord Brancaster still survived in her stupidly ungovernable brain, as if he really had existed and was different from the one to whom poor Violet was married. She could still visit him in memory and see his smile and feel the tender feelings he had aroused. She missed him – or, rather, she missed the feelings she had had about him. She mourned the loss of her idol and the joy of being in love, and wondered more than ever what the rest of her life would hold.

Ever since Christmas, Sir James Reid and the courtiers closest to the King had been urging him to go abroad. The cold and damp and fog of winter were exacerbating his condition; his violent fits of coughing were frightening, leaving him gasping for breath and blue around the lips. But the King would not leave the country during the general election and with the constitutional crisis hanging over it.

The Liberals' reduced majority gave him some small comfort, lessening their ability, he felt, to bully him; and at Windsor he had a happy thought. He confided to Knollys and Overton that as the Prime Minister was effectively proposing to destroy the House of Lords in its long-established state, he felt a matter of such constitutional importance must be put to the country. There must be a second general election fought solely on that issue, before any further action could be taken.

Asquith accepted this, and so at the opening of Parliament in February had to stand up before the House of Commons and admit that he had no pledge from the King, as had been assumed, to create sufficient peers to ensure passing the government's Bills. He added that it was the duty of responsible politicians to keep the Crown out of the realm of party politics.

'To ask, in advance, for a blank authority in regard to a measure which has never been submitted to or approved by the House of Commons, is a request which, in my judgement, no constitutional statesman can properly make,' he said. Since this was exactly what he had done before the election, Venetia, reading the speech in *The Times*, put him down as a hypocrite.

His words were greeted with a frenzy of disappointment from his own party members, who had assumed the battle was as good as over, and now discovered it had barely begun. The speech pleased the King, though it did not make him like Asquith any better. Just after the election, he had invited Asquith down to Windsor, and Asquith had refused, which was not only ill-mannered, but unprecedented. As Knollys said angrily to Venetia, 'It is criminal for a prime minister to refuse the sovereign, because unlike a private person, the sovereign cannot retaliate.'

With matters in this state, the King was persuaded at the beginning of March 1910 to go to Biarritz for a rest. Overton went with him, and he was joined at the Hotel du Palais by Mrs Keppel and his close friend the Marquis de Soveral. But the weather was miserable, and two days after his arrival he became so ill that he remained in his room, while the wind lashed the rain against the windows, rattled the shutters, and flattened the flowers in the municipal gardens.

The first weeks of the new Parliament were as stormy as the weather, with such divisions in Cabinet that Sir Edward Grey, the Foreign Secretary, believed the government would collapse. Lloyd George and Winston Churchill were still making provocative speeches: Churchill had publicly declared that he would not object to the removal of the House of Lords altogether, and government by a single chamber. And the Irish members were threatening to vote against the Budget because of the increase in duty on whiskey, which would damage their trade.

The Irish members were, in fact, much more interested in Home Rule, which would never be carried without a reform of the House of Lords. To appease them, Asquith introduced, not quite a Bill, but three resolutions on Lords reform. He announced that if they were rejected he would feel obliged to advise the Crown on the 'necessary steps' to be taken to ensure that Bills passed in the Commons by large majorities were not rejected by the Lords. He further stated that the measures would have to be taken in that Parliament, ignoring the agreement he had made with the King that it would be put to the people first.

'In fact,' Overton wrote to Venetia, 'what the government means to do is to purchase the assent of the Irish MPs to a Budget they disapprove of by threatening the King. In effect, they want to force His Majesty to assist in a *coup d'état*. If you can think of any more disgraceful an example of blackmail, I'd like to know what it is. I can't think why the moderate Liberals don't stand up and oppose it. It's obvious that Asquith and Co. are in the hands of the Irish and no longer their own masters. The King is disgusted with them. He says they are ruining the country, and so puffed up with conceit they think they can do no wrong.'

The King returned to England on Wednesday the 27th of April, looking little better for his holiday. Still, he went to Covent Garden that evening to see *Rigoletto*, one of his favourite operas, with Tetrazzini singing Gilda. It was his habit to make a public appearance of that sort when returning from abroad, to emphasise that the King was back in the country. There was a great burst of applause as he appeared in his box, showing his enduring popularity.

The following day, the House of Lords passed the Budget, removing one element from the conflict. But the three resolutions on Lords reform had been agreed by the Commons, and the rest of the session promised to be an acrimonious struggle. The House adjourned for the

416

short Easter recess, and the Prime Minister set off in the Admiralty yacht for a holiday in Gibraltar.

On the Friday, the King held a small luncheon at Buckingham Palace to which Venetia and Overton were invited, and to which the Prince of Wales brought his two eldest children, the young princes Edward and Albert, now aged fifteen and fourteen. They were both rather small and slight for their age, but nice-looking boys, particularly the elder, who was very like his mother, with her golden hair and blue eyes, while the younger more resembled his father. They were both having a naval education, like their father before them, Prince Edward at Dartmouth, where his prowess at sports had made him popular, Prince Albert still at Osborne. They had nice manners, and Venetia enjoyed talking to them.

The Queen was still abroad with Princess Victoria, staying with her brother the King of the Hellenes in Corfu, so the King asked Venetia if she would act as his hostess for the weekend at Sandringham: he could never bear solitude. She discovered that as a gesture of thanks to her he had invited her sister Olivia and her husband to join them there. As Eddie was on duty, Venetia for once looked forward to a Sandringham Saturday-to-Monday. 'It will be quite like a family affair,' she said to Overton, as they climbed aboard the train early on Saturday morning.

In fact, it was a very pleasant weekend, though the weather was cold, windy and wet. The King seemed happy, having put aside the troubles for the time being. He enjoyed a lengthy peramble around his gardens with the head gardener and agent, to discuss the alterations that had been put in hand while he was away, and visited his farm and stud. In the evening he was in very good form, and told a string of amusing stories about incidents from the past. On the Sunday he drove to church rather than walking across the park with the others, but after the service, despite the inclement weather, he had another long walk around the gardens and greenhouses. Venetia thought him quieter than usual, but more content than she had seen him for a long while. 'He really is devoted to this place,' she added, with a hint of amazement in her voice that made her husband laugh.

Jack was sitting by the fire in his room, reading. He was feeling quite content. He had done a good piece of work that morning; his shoes were off and his stockinged feet were resting on the fender, toasting nicely; he had just made himself a cup of cocoa in a saucepan on the trivet; and outside the rain was lashing the windows. As a crowning comfort, today being Saturday there would be meat pie for supper, which was one of the better creations of his landlady, Mrs Parsons.

He was half-way down his cocoa when he heard her on the stairs: she breathed like a steam-engine when going up any kind of slope, and it was only her insatiable curiosity that made her bring letters upstairs instead of leaving them on the hallstand to be collected. He was not expecting a letter and thought she would pass his door and go on up, but her steps slowed, the gasping came to a halt, and in a moment there was a tap at his door and her voice called, 'Are you there, Mr Compton?' It was her invariable greeting, though she watched all her lodgers in and out and always knew exactly where everyone was in the house.

Jack put down his cup and padded over to the door to open it. There was no letter in her hand, but instead a folded newspaper. Her face was creased in an expression of such deep concern that he suffered a sinking of his stomach, thinking it must be news of a death. 'What is it, Mrs Parsons? Not bad news, I hope?'

'Well, I don't rightly know, Mr Compton, and I certainly hope not, but I was just having five minutes with the paper when I saw this here, and I thought I ought to show it you, in case you hadn't seen it.' She took his posture as an invitation to come in, and advanced to the centre of the room, her quick eyes darting round to see exactly what he had been doing and whether he had moved anything. She objected violently to the transposition of any article of furniture even by so much as an inch or two.

Jack resignedly shut the door. The paper, he saw, was the local weekly, and it was folded open to the page where they relayed the more important of the announcements from the London papers and the local dailies.

'Here,' said Mrs Parsons, holding out the paper to him and prodding with one forefinger at a paragraph. 'I read this, and straight away I wondered, because it isn't what you'd call a common name, is it?'

Jack read where she was indicating. 'An engagement has been announced between Maud, only daughter of Richard Puddephat, Esq., of Pont Street, London, and Sir Percival Parke, of The Red House, Bishop Winthorpe, Yorkshire. Sir Percival is lately returned from India.'

Mrs Parsons watched his face greedily as he reread the short paragraph, and then prompted him, 'Well? Is it the young lady you've been courting all these months? I did wonder, because I b'lieve you said her name was Maud and, like I said, Puddephat is a queer unusual name. Only I thought p'r'aps there'd been a mistake somewhere, on account of the way you've been walking out with her all this time. P'r'aps the newspaper got it mixed up?'

Jack was trying hard to take it in, staring at the words as if looking could make them different. Maud engaged to Bertie? He had known, of course, that Bertie was coming home earlier than planned, and would be staying with the Puddephats, but he hadn't even known he had arrived yet. He had expected a note from Pont Street announcing the arrival, and perhaps inviting him to call, but none had come. And now this! Unlikely, as Mrs Parsons knew very well, that it was a mistake. Could Bertie and Maud have fallen in love so quickly? Assuming he had arrived at the very beginning of April, that only gave them three weeks. Or was it something that had been arranged between Bertie and Mr Puddephat before he ever came home? That, alas, seemed much more likely.

He had to say something to his landlady. 'I wasn't walking out with her, Mrs Parsons. She was simply a young lady I admired very much.'

Mrs Parsons was not to be cheated of her outrage. She sniffed. 'It's like you to put a good face on it, so good-natured as you are, but if you ask me, there's been some queer goings-on. This Sir What's-his-name, he'd be a wealthy gentleman, I make no doubt. Just back from India, it says. One of them Nabobs, made his fortune out there, and now come back stealing other men's fee-ancies out from under their noses, luring them with his gold, the black-'earted villain! And the way young girls go on these days is shocking! Throwing over a nice honest young gent for the sake of a title – and to do it so fast, as well, the madam. It's what I'd call indecent 'aste.'

The *Daily Mail* and other journals like it had a lot to answer for, Jack reflected. He pushed the paper back at her and said, 'You mustn't speak like that, Mrs Parsons. There was no understanding between Miss Puddephat and me. She was free to give her heart wherever she liked. We were not engaged, nor ever likely to be.'

'No, not with black-'earted villains like this Sir Periwinkle about, or whatever his name is, dazzling young girls with his ill-gotten gains!'

'Miss Puddephat is not a young girl, and Sir Percival is not a black-hearted villain. In fact, he's my cousin.' He was rewarded by seeing Mrs Parsons's jaw drop at this last revelation, and took advantage of her momentary silence to propel her gently but firmly towards the door. 'So, you see, there is nothing underhand going on, and I would be obliged if you did not speak about this matter again.'

Out on the landing, Mrs Parsons recovered the power of speech, and said with paralysing dignity, 'I 'ope I know how to hold my tongue, Mr Compton. I wouldn't have mentioned it at all, even to you, only for thinking there was something going on behind your back, and being fond of you, after all this time, and not wanting you to be 'urt and put upon. But if this fellow really *is* your cousin I daresay it might all be above board, as you say. I'm sure it isn't *my* business, and I shan't mention it again to a soul.'

She flounced off, and Jack had no hope that she would not spread her juicy tale of betrayal and villainy all through the house and her large acquaintance. He would be getting pitying looks from the other lodgers, local traders, and even the slavey who brought up the coals. For a moment the annoyance acted as a counter-irritant; but as it wore off, a deeper pain rose from the depths to the surface. Maud, to marry Bertie! How could it be? If it had been long planned, why hadn't she warned him? If it was not planned, but a sudden thing, was it love, or ambition? He hoped, desperately, that she was not being coerced into it by her father. But, oh, Maud, Maud! He sat down in his chair again and stared unseeingly into the flames, mourning his lost love.

After a restless and miserable night, he woke on the Sunday determined at least to find out what lay behind it all, and after church he excused himself from Mrs Parsons's dinner and set off for the railway station, perfectly aware that she would be sighing and shaking her head and explaining his mission in her own terms to a fascinated audience all afternoon. It was too early to call when he got to London, so he used up some time by taking luncheon at the Victoria Station Hotel: Scotch broth, roast beef, potatoes and cauliflower, apple pie and custard sauce – all a cut above Ma Parsons's efforts – washed down, to the waiter's disappointment, with water, since he did not want to arrive with liquor on his breath. In normal circumstances he would have enjoyed everything about the meal, including the novelty, but now with pain and doubt gnawing at him he ate without relish and left a good deal on his plate.

He left the hotel and walked to Pont Street, but the nearer he came the more uncertain he was of what he would find and what he would say. Would they think it odd of him to call unannounced? But he had often done so before – though less frequently since they had been in mourning. How would he excuse his visit? Should he admit to having seen the announcement, or feign ignorance and wait to see if they told him? When he reached Pont Street he could not bring himself to go up to the door and knock. He tramped around the streets, trying to summon his courage and assemble his sentences. He sat for a long time in Cadogan Square gardens, watching the nursemaids pushing perambulators, and almost went straight back to the station, except that he told himself at the last minute he was being a despicable coward. And suppose Maud *was* being coerced?

So when he finally knocked at the familiar door in the familiar red-and-white façade, it was tea-time. The door was opened by Mr Puddephat's manservant Hobbs, who when the master was at home combined the services of valet and butler. He regarded Jack without surprise, and said, 'The master is in the drawing-room, sir. Will you permit me to shake your jacket a little before you go in? It is rather wet.'

So it was, Jack discovered. A fine mizzle had begun at some point in his wanderings, which he hadn't noticed, and since he had come up without a coat, his jacket was beaded all over with moisture. He took a surreptitious glance in the glass behind the hallstand to see what his hair was doing, and combed it quickly with his fingers. Hobbs helped him back into his jacket, and then preceded him to the drawing-room, announcing him as he opened the door.

Four figures were grouped around the low table in front of the fire on which the tea-things were arranged. Mr Puddephat was to one side, a neighbour, the widowed Mrs Arbuthnot, to the other, and on the sofa between them was Maud, looking ravishingly pretty in an after-noon gown of dove grey over a cream lace guimpe. The fourth person, sitting beside her, who rose when Jack

422

came in, was a stranger, a tall and muscular man with a heavy beard and moustache and a face lined with experience and very tanned, so much so that he looked like a foreigner. It took Jack an instant to understand that this must be Bertie.

The tanned face split into a smile, and before anyone else could say anything, he had crossed the room and seized Jack's hand in both his. 'Jack! Dear old Jack! What a wonderful surprise! You know, I thought about you when I landed, and wanted very much to look you up, but there simply wasn't time, with the horses to see to and everything. But here you are! What a pleasure to see you.'

'I must confess, I hardly recognised you,' Jack said.

'What – the beard, you mean? Or the colour of my face? The one depends on the other at the moment. I mean to shave off the beard and moustache, but I can't until my tan has faded, for the skin will be white underneath and I should look like a clown.'

Jack now made his respects to the others, and was received with the utmost calmness by Mr Puddephat and Mrs Arbuthnot; but Maud looked very conscious, blushed, and would not meet his eyes. His heart twisted in him at the sight of her flushed cheeks and lowered eyelids. Was she ashamed, or only tender for his feelings? At all events, she did not receive him with her usual composure.

But nothing could be more open and affable than Bertie's manner, and it was plain that he did not know Jack had ever been a rival.

'I read about your engagement in the newspaper,' Jack said, by way of advancing a reason for his presence. 'I thought I must come and offer my congratulations. And my felicitations to Miss Maud.'

'You are very good,' Bertie said. 'I'm a lucky fellow.'

Mr Puddephat said, 'Do sit down, Mr Compton. It's kind of you to call. Will you have some tea?'

Hobbs reappeared with the extra crockery. Maud poured out, and Jack took a piece of seed-cake when the plate was handed, without knowing he had done it. He hated seed-cake, as Maud by now very well knew. She looked briefly up at him in surprise and, meeting his eyes, blushed richly again and looked away.

Jack began to speak, had to clear his throat and begin again. 'Is there – have you set a date for the wedding yet?' he asked of the company in general.

Mr Puddephat answered. 'The wedding will take place in three weeks' time, as soon as the banns have been read.'

'So soon?' Jack could not help saying, in dismay.

'There is nothing for either party to wait for,' Mr Puddephat said. 'And as we are still in mourning, it will be a quiet ceremony, with few guests, so no great preparation is needed.'

'I see. Well, I – I wish you very happy,' Jack said, without directing the sentiment at anyone in particular. The questions he wanted to ask were not possible in polite company, and instead he asked Bertie what it was like to be back in England.

'Cold,' said Bertie. 'I'd forgotten how this damp cold of ours sinks into the bones. Back home – back in India, I mean – it's bitterly cold up in the mountains, but it's a dry cold one can bear much more easily.'

'We are having a poor spring,' Jack heard himself saying, 'but I believe it's the same everywhere.'

'I'm beginning to think I shall have to abandon propriety and get out my sheepskins and Afghan coat,' Bertie said good-humouredly. 'Do you think London could bear the sight of me dressed as a tribesman?'

'It might raise eyebrows if you went to the opera dressed like that,' Jack said. 'Perhaps you had better go down to the country. You haven't been to Yorkshire yet?'

'No, not yet. There has been a great deal to arrange in London, but that is my next port of call. I have to go and look at the Red House, and see what condition the estate is in.'

'Everyone at Morland Place will be glad to see you,'

said Jack. 'And the whole of York will turn out for a glimpse of you. You can't think how much speculation there's been since it was known you were coming home.'

'I suppose it will feel like home eventually,' Bertie said, 'but I have to confess that at the moment everything looks very strange to me. I feel as if I'm in a dream. Every time I close my eyes, I think that when I open them again I shall see India, not England. It's very distracting.'

And, yes, Jack could see that in his eyes – a sort of wandering and unease, together with a look of fatigue. The upheaval and the journey must have been taxing.

'So, do you mean to settle in Yorkshire?' he asked. Out of the corner of his eye he saw Maud look up, but at Bertie, not at him. In a sudden, unwelcome flash of imagination, he saw her pale slenderness being engulfed by the big, muscular, tough-skinned brownness of Bertie, and he had to swallow hard. How could it be? It was all wrong!

'Yes, probably,' Bertie said. 'It depends rather on the state of things up there, but it's my intention to take over where my father left off. But I tell you one thing, I am not going to be Sir Percival, as the newspapers have it. I'm Sir Bertie, that's all! And if they don't like it – too bad!'

The talk turned then to the political situation, the weather and its effect on the lambing and the spring crops. Jack didn't say much; Maud did not contribute at all. When tea was over, Mrs Arbuthnot rose to leave, and it became apparent that she was coming back to dinner that evening; but no invitation was made to Jack to join them. He thought that Bertie was just a little puzzled about that, but of course he could not make the suggestion himself, being merely a guest in the house. When the widow had gone, Mr Puddephat said that he had business to discuss with Bertie, and Jack therefore was obliged to say that he must go. He shook hands with the two men, but when he turned to Maud she said quickly, 'Don't ring, Father. I'll see Mr Compton out myself.'

425

Out in the hall, when the drawing-room door was closed, she said in a low, hurried voice, 'Come into the morning-room for a moment. I must speak to you.' And so it was in that chilly room, dark at this time of day, that he had his private conversation with his beloved, the last he would ever have.

'I know you are wondering,' she said, eyes still down, tracing an unhappy pattern with her forefinger on the table. 'I saw the way you looked at me. I couldn't bear you to go away thinking . . .' She paused, and then, looking up, said, 'I don't know, really, what you *are* thinking.'

Meeting her eyes at last, Jack felt all his love and hurt surge up in him. 'Oh, Maud, *why*? I thought you loved me.'

'I never said I did,' she said quickly. 'Now, be fair. I was always fond of you. But I did tell you – I tried to warn you – I *said* Father would never let me marry you.'

'We could have put it to the test.'

'I didn't need to. Besides, I didn't want to marry you.'

'You didn't *then*. But you said you didn't want to marry anyone. And now, suddenly, you're to marry a man you hardly know. You *can't* love him, not in so short a time.'

She sighed. 'Oh, Jack! It isn't a question of love. All I want is a comfortable home, and he can give me that, and a title as well.'

'You'd marry him for his title?'

'Don't speak to me like that. I told you I was happy living at home with Mother and Father, but now Mother's gone, it isn't quite comfortable any more. Father thinks it not right, and wants to see me married. I have to marry to have an establishment of my own, that's all. Love doesn't come into it. Father suggested a long time ago that I might marry Bertie, that it would be convenient all round –'

'*Convenient*?'

'– because they were in business together. And now he's retired – well, he's been talking for years about buying a country estate, and Bertie has one already, which only needs doing up. Father was always going to leave everything to me, but this way, he'll be able to see where and how it will be spent, and have some say in it. And Bertie will have the funds to put his estate in order. So it all works very well.'

'But, Maud, I *love* you! Doesn't that count for anything? And if you don't love Bertie, how can you marry him?'

'I'm not romantic, like you,' Maud said, calmly, but with pity in her eyes. 'I know you love me and I wish you didn't, because there's nothing I can do about it. Even if we could get married, I wouldn't make you happy, because you'd always be wanting me to love you the way you love me, and I couldn't. It's better this way, truly it is. You'll get over me and fall in love with someone else. If we married I would be hurting you all the time, and I don't want to hurt you. I'm very fond of you, Jack dear.'

He seized her hand. 'I know you are, and we could work on that. It would be enough to begin with, and after a while—'

'No, Jack,' she said firmly, pulling her hand away. 'It wouldn't be enough, and I'd never love you enough. I'm much better off marrying Bertie. We'll be comfortable together. And Father has set his heart on it, because Bertie's already like a son to him, and he's always wanted me to have a title. I shall be Lady Parke, and I shall like that.'

'I don't believe it,' Jack said, his eyes stormy. 'I don't believe you feel like that. I know you too well. You're sacrificing yourself for your father's sake.'

'Well, if I am, that's my decision. I'm sorry, Jack, but my mind's made up. The announcement's been made and I'm going to marry Bertie, and I just wish you would forget about me and find some nice girl who will love you properly.'

'I don't want anyone else. I've loved you all my life. I want you.'

'Well, you can't have me,' Maud said. 'And now I think you'd better go, before one of the servants comes in and finds us.'

He gave her one last look of agonised appeal, but her face was firm – so unusually so that he believed her at last and his hope died. He turned away and allowed her to usher him out. At the front door he turned one last time and said softly, 'I will always love you, Maud. Always.'

And she said kindly, 'It will be better if you don't call again. I'm sorry.'

She held out her hand, and he took it and lifted it to his lips, impressed one fervent kiss on it, and left her. He walked away down the street, feeling as though some essential part of him had snapped off inside. His feet moved mechanically, miles away down there on the pavement, but inside his mind he stumbled blindly in the dark, grieving, and not knowing how to think or what to do next.

Chapter Fourteen

Alice's baby was born after a long but straightforward labour on the 14th of April 1910. To Teddy's delight, it was a boy.

'He's small, but perfect. Everything in its right place,' he pronounced when the child was first placed in his arms. 'My clever wife!'

Alice was looking exhausted, with brown circles round her eyes, but happy. In the end it had been Dr Hasty, a midwife and Emma who had attended her: she had finally plucked up courage to beg Teddy not to bring in a specialist to her 'because it would make me nervous'.

'I wanted her to have it on my birthday,' Polly had complained when the labour started. 'I thought it was supposed to come in May.'

Dr Hasty had revised the birth date some months ago, saying these mistakes often happened with older mothers, but Polly had clung in her heart to the first prediction. She was sure the child was being born for her particular benefit. When she was taken up to see him for the first time, she was so enchanted she forgave him for being born on the wrong day. 'I dare say you couldn't help it,' she addressed her brother kindly. 'Can I hold him?'

Emma thought it was never too early to interest girls in babies. 'Be very careful,' she warned. 'That's not a toy, now.'

'Oh, he's heavy!' Polly exclaimed.

'And I was just thinking how tiny he is,' Emma said.

'He's got such a funny little squashed face!' Polly cried, staring intently.

Emma was clearly longing to take him back, but restrained herself nobly. She had thought after Polly there would be no more babies for her nursery, but now here was this little angel – and she was watching Ethel like a hawk. 'He'll look prettier by and by,' she said.

'Oh, I don't mind,' Polly said. 'I rather like his funny face. And look at his tiny hands, and the little fingernails! Much better than a doll. Oh, Em, let me hold him a bit more,' she added, as her rival stooped to take him back.

Teddy had the house bell rung to tell the world that Morland Place had a new heir.

'It's a pity we don't have a flagpole and a Royal Standard,' Henrietta said to Jerome.

The proud father arranged for notices in every newspaper he could think of and, as soon as he could drag himself away, rode down to the village in person to arrange with Mr Grantby for a christening in the chapel.

It took place a week later. Alice, who was still very tired, was carried down in a chair just for the ceremony. Teddy had invited a large number of friends and neighbours, and the chapel was packed full as the child was 'dipped' and given the names James – a Morland family name – and William, after Alice's father. Then as the mother and child disappeared upstairs, Teddy hosted a luncheon of great lavishness. There were lots of christening gifts for the young heir, including a beautiful little Cézanne landscape from the Overtons, and a handsome Carolean silver cup from the Ismays, but there was a present for each of the guests, too: Teddy had called in a photographer from York and had a portrait taken of little James in a lacy robe lying on a velvet cushion, and gave each person a framed copy of it, evidently without the slightest doubt that they would cherish the gift as he would himself.

Ned was slightly alarmed to be summoned to speak to his father in the steward's room: Teddy had never been given to these formal gestures. His apprehension was not alleviated by finding Teddy pacing up and down looking ill at ease; but being a straightforward sort of young man, he posed his question right away.

'Is something wrong, Father? Is it something I've done?'

'No, no,' Teddy said, looking surprised. 'No, not at all. Of course not. I just wanted a word with you in private, without anyone else bursting in on us.' Ned waited with an expression of polite enquiry. 'It's about baby James. You see,' Teddy went on, 'I have an heir now. Morland Place has an heir. But James is your brother by adoption, as well as your cousin by blood, and I could not bear there to be any ill-feeling between you, now or ever. So I wanted to talk to you privately like this, to tell you that I don't regard you as any less my son. I am immensely proud of you, you do understand that?'

'You needn't worry,' Ned said, smiling. 'I understand what you are trying to say, and I assure you that I never for a moment expected you to leave Morland Place to me.'

'Didn't you? But I thought of it, all the same. If I hadn't had children of my own – given that you are the son of my elder brother—'

'The *illegitimate* son,' Ned interposed. 'Father, no-one could have been kinder or more generous than you. You plucked me from destitution and gave me a home, and a name, and the best of education, and I would be a fool and a knave if I were anything but eternally grateful to you. So be easy about me. You've already given me more than enough.'

'You've been a good son to me,' Teddy said, rather huskily, 'and you've amply repaid any kindness on my part. Are you happy at the mill?'

'Yes, very. I enjoy the work very much.'

'From now on, the mill shall be your own.'

'You don't need—'

'Yes, I do. I promised it to you if you made a success of running it, and you have. Did you think I would make no provision for my boy? I shall have the papers drawn up to make it yours entirely. How you develop it will be up to you.'

'I have some ideas already,' Ned said eagerly.

'I hoped you had. Well, it will give you the means to make yourself a respectable living.'

'It's more than a respectable living! I shall be rich.'

Teddy smiled. 'Don't be so sure, my boy! You may feel rich as a bachelor, but once you marry and have children you will look at it very differently.'

'I don't think I shall ever marry,' Ned said.

'Nonsense! You can't say never, young as you are. Good God, look at me! Everyone thought I was a bachelor for life – thought so m'self. Over forty when I tied the knot for the first time. You can never tell with Cupid!'

'Oh, as to Cupid, I'm afraid he has fatally stabbed me already.'

'What, and she won't have you?' Teddy said indignantly. 'Who is the girl?'

'I would rather not say, sir.'

Teddy reflected. 'Quite right. Wouldn't be gentlemanly. Well, she may change her mind. Women do, you know. Or you may fall out of love with her and find someone else. Now, don't shake your head at me. You'll see many things in the course of a long life, and I'm living proof of it.'

'Very well, sir, but I'll hope that she may change her mind, by your leave, because I'm sure I shan't.'

'I hope she does, because she must be very choosy indeed if she don't want you!' Teddy said stoutly.

The King returned to London from Sandringham in the afternoon of Monday, the 2nd of May. It was pouring with rain, and on the journey up he spoke little, only stared out at the sodden fields, wet cattle and dripping trees. It really had been a dreadful spring, Venetia thought. It was plain that the King had caught a chill on one of his long, wet walks in the gardens. Despite that, he dined

432

out that evening with his old friend Sister Agnes Keyser in Grosvenor Crescent; but during the evening she sent round a note to Sir James Reid, who was dining out with Lord Mount Stephen, asking him to be at Buckingham Palace to see the King at 11.15 p.m. Reid found the King very unwell, breathing rapidly, with a high temperature, a racking cough and pain in the chest. He applied poultices, gave him his favourite chlorodyne and morphia tincture to take during the night, and on leaving sent a message to Sir Frederick Laking, the other royal physician, to meet him to see the King the next morning.

The two doctors found the King a little better, though he had had a bad night. They begged him to remain in bed. He agreed only to remain upstairs, and he continued to work. Audiences had been arranged and he would not cancel them, or relax from his personal standards, which said that he must receive them formally dressed in frock coat. He also refused to give up his cigars – which Ponsonby said, curiously enough, seemed to soothe him – but his wonderful appetite had failed at last and he ate little dinner.

In the evening Mrs Keppel sent a note round to the Overtons asking if they would come and play a hand or two of bridge. The King barely spoke except to greet them and, noting how bad his breathing was, Venetia guessed Mrs Keppel had determined on bridge to avoid the necessity of talking, and had chosen them as they would not need to have the matter explained to them. It was a quiet evening, and Venetia felt very sad at the end of it. She could not believe that the King had much longer, and she looked round the Japanese Room as she left it wondering if she would ever sit there again, or, as she touched the King's hand in farewell, if she would ever see him again.

The King had another bad night, and was unable to eat any breakfast, but he insisted the following day on carrying on with business, reading his boxes, signing letters and giving audiences. He was interrupted by terrible fits of coughing, which led him almost to choke, but when those close to him gently remonstrated, he said only, 'I shall work to the end. Of what use is it to be alive if one cannot work?'

After consultation with Reid and Laking, the Prince of Wales had sent to his mother and sister in Corfu asking them to come home. They arrived at Dover in the afternoon of Thursday the 5th, and were met by the Prince and Princess of Wales and their two eldest sons with the news that the King was too ill to meet the Queen himself. The Queen seemed unconcerned, until, at the palace, she saw for herself. The King was unable to walk now, but sat hunched in a chair, a blanket over his knees, grey and gasping for breath.

That evening the first official bulletin was issued about his health. The King had refused to consider it at first, but the Prince of Wales had pointed out that people would wonder why he had not met the Queen at the station that day, as had always been his custom. He yielded at last, and at seven thirty a bulletin was issued saying that the King was suffering from bronchitis and that his condition was causing some anxiety.

On the following morning, the 6th, the King admitted to feeling 'wretchedly ill', could not eat any breakfast, and managed to smoke only half a cigar before putting it aside saying he could not enjoy it. But he insisted on getting up, indignantly rejected the informal clothes the valets had hopefully laid out for him, and struggled into formal frock coat before receiving Lord Knollys to discuss the day's appointments. On leaving him, Knollys scribbled a note to the Overtons saying that if they wished to say goodbye they should not delay calling.

Other friends called at Buckingham Palace that morning, and the King saw some of them for a few moments, including Sir Ernest Cassel and Lord Overton. Venetia sat with the Queen and Princess Victoria while her husband was with the King. Afterwards Overton told her he found the King very feeble in body, but perfectly sharp in mind, and though he could only speak indistinctly, his kind smile had been just the same, and he had insisted on rising to his feet to shake Overton's hand and thank him for all his services. The Overtons took their official leave then, but when they had left the Queen, Lord Knollys invited them to wait in his sitting room for as long as they liked, and he came to them from time to time with bulletins. Reid also looked in, having heard they were there, and said it could not be long now.

The King was served a light luncheon in his room, which he could not eat. He got up and went over to look at his canaries, whose cage stood by the window, and while trying to talk to them, he collapsed and fell to the floor. Still, he would not go to bed, but allowed his attendants to sit him in a chair, protesting, 'I shall not give in. I shall work to the end.' So he sat for the rest of the day, the Queen and the Princess with him, Reid and Laking administering oxygen and injections of strychnine. The Archbishop of Canterbury was sent for, and the Queen herself sent for Mrs Keppel so that she should have the chance to say goodbye – an act of great graciousness, Venetia thought. The King's consciousness was fading, though he was aware enough to understand when the Prince of Wales told him that his horse, Witch of Air, had won the 4.15 race at Kempton Park. 'I am very glad,' he said, but they were the last coherent words he spoke. He lapsed gradually into unconsciousness. Once his heart stopped, and was revived again by Reid and Laking. At 11 p.m. it was decided he was beyond noticing if he was moved from the chair into his bed; and so it was in his bed that he died quietly at 11.45.

A crowd had gathered outside Buckingham Palace since the posting of the first bulletin, but with no more than that to prepare them, they were not ready to hear of his death. When the policeman pinned up the black-bordered notice, the reaction was one of stunned silence. Only those close to him had known of his failing health. To the public at large he had seemed as he always had, a big, bluff, hearty man, too full of the zest for life ever to leave it, their genial King Teddy, the portly man with the ever-present cigar, lifting his hat to all with his old-fashioned courtesy.

Neither the Queen nor the Prince of Wales – now King George V – could bear to part with his body just yet, and could not be brought to think about naming a date for the funeral. The Queen believed his body had been wonderfully preserved by all the oxygen he had been given; and the summer was so cold there seemed no hurry to remove him. So he lay in his bedroom for over a week, while the Queen invited his close friends and attendants to come and take a last look at him before he was put into his coffin.

Venetia and Overton were invited on the Tuesday following his death. When they entered the blinds were drawn and there was a screen around the bed, so nothing could be seen at first. The Queen was there and received them, dressed in a simple black gown, her uncannily youthful beauty untouched. She seemed very calm, thanked them for coming, and led them round the screen. Venetia had seen more dead bodies than she could count in the course of her career, but was unexpectedly moved by this one. The King was lying with his head slightly inclined to one side, looking just as he had in life, and with the peaceful, almost smiling look she had seen before in other cases where death had come quietly. It looked so like the King it was hard to think of this as a corpse, and Venetia was amazed at herself for such a lapse into unprofessional sentimentality. She thought about the man she had known, hard-working, cheerful, immensely brave, unfailingly courteous to high and low alike, generous, truthful, and with that extraordinary ability to make every person he spoke to feel that they were uniquely inter-esting to him.

The Queen moved gently about the room as if he were a child asleep, touched his things and smoothed his counterpane with great tenderness, seeming, oddly, almost happy, as though she were glad to have him completely to herself at last. Venetia did not doubt then that she really had been in love with him all her life. And the King had loved her, too, in his way. Whatever his offences towards her as a husband, he had borne with her faults and caprices with exemplary patience for an impatient man; and for a stubborn man had accorded her the honour of being the only person who could change his mind, once it was made up, the slightest jot.

The Queen said, 'How peaceful he looks! It was very quiet at the end, quite easy. I am glad he suffered no pain. Don't you think he looks younger now?'

Venetia saw that Overton was unable to speak, and answered herself, 'Yes, ma'am, just like his old self. It must be a great comfort to you.' She could not bring herself to speak loudly at such a moment, so the Queen probably did not hear her, but she seemed to gather what had been said.

'To tell the truth,' the Queen said, 'I can't quite grasp it yet, the meaning of it all. I feel as if I am turned to stone – unable to cry at all. Unable to do anything. If only they would leave me alone! But they will come and trouble me and want to take him away from me. I would like to run away to Sandringham and hide there. Sir James says the King caught cold at Sandringham, but to my mind it was that horrid Biarritz that did the damage. He never took any ill from being at Sandringham.'

And she spoke then of the time in the future when they would be together again, and of their ultimate resting-place, and complained about the necessity of 'this terrible State Funeral' and all the dreadful arrangements that would have to be made.

When they left the Queen they called on Francis Knollys and found him bewildered with grief. Lying beside his fire – necessary that cold, wet May – they found the King's little terrier, Caesar.

'I'm taking care of him,' Knollys said. 'He won't go

near the Queen. He waits all day for his master, wandering about the house looking for him.'

Caesar, Venetia thought, observing her old friend, was not the only one.

It was not until Saturday the 14th of May that the King's remains were transferred to an oak coffin, which was placed on a purple-draped catafalque in the Throne Room at the palace. It had never been the custom for English kings to lie in state, but perhaps the new king was responding to the nation's deeply personal sense of loss when he ordered that 'the remains of His late Majesty King Edward VII of blessed memory' should lie in state in Westminster Hall from the 17th of May for three days.

Never before in its history had this ancient building seen so many people pass under its roof in so short a time. Despite the continuing bad weather and unremitting torrential rain, crowds waited in silence for hours, the queue often stretching all the way back to Chelsea Bridge, for their turn to file past the catafalque. More than half a million people paid their respects in this manner. On the first day, the very first to enter, as the newspapers reported, were three seamstresses, very poorly dressed, and very reverent. The conduct of the public was in marked contrast to that of some government ministers. The official in charge of the lying-in-state noted one evening that Mr Asquith was outside Westminster Hall, leaning against a lamp post and watching people pass in a manner he thought offensive. 'I fear he had dined well,' he concluded. On another evening Winston Churchill arrived after the hall had closed for the night with a party in four motor-cars and demanded admittance. When the custodian refused, Churchill argued, shouted and abused him before driving off.

The funeral took place on the 20th of May, a day which, after a stormy night, dawned clear, with brilliant sunshine. People had been gathering all through the night to secure a place from which to watch the procession, and by dawn the streets were lined twenty deep. They were chilled and damp from the rain, but undaunted, grateful for the warmth of the sun, which began to dry them as the morning progressed. The procession was magnificent, and appropriate to a king who had set such store by, and been such a master of, ceremonial. Lord Kinnoull's little daughter, who watched the whole spectacle from a window, refused to say her prayers that night. 'It won't be any use,' she explained, when her father was fetched by the nanny. 'God will be too busy unpacking King Edward.'

By the Queen's orders, the coffin, on its gun-carriage, was followed immediately by the King's favourite horse, Kildare, and the dog Caesar, led by a Highlander. There followed in glittering cavalcade the German Emperor (who said afterwards that he had done many things in his life but had never before been obliged to yield precedence to a dog) and eight kings, all of them related to King Edward, as well as King George and the young princes, and then a procession of twelve carriages. Queen Alexandra rode with her sister the Dowager Empress of Russia; in one of the following coaches were the ex-President of America, Theodore Roosevelt, and the French Foreign Minister, Monsieur Pichon.

In the last carriage Lord Knollys rode with Lord Overton – two figures unknown to the crowd. 'My poor Francis,' Overton said at one point, 'what will become of you? It is half your life gone. Forty years of unstinted devotion.' Knollys shook his head slightly, unable to speak, and Overton went on, 'I hope you can take some comfort from the fact that all your many friends will never forget your devotion to our poor dead king. I think such loyal – and affectionate – service has rarely been given by one man to another.'

'It has been my privilege,' Knollys managed to answer. 'He was always the kindest of masters to me.'

His loyalty was not forgotten by the new king, who appointed Knollys joint private secretary with Arthur Bigge. Fritz Ponsonby was assistant private secretary.

King George also remembered Sir James Reid, and appointed him physician-in-ordinary, making him the first doctor to hold the appointment under three monarchs. Queen Alexandra, with practical kindness, sent Reid two hundred guineas, 'so that you may know Her Majesty fully appreciated your kind and willing services during King Edward's illness'.

There were two other appointments that meant a great deal to the Overtons: Eddie was given the same Court position he had held under King Edward – an act of generosity perhaps similar to the Queen's in inviting Mrs Keppel to the bedside – and Thomas was made a military attaché to the Court of St Petersburg. He had met the Tsar and his family again when they visited Cowes in August 1909, and renewed the favourable impression he had made on Their Majesties. The Tsar had spoken to his cousin, and the thing had been arranged.

'I shall miss you, ma,' Thomas said, 'but – what an adventure! And you know, it is very appropriate, what with Great-Grandpa having been an ambassador and Grandpa an adviser on Russia. It's practically a family post – don't you think?'

It was a three-year appointment initially, and Venetia hoped that her son would come home at the end of the term. It was a tremendous opportunity for him, but things in Europe looked more and more menacing, and she wanted to have Thomas back before anything happened to take him away again. It seemed very ominous that, at the luncheon at Windsor after King Edward's interment, the Kaiser had taken the opportunity – with the King's wine not yet dry on his lips, so to speak – to take the French Ambassador aside and raise the possibility that France might side with Germany in the event of Germany's attacking England. Shocked by the impropriety, but afraid of offending the volatile Emperor, Monsieur Cambon had had to summon all his Gallic wiliness, affect to misunderstand the suggestion, and make his excuses.

Venetia thought of the late King's wide understanding of international affairs, his intimacy with Continental rulers, his tact, his ability to charm, his faultless French and German – in a word, his diplomacy. What will we do without him? she wondered. The world just seemed to have become a more cold and hostile place.

The wedding between Maud and Bertie had been set for Saturday the 7th of May, and although the Puddephats were not in Court circles there could be no question of going ahead even with a quiet wedding at such a moment. It was postponed until the funeral should be over, and a new date was set for the 28th. The delay gave Bertie a chance to go down to Yorkshire, talk to Exelby, the solicitor, inspect the property and see what had to be done, appoint an agent and put the first repairs in hand.

He spent the first night at the Star in York, and the second and third – to the delight of the landlord and the villagers – in the Same Yet, the little village inn in Bishop Winthorpe. It was picturesque and quaint, dripping with wisteria, with a wavy roof and crooked chimneys, and had been the subject of more amateur sketches, watercolours and oil studies than perhaps any other hostelry in Yorkshire. The bedrooms were tiny and low-ceilinged with polished oak floors that billowed like counterpanes, and at the thought of Sir Percival occupying one of them, the landlady was thrown into a flutter so intense and prolonged it looked likely at one point to threaten her life. She had palpitations and had to be sat down, fanned, and given a nip of three-star by her husband, while she gasped 'honour', 'privilege' and 'not worthy', and tried to give orders simultaneously about killing ducks and airing the best sheets.

Sir Percival Parke, Baronet, lord of the manor, master of the Red House and squire of the village, was a person so distinguished that it was impossible for Mrs Outwill to imagine a luxury too great for him. It was not until long afterwards and in retrospect that she was able to enjoy his visit: at the time she was too anxious about falling short of his expectations. She could not know, of course, how often on his up-country trips he had slept in caves, in tribesmen's tents made of imperfectly cured horse-skin, in native inns on straw-filled mattresses that seemed to dance and jig with the multitude of fleas they housed, on the hard ground under the stars, wrapped in a coarse woollen cloak that stank of the sheep-yolk that made it waterproof. The bedroom seemed comfortable to him, and the old feather bed, with the linen sheets newly aired and scented with lavender, was all he could have desired. He enjoyed his first quart of proper Yorkshire ale in many years, only slightly disturbed by the silent crowd of onlookers who gathered in the doorway of the snug to watch each mouthful go down his throat with the same fascination as if he were a mountebank swallowing swords. Each forkful of his dinner was likewise observed with an almost religious awe, and every now and then a little excited whisper of commentary rustled back to those unfortunates at the rear who had no view.

''E's etten all them taties. 'E's a right good trencherman.'

''E's goin' to 'ave cheese now.'

'Nay, wait, it's th'apple pie 'e's after.'

'By 'eck, 'e's tekkin' t'cheese wi' it, jus' like our dad!'

'Did 'e 'ave the Wensleydale?'

It might have put a lesser man off his vittles entirely, but Bertie had often had to eat around a campfire up in the mountains of Tibet or Kashmir under the unwavering gaze of the tribesmen, to whom he was an object of more astonishment and mystery even than to these Yorkshiremen. He enjoyed his dinner, smoked a cigar, and then went for a stroll, followed at a respectful distance as far as the front gate, after which his admirers retired to the public bar to exchange memories. On the second evening he was invited to dine with the rector and his wife, deeply disappointing Mrs Outwill, who had invited both her sisters and their husbands and three bosom friends to the spectacle, and had to satisfy them instead in his absence with a guided tour of his bedchamber.

Bertie left the next day, feeling that he had won a great deal of good will among his people, and took himself over to Morland Place. He was greeted rapturously.

'My dear boy!' Henrietta cried, bathing his neck with tears of joy.

'At last!' Teddy cried. 'I thought you were never coming.'

'How long can you stay? You are staying, aren't you?'

'Of course he is! Where else would he stay? He's not going to take a bed at the Have Another.'

'I've just had a bed at the Same Yet,' Bertie confessed. 'I've been in Bishop Winthorpe for two days, going over everything.'

'You didn't stay in your own house?' Henrietta said, surprised.

'No, thank you! Cold and damp, empty and gloomy – and not a bed fit to be slept in. I should have gone into a decline.'

'Well, if you have developed a taste for inns,' Teddy said, 'I suppose we could speak a bed for you at the Have Another, but otherwise—'

'Otherwise I'll have your old room made up for you,' Henrietta said happily. 'It's so good to see you, Bertie dear! I was quite taken aback by your beard, but I see that underneath you haven't changed a bit.'

Bertie would have liked to return the compliment, but in truth he thought she looked much older, and too thin, and there were deep lines of worry in her face. On the tail of the thought he asked, 'How is Uncle Jerome?'

He read the stark news in her eyes in the instant before she summoned up the calm smile with which troubles always had to be faced. 'Oh, he's as well as can be expected,' she said lightly. 'He'll be delighted to see you. I hope you'll sit with him and tell him all about India. It will be such a treat for him. He always did love to travel.'

There was so much suffering, present and to come, in

this short speech that for a moment Bertie could not answer for the lump in his throat. He swallowed it with an effort and said, 'I dare say I shall bore all of you with my stories long before I tire of telling them.'

Now Polly joined them, having got word up in the schoolroom that there was a visitor and having bullied Miss Mitchell into letting her out. She was in a ferment of excitement and her eyes were on stalks at the sight of him, but she managed to keep a grasp on the essentials. 'Are you my cousin Bertie? I'm Polly. I expect I'm a lot bigger than when you last saw me. I've got a new brother now. Did you bring me a present?'

'I've got presents for everyone in my luggage. Has it arrived?'

'Yes, a box arrived here this morning,' Teddy said. He took Bertie into the drawing-room, where Jerome was lying on the sofa with a rug over his legs; Bertie was able to see for himself at once what the situation was, and his heart turned over with sadness. He was introduced to Ethel (who blushed deeply at the quick, appreciative examination of his experienced eyes) and was soon installed in an armchair with a glass of sherry. His box was brought before him. He opened it with difficulty, as the muzzles of five dogs were everywhere in the way, sniffing ecstatically at his boots, trousers, hands, the box itself and every layer of goods inside it in a kind of exotic nasal Cook's Tour. Ethel's cat, Snowdrop, perched on the high back of his chair and dabbed experimentally at his hair from time to time; and Polly was so eager to help him get to her present she was practically climbing inside the chest. Robbie and Ned were at their respective places of work, of course; Alice was upstairs, not yet having left childbed; and Emma very soon appeared with the baby in her arms and a look of spurious innocence on her face as if she had not known there was a visitor – belied by the fact that James William was in his best silk dress, gleaming with cleanness and with his few wisps of hair brushed up into a silken tunnel on his head.

'But where's Jessie?' Bertie asked, when he had admired the young master and pleased Emma by handling him with the ease and assurance of accustomedness. 'I've seen everyone but her.'

'She's at Twelvetrees,' Henrietta said. 'She went before your box arrived so she had no idea you were coming. But she'll be back for luncheon. Which reminds me, I must go and speak to Mrs Stark about it.' She jumped up with the habit she had acquired during the years of poverty, before there were bells and servants to answer them, with the intention of going to the kitchen in person. But at that moment Sawry came in to see if glasses needed to be refilled, and she recollected herself and took him to one side to give him a detailed series of orders to relay, about the food and where to sit Bertie at the table and which room to make ready for him and what to put in it.

'I'll go up myself after lunch and do the finishing touches but he may want to wash before then so see there's water and that the glass from the Red Room is put in there,' she concluded. Behind her, conversation had grown up and was pleasantly filling the room. As she talked to Sawry she glanced sidelong and saw Jerome looking more animated than for many weeks, with a touch of colour in his cheeks. Polly was hero-worshipping from the far side of the box, whose contents had not yet been fully displayed to her. Snowdrop had fallen asleep on his perilous perch, and the dogs had settled down, with Brach and Bell having won the jostle to sit with their heads on Bertie's knees and have their ears stroked. Muffy had gone off in a sulk and was sitting with her back pointedly turned on the other side of the room, Digby and Danby were behind Teddy's chair washing each other's faces, and Fern had gone back to Jerome.

When Sawry had departed with his instructions, Henrietta stood a moment longer, looking on. Bertie, her extra son! How strong and manly and how much older he looked, with his dark-tanned face and his big beard

445

and muscular shoulders. But the eyes had seemed the same when he smiled down at her. And he was to marry pretty Maud Puddephat. Well, that was nice. She had always liked Teddy's friends, the Puddephats; and it would keep it all in the family, so to speak. Poor Maud must have felt very isolated since her mother died. It would be good for her to have an establishment of her own – though Richard would be lonely without her.

She didn't hear Jessie come in behind her, quietly moving as she always was. It was Jerome's eyes, and Fern's welcoming thump of his tail, that told her; and then she heard a soft indrawn breath, which seemed to be let out in the almost silent shape of 'Bertie!'

Bertie discovered he had lost part of his audience, turned his head, and jumped to his feet, scattering hounds. 'Is that my little Jessie?'

Jessie took a step into the room, and Bertie crossed the space and took both her hands in his, his bearded face splitting in a smile. 'You've grown so much,' he said, looking down at her searchingly. 'You're really a young lady now.'

'I'll be twenty in December,' she said, feeling very odd. This big, bearded, dark-skinned, rather dangerous-looking man her cousin Bertie? She would not have recognised him if she had passed him in the street, and was too shy of his strangeness to study his face and see if she could trace the Bertie she had known in his features. So she felt light and detached and rather bemused, like someone woken too suddenly from a sleep.

He let go of her hands and said, 'Everyone else has had their present. I've got something for you, but now I see you, I wonder if it is the right thing after all.'

'I'm sure it will be,' she said politely. And it was: a bridle of painted leather decorated with studs of gold and blue enamel, the browband hung with long strands of leather threaded with crystal and enamel beads, and thin, flat gold discs that twisted and threw back the light.

'It's beautiful!' she exclaimed.

'It's from the Kush. I got it in the market in Peshawar, up in Frontier Country. Only the wealthiest tribesmen wear them so fine. But you're so grown-up now, perhaps I should have brought you something more ladylike, a scarf or a dress length or something.'

'Don't be silly,' Jessie said, with a laugh that made her feel more natural. 'I still love horses and I ride for most of every day. This will look wonderful on Hotspur. Thank you so much, Bertie – it's the perfect present for me.'

The rest of the day passed as a family celebration with, first of all, the hastily improved luncheon, and then an afternoon of revisiting the house and grounds, paying a formal call on Alice, a walk up to the nearest paddock with Teddy and Jessie to look at some horses, and talking, talking, talking. In the evening Robbie and Ned came home, and everything had to be said all over again, and there was champagne and a fine dinner, to which Mr and Mrs Cornleigh, Miss Angela and the eldest son Mr Hector were summoned to share the treat. The talk went on late into the night, and the younger Cornleighs left with their heads stuffed with dazzling stories of bandits and horse-thieves, tribal customs and village markets, campfires, precipitous trails, rockfalls and sudden wild hailstorms in the high mountains.

Bertie stayed a week, but he was away from the house as much as in it, for he had a great deal of business to put in hand. Teddy supplied him with a road horse and offered the use of the Benz when he was not using it, and Bertie went into York or out to Bishop Winthorpe every day. He spent long hours in consultation with Teddy, and Exelby, and Semper, the land agent he had appointed; and rode out with Teddy to Twelvetrees to inspect the stock. He talked to Jerome about the prevailing political and economic situation and the likelihood of war coming; and to Henrietta about how to improve the Red House and make it fit for a gently raised female to live in.

Henrietta drove over with him to Bishop Winthorpe one day in Teddy's motor car, to inspect the house and give more particular advice, and it was while they were refreshing themselves with a walk around the garden there that Bertie confided in her on the subject of his upcoming marriage.

'Puddephat first suggested it to me last summer, in a letter, and I thought it would be quite a neat solution. I hadn't thought that way about Maud before – in fact, I hardly knew her. She was always so reserved, though of course I'd noticed that she was pretty. But I took it for a fairly idle suggestion and didn't think about it, until I wrote to Puddephat to say I had booked my passage home, and he raised the subject again. It was clear then that he was quite serious about it.'

'It seems an odd way to go about things,' Henrietta said cautiously, not wanting to offend. 'Of course, I know Richard was always determined his daughter should marry well, and he and Aileen were old-fashioned people – in the nicest way. But in these modern times one doesn't really expect marriages to be arranged, except in titled families. Perhaps more of them ought to be,' she added thoughtfully. 'I don't mean to say it's a bad thing, only unusual.'

'Not in India,' Bertie said. 'Even English girls have their husbands chosen for them – though I suppose it's different out there, not so much choice and a way of life not everyone can adapt to. At all events, it seemed quite logical to me when I was in India; and when I got back to England . . .' He hesitated for a moment, frowning in thought. 'I don't know, really,' he went on more slowly. 'I seemed to get caught up in things. What with the journey, and the upheaval, and the almost violent change of scene – London is *so* different from the hill country, even from Darjeeling – I felt rather dazed. Bemused, I suppose, is the word.'

'I don't doubt it,' Henrietta said.

'And there was Maud, looking as pretty as a picture – and between you and me, Aunty, I'd hardly seen a white girl to speak to for months – and there was Puddephat more or less seeming to think it was all settled. What with one thing and another, I found myself engaged before I had time to turn around. It's only since I've come up to Yorkshire that I seem to have had a chance to think.'

'And what have you been thinking?' Henrietta asked, anxious for him that he should not have been trapped into something he did not like. 'Have you changed your mind?'

'Oh, there's no question of that,' he said. 'It's all been announced, and I couldn't back out now if I wanted to.'

'But do you want to?'

'Oh! No, it isn't that. It still makes sense in every way. Puddephat wants a country estate for Maud, and he's prepared to put in the extra money that I need to make the Red House comfortable and bring back the land, rather than wait to leave it to Maud and our children when he hangs up his hat. And I've got the title, of course, which he's taken a fancy to. So all the arguments for it are the same. It's just that, on reflection, it seems a bit of an unusual way to pick a bride. But Maud is a sweet girl and seems to be all for it, and I must marry someone. I owe it to the poor Guv'nor to keep the line going, and this way I can keep the old place going too. So there it is.'

Henrietta said, 'Well, I hope you will be happy together.'

'No reason why we shouldn't,' Bertie said easily, as they turned along the south side of the lawn walk. 'I say, these hedges need cutting, don't they?'

'Yes, but poor old Sutton can't do everything on his own, with the kitchen garden to look after as well.'

'We'll need a lot more staff, inside and out. I must get Semper on to it.'

'But, Bertie, as we were saying,' Henrietta said, anxious not to get off the subject before her curiosity had been satisfied – after all, Jack's happiness had been scuppered by this arrangement, 'about you and Maud. Forgive me for prying, but are you in love?'

Bertie shook his head. 'The sort of life I've been leading

in the hill country and the Himalayas isn't conducive to nice English things like falling in love. I don't think I've ever been in love.' He paused for a moment, thinking of the three-month affair he had had with the wife of Colonel Maltravers in Darjeeling, which had seemed at the time to scorch the very earth around them. But that was not mentionable to his aunt, of course, and he rather doubted it had been love in the way she thought of the thing.

'What about Maud?'

'I don't think she has either. She's a very sensible, level-headed girl, without an ounce of sentiment about her.' He glanced down at Henrietta. 'You're not to be thinking she's being forced into this by her father. He loves her too much to dream of trying to make her marry against her will. She wants the marriage as much as he does, and for just the same reasons. I think we probably suit each other. I'm sure it will work out very well.'

He had changed, Henrietta thought as they walked on; but that was hardly surprising given his experiences, and if she missed the passionate, headstrong boy just a little, the rock-solid man he had become would get into far less trouble. At least it did look as though poor Jack had never had a chance with Maud, and that she had not deceived him in any way, which was a comfort of sorts. She would not have liked to think anything ill of dear Maud, whom she had known for over ten years. And if Bertie was to travel a great deal in future, this rather cool-headed arrangement of theirs was probably for the best. It would not have suited her and Jerome to be often apart, but Maud and Bertie might take it in their stride.

The black-bordered newspapers, and all the accoutrements of public mourning – black clothes, black armbands, black ribbons on hats, black-festooned displays in shop windows (one grocer in Jermyn Street filled his window with black Bradenham hams, appropriate salute to the passing of a noted trencherman) – suited Jack's mood. He felt as if the whole nation had chosen to display its sympathy with his misfortune. The fact that the wedding was put off because of the King's death was somehow part of it. He tried not to allow himself to think of it as an omen for Bertie and Maud – tried with all his heart to wish them well – but it wasn't easy. All his plans and hopes for years past had been bound up with Miss Puddephat. He had admired her as long as he had known her, and had loved her almost as long. And Bertie, of all people – Bertie who was practically a brother, whom he had looked up to, whose cricketing style he had consciously emulated! Well, he supposed he would not see very much of them when they were married and living in Yorkshire. Once a year at Morland Place, perhaps. Their lives would be carried on in a very different sphere from his.

In his unhappiness over Maud, he found himself feeling restless and wanting change. His lodgings had become unbearable owing to Mrs Parsons's continuing sympathy for his plight, the pitying looks the other lodgers gave him, the whispered conversations that stopped as soon as he entered the dining-room. The King's death did give him some slight relief, diverting sentimental attention, giving Mrs P another tragedy to pursue, and another object of pity in the Queen: 'Whatever will she do without him, poor lady! Devoted, she was, and no wonder, after forty-five years of marriage, and her a child bride!' But when that had run its course she would come back to him, with the satisfaction of a dog remembering where it had left a bone, coming back from a boiled rabbit supper to dig it up again.

He would have to find new lodgings before that happened, that was for sure. It was a bore, but apart from the peril of Mrs Parsons, there was the unmarried half-sister of Mr Scruton – another of the lodgers – who had been introduced to him after supper one evening with a good deal of significance by Scruton, and fond onlookings from the others. He had nothing against Miss Perry, but he had no wish to arouse expectations in her breast.

451

He took to walking about the streets in the evening, looking for 'rooms to let' notices – though with a listlessness that prevented him from following up any he saw for a variety of reasons: this one had an aspidistra in the window, and he hated aspidistras; that one had unpleasant-coloured curtains, the other had a shaggy dog lying across the doorstep and the rooms were bound to smell of it. At least the long walks kept him out of reach of the Parsons-Perry pincer movement; and the exercise tired him out, so that with the aid of a pint of beer at one of the pubs he passed, he was able to fall dreamlessly asleep as soon as he was in bed.

On the Saturday on which Miss Puddephat was married, he took a train to Bournemouth and in the afternoon walked along the clifftop, looking out at the sea – blue-green, with white 'force three' caps – and the cloud-blown sky, and the gulls wheeling about and making their unearthly cries. He was conscious for the first time in his life of feeling lonely. Work had always been enough for him, work and the knowledge of family in the background and his plans for life with Miss Puddephat. But she had not loved him after all, had married another man, and he felt the loss of her as if she had been a physical presence in his life. His family was far away and (he told himself in a fit of self-pity) didn't care a jot for his broken heart. He had acquaintances, but no close friends. He hadn't seen his friend Sopwith for ages, for he had finished at college and had been busying himself since with his wealthy friends and his motor-bicycles and speed-boats.

What I need, he thought, watching a gull hovering against the westering sun, is a complete change. Mr Rankin has been good to me, but I think it's time to look for a new challenge. And as soon as he thought it, everything seemed much more hopeful. The fact of the matter, he saw it now, was that he was bored at Rankin Marine. As he watched the way the edges of the gull's wings flexed and adjusted to the airflow under them, to keep it perfectly poised and in the same position, he thought about aeroplanes and the blood began to run hotter under his skin. Part of the reason he had stayed at Rankin Marine so long was that the salary was good, the prospects were secure, and he was saving a lot of money towards getting married. But without Maud to work and plan for, he had no need of such security. A bachelor could live on next to nothing. He could please himself, take risks, use up his savings, follow his interests even if they were not immediately lucrative.

He would fly! The gull banked suddenly and dropped away, flashing towards the water. He had so many books of drawings now, so many ideas he wanted to try out, and surely there would never be a better time for him to strike out in a new direction. Since the meeting at Rheims, the whole of Europe seemed to have gone aviation mad. The success there had led other newspaper proprietors – locked in permanent battle for circulation – to offer prizes for flying feats. There had been aviation meetings in Italy, Germany, Russia, Spain, France and England. Lord Northcliffe had offered a £10,000 prize in April of that year for the first flight from London to Manchester – a distance of 185 miles. In the end just two flyers, an Englishman and a Frenchman, had battled it out, following the railway lines and setting down beside them for the night when darkness fell.

The Rheims meeting was to be repeated in August and was intended to become an annual event. There had been an 'aviation week' at Blackpool. A Parisian, Georges Chavez, was setting and breaking records for high altitude flying, and was planning later that year to fly across the Alps from Switzerland to Italy – a feat unimaginable only a year ago when the highest ever flight had only been 500 feet, and given that most flyers still stayed close to the ground. There were aero clubs in Milan, Florence, Munich and Paris. The British one was called the Royal Aero Club, because of the interest of the late King Edward, who had seen Wilbur Wright fly when holidaying in France in March 1909.

And with all this mania for flying, wealthy young men all over Europe were wanting to buy an aeroplane of their own, and manufacturing companies were being set up to provide them. The field, it seemed to him suddenly, was wide open. There must be a place for him somewhere. On Sundays, when he was not able to go and see Maud, he had sometimes gone down to Brooklands in Surrey, where an airfield had been established. Inevitably when there he had got talking to the flyers and mechanics, and had always ended up with his head inside an engine and grease on his hands, a condition that to him spelled almost perfect happiness. Flying was a new field, a young man's sport, and had all the friendliness and instant intimacy of young men bound together by a single passion for machinery.

The other thing that Brooklands had was a flying school, where Gustav Blondeau gave lessons on a Farman owned by Mrs Maurice Hewlett: here one could take one's 'ticket'. To obtain the Royal Aero Club aviator's certificate one had to fly three circuits of three miles each – though they need not be on the same day – and on completion of each cut the engine and land within 150 yards of a designated spot. Jack felt in his bones that he could do this with ease. Ever since he had been taken up by Henri Farman, he had longed to fly. His dreams had been haunted with the sensation and the image of it. Well, now was his chance to realise those dreams! His heart was broken, love and marriage were no longer in his future, but he had money put by and no-one to please but himself. He determined then and there that he would go to Brooklands and take his 'ticket' – and while he was there make enquiries about the possibility of a job as an aeroplane engineer. Flying was a small world, and if there was an opening, someone would know about it.

His mind made up, he turned at last and walked back towards the town, and promised himself a pleasant supper somewhere, with perhaps half a bottle of wine by way of celebration. The wind had dropped and the clouds had thinned, and the evening sunshine was really lovely, making the fields to either side of him shine like gold. In the rough-bitten pasture on the right, rabbits had come out from their holes and were sitting up on their shadows, cleaning their ears and whiskers, blinking in the warmth. Everyone has a mate but me, he thought, and then dismissed it as silly and self-pitying. I have something better, he told the rabbits as he passed: I have a dream. The rabbits dashed away from him, but it was too warm and delightful in the meadow for them to be really afraid, and they only ran a little way before stopping to resume their grooming.

It all happened much more quickly than he would have expected – except that everything in the world of flying seemed to happen quickly. With a young man's impulsiveness, Jack did not wait to find a new position before giving his notice to Mr Rankin – who was so far distressed that, after a long moment of silence, he actually begged Jack to change his mind and stay. But Jack, though grateful, was adamant. 'You've been more than generous to me, sir, and I shall never forget all you've done and all I've learned while I've been here. But it's aeroplanes for me, now. I've got the itch, and I can't rest until I've tried my hand at them. I know there's a great future for aviation, and I want to be part of it.'

Rankin, who understood more about Jack's private disappointment than Jack realised, sighed and accepted the inevitable. 'But don't forget us,' he said. 'Come and see us from time to time. I shall follow your career with interest, my boy, and if you should ever change your mind and want to come back, you have only to let me know.'

Jack thanked him again, and in many ways was sorry to leave; but with savings in the bank he could not feel any apprehension about his future. In fact, he could not feel anything but excitement. He left his lodgings with relief, though he could not avoid Mrs Parsons's loud laments and tearful embraces, conducted on the front step under the interested gaze of the man with the barrow waiting to take Jack's luggage to the station, a dozen female neighbours, two loiterers, six boys and three passing dogs. Having escaped, he made his way to Weybridge where he took a room at the Ship, and the following day he went out to Brooklands.

'Ah, I didn't think it would be long before you asked me that,' said Mrs Hewlett. 'Yes, of course we can help you take your ticket. I don't suppose there's much we can teach you, though. You must know it all already.'

'I think I have a fair grasp of the theory,' Jack said modestly.

'More than fair!' she laughed. 'But Gustav can take you up and show you the controls in action, and then it's just a matter of trial and error.'

So in a little while Jack was in the air again, crouching behind Blondeau just as he had crouched behind Farman, reliving the experience of the year before. There was that same exquisite little tug as they left the ground, the same sense of astonishment on looking over the side to find that the ground had gone, the same half-fearful exhilaration at the knowledge and sensation that one was travelling through the empty air. Jack watched carefully what Blondeau did, listened to his shouted instructions. The controls could not have been more simple – a control column to go up and down, a rudder bar to go left and right – he knew about them already. What a flyer had to do, he had learned from many conversations, was to develop a 'feel for flying', and that was something that could not be taught.

After these two trial flights, the next stage was for him to sit in the control seat himself and 'roll' the aeroplane up and down the field, discovering how to increase the speed and how to keep it going straight. The touch on the controls had to be delicate and, when one was in the air, continuous. Air was not a smooth, flat thing like a good tar-macadamed road, and constant adjustments had to be made to keep the aeroplane level. He trundled up and down, with the mechanic pulling him round at each end. Then it was time to get into the air.

'Don't try to go very high,' Mrs Hewlett advised him. 'You're bound to have a crash or two and you'll do less damage to the aeroplane if you're only a few feet up.'

'The aeroplane? What about damage to me?' Jack protested, laughing.

'Oh, flyers are all made of india-rubber, didn't you know?' she said. It was not quite true, and they both knew it. Already that year a dozen aviators had been killed; but flying was a young man's sport, and the risk only added to the excitement. Besides, Jack felt instinctively that he *belonged* up in the air, and that flying could never really hurt him.

His first attempts were merely hops. These developed into short, straight flights a few feet up – longer hops, in fact. Then Mrs Hewlett advised him to make a single circuit so that he could try the tricky landing technique. The angle of descent and the speed had to be just right to make a smooth landing. Coming in too fast or too steeply would result in alarming bounces; too slowly risked 'pancaking', which was very destructive of the undercarriage. The only way of modulating speed was turning off the engine and 'vol-planing' in, as the French called it. It took experience to get it just right. Skilled flyers, he knew, switched the engine on and off several times in an approach to reduce speed, but for him now it was a matter of trial and error.

On his first landing he came in too fast and suffered a series of spine-jolting bounces while he struggled to keep the machine from slewing sideways and digging a wing into the grass, which could badly damage it. On the second he over-compensated, came in too slowly and too shallowly and pancaked, dropping the last ten feet – a horrid sensation that made the stomach rise – which almost tipped him out on his nose.

'No harm done, sir!' the mechanic called to him, when he had inspected the elevators and undercarriage.

457

'I know what I did wrong,' Jack called down to Blondeau, who had come across to talk to him. 'I shall get it right next time.'

But there was no next time that day, for the weather, which had been darkening, broke at last, and a veil of chilly rain rushed across the airfield, with every appearance of settling in for the day.

The weather remained bad for three days, with squalls of blustery rain following each other like migrating animals sweeping across Surrey, and there was no flying from Brooklands. It was hugely frustrating for Jack, who was sure he had been on the brink of mastering the air, and was so infected with flying-fever he felt that every moment out of an aeroplane was a moment wasted. He hung scowling about the hotel; mooched about the shops in Weybridge, seeing nothing in any of the windows he stared at; he stood in a doorway watching the rain sweep by and willing it to stop. He tried to be sensible and use his time more constructively, sitting in the hotel's parlour and drawing aeroplanes and engines and planning modifications he'd like to experiment with, but his heart wasn't in it. Finally he went out to Brooklands and hung about the sheds, talking to the mechanics and helping them with their endless tinkering.

On Friday the rain stopped, though the sky was still grey with fast-moving clouds, and there was a stiff breeze. Jack was out at Brooklands all morning, and in the afternoon, when the wind had dried out the ground considerably, he persuaded Mrs Hewlett to let him take the Farman up.

'I know it's windy, but it's a steady wind, not gusty, and it will be useful for me to learn how it affects the aeroplane.' And then, 'If I damage anything, I'll repair it myself.'

'Well, you can try a few hops, and we'll see,' she said at last. He spent the morning doing hops, discovering how to rebalance in a cross-draught, how to adjust to the extra lift or drag. In the afternoon the sun came out and the breeze moderated, and seeing how well he had managed in the morning, Mrs Hewlett had no qualms about letting him fly some circuits.

Blondeau agreed. 'He is a natural aviator, that one,' he said to Mrs Hewlett, in Jack's hearing. 'It is what one cannot learn, it is the instinct, to know how an aeroplane will behave and adjust almost before it happens.'

Bolstered by this good opinion, Jack took the Farman up and enjoyed himself enormously, flying ever larger circuits, round the airfield and round the sewage farm at the back of the sheds, experimenting with speed and height and turns, learning how to bank more tightly, growing more accomplished at landing. Switching off the engine at the right moment, he thought, was rather like riding a horse at a jump: something inside you knew how to count the lengths back from the jump so that you could adjust the horse's stride, give the command to take off at the right moment, and go with him instead of being 'left behind' or going forward too early and hitting your nose on the animal's neck. In the same way, he discovered that something inside you could calculate the distance from the ground, the angle and the speed of approach so that you could make the adjustments without even thinking and put the areoplane down smoothly.

At the end of the session he told Mrs Hewlett and Blondeau that he felt ready to take the Royal Aero Club certificate, and they agreed. 'I'll let the examiners know, and you can do it on Sunday,' Mrs Hewlett said. Sunday was a favourite flying day. 'We must hope that the weather holds up.'

The wind continued to modify, but as it did so, it grew more gusty. Saturday was cold and marred by intermittent showers. Jack managed to fly a few circuits, but his feet, pushed out in front of him on the rudder bar taking the full force of the wind during flight, grew numb with cold, and eventually the pain forced him to give up. On the Sunday morning he jumped out of bed and rushed to the window as soon as he woke. The sky was an overall grey, but it was not raining and the cloud-cover seemed quite high. He studied the trees and the chimney-smoke within his range of vision, and the wind seemed to be moderate and steady, coming from the south-west. His spirits rose. He would do it today! He opened the window with difficulty – it was a sash and had warped in all the wet of this dismal year – and stuck his head out. Without sunshine to warm it, the air felt very cool. He must do something to protect his feet and legs, he decided. He did not want to be hampered by loss of feeling. Two pairs of stockings inside his stoutest winter boots, to begin with; and then – an inspiration – several layers of newspaper around his legs under the stockings as a kind of makeshift puttee.

Out at Brooklands there was quite a Sunday crowd of air-enthusiasts – mostly men, of course, but with one or two wives and sweethearts who had been brought along in varying degrees of unwillingness to this damp field. Waiting for Jack were not only Blondeau, Mrs Hewlett and the mechanics, but the Royal Aero Club examiners and a reporter from the *Aero* magazine, John Farley, who intercepted him and asked him questions about himself for an article he meant to include in the next edition.

'Don't you think you ought to wait until I've taken the test?' Jack said good-humouredly. 'You won't want to write about me if I fail.'

'Oh, everybody says there's no danger of that,' said Farley. 'They say you're a natural flyer. Foregone conclusion you'll get your ticket today.'

'Are you trying to make me nervous?' Jack said.

'All right,' said Farley, with a grin. 'Will you let me interview you afterwards?'

'Fair enough,' Jack said. 'If I pass you can ask me as many questions as you like.'

When shaking hands with examiners and being reminded of the test conditions he did feel a little nervous, but as soon as he approached the Farman – 'the dear old bus' as he thought about it now – any anxiety vanished and he simply felt happy and hopeful, as he might have back home at Morland Place contemplating a ride on a good horse. He took his seat, the engine revved, the mechanics removed the drags, and he rolled forward, increased speed, and his heart lifted as he and his machine jumped into the air. There was no feeling in the world better than this, he thought, to be skimming through the air as the birds do. The Farman felt like an extension of his own body; he could control it as he controlled his own limbs, so that flying seemed to happen by his simple volition. He banked joyfully at the end of the field and flew out over the sewage farm, climbing steadily, feeling the wind under his wings and adjusting constantly and without thought, just as he had observed the seagull doing on that day in Bournemouth. Below him was the earth as still very few men had ever seen it, green and brown and divided into patches, seamed with roads and hedges and streams, studded with buildings, like that model Jessie had made years ago of the South African war. The sky was his, shared only with the birds and insects. He skimmed over the heads of the watching crowd and felt utterly happy.

He did his three circuits and three landings – the best three he had ever done, he felt, managing to put down well within the 150 yards of the marked spot. When he rolled to a halt after the third he felt only disappointment that it was over. But there was pleasure in the applause of the onlookers, in the proud smiles of Blondeau and Mrs Hewlett and the mechanics, in the congratulations of the examiners, who confirmed that he had satisfied them in his aviator's skills. One of the most enthusiastic welcomes came from Farley – perhaps because he would have something to write after all. Jack invited him to come back to the hotel with him and conduct his interview over a celebration dinner, and by the end of the evening they were calling each other 'Jack' and 'Johnny'.

'So, what now?' Farley asked at the end of the meal, as they lit cigarettes.

Jack told him about his wish to find a new position in the aviation world. 'I've got so many ideas I want to try

461

out. If I were a rich man I'd start my own company, but as it is . . .'

'You're talking to the right man,' Farley said eagerly. 'Working for the good old *Aero* keeps me in touch with everything that's going on, and I happen to know of just the right billet for you. What luck we met! You know, the more I think about it, the surer I am it will suit you down to the ground.'

'I'd rather be suited up into the sky,' Jack said, laughing, 'but tell me about it.'

As a result of his conversation with Farley, Jack went up to London the next day with a portfolio of drawings, and made enquiries at 110 Marylebone High Street, the offices of Howard T. Wright (no relation to the Wright brothers). An hour later he had secured his new billet as chief design engineer, with full permission to try out his ideas. The Howard Wright workshop was in Battersea, and on Wright's suggestion Jack looked for new lodgings in Chelsea – handy for both office and workshop and not too expensive. He found a pleasant room in Oakley Street, settled in, wrote some letters, and went to sleep to dream of flying – but now his dreams were not clouded with wistfulness.

A day or two later his 'ticket' arrived, a little bound folder with his photograph on one side, and on the other the information, printed in English and French like a passport, that J. Compton had satisfied the conditions and been granted an aviator's certificate by the Royal Aero Club of the United Kingdom. There followed the signatures of the chairman and secretary, and at the bottom was the date of his test and the serial number. The very first ticket, Certificate No. 1, had been issued on the 8th of March 1910 to J.T.C. Moore-Brabazon, who was just two years older than Jack. Jack's certificate was No. 23. He had entered, he thought, a small band of brothers, and he felt immensely proud to be one of them.

Chapter Fifteen

Lord Holkam died a week after the King. Oddly, it affected Violet much more than Brancaster: he had gone through his grief when his father suffered the stroke, and Lord Holkam had been lost to him for so long that his final death was nothing but a relief. But Violet, who had never known Holkam when well and so had had no affection for him alive, had developed a warmth towards the helpless and possibly conscious man trapped in the immobile body.

She cried a great deal, immediately afterwards, and at the funeral – though that might have been something to do with her condition. In consequence of a visit to her bedroom by Lord Brancaster in April, on the day Jessie went home, she was pregnant again. Though she was suffering almost constant nausea, she was delighted to be expecting another child, and hoped it would be a boy. She knew it was her duty to provide 'an heir and a spare', and would be glad to get that done, after which perhaps she could have a little girl for her own pleasure. She adored Robert, but now that he was weaned Nanny had been firm in making it clear to Violet that the heir to the House belonged to her, and that she should not visit the nursery except at certain fixed times.

A large number of guests came for the funeral, many of whom arrived the day before and stayed for several days afterwards. There were friends of Lord Holkam and distant relatives, some of whom were so old Violet was in a ferment of anxiety lest one or more of them should succumb during the ceremonials. The passing of an earl of Lord Holkam's generation seemed to be a matter of great moment. The servants did not just wear bands but were all put into full mourning livery, and since it had all been packed away in the attics for many years there was a stronger smell of camphor in the air than ever. Every looking-glass and picture in the house was turned face-to-the-wall; the overmantles in every public room had a covering of fringed black plush; every statue and figurine had a black holland bag put over it; black muslin was hung at the windows of the main rooms. The servants were deeply affected by their master's passing, and red eyes and constant sniffing attended all their duties.

There was a stream of visitors to the house to convey their condolences, some of whom were thanked and sent away and some seen by Brancaster, while the intermediate sort fell to Violet's part. It was the first time she had ever been allowed to do anything Holkamish, and she was pleased by the implied trust, though constantly afraid lest she should have to run out in the middle of a speech to vomit. Pale in her mourning clothes, and with an air of inner preoccupation, she made a very pretty effect on the visitors, who were touched by what they took to be her deep feeling.

The funeral itself was a tremendous spectacle. The family hearse had been dragged out from the back of the coach-house where it had been mouldering for years and hastily repaired. It was given a vigorous cleaning, the gilding retouched, and the box cloths unearthed after a long and increasingly frantic search, for they had not been put away in the right place. New ostrich plumes were bought, along with new black rosettes and ribbons; and when so bedecked, with the earl's coffin inside draped in his standard, and harnessed with six black horses superbly accoutred and plumed, it looked magnificent. At the appointed time it set off at the slowest of walks to the doleful tolling of the tenor bell from the church at the estate gates. Behind came a procession of carriages, followed by servants, tenants and villagers on foot, a train so long that the last mourner had not left the house when the first reached the church. After the ceremony everyone returned to the house where there was a vast spread of delicacies, with wine, in the state dining room for the relatives and friends, and a lavish cold repast, with beer, in a marquee in the garden for the tenants, workers and pensioners.

At the funeral, in the family pew, Violet realised that she was now Lady Holkam; that Brancaster was now an earl, and that her small son had become Lord Brancaster in his turn. She wondered how life would change. She hoped there would now be refurbishment of Brancaster Hall, not to mention repairs. She did not dare to hope it would have central heating installed, like the home of a certain lord who had married an American heiress, but perhaps if the leaks in the roof were stopped and the worst of the warped window-frames replaced, the fires might have more chance of warming the place.

And at the funeral feast she allowed herself to think that she might now be able to have her family to stay, and to go and stay with them in return. There might be entertainments, and visits to friends' houses – supposing Brancaster had friends, which he surely must? She thought longingly of London, and of plays, concerts, balls and dinners. Brancaster (she still thought of him that way) would have to take his seat, and would presumably want to keep a house in Town while the Lords were in session. The prospect of a change of scene, of pleasure and gaiety – of freedom! – excited her so much she had to study to keep her expression such as befitted a funeral.

As soon as the last guest was gone, the new earl announced his intention of going to London; but when Violet said eagerly, 'Shall I come with you?' her first hopes were dashed when he raised his eyebrows in faint surprise and said, 'Of course not. It is not a visit of pleasure. I have a great deal of business to conclude.'

For once she dared to argue with him, though in the

mildest manner, for there were servants present. 'I understand that,' she said. 'I should not expect you to take me
about.'

'Take you about?' he said. 'There is no question of your
going about. We are in deep mourning. It will not be seemly
for you to go into public at all until six weeks have passed
at least. I should not go myself if it weren't necessary.'

'I see. I'm sorry,' she said; and then because it was so
important to her, she added, 'But after six weeks, may I
go to London then?'

'There will be no Season this year, because of Court
mourning,' he said. 'Your presentation as Countess of
Holkam won't take place until next year, after the
Coronation.'

'Oh, I understand that,' Violet said. 'It's just that I
should like to see my mother.'

She thought she saw a negative on his lips, but at the
last minute he seemed to relent. 'It might be possible for
you to accompany me to Town in, say, July. One of the
things I have to go up for now is to see what state the
house is in. If there is not too much dilapidation, we
could open it for a month.'

Her heart leaped. 'House?' she queried. 'What house
do you mean?'

'The London house,' he said. 'Fitzjames House, in St
James's Square. It hasn't been used since Father last went
to a debate, which was in – oh – 1902, I think. There's
a caretaker, of course, but it will all have to be done up
freshly before we can entertain in it. Really, this Court
mourning is rather convenient. It will give me time to
put work in hand, and everything can be ready to open
it for the Coronation. But there might be a room or two
we can use for a short time in July.'

So Violet had something pleasant to think about during
the dull weeks she spent alone while Holkam (as she must
get used to calling him) was in London. It was *very* dull,
as everyone and everything was draped in black, and
because of their mourning there weren't even the usual

466

callers. She was nineteen and longed for dancing and company and fun, but here she was shut up alone in a horrid old house in the country and feeling sick all the time. She couldn't even work in her garden, because bending made her feel dizzy and nauseous. But at least she could sit out of doors when the weather was fine and think that in a few weeks she might see her beloved mother again; and that next year they would be in London for the Season, and that she would entertain as Lady Holkam, with a house of her own in St James's Square. Perhaps they would give a Coronation ball. She wondered if Fitzjames House had a ballroom.

It was during one of these musing moments, sitting on the seat fixed round the trunk of the catalpa, that she was approached by Scole.

'I've something to tell you, my lady,' she said, looking grim, 'and I thought it had better be out here, where there aren't so many spying eyes and listening ears.'

'What can you mean?' Violet said, surprised. 'What can you have to say to me that is so secret?'

'It's not my secret, my lady, but Betsey's.'

'Betsey has a secret? But why does that concern me, Martha? You look worried. Sit down.' She patted the seat beside her.

'Best not, my lady. You can see this place from the house. And, if you'll forgive me, best you don't call me Martha. You might forget and do it in front of one of the other servants, and they wouldn't like it.'

Violet smiled. 'I shan't forget. And I like to call you Martha when we're alone, because it makes me feel you are my friend.'

'I hope I am your friend, my lady,' said Scole. 'I try to keep an eye out for your interest, and I've been watching young Betsey for a while now. There was something about her I didn't like. At any rate, I cornered her this morning and after a bit she gave up and admitted it. She's with child, my lady, and three months gone.'

Violet looked upset. 'Betsey? I would never have

thought it of her. Oh dear! How very difficult. Who is the father?'

'She wouldn't say, my lady, though I've an idea of my own,' Scole said grimly. 'But that hardly matters—'

'I should have thought it mattered a great deal,' Violet interrupted. 'He must marry her, whoever he is, and make her respectable.'

'There's no question of that, my lady.'

'Are you sure? Who is he?'

'Betsey won't name him, my lady, and I'll keep my suspicions to myself, by your leave. But she says he won't marry her, and she should know. In any case, that's her problem, and hers alone. Yours is to get rid of her as soon as possible, before word of this gets out.'

'Well, of course, I agree she has to go, but I don't think I should act in haste,' said Violet. 'Even though she has done wrong, I wouldn't want to send her away without being sure someone will take care of her. She could be found some work about the house for a week or two, while enquiries are made. Perhaps the father can be persuaded to marry her after all.'

He's not in a position to,' Scole said impatiently.

'He's *married*?' Violet was shocked.

'So I understand. But that's not to the point. You must send her away, my lady, before his lordship comes back.'

'He brought Betsey here in the first place,' Violet said. 'He'll be very disappointed in her.'

'Just so, my lady. Much better have it all done with while he's away.'

'I suppose it would be less painful for him that way.' She pondered, and then said doubtfully. 'But as he did recruit her himself, perhaps he would be angry if I sent her away without consulting him.'

'No, no, believe me, my lady, he'll be glad not to have to think about it,' Scole said urgently. 'Gentlemen don't like servant bother, I promise you. He won't mind if he finds she's gone when he comes home and there's nothing he can do about it.'

'A *fait accompli*, you mean,' Violet said.

'He might never even notice she's gone,' Scole added, 'and if I were you, my lady, I wouldn't mention it at all unless he asks directly.'

'Very well. But I would like to know what is to happen to her. And who is to look after Robert? I don't want Nanny to have to pick him up and bathe him and so on. She might drop him.'

'I've an idea about that. Sibsey says she doesn't mind looking after him for a while, until we can get the agency to send a new nurse. She's very fond of his little lordship, and Nanny seems to like her. As to Betsey, I've questioned her pretty sharp, and she says she's got an aunt married to a farmer near Wisbech who would take her until the baby's born. After that, it's up to her, and no worry of yours.'

'All the same,' Violet said firmly, 'I will give her some money, to buy clothes for the baby if nothing else. Whatever she has done, it's no fault of the poor child.'

'Whatever you say, my lady,' said Scole. 'Give her something if you like, as long as it's kept a secret – the other servants wouldn't like to know vice was being rewarded, which is how they'd see it. But she goes right away, today.'

'Very well. There's twenty pounds of my allowance left in my box in my wardrobe. She can have that.'

'That's far too much, my lady,' Scoles said, shocked. 'Five pounds is more than enough.'

'But five pounds won't keep her and a baby for long. Give her ten.'

'She doesn't deserve it, the way she's betrayed you.'

'Nevertheless, I shouldn't feel easy about doing less.'

'If you insist, my lady.'

'I do,' Violet said firmly. 'You can send her to me now.'

'Oh, no, that would never do. Now, I must insist, my lady! His lordship wouldn't like to hear you had spoke to her yourself, knowing what she's done – and you in your condition. Let me do it for you. I'll give her the

469

money, just like you said, and have her out of the house and gone before you're back in it.'

Violet was glad enough to be spared the embarrassment and trouble, and to be given a good excuse for what she would otherwise have suspected was cowardice on her part. 'Very well,' she said. Scole turned away, and Violet called her back. 'Oh – and, Martha, thank you. It's good to know that you are looking after me.'

'It's what your mother wanted me to do, my lady,' Scole said, and went briskly away.

The death of King Edward obliged the opposing parties in Parliament to suspend hostilities over the constitutional crisis. There was a strong feeling in the country that the new king was a decent chap who should be given a fair chance. When he enquired of the leaders on both sides of the debate whether they would try to settle matters by an all-parties conference, they felt obliged to agree. The alternative would be an immediate second general election, which would be extremely unpopular.

With the major question being discussed behind closed doors, there was very little to do in Parliament, and on some days the House rose early for lack of business. The Suffragettes were therefore very hopeful about the Conciliation Bill, and their truce also held. They concentrated on keeping up momentum with meetings, speeches, and peaceful demonstrations like bicycle parades, which were always popular. There was a general need in the WSPU for recuperation. The Pethick-Lawrences had groups of weary workers down to their country house; Christabel and Annie Kenney went on holiday together to Sark; Mrs Pethick-Lawrence took Sylvia to Oberammergau; other Suffragettes went to stay with the Blaythwaites at Batheaston, where each of them who had been to prison for the Cause was invited to plant a tree in the arboretum the Colonel had begun as a commemoration.

A grand parade was planned for the 18th of June, 1910,

when national mourning would be over, and ten thousand were expected to march from Victoria Embankment to the Albert Hall where there would be a rally and speeches. The parade was called 'From Prison to Citizenship'. It was led by Mrs Pankhurst and 617 women, each representing a term of Suffragette imprisonment. They were dressed in white and carried wands tipped with silver arrowheads to represent the broad arrows on prison clothing. Behind them came the suffrage pioneers, many of them white-haired old ladies now; and the graduate contingent, in which Venetia marched (now that King Edward could no longer be offended), persuaded to it by her old friend and colleague Dr Elizabeth Garrett Anderson. Mrs Anderson was retired from medicine, but still involved in public service as mayor of Aldeburgh, the first woman ever to be elected a mayor. She was over seventy, and a little bent at the neck, but she kept up a brisk pace at the head of the 'Regiment of Portias'. It was remarked in the newspapers afterwards that all the eight hundred graduates marched with military precision, in contrast with a detachment of male supporters behind them who shambled along in an apologetic, almost furtive way.

There were forty bands, and a hundred and thirty contingents from various nations and all ranks of society. The Actresses' Franchise League were all in pink and green and carrying rose-twined staffs; the gymnasts kept perfect step with each other, marking time with high-lifted knees and pointed toes whenever the procession halted; the sweated workers in their Sunday best looked pale and haggard under the fortuitous sunshine. The American contingent was led by Miss M. Roosevelt, second cousin to the former President. The Men's Political Union, led by Henry Brailsford, carried a banner saying 'We Fight the Government that Refuses to Give Women the Vote', and among them was the cricketer A. J. Webbe, who had actually left a match in progress at Lord's to join the march.

There were glowing reports in the newspapers on Monday, but Venetia said sadly that she thought people were more impressed with the picturesqueness of the procession than with its purpose.

'Well, Mum, what do you expect?' said Oliver, who had marched with a group of medical students. 'It's bound to take time to change the minds of a whole nation. Even the French Revolution took twenty or thirty years, and they were allowed to execute anyone who disagreed!'

Venetia was pleased that she still had her younger son at home to keep her and Overton lively, and in particular to keep her mind active as he studied afresh what was old knowledge to her, and brought her news of the latest discoveries and new thinking. In return she helped him, not only directly with his studies but indirectly by her influence in the medical world. She had arranged for him to accompany her old friend Mark Darroway on his rounds during the long vacation; and had also persuaded some surgical colleagues to let him observe their operations at close quarters.

Anne Farraline did not take part in the march. Venetia was a little surprised, and sent round to Bedford Square to ask if she was quite well, but a message came back from Miss Vaughan to say that Lady Anne was still in the country. Further enquiry elicited the information that, after a spell at Wolvercote with the cousins, Anne had gone down to her brother's place for the end of the hunting season, and thence to Liverpool to stay with a Suffragette acquaintance, Miss Dancey, for Easter. What had happened there was a little unclear, but it seemed that instead of coming back to London, as Miss Vaughan expected, she had written to say that she was renting a cottage in the Lake District and was expecting to remain there, touring the lakes, until the end of summer.

It seemed a little odd to Venetia, but she supposed that Anne had been badly shaken by her experience in prison and was in need of rest. She felt vaguely glad to think of her cousin's being steeped in so much peaceful beauty and fresh air, and hoped she would come back in a calmer frame of mind. It was only later, when speaking to Lizzie, that she discovered Anne had not gone to the Lakes alone.

Lizzie had come to visit and brought Rose with her, confident in the assumption that everyone must want to see her remarkable daughter. Rose was a very pretty child, and at sixteen months was running everywhere and had quite an extensive vocabulary, though she could not yet join her words into sentences. Venetia kept an anxious eye on ornaments at child-level, but Lizzie seemed quite accustomed to jumping up and rescuing delicate objects, which made conversation rather jerky but at least relieved Venetia's mind somewhat.

When she asked Lizzie if she knew anything of Anne's whereabouts, Lizzie made a face and said, 'Oh, yes, I'm afraid there's a lot of talk about it at Clement's Inn – though, really, I can't see what business it is of anyone's. But it seems she's gone off with her new friend.'

Lizzie told what she knew – that in Liverpool, while staying with Miss Dancey, Anne had met a young girl called Vera Polk, just eighteen, daughter of a widowed shoemaker, who had been recruited into the Cause and become one of its most fervent adherents. She had taken part in the demonstration outside Walton gaol and had been struck then with Lady Anne's beauty, nobility, courage and spirit. Meeting her in the flesh at Easter she had fallen into a daze of hero-worship, and Anne had 'taken her under her wing', as Lizzie put it.

'I can't quite tell why this Miss Polk stood out from the others. I know there's a lot of hero-worship of Anne among the younger Hot-Bloods, but she has always rather dismissed it and laughed it off as nonsensical. But whatever the reason, it seems that Anne took a fancy to her.'

Miss Polk, though very young, had had a lot of experience among the Suffragettes. Though ill-educated, she was a bright girl and very spirited, and her father, poor and desperately hard working, was quite unable to control her. She had attracted the attention of two WSPU workers in Liverpool when she was only sixteen, and ought not to have been allowed to put herself into danger. But she had no-one to look after her, and she was so eager for the Cause that Miss Dancey, and the friend she lived with, Miss Oliphant, had decided she was safer with them than following a lone and impetuous path. So, under their guidance and care, Miss Polk had worked her way into the centre of the local organisation by the time she came to Anne's notice.

'And immediately after Easter, Anne decided to go on a holiday to the Lakes, and took Miss Polk with her. And there they are still, from all I can understand. There's a lot of unkind whispering about it around the Union but, really, I'm surprised our colleagues should go in for that sort of thing. As if we didn't have enough to fight without that!'

'What sort of thing?' Venetia asked.

'Well,' Lizzie said, picking up Rose and sitting her on her lap, 'I suppose it must be snobbery that makes people object to their friendship, because Anne is an earl's daughter and Miss Polk's father is poor and only an artisan. I can't think what else it can be. But I think it's dreadful nonsense, and not at all in the spirit of the WSPU. We are all women together, surely, no matter what class we were born into?'

The Conciliation Bill had its first reading in June and was passed without division; but though Parliamentary time was not in short supply, Asquith refused to commit the government to a second reading. As Lord Lytton told a WSPU meeting, 'The answer really in effect comes to this: "We have for so long fallen into the habit of trifling with this question that we are going to trifle with it a little longer."'

However, after constant lobbying and pressure from every group and individual, Asquith was at last persuaded to name the 11th and 12th of July for the second reading, and the suffrage groups at once went into a flurry of activity to secure promises of votes from MPs. So many letters were written that it even came to the attention of the newspapers. The *Daily Mail* wrote: 'A prominent politician, who has sat in the House for over a quarter of a century, has received more correspondence on this subject than on any other since he entered public life.'

But when the debate began, the speeches were almost all against the Bill. One MP said that votes for women would overturn the marriage vow and bring trouble and discord to family life. Another said that the actions of the Suffragettes had shown that the granting of the franchise would bring about 'a far-reaching and regrettable alteration in the habits of the people'.

Churchill objected that under the Bill a rich man could set up his wife and daughters as 'occupiers' and get them votes – effectively extra votes for himself – while a poor man could not do so. Also, it would deny the vote to respectable older married women but give it to irresponsible girls of twenty-one. He pointed out that it would give the vote to a prostitute, but if she made herself an honest woman through marriage she would lose the vote again, and only regain it if she became a divorcée.

He, Lloyd George and Asquith, who had all vehemently opposed giving the vote to women on the same terms as men, now opposed the Conciliation Bill because it did not do so. Asquith said, 'No suffrage measure will be satisfactory which does not give women votes on precisely the same terms as men.' It seemed to supporters of the Cause a breathtaking hypocrisy.

In his speech, the Prime Minister also gave a stern warning to the Suffragettes. 'Those who take the sword shall perish by the sword. A cause which cannot win its way to public acceptance by persuasion, by argument, by organisation, by peaceful methods, is a cause which already, and in advance, has pronounced on itself its own sentence of death.'

Reading the debate in the newspapers, Lizzie protested to her husband, 'How can he say that? They would never listen to us when we used persuasion. They would not receive our letters, our deputations – the newspapers did not even report our meetings. What choice did we have? It's a wicked thing to say.'

All the same, those MPs who had promised to vote for the Bill kept their promise, and it was passed by a majority of 109 votes. Now a decision had to be made as to whether the committee stage would take place 'upstairs', with a standing committee, or on the floor of the House, where it would have to take its turn with all the rest of the Parliamentary business, and would inevitably be pushed to the back of the queue until time ran out. Those MPs who had voted for the Bill against their inner feelings now saw the chance to get out of it. When the vote was taken it was decided by a majority of 145 to keep the Bill on the floor of the House.

'Well,' said Venetia, 'that is that. The Bill is a dead thing.'

'Asquith hasn't said he won't give it time,' Overton pointed out.

'Oh, Beauty, you know as well as I do what comes next. Refusal to make a commitment – more "trifling", in fact – followed by vague promises about a *possibility* of *perhaps* thinking about it next session. Another disappointment, and the hotheads will go back to violence,' Venetia said sadly. 'It will all go on as before until someone will be killed at last.'

He looked at her in concern, and thought of asking her not to become involved; but realised before he spoke that she would not do anything like that, not now. It was Anne she was worried about. He said nothing, but placed his hand over hers in silent sympathy, and when her fingers curled round his, squeezed them back. Strong fingers, he thought, skilled, knowing a man's work, but still capable of a woman's caresses. He saw her suddenly as a separate being, as one hardly ever sees the spouse of a long marriage. The beautiful, vivacious and too-clever girl he had loved as an idle young officer had matured into someone much greater, he acknowledged, than himself. He felt a huge love for her, and a correspondingly huge pity for womankind, whose abilities and minds and ambitions were for ever trapped by the simple fact of their sex. Venetia had achieved so much, but had been thwarted in so much. She had settled for what she had, and he knew she was not unhappy, not now – but, oh, she had been! And how many others would suffer as she had, and worse, because they belonged to the female half of the human race?

He thought of all these things in a rush of images, but had no words to express them. Instead he enquired gently, 'Shall we have tea? Shall I ring?'

And her eyes came up to his sharply, then softened into a smile, understanding all he had not said. 'Dear Beauty,' she said. 'What would I ever have done without you? Yes, ring by all means. I believe there may be short-cake.'

'Shortcake!'

'Ordered for your benefit, of course,' Venetia said. 'I am womanly enough for that. And I can't really be unhappy about anything, now that I've seen Violet again. I'm sorry to say it, but nothing in life became the old earl so much as leaving it!'

'I just wish she had stayed with us, so that we could have seen more of her,' said Overton.

'Yes. I'm sure that house in St James's Square can't be fit to live in,' Venetia agreed. 'Who would have thought Holkam would turn out such a stickler as to say she must be under his roof while they're in mourning? I always thought it was the old earl who made those preposterous rules, but it seems the young earl is just as fusty as his father.'

'Never mind, it will all be different next year. It was good to see her so happy – and looking well, don't you think?'

'I thought she was a little pale. But as long as she has Scole with her, I shan't worry too much. And perhaps

477

we shall be allowed to go and stay with her in Lincolnshire this winter.'

Overton smiled. 'After all the complaints you made about being in Sandringham in winter, with those icy winds, I never thought to hear you *hoping* for a visit to the fens.'

The new king was almost the same height as his father, but being very slight in build and scorning the raised heels King Edward had employed, he did not have his commanding presence. 'He ain't such a fine man as Teddy,' was the general opinion. However, he copied his father's care in dressing, making the most of what he had. His hair and beard were always neatly trimmed, brushed and anointed with lavender water, his hands beautifully manicured, his clothes formal, exquisitely cut and perfectly kept, his boots polished to a high gloss. From long naval habit he wore his trousers creased down the side; he did not knot his ties but pulled them through a ring and fastened them down with a jewelled pin. He always wore gloves out of doors, even when shooting, and always carried a stick. He had not the exotic tastes of his restless, cosmopolitan father, but he liked everything to be of the best: not only his clothes but his Purdey guns, his food, his stationery, his cigarette cases by Fabergé. He liked order, elegance, perfection of detail.

Out of doors he liked shooting, and was an excellent shot; within doors he liked the quiet wholesomeness of family life, small parties of respectable people, naval punctuality, and early bed. He did not care for bridge – still less gambling – of an evening: the Queen liked to knit or sew, and the King had an extensive stamp collection, about which he was very knowledgeable. After the glittering, 'racy' days of Edward, the Court seemed to be reverting to the dull domesticity of Victoria and Albert.

The new queen, though she had been known by friends and family as May, had always signed herself officially with both her given names, Victoria Mary. But double names were not acceptable in England, and since she could hardly call herself Queen Victoria, she took the style of Queen Mary, and grumbled a little at being rechristened at the age of forty-three. She was exactly the same height as her husband, but with her rigidly straight back, long gowns, raised heels and large hats, she appeared to tower over him. Saloon bar wits talked about 'King George the Fifth and Queen Mary the Four-Fifths.' She had as strong a sense of duty as the King, in consequence of which she never forgot he was her sovereign as well as her husband, and was obedient to him in everything, even allowing him to dictate what styles and colours she might wear. As his taste was deeply conservative and old-fashioned, she dressed the same year after year, adding to the general perception of the dullness of Court.

The new reign was marked with an internal difficulty. Queen Alexandra's widowed sister, the Empress Dowager, arrived soon after the death of King Edward to comfort her, and remained for three months. Her influence over her sister was considerable and unfortunate. At the funeral she persuaded the Queen Dowager to adopt the custom of the Russian court, and take precedence of the new king and queen. Then she encouraged Queen Alexandra not to move out of Buckingham Palace, and to continue to fly the Royal Standard, where she should have used a standard impaled with her maiden arms. When Queen Alexandra wrote to her son she refused to address him as 'The King', but marked the envelopes 'King George', as though he were only standing in for his father. And when at last, in December 1910, she consented to move to Marlborough House, she gave away a large number of royal heirlooms as presents, which Lord Esher had tactfully to retrieve from the bemused recipients.

The private family retreat of Sandringham had been left by King Edward to Queen Alexandra for her lifetime, and she saw no reason to quit it for the convenience of her son. So King George and Queen Mary continued to live at York Cottage, a small, plain and rather ugly villa on the estate, which had been cramped enough when they were Prince and Princess of Wales, with their six children and the servants, but was even worse with the business of monarch to carry on. The rooms were inadequate – some bedrooms were as small as cupboards – the dark stairs and narrow passages were inconvenient, and the place certainly had no look of a king's establishment, with its furniture from Maples and coloured prints of old masters on the walls. The private secretary had to conduct business in the King's bedroom, while visitors waited on a hard chair in the passage outside the door.

But the shadow that hung over the King in his first year of reign was the constitutional crisis. The conference that had been going on since May had been unable to come to any conclusion, and on the 11th of November Mr Asquith travelled down to Sandringham to wait on the King at York Cottage and ask him to dissolve Parliament as a preliminary to a general election. He said he would like to get it over with before Christmas. The King was relieved that he had not been asked to pledge the creation of peers, and thought better of Asquith.

However, only three days later, Lord Knollys was summoned to Downing Street and told that the Prime Minister required the King to give an immediate guarantee to create enough peers in the next Parliament to push through the Lords reform.

Afterward, Knollys went to see Venetia, and walked about her sitting-room in an uncharacteristic state of agitation.

'Why did Asquith change his mind about it?' she asked him.

'He says he didn't. He says that he didn't go to Sandringham to tender any specific proposal, only to acquaint the King with the general situation.'

'Ah! And in the mean time, he has been bullied by his more radical colleagues, you think?'

'I would not be surprised – would you?'

'But it's quite outrageous,' Venetia said. 'Bad enough to try to force King Edward to make guarantees, but a new, untried king! Besides, Asquith has said publicly that it's a request no statesman could properly make.'

'Just so. The Parliament Bill has only just had its first reading: the Upper House hasn't even had a chance to consider it, let alone reject it. But of course Asquith made that rash promise to the Lower House in April to placate the Irish and Socialist members, and now they've come to collect their dues.'

'But what will you advise the King, Francis? He must not give in.'

'Ah, you don't know the half of it,' Knollys said, and stopped his pacing to turn and face her, his expression grave. 'This is in absolute confidence?'

'Of course,' she said. 'You know you can trust me, my dear.'

'Well, then, I told Asquith that the King was adamant about not giving a guarantee in advance of the election, and Asquith said that if the King refused he would immediately resign and fight the election on the issue "The King and the Peers against the people".'

'Francis, no!'

'He is quite serious. I put up every argument I know, but he would not shift. He means to blackmail the King. He advised me to persuade His Majesty rather than let it come to that.'

Venetia was shocked. Knollys was now in a position of having to persuade the King to do something he did not want to do, and which he, Knollys, thought he ought not to do. It was blackmail of the lowest kind. 'It is a dirty trick!' she exclaimed indignantly.

'The worst,' Knollys agreed. 'And for such a paltry reason – to protect the cabinet from the consequences of a rash promise they made only to sustain the government's majority.'

'Is there no alternative? Surely the King can allow the Liberals to resign without calling an election? He can

481

send for Balfour. Balfour and Lansdowne told King Edward they would serve.'

'Balfour wouldn't be able to command a majority in the Lower House,' said Knollys. 'He would have to ask for a dissolution, and then the election would be fought not only on the Lords reform but on the King's conduct. If the Liberals won he would be left completely defenceless in their hands, and if the Conservatives won he would have been made to look like a party-political pawn. Either way his impartiality would be compromised, and the Crown would suffer. It would make the Liberals feel justified in pressing for even more radical and – dare I say it? – revolutionary changes.'

'It's an utter disgrace,' Venetia said warmly, 'for Asquith to impose on an inexperienced king for his own political ends.'

Knollys nodded glumly, rubbing his hands together as his brows bent in thought. 'I can't see any way out,' he said at last. 'I shall have to try to persuade the King. We can't possibly allow an election to be fought on the lines Asquith proposes. Setting class against class – setting the people against the King. The damage that would do! It could lead to full-scale revolution. God knows, there are plenty of factions hovering on the brink of violence, plenty of individuals longing for an excuse to riot, burn and destroy. God, Venetia, what times we live in! The whole of Europe is a tinder-box, but I hoped we might avoid that sort of thing here. How I miss my old master! The new king is a good man, but just now above all we need experienced hands on the reins.'

'My poor Francis,' Venetia said, 'I do feel for you. Everything's changing so fast these days.'

He was silent a while, and then sighed, and said, 'Thank you for letting me unburden myself. I feel a little better now.'

'What will you do?'

'My duty. Try to persuade the King to yield, but without telling him why. It will be difficult.'

It proved not difficult but impossible. The King refused to be persuaded. He wrote to the Prime Minister that while he fully recognised what must be the ultimate solution of the political situation if an election took place and the government were returned by an adequate majority, he saw no reason why he should give guarantees in advance. Indeed, he doubted that giving such guarantees would be constitutional.

The result was a meeting at Buckingham Palace on the 16th of November at which Mr Asquith and Lord Crewe, the leader of the House of Lords, repeated to the King the threats they had previously made to Knollys and, after an hour and a half of bullying, persuaded him to give his secret pledge. The King was deeply angry and resentful about it, Knollys told Venetia afterwards: the indignity of having been browbeaten, of not having been trusted to do his duty when the time came, rankled with him. Furthermore, he was shocked by Asquith's insistence on secrecy. He said to Knollys, 'I have never in my life done anything I was ashamed to confess.' Concealment was not in his nature, and it hurt him to be forced to practise it.

When Lord Knollys had referred to the troubled times they were living in, he did not only mean the constitutional crisis. Of late the trades unions had abandoned Parliamentary means and turned to 'direct action', as they called it. This was on the wave of an idea imported from France called Syndicalism, which decreed that the working classes were locked in a class struggle that equated to war, and that it should therefore be carried out by frankly violent means. Syndicalism proposed varying types of strike, aggressive demonstrations, and sabotage leading up to a general strike that would 'bring the country to its knees'. The constitutional crisis gave encouragement to the leaders of the movement, who said that if the Commons were sabotaging the Constitution for their own purposes, why shouldn't they do the same?

In July 1910 there had been a four-day railway strike in the Newcastle area; in September a strike of 120,000 workers in the cotton industry in Lancashire. A lock-out of boilermakers in the north-east in September affected ironworkers and shipbuilders and lasted fourteen weeks. In October a railway strike in France paralysed that country and the Channel and North Sea ports, and was only crushed by the French government's employing soldiers to do the strikers' jobs.

And then in November a strike of 30,000 coal-miners took place in South Wales. It began in sympathy with a handful of miners who were complaining about the rate of pay for a particular seam, but it soon escalated. On the 7th of November a gang of strikers attacked the pithead at Ton-y-pandy and destroyed the ventilating machinery to stop the pit being used. From that beginning a violent mob went on to loot and terrorise the area for three days. Police were brought in from Swansea and Bristol but were unable to control the situation and the chief constable of Glamorgan asked for troops. Hussars and infantry were sent from Salisbury Plain but Mr Churchill, the Home Secretary, had them stopped at Swindon while he urged the leaders of the mob to stop rioting. The disturbances went on, and the troops were marched in, backed up with a large force of Metropolitan Police. There was terrible damage to property before things were quietened down, and respectable people of all degrees were in fear of further disturbances.

Against this background, it was hardly likely that the Suffragettes would be able to command much attention. It was known that when Parliament assembled on the 22nd of November, Asquith was likely to announce an immediate general election on the Parliament Bill issue, in which case there would be no time for the Conciliation Bill. It was further believed, with grim reason, that if Parliament dissolved without having made firm promises about the future of the Conciliation Bill, it would be a dead letter, and all the negotiations would have to start again from the beginning, which would mean a setback of years, given the other matters clamouring for Parliamentary time.

So it was decided that there must be a deputation to Asquith at the House to extract a promise from him. No-one knew when the dissolution would be – Asquith had not made an announcement – and London was filling up with Suffragettes from all over the country, buzzing like hornets with their anxiety not to miss their chance. It was decided, therefore, to mount the deputation on Friday the 18th of November.

On the 17th, Venetia received another visit from Mrs Anderson, who asked her to join the deputation on the next day. 'We want a small group of distinguished women to lead the others – there will be more chance of getting through in that way. I shall walk at the head with Mrs Pankhurst, and we would very much like you to make a third.'

Venetia was doubtful. 'I'm rather afraid there may be some violence planned by the authorities,' she said.

'They will hardly use violence on *me*,' said Mrs Anderson. 'That is why I would like you to be at my side. If I can get through with Mrs Pankhurst we can at least put our case, but as you know Mr Asquith personally—'

'Not well.'

'Even so, he must listen to you. And we *must* make a push now, or lose the progress of the last year.'

Venetia said, 'I hate to deny you anything, considering how much I owe you—'

Mrs Anderson interrupted her with a beguiling smile. 'Ah, now don't say no! We women who have broken through the barrier owe it to the younger ones to continue the campaign. Think how much good your presence can do, a woman of rank, and of personal achievement.'

'But that's the problem,' Venetia said. 'I don't believe I can do any good. This is not the time, with the Parliament Bill and the riots in South Wales, to catch the government's attention. And, frankly, the Conciliation Bill

485

is not the right Bill. We ought to be campaigning for the vote for all women.'

'But you know that is a practical impossibility,' Mrs Anderson said. 'We must work with what we have, and consolidate our gains step by step. It's what we have always done, you and I. Won't you join us tomorrow? It will make it very uncomfortable for Asquith to refuse to receive us.'

Venetia yielded. 'Very well. If it is a question of making Asquith uncomfortable, I can't refuse.'

Venetia rang for the maid to show her out, and while they were waiting, Mrs Anderson said, 'By the way, is your cousin, Lady Anne Farraline, back in Town? I thought I might see her at Clement's Inn – she is usually at the centre of things – but she was not there.'

'I haven't seen her, but she left her card at the beginning of the week,' said Venetia.

'Ah. Perhaps she was busy somewhere else,' said Mrs Anderson.

When she had gone, Venetia thought about her cousin, and wondered why, if she was back in Town, she had not called to try to recruit Venetia for the demonstration. She returned to her work, but the question kept recurring to her, interrupting her study of the effects of injections of gold on tuberculous cells. At last she gave in to curiosity and drove round to Bedford Square.

The door was answered by a footman Venetia did not know. He was new since she had last called, and did not recognise her, did not even seem to know who she was after studying her card. He disappeared upstairs, much to Venetia's annoyance. She did not expect to be kept waiting in the hall, especially in the house of a relative. However, he came back quite soon and invited her in a casual manner to go up to the drawing-room, and she followed him, reflecting that Anne's standards had slipped if she was willing to be served by servants as poorly trained as this one.

He mumbled her announcement, and did not stand

sufficiently out of the way, so that she almost had to squeeze past him into the drawing-room; and as he closed the door behind her far from silently, she saw that Anne was not present. Instead there was a small, slight, dark-haired young woman sitting with her legs curled under her in one corner of a sofa with a magazine in her hands. She jumped up and stood surveying Venetia with an intensity that would have been impertinent if it had not seemed so innocent and childlike.

'Good afternoon,' she said. 'Lady Overton? You're Anne's cousin, aren't you? She has spoken about you such a lot, I almost feel I know you. I'm Vera Polk. How do you do?'

It would have been churlish to refuse the frankly outstretched hand, and Venetia reflected on what she knew about Miss Polk's background and forgave her a lack of knowledge of the correct forms.

'Is Lady Anne not at home? The manservant did not say.'

'Oh, Vicars is hopeless! Anne says so, anyway. She only took him on as a favour to a friend. I suppose he ought to have said Anne was out, but she should be home soon, and I know she would like to see you, so please wait. Won't you sit down? Shall I ring for some tea?'

'No, thank you, no tea,' Venetia said; but she sat down. It was hardly proper for Miss Polk to assume the rights of hostess in Anne's absence, but there was something almost comical about the informality of this young woman's manner, though her lack of deference would have offended someone more on her dignity than Venetia. She spoke and behaved with a kind of childish impulsiveness, and indeed she looked very young, closer to sixteen than eighteen. She had small, sharp features, a pointed chin, dark hair that curled softly like duck's feathers all over her head. She was dressed in a navy serge skirt of the currently fashionable length, which cleared the ground by two inches, and a white blouse: though plain, both were of good quality, and she was wearing on

487

the third finger of her right hand what looked like an expensive gold and diamond ring.

Yet for all her apparent innocence, there was something in the regard of her dark eyes that struck a false note with Venetia. They were too watchful, too noticing and sharp. She could not get over the feeling that Miss Polk was *playing* the kitten, and that in fact there was something unexpectedly old and knowing about her; that her lack of deference and ignorance of form were manipulatory; that she *pretended* not to know how she ought to address Venetia so that Venetia could not object to being addressed in this egalitarian way.

She had not said where Anne was, and Venetia would not dignify her position by asking; but they did not sit in silence. Miss Polk chatted with that same spritely innocence about the weather and the new play at Drury Lane, not seeming to need any encouragement or even reply. After a few moments Venetia rose to her feet again, intending to leave, but Miss Polk said, 'Oh, don't go. Anne will be back very soon. Honestly, she will be furious with me if I let you go without seeing her.'

This was too much, and Venetia drew on a freezing manner she had not used for a long time. 'Miss Polk,' she said coldly, 'I do not know who you are—'

She got no further. Miss Polk said, 'I'm Anne's friend. I thought you realised that.'

'Forgive me, but you are not mistress of this house and for you to assume the rôle of hostess is not appropriate.'

Miss Polk remained unfrozen. 'Oh, that's all right. I live here,' she said.

Venetia was taken aback. She did not know how to counter someone who had so little regard for the social niceties. 'Is Miss Vaughan at home? Perhaps I can speak to her,' she said.

'Miss Vaughan's gone,' said Miss Polk.

'Gone?'

'Left. Gone away. She doesn't live here any more,' said Miss Polk, and there was no mistaking now the gleam

488

of satisfaction in her eyes, or the hard edge to her voice. 'She wasn't needed any more, now Anne's got me. So it's just the two of us. I hope you've got no objection to that?'

'It is not my business to object or otherwise,' Venetia began.

'That's right,' said Miss Polk. 'I'm glad you realise that. Some of her other friends have been stuck-up about it.'

'Stuck-up?' Was there nothing this young woman would not say?

'Don't you know what stuck-up means?'

At this dangerous moment the door opened and Anne came in, seeming a little out of breath as though she had run up the stairs, her hair slightly disordered, and fog jewels still glinting on it. She flashed a look from Venetia to Miss Polk, assessing the situation, and having made a small, quelling gesture of her hand towards the latter, she advanced on Venetia with a rather nervous smile. 'I'm sorry I wasn't here to receive you. I didn't know you were going to call or I shouldn't have gone out.'

'It wasn't a planned visit. I called on the spur of the moment,' Venetia said. Anne was looking well, she thought: a little plumper in the face, and with a flush of health in her cheeks. She had dressed her hair differently, too, in a softer style that suited her.

'Oh,' said Anne. She moved her hands about nervously, an uncharacteristic fidget. 'Of course you've met Miss Polk now. I'm sorry I wasn't here to introduce her.'

'Miss Polk introduced herself quite efficiently,' Venetia said.

Anne took the rebuke with unprecedented meekness. 'Miss Polk is my new companion, in place of Miss Vaughan,' she said. 'Vera, did you ring for tea?'

'She didn't want any,' said Miss Polk.

Anne flinched at the 'she'. Venetia was amazed that her cousin did not say anything to the girl, nor yet ask her to leave them alone. Was this her proud, haughty, fiery Anne, this woman who looked at Miss Polk with placatory nervousness? 'Well, I want some. Be a dear and ring, won't you?'

'Anne, I would like to speak to you alone,' Venetia interrupted.

Miss Polk abandoned all pretence. 'Whatever you've got to say to her you can say in front of me,' she said sharply. 'I'm not having you discussing me behind my back.'

'Vera, don't,' Anne protested, but weakly.

Venetia breathed hard, and said coldly, 'I have no wish to discuss you, Miss Polk. I do not know you.'

'Don't take me for a fool,' said Miss Polk. 'You were going to tell her she ought to get rid of me – I know!'

'Lady Anne can choose her own friends without help from me,' Venetia said.

'Vera, please be quiet,' Anne begged. 'We're not going to discuss you. Ring for tea, there's a dear, and sit over there quietly while I talk to Lady Overton.'

For a wonder, Miss Polk did as she was told, though with a certain amount of head-tossing and a few burning looks. Venetia did not use the degree of privacy so attained to mention the matter. She understood now why there had been talk. Anne had got rid of Miss Vaughan and even in these enlightened days it was not usual for a woman of Anne's rank to live without a companion. Miss Polk was far too young to qualify; and if Miss Polk regularly behaved like this in company, a lot of people would be offended. What might pass at Suffragette meetings in Liverpool would not do for London drawing-rooms, or even, let it be said, Clement's Inn. She was sorry to see her cousin so humbled, in thrall to a capricious young woman who seemed to have an unwholesomely strong influence over her, but she had no wish to discuss it. She saw from Anne's eyes that there was nothing she might have said that Anne had not already heard or anticipated. Anne must find her own way out of the situation.

Anne said, 'I'm sorry about that. Vera is rather sensitive, and some people have been unkind to her.'

490

'I only called to see how you were,' Venetia said, striving for a normal tone of voice. 'You were away for so long.'

'Yes, I was in the lake country all summer,' Anne began, and fearing there might be a confession on its way, Venetia jumped in quickly with an exposition of Mrs Anderson's visit.

'I wondered if you were going to be part of the deputation,' she concluded.

'I did offer, but they turned me down,' Anne said.

'Turned you down?' Venetia was surprised.

'WSPU rules. They're afraid there might be violence. Something is going on, you know. I've heard that Inspector Jarvis has been sent away for the day, and a stranger brought in to run the operation, because Jarvis is too much of a friend to the WSPU. So they aren't allowing any girls under twenty-one to join in this time. Some of the very old women and others who aren't strong have been refused too.'

'But why does that affect you?'

'Miss Polk is under twenty-one.' Anne looked defiant. 'I told them that where I go, she goes, and if they won't take her they can't have me. But don't worry – Vera and I will have our own demonstration. We would have volunteered for "danger duty" if they'd have us. As it is we shall have to do what we can to get arrested on our own.' Anne met Venetia's eyes, and lowered her voice and said, 'Don't blame me. I didn't realise until this summer how lonely I've been. I needed a friend who was interested in the same things as me.'

Venetia couldn't help saying, 'I should have thought there were plenty of suitable people in the WSPU – people closer to your age and rank.'

Anne sighed and shook her head, looking away. 'It doesn't seem to work that way,' she said. 'Suitability doesn't seem to come into it. I wish you could understand.'

'I understand better than you think,' Venetia said.

Anne looked up briefly, then down again. 'Perhaps you do,' she said.

491

'Well, I've no more to say,' Venetia said. 'Perhaps you'd ring for the servant to show me out.'

When the footman appeared, Venetia bowed her head to Miss Polk, and Anne walked with her to the door. She touched her arm. 'I'm happy, you know,' she said in a low voice, 'for the first time in years. I thought you'd be glad for me.'

'I am,' said Venetia.

Chapter Sixteen

On the 18th of November the Suffragettes who were to demonstrate gathered at Caxton Hall, wearing white satin badges inscribed 'Deputation 1910'. The cabinet was meeting at Westminster, and the intention was to ask Asquith to guarantee time for the Conciliation Bill in the next session. The women were to go in groups of twelve, the first group led by Mrs Pankhurst, Mrs Anderson and Lady Overton and including other distinguished women such as Mrs Cobden Sanderson, Dr Louisa Garrett Anderson (Mrs Anderson's daughter) and Mrs Hertha Ayrton, the scientist.

Mrs Pankhurst made a speech before they set out. 'In quietness and assurance shall be your strength. You are acting legally in persistently endeavouring to see Mr Asquith. All other kinds of effort having failed, you will now press forward in quietness and peaceableness, offending none and blaming none,' she said, and finished – rather melodramatically, Venetia thought, 'ready to sacrifice yourselves unto death if need be, in the cause of freedom.'

There had been persistent rumours that some particular violence was expected against the women, but nothing definite was known. The leading deputation set out, with Venetia walking in front with Mrs Anderson and Mrs Pankhurst, along Victoria Street with an escort of police. There were cheers from passers-by, and from people in omnibuses on their way home. It was a cold evening, and Mrs Anderson was wearing a fur bonnet and a seal-skin jacket with a sable border. At seventy-four she had shrunk with age, and glancing down at her Venetia felt tall and vigorous by comparison. But the face peeping out from its encircling fur was firm with determination and the pioneer doctor walked at a brisk pace, which was somehow comforting. Venetia rehearsed in her head what she would say to Asquith if they should manage to see him, and thus engaged did not much notice her surroundings until they were almost at Parliament Square. Then she saw ahead a dense crowd; and at the same moment Anne suddenly appeared at her side, having struggled through until she was close enough to speak to her.

'I know what's happening,' she said, breathless with the effort. 'They've sent away the usual police because they're too sympathetic to us, and called in a contingent from the East End. Churchill's told them to do as they like, as long as we don't get through. He's told them no arrests. *No arrests!*' she repeated frantically as an arm came out from the press of bodies and restrained her, and Venetia and her two companions moved ahead, leaving her behind.

No arrests, Venetia thought with alarm. She knew what that meant. On other occasions demonstrators had been able to protect themselves to an extent by provoking the police to arrest them if things became too violent. But if arrest was specifically ruled out . . . She looked around. Two of their original police escort remained, and a path was being made ahead of the three leaders, evidently by some prior arrangement. But the remainder of the escort had disappeared, and the rest of the deputation had been swallowed by the crowd. The square was filled with people, among whom there were hundreds of policemen in uniform, and an equal number of large, tough-looking men in the clothes of East End working men. Venetia had spent many years working with the police and knew the look of a constable in plain clothes. As she contemplated why they should be wearing plain clothes, she felt a thrill of fear.

But no insult was offered the three of them, and a way was thrust through for them until they reached the steps of the Strangers' Entrance, where a line of police parted to let them through and closed again. They were breathless from the crush of bodies, but otherwise unharmed, and it was obvious that orders had been given that they were to be kept safe. They sent a message by a House of Commons servant to the Prime Minister requesting an audience, and then had nothing to do but wait, and view with increasing horror the events that were unfolding beyond their protective cordon.

The East End bobbies, with their instruction to do as they liked, were treating the women trying to get through to the House as they would have treated rioting men on their own ground. They kicked them with feet and knees, punched them, twisted their arms behind them, knocked them to the ground, dragged them by the hair, tossed them from one to another, threw them against railings and against members of the crowd. They seemed to take particular delight in seizing the women by the breasts and wrenching them. Some of the crowd were sympathetic to the women, and shouted in protest. But there were a lot of toughs there, and a large contingent of sailors, most of whom were drunk, who whistled and bellowed and encouraged the police to 'Go it!'

Venetia and her companions could do nothing but look on in horror. Their protests were ignored; they were not allowed to leave – 'for your own protection' – or admitted to the House. The Prime Minister did not come. His secretary appeared briefly with an excuse and said that he would pass on a message, but he seemed offhand and distracted – perhaps because of the ghastly scenes being enacted in the square – and soon hurried away.

The battle went on for six hours. Venetia saw women bleeding, women with their clothes torn almost from them, women lying on the ground being kicked, women thrown through the air like sacks. Seeing one woman sprawled in the gutter not far away, apparently unconscious, Venetia demanded to be allowed to go to her. 'I am a doctor,' she said, her voice trembling with rage and horror. 'She may need help.' But the policemen merely stared at her stolidly and shook their heads. 'Have you no humanity?' she cried, and one of them said, 'She asked for it. She knew what she was getting into.' There was a flash of light as a photographer took a picture of the fallen woman, and in a moment she struggled to her feet and leaned weakly against the railings. Venetia shouted to her, 'Are you all right?' but in the prevailing noise she did not hear, and a moment later a surge of bodies hid her from sight.

At last, after midnight, the battle died down, the crowds dispersed, and a message came to their police guardians that they could be allowed to go.

'We had better go to Caxton Hall and see what's happening,' said Mrs Pankhurst. 'Will you come? I expect they will have taken the injured there. You may be needed.'

'Of course,' Venetia said. She was extremely shaken, and saw that Mrs Anderson was too.

'This is horrible,' she said quietly to Venetia, as Mrs Pankhurst marched ahead. 'This is all wrong. I cannot think these tactics are right.'

'They won't get away with it. There were press photographers there. It will be in the papers tomorrow,' Venetia said.

'It was like a war,' Mrs Anderson said. 'A war on women. I begin to wonder whether Millie is right.' Her sister, Mrs Fawcett, had always been against violent methods and was the leader of the NUWSS, the 'nice' Suffragettes. 'What has this achieved except to hurt and humiliate a large number of women?'

At Caxton Hall an ante-room was serving as a makeshift hospital. Most of the injuries had been attended to by the time the two doctors arrived, but they took off their coats to help those still waiting. Two of the women had been indecently assaulted, and the word went round that they were not the only ones to have suffered in that way. In an atmosphere where violence towards women was tacitly encouraged, it was not surprising.

The following day, the early edition of the *Daily Mail* bore the headline 'BLACK FRIDAY' above a photograph of the woman Venetia had seen lying in the gutter, but as soon as it was known about, the government made an order that the picture and the story were to be suppressed. The edition was withdrawn and destroyed, and only those copies already sold reached the public gaze. Despite the order that no arrests were to be made, a hundred and fifteen women had been taken up. Now the order went forth that they were not to be tried. In batches they were taken before a magistrate and discharged.

Anne came alone to visit Venetia in the afternoon of the next day. She was pale and seemed shaken, and pulled back her hair to show a cut on her forehead, and rolled up her sleeve to show some of her bruises. 'If they want war they shall have it,' she said. 'Vera and I were arrested, but of course they let us all go. The magistrate said it was on the Home Secretary's order.'

'I heard that. I wonder why?'

'Don't you know? Because if we were tried, the story would come out about the methods used that night. Churchill's a clever devil – but if he thinks we can be intimidated by violence he is very much mistaken.'

'Was Miss Polk hurt?' Venetia asked.

'Yes,' Anne said shortly.

'I hope not badly?'

'Thank you, no,' Anne said, a little stiffly, as if unable to accept any mention of Miss Polk as friendly.

Venetia remembered her conversation with Mrs Anderson the night before and said, 'You know, I wonder if this violence is not counter-productive. You – we – have sacrificed the right to chivalry, without any compensatory gain.'

'Chivalry!' Anne said, with a short, harsh laugh. 'All we ever asked was to be treated as equals. Now they kick us like dogs. That is what we get for trying to demonstrate peacefully! Well, we shall have to change our tactics. Christabel says that in future, if they are going to use crude violence on us, we must commit offences against property so as to get ourselves arrested quickly. They care about their windows and motor-cars – they don't care about us. You didn't get to see Asquith?'

'No, he didn't come out, and we weren't admitted. But it was announced this morning that he is going to say something about the Conciliation Bill on Tuesday.'

'We'll be waiting for him,' Anne said grimly. 'He is not to think we are cowed by yesterday's proceedings. We'll make him know he still has to answer to us, no matter what his methods.'

There was nothing Venetia could say; but she decided then that she could not take part in any more demonstrations. It was not fair to her family. As Anne was leaving, however, she did ask, out of her own curiosity, 'If you care for Miss Polk, how can you let her put herself in danger?'

'*Let* her?' Anne said in surprise.

'She is very young,' Venetia reminded her.

'She is old enough to make up her own mind. It's what we are fighting for, Venetia, haven't you grasped that yet? The right to decide for ourselves, not to be patronised and protected and looked after and hidden away. Vera knows what the dangers are, and I have no right to try to stop her doing what she wants. She's as brave as a lion – the bravest person I've ever met. We fight side by side, or not at all.'

Venetia said no more, but in her quiet moments afterwards she could not help wondering where all this freedom would ultimately lead. If everyone had the right to do exactly as they pleased, and no-one had the right to care for or try to protect anyone else, would civilisation be able to survive?

On the Tuesday, when Parliament assembled, all MPs were eager to be done with the remaining business as quickly as possible, and the session lasted less than an hour. There was a noncommittal statement from the Prime Minister over the Conciliation Bill. Three hundred Suffragettes were waiting at Caxton Hall, and when they heard what he had said – and, indeed, what he had not said – they marched on Downing Street. There were more violent and dangerous scenes, in the course of which windows were broken and Asquith's motor-car damaged. A hundred and seventy-seven women were arrested, but Churchill ordered that all except those who had damaged property were to be released. Seventy-five women were tried and given fines, but elected to go to prison. The newspapers were not allowed to publish the names of those imprisoned, but privately it was known that they included Mrs Pankhurst's sister, Mrs Clarke – and Lady Anne Farraline and Miss Polk. They were each given one month.

Mrs Pankhurst's speech on Black Friday turned out to be prophetic, for the events of the day claimed the first two martyrs for the Cause. The Downing Street prisoners were released just before Christmas. Mrs Clarke was spending Christmas Day with the Pankhursts when she collapsed and died of a brain haemorrhage; a week later, another of the released prisoners, Henria Williams, died of heart failure.

'You said that someone would get killed sooner or later,' Lord Overton said when he heard the news.

'I wish I had not been right,' Venetia said. 'I can only be glad it was not Anne. The WSPU *must* restore the truce now.'

'Perhaps Asquith will give the Bill time next year.'

'With the Parliament Bill still to push through, and all the strikes, and the Coronation coming up, I don't have much hope.'

'The Coronation may work in your favour. Asquith may be afraid of some outrage being perpetrated during it and give the Bill time for that reason.'

'Certainly the hotheads like Anne would be capable of disrupting even a Coronation,' Venetia agreed. 'Well, we shall wait and see. But I'm not going to get sucked in again, that's certain.'

'I can't tell you how glad I am to hear it,' Overton said.

Jack loved his new job from the first day. Now he was 'messing about' with aeroplanes all day long, given the freedom of the workshops, encouraged to think of new ideas and improvements and allowed to try them out. Howard Wright was, like Jack, a believer in the ultimate superiority of the monoplane, though for the moment the design problems made the biplane more practical: it was far stronger, and the double wings gave more lift – though equally they gave more drag. If the strength-to-weight ratio problem of the monoplane could be solved, it would be much faster and more manoeuvrable. Though nothing was said about it, and there had been no interest from government departments, Jack was thinking about the war with Germany that now seemed inevitable sooner or later. The aeroplane might well play a part in such a war, not only for reconnaissance but even, perhaps, for fighting. It had occurred to him that it would be possible to drop explosives from an aeroplane; and if that had occurred to him, it would surely have occurred to someone in Germany, too.

But for the moment he was simply happy to be involved with aeroplanes, and the fact that he could – and did – take part in every stage of the manufacture helped his understanding and thus his designing. He had not even sacrificed any salary for the pleasure of doing what he liked all day long. His new boss paid him generously, saying that in him he had not only a designer but an engineer and an aviator, three men rolled into one, all for one salary.

'I ought really to pay you three times as much,' he said, 'and I'm only grateful you're willing to stay with me at all!'

From a business point of view, Jack thought, it was a good thing that aviators had so many crashes, for they were always coming back for repairs or new aeroplanes. Business was particularly brisk with monoplanes because they were not strong enough to lift two people into the air, so would-be aviators had to teach themselves to fly in them by trial and error – mostly error. Fortunately the machines were so light that a fall from forty or fifty feet usually resulted in no more than a few bruises for the flyer, even if the wings, propellor and undercarriage of his vehicle were smashed in the process.

It was in late September at Brooklands that he met his friend Tom Sopwith again. Sopwith had been spending all his time that summer on boats, both motor-boats and sailing boats; he owned a half-share in a 166-ton schooner with his friend William Eyre, and had won races with it.

'It's a wonderful sensation, flying along over the water with all sail set, you know,' he said to Jack.

Jack was amazed. 'I don't doubt it, but can it hope to compare with flying along through the air?'

'Well, perhaps not. That's what I'm here to find out,' Sopwith said. 'You see, Eyre and I were tooling around in the Channel on the *Neva* a couple of weeks ago, and we happened to put into Dover just after Johnny Moisant had flown across from France, and put down on his way to London.'

'Oh, yes, I read about it. First flight across the Channel with a passenger,' said Jack.

'And what a passenger! It was his mechanic – wise choice, given how much engine trouble he had – but you never saw such a hefty, beefy fellow! He'd have made the average horse sag at the knees just to look at him.'

'You saw them, then?'

'Well, everyone in Dover was talking about it, and we were rather fed up because our sailing had been so slow, so we decided to trot off and have a look. You never saw such a frail, rickety-looking thing as that aeroplane, but it had come all that way with two passengers, one of them the size of a barn, and I began to think there must be something in this flying after all. So here I am.'

'I'm jolly pleased to see you,' Jack said. 'I promise you, once you've tried it, there'll be nothing but flying for you. Everything else pales into insignificance.'

Sopwith laughed. 'I'm ready to be convinced. But what are you doing here?'

So Jack told him his story, and the two men exchanged all their news over a couple of cigarettes. When he heard Jack was living in Oakley Street, Sopwith said, 'There's a coincidence! I've got a little place in Draycott Avenue, practically round the corner. How is it we've never bumped into each other?'

'Probably because neither of us is ever there,' Jack laughed. 'Ah, here's Mrs Hewlett. Are you going up in the Farman?' he asked Sopwith.

'Yes, Blondeau's going to take me up, just to see what it's like. And if I like it, I might get a little bus of my own.'

'You want to buy an aeroplane?'

'Hold hard, I said "if"! I may not like it. It might make me sick. But if I do like it – well, you know me! When it was ballooning, I had to have a balloon, and when it was motoring, I had to have a motor-car.'

'Well,' said Jack, 'if you do decide to buy your own bus, do come to me. I'm working on the nicest little machine you ever saw. Modifications of my own, including my latest redesigned propellor, and—'

'Whoa! Steady on! Let me try to get off the ground first and then, if I do catch the fever that obviously has you in its grip, I promise I'll come to you first.'

It only took two circuits in the Farman to convince Sopwith, as it had Jack before him, that life on earth was stale by comparison. 'Best fiver I ever spent,' he said breathlessly when he climbed down from the wing after-wards. A week later he had visited the Howard Wright office in Marylebone High Street, and a few days after that he met Jack in the evening and went with him to the workshop in Battersea to look at a monoplane. He bought the latest model for £630, to be delivered to the sheds at Brooklands, and Jack undertook to go down and assemble it himself and be there when his friend took his first flight.

It proved a short one. After rolling about for a while, getting the feel of it, Sopwith decided to try to get airborne. He increased speed, but as the machine began to rise he pulled the stick back too sharply, and it shot forty feet into the air, stalled, and fell back to earth. Jack went running, but Sopwith was unharmed, though looking rather surprised.

'What happened?' Jack asked.

'I was so astonished when I looked down and saw the ground had gone, I suppose I pulled the stick too hard,' Sopwith said. 'How bad is the bus?'

It was not good. The propellor was snapped in half, the undercarriage was a splintery mess, and one of the wings was crumpled.

'It'll take a bit of work,' Jack said.

'How long before I can try again?' Sopwith asked, with the eagerness of an addict craving his pipe of cocaine.

Jack grinned. 'Flying has hooked you, all right, hasn't it?'

He had the aeroplane ready by the beginning of November, and on the 4th the weather was fine, bright and still – perfect for flying. Sopwith spent the morning rolling and making short hops; then after lunch these developed into short, straight flights, and finally into circuits. Jack watched the whole thing – for such a potentially valuable client, Howard Wright had made it clear, no attention was too great. John Farley, the *Aero* reporter, was also there, and said to Jack, 'Who is that fellow? I thought you were a gifted aviator, but I've never seen anyone make so much progress so quickly.'

'He has a knack for all sorts of machines,' Jack said. 'But you're right – he beats my record hollow.'

'Well, I shall write him up – and keep an eye on him for the future,' said Farley. 'I wonder if he'd let me interview him for the magazine. Do you think he'd be willing to take a spot of supper this evening? I know a nice little inn where they do an excellent beefsteak pie. I'd like you to come along too, if you would. A conversation between you two would be something!'

Through November Sopwith spent most of his time at Brooklands, much of it waiting for suitable flying weather. He managed to get airborne from time to time, but nothing like often enough for the fever inside him. Half-way through the month he decided that the monoplane was underpowered with its 40 h.p. engine, and was back at the workshop to talk about buying a Howard Wright biplane with a 60 h.p. engine. Before the end of the month, and within hours of first taking up the biplane, he took his aviator's test and was awarded his ticket – Certificate No. 31.

At a celebration supper that night, Jack said, 'Well, you've broken all records, I should think, for learning to fly in the shortest time ever. What mountain will you scale next?'

Sopwith was ready with his answer. 'I saw it in the *Aero* magazine – that old number you left lying around at the workshop. I was browsing on it while I waited for you last week. The British Empire Michelin Cup competition. There's a five-hundred-pound prize, which would come in handy, and a month left to compete in, which ought to provide one day at least when the weather will be kind.'

The Michelin Tyre Company had offered the prize for the longest non-stop flight made up to the 31st of December, by a British subject in a British-made aero-plane. The flight was to be done in circuits, observed by timekeepers from the Royal Aero Club – it was thought that a point-to-point flight might provoke suspicions of a landing on the way that would be hard to prove or disprove. Circuits were deemed to be fairer.

'You'd have to do pretty well,' Jack said. 'Bill Cody's got the record so far, and that was for ninety-four and a half miles, in two hours twenty-four minutes.'

'Trust you to have the numbers in your head! Still, if

504

the weather's right and the bus doesn't run out of petrol, I see no difficulty about breaking that,' said Sopwith.

Jack grinned. 'I shouldn't mind having a pound or two on you, if anyone could be found to take the bet! But be sure you put on plenty of warm clothing. You're even more exposed on the biplane than on the monoplane, especially about the feet. It would be a pity if you were forced down by frostbite.'

'I'll make a point of bundling up,' Sopwith promised. 'Will you be present for the attempt? I'd like you to give the aeroplane a thorough overhaul beforehand, so I'll know it won't let me down.'

Jack was only too pleased to be involved, and on the 10th of December the attempt took place at Brooklands, around a circuit marked out with poles. Howard Wright himself came down with Jack, and as well as the observers and timekeepers, the secretary of the Royal Aero Club had come to watch, along with several reporters and the usual crowd of onlookers, flyers, mechanics and aviation-mad locals. There was already a great deal of interest in this man who had progressed so fast in flying. Though most of the crowd was male, of course, there were two females present. One was Miss Ormerod, a cousin of Mrs Hewlett who was quite often around the sheds when Jack was there. She was surprisingly knowledgeable about aeroplanes, and Jack often had conversations with her, and thought her quite sensible, though rather plain in looks. Sopwith brought his older sister May, a friendly, sensible, intelligent woman with a definitely motherly streak towards her brilliant little brother. She greeted Jack kindly, having met him before at the family house, and asked after Maud. Jack told her as briefly as possible what had happened, and she was instantly full of compassion.

'But there are plenty more nice girls in the world,' she said. 'I expect you think just now that you will never fall in love again, but it's surprising how the human heart mends.' And the humour in her warm eyes suggested to him that she knew whereof she spoke.

'I shan't *refuse* to fall in love again,' he assured her with a smile. 'It's just that it doesn't feel likely at the moment.'

Miss Sopwith and Miss Ormerod seemed to take to each other, and when May said she was glad to have another female to keep her company, Miss Ormerod seemed to feel the same.

It was a cold day, but dry, and the breeze was light – good flying weather. Sopwith had fortified himself with a large breakfast, followed by a good pipe of 'baccy' (to his sister's disapproval: she thought the habit unhealthy), and at ten o'clock, wearing, as promised, several layers of clothes, he took to the air. On the ground, Jack, May, Miss Ormerod and the mechanics had a scoreboard on which they changed the number after each lap so that Sopwith could see it and not have to keep count himself. Each lap was a little over a mile, to be on the safe side.

Time ticked by. The aeroplane was going well, and Jack's anxious ear could hear no untoward sound that might necessitate a forced landing. The breeze died during the morning and it became perfectly still; a little reddish sunshine struggled through low on the misty horizon, but there was no warmth to it, and the day remained very cold. Down on the ground they stuffed their hands into their pockets, stamped their feet on the frozen grass, lit cigarettes, even had mugs of tea to keep them going; but up in the aeroplane there was nothing to comfort the aviator. Jack knew how cold it must be up there. In the biplane, the flyer sat on a flat seat between the wings with his knees bent up and his feet on the rudder bar in front of him. In this position, with no wind-shielding at all – immobile for hours and with the icy air rushing past – the cold had to be experienced to be believed. It was the feet and hands, of course, that suffered the worst. After an hour or so it would be an agony.

It was after midday when they put '95' on the board, which meant Sopwith had beaten Cody, and they gave a wave as he went over, to draw his attention to it. At one o'clock it was 100 – always a milestone in any scoring –

and a press photographer took a picture of May putting the number on the board.

'He said this morning that if he reached a hundred, he would still go on as long as possible in case someone else tries for the record before the end of the year,' May said.

'Very wise,' said Jack. 'Like having savings in the bank.' But he could guess that now the record was broken it would be harder to bear the pain of the cold; and in fact about a quarter of an hour later Sopwith brought the Wright in to land, having done just under 108 laps in three hours and twelve minutes. In fact, the lap being slightly longer than a mile, Jack calculated that he had done close to a hundred and twenty miles, but the official record was 107¾.

Miss Ormerod, who had gained Jack's respect by sticking it out to the end despite the cold, shoved a mug of tea into his hands and said, 'For the driver. He must be frozen!'

Jack thanked her and managed to force his way through the admiring onlookers and the eager pressmen and photographers to his friend's side. He held out the tea, saying, 'I should think you need this.'

Sopwith smiled. 'Thanks, but you'll have to hold it to my lips for me. I'll never be able to grip it with these.' He held up his hands helplessly. 'Dead after the first half-hour.'

'It's my ambition,' Jack said, 'to design an aeroplane on which one can let go of the controls.'

'All very fine, old man, but that's in the future. For the moment, we might concentrate on rigging up some sort of a windscreen before my next effort. This flying is good fun, but it's bloody cold!'

'Next effort?' Jack caught the important part. 'What effort is that?'

'Well, there's a couple of weeks of December left, and someone might easily beat me for the Michelin Cup. Besides, flying round in circles is rather boring. I thought I'd have a crack at the De Forest prize – longest flight

507

from England to the Continent before the 31st of December. Of course, I'll need a larger petrol tank for that.'

Jack laughed at all this enthusiasm. He had to remind himself that this was a man who had flown for the first time only a little more than a month ago. But if he himself had been a rich man with a private income, he would have been just the same. To fly at all was glorious, but to be pioneering, creating and breaking records, testing the bounds of what could be done was the ultimate thrill! He bent his mind to the new problem. 'Windshield, larger petrol tank. What else? You'll need a compass,' he said.

'Gosh, yes, I don't want to go flying up the Channel instead of across, and end up in the Atlantic!'

'We'll have to think of a way of suspending it on gimbals, or something, so that it stays true.'

Sopwith put an arm across Jack's shoulder. 'Let's go and have a bite to eat and talk about it. You must be nearly as cold as I am, my faithful friend.'

Jessie left her horse at the new stables – which was what they still called the block built by her late uncle George along the track beyond the barns – and walked the short distance home. The December day was closing already, the sun gone behind the trees, showing its glints of swollen red through the black filigree of bare branches. In the hedges, which still gleamed here and there with the red of hips and haws, sparrows were gathering for the night, carrying on their cheerful, secret lives deep in the uncut heart, with only the noise and the occasional popping out to tell they were there. Jessie smiled at their racket. She liked sparrows, perhaps best of all the birds, though the farmers' hands were against them.

There was a smell of mist in the air, but nothing else: it was too cold for any scent of earth or grass. But the ground under her booted feet still had a little give in it, for which she was grateful. She would be hunting tomorrow, taking out a promising but very hot youngster, and if he had her off, as she suspected he might, she would sooner land on something without the bone in it. A fracture would be a severe complication in her busy life.

She reflected on the difference between her life and Violet's – though, of course, there had never been any doubt that they would be different, coming from backgrounds so far apart. She had gone to stay with Violet again, at Violet's urgent request, for a month from mid-August to mid-September. Brancaster (Holkam, she corrected herself irritably) had been away the whole time, for which Jessie had been grateful – visiting various friends for the shooting. In as tactful a way as possible, Jessie had asked why Violet had not gone with him, and received only a muddled explanation about being in mourning and with child, which apparently made it impossible for her to be seen to be enjoying herself at house parties. Such an embargo did not apply to a man in mourning, it appeared, as long as he was *en garçon* and did not do anything outrageous such as dance. There was nothing frivolous, Jessie had to admit, about a man shooting, but she could not help thinking that Holkam was playing on his wife's innocence and pliant temper.

Still, it could not be said that Violet was unhappy, and she said she was glad not to have to go to a shooting party. 'Mama always said they were the worst thing, and she would do anything to get out of them. So boring, she said.'

Jessie was a fair shot herself, and often brought things home for the larder, but couldn't see the sport in slaughtering birds that were driven across right in front of your nose where you couldn't miss, and had often wondered what it was about men that made them enjoy it.

'And besides,' Violet said with a faint blush, 'I'm beginning to show now, and I should hate people to stare at me.'

'But, darling, you've told me you want lots of children. Are you going to shut yourself away for the best part of a year every time you have a baby?'

'Yes,' said Violet. 'So I hope you will keep that in mind and remember you must come and stay with me every time.'

It was a quiet month she spent with Violet, very different from her usual pace of life, and she thought that perhaps it did her good, like a rest cure – not that there was anything in particular she needed curing of. They sat a lot (which made her restless at first, until she got used to it) and talked for hours. Violet was eager to tell her about Fitzjames House, where she had spent several weeks in July.

'It's very grand inside, only very shabby. Nothing's been done to it for years and years. Lord Holkam – the old lord – used to stay there when Parliament was sitting, but he hadn't been up for a long time because of his illness, and it was even longer since any woman stayed there or he entertained or anything, so I suppose he didn't mind about the peeling plaster and the damp and the scuffed paintwork, and holes in the carpets and the curtains falling to bits. But Holkam's having it all done up now, and next year we are going to open the house for the Coronation and have all sorts of entertainments. It will be in June, of course, so I should be well recovered by then.'

She described the house in some detail, then said proudly, 'Holkam showed me three rooms and said I could have my choice of them for my own sitting-room, so I have chosen a pretty-shaped room on the garden front – not that there's a garden, just a small courtyard, but there's a lovely old tree in it and it's quieter than the street side. And Holkam said I may decorate it myself, and choose my own things to go in it, so it will really be mine.'

'Will you not have any say in how the rest of the house is decorated?' Jessie asked, thinking that that would not suit her – and suspecting it would not have suited Cousin Venetia either.

But Violet did not seem at all put out. 'Oh, no,' she

said calmly. 'That isn't the way it works. It's for Holkam to provide a home for me, and everything in it, not the other way round. And it's his house after all, and will be Robert's afterwards. I'm just . . .' She paused, seeming unsure what word would describe her status.

'A visitor?' Jessie suggested.

'Oh, I don't mean that. But I'm not a Fitzjames Howard, am I? I was brought into the family for a purpose, that's all, like a – like a . . .'

'Piano tuner?' Jessie said innocently, and they both burst into laughter. 'Do you remember when we were children,' she said at last, 'and we used to talk about what we'd do when we grew up? And you said you wanted a little white house with green shutters like Mrs Parry's in the village.'

'And six children,' Violet concluded. 'I still want the six children.'

'All this,' Jessie waved a hand, 'is rather far from Mrs Parry's cottage.'

'And you said you wanted to do something exciting.'

'Yes. Well, I suppose I may still do, one day. My life is pretty nice as it is, but who knows what may be round the corner?' They were silent a while, following their own thoughts.

Then Violet asked diffidently, 'Are you in love with anyone?'

'No,' Jessie said, and, almost without meaning to, 'Are you?'

'It isn't the same,' Violet said. 'I mean, it's not like being in love before you're married. You know, that sort of terrible excitement – half nice and half frightening? But there's a different sort of niceness about it.' She thought a moment and added, 'Holkam and I are – *comfortable* together.'

It seemed to Jessie that Violet and Holkam weren't often anything together, that they spent most of their time apart, and she wondered whether that was the conse- quence of rank and wealth. And it seemed to her that if the 'terrible' feeling of being in love stopped so entirely when you were married it was hardly worth being married at all. Was Violet really content, or was she putting a brave face on it? Perhaps she would never know. If Violet did regret marrying Holkam, probably Jessie would be the last person she would admit it to. But Jessie could see now that this life – as Holkam's wife – would never have suited her. Lacking Violet's early training she could not have fitted into this world, this house, this scheme of things. It came to her then what Violet was, what the word ought to have been that she had been seeking. She was a vessel: brought into the Fitzjames Howard circle to bear it sons, to do the one thing the male succession could not do for itself. Violet had only ever wanted a house and children, so perhaps it really did suit her. But when the childbearing was all done, what then? What would Violet find to fill her days?

She thought about all this as she walked home that December day. She thought about marriage, and whether it would ever happen to her. She had her admirers. George Ayliffe had dropped out: having asked her to marry him and been refused he had hung about looking mournful for a while, but then his attention had been seized by another girl and he was now engaged to her. But Frank Winbolt was rather pathetically faithful, and Peter Firmstone was still a regular suitor (though she suspected he was rather glad she didn't want to marry him, and paid his attentions to her somewhat on that under-standing); and they now had a rival in David Cornleigh, one of Ethel's brothers, who seemed very much in love with Jessie. He had taken secret riding lessons (Angela, rather reprehensibly, had 'told') to impress her. And, of course, there was still dear, faithful Ned, whose company she enjoyed more than the others because they had more memories in common, and there was so much she didn't have to explain to him.

Her twentieth birthday was past, and she was female enough to be glad that she had enough admirers to satisfy a girl's vanity and assure her that age had not yet withered her attractions. And in spite of what Violet had said and her own response to it, there was something in her that wanted to get married. She felt a restlessness, an urge towards it, which she didn't understand but could not deny. It was not that she wanted to marry any specific person of her acquaintance, but the idea of never marrying at all seemed to have become unthinkable. To die an old maid, never having known what went on behind those closed doors – not just bedroom doors, of course, but all the other secret rooms married people inhabited together; to die never having known what it was all the rest of the world knew? No, that was impossible. She wanted – oh, *something*, she didn't know what; but she felt she would know it when she had it, and that marriage was where she would find it. It was that, she thought now, which had made her fall in love with Brancaster. He had seemed to promise the thing she sought. That she had been mistaken was alarming – suppose she made the same mistake about someone else, someone she *could* marry? You only had one chance to get it right, after all, which made the whole thing seem perilous.

Puzzling on these matters, she passed through the barbican and across the yard into the house. The great hall was in dusk, with only the glow of the fire to augment the feeble light from the windows, for the lamps had not been lit yet; but it was cosy, and the red fire gleam picked out surfaces and objects that were familiar and dear, and glinted off metal corners and gilded decorations. The long clock in the dark corner beside the chimney gave its slow, heavy beat – so slow that after each *tick* there seemed a breathless moment when you wondered if indeed there would be a *tock*. It was like the heartbeat of the house; and the house was like a living thing, she felt just then: a person – a dear, familiar person – one could always come home to, and who would always be glad. She understood why her mother loved it so much.

She dropped her hat, crop and gloves on the table by

the door, and spoke to the dogs, who were too comfort-ably sprawled to get up, and thumped their tails apolo-getically to explain the matter. She noticed with amusement that Ethel's cat, Snowdrop, had comman-deered the best place of all, and was reclining in a lordly way with his back supported by Bell's flank, his white fur turned to rich imperial red and gold by the fireglow.

And then there was the familiar flip-flap sound of the kitchen passage door and a footstep on the marble, and Jessie turned her head to see one of the maids – Peggy – starting across the hall with a tray in her hands.

'Is that for my father?' she asked.

Peggy obviously had not seen her in the gloaming because she started at the sound of her voice, making the china rattle. 'Oh! Yes, Miss Jessie. Mr Sawry said you were out.'

'I was. I've just come back in,' Jessie said patiently. 'I'll take that.'

'Very good, miss,' Peggy said. 'Should I tell Mr Sawry you're back? Will you want your water sent up?'

'Not yet. I'll ring when I'm ready.'

'It's only tea for one,' Peggy said, handing the tray over. 'Mrs Compton's still out. Shall I bring you something, miss?' she offered kindly.

Jessie looked at the thinly sliced bread and butter, the best strawberry jam, the scones, the Viennese fingers, all chosen to tempt the invalid's appetite, almost all of which would be left if she did not eat it, and said, 'No, don't bother.'

In the drawing-room the fire must have been made up recently, for it was leaping and cracking with young vigour; and whoever had refreshed it had lit the candles in the chimney sconces, though the central lamp was still dark. In this pleasant, soft light – which seemed somehow to be all-of-a-piece with the shadows of the room, rather than their antithesis – she could see her father lying on the day-bed drawn up under one of the south windows. It was where he liked to be during the day, where he could see something of the outdoors (the house had been built at a time when windows were a weakness, and views had not been provided from most of them). Sitting up he could see the other bank of the moat, where sometimes the swans got out to preen themselves, and the hedges of the rose garden and the Italian garden, which were generally full of birds. Even lying down he could see a little bit of the sky.

She put down the tray on the table, and walked across to look at him. He was asleep – at least, his eyes were closed and he had not stirred. She stared at his face, noting how the flesh had fallen away, leaving his nose strangely prominent, his cheeks hollow under sharp cheekbones. His fine hair had receded, giving him a noble brow; there were delicate shadows under his eyes, and his skin was very pale. In the uncertain light he looked somehow transparent: not solid, but a trick of the eye, or the after-image left by staring at a lamp. It came to her then how little stood between someone being there and not being there. He was so still under the tartan rug: she could not see any movement of his chest. A sudden fear gripped her.

Something cold touched her hand and she let out a little shriek, and her father opened his eyes. Fern shoved past her to put his great, heavy head on Jerome's lap, and his hands moved automatically to stroke the rough brow and unexpectedly soft ears. Jessie felt her heart fluttering with the remains of its panic, and drew a steadying breath.

'Is that a ministering angel I see?' Jerome said, and his voice sounded to Jessie as if it came from a great distance.

'No, it's a daughter bringing tea,' she said, trying for lightness.

He smiled, a smile that seemed painlessly to enter her breast and squeeze her heart, and she was speechless for a moment with love for him.

'Let me help you sit up a little more,' she said, when she could find a voice.

'I can manage that myself,' he said. 'I'm not helpless yet.' He shifted himself, and she snatched out his pillows quickly from behind him to reinsert them in a better position. Then she brought up the small table he used beside him and transferred the tea tray.

'Mother not home yet?' he said, watching her pour his tea with the indifference of the invalid.

'No. It's not late, just dark early,' she said, concentrating on not spilling. He hated slops in his saucer. She handed the cup. 'Will you have bread-and-butter, or shall I spread jam on a scone for you? It's strawberry.'

'Nothing to eat. I only want tea.'

'Cook will be upset. Look how nice and thin the bread-and-butter is.'

He gave a tired smile. 'You eat it. Don't want to be responsible for breaking the cook's heart.'

She felt her lips quivering. 'Oh, Papa!'

'Oh, Jess!' He gave her her tone back, but with a gentle glow of teasing in his eyes. 'You look so beautiful in this light,' he went on. 'My lovely girl! I suppose I oughtn't to say it, but I'm glad you didn't fall in love in your London Season and get married. I've been so glad of having this time with you. Selfish of me.'

She shook her head, and could only manage to say, 'Drink your tea.'

'Yes, Mama,' he said, and sipped it. He set the cup down in the saucer with delicate care and went on, 'It has been wonderful having you at home, but now I wish I might see you married and settled before I go.'

'You're not to talk of going,' she said, and though she had wanted it to sound light and joking, when it came out it only sounded like a little girl, frightened.

He looked at her kindly. 'Oh, Jess, darling, you're old enough now for us to have the truth between us. I never thought to have so long – two years! Hasty says it's a miracle I've lasted so long, and only the finest nursing could have done it.'

'But, Papa—'

His hand came out and folded over hers – such a thin hand! – and he said, in a voice that was unsteady for a moment, 'It makes my heart turn over when you call me that, the way you used to when you were very little. My golden girl! A father shouldn't have favourites, I suppose, and I love the boys, but I always felt you were my finest achievement.'

She couldn't speak, struggling with tears. He sipped his tea again, to give her time. In the quietness Fern sighed, a sound of content, his head on his master's lap, his eyebrows twitching as his eyes moved from one face to the other. Jerome said, 'So if there is some fellow you have in mind, someone you like, I'd be glad to know about it.'

'No,' she said. 'I don't love anyone that way. But I don't want to get married. I don't want to leave you.'

'My darling, soon *I'll* be leaving *you*.'

'No—'

'I want you to be ready,' he said seriously. 'I don't feel close to death this minute, but you know that it could happen any time, without warning, and I want to know that you are ready.'

'I can't be ready. Not ever.'

'Yes, you can. You have to be the strong one. You'll have to take care of your mother. And – and I need to know you can bear it, for my own selfish sake. I need to know you'll be all right.'

She nodded, her throat so tight with tears it was an agony. She understood; she loved him so much, she had to give him what he wanted. She said, 'I'll be all right.'

'Yes,' he said, and the word was a sigh as he relaxed a little against the pillows.

'Papa, please try—' The words seized up.

He understood. 'I'll hold on as long as possible,' he said. 'I don't want to leave you, or your mother, or any of this.'

They were silent a little while, as the crackling fire and the light, fast ticking of the mantel clock informed the shadowy room. At the farthest reach of the firelight, the canary was asleep in its cage, head buried in its back, and the flickering light threw its shadow now on the wall, now on the cornice. Jessie took her father's neglected cup from him – half full, still – and put it aside, and his freed hand reached for hers and brought it back to rest on his chest, fingers interlocked. It felt warm and strong, she thought – surely not near death. She couldn't part with him, not yet. Oh, please, God, not yet!

At last he said, 'You will marry one day. I hope I am here to see it, but if not – choose wisely, won't you? Don't marry some paltry fellow just because he asks, or because he has a handsome face. I know you won't,' he added apologetically, 'but I feel I must say it. When you choose someone, imagine you are introducing him to me, imagine us talking together. If you can't see me smiling—'

'I'll be careful,' she said. 'But perhaps no-one will ask me.'

'Don't fish for compliments,' he said, with mock stern-ness. 'If you think I don't know about all your suitors, you are taking your father for a fool!'

She smiled. 'Well, I don't love any of them.'

'Not even Ned?'

'I've sometimes thought that in the end I might marry him. But I don't know whether that's what marriage ought to feel like – just thinking it would be all right. How did you feel about Mother?'

'I thought it would be all right. But I loved her madly, too.'

'Well, I don't love Ned madly.' She sighed, and he watched her thoughtful face fondly. He squeezed her hand.

'You'll be all right,' he said. 'Are you hunting tomorrow?'

'Yes. I'm taking out Hat Trick.'

'Is he ready?'

'Well, I'd sooner give him longer, but I'd like to sell him this season, so I've got to get him used to hounds.

518

Otherwise it's another year with him eating his head off, and taking up my time.'

'I ought to worry about you, going out on a hot youngster like that, but I'm so comfortable I can't.'

'I'll be careful,' she said, and then, with a teasing smile, 'David Cornleigh asked if he could ride beside me. He'll look after me.'

Jerome laughed. 'Ha! If he sees you after the first hound speaks, it will be as a vanishing cloud of dust.'

The door opened, and John the footman came in to light the lamps, closely followed by Henrietta, bringing the evening cold and fog smell in a little halation around her. 'Sitting in the dark?' she said cheerfully. 'I'm sorry I was late, but there was a horrid creak coming from under the phaeton and I was afraid an axle was going to break, so I didn't dare go out of a walk.'

'You should learn to drive a motor-car,' Jessie said. Teddy had recently bought a little second-hand Renault for £150, in which he occasionally drove himself, and which Jessie had mastered in a day.

'No thank you,' Henrietta said, with a shudder. 'At least a pony doesn't walk blindly into ditches or run headlong into walls. Jessie, darling, you smell of horses. You'd better go up and change before your uncle gets back.'

Everybody came home for Christmas, 1910. Lizzie and the children travelled up with Frank two days beforehand; Ashley and Jack arrived on Christmas Eve. Jack was full of talk about his new job, which he said was much more free and easy than the old one.

'It's almost like working for myself. I can pretty much do as I please, you know. Wright is a topping fellow and trusts me absolutely.' He managed to get in quite a bit of flying, testing out new ideas, and trying the machines of rivals, 'though never as much as I'd like,' he added.

He had also a great deal to say about his friend Sopwith, who was hoping to win the De Forest prize with the flight he had made in mid-December. He had taken off from Eastchurch rather than Dover, because, as Jack had pointed out, difficulties were most likely to occur in the first few minutes, and if he were to crash it would be better to do it over land than over the sea. He had intended heading for Châlons, but the compass had stuck, and visibility was so poor, all he could do was to keep flying for as long as possible over unknown fields and villages, until violent gusts of wind forced him to look for a landing-place. He eventually came down in a field and on enquiring at the nearest village found he was in Belgium. Jack and Fred Sigrist, the mechanic, had gone over to disassemble the aeroplane and bring it back. The flight was officially agreed at 177 miles in three hours and forty minutes, much the longest so far.

'But there's always the possibility someone may over-take that,' Jack concluded, 'so he's standing by to do another if necessary before the end of the year. I may have to leave at a moment's notice,' he apologised. 'Wright is very keen an aeroplane of ours should win the prize. It would be such good advertisement.'

Frank had graduated that summer, but had remained in London, taking up a position as assistant librarian at the London School of Economics. He was still living in Endsleigh Gardens.

'Ashley and I don't mind having Frank living with us,' Lizzie confirmed. 'He can stay as long as he likes. The boys love him.' Privately, to Henrietta, she confided, 'He doesn't much like his librarian job, and Ashley's offered to find him a position at Culpepper's, but he doesn't want that. And he says he doesn't want to teach. He doesn't seem to know what he wants to do.'

'He had better make up his mind,' Henrietta said, less indulgent than a fond sister. 'And you mustn't let him sponge on you and Ashley, dear. That would be fatal. Young men can be so lazy – and it would be a bad example to your boys.'

'Oh, I've no fear of that. He pays his way. And I don't

520

think he's lazy at all. He just wants the right position at last.'

There was good family news, for Ethel had discovered she was pregnant, which thrilled and alarmed Robbie in almost equal degrees; but when the alarm wore off, he seemed to want to talk about it all the time, and his plans for the future of his firstborn competed with Jack's talk of aeroplanes and Lizzie's about the cleverness of baby Rose, so that a very pleasant bedlam reigned. Teddy had been afraid at first that Ethel's interesting condition would prompt the young Comptons to want to find a home of their own; but it soon became apparent that the thought was not in their minds. They were completely happy living at Morland Place, and Ethel was already discussing with Emma the care of the new baby and whether James William's first things would do.

'Napkins and binders you'll need,' Emma said, 'but his dresses and caps and such are as good as perfect, and babies grow out of everything so quick at that age it'd be wicked to buy new.'

And further pleasant news was that the refurbishment of the Red House was almost complete and that it would be occupied for the Christmas season. Bertie and Maud had been living in Pont Street since coming back from their honeymoon – or, at least, Maud had, since Bertie had been away on business almost as much as he had been at home. But they travelled up together to take possession of their new home two weeks before Christmas. A week later Richard Puddephat joined them, and they had invited everyone at Morland Place to visit. The invitation was for Sunday (so that Robbie and Ned would be able to come), to have tea, a tour round the house and grounds to see what had been done, and then an early dinner. Henrietta very much wanted to go, and Jessie offered to stay at home with her father; but in the end Alice said that she ought to be the one to stay, since she was not a blood relative and had, moreover, the beginnings of a cold in the head, which she didn't think she ought to inflict on anyone else. Teddy was not happy about her being left out, but he knew that she was shy, and when she said she had just as soon stay quietly at home, he had to admit that it was probably true.

So seven of them were driven by Simmons in the Benz, on a cold, foggy day that never seem to grow properly daylight, over to Bishop Winthorpe. As they drove up the village street, everything looked painfully familiar to Henrietta, and she spared a long look for the Rectory as they chugged past, thinking how long ago it all was, and wishing Jerome was at her side just then to support her against her memories. As the motor drew up on the fore-court of the Red House, she reflected that it was in the great hall here that she had first set eyes on him so very many years ago – and probably fallen in love with him the same instant, though as a married woman she couldn't then admit it to herself.

But as the door was flung open there seemed very little about the great hall that was familiar. The old red flock wallpaper was gone, which had been there since Perry's father was master. Everything seemed very light and bright without it, there was a large new carpet on the floor, and a strong smell of fresh paint. Most of all, as Polly exclaimed perfectly audibly, 'Daddy, it's boiling *hot*!' Those large, square, flattish boxes with the strapwork fronts that were fixed to the walls, and from which the strongest paint-smell seemed to be emerging, must be radiators, Henrietta thought. Bertie had had central heating installed!

And there was Bertie waiting to meet them, with Maud by his side – Maud looking every inch the chatelaine, in a lilac silk gown that went all the way to the ground and swept a little behind – no modern lengths for her. Mr Puddephat stood at her other side, beaming proudly, greeting everyone rather as though he were the master of the house, Jessie thought.

But what took Jessie's attention most was Bertie. 'You've shaved off your beard!' she exclaimed. 'Bertie, how nice! You look like yourself again.'

'I always said I would,' he replied, 'when I got my English pallor back. Welcome to the Red House.'

'Welcome to our home,' Maud said, very graciously. She seemed absolutely at ease, Jessie thought. Bertie, on the other hand, seemed a little nervous. She could not take her eyes from him. The bearded stranger who had disconcerted her was gone, and this dear and familiar Bertie, suddenly resurrected, was disconcerting her in a different way. She stared and stared, knowing it was rude, but unable to help herself. Her eyes found such accustomed pleasure in him that it seemed somehow more than just meeting again someone she had known. It was almost like – oh – like finding *herself* again. He was shaking hands and kissing along the line, and when he got to her he looked down with a quizzical half-smile and said, 'You'll wear me out with looking at me. Am I such a guy? I could grow it again.'

'Oh, *no*!' she said quickly. 'You've such a nice face, it was a shame to hide it.' She turned up her cheek and he kissed it, and she felt a small, sharp pang somewhere deep inside her at the touch of his lips and the unexpectedly familiar scent of him when he stooped near. She had not known that she remembered it, but now she caught it she knew it of old.

He shook hands with Ned last, and then enquired after the absentees.

'What a shame. I did so want Uncle Jerome to see everything. After all, he knew the Red House before I did. Could he really not come, even in the motor-car?'

'It would have been too much for him, with so many people,' Henrietta said. 'And the cold of the journey would have tried him. Perhaps when the weather is warmer he might be able to come for a quiet look round, with just him and me.'

'Of course. I must ride over soon and pay my respects,' Bertie said. 'And to Aunt Alice. Is she well? How is the young sprig?'

'Do you mean James William?' Polly said, feeling she

was not having enough of the conversation. She always used both his names and the habit was rather sticking with everyone else, too. 'He's going to have his first Christmas, and a Christmas present to unwrap just like the rest of us. He loves to play with paper. Aunt Henrietta says it's the crackly sound he likes. When Jessie had her birthday, James William got hold of some of her presents and tore the paper right off one of them.'

'Was it your birthday recently?' Bertie asked, turning to Jessie.

'The twelfth of December,' Jessie said. Well, there was no reason why he should have remembered. 'I was twenty.'

'Twenty!' Bertie stared at her, looking suddenly stricken. 'Not really? Where does time go to?'

At that moment Maud interrupted. 'My dear, shall we go into the drawing-room?'

'Yes, yes,' said Puddephat, 'don't keep our guests standing in the hall. Come this way – Mrs Compton, Miss Compton – everyone. I think you'll like what we have done with the drawing-room. The drapery was Maud's own thought.'

Jessie dragged her eyes away from Bertie's, and allowed herself to be ushered by Mr Puddephat, who was evidently very proud of his daughter's taste. She thought of Violet, with no say in how her house was decorated, because it was not really her house, and wondered if the difference was to do with class, or because it was Mr Puddephat's money, mostly, that had paid for the doing-up.

It was a very pleasant visit. After tea in the drawing-room they were invited to look at the gardens before it got dark (though Jessie thought there was not much to see in December, and it was hard to be enthusiastic about the description of what would be there in spring and summer) and then were shown all over the house, to the point where Bertie grew embarrassed about the detail in which everything was being described, and suggested there was no need to inspect *all* the plumbing *and* the patent soot-traps on the chimneys *and* the new boiler.

Teddy, however, expressed a deep interest in boilers, and so the party split, with Puddephat taking Teddy, Robbie and Ned for the full excursion while Bertie and Maud escorted the others back to the drawing-room. There Ethel, who had pretty manners, asked Maud if she would play to them on the pianoforte, and so they were happily occupied until dinner, for which the rector and his wife, Mr and Mrs Chase, had also been invited.

Jessie did not eat out very often, so was always interested to taste other people's food. She found her dinner interesting, especially a spicy dish Maud had instructed the cook to prepare to a description of Bertie's of something he had had in Jungaipur. This led to questions from Ned and Robbie about life in India, and demands from Polly, who was rather excited at being at a proper grown-up dinner party, to know whether Bertie had ever ridden an elephant, and what it was like. The Chases asked after Lizzie, who had been a pupil of the rector's, and then Mrs Chase wanted to talk about babies, Henrietta wanted to hear about village matters and former tenants, and Mr Chase wanted to talk politics with Mr Puddephat. Between savouring the food and listening to all the conversation, Jessie said very little. She found her eyes drawn again and again to Bertie's face; and often when she looked at him, she would find him looking at her, with an intent, half-puzzled look.

Bertie did ride over before Christmas to see Jerome, but Jessie was out at Twelvetrees at the time, and when she came back to the house he had gone, winter visits having to be short because of the light. So the next time she saw him was at the Boxing Day hunt. This year there was a lawn meet at Lord Lambert's house, which was about three miles away as the crow flew. Teddy, Polly, Ned and Jessie were hunting, but on Christmas Day Jack said he would like to go out too, if there was something for him to ride. Jessie said he could have her hunter, Bay Rum.

'He's going well, and a child could handle him, so it

won't matter that you haven't been on a horse for a year,' she said.

'Thank you. You give me great confidence,' Jack said. 'One never forgets how to ride, you know.'

'As long as you remember horses can't fly,' she retorted.

'But what will you ride?' Ned asked her.

'Oh, I'll take the opportunity of giving Hat Trick another outing. He needs more experience.'

The Boxing Day hunt was always well attended, being one of the social high spots of the winter. A large number of non-hunters always turned up for the meet, and the numbers were especially large this year because Lord Lambert always served excellent food and drinks. It was a dark, clammy and misty day, damp enough for good scent but cold enough to make the less dedicated hunters linger by the fire until the last moment. Teddy's groom held his horse and Polly's pony so that they could go inside, and Jack offered to hold Hat Trick, but Jessie laughed and said he didn't know what he was offering, and that she preferred to keep him walking about. Servants, looking a little blue about the nose and fingers, circulated freely with trays of hot oyster, lobster and venison pasties and tots of sherry and cherry brandy, so they did not miss anything.

At last there was a stir and a cry of 'Hounds, please!' and round the side of the house came the hunt servants, with the pack all smiles, sterns waving. There was a flurry of mounting and the indoor lingerers hurried out. Hat Trick was very excited, staring at hounds, nostrils wide, twirling on the spot to try to look at every one individually. Jessie had no attention for anything but him, until someone came up beside her and she glanced up and saw it was Bertie, on a big brown hunter. Her heart tripped at the sight of him, and she felt her cheeks burn in the cold air.

'Hello,' he said, looking at her keenly. 'That's a hot-looking youngster. Isn't he a bit strong for you?'

'He's just rather excitable. I'm trying to get him used

to hounds so that we can sell him this winter. I like your horse. Is he new?'

'Yes. Barnabas. I bought him in Ireland in the summer, but I've only had him out a couple of times. I'm trying to get used to the size of him – I've been riding ponies for the last eight years.' He continued his slightly puzzled scrutiny of her face; and though part of her wished he wouldn't, another part liked the fact of his eyes on her, wouldn't have wanted them to look away.

'The scent should be good,' she said. 'I was talking to one of the groundsmen just now and he said they've stopped half a dozen earths, so we should have a good run.' From the corner of her eye she saw Ned approaching, coming, she supposed, to express his intention of looking after her, and for once she wished he wouldn't. David Cornleigh and Jack were also hovering; and then from her other side Peter Firmstone rode up, looking young, dashing and handsome on his lean dappled grey, his top hat tipped at a rakish angle.

'Miss Compton! So glad you are here – I hardly dared hope when I saw your brother on Bay Rum. Taking your tiger out for a walk, I see. Will you let me ride beside you? Someone ought to be on hand to pick up the pieces.'

He said it in a light and amusing way, but with such an expectation of the answer 'yes' that for an instant Jessie felt annoyed, though she didn't know why. Firmstone was looking curiously at Bertie, and she felt she had to introduce them.

'My cousin, Sir Percival Parke – Mr Firmstone.'

'Honoured to make your acquaintance, sir,' said Firmstone, taking up his place at Jessie's side as of right.

Bertie touched his hat and said, 'Servant, sir.' And to Jessie, 'Well, I see you are in safe hands.' And he turned his horse away and rode off.

'Good-looking horse, that,' Firmstone said, watching his retreat; but the hunt was moving off and there was no time for more conversation.

Soon Jessie forgot everything but the fascination of

watching hounds working. They found at the first covert, the huntsman blew 'gone away' and 'cope forrard', and soon they were streaming away across the fields. There was nothing in the world then but the sound of hoofs thudding on green turf, of blood pounding in the veins, the cold air rushing past, the pricked ears and snorting breath before one and the misty, tree-sketched horizon beyond. Firmstone was at her side the length of the first field, but at the hedge his grey pecked on taking off, crashed through the top of it in a welter of flying twigs and fell heavily on the far side. Hat Trick jumped cleanly, and when they had landed Jessie took a quick look back to see that both Firmstone and the horse were up and apparently unhurt, and then concentrated again on her own mount. He was very excited, but still in hand. They cleared a second bullfinch with inches to spare and hit plough, which slowed them somewhat, and then came to a spinney, where the fox disappeared and hounds were checked.

Jessie gave Hat Trick a long rein and he stretched his neck. The steam clouded the air from his hot body. In the spinney the huntsman blew a short toot of encouragement, and his cries of 'Leu in there, leu in! Ki try for 'im, try!' echoed off the bare trees as hounds crashed about in the undergrowth.

Bertie came up beside her, Barnabas hardly panting. 'Your escort has got lost, I see,' he said.

'He took a fall,' said Jessie. Why was it whenever Bertie came near her she found her eyes on his face as though they were stuck fast and couldn't be moved?

'Not much of a guardian,' he said, staring at her in the way he had at the Red House.

'I don't need one,' she said. 'Hat Trick's all right.' A hound spoke from within the spinney, and the huntsman cried, 'Hike, hike to Valiant!' Hat Trick spun round on the spot three times with excitement.

'He's a whirling dervish,' Bertie said.

There was a burst of hound music from the side of the

spinney, and out of sight in that direction one of the whips shouted the view holloa. Hat Trick spun four more times, Barnabas snorted like a dragon, his whole body quivering with excitement. Then the huntsman shouted, 'Cope forrard, away!' and the field sprang into action. As Jessie gave him the office, Hat Trick leaped forward with a bound that almost unseated her. She recovered herself quickly, but felt that he was getting away from her. He was galloping so fast that the ground was a blur beneath her. It was faster than she had ever gone before, and she was intoxicated with the speed, and only a tiny bit afraid. As long as they were in the open it didn't matter that she couldn't stop him; and sooner or later he would tire and slow. They pounded across a field, snippets of turf flying from his hoofs; soared over a hedge as if they had wings. They were going so fast they had left the rest of the field behind; a sneaked look backwards saw that only Bertie was anywhere near, leaning low over his brown's neck and urging it on. She looked forward again. They were almost up with the huntsman and whips, and hounds weren't too far ahead, approaching a belt of trees.

She sat down harder and tried to take a pull on him, and after a moment felt him coming back to hand. A labourer was standing at the edge of the trees, waving his cap, presumably having headed the fox off, for hounds did not go into the trees but skirted them. He was heading for the river, Jessie thought. The quickest line was the one hounds had taken, along the wood edge; but just as they reached the trees a gun went off somewhere close by, inside the copse. Hat Trick started almost out of his skin, twisted round with an unseating leap, and thundered off at right-angles to the line of the hunt. If Jessie had thought she was going fast before, it was nothing to this. She knew she had lost him: there was no connection between her hands and his mouth, and he was in a blind panic. She could only sit down and go with him. He galloped madly across the field, swerved violently round a gorse clump, and pounded on towards a blackthorn hedge that looked as big and solid as a train. That would stop him, she thought with relief.

She had been talking to him the whole time, trying to reassure him; now, with the hedge ahead to help her, she made a strong effort to stop him, giving and taking on the reins, crying 'Whoa!' in her longest and calmest tones. She felt him listen to her a moment: his ears, which had been flat down, lifted a little to her voice. Then they pricked sharply ahead. Hat Trick loved to jump, and he had no wish to stop with pursuing devils behind him. She realised simultaneously that he was going to jump the blackthorn, and that it was too high for him; but there was nothing she could do, no time left. They were upon it. He dug down and sprang, going up almost vertically, with a wonderful coiled strength so powerful that she thought for a moment they might make it. But her judgement had been right – it was too high for him, for any horse. He crashed into it, not into the thin twigs at the top but the unyielding bulk a foot below the crest; crashed into it forelegs and shoulders, was stopped, and with his huge momentum almost bounced back, falling sideways. Jessie was half in the hedge before she fell too, feeling sharp thorny nails scratching her face like angry cats, trying to free her foot from the stirrup as she and the horse crashed down from what felt like a huge height. Her foot came free at the last moment, the ground came up and smacked the breath out of her with a sickening *whoomph*, and she felt the wind and weight of the horse just missing her as he hit and rolled over.

She was not knocked unconscious, but had hit the earth so hard that for a moment she could not move, breathe or see, only hear the threshing and snorting of her horse trying to get up, and feel the clods of earth hitting her face. Then breath and sight came back to her. Hat Trick was on his feet, trembling, towering above her with the saddle pulled half round, blowing great snorts of distress. From old instinct she had not let go of the reins. He had no wish to run off just at the moment, but she was not in the best position to stop him if he did; and besides, she knew she ought to get up and comfort him. But she did not seem to be able to move. Her head was giving instructions that her body was choosing to ignore. I've broken my back, she thought. I'm paralysed. I shall never walk again. Oddly enough, the thought did not frighten her as it should. Shock, she thought dispassionately. She wondered if she would die.

And then there was the sound of more hoofs – someone riding to her rescue – coming up very fast. She heard the horse scrabble to a stop, saw Hat Trick jerk his head back at the approach, heard the thump of booted feet hitting the ground, and then someone's knees landed beside her, and Bertie's face loomed over her, wild with panic.

'Jessie, Jessie,' he said. He didn't seem to have any other words, but she liked her name on his lips.

'Hello, Bertie,' she said, in a peculiar croak.

His eyes were panicking as he said, 'Are you hurt? Where are you hurt? My God, I never saw such a fall! I thought you'd be dead for sure!'

'I'm all right,' she heard herself say, and began to sit up – as though the command to her body, long delayed, had just got through.

He tried to push her back. 'Don't move! You may have broken something. Dear God, what a fall!'

'Let me get up. I'm all right. I haven't broken anything.' She struggled over onto her knees, took his arm, and got to her feet. She swayed dizzily for a moment, but then her stomach and the contents of her head swapped places for the better, everything sank back into its proper position, and she really was all right. Her first thought was for the horse. 'Oh, poor Hat Trick! There, my boy, hoah, hoah. Steady now.' Holding his reins, she stroked his cheeks and neck until he lowered his head and the trembling grew less. 'Have a look at his legs, will you?' she said to Bertie. 'Give me your reins.'

She took both horses and he stripped off his gloves and obeyed her in silence, perhaps too shocked to speak yet. Hat Trick fidgeted under the examination but did not flinch. 'He seems to be all right. Just a few scratches, none of them deep. I think he's got away with it. It's a miracle.' He straightened up and turned to her, and they stood just a foot apart, looking into each other's faces with the same strained and searching look. 'My God, Jessie,' he said at last in a low voice, 'you frightened me. Why in hell did you try to jump it?'

'I didn't. *He* did.'

'I said he was too strong for you.'

'He's not really,' she said, and then, 'I'm sorry. It must have looked worse than it was.'

'You've scratched yourself,' he said. She could feel it now, the little hot stinging paths coming to life in her cold face.

'Do I look dreadful?' she asked.

He gave a shaky laugh. 'Dreadful? My God, no! No, you don't look dreadful.' He reached out and cupped her cheek with a hand that trembled worse than her legs were doing. 'Not dreadful,' he said, his voice almost failing.

She knew it when he touched her, when his warm hand curved to the shape of her face; knew at the touch of him that she wanted it never to stop; wanted with a fierceness she had never known before to press herself against him, to hold him and never to be apart from him again. It was love, she thought, the seed of which had been planted years before, when she was only a little girl, when her yearning for him had been called 'just a crush'. But it had been a true thing, she saw now – a rehearsal for this. Something in her had known all along that she was meant for him; she had always been his, from the very beginning.

That seed had grown in secret, unnoticed; grown strong, flowered and fruited, and now there was no mistaking it. It was love, terrible and lovely; she wanted him so desperately she felt she might die of it. She wondered then that she could ever have mistaken anything else for it, because it was so unmistakably the real thing:

as different as being awake was from dreaming.

She felt her heart lift with triumph and joy in the recognition; but then his hand dropped to his side, letting the cold air back. There was no triumph and joy in his expression. He said again, 'My God, Jessie,' and she remembered, with a sickening thump of her heart back to earth, that he was married, married to Maud, a married man, Bertie was married and could never be hers. Married, married, married. It was like a mad yammering taunting voice in her head. With an effort that felt as though it must wrench something vital loose inside her, she dragged her eyes from his face and turned away.

'If I hold them, do you think you can put my saddle right for me?'

She was amazed to hear how normal her voice sounded. It must be someone else doing all this, she thought. It can't be me. Dazed and bruised and drowned she stood outside herself watching, and wondering how she was going to be able to go on with life from here.

Chapter Seventeen

Tom Sopwith's record for the Michelin Cup was broken on the 28th of December when Alec Ogilvie flew 130 miles at Rye. Sopwith called at Jack's lodgings that evening and said, 'We've three days left before the end of the year. I mean to have another crack at it tomorrow. Will you come with me?'

'Of course,' Jack said, 'if Mr Wright doesn't mind.'

The next morning at Brooklands Sopwith took off at nine in the morning, but the wind was strong and gusty and the effort of holding the aeroplane steady was exhausting, forcing him to land after only managing seventy miles. 'Good thing there are another two days to go,' he said, as Jack pulled the gauntlets from his numb hands.

The next day the weather was much the same, and again he had to land after seventy miles. But on the last day of the year, the wind had moderated, and Sopwith was hopeful. He made an early start, but after only a few circuits had to land with engine trouble. Jack and Fred Sigrist worked frantically on the aeroplane, and managed to put the fault right by half past nine. 'This really is my last chance,' Sopwith said, with grim determination. About five hours of flying were needed to cover the distance, and there weren't many more than five hours of daylight left. 'I'm not going to be beaten this time. I'm not coming down for anything less than complete engine failure!'

So the cold winter day wore on, with the little machine circling the pylons and the team on the ground changing the numbers on the board. In the late morning Mrs Hewlett came over to join them, accompanied by Miss Ormerod. After chatting a while Mrs Hewlett went away to her office, but Miss Ormerod stayed, impressing Jack with her enthusiasm and, not least, her endurance. It was bitter down on the ground, and they were all stamping their feet and beating their arms against the cold, all the while knowing that the man in the sky was enduring agonies beside which theirs were mere pinpricks.

At last after four hours and seven minutes the 150 went up on the board, and with a twenty-mile superiority over Ogilvie, Sopwith landed. All the onlookers, even the brave Miss Ormerod, had gone by then, and Sopwith himself was almost paralysed with cold, but he and Jack were happy and pretty confident of winning the Michelin prize. It was deeply disappointing to learn later that on the same day Bill Cody had been taking another shot at it at Laffan's Plain, and had done 195 miles. The cup was his.

But at least Sopwith had won the De Forest prize. On the day he had made his flight, the other contestants, who had chosen Dover for their take-off place, had found their machines damaged during the previous night by gales. The only one that was repairable belonged to Graham-White, who took off eventually, but was unable to control it in the buffeting wind, tried to land again, and crashed. He was taken to hospital, but his injuries proved, fortunately, to be superficial. After that day the weather over the Channel remained too rough for anyone to break Sopwith's record; and tragedy ended one effort. Cecil Grace did not take a compass with him, and suffered the fate Sopwith had jokingly feared for himself: he lost his bearings and was last seen flying out to sea by the men manning the East Goodwin lightship. Neither his body nor his aeroplane was ever found. On the last day of the year, when Sopwith was flying at Brooklands, thick fog over the Channel prevented the remaining flyers in the running from making any attempt, and on the following day Sopwith received a telephone call from the secretary of the Royal Aero Club, saying, simply, 'It's yours!'

Howard Wright was delighted that his machine had won this important prize, which was a wonderful advertisement for him. A number of orders for aeroplanes followed, and he told Jack that it was worth every moment he had spent at Brooklands. 'Any help Mr Sopwith wants, you give it to him,' he said.

On the 31st of January the Royal Aero Club held its annual dinner, at which Sopwith was to be presented with the prize. Howard Wright acquired a ticket for Jack at the same table. Jack had never been to an occasion like this, and felt very proud to be included. There was a great deal of what he felt was reflected glory, but it was flattering all the same to have people pass his name among them and want to shake his hand; and fascinating to be among so many aviation enthusiasts and be able to talk unchecked about aeroplanes.

The speeches were interesting. The chairman, the Duke of Atholl, gave the opening one about the importance of aviation to the nation and the Empire, and said that all efforts must be made to improve the stability and safety of the aeroplane, suggesting a prize should be offered in that field as well as the more adventuresome ones. He also suggested that in view of the number of crashes there had been, some thought ought to be given to a device that would allow the driver of the aeroplane to jump out and descend safely by parachute.

The second speech, by Major Sir Alexander Bannerman, commandant of the Balloon Corps, seemed to be invested with some institutional jealousy, for he played down the importance of the aeroplane. It would not, as had often been suggested, revolutionise warfare. In fact, he saw little use for it that could not equally be served by the balloon. Moreover, the aeroplane was a crude instrument, which had not advanced much since Wright had first flown in France.

There were several outraged cries of 'Oh!' when he said that.

When the prize was presented, Sopwith made a short speech. First, with proper modesty, he attributed his success to the misfortunes of his colleagues in meeting bad weather. Then he went on to say that he hoped he was speaking for most aviators when he said he would be pleased to help the army or navy if they were to take an interest in aeroplanes. This was already something of a hobby-horse with Jack, who thought that with the general expectation of war some time soon, the government's ignoring of aviation was unforgivable. Sopwith went on to say that what was most wanted was a lighter British engine, for those currently used were the equivalent in weight to an extra passenger compared with the French rotary engine.

Then Baron de Forest made a speech complimenting the winner, and saying that it was one of the pluckiest efforts ever seen in any sport or industry. He was a millionaire, a naturalised British subject who had been educated at Eton and the House and had been a close friend of King Edward. He could therefore speak with some authority when he said that Sopwith's achievement had not gone unnoticed in royal circles.

Jack was very happy with life that January. His new job was proving thoroughly absorbing; he was getting quite a bit of flying; his friend had won the De Forest prize. He had acquired a dog (most flyers seemed to have pets, he didn't know why – Sopwith had a monkey). It was a little rough-coated mongrel called Rug, who went everywhere with him and very much enhanced his life. And through Sopwith he had gained a much wider and more varied circle of friends. He had been introduced by them to the amusement of roller-skating, which was an agreeable way to spend a winter evening in London when one felt too restless for sedentary pastimes. And at the Aldwych skating rink he had met a Miss Florence Airdrie, who had curly brown hair and an impish smile. Miss

Airdrie and Rug took an immediate liking to each other. She lived with her family in Queen's Gate Terrace and revealed that she and her elder sister often walked the family's dog in Kensington Gardens. Jack suddenly found it convenient to exercise Rug there, too, and it was not long before Rug and Prince were on the way to being the firmest of friends. Altogether, Jack thought, life was very good.

Against expectations, Jessie was happy to be in love. She woke every morning to the Christmas feeling of something exciting having happened, and then Bertie would come into her mind with her first conscious thought, and she would snuggle back down under the covers to indulge a few minutes' daydream. Love, even hopeless love, seemed exhilarating after the dry months of disillusion. Her mind sang with it all day, with a high, strong sweetness like the wind in the telegraph wires. It seemed a blessed thing just to be in the same world with him, to know he was seeing the same sunrise, breathing the same air, going about his daily tasks in the same green county. All day she would imagine what he might be doing. She could picture him riding, eating, reading the newspaper, and her mind caressed the images. Most of all, she revisited the memory of his touching her cheek, and the way he had looked at her then. Long after her bruises had faded and the scratches were healed, she could feel in memory the warmth of his hand on her skin, and see the surprised tenderness of his eyes.

It was wonderful knowing that, because he was her cousin, there could never be a time when she lost him absolutely. She was entitled to speak about him, to know about his life. She might legitimately wonder when she would see him again. And, best of all, was that she *did* see him. He rode over to Morland Place; they were invited to the Red House; occasionally they met in other locations. Just to be with him and indulge her longing to look at him would have been wonderful, but as a cousin she was entitled to talk to him and smile and laugh with him. That he was a married man she managed to keep locked away in a separate compartment of her mind. She told herself that there was no harm in her loving him as long as no-one knew about it. She had no expectations. She just wanted to be able to see him.

This state of happy folly lasted a month. At the end of January Teddy had a houseful of weekend guests for the hunting, and decided to have a dinner party and ball on the Saturday evening. He loved to plan and execute such festivities, and if it was no-one's birthday, he could be relied on to think up an excuse of some sort about once a month. Jessie once asked Emma if the servants minded all the extra work it caused, but Emma said, 'Lord, no, Miss Jessie. What servants hate moost is not hard work, it's boredom. That livens us up, to have parties. Cook likes to show off with fancy dishes, and Mr Sawry likes to show off how well everything runs, and the girls like all the new gossip that comes with visitors, and we all like new faces in the servants' hall. And there's no doubt about it, the master is very 'preciative, and never forgets to say thank you after, which is nice.'

Jessie liked having people to stay, and was particularly glad this time as she sold Hat Trick to one of them: George Laxton, of the banking family, who liked the look of him on Friday, asked to try him out on Saturday, and was so taken with him he closed with Jessie when hounds checked at Wilstrop Wood. She went up to change for dinner feeling very well with the world, with her mind tingling from the thought that Bertie and Maud were coming to dinner, so in a very short time she would see him again. Tomlinson came up to help her dress, as she always did when it was a special occasion (Jessie liked to manage for herself on common days), and even she noticed her young lady's high spirits.

'Looking forward to the ball, miss?' she asked, as she arranged Jessie's hair.

Jessie stared into her own bright eyes in the glass, and

moved her head slightly to see if her scar was obvious. 'Oh, yes,' she said. 'I really feel like dancing tonight. Mary, do you think it matters? This, I mean.' And she touched the faint mark with a finger.

'No, miss,' Tomlinson said loyally. 'It doesn't hardly show at all. And, besides, if a person loves you, he won't care about such things as that.'

Jessie smiled. 'Absurd of me to ask. Of course you'd say that.'

Tomlinson met her eyes seriously. 'I tell you what, Miss Jessie – I've never seen you in such looks, and that's the truth. There's been a kind of glow about you this last week or so, and tonight you look like an angel – and that's the truth, too, if I was to die tomorrow!'

Jessie had on her new evening-dress. She had had it from Uncle Teddy for Christmas. It was in old-rose taffeta with a beaded chiffon over-bodice and a short train, with a very straight, narrow skirt and high waistline. The style suited Jessie's slenderness, and when Tomlinson had dressed her hair wide and low, with a large chignon at the back and a profusion of soft curls at the front and sides, she really did think she looked at her best. Would he notice? Would he say anything? She went down to the drawing-room a little while later in a happy dream, enjoying the sound of the weights in her train clicking down the stairs behind her, thinking of the evening and dancing to come. He might ask her to dance. There was no reason why not. She was sure, really, that he would.

In the drawing-room she attended to the guests efficiently, but her mind was not with them: she was listening for arrivals. At last she couldn't bear it any longer, and making an excuse she left the group she was talking to and slipped through the crowd to the door and out into the staircase hall. Her face was hot, and she paused a moment to let it cool down. The closed drawing-room door cut the conversational noise to a murmur, and she heard carriage wheels outside quite clearly. Irrationally, she knew it was him. She crossed the staircase hall and reached the great hall just as Sawry opened the door.

Bertie and Maud came in from the night into the lamplit warmth, he in tall hat and overcoat, she in a hooded evening cloak. Jessie's heart lurched at the sight of him, and she stopped in the shadow of the archway to watch. John the footman and Mabel, one of the house-maids, came forward to take their outer things. Bertie unfastened Maud's cloak for her, for she seemed to be fumbling with the clasp. Perhaps her hands were cold, Jessie thought distantly. The sight of his gentle attention to Maud troubled her. And when they had shed their outer garments and stood together side by side in evening clothes, it suddenly came to her with the full force of reality that they were husband and wife. Maud was not an inconvenient fact she could ignore. Maud *owned* him: he was hers for ever and ever, and there was nothing to be done about it. And, worst of all, she liked Maud. She had been wrong, she realised, to think her secret fantasies did not hurt anyone: they hurt her, Jessie. Her cheeks burned with guilt and confusion as if she had been caught out. Maud, in a midnight blue velvet gown, looked very handsome, and as calm and confident as she always did. Now Jessie hardly dared look at Bertie – but it didn't matter whether she looked or not: his face was burned into her memory. She didn't think they had seen her. She backed through into the staircase hall and then ran up the stairs as fast and as quietly as she could. From the safety of the turn of the stairs she watched them go by in Sawry's wake towards the drawing-room; heard the noise of voices jump up suddenly in volume as the door was opened, and Sawry's most sonorous tones announcing, 'Sir Percival and Lady Parke.'

Lady Parke. Jessie sat down on the stairs, her knees feeling suddenly weak. Love welled up in her, and sorrow, deep and broad as a calm sea. She loved him absolutely and for ever, but he was married, and loving him she had to accept Maud as part of him. She could not hate her or feel jealous of her. She could not indulge in any of the imaginings that as a young girl she might have thought would help, of Maud's magical disappearance or painless and sudden departure to a better world. She was wiser now, and this was the real world. Things were as they were. She realised now that she had loved Bertie always, that he had been that thing she had waited for, the reason other men seemed to fall short, to amuse her but not engage her. She had been safe from them because a vital part of her had been already gone. She would always love him; and he would never be hers.

It was a huge thing to swallow, and it took her a moment. Tears wanted to well up and she would not let them. He must never know, no-one must ever know, how she felt. If she kept nothing else, she would keep her pride. For a moment she saw the rest of her life stretch before her, a vast, shadowless plain to be crossed, as without water, without love or the hope of it. She took a long, trembling breath, and then stood up, smoothed her skirt, and walked down the stairs. It seemed a thousand years ago that she had been able to be amused by something as simple as the sound of her train following her. She was so much older now, as old as sadness itself.

She opened the drawing-room door, and the first thing she saw was Bertie, his back to her, standing just inside, talking to Uncle Teddy. Maud, beyond him, was facing Jessie's way, and she smiled in greeting. Bertie must have seen it, for he broke off and turned. For a moment they faced each other, and the rest of the room seemed in Jessie's mind to fall silent; everything stopped, time stopped, and she allowed herself one last, long stare, looked into Bertie's eyes and said goodbye. He had no way to know what she was thinking, of course. Through the drag of slowed time he stretched out a hand to her, took her hand in his, leaned down to kiss her cheek. Her eyes closed against tears at the touch of his lips, and inside her mind she whispered, *Goodbye, my love*.

Then he straightened up; time jerked into motion again

and the noise sprang back into the space like water into a hole.

'Jessie, my dear,' Bertie said. 'You look so charming tonight. I like the way you've done your hair. Doesn't she look pretty, Maud?' he appealed to his wife, expertly drawing Jessie into the group.

'Very pretty,' said Maud.

And Jessie, her heart breaking, said, 'Thank you. You look lovely too.'

A large family learns how to give and acquire privacy, and in the drawing-room in the evening there were generally several little self-contained groups and the odd individual, each pursuing different activities. February Fill-dyke was living up to its name, and the rain teemed down relentlessly outside, squalling sometimes with the gusty wind. The sound of it gurgling in the down-pipes was quite audible inside, together with a steady drip-drip-drip from somewhere – probably a leaking gutter – and there was a dampish smell that always became apparent when the moat rose to a certain level. But it was cosy in the drawing-room, with the fire heaped high and the lamps and candles lit. Teddy was still talking about having gas laid in, but never quite got round to it. The cost of laying a private pipe-line all the way out here would be very large, and no-one in the house was pressing hard enough for it to counter that drawback. Jessie was glad, really. There was something so comforting about lamp-light, something that seemed to suit Morland Place. She had been in enough gas-lit houses and disliked the hardness and hiss of it, and the disappearance of shadows. Here shadows seemed part of the house – friendly, known, hanging around behind and under things like dear old dogs.

She was playing chess with her father. His chair was pulled up close to the fire, and Snowdrop was curled on his lap; Jessie was sitting on a little footstool drawn up on the other side of the chess table. She was getting better at chess, but he nearly always won, and the times when

543

she won, she suspected he had let her. She had the feeling that where she had to work out the consequences of any particular move laboriously and step by step, he saw them all in one wonderful flash. She had been staring at her endangered knight for some time now without coming to any conclusion about his future, partly because looking at a horseman made her think about Bertie on horseback – a position in which she thought he always looked his best.

Bell, hogging the fire as usual, stirred and moaned with pleasure, and Brach, who was using him as a cushion, sat up, yawned mightily until her ears touched behind, and lay down again in a minutely different but preferable position.

Jerome said, 'Your move. Are you thinking or had you forgotten?'

'I was thinking,' Jessie said.

'But not about chess, I fancy.' She didn't answer. 'You've been rather quiet lately.'

'Have I?'

'There's an evasive answer if ever I heard one. You know you have – not your usual energetic, cheerful self.'

She moved her knight pretty much at random.

He took it with a little sigh. 'Now why did you do that? Check.'

She looked up with a rueful smile. 'Sorry.'

'Your mind's not on the game. What is it, Jess?' he asked tenderly. 'Distraction in a girl of your age is usually a sign of falling in love. Are you in love with someone?'

She could not lie to him, and sought an answer that would be true without admitting anything. 'Not any more than usual,' she said at last. She thought it a clever answer, but perhaps she had hesitated too long. At any rate, he looked as though he knew it for a prevarication.

He said, 'I hope you'll remember what I said about giving your heart to someone unworthy?'

She looked down, unable to meet his eyes with composure. 'I'll remember,' she said, and even to herself her voice was a betrayal.

He sighed again, and said, 'Sometimes things take time, chick. You can't always see what God has planned, but it turns out the right way in the end.'

'P'r'aps it doesn't always,' she said. 'There must be sad endings as well as happy ones.'

'It won't be that way for you. I know. I promise.' He looked down at her bent head, and saw something glisten in the firelight on her cheek. His heart ached for her. He wanted to stroke her head, take her in his arms like a little girl. He spoke again, very softly, though no-one was near enough to overhear them. 'I've had a long and rich life, and it would be a poor thing if I could not take what comes at the end of it without a heart full of thankfulness for all my blessings. I don't want anything more for myself; but if I could ask one thing, it would be to see you happy before I go.'

'I am happy,' she said. She swallowed and made herself look up, made herself meet his eyes steadily. 'I'm happy here at Morland Place. I don't ever want to leave. Don't worry about me, Dad. I have everything in the world I want.' Everything I can have, anyway, she added silently.

'My brave girl,' he said.

She reached her hand across the table to rest it over his. A shadow crossed them, and there was a rustle of skirts, and Henrietta was there, bending over her husband.

'This game doesn't seem to be progressing very fast.'

'Dad has me beat to flinders,' Jessie said.

'Checkmate in three moves,' he admitted. 'I didn't know you'd realised.'

She grinned. 'Just a wild guess.'

'I came to see if you'd like a nightcap,' Henrietta said. 'A little brandy in some hot milk, perhaps?'

'She means me, not you,' Jerome told his daughter. 'Thank you, my love, that will be very nice.'

Jessie was getting up to reach for the bell, but Henrietta said, 'No, don't move, I'll go and get it. I've been sitting still too long.'

Jerome's fond eyes followed her out of the room, and

when he turned back to Jessie, he saw her watching him with a great wistfulness. In a moment of intuition it came to him: that she had fallen in love with someone already married. A great sadness weighted his chest so that for a moment he struggled to draw a breath. It was worse than he feared, then – and there was nothing in the world he could do about it, except pray that everything would work out for her in the end, as it had for him.

During the evening the wind changed direction and dropped to nothing, the rain stopped, and by the time Jessie went to bed there was a clear sky, the first for a week. She stopped on the landing to look out and saw the blue-white stars blinking gently in the dark sky. It would be cold later, she thought. A still, clear night like this in February would mean a sharp frost. Her mind was restless, and when she got into bed she knew she wouldn't sleep, so she put a shawl round her shoulders and sat up to read. It began to get very cold in the room – the tip of her nose told her, and the chill of the fingers holding the book. Her fire had died down, and she got up, reluctantly, and hopped shivering across the room to make it up again with the last of the coal.

The house was still, and she thought it must be nearly one o'clock – it was a long time since she had heard any clock strike twelve. Against her curtains she could see the brightness of moonlight, and she thought again of the frost of a still clear night. It was just past the full moon, she knew, though there had been no moon to be seen for a week past. She longed suddenly to see it. Outside, quite close, she heard a fox bark sharply, that unearthly sound; and, as if it were in reply, somewhere in the house a dog howled, just once. Pulling the shawl tightly round her she went on flinching toes across the chilly floor to the window, and drew the curtain back.

It was a magical scene, everything frosted in sparkling white, like an illustration she had seen once in a story book. The moon sailed high and serene in a black sky, too bright for stars; a gibbous moon, white and hard, laying dappled silver over the water of the moat like shining metallic fish-scales. And then she saw the foxes: two of them, sitting on the far bank of the moat, side by side; sitting quite still, staring at the house. She wondered what they could be looking at. There was no light on downstairs, or she would have seen the shine of it on the grass or the moat. They sat quite still for a long time, and she remained, shivering, watching them; until at last one of them barked again, and as if at some signal they stood up and trotted away, one behind the other, and disappeared out of sight behind the bushes. It was the oddest thing, like something in a dream.

She dropped the curtain and was heading back for the warmth of her bed when she thought she heard a sound outside the door. She opened it, and in the shadowy dimness in the corridor she could just make out the shape of a dog lying in front of the door to her parents' bedroom. She went across and hunkered down. It was Fern, and he was so cold to the touch she thought for an awful moment that he was dead, but as she stroked his head he lifted it a little and she saw him looking at her. All the dogs slept together in the great hall in front of the fire, keeping each other warm. Why had he left them? Poor old thing, she thought. Perhaps Bell had pushed him out and he had come upstairs looking for warmth.

'Come on,' she whispered, pulling at his collar. 'Come to my fire. Come on, old boy. You can't stay here. You'll freeze.'

It was hard to move him, but at last he got to his feet and she led him into her room, closed the door, and went with him to the fire. It had burned up nicely now, and he sat down before it with a sigh, and looked into the flames. She stood there a while, warming her hands and legs, and then left him and went back to bed. She still felt wakeful, but almost as soon as her head was on the pillow, she fell asleep.

When she woke the moon was down and it was pitch

black in the room, with only the slightest red glim from the fire. It was Fern who had woken her, she realised. She heard him whimpering, and now felt him pawing at her through the blankets. He wanted to go out, she supposed, and sat up in bed, feeling for her candle and matches. With the candle lit, she looked at the clock on the mantel, and saw it was half past five. The maids would be up soon. It was bitterly cold in the room. She got up, pulled on her dressing-gown and went to the door, Fern following her so closely he was pressing against her legs. When she opened it she thought he would push past her and run off down the stairs to join the others, but instead he went to her parents' bedroom door again, and sat down, looking at it as if willing it to open.

'No good. They won't be awake yet,' she told him in a whisper. 'Go on downstairs, fool.'

She tried to pull him and then push him, but he had nailed himself to the floor, an immovable weight, and in the end she shrugged over his fate and went back to bed. The maids would be astir soon and half an hour in a cold corridor couldn't kill the old dog now.

In the warmth of her bed she dozed off again, to be woken from the black depths of a new sleep by an unusual activity somewhere nearby. And soon afterwards Mary Tomlinson came in, looking very shaken: not to make up her fire, but to tell her that her father had died during the night.

Work helped, routine helped. Henrietta, looking white and lost, went about her normal tasks, to which were added receiving visits of condolence, and answering letters. Alice and Ethel were both a great comfort to her – Alice with her quiet kindness, Ethel with her cheerful fecundity which seemed to be a pledge that winter could not last and that spring would come again. And it did, of course – outside, at least. The blackthorn burst into tender green, the fields were white with lambs, new foals raced about on their stilt-legs, absurd tails cocked, little nests of primroses and drifts of sweet violets appeared on banks and under hedgerows.

One day when she was sitting at the table in the dining parlour writing menus, Teddy came to find her.

'Ah, there you are,' he said. 'May I sit down? I'd like to talk to you about something.'

She looked up, patient in her sorrow, and he was touched all over again.

'I wanted to tell you – well, I hoped it didn't need saying, but Alice said I should say it anyway, so that you know. I want to tell you that Morland Place is your home, and always will be. Jerome and I talked about it last year, about what would happen when he was gone, and I told him the same that I've just told you. On his advice, I've had a codicil added to my will. So no matter when James inherits, it's all in black and white. You are to stay here as long as you live, bed and board and everything provided, so you need never worry about anything on that score, Hen.'

'Oh, Ted, you are so good,' she said. 'There never was such a kind and generous brother.'

'Oh, tosh! Couldn't do less for my own sister,' he said.

'You could have done very much less. Thank you, my dear – and thank you for easing Jerome's mind about it, too.'

Teddy looked bleak. 'I miss him. Not just all the things he did – I never realised, you know, how much there was until he had to stop doing it – but I miss *him*. No-one else made me laugh as he did, or showed me my faults and follies in just that way.' He pulled out his handkerchief and blew his nose briskly. 'But here's me talking to you about missing him!'

Jessie found work a distraction too, and threw herself into it. It was the only thing that made the slowly passing days bearable at first. She refused kind offers from the Cornleighs for all sorts of diversions, and sent a grateful refusal to Violet (recovering from the birth of her second son, Richard), who invited her to come and stay for as long as she liked. Work was her drug. She took on extra tasks, doing jobs normally left to the grooms so that she could tire herself out enough to sleep. She was at Twelvetrees all day, grooming, exercising, schooling, helping with the feeding, even sometimes cleaning tack. That day-end ritual in the tack-room, when tea was brewed and the lamp lit, when a cosy fug built up as the grooms rubbed and polished in rhythm with their chat, was as soothing as a bedtime story to a child. It was not seemly for Miss Jessie to do such work, but the first time she appeared in the doorway there was only a brief pause and surprised look before Harold, the oldest of the grooms, shifted up on his bench and made room for her and, after a further hesitation, offered her Nagira's bridle. In a little while, one of the younger ones dared to hand her, with a slightly apologetic look, strong orange tea in one of their great white enamel mugs. The talk gradually drifted back into the space it had vacated, while Jessie silently, but feeling accepted by them, polished the bits and rubbed up the leather to a soft gleam.

Her favourite jobs were breaking the foals to halter – which she thought, as her father had, of vital importance, being the foundation of the animal's entire relationship with man all its life long – and schooling the polo ponies. She also liked to be around for the first backing of any horse that was more than usually nervous or spirited; and the schooling of riding horses being trained to carry side-saddle. Over the two years of her father's illness even Lelliott, the head man, had come to accept her, and her orders were obeyed now without demur, questions and problems brought to her quite naturally. It was as well there had been this time during which to build up her authority, for in his will Jerome had left his entire interest in the horse business to her. She had been as much shocked as pleased when she first heard, and looked at her mother with stricken eyes.

But Henrietta had said, 'Don't worry, darling. Your father and I talked about it. You are the one who loves the horses and does all the work, and the boys and I are taken care of. No-one will feel aggrieved, I promise you.'

'But, Mother – all of it?'

'No sense in sharing it. And your father wanted you to be secure, so that you never need worry or . . .' She hesitated.

Jessie understood. 'Feel I had to marry someone, just to be taken care of?'

It was a long time before she could come to terms with being an heiress (the interest in the business was to be held in trust until she was twenty-one) and even longer before it gave her pleasure. She was too swallowed up in loss – a double loss for her, publicly of her father and hidden and unspoken of Bertie. She could not cry for her father – had not cried even at his funeral, though nearly everyone else had. She came close to tears when, a week after his death, Fern died: the old dog had spent the week miserably looking for his master, and at the end had taken to lying across the bedroom doorway as he had that last night, refusing to eat. Jessie had carried choice morsels up to him and tried to feed him by hand, but he had only looked up at her, nose on paws, with lonely eyes, and beat his tail against the ground in apology. It was Fern's death that had made Robbie break and cry for his father, but Jessie's loss was too deep for tears.

But when Bertie had come to express his condolences, had ridden out to Twelvetrees on purpose to see her, his tenderness, his understanding had almost done it. He had laid a hand on her shoulder and said he knew how much she would miss him. 'He was a wonderful man, a fine man, and I feel honoured to have known him. I liked and admired him enormously.'

'He liked you very much, Bertie,' she had said, and thought of her father's words to her, and how glad he would have been if she could have brought him Bertie as her suitor. She was very conscious of the warmth and weight of his hand on her shoulder, the closeness of him; the mad desire to fling herself against him and cry out,

551

'Love me or I shall die!' And that night, in bed, she cried at last, muffling her sobs with her pillow in case her mother – sleepless, she knew – should hear her. She cried for the loss of her father, who had been friend and companion and wise mentor, for the tender love there had been between them, and for the lost love that might have taken its place, if Fate had not decreed otherwise.

Perhaps it was that storm of tears that began the healing; or perhaps it was the coming of spring, the new leaves and grass, the occasional warmth of sunshine, the excited racket of birds in every tree and hedge – all things it was hard not to be cheered by. It did not happen all at once, and there were often occasions when she felt wretchedly low and life seemed weary. It was wicked, she thought, to feel lonely in a houseful of people who all cared about her, but lonely she was. Of late she had shared an intimacy with her father that had been special to her; much as she loved her mother, she knew instinctively that no member of her own sex could replace what he had been to her.

When she had her fits of misery, the difficulty was to find somewhere private to cry, for she did not want to inflict her tears on the rest of the family. One evening she slipped out, unnoticed, she thought, to the yard stable, where lived the pony Dunnock and her father's old horse Minstrel, who were eking out their retirement doing light chores. A horse is a good friend to someone who wants to cry – solid and warm, uncomplaining and friendly, and just the right height to lean on. She wept against Minstrel's withers, and he stood quietly and let her, only turning his head curiously from time to time and touching her with his muzzle. When she had got to the messy, hiccuping stage, she went and sat on the manger and stroked his face and broke up the apple she had taken from the bowl in the dining parlour on her way out and gave it to him.

'I'm sorry, old boy,' she said. 'You must miss him too.' She fumbled her handkerchief out of her pocket and wiped her face and blew her nose, while Minstrel tossed his head up and down to get the last sweet fragments from behind his teeth, then nuzzled at her hands with his sensitive lips to see if he had perhaps missed anything. She stroked him again, rearranging his forelock neatly between his eyes, and carried on talking to him; and it was thus that Ned found her.

'I've been looking for you,' he said. 'I saw you slip out. It should have been the first place I looked, I suppose, but it wasn't – alas.'

'Why "alas"?' she said.

'Because if I'd found you sooner, it would have been my shoulder that received your tears and not the horse's.'

'How did you know I came here to cry? I might just have come to see him settled for the night.'

'I knew,' he said.

She looked away from him. 'I must look terrible.'

'You look lovely.'

'Nonsense! Red eyes, and a red nose.'

He didn't argue with her. He said, 'You're cold.'

She was, now she noticed it. 'A little.' He began to take off his jacket and she said, 'Don't.'

He desisted, but then, after a hesitation during which she could feel his eyes on her face, examining, probing, perhaps calculating, he moved closer and said, in a voice that just barely trembled, 'Let me warm you.'

She said nothing, and did not move, her head still turned away; but she did not resist as he put his arms round her and drew her against his chest. After a moment she put her arms round his waist, glad of the warmth, the sympathy, glad – she had to acknowledge it – of the touch of a man. In the darkness of her closed eyes she thought about Ned, visualised his face, his firm handsomeness, his kind smile. Now it was she who was trembling. He wanted nothing more of life than to love her and marry her, and how easy – how easy! – it would be to give in, to grant him that, to take the comfort he offered. She even knew that she could be happy with him in a way; that he would make a good husband and a good companion and that she would never have to feel alone again.

But I would be alone, a deeper voice said. Was it true, she wondered. Were there ways in which he could never touch her, or was that romantic folly, a childish dream? And if it was true, was it important? She didn't know enough to be able to tell. How many people married their one true love? Were all the others unhappy? Was there even such a thing as a one true love?

She felt his lips touch the top of her head. 'I love you, Jess,' he said. She didn't answer. What could she say? 'Are you warmer now?' he asked, in a different voice, a more everyday voice.

'Yes,' she said, and gently freed herself from him. She stood up and he moved back a little to let her, but not very much, so that when she was upright she was still very close to him, their bodies only just not touching.

'I want to ask you something,' he said. 'You know all about me. You know what I am. My father adopted me and gave me a name, and now he's given me a business of my own, so that I can be respectable and support myself and have a place in the world. I could take a house for myself, set up my household, but I stay here so that I can be near you. I love you, I've loved you for years. I know you like me, and we're always good company for each other. I think it could be enough. I know that you're not just sad because of your father . . .'

How did he know that, she wondered, startled. He couldn't know about Bertie. He must be thinking of her crush on Lord Brancaster, she decided. That must be it – mustn't it?

' . . . but I believe that will fade in time. We could have a good marriage, Jess. We could be happy.'

He stopped then, and although he had asked no question, he plainly wanted an answer. She examined his face, thought about what he had said. It was all true. She opened her mouth without fully knowing what she was going to say, and what came out was, 'Don't ask me yet, Ned. Not yet. Wait just a little.'

He studied her, trying to understand. She hardly

understood herself. She had no hopes of Bertie – indeed, it would be wicked to harbour them, and she didn't, truly she didn't. But it seemed just now too much like giving up to be bearable. She knew it was possible, that she *could* marry Ned, but she didn't want to do it in a spirit of sacrifice. She needed time to settle her heart, to have it understand as well as her mind did, that there was no hope.

'I can wait,' he said at last. 'I've waited this long, I can wait a little longer.'

'Until the summer,' she said. 'Give me until then.'

'And then?'

'You can ask me again in the summer,' she said.

He nodded, gravely. 'Whatever you say, Jess.'

'Go back now,' she said. 'I have to wait a little longer until my face goes down.'

'Don't get cold,' he said doubtfully, but he obeyed her, and left.

The second general election of 1910 delivered results almost exactly the same as the first. In January 1911 it was known that the Liberals had won 272 seats, the Conservative Unionists 272, the Irish members 84 and the Labour Party 42. This meant that, counting in the Irish, the Liberals had an overall majority of 126, four more than before. As an answer to King Edward's question it seemed decisive. There could be no thought of holding another election, and the Parliament Bill would have to be fought through the two Houses, with, if necessary, the promised intervention from the King.

Since the Black Friday and Downing Street outbreaks, the Suffragette truce had held, in the hope that the Conciliation Bill would have another chance in the new session. But every MP they approached said that the woman question would have to wait until the constitutional crisis had been resolved.

'But there will always be something that has to be settled first,' Anne said, on one of her now rare visits to

Venetia. 'If we sit and wait, they will never stir themselves to action. The only thing that counts is militancy, because it is the only thing that makes them notice us. And yet . . .'

'And yet?' Venetia asked, seeing her cousin's fierce expression fade to one of despondency.

'Every time, with every new stage of the struggle, I think, This must move them, and every time I'm disappointed. So many of us have suffered – two of us have died – and still they are not really moved. I look ahead and I can't any more see the end of it.'

There was no mention of the Conciliation Bill in the King's Speech on the 5th of February, which seemed to support Anne's view. However, the Private Member's Ballot was won by Sir George Kemp, who was a Liberal member and a firm suffragist, and he chose to bring the Conciliation Bill for its second reading debate on the 5th of May. After the debate it won a majority of 255 votes to 88, and though at first Asquith would not give any commitment to further time for the Bill, he eventually said in a letter to Mrs Pankhurst that he would grant facilities during a week in the next Parliamentary year.

Anne was sceptical about this statement, though it seemed on the face of it an unequivocal promise. 'We are going to do everything we can to keep him up to the mark by mentioning the contents of his letter in every public speech between now and then. If the whole country knows he has promised, he'll find it more difficult to wriggle out of it.'

The truce was therefore extended, and it was announced that in view of Asquith's promise, only Liberals who had voted against would be challenged by the WSPU in by-elections. Anne was not entirely happy about the truce. It seemed to her that they were losing the momentum they had built up. Without the militant action there were hardly ever any headlines about the Suffragettes, or indeed any mentions at all in the press, and this was allowing their public support to slip away.

Meetings drew smaller audiences, and the stream of donations coming in was slackening. If things continued in that way, the truce could prove very damaging.

But there was a benefit to it, which was that after an exhausting time she was able to rest, recuperate, and even take an interest in other things from time to time. She played the piano more regularly, and felt the improvement in her fingering and execution. She had time to go riding, and to accompany Miss Polk when she went for lessons (paid for by Anne, of course) so that one day they would be able to ride together. Vera had a great desire to go to the theatre, which she knew nothing of, and when Anne took her, she delighted in it so much that there were thereafter regular visits to plays and concerts. Anne took her to art galleries, too, though Miss Polk was not nearly so quick to appreciate paintings, and went to exhibitions more to please Anne than herself.

And there were regular trips away, to stay in the country or at the seaside, to visit famous beauty spots, historic houses and cities, and tour lovely districts – the Peaks, the Cotswolds, Cornwall. Anne bought a motor-car – a Wolseley M5 limousine – which cost her £803 15/-. Anne had never lived up to her income, her greatest expenditure until now having been donations to the Cause, and her own action rather surprised her. But it also pleased her to be the owner of such a thing. It was a great, shiny, dark blue monster with every handsome fitting of chrome or leather in the catalogue, and since neither of them could drive, Anne hired a lady-chauffeur, a fellow Suffragette, who was the second woman ever to qualify for the Automobile Association Certificate in Driving (the first was Aileen Preston, who drove for Mrs Pankhurst). Anne paid her Mary Taylor a pound a week, and bought her a livery of a serge skirt with a jacket of military cut and a peaked cap. They caused a sensation wherever they went, what with the size of the car, Anne's beauty and grandeur, and the female driver. Mary Taylor cut her hair very short, and once for a joke she drew a black

557

moustache on her upper lip and spoke in a gruff voice, much to the consternation of onlookers when she climbed out and proved to be wearing a skirt. The spring and early summer were a wonderful time for Anne, who enjoyed Vera's company and her life of idleness and travel so much that she sometimes almost hoped the truce would last for ever, almost felt she could give up the Cause and the agonising battle, and give herself over to pleasure.

They had to be back in London for the 17th of June when there was to be a grand procession through London, to keep the Cause in the public mind and to benefit from the presence in the capital of all the foreign visitors come for the Coronation, which was to be on Thursday the 22nd of June. The Coronation March was, in the opinion of many, the finest thing the Suffragettes had done: forty thousand people in a procession that stretched seven miles, marching from the Embankment to the Albert Hall, most of the women in white, carrying banners beautifully painted, their eyes bright and their faces hopeful, to the tremendous cheers of enormous crowds.

Anne would have liked to go away again immediately after the march, but both Miss Polk and Miss Taylor cried out at the suggestion that they should miss the Coronation and attendant celebrations. So it was not until the beginning of July that the Wolseley set off with its roof laden with luggage to drive down to Dover. Miss Polk had never been to France, and Anne intended to make that good with a tour of three months.

Bertie and Maud came to London in mid-May, and they made a courtesy call on Lizzie at a time when Jack happened to be there. It was exquisitely painful for Jack to be in Maud's company, and for the first few moments he could not bring himself even to look at her. But after a quarter of an hour, when they were all seated in the drawing-room and general conversation was going on, he managed a glance and then a longer look, while her eyes were on someone else. She was beautiful, of course, and elegantly dressed, and sat and moved with her usual poise; but after a little study Jack found himself, to his own puzzlement, thinking that she was somehow less beautiful than before. He admired her, but she did not stir his heart in the same way. What was it, he wondered. He could not detect any fault in her looks or her dress: she seemed exactly like any other handsome young matron. And then he thought perhaps that was what it was. She was a married woman. There was a worldly confidence about her. She was no longer serenely withdrawn, but chatted in a very ordinary way to Lizzie about household things and played with little Rose as if she were a mother herself. Her mystery had been dispersed like a magical fog, revealing not a goddess or a fairy queen but an ordinary human being. The discovery ought to have pleased him, releasing him from his long worship, but at first he found it as painful to stop loving her as it had been to love her.

His visits to Lizzie were frequent at this time – Tom Sopwith was away on an extended trip to America and would not be back until the late autumn, so many of his social engagements had collapsed – and as Maud was often there too, he began to grow accustomed to the new situation. Bertie stayed only a few days before returning to Yorkshire, for there was too much to do about his new estate for him to be long absent from it; but Maud was intending to stay for the Season at her father's house, and Bertie had promised to come up as often as he could – though from the way he said it Jack guessed it would not be often. Maud was therefore frequently in need of a more equal companionship than her father could offer, and she had taken a great liking to Lizzie's house and Lizzie's baby. Jack had plenty of opportunity to see the change in her, and listen to her conversation. In place of those serene silences there was domestic talk. Maud had no difficulty in finding things to say about the refurbishment of the Red House and her future plans in that direction, of the difficulties of finding good servants and keeping them, and of the iniquities of bad servants – the latter a subject without end. She talked of future visits to London, when she and Bertie would take a house of their own, and hinted that Bertie ought to think of buying a London house so that they could come up whenever they wanted and entertain in more style than Pont Street allowed. It seemed to Jack that she had large ambitions in the social field, and more than once she wondered aloud what one did to be able to be presented, and whether Lady Overton would supply the information and even the patronage. Lizzie seemed obtuse when these hints were dropped and did not respond in a way that satisfied Maud, so that the subject returned, wistfully, at regular intervals. Jack gathered from her conversation that London held her heart and that the country was to her only a place to be visited in August and September when London closed. She liked to talk about the Red House, but she never called it 'home'.

The *coup de grâce* to his infatuation was the discovery that Maud did not like Rug. She drew her skirts aside from him if the friendly little fellow came near, and one fatal day confessed that she did not like mongrels and that she had hinted to Bertie that she would like a gazelle-hound for her birthday, because she had seen a picture in a magazine of a French countess with a Saluki, and it was *so* elegant and beautiful – quite different from horrid little *common* dogs.

The pain of losing Maud faded under this clear light of day, and he found his thoughts lingering much more on Miss Airdrie. One evening when he and Lizzie were alone at her house, he told her about her, and Lizzie's immediate reaction was to suggest that he brought Miss Airdrie to visit one day. 'She sounds sweet. I'd love to meet her,' she said; and then, with an innocent air, 'Why not bring her to dinner one evening? I could invite Maud and her father as well, and make a little party of it. I'm sure Maud would love to meet her too.'

Jack looked at her closely for a moment, and then saw the gleam in her eyes. 'Lizzie!'

Lizzie began to laugh. 'Oh dear, Jack, your face is such a window! I've been watching you fall out of love with Maud in stages and it couldn't have been clearer if you had written out a statement and read it to us!'

Jack tried not to look sulky at being found so transparent, and at having his tenderest feelings laughed at. 'Do you think Maud . . . ?'

'No, Jackie darling, I don't think she noticed. To be quite frank, Maud is a dear and I'm very fond of her, but at the moment she's so wrapped up with being Lady Parke she doesn't notice anything or anyone else. But I'm quite serious about your bringing your Miss Airdrie to dinner.'

'Not *my* Miss Airdrie,' Jack said. 'Not yet, anyway.'

'Well, perhaps if you have her at the same table with Maud, the comparison might make up your mind for you,' Lizzie said. 'I leave it to you, but any time you want to bring her to see me, please do.'

Lord and Lady Holkam also came to London that summer. Holkam came first, in May 1911, to take his seat and talk with Lansdowne in advance of the Parliament Bill's being presented to the Lords. Violet came up to London at the beginning of June. She would have liked to come earlier, but had not realised that she would have to leave the children in Lincolnshire. Holkam was astonished when her conversation revealed she expected to bring them with her, and he told her firmly that it was simply not done, and that the country was the place for children.

'I was brought up in London,' she pointed out.

'Your parents are eccentrics,' he told her. 'You must not judge by their actions. You must be guided by me as to how a countess behaves. Your mother, in particular, is no sound template for a gentlewoman, let alone a peer's wife and daughter.'

Violet was hurt by this, and said no more. At first she thought of punishing Holkam by saying that she would sooner stay in the country with her children than go to London without them. But the fact was that she *did* want to go to London: she wanted to see her mother, she wanted to see the Coronation, she wanted to take part in the London Season, and be presented, and act as hostess in her own newly refurbished house. To be Lady Holkam and hold a ball at Fitzjames House and be photographed for the illustrated magazines were the rewards for the long months she had spent exiled in the fens, recompense for the ways in which marriage had fallen short of her dreams. It would be foolish to balk now at a few weeks' separation from her darlings and, after all, no harm could come to them without her. She was twenty years old and beautiful and she *wanted* to wear a tiara and go to the Abbey and dance and have everyone admire her and talk about her. So instead of cutting off her nose to spite her face, she went instead about hastily weaning baby Richard and sorting through her clothes. She would buy new things in London, she decided, but she needed some things for immediate wear. She wrote to her mother that she was coming up, and her mother suggested that she immediately put in an order with her dressmaker for Violet's gown for the Coronation itself, since all dressmakers would be so busy that placing an order in June when she arrived would be quite pointless.

As a peeress, Violet would have a place in the Abbey for the ceremony, and Venetia spoke to her old friend Cocky Lansdowne and asked him to use his influence so that they could sit together. Lord Overton had been honoured by a place in the actual procession: he was to carry the golden spurs, part of the King's Regalia, and was deeply moved by King George's having asked him, 'as a token of my gratitude for your long and faithful service to my father'. This was more reason than ever for Violet to be there, and when the time came she parted from her babies with a pang, but with no real doubt that she was doing the right thing.

*   *   *

562

Lizzie had issued a blanket invitation to everyone at Morland Place to come and stay for the Coronation, though where everyone was to sleep if all accepted she had never made clear even to herself. Venetia, independently, had invited Henrietta and Jessie to come and stay with her for the occasion, reminding them that Jessie's three months of deep mourning would be well over by then, and Henrietta's six months almost over, that it would be good for them to have a change of scene, and that Violet would love to see Jessie. Henrietta and Jessie could avoid the more public celebrations, but still have a great deal of quiet pleasure in the company of people who loved them.

Henrietta put it to Jessie in these terms, concealing her own feelings and prepared to go herself, though she did not want to, if that was what it took to be sure that Jessie went. She did not like to see her daughter work so hard and smile so little; and in spite of the previous failure she still had the feeling that the London Season might produce a suitor who would engage Jessie as the local boys did not seem able to. But Jessie did not want to go, not even to see Violet – 'I can see her in the summer in the country. That would be much better than a hurried call in Town, which is all she'd be able to spare me.' She wanted to stay at home, and she assured her mother she was perfectly happy – or at least, as happy as she would be anywhere.

Robbie and Ethel really wanted to go, but Ethel would be too large with child in June to make the journey or to appear in public, and with many regretful sighs they refused Lizzie's kind offer. So the party was reduced to Teddy, Alice, Ned and Polly, which would put much less of a strain on Lizzie's household. Teddy and Alice could have the guest room, Ned could sleep in with the boys, and Polly agreed in such a great cause to leave off some of her dignity and sleep in the nursery with Rose, as long as it was thoroughly understood that she was not a child but a young lady, and that she would have to have several new dresses for the occasion.

Before the departure for London, Teddy had another engagement to fulfil: he was invited to witness the launch of the second of the White Star's new super-liners. Consequently, on Wednesday the 31st of May he was in Belfast in the company of Bruce Ismay, Thomas Andrews and Lord Pirrie to watch Hull 401 slip into the water. It was a clear, bright day, with a sharp breeze that whipped out the flags on the gantry tops and made them crack like whips, and ruffled the surface of the Lough. White Star did not traditionally have a christening ceremony – as one worker said in Teddy's hearing, 'They just builds 'em and shoves 'em in' – but all the same there was a huge crowd assembled, perhaps as many as a hundred thousand people, for Belfast was deeply engaged with the shipping business, and there was no-one in the city who had not followed White Star's venture with interest. The men who actually worked on the ships were intensely proud of their involvement, and none of them would have missed this moment for anything. Hull 401 was the biggest ship ever made, bigger even than the *Olympic*, so the launch would be an historic moment that they could tell their children and grandchildren about.

At 12.05 two rockets were fired, initiating the ceremony, followed by a third at 12.10; and then at 12.13 the huge hull, weighing 26,000 tons, began to move down the slipway under its own weight. In awed silence the onlookers watched it gather speed – reaching, Teddy learned afterwards, twelve knots, though he was never sure how anyone knew that – and hit the water with a great fountain of a bow-wave. Then its tail of six anchor chains and two piles of cable drag chains, together weighing eighty tons, brought it to a halt. Now it was no longer an it, but a she, no longer Hull 401 but the *Titanic*.

Lord Pirrie closed his watch with a snap and said, 'Sixty-two seconds from start to finish.'

And that was all there was to it, Teddy thought. Now the tugs would come and tow her to the fitting-out basin, where she would have her internal spaces built, the cabins, dining-rooms, galleys, store-rooms and so on. Carpenters, electricians, metalworkers, steam-fitters – all the craftsmen and tradesmen would go in and turn her from a hull to a living space. And then in time carpet-layers, painters, plumbers, interior fitters and so on, and the installation of the furnishings and equipment, would turn the living space into a luxurious floating hotel. The process, perhaps unsurprisingly given the extent of it, would take almost a year.

The crowds of onlookers were filtering away, returning to their daily rounds.

'Luncheon, gentlemen?' said Lord Pirrie, and they retired to the offices of Harland and Wolff for a mildly celebratory lunch, preceded by a glass or two of champagne to raise to the glorious future of the most magnificent ship ever to sail the seas. It was during the fitting-out stage that Teddy would be most involved, and there was much to discuss over the meal, at which they were joined by Edward Wilding, Andrews's assistant. But there was another small ceremony to be performed before they sat down at the table, and that was the formal signing-off by Harland and Wolff of the *Olympic*, making over ownership to the White Star Line. She was about to start her sea-trials, and when those were complete and she had her Board of Trade approval, she would sail to Southampton to take on passengers for her maiden voyage to New York.

'It has always been my custom to go with each of my ships on her maiden voyage,' Ismay said to Teddy over the turtle soup. 'There is a great deal to be learned in that way.'

'About the handling of the ship?'

'Yes, that of course, but I am not an engineer and such technical matters are not my province. What interests me more particularly is how she functions internally. One can see instantly by the reaction of the passengers during the voyage whether their comfort or satisfaction is compromised in any way. It becomes obvious where there is an awkwardness or deficiency that was not at all apparent on paper.'

Teddy agreed that it must be so. 'I was just now thinking the same thing, that it would be useful to see how the *Olympic* performed before fitting out the *Titanic*. To correct the mistakes in her before they happen, so to speak.'

'I'm glad you think so, because I would like to ask you to come with me,' Ismay said. 'At my expense, of course. It would be agreeable to me to have your company on the voyage, and I would also be glad of your observations and opinions on how she functions. The *Olympic* is a beautiful ship, but I want the *Titanic* to benefit from her sister ship's experience and begin life as close to perfection as human ingenuity can make her.'

'I am very flattered to be asked. When do you sail?' said Teddy.

'We sail from Southampton on June the fourteenth,' Ismay said. 'The return voyage will begin on July the twenty-eighth, but of course if you do not care to remain in America for that length of time, I can arrange a return passage for you on another ship.'

'Ah! You are very kind,' Teddy said, 'but June the fourteenth? It would mean missing the Coronation. I could never be back in time, and my wife and I are engaged to stay in London for the event. I'm afraid I could not alter the arrangements now.'

'Very well,' said Ismay. 'I will not press you.' He gave a faint smile and added, 'Though the maiden voyage of a ship like the *Olympic* is a once-in-a-lifetime thing, and we cannot quite say the same of a coronation.'

'True – but my wife would never forgive me if I denied her this one.'

'Far be it from me to come between a man and his wife,' Ismay laughed. 'Perhaps you will engage now to come with me on the *Titanic*'s maiden voyage instead? Some time in April next year – the date is not fixed yet, but it will certainly be in April, unless she fails her sea-trials.'

Teddy smiled. 'That I think I can promise you,' he said.

'It's unlikely that we will have another new king by then, and even if we do, there can't possibly be another coronation so soon. I think I can safely promise you to accept your kind invitation for April next year.'

Chapter Eighteen

On the 13th of July, 1911 – the same day on which the young Prince Edward (or David as his family called him) was invested as Prince of Wales – Ethel's baby was born. The Cornleighs were a practical, efficient race, and Ethel got down to childbirth in an almost businesslike way, producing in a remarkably short time, and apparently without effort, a small, red baby girl. By the time she made her appearance, the house was full of Cornleighs, and the rejoicing was very great. Even Cornleigh *père*, who had badly wanted his first grandchild to be a boy, was delighted enough almost to caper on the spot and deal Teddy a blow on the back that knocked his cigarillo flying. Within minutes of the birth, Emma was calling the newcomer 'my baby', and Jessie said it would be a poor look-out for James William. 'Fancy being past your best when you're not even a year old!'

By the end of the first day, Robbie and Ethel had decided to call their new daughter Roberta, after her father. Jessie suppressed a smile at the news, and suddenly missed her own father with a sharp pang, thinking how he would have laughed at the choice. She could almost hear his voice saying, 'If the next is a boy, will they name it after Ethel? What will it be called – Ethelburga?' She would have liked to share the joke with him.

Teddy sent telegrams to everyone he could think of, in a burst of pride that made him seem much more like Robbie's father than his uncle. But as the years passed

Teddy was becoming more of a patriarch all the time. The house bell was rung for Roberta's arrival, and Teddy often referred to her as 'the new Morland', blithely ignoring the fact that her name was Compton.

Bertie was at the Red House and one of the telegrams brought him on a congratulatory visit. He paid homage, found something pleasant and complimentary to say about the baby to all the interested parties, and then stepped aside to talk to Jessie about horses.

His visits were a sweet torment to Jessie, an exquisite mixture of pain and pleasure that she would not have given up for her life. It was one of the reasons she had not wanted to go to London for the Coronation, for at least here at Morland Place she could see him sometimes. He came over two or three times a week when he was at home, and since she was now virtually in sole charge of Twelvetrees, and in the frequent absence of Teddy, it was her he generally came to see. Maud was still in London, apparently planning to spend the whole of the Season there, and Bertie went up from time to time for a day or two, but seemed much to prefer Yorkshire, and not to mind being separated from his wife.

Just to see him eased something in Jessie. It was as if there was an aura around him, a bubble which, when she got within it, allowed her to breathe more easily and feel comfortable. She thought he seemed happier when he was with her, too. Age or marriage or living abroad or something had made him more serious, but she thought that he laughed more often when they were together, seemed younger, more boyish, made silly jokes and teased her a little in the old way. She loved to see him laugh; she loved to feel that, in some small way, she was important to him.

But there was no future for her with him, and some time soon, Ned was going to ask her again to marry him. She knew he was thinking about it all the time, while she was thinking about Bertie. She caught him looking at her, and already several times had managed to stop him resurrecting the subject by an impassioned look, a shake of the head, a few pleading words. But she had told him he could ask her again in the summer, and summer was passing fast. And when she could put it off no longer, and he did ask her, what would she answer? It would be better for her in the long run if she did marry him. Perhaps married to kind Ned she would gradually come out from under Bertie's spell, perhaps one day learn to think of him as just another member of the family, a cousin she was fond of. One thing she knew for sure: there was no-one other than Ned that she *could* marry, if she was never to have Bertie. To give herself to a stranger was unthinkable, but she thought that Ned would make it tolerable for her. It was foolish to hesitate, really. It would be as well to do it and get it over with. Yet, illogical though it was, accepting Ned felt like putting Bertie out of reach for ever. She wondered if *he* would mind, too. She ought not to wonder, but she did.

The summer was a hot one, day after day of bright blue skies and strong sunshine. The hay harvest was early, and the cereals were ripening fast in the fields. Bertie, when he came over, talked to her about his own fields, how it was too late to take any corn crops this year, but that he hoped to get two cuts of hay, which would help the winter feed problem.

'This year has gone so fast,' he said one day – gravely, as though the thought was not a happy one. 'Here we are in July already. Before you know it, the grouse-shooting will be starting. My father-in-law wants to take a house up on the North York moors and have a shooting-party.'

'He's very sociable, isn't he?' Jessie said politely. She didn't really want to talk about Mr Puddephat – it was too close to talking about Maud.

Perhaps Bertie didn't want to either. He said, 'Yes, he—' and then stopped and did not resume.

They were riding along the track going towards one of the top fields, to look at some youngsters. Bertie had not yet quite decided what to do with his estate. He wanted to do something with horses, but did not want to set up in competition with Morland Place. As they rode, he talked about various ideas, but without any sense of urgency, as though the Red House were a place far away and unimportant. It was too beautiful a day, Jessie thought, to think anything very vehemently. The sky was flawless, the air crystal clear, and a tiny grass-scented breeze kept the sunshine from being too hot. The horses' hoofs were almost silent on the grey-white dust of the dry path; birds were calling and bickering in the hedges, and a skylark, so high he was just a black speck, was throbbing his sweet, piercing joy against the great blue bowl of the sky. There was a scent of honeysuckle, and the hedges were tangled with wild roses, lifting their flat, pale-pink faces to the sun.

Bertie was riding his new young horse, on which he had hacked over from Bishop Winthorpe, saying that it needed lots more steady work. Kestrel had been fidgety at first, but he had calmed down and seemed to be enjoying Hotspur's company, pacing along in step, with his neck nicely flexed.

Now Bertie said, in a different kind of voice, 'It's been a strange year.'

It had, Jessie thought. When it began, Dad had still been alive, and she had not known she was in love with Bertie. Hotspur shook his head, so that the leather fringe on his browband drove away the flies from his face, and the gold discs at the corners chimed softly.

'Hotspur looks very fine in his chieftain's bridle,' Bertie said quietly. There was something in his voice that made her look round, startled, to meet an odd expression in his eyes. But before she could wonder what it meant, a pheasant rattled out of the hedge right under the horses' noses and shot across the track squawking an alarm. Hotspur snorted and jerked back his head, but Kestrel almost jumped out of his skin, and then stood up on his hind legs in protest. Bertie had not been paying attention, and for once in his life he was thrown, landing awkwardly with a sharp cry of pain.

Jessie reached out automatically and caught Kestrel's rein, and there was a snorting and stamping moment before Hotspur's calm communicated itself to the young horse and he consented to stand still.

'Are you all right?' Jessie called to Bertie, who was still sitting on the ground. Now she had attention to spare, she could hear that he was cursing steadily under his breath.

'Hurt – my ankle,' he ground out, between his teeth. 'Bent under me. Hurts – like hell.'

Jessie slithered down, slipped both sets of reins over her arm and crouched down by him. She saw now that he was sweating with pain. 'Have you broken it?' she said.

'Dunno. May have,' he said. He was white under his tan.

'You'd better get the boot off and have a look,' she said. 'Wait, I'll tie these two somewhere and help you.' Kestrel did not want to get too near his master in this unexpected posture, and was pulling her backwards. She walked the two of them a little down the track and hung their reins over suitably stout stems of hedge, and prayed that Kestrel would stand and not break them. When she got back to Bertie he had stopped cursing and his colour had come back a little, but she could see he was still in pain. She knelt before him and took hold of his boot.

'You hold the leg and I'll try and work it off.'

'No, don't,' he said. 'It'll hurt.'

'I must have a look at it. Don't be such a baby,' she said shortly.

'I can get the boot off at home.'

'Look,' she said, 'if you don't get it off now, your foot will swell and then you'll have to cut it off later. Why ruin a perfectly good pair of boots? Does it hurt a lot?' she added more kindly.

'Damnably,' he said.

'I'll be as gentle as I can,' she said. It was a horrid few minutes, and Bertie bore it stoically. When the boot was off, it was clear she had not acted a moment too soon, for the ankle and foot were already swollen. He made no protest as she rolled off his stocking to reveal the foot already blackening. 'It looks nasty,' she said. 'Let me just feel it.' She ran her hands over his flinching skin, but at the end of her examination was able to say, 'Well, I don't *think* it's broken. Can you wiggle your toes? I think it's just badly twisted.'

'I landed on top of it,' he said. 'It's going off a bit now.' He peered at it nervously. 'It's turning black.' She concealed a smile, remembering the times her father had brought her a gashed finger with the request '*You* look.' Men would bear great hardship with enormous stoicism, but sometimes just the look of a minor injury unmanned them.

'If I help you up, do you think you can hop as far as the gate up there? Then I can help you mount.'

'Of course,' he said. He held out a hand, and as she took it he winced and said, 'Seem to have twisted my wrist as well.'

'Yes, I can see it's swelling too.'

'Damn' foolish, for such a piffling fall,' he said, with a rueful smile. 'Fact is, I had my mind on other things.'

'I think you'd better ride Hotspur, and I'll take Kestrel. I don't think you'll manage him one-handed.'

She helped him up by his other hand, took his arm over her shoulder and supported him as he hopped to the gate. Then she brought up Hotspur and held him while Bertie hitched himself onto the top bar and scrambled across into the saddle. It wasn't easy, for Hotspur did not understand what was wanted of him, and kept swinging his quarters away just as Bertie was about to cross the gap. But they managed it at last, and she went back for Kestrel.

'Are you going to be able to mount on your own?' Bertie asked.

'If you walk on a bit, I can use the same gate,' she said. Fortunately she was wearing breeches and boots under a split skirt – her usual workday garb – so once she had got a foot in the stirrup she was able to swing herself up and across. Kestrel twirled round and round on the spot as she found her other stirrup, resenting the change of rider, but Bertie, watching her anxiously, saw she was not unseated by this. For himself, the horns of the sidesaddle gave him something to hold on to, to compensate for the lack of an offside stirrup. It was his right foot that was damaged, and he was glad to be allowed to let it hang loose. It was throbbing like the devil and very swollen, and he would not have wanted to try thrusting it into a stirrup. Jessie was managing Kestrel very well, and with an offhand grace that showed she did not know she was doing anything unusually skilful. Bertie was glad to have the quieter Hotspur to carry him.

At Morland Place, Henrietta rushed for water and herbs and arnica and bandages and tended him, while Alice hovered, offering hot tea, and Jessie went quietly for a more manly restorative, and brought him a glass of port from the dining-parlour sideboard. Henrietta agreed with Jessie's diagnosis that the ankle wasn't broken, but said, 'It's quite obvious you can't ride back in this condition. You'll have to stay here, at least for tonight.'

Bertie said, 'I'd love to stay at any time and for any reason, you know that, Aunty, but I have to go home. I've my bailiff coming round this evening, and the solicitor tomorrow morning.'

'You can put them off.'

'I'd rather not. If there was some way to get me a taxi-cab . . .'

'There!' said Henrietta. 'Teddy is always saying we ought to have a telephone machine fitted, and here's one time when we could have used it. But I can send someone down to the Have Another – they have the telephone there.'

'Nonsense, Mother,' said Jessie. 'A taxi-cab all that way? I can drive him home in the Renault.'

'Oh yes, of course, I was forgetting that.' She did not really like Jessie to drive, sure it was dangerous. 'But will

Bertie want to go in it with you driving? Oh dear, if only your uncle were home, or Simmons.'

'I'm as good a driver as Simmons and ten times better than Uncle Teddy,' Jessie said, 'but if Bertie doesn't trust me—'

'Of course I do,' Bertie said hastily. 'I'm sure you're an excellent driver. You do everything well.'

Jessie's prickles were laid, and in another half-hour they were on their way. Kestrel was stabled with Hotspur with the promise that someone would lead him over the next day, and Bertie, despite his protests, was virtually carried and lifted into the Renault by Sawry and John the footman. The first part of the drive, over the track, was rough and jolting and obviously tried Bertie somewhat; but once they were on the road proper, all became smooth, and they went along in companionable silence. Jessie was very conscious of his nearness, could see every line of his lounging body whether she looked at it or not – his muscular legs stretched out, his big hands resting on his thighs, his shoulder so near to hers. She could feel him like a heat all down one side of her, as though he were a roaring fire. She knew he was looking at her, and became conscious in turn of herself, of her hands on the wheel and her body braced against the vibration and her eyes on the road ahead. She felt strong and capable, skilful in her handling of the heavy machine; she felt he must admire her. She glanced sideways at him, like someone taking sips of refreshment, and every time she looked at him, he was looking at her. She felt she ought to say something, chat to him to make everything seem more ordinary; but it didn't *feel* ordinary, and she couldn't think of a thing to say. Her mouth was dry and her cheeks felt hot, and there was a tingling all over her that was nothing to do with the engine's vibration.

When they turned off the main road at the signpost for the village, she said, 'Still hurting?'

'No,' he said. 'Not much now, as long as I keep it still.'

'You probably won't be able to walk on it tomorrow.'

575

'Tomorrow? It's hard to believe in tomorrow,' he said. She didn't understand why he said it, but it perfectly reflected her mood. The afternoon was slipping towards evening now, the sunshine ripening to gold, the sky's deep blue paling to a tender milkiness. The birds were singing, but quietly as they do late in the day: blackbird and wren, greenfinch and robin, and a great tit high in a hedgerow elm crying, 'Me too, me too!' The ditches were full of flowering sweet-nettle, the smell pungent and poignant in the warm evening air, and through the hedges could be seen a glimpse of tall dry fairness, green wheat stems bleaching to blonde.

Bertie said, 'Turn left here.'

It was a narrow lane off to the side of the road that led to the village. She thought of asking him why, but then, her heart beating all over the place, did not. She slowed the car and swung it carefully into the lane.

'Just along on the left there's a gateway. Pull in there,' he said.

It was a big gate, set back from the road, and a widely splayed gateway, so that she was able to get the Renault right off the road. She put on the brake, and turned off the engine, and as it jolted into silence, the birdsong came rushing into the space left like a clear, cool torrent. Now she did not dare look at him. Her heart was beating so fast she could hardly catch her breath, and she was so conscious of his nearness her skin seemed all nerve-endings. Over the gate was a view across the cornfield to a hedge, with a pasture and a little wood beyond; a lark was still up in the transparent sky somewhere nearby, and in the middle of the field was a clump of tall elms in which a rook colony was gathering for the evening's conversation.

'A conversation of rooks,' she said. 'That would be a good collective noun.' He didn't speak, and she said, in a voice that only just didn't sound natural, 'It's a nice view. Thank you for showing it to me.'

'Jessie,' he said.

'Yes?'

'Jessie, look at me.'

She had to pull her head round against what felt like rusty hinges, because she knew if she looked at him she was undone. He was gazing at her, and seemed to be breathing too quickly, as though he had been hurrying. Every part of her tingled, and she felt his eyes on her face as though they were a physical touch, on her eyes, on her lips, on every part of her.

'You know what's happened, don't you?' he said, his voice different from any he had ever used to her, and she knew she would never forget the sound of it, never forget through the desert of time to come – why was she thinking that? She couldn't speak. She couldn't take her eyes from him.

'I've fallen in love with you,' he said.

The words hit her like a jolt of electricity. 'Bertie, no. You mustn't,' she said, her voice only a husk; but everything inside her was singing, throbbing with joy like the lark.

'I can't help it,' he said. 'I think I must have been a little bit in love with you all along, only I didn't realise it until – well, it was at Christmas it suddenly struck me, at the Boxing Day hunt. It was as though I'd never seen you before. I've fought against it, I've tried not to love you, I've really tried, but I can't help it. You're so lovely . . .'

She was staring into his eyes, almost straining to hear his words, though he was so close, only a breath from her. 'Oh, Bertie!' Her lips moved only, she made no sound.

And then he was kissing her. It seemed, the moment it happened, as if it had been inevitable, as if everything in her life had been gathering to this one point. As his lips touched hers everything inside her seemed to swoon; she felt blown to pieces by a great, painless explosion. *Bertie*, her mind said, in faint, stunned ecstasy.

They kissed and kissed. His right hand was round the back of her neck, and she loved the touch of it with a fierceness that surprised her. She wanted more, more kisses, more of him, wanted that thing she had the instinct for but no knowledge of: her body yearned and ached towards him, and she knew, without knowing how she knew, that he wanted the same thing. She seemed to become boneless in his arms. Her head was on his shoulder now, he was hanging over her, kissing her with a wildness that thrilled her, and she wanted to lie down under him – it seemed natural that he should be over her, as if this were the right, the only proper way to kiss.

Then in his passion he made an unguarded movement and she felt it hurt him, and instantly the wonderful madness ebbed, and he began to withdraw from her, and she from him. Their lips parted, she moved back, sat up. His eyes were very bright, his hair was tousled, and at the sight of it she remembered she had done that, that her fingers had an exact memory of the feeling of his hair and the shape of his skull under it.

He tried to smile. 'My damned foot. I knocked it against something.' He drew a long, shuddering breath. 'Just as well, perhaps. I was on the verge of losing control.'

She didn't know what to say. Her lips rehearsed soundlessly, but all that was in her mind was *I love you, I love you, I love you,* and it did not seem right to say that.

He said, 'Are you shocked? Did I shock you? Oh, Jess, I'm sorry, I shouldn't have done that, but I thought – I felt—' Another shaky breath, and then, with a twisted smile, 'For God's sake say *something*. I'm drowning here. Tell me I'm a beast and a cad, or—'

'Or what?' Yes, that was her voice: it had spoken at last.

'Or tell me that I wasn't mistaken,' he said, almost humbly.

'You weren't mistaken,' she said.

'Oh, God, Jess. Oh, God. Darling, will you – will you say it? I want to hear you say it.'

'I love you,' she said, and there was a release in the words. There seemed to be something loosened inside her, a gushing like pent-up water. She was loose and wet, boneless again, wanting him so much she felt she might faint away, from the effort of it. 'I love you, Bertie. I love you.' She couldn't stop saying it now; wanted to go on saying it. 'I love you. I love you.'

He gave a shaky laugh, and took her in his arms again (carefully with his right hand, the hurt one) and kissed her, her lips but then her face, her eyes, her throat. She felt the passion mount again between them, and now she wanted all of him, and wanted it so much she did not care about anything, had no fear or shame, would have lain down there and then with him if she died for it the next minute.

There was a sharp bark somewhere nearby, and Bertie pulled back from her again. She was so out of herself that for a moment she couldn't see; then she heard a pattering sound, and as she sat up straight again, saw sheep coming down the lane, coming into sight round the bend, a dozen ewes pattering along, the leaders' heads going up as they saw the car. A black and white sheepdog was running about behind and alongside them, keeping them close together; and last of all round the bend came the shepherd, an old man in shapeless brown clothes and a cap pulled low over his eyes against the westering sun, walking in measured strides with his crook in his hand.

The sheep jostled, unwilling to pass the car but pressed by the dog. Bertie, wonderfully composed, called out, 'Is the bus in your way?'

'No, maister, thank'ee. We can manage,' the old man said. He uttered a sharp command to the dog. The sheep teetered on the spot, and then the leader took courage and dashed forward, keeping well to the other side of the lane, and the others followed in a bunch as though they were stuck together. Jessie looked down and saw their strange yellow eyes turning up at her from their dark faces, saw their jouncing woolly backs pass below, saw the sharp, foxy muzzle and quick glance of the dog, the steady, uncaring pace of the man, who touched his cap to them but did not move his eyes from the distant horizon. 'Get by, dog!' he said sharply, and gave a whistle. And then the pattering faded and they were gone, turning into the village road.

'There's another collective noun for you,' Bertie's voice said. 'An interruption of sheep.'

Slowly she turned her head back to him. The air was cooler now, the sun having gone lower, and their passion had passed, too – not faded, but gone back into its lair. He looked at her, troubled. 'I shouldn't have done that. I shouldn't have told you.'

'It was my fault too,' she said. All the hopelessness of the situation was in her look. 'Oh, Bertie!'

'I know.'

'We can't do this. We mustn't. It's wrong.'

'Yes, it is.'

'You're a married man.' She felt her eyes burn with tears, and lowered her head. He put out his hand to take hers and she pretended not to see it, kept hers out of its way.

'I know,' he said again. 'Do you think I don't know that? Oh, God, it's a damnable situation! What are we to do?'

'I can't stop loving you,' she said, in a small voice. 'I know it's wrong but I can't stop. But we must never – do this again.'

'No, you're right. We must keep it a secret, and then no-one will be hurt. But – Jess?'

Now she looked at him. She couldn't help it. Love surged up again, and she wanted to be kissing him, wanted it so badly. 'Yes?' she managed to say.

'I can see you? I must see you – just that. Come over, the way I have been doing. If I can't see you, I don't think I can go on.'

She said carefully, 'It would look very odd if you *stopped* coming over. After all—' She waved her hand, incapable of expressing all the ways in which their lives were interconnected.

'Yes, you're right.'

'But – can we manage just to be ordinary?'

'We'll have to,' he said. 'We'll just have to. But, oh my darling—'

'You'll have to stop calling me that,' she said shakily. 'I love it, I love you to call me darling, but you mustn't, or I can't be ordinary. You mustn't say it again. It's wrong. We can't do wrong things, or I won't be able to see you at all. I'll have to go away.'

'No, you mustn't do that,' he said quickly. 'I have to see you. I won't do or say anything, I promise – not after this. Let me just say goodbye to you, my love, and then I'll be Cousin Bertie again.'

She nodded, and he reached out his hand, very gently, and stroked her face, a touch so loving it almost broke her heart. He gazed at her a long time, and then leaned forward to touch his lips very gently to her mouth, and then her brow. She closed her eyes and tears squeezed out past her lashes. She felt his breath stir her hair. And then his touch was gone.

Without looking at him, she started the motor again, took off the brake, and turned the car with some difficulty across the narrow lane. They drove in silence down the road into the village, along the village street, and into the gravelled drive of the Red House. 'I won't come in, if you don't mind,' she said. 'I had better be getting back – Mother worries. You can manage all right now, can't you?'

'With a houseful of servants? Of course.' He opened the door and began to climb down.

'Take care of your poor foot and hand. Someone will bring Kestrel over tomorrow.'

Behind him the door had opened and his butler stood there, hovering, wondering what was wanted of him. Bertie looked up, a flash of blue in his summer-brown face. 'You could bring him yourself,' he said.

Her heart jumped at the thought of seeing him again so soon. But, 'I'd better not,' she said.

'No-one would think anything of it,' he said. And then,

very low, 'Just to *see* you. I promise that's all.'

'I'd better not,' she said again. But as she drove away – her heart singing like the skylark because he loved her, he loved her! – she knew that she would come, whatever she said. And she knew he knew it, too.

The Parliament Bill went up to the Lords on the 23rd of May 1911. Consensus had largely been reached at the conference the year before. Reform of the Lords had been under discussion for many years, as the logical consequence of the increased franchise of 1885, and most peers accepted that, sooner or later, there must be some adjustment of power between the houses. It might have hung fire for longer, but in recent years the Lords had taken to routinely rejecting all sorts of Liberal Bills on relatively trivial subjects, and to be so thwarting a popular government with a large majority was tempting reprisals.

'It's our own fault,' Overton said. 'We overstepped the mark by rejecting the Budget.'

'You said it was an iniquitous piece of legislation and nothing more than class warfare,' Venetia reminded him.

'So it was. But was it worth dying for? If we lose our veto altogether, it will be worse than having let the Finance Bill go through on the nod.'

'Will you lose it?'

'It's only a matter of time now, since the King has given his word to flood the House with new peers.'

The three main measures of the Parliament Bill were that 'Money Bills' should not be capable of veto by the Lords, with the decision left in the hands of the Speaker whether any particular Bill came under that heading; that any other Bill passed by the Commons in three successive sessions and rejected by the Lords should nevertheless become law two years after its introduction; and that the maximum duration of a parliament should be reduced from seven to five years.

At the conference, the Lords had agreed to give up the veto on Money Bills, provided nothing extra was 'tacked

582

on' to them, but wanted the decision as to what was a qualifying Bill to be taken by a joint committee of the two Houses, rather than the Speaker. They had agreed on the reduction of a parliament's span.

It was on the second point that there was difficulty. The Lords wanted to except from the automatic passing rule any Bill that was of a constitutional nature, and have it put instead to a referendum. The Liberal government had been willing to allow an exception for Bills concerning the succession, but would go no further. The unspoken issue in either case was Irish Home Rule, which the Liberals were determined to get through, and which the Lords were determined to block.

'It is fantastic,' Overton said gloomily, 'that the future of the Constitution should come down to this one question. Far more important matters are at stake. If the House of Lords loses the veto, it will mean a virtual dictatorship of the Commons.'

'But the Commons expresses the will of the people,' Venetia began.

'Does it?' Overton said, raising his eyebrows.

'Well, of course, it doesn't represent womankind,' she amended hastily.

'Nor even all of mankind. The electorate now stands at between a quarter and a third of the population – not even a majority. And how many of them really understand what they are voting for? They are swayed by plausible rogues and popular agitation and the hope of short-term gain. Only we – the Lords – have the long view. We were the guardians of the country, before even there were kings. Who takes more care of a thing, the man who owns it or the man who merely borrows it?'

'So you wouldn't have the Commons at all?' Venetia asked.

'Of course I would. There must be checks and balances. The Commons was created as a check on the power of the Lords, and that was right and good. Then we became a check on their power, which was tolerable. But now

583

even that is under threat, and the whole structure of society is cracking. It will all be change, change, and the tyranny of the new. You can get a fool to vote for anything, even his own enslavement, if you tell him it's a new idea.'

Venetia privately thought Overton's views were rather overheated, for as a woman and a doctor she could not help feeling that life went on despite anything that men might talk about in Parliament. But she had to admit that it was hard to take the overview when your head was down, concentrating on the day-to-day of ordinary life. It was clear that to the male part of creation the constitutional crisis was of the gravest importance, and that in the long term very serious consequences to the whole of society were implied.

She met her old friend Lord Lansdowne, the leader of the Lords, at dinner one evening during the Coronation truce, and he told her that he knew the game was up, and that it was only a matter of time before they would be forced to accept the Parliament Bill. His plan was to delay the moment as long as possible in the hope of winning over the core of 'diehard' opponents, or perhaps of exhausting them into surrender. For this reason he and his adherents debated the Bill at length and passed a long list of amendments in committee stage, sending the Bill back to the Commons in July transformed.

But time did not soften the diehards. They coalesced into a fiercely determined 'no surrender' group, led by young Lord Willoughby de Broke, a well-known neck-or-nothing rider in the hunting field. In the Commons, meanwhile, the Government had no intention of allowing the Bill to be rejected or emasculated when they had fought two general elections for it and were sitting on a majority of 121.

On the 20th of July Lloyd George saw Lansdowne and Balfour privately to tell them about the King's pledge – which, amazingly, had been kept secret since November, despite the notorious indiscretion of Liberal ministers. (It was said that you should never tell a Liberal minister anything because he always told his wife – except for Asquith, who told other people's wives.) Balfour, who dined out everywhere, only heard of it a few days before he was told officially.

So on the Friday the 21st of July, Lansdowne called a meeting at his house of two hundred Unionist peers. He read out to them a letter from Asquith about his intention to reject the amendments, and to call on the King to honour his pledge. The reaction was violent. The peers were furious that the royal prerogative was being harnessed to party-political benefit, and that the King was being blackmailed into humiliating himself and the Crown in the eyes of foreign potentates by giving peerages to five hundred unknowns selected by a lawyer.

Lansdowne urged the Unionists, in the face of this threat, to follow his example and abstain from voting. It would no longer be possible to offer effectual resistance, and to persist would render the Upper House ridiculous and destroy for ever what power and prestige might remain to it. Lord Curzon and others supported him, but the 'no surrender' group said they would rather 'die in the last ditch'. A newspaper the next day dubbed them the 'ditchers', and called Lansdowne's following the 'hedgers'.

On Monday the 24th Asquith rose in the House to announce that if the Upper House did not pass the Bill in its original form, the creation of new peers would be demanded forthwith. The ditchers had a band of ardent followers in the Commons, and Asquith was howled down with such fury, and such scenes of disorder ensued, that the Speaker felt obliged to adjourn the House.

Campaigning in the Lords began, trying to win over the undecided and change the minds of the decided. Feeling on both sides was bitter, apprehension was acute, and the ditchers' language was violent, speaking of a 'revolution, nurtured in lies, promoted by fraud'. The Prime Minister, they said, had tricked the opposition, entrapped the Crown, and deceived the people. The government's action in forcing a promise from the King was a 'gross violation of Constitutional liberty'.

Overton was doing his best to persuade Unionist peers to abstain, promoting it as the only honourable compromise. Much as he hated the situation, he agreed with Lansdowne: to vote for the Bill was unthinkable; to vote against would risk destroying the Upper House entirely, with the gravest consequences for liberty. He called on his son-in-law, Lord Holkam, almost as a matter of courtesy, taking it for granted he was in the Lansdowne camp, and was shocked at his reception. Holkam, cold and angry, expressed astonished disgust that Overton could think of abstaining on such an issue.

'To be giving in to this most base and paltry of attempts at blackmail? To be handing over the veto without the vestige of a fight? I hesitate to use the word cowardice—'

'I hope you continue to hesitate,' Overton said, more surprised than angry. 'What can you be thinking of? I am your father-in-law.'

'I owe you respect on that account, but there are some things that are too important to be suppressed by mere form. This Bill is an abomination, a violation of principle, of decency, of freedom!'

'I agree with you, it is. Did you think for a moment that I like it?'

'I am forced to wonder, sir, when you talk of compromise. To allow the Bill to pass is to surrender our birthright and betray our heritage and our children. It will be the end of everything we hold dear. Good God, sir, you must know that! Today the House of Lords, tomorrow the Crown! We will be overrun with bloody revolution. It will mean the destruction of society, the end of England herself! Honest men will be slaughtered in the streets by fanatics preaching socialism and atheism and every vile creed of slavery and oppression.'

Overton was taken aback at his vehemence. He had thought all these things himself in his darkest moments, but would not have dreamed of expressing them in these terms to Holkam. But of course, Holkam was young, and level-headedness is an old man's trait. At Holkam's age, he might well have said the same sort of things – though not to *his* father-in-law, the terrifying Duke of Southport!

'I'm not asking you to vote for the Bill,' he said, trying for an even tone, 'but simply to abstain.'

'So that the Bill will go through! That is the purpose of your abstention.'

'Yes, but—'

'It is a distinction without a difference to me, sir,' Holkam said angrily. 'I will not consent to the Bill by any means.'

'You don't understand: Asquith has the King's promise to force the Bill through if necessary. Do you want to see the House made ridiculous, to have the chamber polluted with hundreds of inferior men made up solely to take the Liberal whip?'

'It could never happen,' said Holkam. 'The King would not do it. He would not betray us or himself in that manner.'

'I assure you, he will do it – reluctantly, I grant you, but he will do it. He has promised and will keep his word.'

'*If* he gave his promise, it was under duress – but I am not convinced that he did. I don't trust Asquith and his cabinet: they would say anything to get their own way. But in any case, the King will not do this appalling thing. If we stand fast, the government will back down, as all bullies do when you stand up to them.'

'How can I convince you?' Overton said despairingly. 'Consider, I move in Court circles, I am on close terms with the King's secretaries. I *know* whereof I speak. I must beg you to abstain when the moment comes.'

'And I must demand that you vote against the Bill, as every man of honour must do,' said Holkam. 'This is not a matter for compromise. Consider my wife and your grandchildren, if you have no care for yourself or for me. You must vote against. You must join us!'

'I can't. For God's sake, Holkam, you must see—'

'I see that my father-in-law has no care for what happens to me or my sons or my sons' sons,' Holkam said harshly. 'I should have known what manner of a man you were.'

Overton stared. 'What do you mean by that?'

'Your views were known to me long ago. My father told me that you were a supporter of the female suffrage – and indeed, you betrayed yourself when you chose for a wife someone who had so outraged her sex—'

'Be silent, sir! This I cannot allow. If this were fifty years ago I would have called you out for such words.'

'You cannot regret any more than I do the difference in our opinions,' said Holkam. 'But the situation is what it is. I suggest we end this painful conversation.'

Overton returned home seething. He tried to moderate his account of what had been said when he told Venetia, but it alarmed her all the same. The thought of her daughter's being married to someone who was a political enemy, who disliked and despised his wife's family and interest was horrible. It might lead to a split, an estrangement, and she could not bear the thought of it. But perhaps it would all blow over. Men spoke hotly on these occasions, but when the situation was resolved they would forget it all and be friends again – wouldn't they?

The summer had been the hottest ever recorded, and on the 9th of August, when the two-day debate in the Lords opened, the temperature measured at Greenwich Observatory touched 100°. The ditchers were still clinging to the obstinate belief that the government was bluffing and that the King would refuse to create peers, no matter how Lord Curzon and others tried to persuade them otherwise. The 10th of August was even hotter, and damp and sultry into the bargain, and matters were not helped inside the Chamber by the unprecedented number of peers who were packing the benches. Through the stifling evening the debate continued, as one peer after another rose to state his side of the argument yet again. Lord Curzon and the Archbishop of Canterbury made powerful speeches for accepting the Bill; the eighty-seven-year-old Lord Halsbury and young Lord Holkam were eloquent for rejection. The result remained in doubt: so far about three hundred Unionist peers had agreed to abstain, but there were a hundred ditchers determined to vote against, and as the Liberal peers only numbered eighty, disaster seemed inevitable.

Overton, like others on the hedgers' side, had done his best right up to the last, going round anyone he thought might waver and trying to persuade him to abstain. During the evening the former prime minister Lord Rosebery, an old friend, met him in the corridor on the way back into the chamber and said, 'I've decided to vote with the government. I dislike Asquith and all his ways, and this is a vile situation, but the alternative is worse. Can't have the Crown humiliated and the King put on the rack. Tell Curzon, will you, there's a good fellow?'

'I will. And thank you,' said Overton. Rosebery gave him a nod, and returned to his seat.

The division began in an atmosphere of strained excitement, and though voices were kept low, the vehemence of the conversations still going on could not be doubted from the expressions on the noble lords' faces. Overton was determined until the last moment to abstain, but when he saw Lord Rosebery going into the government lobby, and thought of the King, who had asked him to carry his spurs at the Coronation, not to mention King Edward, whom Overton had served and loved, he felt guilty. Then when he saw his son-in-law stalking into the other lobby, with a glare around him as if daring anyone to neglect his example, Overton's choler rose. It was abominably hot, his collar was chafing him, his nose felt as though it had been stuffed with cotton wool, his feet were swollen, and his country was in danger. It was a situation in which there was no winning, but there were bad and worse ways of losing. Before he had a chance to talk himself out of it, he stood up and followed Rosebery into the government lobby.

It was not until 10.40 p.m. that the tellers came out to announce the final figures. The government had won by a majority of seventeen votes. The news was greeted by a moan from the ditchers, and in a rather stunned silence by the hedgers. The Liberal peers congratulated each other quietly, and a buzz of conversation broke out all round as everyone speculated on how the vote had gone and names were passed from person to person. There was little feeling of triumph, even for those who had won the day. The overall sensation was one of relief that it was over, and a vague apprehension about what was to come next.

Lansdowne came over to Overton and shook his hand. 'Thank God,' he said; and then, curiously, 'Why did you do it?'

Overton shook his head, too tired to go into explanations.

Curzon joined them, having been talking to the tellers. 'Cantuar swung the day,' he said. 'Took twelve of his episcopal brethren through the government lobby. And Rosebery took a number of Unionists with him.'

'Yes. He took Beauty, here, for one,' said Lansdowne.

Curzon raised his eyebrows. 'Is that right, Overton? I didn't see. Damme, that was brave of you.'

'I did it for the sake of the Crown and the country,' Overton said wearily. 'No doubt there will be those who revile me, but if the vote had gone the other way . . .'

'Doesn't bear thinking about,' Curzon said, shaking his head. 'Asquith had a list all ready, you know – Morley told me. Two hundred and forty-five men all ready to be shovelled into the ermine. Poets and playwrights and bankers and grocers. Ghastly! He was going to put up Sir George Lewis, dammit!' Lewis was the Society solicitor who had handled the eminent and scandalous cases of the rich and titled for years. 'Knows more shocking secrets than a Catholic confessor. Imagine sitting next to him! Damned uncomfortable.'

One of the ditchers walked past at that moment, glared

at the group, and then, seeing Overton, hissed, 'Betrayer! You have made yourself Redmond's helot, sir!'

Overton blinked, but said nothing. The angry lord walked on, and he said quietly, 'I had to do it, or it would have been the end of us. I have a son . . .'

'We all have sons,' said Lansdowne. 'Well, I must go and find my secretary. The King will be pleased, anyway. He ought to know by now.'

Curzon smiled. 'That's right. Old Bigge denied himself the excitement of the chamber to stay by the telephone room all evening. He'll have rung up the palace right away.' Sir Arthur Bigge had been created Lord Stamfordham in the Coronation Honours, but his old name came more easily to the tongue still.

'I must be off,' said Lansdowne. 'Are you coming, Curzon? My respects to Venetia, Overton.'

They left him. In a moment Lord Rosebery passed him, and paused to touch his shoulder lightly. 'You did a brave thing,' he said. 'Can't have been easy, but there are plenty here who will thank you.'

'Plenty who won't,' Overton observed.

'Never mind. Can't take account of the opinion of fools. Your father-in-law would have been proud of you, I think,' he added, and went on his way.

The chamber was emptying, except for close-knit groups of mutterers here and there. Overton was tired and wanted his bed. He headed for the door, but before he got there he was buttonholed again, this time by Lord Holkam.

'I find it hard to believe,' he said, staring down at Overton with glinting eyes, 'that you did what you did. You have betrayed us all, sir. You have taken the most ignoble part. I am ashamed to be associated with you.'

'You had better guard your tongue, sir,' Overton said wearily. 'Speaking in the heat of the moment you may say things you will regret later. Consider our relationship. It is not fitting—'

'No, sir, it is not,' Holkam interrupted. 'I had some

doubts from the beginning about allying myself with a family of such irregular habits, and I can tell you now that my father was very much against the match, and only gave his consent on my insistence. He has been proved right in the event, though I think even he would have been surprised by this day's events.'

'No more,' Overton said shortly. 'You have said enough. I shall try to forget all this tomorrow.'

'That you will not do,' Holkam said. 'The consequences of this day's action will haunt you for the rest of your life. I hope your grandson is not required to pay the price of your betrayal. We are strangers from this moment, sir. I hereby end all intercourse between my family and yours. But I assure you,' he added, with dignity, as Overton opened his mouth to bark in exasperation, 'that I shall never hold any grudge against your daughter on this account.' And he walked away.

Afterwards, telling Venetia about it, Overton wondered that he had been so tongue-tied and had not defended himself more.

'But you were tired,' she excused him. 'And unlike that fool of a son-in-law of ours, you did not want to start a family feud. Oh, Beauty, what will happen now?'

'In the Lords, do you mean, or in our family?'

'In our family, of course,' said Venetia. 'Poor Violet, caught between us! He won't stop her seeing us, will he?'

'I think he means to,' Overton said miserably. 'Oh, this is a bad business! But what else could I have done?'

'You followed your conscience. I'm sure Papa would have done the same in your shoes.'

'That's more or less what Rosebery said. Oh, Venetia, let's go to bed. I'm tired to death. I must sleep.'

'If you can sleep in this awful heat,' Venetia said. 'Well, at least now it's all over we can go down to the country. London is impossible in August. I always said so.'

Violet listened in blank incomprehension to Holkam's exposition. She did not read newspapers and regarded politics as something that only interested men, so she had no idea what the debate had been all about. She did not understand what the constitutional crisis was, who had won what, or what the consequences might be. What she did grasp quite clearly was that Holkam and her father had been on opposite sides, that Holkam had lost, and that he was very angry about it and blamed her father.

As he paced about the room, pouring out a flood of hot words like Mount Etna erupting, her eyes followed him up and down. She was afraid of him – not physically, for she had never been struck in her life, and was unaware that such a thing was a possibility – but as a gentle and unassertive person is of a stronger personality. At last, into a pause, she inserted the words, shyly, 'I'm sure Papa didn't mean—'

Holkam rounded on her. 'Of course he did! Good God, haven't you understood *anything*? I told you, he did not abstain, which would have been bad enough, he voted *for* the Bill.'

'I'm sorry,' Violet said in a voice that trembled. 'I don't understand politics.'

Her words seemed to calm him a little. 'No, of course not. Nor should you,' he said, with a more approving look. 'Politics is a man's business. Thank God you are a proper, womanly woman, and not one of these vile feminists. I was right *there*, at least. I told my father you were not like your mother. He hardly believed me, but I'm proved to have judged you correctly.'

Violet frowned, trying to untangle the ideas. She gathered that there was a criticism of her mother implied. 'But my mother is a good person. She does wonderful work, and helps the poor and neglected. She's a fine doctor.'

'Exactly so,' he said triumphantly. 'She has no business being a doctor. For a female to visit sick tenants or poor villagers is one thing, but to be doing a man's work, especially of such a coarsening nature, is past comprehension.'

'I don't understand, I don't understand,' cried poor Violet.

'Of course you don't, and that is entirely to your credit,' said Holkam. 'But you must be guided by me now, and accept what I tell you. Will you do that?'

'Of course, but—'

'No "buts", please. You must believe what I say when I tell you that your father has betrayed us all – you included – and that your mother is a disgrace to her sex. From now on there can be no more intercourse between our two families.'

'But they *are* my family,' she said, bewildered.

'Not any more. I am your family now. You are my wife. You are not a child, to be running to Mummy and Daddy every minute. You must grow up, Violet. You are a wife and mother, you are Countess of Holkam. My interest is yours, and there can be no other. Your loyalty must be to me.'

'Oh, but it is! I mean, of course I am loyal to you, but I love Mama and Papa. You can't ask me not to.'

'I am not concerned with your feelings, but with your actions. I have told Lord Overton that all communication is at an end between us, and I expect you to abide by that.'

'Not see them any more?' Tears rose in Violet's eyes at the thought. 'Mama and Papa? And the boys?'

Holkam grew impatient. 'For God's sake, are you on my side or not? Are you my wife or their daughter? You can't be both.'

Violet thought that, on the contrary, she couldn't help being both; but she understood that he was asking her to choose – or, rather, demanding that she choose him. And what else could she do? She was his wife, mother of his children. She belonged to him now, and nothing could change that. She had married him of her own free will, and in so doing had chosen what side her loyalty must fall – though she could never have anticipated that such a rift would occur.

'I'm your wife,' she said, in a low voice, trying not to let the tears overpower her. 'What must I do?'

'Be guided by me. They will not come to any of our houses, nor will we go to theirs. We will not accept invitations if they will be present. There will be no communication between us.'

Violet couldn't help it. The tears rolled over her eyelids and shone on her cheeks, as she bowed her head and held her lower lip in her teeth in the effort not to sob. Holkam was moved by the sight. He felt a thrill of power over her. He spoke more gently. 'Birds outgrow the nest and all girls have to leave their parents sooner or later. You know that, or if you don't you should. And your mother has been a thoroughly bad influence. It is to your credit, my dear, that you have resisted it so successfully.' He laid a hand on her shoulder, and then brought out his handkerchief and pushed it into her hand. 'Stop crying now. Dry your face. We shall be going down to the country tomorrow in any case. You will like to see the children again, won't you?'

She nodded, and drew a little hitching breath. She longed to get back to her babies. Suddenly Brancaster Hall seemed the most inviting place on earth.

'And then we've a summer of engagements ahead of us,' he said. 'Grouse-shooting, house parties. The Palgraves have invited us on their yacht in September. The Dungarvons have asked us to Locheish for the shooting. And Willoughby de Broke mentioned something about a hunting party in Leicestershire. There's no harm in encouraging that connection, even if we don't hunt. My dear, you won't have time to miss your former family.'

That night he came to her bed for the first time in almost a year, and made love to her with an enthusiasm that was almost violent. He did not leave her until dawn, and during that time she hardly slept. Sibsey woke her at half past nine with her morning tea and the excitement of having heard the news that they were to go down to the country that day. Violet sat up, and in moving found that she was quite sore *down there*. The memory of the night before came flooding back to her, the horrible embargo on her mother and father, and then the long uxorial passion, and they were in some way entangled in her mind, the one depending on the other. It was as if he had removed her physically from her parents' camp to his. She was Holkam's wife, that was certain – and from his visit to her bed she assumed he meant her to have another baby. Indeed, she thought with a tremor of excitement, she might be pregnant already, *this very minute*! And later today she would see her dear babies. She suddenly felt full of energy.

She did not give up her parents in her mind, only put them away carefully and tried not to think of them. She had a family of her own now. In any case, men were full of inexplicable moods, and as she did not understand why he had taken against Mama and Papa, she believed that he might just as easily change his mind in the future and accept them back. All she had to do was to keep her counsel and bide her time.

Chapter Nineteen

For a few weeks, Jessie retreated into what she thought of afterwards as her fool's paradise. Bertie came to Morland Place as before – perhaps a little more often – and they kept their word: they behaved normally, even when they were alone together. No special words passed between them; they were careful to act like nothing more than friends and cousins – in fact, they were probably more formal with each other than at any time in their lives. But there was no force on earth that could have stopped them looking at each other, and when their eyes met, a world of messages passed between them. To know that he loved her was the greatest joy of her life, and for those few weeks she refused to look at the accompanying shadow: that the same joy would bring her an equivalent sorrow.

For now, she was glad just to be near him. Once, when they were inspecting a horse in a loose-box, his hand touched hers resting on the animal's withers, and though neither of them moved to break the contact, she did not know whether it was accidental or not. She lived for such moments, for when they brushed past each other in a doorway, or he helped her off her horse, or she brought him a glass of wine as he sat chatting to Henrietta in the drawing-room. But she did not try to engineer them. As she had said to herself before that her love hurt no-one as long as no-one knew, now she told herself that as long as they *did* nothing wrong, their thoughts could hurt no-one.

Yet even as she comforted herself thus, there was a part of her that knew it was a delusion. Asleep, she dreamed of him, and in her dreams she ached with longing as she did in waking life, and he was always going away from her, calling to her but just out of reach. Her dreams were of sadness and loss, and she woke from them sometimes with tears on her cheeks. She saw sometimes from his shadowed eyes that he dreamed, too. She did not know how they could go on like this, but every day she prayed silently that it would last just a little longer. It was all she could hope for.

Then August came, and Maud and her father came down to Yorkshire. For almost a week Bertie did not appear at Morland Place, and Jessie pretended cheerfulness and sang about her work, while inside she drooped, sick with longing, and sometimes rode off to be alone so that she could weep in private against Hotspur's accommodating neck. Then all three of them made a formal call.

Maud excused herself to Henrietta for not having come before on the grounds that she had returned to Bishop Winthorpe with a summer cold. 'Of all ridiculous things – in this hot weather!'

'Summer colds are the most tiresome,' Henrietta said. 'Alice had one a fortnight ago – didn't you, Alice?'

Across the room Teddy, Bertie and Richard Puddephat were deep in man's talk. Jessie was stuck here on the distaff side with her mother, Ethel and Aunt Alice to entertain Maud. She stared at Maud because her eyes longed to go to Bertie and it was the only way she could stop them. Maud looked beautiful and content – happy, even. Jessie's thoughts were poisoning her, so that she felt physically sick. This was Maud, whom she had known since she was a little girl; practically one of the family; nice Maud, good Maud. She liked her, and, oh, little bits of her hated her, and she couldn't bear it! Lucky Maud was married to Bertie. Had he kissed her this morning? Was she looking so happy because he had been particularly nice to her? Yet she could not want him *not* to be nice to Maud. There was nothing she could think about the situation that did not make her feel bad.

At the end of the visit they all stood up and now she could not help looking at Bertie. His eyes leaped to hers on the instant, and the flash between them was as fast and all-consuming as wildfire. I love you, she thought despairingly. She could not make herself look away, and it was well that Uncle Teddy moved between them just then, cutting the connection. She made herself listen to what Maud was saying. It seemed that Mr Puddephat was indeed taking a house for the grouse-shooting, up on the moors above Hawnby. They were taking it for the whole of August, and were going to play host to a succession of friends.

'I haven't seen it myself,' Maud was saying, 'but Father says it's a very large place, with stables and kennels attached. Rather isolated, but we shall take a full household with us, so we shall be comfortable.'

'What's the house called?' Teddy asked.

'It has a rather funny name,' Maud said. 'Crow's Nest Castle.'

'Oh, I know it,' Teddy said. 'I've seen it in a book somewhere. It isn't really a castle, just a large house with crenellations round the roof. Twenty bedrooms, if I don't mistake.'

'We hope to be able to invite all of you during the month,' Puddephat said.

There was a flurry of movement and goodbyes. Bertie was there before her, his eyes holding hers for a second, before he stooped to touch his lips to her cheek. Then he moved on and was kissing Henrietta. 'You will come, won't you?' he said, and Jessie knew the words were for her.

After they had gone, Henrietta said that it seemed rather a waste for the Parkes to be hiring a house so near when they had one already.

'Maudie's enjoying playing the hostess,' Teddy said

indulgently. 'And, of course, if you want to shoot grouse you have to go where the grouse are. They couldn't shoot on Hawnby Moor and go home at night, you know. It's further than you think. It must be ten miles or so above Helmsley – and on bad road – and Helmsley's twenty miles away.'

'Oh,' said Henrietta; and then, 'Well, I suppose we must go if they ask, but shooting parties are really for men. I don't know what we women would do.'

'There will be lovely walks up there,' Teddy said. 'And wonderful views. And Jessie could take a gun out – you're a very decent shot, Jess, better than some men I know.'

Jessie answered him – she never knew what she said – and then made an excuse and hurried from the room. She needed privacy to gain command of her face and voice. She didn't want to go and stay with Maud and Bertie. She was afraid of what she might feel. Behind her she heard her mother say, 'I wonder who else they will ask. Maud is getting very smart, isn't she? She really did look the baronet's wife.'

So Bertie disappeared temporarily from Jessie's life. Teddy and Alice were asked for the weekend of the Glorious Twelfth, to which all the wealthiest and most important of Puddephat connections were invited. The fine weather continued, and they returned with Teddy talking about good sport, and Alice quite animated by the change of scene and company. She had been most impressed by the conservatory at the back of the house, a bower of ferns and tropical greenery. 'Like being out of doors *indoors*, if you understand me. Maud was talking of having one built at the Red House. What a pity we can't have one here.'

'You'd have to fill in the moat,' Henrietta said, meaning it was an impossibility. But Alice talked for some time about how much it would cost to do that, and whether you would have to knock down some outer walls as well.

Later in the month they were invited again, this time with Henrietta and Jessie too. Henrietta accepted dutifully, but Jessie pleaded off, saying she had too much to do.

'You must have some pleasures, darling,' Henrietta said. 'It isn't natural for a girl your age to be working so hard all the time.'

'But I like doing what I do,' she said, 'and I shouldn't like to go to a shooting party. I wouldn't know anyone there. And I've got Pulcinella to school. I was meaning to work really hard on her for the next few days to get her ready. Mrs Raynham wants to cub-hunt on her, and she'll need her for a few weeks beforehand so as to get used to her.'

'Well, if you insist, I'll make your excuses,' Henrietta said. 'I rather wish I could make mine,' she added, 'but it would be too hard on poor Maud for everyone to cry off.'

'I'm sure "poor Maud" has no difficulty in filling her house,' Jessie said. 'If she had, we would all have been asked, and a lot sooner.'

She was afraid that she had sounded rather sharp, but Henrietta didn't seem to notice. When she came back from her visit, she told Jessie that she was sure she'd have enjoyed it, because the country was wonderful, and she'd have been able to go out for long walks. 'And the company was very nice – quite a few young people. Really, I ought to insist on your going if there are any more invitations like that. You must get about more. Papa's been gone six months now, and he wouldn't want you to mourn for ever and become an old maid.'

Maud sent a formal note to Henrietta when they gave up the house to say they were back at the Red House, but she did not call; and a few days later a note came to say that they were all going over to Ireland to stay with friends of Richard's, for three or perhaps four weeks. There had been a long-standing invitation to go, and Bertie, who had seemed very restless on his return from Hawnby, had suddenly suggested they take it up. It had all been arranged in a trice, by telegram, so Maud hoped

Henrietta would excuse her not calling, as there had been so little time to do everything.

Jessie listened to all of this, as Henrietta relayed it, with a dull sense of loss. He was avoiding her, she thought. He had found it too difficult and had taken himself out of her way. Probably he was right. His face came clearly before her mind's eye, and she could hear his voice saying, *It's better this way*. Oh, but she would miss him! To see him now and then was her only comfort. The days stretched ahead in dreary monochrome.

The fine weather continued, the harvests were all in, cub-hunting began, sheep were turned onto the stubble, last January's foals were brought up to be blanket-broken. Jessie was as busy as ever; but the one person who observed her constantly and closely noted a grimness to the line of her mouth and a frequent absence in her eyes.

In October Mrs Pankhurst left for New York on White Star's *Oceanic* to begin a lecture tour of America. There was a farewell ceremony at Waterloo, where the engine of her train was draped in a large purple, green and white flag, and a crowd of supporters, many of them wearing the colours, gathered to hear her speech from her carriage window.

'We mean to have the vote next session!' she cried, to enormous cheers. 'Prospects have never been so bright. The Prime Minister has given us the most definite promises that full facilities shall be given to the Conciliation Bill, and we are going to make the most of them.'

At the end of the month Anne returned to Bedford Square. She made her formal call on Venetia.

'I don't believe for a moment Asquith will keep his promise,' Anne said. 'There are dark forces at work – a conspiracy of wreckers and reactionaries within the Liberal Party who are bent on destroying the Bill.'

'My dear Anne, there have always been those against it. Why must it be a conspiracy?' Venetia said.

'Because the chief agent of the dark forces is the man who pretends to be such a reformer and a friend to women, Mr David Lloyd George! I have it on good authority he has been going about behind the scenes trying to persuade his colleagues that the Bill would do nothing but give thousands more votes to the Tories!'

'Well, you know, that objection was raised quite openly,' Venetia said. 'I seem to remember he said there should be enfranchisement of all women or none at all.'

'He only said that in the hope that we would be deceived into thinking he is on our side. "None at all" is what he hopes and works for!'

'You always said the Conciliation Bill lacked intellectual rigour. I half think the WSPU was mistaken in deciding to back it, rather than holding out for equality.'

'All very well to say that now,' said Anne gloomily. 'It was our only hope, our foot in the door, and now it will be snatched from us.'

'Who is your "good authority" – may one ask?' Venetia said.

'Peter Padstowe,' Anne said. 'He had it from one of the whips. The chief whip has been canvassing the opinion of the Liberal regional agents on the subject of whether the Bill would make them more or less likely to win future elections. And they agree with Lloyd George that it would give votes to the Tories. God, there never was such a rabble as this present government, putting party before country! Our common grandfather would have a fit if he were alive today.'

'Yes, I'm afraid politics is a very unpleasant business these days,' Venetia said.

Anne eyed her a moment and then, divining her thoughts, said, 'What's this I hear about a rift between Overton and Holkam? Peter said something about Violet being forbidden to see you.'

'Oh, has it become common knowledge?' Venetia said, with distaste.

'Hardly common, darling,' Anne said. 'Peter's as silent as the grave. He only told me because you and I are cousins and friends.'

'Yes, but where did he get it from?'

'Oh, I see what you mean. I've no idea – but a feud can't be kept quiet, can it?'

'It's not a feud. Overton had no spleen against Holkam – it was all on his side.'

'I'm sorry,' Anne said. 'It must be distressing for you. How is Violet taking it?'

'Stoically. She says she must support her husband, and I agree with her. Her first loyalty must be to him now, not to us, hard though it is to bear. I wouldn't do anything to make matters more difficult for her, in any case. But he hasn't forbidden her to write to me, so we are not entirely cut off from each other.'

'Holkam's a fool,' Anne said, 'and a fossil and a beastly prig, like his father. I wonder you let Violet marry someone so anti-suffrage as him.'

'None of us knew he was,' Venetia pointed out. 'Why should he have wanted the daughter of a suffrage pioneer, for that matter?'

'Money,' Anne said.

'It was a love match,' Venetia said defensively. 'And it still is.' The last letter from Violet said that she was pregnant again. 'Violet's happy, and she's sure this bad feeling will blow over.'

'Perhaps,' Anne said. 'Men are as inconsistent as the weather.'

'Women are too,' Venetia said, annoyed at being put on the spot. 'You seem to be on good terms with Peter Padstowe again.'

'I always liked him,' Anne said, 'and now he's married and doesn't gaze at me like a sick spaniel all the time, he's very sensible and makes a splendid friend. I dined there last night and had an excellent evening of talk.'

'I'm glad to hear you're dining at respectable houses again,' Venetia said. 'Come and dine with us next week. I've invited Balfour and some other interesting people with a lot to say about the Lords' reform.'

Anne looked grave. 'I should love to come and dine

with you, but only if you invite Vera as well.'

Venetia was taken aback. She had forgotten Anne's friend in the course of the conversation, and now said, 'You are not serious?'

'Of course I am. Why should you doubt it?'

'But, my dear, Miss Polk may be a very nice girl, but who is she? I can't ask my guests to meet a cobbler's daughter.'

Anne's mouth turned down in distaste. 'Oh, you're there, are you? To me it's what a person is in themselves that matters, not whose daughter they are.'

'Don't lecture me,' Venetia said tautly. 'You never refused to dine here without Miss Vaughan.'

Anne flushed slightly. 'Miss Vaughan wasn't—'

'Yes? Wasn't what?'

'Never mind,' Anne growled.

Venetia sighed, and said, 'I don't really know Miss Polk. Why don't you bring her round to see me one afternoon? Bring her to tea.'

'And have you sneer at her and make her feel small? No thank you.'

Venetia was angry at that. 'What do you take me for? You know who I am, how I have lived, what I stand for. I should like to get to know your Miss Polk; but I cannot impose her on guests who would object to her origins, and if you care for her you should not wish to embarrass her in that way either.'

Anne looked mutinous for a moment, but then her jaw relaxed, and she said. 'Very well. As you please. I shall bring her to tea. And – thank you.'

The last was a great concession from Anne, and Venetia smiled, though foreseeing trouble. She had begun to suspect that the gossip Lizzie had half heard about Anne and Miss Polk was not about social origins, but something else entirely. There were a great many passionate friendships and pairings-off among the WSPU women, and Venetia believed the vast majority of them were quite innocent, if rather sentimentally overwrought. But it was not surprising that the franchise movement had attracted a few of another sort of woman, who loved other women not just sentimentally but physically.

Venetia's wide and worldly experience as a doctor had brought her in contact from time to time with sapphics, as they were generally called, after the classical poet Sappho. When the laws on homosexuality had been hardened twenty-odd years back, women had not been included in the legislation because most people had not the slightest notion that female homosexuality could exist – and if told about it, generally did not believe it. This ignorance worked in the sapphics' favour, since it meant that women could speak openly of their love for other women, whereas men had had to become more cautious in their dealings, however innocent, with friends of the same sex. It was ironic, Venetia thought, that letters were passed between women friends, couched in the same sort of high-flown language of love as those that had helped to condemn Oscar Wilde to prison and exile.

Venetia had heard something of the Miss Dancey and Miss Oliphant who had 'adopted' Miss Polk; and what she knew of Miss Polk suggested she was just the sort of girl to be vulnerable to them – high-spirited, motherless, lacking a father's care and guidance. Much the same, of course, could be said of Anne. Perhaps that was what had attracted them to each other. Public ignorance might well work in Anne's favour too – but only if she was discreet. If she made a point of forcing Miss Polk on people, made defiant declarations of her devotion to her, gossip would eventually spread from the confines of the women's movement to society at large, and there would be a scandal. Lady Anne Farraline was not a nobody, and Venetia doubted whether even she would relish veiled speculations about her and her friend in the newspapers. But it was never any use urging discretion on Anne. All Venetia could do was to worry about it – which never did any good either.

Anne's information about the Conciliation Bill proved

right. The new session of Parliament opened, and on the 7th of November, Asquith announced that the government would be introducing a Manhood Suffrage Bill, to clear up the mess of the present electoral system, with its property qualifications and plural voting. The Bill would give the vote to all men over twenty-one on an equal footing, and so would effectively scupper the Conciliation Bill, which was based on present franchise rules.

'Give the vote to all *men*, you notice,' Anne said angrily, when she called on Venetia to let off steam. 'Four million men who are currently excluded from voting will be given this great boon, though they have never asked for it, though there has never been the slightest popular agitation or demand for reform. Nobody thought them worth a jot until *we* drew attention to ourselves!'

'It is a logical step, following on the reform of the Lords,' Venetia pointed out, as Overton had pointed out to her. 'If the Commons is to be the ruling authority it must have a proper electoral basis.'

'Yes, the votes of the ruling caste,' Anne said bitterly. 'The male sex alone are considered human beings with the right to elect their government. Women are classed with the dumb beasts of the field! Women are cattle over whom men have dominion, as granted by God in the beginning, for ever and ever, amen.'

'Oh, Anne! You do exaggerate.'

'Do I? I smell Lloyd George behind this. The whole crooked and discreditable scheme is characteristic of the man. Asquith has broken his word and blown us out of the water. Well, they will see what we shall do!'

The Suffragette howl of rage was heard all over the country. Perhaps alarmed by it, or perhaps to disarm and outmanoeuvre them, Asquith agreed, suddenly and unexpectedly, to Mrs Pethick-Lawrence's almost routine demand for an audience. The demand had so expected the answer 'no' that assent took the movement aback. The deputation took place on the 17th of November, with delegates drawn from all varieties of suffragists, militant and constitutional, Liberal and Conservative, and perhaps because of that its tone was rather more muted than might have been expected. Asquith seemed in comfortable, even benevolent mood. He invited the thirty women to speak freely and listened to the speeches in silence.

At the end of it he said, 'I am not convinced. You may think it deplorable, but that is the fact, and I have colleagues who are like-minded. As head of government I have no intention of bringing in any measure which I do not believe to be in the interests of the country.'

At this Christabel's fury broke through. 'Then you can go, and we shall get another head!'

Asquith was unmoved. He almost shrugged. 'Get rid of me by all means, if you can. But at the moment I am head of the government and I am not convinced.' And he closed the interview.

Before the deputation took place it had been announced that whatever the result, there would be a WSPU meeting at Caxton Hall on the 21st of November to take what action was necessary. The feeling of betrayal and the mood of anger were so strong that there was no dissent from the decision to end the truce forthwith. The resumption of violence had, of course, long been anticipated, and Anne had agreed with Christabel that if – when – it came, the women should not expose themselves to another Black Friday. They would get themselves arrested as quickly as possible, having done as much as possible to inconvenience the world of men. Consequently an organised window-smashing took place, on a scale not seen before. Armed with hammers and bags of stones, women set out in groups from separate locations. They smashed the windows of the Home Office, the Treasury, the Local Government Board, Somerset House, the National Liberal Federation, the Guards' Club, the *Daily Mail*, the *Daily News*, Swan and Edgar's, Lyon's Corner House, Dunn's Hat Shop, and other shops, commercial premises and post offices along the Strand.

Two hundred and twenty-three women were arrested, including Anne and Miss Polk. They were put up before a magistrate and given two months. Venetia heard the news with resignation. This time they had been sent to the first division, so at least there would be no hunger strike.

In November, Jack arrived at Morland Place for a holiday. He had not been home in August as in other years, and everyone assumed that this visit was in place of the August week. He was full of the exploits of Tom Sopwith in America. Sopwith had had such success, and received so much attention from the press, that at one point the Wright brothers, Wilbur and Orville, tried to prevent his flying by filing a legal action against him, on the grounds that they had invented heavier-than-air machines, so he was in breach of their patent. He had to placate them by buying one of their aeroplanes to add to the Howard Wright and the Blériot he had brought with him.

As well as taking part in competitions he had given exhibitions, and taken passengers up for five-minute flights. One newspaper noted that Americans returning from England, where they had gone for the Coronation, had reported that just such a ride in a flying-machine could be had from Hendon aerodrome for the equivalent of twenty dollars, whereas Mr Sopwith charged fifty. The newspaper clearly resented such financial enterprise – usually thought to be a Yankee trait – and suggested that a more thrifty person might take a steerage passage to England and a flight at Hendon and still have change out of his fifty dollars.

At one exhibition, at the Columbus, Ohio, Aviation Week, Sopwith and other flyers had demonstrated throwing small bombs from the air onto make-believe battleships marked out on the field below; and later target-shooting with pistols while in flight. Most pioneer flyers felt frustrated that the authorities in both England and America could not be made to see the military potential of flying.

Teddy was most interested in a particular undertaking

by Sopwith – what Americans called a 'stunt' – which involved White Star's magnificent *Olympic* on the day she sailed for her return journey to Europe.

The ship was installed with the latest of all luxuries, including the wireless telegraph, which sent messages through the air by radiative propagation instead of through cables. When it had first been demonstrated in December 1901 by its inventor, Guglielmo Marconi, by sending a Morse-code signal from Cornwall to Newfoundland, it had been received with much scepticism. The *Daily Telegraph* – the paper named, of course, for that previous wonder of communication – had reported, 'It may be very pretty science, but it is not business.' However, its applications had soon become apparent.

Wireless telegraphy had come to popular fame and reached newspaper headlines in 1910 when it had been instrumental in the arrest of the murderer Dr Crippen. He had poisoned his wife and fled with his mistress, Ethel Le Neve, aboard White Star's *Montrose*, bound from Antwerp to Quebec. Miss Le Neve was disguised as a boy, so that she could share her lover's cabin, but the captain of the ship grew suspicious about her odd appearance. Having compared the face of the 'boy' with a photograph of the murderer's mistress in a newspaper he had brought with him, he used the Marconi wireless to signal to White Star's office in Liverpool with a message for the police. As a result, the detective inspector leading the investigation sailed in pursuit, accompanied by a sergeant and two wardresses, on the White Star's *Laurentic*. She was a faster ship and arrived a day earlier than the *Montrose*, so the police were there waiting as the *Montrose* entered the St Lawrence river. Inspector Dew went aboard from the pilot launch and the murderer and his accomplice were arrested.

Teddy was interested in anything to do with White Star, and he was also intrigued by the new invention. It was obvious that telegraph signals could be passed along a wire, but wire-less telegraphy seemed, even to a sensible businessman, like a species of magic. So Jack's story about Sopwith's stunt, combining both elements, was one that had him enthralled.

It seemed that a passenger on board the *Olympic* had discovered almost as soon as the ship left her berth that his eyeglasses were broken. He had used the Marconi wireless to send a message from the ship to the Wanamaker department store in New York, which had a Marconi station installed on its roof. He asked for a new spring for his pince-nez to be sent to him at his hotel in London by the next available steamer.

It happened that Sopwith had planned to fly out to meet the *Olympic* on her arrival but had been prevented by fog. Now the manager of Wanamaker's saw the opportunity for some advertisement, telephoned Sopwith and asked if he would like to fly the replacement spring out to the ship. Sopwith agreed, took the package and flew his Howard Wright out in the early afternoon. He sighted the *Olympic* nearing the Narrows, and descended from a thousand feet to fly over the great ocean-racer, on whose decks the excited passengers had crowded to see the fun. Unfortunately the smoke from the four stacks obscured the field from above, and the warm air rising from them made the aeroplane hard to handle. The package was dropped but it was not possible to see where it landed. Back on shore, Sopwith learned that the package had fallen not on deck but into the water; and by then the *Olympic* was too far out to sea for a second attempt to be made. So the passenger, who rejoiced in the name of W. Atlee Burpee, had to wait until London for his repair. Wanamaker's and the aviation fraternity generally were very pleased with the publicity, however, and at a special dinner that evening, Sopwith was presented with a silver cup from the Aero Club of New York, inscribed 'To Thomas Sopwith in commemoration of his flight to the *Olympic*'.

Sopwith had come back to England in October, primed

with his new experiences and more enthusiastic than ever about aviation. It was fortunate for Jack that his fertile mind was always looking for new fields to explore, because his own career was in jeopardy. Howard Wright had been offered the opportunity to amalgamate his business with the Coventry Ordnance Works, who wanted to take a first step into aeroplane manufacture. They had offered Wright the position of aeroplane department manager, but they already had a designer – W. O. Manning – and so did not need Jack's services.

'It looked as though I was going to find myself out on my ear,' Jack explained, 'until good old Sopwith came up trumps. He's going to start a flying school at Brooklands, and when he heard I was out of a position he said what a good thing it was, because he'd wanted for ages for me to come in with him on something. So he's asked me to be one of the instructors.'

Being a naturally modest man, Jack did not mention that Sopwith had said many complimentary things about his abilities, and added, 'I know teaching in the school probably isn't the best use of them, but that won't be the beginning and end of it. There are so many exciting things happening I can hardly predict what direction I shall go in next, but I do know I want to have you along with me, old man. Will you come in with me?'

Jack had shaken hands gladly. The school was to open on the 1st of February 1912, and there would be four machines in use: the Howard Wright biplane, a Blériot monoplane, the American Wright biplane Sopwith had bought in the United States, and a new Martin-Handasyde monoplane he had just purchased. Sopwith's view was that men would be better flyers if they learned on a variety of machines. He had taken every opportunity in the States to try out different ones, and was eager to develop a better aeroplane.

'That chain from the engine to the propellor on the Howard Wright, for instance – it's a monstrosity!'

'Yes,' Jack agreed, 'I've been thinking for a long time

how to get around that. Of course, it makes up for it in the slow propellor speed, but we must be able to do better. And I've been working on how to reduce the weight of a larger engine.'

'Excellent man! Well, don't worry, I know you are principally a designer, and I won't waste that. To begin with, you might put your mind to designing a dual-control for the old Wright for the school. It would help enormously to be able to take people up and teach them in the air.'

So that he should not suffer a period of unemployment between leaving Howard Wright and joining the school in February, Sopwith, ever generous, had taken him on at once. 'And he suggested that as there wasn't a great deal to do just now, I might as well take the chance to come up to Morland Place for a few days. So here I am.'

Jessie was delighted to have her favourite brother home again. They had long talks, and she took him to the stables and found him a horse so that they could go out riding together. Jack asked her if she was in love with anyone, and she laughed and said no, and changed the subject. She seemed just the same brisk, efficient, affectionate, amusing Jessie as always, very loving to him, interested in everything he had to say. But he sensed that there was something missing. Somewhere inside her there was a blank space, and he did not know what it was or why, only that every now and then he struck it, like a cold patch of air in a warm room.

She asked him about Miss Airdrie. He made a face, and said, 'Gone the way of all others, I'm afraid. She's walking out with a fellow from a City lawyer's firm – steady work and fine prospects. I couldn't blame her. She might almost have been prescient – a week after she told me kindly to go away, I was out of work.'

'Back in it now,' Jessie said. 'Silly girl. She doesn't know what she's missing.'

'Oh, it's all right, sissy. I wasn't mad in love with her, you know. She was a nice girl, but . . .' He shrugged.

Jessie eyed him with sympathy. 'Is there always a "but",
Jackie dear?'

'So far,' he admitted. 'I haven't met the girl who could
hold my heart for a lifetime.'

He had been upset when Miss Aidrie went out of his
life – more so than he had realised, until Miss Ormerod
had spoken to him diffidently one day at Brooklands and
asked if he had had bad news, because he looked so
unhappy. She had been so kind and sympathetic he had
blurted out the whole story to her before he knew what
he was doing – unlike him, because he was usually quite
a private person. But she didn't seem to think any the
less of him for it. He had thought she might be embarrassed the next time he appeared, but she had smiled her
nice, sensible smile of welcome just the same, and brought
a chocolate drop out of her pocket for Rug, who adored
her. He always left the little dog with her when he went
up, if she was on the field.

He went on to Jessie, 'Don't fret for me. Aeroplanes
are much more interesting. To be honest, I don't feel I
really have time for a girl at the moment.'

'Mother will be disappointed. She wants a grandson.'

'Oh, Rob will do the honours for that.'

'Yes, isn't it wonderful that Ethel's pregnant again?
Perhaps it will be a boy this time.'

The baby was expected in June 1912. Emma was especially delighted, for her brood had been depleted by
Polly's having started as a boarder at a very expensive
school in Scarborough. Polly had been clamouring for
school for some time, and was thrilled by everything about
it: the uniform, the dormitory, the games. She had already
acquired the obligatory 'crush' on a mistress and the 'best
chum' – Ethel's younger sister Eileen, who had started
school at the same time. Her letters home were a great
amusement to everyone. Teddy missed her, but had felt
it was right for her to have the experience, and hoped it
would give her a little polish.

★   ★   ★

On the day that Jack returned to London, a letter arrived for Henrietta from Lizzie containing momentous news. It began, 'I've got something very exciting to tell you,' and Henrietta's mind jumped immediately to pregnancy, but it was not that.

Ashley and Lizzie had long dreamed of taking a trip to America, though without a great deal of hope that it would happen. Ashley wanted to see his brothers again, and wanted to show his wife and children something of the wonders of his home country. Lizzie had always wanted to travel, though she had set her sights rather more modestly on perhaps seeing Paris before she was too old to enjoy it.

But now it seemed that Ashley's employer, Mr Culpepper, was to make the dream come true for them. He not only owned a shipping line, but had many other interests in America – wheat and railways, for instance – and he had just acquired a large new interest in cattle and timber in Arizona. Knowing of Ashley's desire to visit the country, he had asked him if he would go out there and set up the business and get everything running smoothly.

It will mean living there for two or three years [Lizzie said in her letter], so naturally we are all to go with him. I can't tell you how excited I am! I thought at first when Ashley told me Arizona is out in the west that we would be living in a log cabin and have to fight Indians and buffaloes. But Ashley says it is not at all like 'Wild West' stories, but quite civilised. We will live in an ordinary town, with electricity and trains and shops and schools, just like here, except that he says we will have a much larger house, because everything is bigger in America.

Henrietta was stunned – and dismayed. Her daughter and grandchildren to go to America? Not to see them for several years? She tried hard to be pleased about it for

Lizzie's sake, but the fact was that she did not want her to go. It was so far away. And she had heard so much about America being the land of opportunity, she wondered whether the boys, spending three years there at an impressionable age, might not decide to stay and make their lives there. And if they stayed, no doubt Lizzie and Ashley would too. She suspected Ashley had always hankered after America, but had stayed in England for Lizzie's sake. No, she didn't think it would be a hardship for Ashley to resettle in the land of his birth – but if he did, she might never see Lizzie again.

She read on. Their departure was set for April, which Lizzie thought was good because the boys would have the summer out there before having to settle into a school.

And Mr Culpepper is so generous: he is allowing Ashley a whole month when we get there for seeing his brothers and showing me something of the east coast, before we go out west. Dan is in Boston and Nat in New York, so we shall stay with each of them, and do some sightseeing. Then we go by railway to a place called Flagstaff – isn't that a nice name? – where a house will be waiting for us. I'm going to be so busy, trying to get everything packed up before April! I do hope you will come and stay and help me.

The news had to be passed on, of course, the letter read out, and reread, and everything exclaimed over in detail by every member of the family. There was nothing but interest and excitement from everyone else: only a mother would see a negative side to it. But Jessie at least understood, and leaning on her mother's shoulder kissed her cheek and said, 'We'll miss them. But what an opportunity!'

Teddy was delighted for them, and most pleased of all by the paragraph further down the letter where Lizzie said,

Mr Culpepper is paying all our fares and expenses, of course – which makes it better than a holiday! – and he has booked our passage on Uncle Teddy's *Titanic* for her maiden voyage. Not first class, of course – too expensive, and in any case all booked up already – but everyone says second class on *Titanic* is as good as first class on any other ship. I'm terribly thrilled, and Ashley looked almost worried when he heard, because he thinks Mr Culpepper is being *too* kind – isn't that absurd of him? But of course it *is* just kindness on Mr C's part, because he could have sent us on any other ship, but he knows Uncle Teddy is going and thinks it will be nice for us and a once in a lifetime experience. I dare say despite not being first class we might see something of Uncle Teddy on the trip – perhaps he will come and dine with us, if it's not too far beneath him!

Teddy was terribly proud of his part in the *Titanic*'s potential wonderfulness, and covered up his pleasure in the idea of showing it off to the Ashley Morlands by saying gruffly that his would be a business trip, and he wouldn't have time for enjoying himself. No-one believed a word of it, of course.

Henrietta folded the letter up at last – knowing she would read it many, many more times – and sighed, and said, 'Well, we must make sure that this Christmas is the best ever, and that everyone comes home for it.'

'I wonder what Frank will do,' Rob said idly. 'He'll have to find himself lodgings, I suppose. He won't like that, after Lizzie's home comforts.'

One day in late November, Jessie was out for a ride. She had been up at Twelvetrees in the morning, and in the middle of a conversation about shoeing she had suddenly been overcome with a desire to be alone. It was something that happened to her quite often: a mixture of sorrow, weariness and loneliness would rush over her, for which there was no antidote but quiet and solitude. She rode out to Marston Moor, and galloped until she and Hotspur were both winded. Then she rode up on to Cromwell's Plump, dismounted and sat on the grass, holding his reins and staring out over the moor.

After a while, her mind became mute, her thoughts quieted, and she stared at nothing, glad of the respite. The weather had been exceptionally mild, and apart from the autumn smell in the air and the gold of the distant trees, it might have been a spring day. It was quite idly that she noticed a horseman approaching from the Hessay direction; but as he came closer, Hotspur put up his head and whinnied, and the rider raised his hand in greeting. It was Bertie. She had thought him still in Ireland. She rose to her feet, her heart pounding. What was he *doing* here? Had he come for her? No, ridiculous thought. Nothing had changed. It was still impossible.

When he was near enough she tried for a normal voice and said, 'I thought you were in Ireland.'

'I came back,' he said reasonably. 'We arrived yesterday.' He reined in and slid from the saddle. 'Hello.'

'Hello,' she said, her eyes drinking in his face like someone dying of thirst. 'How did you know I was here?'

'I called at Twelvetrees to see Lelliott. Asked in a casual way where you were. Gone riding on Marston Moor, said he. I pretended to be going home and came here instead. No-one knows I'm here, you see.'

'No-one within ten miles without a pair of field-glasses,' she said. 'We are rather conspicuous.'

'Like Boers against the skyline,' he agreed. 'Shall we go and find a wood?' She didn't answer, seeming rather bemused. He said, 'You didn't come to Hawnby. You were invited and you didn't come.'

'I couldn't bear to. I didn't want to see you there, like that.'

'I thought that might be it. I was disappointed at the time. I wanted to see you and I didn't care where it was. But afterwards I decided perhaps you were wise.'

'That's why you went to Ireland?'

'Yes. I thought I had better put myself out of temptation's way. I hoped the feeling might fade in time.'

'And did it?'

He shook his head. 'I just want to see you more and more. It's like a sickness I can't shake off.'

She stared at him despairingly. 'We said we wouldn't do this.'

'I know. I thought I could manage it, knowing—'

'Knowing you had to.'

'Jessie, I love you so. I think about you all the time. I want you so much I can't eat or sleep or work or play. Do you know what I mean? Is it the same for you?'

'You know it is.'

'It feels so *right*, being with you. So natural. As if – as if it's what God *meant* to happen, only we foolish humans managed to spoil it.'

She turned her head away, looking out at the distant grazing sheep, flecks of cream on the green moor. She thought of the ewes passing the car the time he had kissed her. No, she mustn't think of kissing him. 'I know. I want you so much I'm sick with it, too. But there's nothing we can do about it.'

'No,' he said heavily. 'I didn't come to try to persuade you to anything. I'm not that much of a cad.'

There was a part of her that wished he would. She tried to ignore it. 'Then why did you come?'

'There's something I have to tell you. I wanted to tell you myself, alone. I didn't want you to hear it first in front of everyone else.'

She searched his face. 'Is it bad news?'

He didn't answer that. He seemed to be gathering himself for an effort. Then he said, quite baldly, 'Maud is having a baby.'

She stared and stared, her mind in a swoon, understanding all the implications. She knew she ought to say something congratulatory, but her tongue seemed to be stuck to the roof of her mouth.

'Jessie, I'm sorry,' he said at last.

She found speech. 'No, you mustn't say that. You have to be glad about it. Poor baby!'

'I didn't mean that.'

'I know what you meant.' She drew a shuddering sigh. 'It's all right,' she said quietly. 'I – I understand. What were you to do? It would have been odd if—' No way to end that sentence.

'I don't want you to understand,' he cried suddenly. 'I want you to be angry.'

'What were you to do?' she said again. 'You're married to her. You couldn't never touch her again.'

'Jessie!' he cried, and took her in his arms. She clung to him while he wrapped his arms so tightly round her she could hardly breathe. She didn't really want to breathe. She would have liked to die right then, that minute, so that she would never be apart from him again. They were silent a long time, while the horses watched them with pricked ears, and a little breeze ruffled their hair.

'It doesn't change anything,' he said at last, muffled, into her neck.

'It changes everything,' she said.

'It doesn't change the way I feel.'

'No, not that,' she said sadly.

'I love you.'

'I love you too.'

He lifted his head and looked at her. 'I'll love you always,' he said, and she knew that these words were a kind of farewell. He knew, really, that everything *was* changed now.

With a terrible courage she pushed herself back from him, and they stood apart, staring at each other, defeated.

'Tell me something,' she said.

'Anything.'

'Why *did* you marry her?'

'I wish I hadn't. Why did I do everything in such a rush? If I'd waited just a few months—'

'But you must have loved her a *bit*,' Jessie said.

'I was attracted to her. It wasn't love. Oh, how can I explain it to you?' he said. 'You're so innocent.'

'Perhaps not as innocent as you think. You're talking about – about animal attraction, aren't you? Physical feelings.'

'Yes,' he said, 'but—'

'I know about that. I had them too for someone. I thought it was love, but I know now it wasn't.'

'I never thought it was love,' he said. 'But I didn't think it mattered. I didn't expect ever to fall in love. I was past thirty and I'd never felt anything more than that for anyone. I had to marry someone and I thought she would do, God forgive me. But now . . .' He put out his hand and gently cupped her cheek, as he had done before, and she leaned into the touch. 'Now I know what there can be between two people.'

Far off a dog barked, the sound brought tiny and clear on the breeze. The horses were grazing, with a steady tearing sound and a rattle of bit-rings; and in her memory there was a lark, singing as though joy were never-ending. The moment seemed to Jessie to be rimmed with a doomed light, like the silvery storm sun that parts the gathering clouds. In a moment he would go, and it would all be over.

His hand dropped to his side. She said, 'When will you tell?'

'I shall ride over tomorrow with the glad tidings,' he said.

'I'll be happy for you,' she said.

'Will you?'

'It's all I can do now.'

Her calm seemed to make him uneasy. 'I suppose I'd better go.'

'Yes, go. We'll be just ordinary friends and cousins. We'll love each other as cousins.'

He couldn't think of anything more to say, and 'goodbye' seemed too ridiculously dramatic. In silence he

621

picked up her hand and kissed it, then turned away, pulled up his horse's head, mounted, and rode off. She watched him dwindling with distance into a speck until he was hidden from view; and then Hotspur drew a great horse-sigh and shook his head hard, making his bridle rattle. At this hint she mounted too, and turned his head for home. There was a great weight of tears in her chest, but she would have to face people when she got home, and they must wait for the solitude of her bed to be let out.

It did change everything. She realised now how there had been a part of her mind that would not accept that he was really and truly married, that had thought there might still be a wave of a magic wand, or that it might turn out to have been a dream from which she would wake with relief and run to him. But now, with a child coming, there was no room for magic. She did not blame him for having been a husband to Maud. Oddly, she felt no jealousy on that score. It was everything else Maud had that tore at her inside.

She got through the rest of the day pretty well, she thought, talking normally, paying attention to people. It was the benefit of having a large family, that there were generally no awkward silences. But the feeling of oppression grew as dinner wore on, and she was glad when the moment came to quit the table. Ned rose and held the door for the women, and she felt his eyes on her as she went past, but would not meet them. When they reached the drawing-room, she asked Alice to play so that there would be no more conversation. By the fire Henrietta and Ethel carried on a domestic chat in low voices. Jessie retreated to the far end, to the day-bed under the window where her father had spent his last weeks. She sat, her elbow on the seat-back, her head turned away from the room, staring at the blackness outside the window, trying not to think.

The music soothed her. She felt more than anything tired now, wanting sleep. The reflected candles dipped and swayed gently, the room limned ghostly on the glass, broken up by the diamond panes like a prism. She saw a movement, heard at the same time her uncle's voice, and Robbie answering him, and then Ned was there. He sat down on the day-bed beside her. She looked at him, heavy eyed, in silence for a moment, while he scanned her face.

'You were quiet at dinner,' he said.

'Was I? I thought I talked.'

'Is something wrong?' She shook her head, unable to voice the lie. He was silent a while, looking down at his hands clasped between his knees. She looked too – strong, capable hands – and then at the line of his bent neck, the curve of his jaw, picked out by candlelight; and she shivered. As if at this signal he looked up, and meeting his eyes she felt a thin blush run under her cheeks.

'Jessie,' he said, 'I've waited, as you asked me, and not pressed you. Summer's long over, and you said I could ask you in the summer, but I felt you weren't ready. Now I begin to think that perhaps I'm more of a nuisance to you than a comfort, and I never wanted that. I've only ever wanted to make you happy.'

She felt tears starting at those words and fought them down. *Not now*! *You are not to cry now*!

He went on, 'So I will ask you now, one last time, and after this I won't bother you again. If you want, you can forget all about it, and I'll be your friend without any obligation on your part. You needn't have a conscience about me – do you believe that?' She nodded again. And, very low, so that no-one but her would hear, he said, 'Will you marry me, Jess?'

Her mind cried out Bertie's name; but Bertie was lost to her, and nothing she did would make that any more so. *Physical feelings*, she thought. Bertie had married Maud with them; and she had felt, more than once, tremors of them for Ned. Could it be enough? Or if not enough, could it be a foundation for happiness? She wanted love so badly, and she wanted to be held in a man's arms.

Those things seemed to exist outside her love for Bertie, requirements of her body that nagged at her like a hungry child asking for food when there was none, half heeded in the business of the day but never completely to be shut out. She *could* marry Ned; and it would make things easier. It would take her out of Bertie's way, make it easier to meet him again when they did meet, as they must for the rest of their lives.

She said, 'But will it be enough for you?' As the only thing she had said aloud, it didn't make sense, but Ned accepted it as if he had heard all her thoughts.

'I love you,' he said. 'I can make you happy. That's all I ask. Will you marry me?'

And she said, 'Yes.'

He didn't seem to understand at first, probably having expected 'no' so surely that the other word made no impact. And then his face lit as though there were candles inside him, and he took her hand and lifted it to his lips, as Bertie had done a thousand years ago, that afternoon. But, honourably, he asked, 'Do you want time to think about it?'

'No,' she said. 'I've said yes and I mean it. I don't want to wait. I'd like to be married as soon as possible – if that's what you want?'

'I'd like nothing better. Oh, Jessie, you won't regret this, I swear to you. You do love me a little, then?'

'I love you a lot,' she said. 'I always have.' And he pressed her hand and kissed it again, and gazed at her with such happiness she felt ashamed and guilty and then glad, all in quick succession.

Alice finished a piece and paused, looking towards the group at the fire; from which Teddy, seeing her look, called, 'Yes, another – if you don't mind, my dear. If it won't tire you.' Alice changed the music in front of her and began again.

Ned said, 'When shall we tell them? Shall we say something now?'

'Tomorrow,' she said. 'I feel too – disturbed tonight.

624

Tomorrow at breakfast, if you like, and then Uncle Teddy will have time to plan a special dinner.'

Ned laughed, softly. He had beautiful teeth, she noticed, and a cold finger seemed to run down her spine. She was really going to do this. She was going to be – his *wife*. 'There'll be champagne for sure,' he said. 'Father will be so pleased. We are going to make so many people happy, you know.'

It was true. It was something to think about later, in bed, when the turmoil of her thoughts rushed through her like great gusty squalls, first misery, then curiosity, grief, then excitement, bewilderment that she had done this thing, great gasping shock at the ups and downs one day had brought her. But she did not cry. She had waited all those hours to be alone so that the flood of tears could be let out, but the pressure had gone, and she could not cry for Bertie now. The time would come, she knew – there had to be that reckoning – but it did not seem to be now.

Everyone was pleased by the news that Ned and Jessie were to marry. Teddy, in particular, was brought almost to tears between wringing Ned's hand and engulfing Jessie in bear-hugs. 'I've felt like a father towards you since your own dear pa died,' he said, 'and now I can be a father in truth. My dear, dear daughter!'

Henrietta said, 'I'm so happy! I was afraid you were going to be alone. I was afraid you'd never find anyone you liked.'

'I shall be married before I'm twenty-one,' Jessie said, 'so there will be no disgrace.'

'Disgrace! What silly talk. Ned is a fine man, and he'll make a fine husband. You do love him, darling?'

'Would I marry him if I didn't? Don't fret, Mother. Everything is all right.'

It had not occurred to her, when telling Ned the night he proposed that they would announce it the next day, that that was also the day Bertie was to come and tell his news. Bertie and Maud came together in the late afternoon in the carriage, and were instantly invited by Teddy to stay to dinner, with no excuses accepted. And then Teddy told the news. Jessie was beside Ned on the other side of the room from Bertie. They looked at each other across a desert of silence, too far apart to speak, out of reach. *It's better this way*, she said, and he said, *Yes, you're right*. No words were spoken, but it was there in the air between them.

Bertie came over to shake Ned's hand and tell him he was a lucky fellow, and then stood before Jessie, looking down. She gave him her hand – small and cold in his large, warm palm – and he stooped and kissed her cheek, a touch as light as a moth's wing. 'Be happy,' he said tenderly. She could not speak for the pain in her throat, only looked everything she could not say for the instant her hand rested in his. Then he turned away; Ned's hand came down on her shoulder, pressing it comfortingly; Bertie said to the company at large, 'I have good news too. A double celebration, Uncle Teddy – your favourite kind! We've come to tell you that clever Maud is going to make me a papa.'

More outcry; more laughter, words, kisses, congratulations. The champagne was brought forth and toasts were drunk to the two couples standing across the room from each other, *To Jessie and Ned*! and *To Maud and Bertie*!. And of all the people in the room the quietest were those four, two in a daze of happiness, two in a daze of loss.

That evening was perhaps the hardest part for Jessie. After that, the wedding plans took over, and there was too much to do to think about anything deeply. Jessie would not have been a normal girl if she had not found it exciting. She was going to be married, after all. A girl only has one wedding, and it had better be a good one. She missed her father, but Teddy threw himself into the breach with enormous energy. He and Henrietta had their heads together at all hours. The wedding was to take place in the chapel (Teddy grew quite moist about the eyes, talking about their dead brother George, and how if things had been only a little different, Ned would have been heir to Morland Place). He insisted on paying for Jessie's wedding dress and other outfits, which were to be made by his tailoress, and would have paid for Ned's too, but Ned was quietly firm about it.

'Then you must think of something really grand for a wedding present,' Teddy said.

'You've given me so much already,' Ned objected. 'Meynell's Mill is present enough for a lifetime.'

'You ought to change the name, now. Morland's Mill sounds pretty well, don't you think?'

'I don't want to compete with you, Father,' he said. 'I think I'll leave it as it is.'

'Until you have a son of your own,' Teddy said. 'Then you'll think differently. Oh, think of that! Grandsons! By Jove, I'm so happy about this wedding, I can't tell you! You couldn't have chosen better from my point of view. It's a match made in heaven! And in a couple of weeks Jessie will be twenty-one, the trust will be wound up, and you'll have a half share in the horse business too.'

'I don't think Jessie's share is quite half, is it?' Ned said diffidently.

'Tush!' said Teddy. 'It is now. Wedding present to my favourite niece. Not a word more! Glad to do it. Damme, I wish old Jerome was here! He'd turn cartwheels for joy.'

Teddy was being so kind and generous that it was hard for both Ned and Jessie to break his heart by telling him they were not going to live at Morland Place after the wedding. Ned wanted to take his bride to a house of his own, and Jessie thought it would be easier to start afresh with Ned in a place with no memories or associations to haunt her. Layerthorpe, where the mill stood, was not the sort of area for a couple in their position to live. Ned found a house in Clifton, a nice area, and handy both for Layerthorpe and Twelvetrees – for Jessie had no intention of giving up her supervision of the stables.

'Not at first, anyway,' Ned agreed, and she let it pass for the time being.

So now there was a house to have decorated and furnished. There were fabrics and carpets to choose, linens and pots and pans to buy, servants to interview. Jessie discovered, as many a young woman before her, how much fun it is to play house for the first time with the real thing, to choose for yourself exactly how every-thing will look and where things will be placed. Maystone Villa was a nice, square stone house with large windows, high ceilings and good-sized rooms, which had the added advantage of a stable and coach-house to the side. The garden was pleasant, though not large, but there was a paddock attached, which would be useful. Jessie soon began to feel fond of the house, and said, 'I'm going over to Maystone,' with a delightful sense of ownership.

They were starting life with a small staff, as she felt that would be all she would be able to command without bursting into laughter. (How she wished she had paid more attention to what her mother did about the house; how many questions she put to dear, kind Emma about the right way to do this and that!) They were to have a cook, kitchen maid and two housemaids to begin with; a man who would also valet Ned; and Mary Tomlinson, who was to go with Jessie as her lady's maid and 'general factotal', as Emma put it. When she had a moment, Jessie backed her mother into a seat and made her dictate a dozen suitable menus for a young wife to order.

'I mean to do the thing properly, and have Ned be comfortable,' she said.

'Of course you do, darling,' Henrietta said, puzzled that it needed saying, 'but you know, I'll be here and you can always run over and ask me things.'

'If Uncle Teddy would have the telephone put in, I could even call you with it and save the running,' Jessie said. Ned was having the telephone put into Maystone – 'in case there's an emergency at the mill at any time'. And Ned was going to buy a motor, too, to get him to and from the mill, and for them to go visiting in.

Time ran away quickly. The gown came home, and Alice at the last minute offered her own wedding lace, which was very beautiful. Polly came home from Scarborough, and ran wild about the house with excitement. Lizzie arrived with the children; Ashley, Jack and Frank were coming on the day. Eileen Cornleigh and Polly were to be bridesmaids (Jessie thought two quite enough), and little Rose was to walk in front scattering rose petals from a basket. Lizzie had made her practise at home, and hoped fervently that she could do it now without giggling.

Jessie was married a week after her birthday. The house was full of people and bustle, and waking in it, realising it would not be her home from now on, Jessie suddenly felt very odd, as if she had come loose from the world and was floating. The sensation stayed with her through breakfast (Ned was sleeping at the Cornleighs' house so that he should not see her until the wedding began), through checking the flowers in the chapel, and going over the finer points of the feast with her mother, and then climbing the stair to be dressed by Sweetlove and Tomlinson. When she was ready, they made her look in the glass. She looked to herself like a ghost: there seemed no connection between that vision and the Jessie who lived inside her skin.

Downstairs to the drawing-room: Uncle Teddy, bursting with pride, ready to give her away; Mother already in tears, handing her the bouquet – heather and Christmas roses. Guests – lots of guests – with smiles on their faces and their mouths moving, opening and shutting, though Jessie could not distinguish a word. Eileen and Polly, in cream taffeta, having their sashes tweaked by Ethel. Lizzie holding little Rose in her arms, Rose's thumb plugged firmly into her mouth against the stares of all these strangers, her petal basket gripped in the other hand so tightly her knuckles were white. Bertie and Maud were there, among the guests, and Jessie tried not to look at them, but she felt Bertie's eyes on her, caught a disturbing glimpse of his face now and then when the crowds parted.

And then it was time to go. Uncle Teddy loomed over her, offering his arm. The guests crowded out to fill the chapel, and the room became quiet, so that she could hear the clock ticking again, and the canary trilling softly to itself in the winter sunshine from the window. She remembered the day she had come in and found her father asleep on the day-bed, and she suddenly had the strongest feeling of his presence, so that for a moment the back of her neck prickled and she *knew* that if she turned round he would be there, smiling at her. She did not look, of course: it would have been to court disappointment.

Then Uncle Teddy said, 'Ready?' She nodded. 'You look beautiful,' he said, and, his voice missing a little, 'He would have been so proud of you.'

Afterwards, she felt that that was the critical moment, the point when everything changed and there was no going back. The quiet, reverent ceremony in the chapel, the words exchanged, the ring placed, the sacrament taken, the noisy, happy feast afterwards – none of those had the same weight in her mind as the first step forward with her hand on Uncle Teddy's arm. That was the beginning of the journey.

And the end of it was in a bedroom in the Savoy Hotel in London, at the end of a long day, after a 'send-off', as Emma called it, from Morland Place, a drive in Uncle Teddy's motor to the station, a train journey to King's Cross, and a taxi-meter through London's dark, wet streets. On the following day they were to travel to Paris for their honeymoon. Jessie, who had never been abroad, found that one piece of excitement too much, and felt too tired and overwrought to think about it. She had hardly exchanged a word with Ned all day, it not seeming to be necessary at a wedding that the principals should converse. She felt she hardly knew what he looked like. During the journey there were her maid and his man present to stem any exchange of intimacies, and when they got to the hotel they had to part again to change for dinner. Then there was dinner in the dining-room, surrounded by other people, neither of them with anything much to say. And then Ned suggested they went to bed as it would be an early start the next day. She left him once more to be undressed by Tomlinson and get into bed to await her fate.

He came at last, pink and scrubbed about the face (Daltry, his man, must have shaved him again, she thought, and was touched) and looking rather apologetic in a spotted brown silk dressing-gown. She watched him cross the room, hardly knowing how to think about him. She was a battlefield of thoughts. How vulnerable men looked out of their daytime suits. But this was a man, a man's body under the silk – how frightening! He was going to get into the same bed with her – how embarrassing! It was Ned, she was married to Ned – how odd! Would he know what to do? She prayed he would. It would be too dreadful if they were both ignorant.

And then suddenly she relaxed. This was Ned, whom she had known most of her life. He would look after her. She could trust him. She was not alone any more – she had someone of her own, who would care for her. She smiled, and saw the rather tense expression on his face soften.

'Shall I turn out the light?' he asked, almost in a whisper.

'Yes, please,' she said.

He reached for the switch, and at the last moment turned his face to look at her, a look of tenderness and happiness, and he said, 'Don't be afraid. I shall always take care of you.'

It was her own thought, given back to her. He pressed the switch and the darkness snapped over them, and in the darkness he came to her, not cousin or brother or friend but lover. He took his rightful place in her bed, and gently, lovingly, made her his own. And there was no thought in Jessie's mind at all, nothing to disturb or jar or make her want to weep. There was nothing in the darkness but sensation, warmth, kisses, physical delight. He loved her, and they slept a little, and he loved her again, and they slept; and in the early hours, before dawn, when the first blackbird was hesitantly trying the darkness with a phrase or two, he woke her and took her in his arms, and this time she knew what to do, and she loved him back. Her nightgown had long since disappeared into the general tangle of the bedding, and as she lay naked in his arms, suffused with drowsy satisfaction, she thought, So that's what it's all about.

In the darkness, just beginning to pale into grey, he said, 'Are you happy?'

'Yes,' she said. 'Are you?'

He gave a little laugh by way of answer, and said, 'This is only the beginning.'

When morning came it was rather embarrassing just at first to look at him after what had passed, to meet his eyes and see not dear old cousin Ned but the man who had done those things to her. He seemed taller this morning, she thought, laughing at herself but still acknowledging the truth. He *was* taller, and broader in the shoulders, and he spoke to the hotel staff with an extra authority. *He's a husband*, she thought, with an inward smile. She did not think she was yet a wife; but it would come. Downstairs in the dining-room she asked him to order breakfast for her, and enjoyed every moment of seeing him study the menu, consider, choose and give the waiter the command in firm, manly tones.